The Road to Kotaishi

Dear Mike —
Thank you, and I do hope you enjoy the book!
(It's not Gladiator, but then it's not Arthur, either...)

[signed]

The Road to Kotaishi

Kevin Radthorne

Writers Club Press
San Jose New York Lincoln Shanghai

The Road to Kotaishi

All Rights Reserved © 2001 by Kevin Radthorne

No part of this book may be reproduced or transmitted in any form or by any means, graphic, electronic, or mechanical, including photocopying, recording, taping, or by any information storage retrieval system, without the permission in writing from the publisher.

Writers Club Press
an imprint of iUniverse.com, Inc.

For information address:
iUniverse.com, Inc.
5220 S 16th, Ste. 200
Lincoln, NE 68512
www.iuniverse.com

ISBN: 0-595-18368-9

Printed in the United States of America

For Lise, the Hikari who lights my soul

Acknowledgements

This is one of the really fun parts. First I get to thank Mom, because of course without her there would be no Kevin, and thus no book! And Mr. Meeks, the one who got me started all those years ago. And my son Daniel, who has within him a kind and generous heart.

Thanks as well to Margaret Organ-Kean, fantasy artist extraordinaire, who was networking contact number one. And to Honna Swenson, Lori Ann White, and Irene Radford, who took the time at Orycon 21 to provide me with detailed feedback.

I created the cover illustration using Bryce and Photoshop, and some of the objects were modified from those available on the web. Specifically, the originals of the pavilion and the bell came from Terragraphica, and the bridge from Romain Guillard.

Many writers have been inspiring to me over the years but several in particular were quite influential, including Katherine Kurtz, Sean Russell, Janny Wurts, Jane Fancher, and especially Diane Duane. My thanks to each of them for many hours of pleasurable reading. I highly recommend them all.

My dear friend Sofia Krasnovskaya deserves particular mention, not only for her help with the cover, including that nifty starburst over the lantern, but because she is also a very special person whose engaging personality even found its way into the book. And to her wonderful family, Dmitri, Irina, Elsie, and George, who have made my wife and me feel as if we were part of their family too.

And most importantly to Lise, who not only put up with all the ups and downs of this long road of writing, but who contributed her superb editing skills to the final result. The book is far, far better for her attention. None of the words would be here without her help and support. She is truly a remarkable woman.

1

The rain pelted down so hard that it bounced, each drop performing a final pirouette before merging again with its comrades along the wooden planks of the bridge.

As the rain dripped off the edges of his helmet the guard sighed, wishing he could re-join his own comrades back in the barracks. But he was a soldier, and tonight it was his duty to watch the bridge, so watch he would. Not, he thought, that anyone in his right mind would be out on such a gods-forsaken night. Much better to be somewhere around a warm fire. Perhaps with some strong wine. Yes, that would be nice, he decided, as he watched the raindrops roll off the edge of the bridge down to the river below. A good strong wine, the type to put a man to sleep after too much time spent standing in the rain.

The guard stood at the far end of the bridge marking the boundary of Hajimeshi with the territory of its neighbor, the trading kingdom of Yutakashi. A single hooded torch mounted on a post provided him with some light, if no heat. The stone arches of the bridge were quite ancient; the wooden planks and railings had been replaced several times, usually from old age and rot, occasionally from damage in war. There was no war now but the thinly veiled threats issued by Yutakashi toward its neighbors had recently heightened tensions. Hence the call for a watch on the bridge.

Fat lot of good one man does, thought the guard, leaning on his spear as if it were no more than a prop to hold him up. If an army comes marching down that road, they can have the bridge.

Looking over the railing, his thoughts began to wander, drifting aimlessly like the water down below. They would be the last thoughts he would have.

Silently, like a cat stalking its prey, a figure climbed up from underneath the bridge, using the stonework of the arches for handholds. He was dressed in black from head to foot, only a small band of flesh visible where his eyes appeared from below a dark, close-fitting hood. The only thing that gave a hint to his purpose was the curved sword in its sheath strapped across his back, where it would not interfere with his movements. Emerging on the opposite side of the bridge from where the guard stood staring down into the water, the black-clad figure quietly pulled himself over the edge of the railing. His padded shoes and the sound of the rain striking the planks masked the noise of his footfalls. Once on the bridge itself, in two quick steps he was behind the guard and whipping a thin wire around the man's neck.

With not even time for a choking gasp the guard dropped his spear and clutched ineffectually at his throat where the wire bit into his flesh. As he struggled to breathe, the pounding of the rain on the deck merged inside his skull with the pounding of his heart. He never saw his killer as the attacker twisted the wire tight, choking off all air, and finally, all life.

The figure in black let the body fall to the deck. Verifying that the man was dead, he quickly retrieved his wire and slid it into a hidden recess of his tunic. He picked up the guard's spear and threw it into the river. Then he rolled the body under the railing and pushed it off into the water to follow its erstwhile support. The small amount of blood left on the planks from where the wire had cut through the guard's skin mingled with the rain that still fell, and together they washed away off the edge of the bridge.

The assassin watched but a moment to make sure that the body floated down the river. Certain now that he would not be observed, he started at a slow trot across the bridge. Dawn was not too far off and he still had much ground to cover. He would then have many hours of waiting once he arrived.

Some distance away, perched atop one of the trees that grew down along the river's edge, a lone owl watched. The torch on the bridge, with no one to tend it, slowly began to gutter, until it finally went out.

*   *   *

Toshi-hito felt the warmth on his back as the morning sun rose above the trees and spread its light out across Hajimeshi castle and its adjoining grounds. The previous night's rain had left the walls of the castle glistening, the rough texture of the stones painted in colorful little rainbows. The castle itself was perched like a beacon, reflecting the sun out across the plains below the hill. It was, mused Toshi-hito, quite beautiful.

He sat in an open field below the castle, watching the rising sun as it changed the colors in small increments. While he watched he continued to listen with one ear to the voices of his students, who were arranged before him. They were engaged in their daily discourse: exchanging questions and answers on a topic chosen by him, so that all of the students might know what each of them knew.

Strange, he wondered, continuing to watch the sunrise. *Such beauty is usually comforting to the spirit. Why then are my thoughts so troubled?*

One of the younger students was asking, "Why is the Kojuro always called Kojuro? I mean, why does he not just keep using his own name, instead of being called the Kojuro?"

"Kojuro is not just a name," answered Shiko, one of the older boys. "It is the symbol of our connection with Hajimeshi." He, like the other students, was an apprentice Deshi, a member of the monastic order that served as the spiritual guides for Hajimeshi. Tilling their own soil at their priory, and meditating on the ways of the world around them, the Deshi lived simple, uncomplicated lives, working in the fields or studying in their vast Archives. When called upon they served as guides for those who sought answers; and always they pursued knowledge as their staff of life. Learning being a never-ending pursuit, eventually a Deshi might obtain sufficient wisdom to become a Master Deshi, like Toshi-hito. Shiko, approaching the time when he would become a full Deshi, had only recently donned the plain brown tunic that marked him as being of age.

"The Kojuro is always referred to by his title," continued Shiko, "because he is more than just our sovereign; he is also the conduit for our understanding of the world. He alone may enter the Sacred Grove of Shizen." He pointed to the far side of the castle grounds where the students could see the familiar line of trees that nestled incongruously up against the castle walls: the home of the Shizen, the mysterious spirits that had been central to the founding of Hajimeshi.

"More than anything," Shiko continued, "that makes whoever is the Kojuro key to the future of Hajimeshi."

Toshi-hito glanced at the young man before returning his steady gaze to the rain-washed walls of the castle. The Deshi Master sat unobtrusively; apart from the discussion, but always with his reassuring presence close to hand. Nearly all of his forty years had been spent among the Deshi, and yet he still recalled what it was like to be an apprentice. He listened attentively, without seeming to, as Shiko went on.

Having known the boy since he was but a toddler, Toshi-hito always found it somewhat of a surprise to look at the apprentice and realize that the toddler had almost grown into a man. True, the boy was still a bit thin, but his height matched his fellows well. And the results of his Deshi training were certainly exemplary, far surpassing his peers. Beyond all that, one had only to look into the young man's face and notice that calm gaze which held one's own with confidence, which certainly marked the apprentice as someone apart from the others. Or was it perhaps only Toshi-hito's knowledge of the young man's history that caused the elder Deshi to feel this way?

Mentally Toshi-hito shook his head, although outwardly he remained perfectly still. You're getting old, he told himself; you're letting your thoughts wander. Now what would the apprentices think if one of them asked you a question and you failed to respond as a result of such idle daydreaming?

Shiko was still answering the younger student's question. "Since only the Kojuro may enter the Grove," he continued, "and hear the wisdom of the Shizen, it is vital that there be an unbroken line of succession, regardless of the person's suitability for the task."

Ah, thought Toshi-hito with satisfaction, still gazing off toward the castle. Let us see where this thread is woven.

Shiko gestured toward the opposite side of the castle, toward the burial ground reserved for the Kojuro and his family members. "The elder brother of our current Kojuro held the same title, as had their father before them. Our traditions hold that the oldest son inherits, even if he does not possess the good sense to use his influence wisely. The elder brother, Fugawari, neglected his responsibilities when he became Kojuro, and Hajimeshi declined as a result. When he died, his younger brother Kimeru was declared our current Kojuro. Since then, the land has enjoyed greater prosperity."

Another of the older apprentices whispered a fierce admonishment, jabbing Shiko with a finger. "Do not say slanderous things about the Kojuro. It is not right!"

Before Shiko could answer, Toshi-hito spoke: "Do you say so, Hotanu? And why is this so?"

Toshi-hito rarely interrupted the student's dialogues, usually allowing them free discourse on their own terms. Thus it was significant that he had chosen to intercede. Slightly unnerved, Hotanu replied, "Because—well, because the Kojuro is our leader. He decides what is best for our people, and has much responsibility." He swallowed hard. "So—so he deserves our respect," he added, trying to end on a firmer note.

"Ah, respect," said Toshi-hito. "And did you note any disrespect in Shiko's evaluation of the importance of the Kojuro to Hajimeshi?"

"Well, n-no, but—but he said things about the former Kojuro that—that shouldn't be discussed in front of the younger students."

Toshi-hito's voice altered imperceptibly from summer stream to winter ice. "And does Hotanu decide what the younger students may safely hear? Do I? Does even the Kojuro?" Hotanu did not answer but hunched down as if to try and appear invisible. Toshi-hito went on: "Would you deny the blind man his cane? We are all blind when it comes to knowledge; we can never know how much we have not yet learned. To ignore a truth, no matter how undesirable, strips you of that which helps you to see the world for what it really is. And a blind man without a cane is poor at guiding himself, let alone guiding others."

After letting this sink in for a moment, Toshi-hito said quietly to the group, "As Hotanu appears to have sincere respect for the heritage of the Kojuro, perhaps he will share with us his knowledge of the Kojuro's lineage, starting with the First from the Time of Founding. I'm sure the younger students will benefit from the history."

With a groan Hotanu rose, and as he started reciting the history of the Kojuro's line the older students settled in for a long discourse.

Shiko watched Toshi-hito, as the Master once again appeared to drift off into meditation. The Master never really 'left' the discussions, thought Shiko; but he always seemed to be able to do several things at once. His powers of concentration were quite remarkable.

"After the First," droned Hotanu, "there was a period of disagreement over who should succeed him as Kojuro…"

Shiko tried listening with half an ear, as Toshi-hito did, and concentrating the rest of his mind on other things. He focused on the Master's face, as something to anchor his thoughts to while he explored elsewhere.

Watching his Master's eyes as they stared fixedly off into the distance, Shiko pondered Toshi-hito's curious behavior. It was, he thought, quite unlike the Master to interject his comments during the student's dialogue period. But then, Shiko too had been perplexed by Hotanu's objections. It was uncommon for Deshi to publicly contradict one another; usually they discussed differing points of view quietly, coming to a consensus of opinion. Perhaps, reflected Shiko, it was a sign of the current times. Many of the 'civil' ways that used to govern how people, and kingdoms, behaved had become eroded over the last few years, and replaced by raised voices and strength of arms. He found it very sad.

"...and the Fifth Kojuro, and his consort, embarked on a journey across all of Hajimeshi..."

Toshi-hito had returned his gaze to the nearby castle walls, which the sun had now dried out. As Shiko watched, a change seemed to come over the Master's face. His eyes grew focused, and then a frown appeared. Shiko turned to see what had drawn Toshi-hito's attention.

An owl had alighted, silently, on the ground some distance away. Odd, Shiko thought, for a night bird to be out at this time of day. As he looked back and forth between the bird and Toshi-hito, it almost seemed as if the owl and the Master were actually staring at each other...

"When the Tenth Kojuro left only an infant son, a regent was appointed—"

Abruptly Toshi-hito said, "Thank you, Hotanu. That will be sufficient for today." He rose, and the students scrambled to their feet. "We will resume from this point tomorrow." Awkwardly, all of the students bowed quickly to their Master, who gave a short bow in return. As the group, including a slightly confused Hotanu, began to disperse, Toshi-hito intercepted Shiko. "A moment, please," he said, and the apprentice dutifully remained behind as his fellow students went off to their morning chores.

"Shiko," said Toshi-hito quietly once the other boys were gone, "you are familiar with the Hikari Pilgrimage?"

The apprentice was used to Toshi-hito's habit of asking unexpected questions; the Master held that a Deshi should always be prepared to impart whatever knowledge he possessed. Shiko thought quickly, managing to recall from some long-past lecture that the Hikari Pilgrimage had something to do with a special lantern. It was carried throughout the pilgrimage, providing symbolic protection while on the quest. "Yes, Master, I—I believe I have read about it."

"Good. I have a special task for you. I want you to update your research, and find out all that one might need to know about the actual commencement of such a journey."

When Toshi-hito did not elaborate on why he wished such information, Shiko bowed. "Certainly, Master. I will report my findings when I am done." With that, he turned and began walking down the path that led to the Deshi Archive in the priory.

Toshi-hito watched as his young charge set off across the field. He smiled to himself, reflecting with satisfaction on how a promising sapling had grown into a fine tree.

A soft 'hoot' from the still-present owl reminded him of the message he had just received. With an inward frown, he set off in the direction of the castle.

* * *

Shiko's path to the priory took him along the edge of the fields that lay outside the town of Hajimeshi. The farmers there were already hard at their day's work, but still had time to give a friendly wave as Shiko passed.

The farmers and townspeople always welcomed the Deshi. Besides the order's role in helping the people with meditation, and providing knowledge to all who asked, the Deshi were always willing to pitch in and lend a hand with communal projects, be it digging wells, or repairing the thatch covering the town's market shelter. As a result the Deshi enjoyed a high standing among the people of Hajimeshi.

The apprentice smiled and waved back to the farmers as he passed, the movement swirling the still-cool morning air up the wide arms of his Deshi robe. The robe, still new and not 'roughed in' like those worn by the Masters, lacked only the light brown sash about the waist that would mark his full accession to the Deshi order. Shiko still found it odd to wake in the morning and put on this dusky robe instead of his junior apprentice's tunic. Mixed with that feeling was also a small amount of pride, although it was nothing that he would ever show to his fellow students.

Shiko was the first to have reached this level among the Deshi at such an early age. In less than a week he was due to sit before the Senior Masters for the Oral Questioning, held once every three years. If he could satisfy the Senior Masters that he was ready to don the sash, he would be the youngest full Deshi in the order's history. The current holder of that distinction, an apprentice named Utaka, had lived some 200 years earlier, and ever since had been used as an example to Deshi apprentices to encourage them to study hard and to achieve their goals.

Utaka had been an inspiration to Shiko too. Although he had not set out to 'outdo' Utaka's achievement, once it was clear to Shiko that it was a possibility, it had become his singular goal to become the youngest Deshi. It was silly, he knew; and yet to be considered an example to others, perhaps for hundreds of years, was something he found very inspiring. He used it as his own motivation during those cold nights spent huddled before a single candle, trying to decipher the writing of a long-dead scribe on some arcane subject prescribed by one of the Masters.

Shiko's route skirted the stable area that lay outside the castle walls. It was a path so familiar to him from his years of study with Toshi-hito that he padded along it without paying any attention to the way. As he walked he reached up and grasped the honsho he wore around his neck. The small pendant had been with him since the day he had been left on the Deshi Priory's doorstep as a toddler. Usually he didn't even realize that he was holding it, but today, as he looked down at the small medallion wrapped in his fingers, its cool metal felt odd to his touch. It prompted him to wonder again about who had left him at the Priory, and what the medallion meant…

But the question was immediately forgotten as soon as he rounded the corner of the castle battlements. Here, where the path led past the main gate, he had to stop abruptly. A large and colorful entourage was proceeding down the road leading to the gate, stretching so far in either direction that he would have to wait for it to pass in order to get to the priory.

There were at least thirty horses in the group, their riders bearing staffs from which long pennants flapped lazily in the breeze. Shiko had walked up just as the center of the entourage was passing. Directly before him were two ornate palanquins, each one borne by muscular, sweating men who stoically carried their burden onward toward the castle gate. The two palanquins concealed their occupants behind expensive silk curtains, so Shiko could not see who was arriving in such conspicuous style. Horses and riders alike were all festooned with a riot of flying tassels and jingling bells.

Not a typical group of Hajimeshi, thought Shiko. From their ostentation he surmised that they must be from Yutakashi, the wealthy trading city to the west. If so, their visit was undoubtedly related to the current tensions between the two kingdoms.

The tail end of the column was not yet past him when the lead horses stopped at the gate. Shiko could see the riders being greeted by Himitsu, the Kojuro's chamberlain. After much bowing and exchange of pleasantries the entourage resumed its march as it was led into the castle.

Once his way was clear Shiko continued on, filing away in his mind the curious sight of the Yutakashi visitors. He was exceedingly interested to know what had brought them to Hajimeshi, but that was a question for another time. For now, Master Toshi-hito had set him to a task.

* * *

The entourage from Yutakashi wound its way up the switch-backed path from the outer keep of the castle, slowly working its way toward the inner keep. The route was lined with rows of Hajimeshi soldiers, each wearing the sword of a warrior tucked into the sash of his uniform. The soldiers stood rigidly at ceremonial attention, staring straight before them and appearing to take no notice of the passing group of visitors.

Their stillness was but a façade, however, as at a single command the Hajimeshi soldiers could have moved as one body, drawing their swords and cutting down those that passed before them in less than a heartbeat.

These were the Castle Guard, reporting directly to Lord Itachi, the Kojuro's brother. Itachi was in charge of all of Hajimeshi's armies, but the Castle Guard formed an elite troop. Each man was hand picked, and while the Guard's role was ostensibly to protect Kimeru, in fact they operated almost as Itachi's personal escort. Their somber grey uniforms, bearing Itachi's distinctive crest, contrasted sharply with the colorful vestments of the Yutakashi, all of whom rode in silence as the group made its way into the heart of the castle. The Yutakashi escort, likewise handpicked men, and as well trained as the Castle Guard, kept their gazes turned directly forward, ignoring the ranks of grey that outnumbered them many times over.

Himitsu, the elderly chamberlain, led the visitors on foot. At each of the many gates that separated parts of the castle the local Captain of the Guard would formally bow to Himitsu, who would bow in return, and the Captain would signal his men to open the heavy wooden doors that led to the next section. It was a conspicuously ceremonial approach, designed to impress upon the visitors both the refinement of Hajimeshi, as well as its military preparedness.

Not that the Yutakashi, thought Himitsu, would have been uninformed on either point already. However, he reflected, it never does any harm to live up to people's expectations. Then they become complacent. Which makes them more easily surprised should one choose to deviate from those expectations…

Finally the entourage came to a halt before the entrance to the guest quarters. A double team of bearers supporting the lead palanquin was the first clue that its occupant was of larger-than-normal girth. As the exhausted bearers set their burden down gently upon the flagstones of the courtyard, Himitsu waited patiently for the visitor from Yutakashi to alight from his palanquin.

Despite his years the lanky Himitsu was not in the least winded from the long walk up the hill; in fact, he found such excursions exhilarating.

Many of the younger courtiers, freshly arrived for a season of service at the capital, were astounded when old Himitsu would invite them for early morning walks in the castle. He invariably left them quickly behind as he paced rapidly up the winding pathways, his long white beard flowing behind him over his shoulder.

Now he waited, with feigned cordiality, for fat old Lord Choshuka to heave his bulk down out of the palanquin. The two of them had met before and never under happy circumstances. But, thought Himitsu, those hands have long since been played; now a new game was being dealt.

As Choshuka finally managed to plant both feet upon the pavement in front of the chamberlain, Himitsu bowed before the corpulent envoy. "Welcome to Hajimeshi, Lord Choshuka," he said. "I hope your journey to us was a pleasant one?"

Choshuka, in a manner calculated to just border on offensive without appearing so, returned a slight bow to Himitsu. "I have had quite enough of being carried about. An active person such as myself finds it difficult to be restrained for so long. I must be up and about. I like to keep myself fit; no telling when one might have to take the field...or take the ladies, for that matter..." Himitsu, of course, maintained complete composure throughout this declaration, even though some of Choshuka's own retainers had difficulty in keeping a straight face. Choshuka tugged and adjusted his tight-fitting tunic. "Your roads are abominable. I will complain to the Kojuro that he really must improve them if he wants to benefit from Yutakashi trade."

As the visiting lord waxed on with his complaints, the other palanquin was deposited on the ground next to the first. With a whelp of protest, a pudgy, anxious face popped out from between the curtains. Its owner, a youth whose voice was yet to completely change, squeaked, "You dropped me! You barbarians, you dropped me!" The boy turned his head. "Dada! Did you see what they did? They—they—" The whining voice tapered off as its owner finally noticed Himitsu and the other Hajimeshi standing in the courtyard. "Oh...are we there?"

With a look of extreme annoyance Choshuka motioned sharply for the boy to alight from his palanquin and come stand beside him. To Himitsu he said stiffly, "My son, Choja."

Keeping his face perfectly still, Himitsu bowed to the chubby young man struggling his way out of the palanquin. "Welcome to Hajimeshi, master Choja." Inwardly he sighed. The Kojuro, he knew, would not be pleased with this one. Nor, he thought, would the Princess Mikasama. But then again, she had not been pleased with any of them...

Choshuka looked about impatiently. "As the Kojuro has not seen fit to greet me here, you may lead me to him now."

Ignoring the stated and implied insults, Himitsu said smoothly, "His Majesty is presently meeting with his Council of Ministers, attending to the daily needs of his people. Once he has fulfilled his obligations, I am sure he will be ready to welcome you formally." Choshuka huffed, and opened his mouth to retort, but was forestalled by the chamberlain saying, "It the meantime, I have prepared the Ambassadorial Quarters for you and your entourage. Knowing that you have been on the road for no little while, I have taken the liberty of preparing a small feast for our friends of Yutakashi." Choshuka closed his mouth at that, simply raising an eyebrow in inquiry. Himitsu continued softly, "Roasted mutaso. Sunaka with red sauce. And kuso wadimasa..." This last was a rare delicacy, usually reserved only for state occasions.

Choshuka sniffed, making a show of looking over his shoulder at his followers. How transparent he is, pondered Himitsu; not for a moment is he concerned with those unfortunates in his service.

"Yes, well," said Choshuka, "my people have served beyond the normal call of duty, having to put up with your terrible roads. They deserve some small reward. A light meal would do them some good. We will accept your invitation."

Himitsu bowed, which allowed him to hide a small smile. So easy, he thought. The more avaricious the mind, the simpler to manipulate.

Bravado notwithstanding, the noble lord had not, Himitsu knew, set foot outside his own palatial compound in Yutakashi for over two years. The chamberlain's spies always kept him well informed of the status of all of the powers that be, or would be, in the neighboring mercantile kingdom. Further, Himitsu was aware that Choshuka was a gastronome of unbridled proportions. It had been a simple matter to create an incomparable feast with which to divert his attention.

As the Hajimeshi grooms led the horses away to the stables, Himitsu led the Yutakashi party inside to the guest quarters.

* * *

As Shiko arrived at the priory he walked through the great open gate, always open to all that came seeking knowledge. He crossed the large courtyard, busy with activity at this hour of the morning as many of the apprentices trained at their daily martial arts exercises. It was not so long ago, Shiko reflected, that the martial instruction had simply been considered an effective means for focusing one's energy and concentration. Of late, however, it had seemed to take on a more practical importance, given the dangerous nature of solitary travel in the countryside where the Deshi frequently journeyed.

Across the whole northern length of the courtyard stretched the building that housed the Archive. A large, two-storied timber building, it was one of the largest structures outside of Hajimeshi castle. Shiko approached the sliding doors fronting the covered walkway along the courtyard, and knelt down to open them.

Ordinarily in Hajimeshi society one knelt to slide open a door if one knew that the occupier of the room was of a higher rank, for it was customary to then immediately bow. Among the Deshi, there was nothing considered of higher importance than the body of knowledge contained in the Archive, and thus the room itself was the recipient of Deshi respect. As Shiko opened the large door he dutifully bowed to its contents, which contained the fruits of hundreds of years of research from Deshi all over Tonogato.

Entering the room and closing the door behind him, Shiko drank in the familiar smell of parchment, ink, and candle smoke. He had spent many days and nights in the Archive; probably, he reflected, more time than he had spent in his own room.

The Archive was a single large chamber, its roof supported by massive curved beams. At regular intervals along the walls were huge window openings, running nearly from floor to ceiling, their many-paned surfaces letting in an abundance of natural light. Nearly every other inch of wall space was covered with rows of square openings, from which Shiko could see the rolled up ends of parchments: the books of the Deshi. Contained within the scrolls was the knowledge of many ages, and a Deshi could spend his entire life immersed in reading them. Quite a few of them did; there were those who never left the priory at all but instead served here in the Archive in the pursuit of knowledge or in the imparting of it to their fellow Deshi.

One such was Master Nobaka, the head archivist, and keeper of the Great Index. Hunched as always on his stool by the Index, he would look up from his work and cast a wary glance at anyone approaching the precious parchment stretched upon its frame. It mattered little whether one was apprentice or Master; Nobaka's protective gaze assessed one and all before allowing them close to the Index.

And with good reason, figured Shiko, for without the Index it would be next to impossible to find anything within the vast Archive. Across its surface the Index contained hundreds of little hand-drawn boxes, numbered and cross-numbered to match the parchment holes along the walls of the Archive. It was the work of many hands, numerous Deshi having spent years categorizing and filing the scrolls. A familiar 'customer' of the Archive, Shiko received the usual unsmiling nod from Nobaka that he knew was his signal to proceed, before the older man craned his long neck back over the scroll in front of him.

Shiko grinned to himself. He had spent many nights with the old archivist, listening as Nobaka had talked for hours about one obscure body of knowledge or another. Thus he knew that beneath the grim exterior, Nobaka's love of learning fired the man's passion as much as that of any artist.

As Shiko studied the Index, looking for references to the Hikari, he pondered the Master's question. Now why in the world, he wondered, did Toshi-hito want to know about a Hikari Pilgrimage?

Now that he had more time to think about it, more facts about the Hikari slipped into his head. He remembered, from some of his earlier lectures, that such a pilgrimage was once considered a sacred journey. Each of the kingdoms of Tonogato, including Hajimeshi, and all of their rulers and subjects, were bound by ancient tradition to respect the sanctity of the Hikari. If he recalled correctly, though, no such pilgrimages had taken place for a long time, since probably well before the days of Toshi-hito's great-grandfather. It wasn't too hard to figure out why, either. The increasing isolation of the kingdoms from one another in recent years, the rising lawlessness spreading unchecked in the hinterlands, and the typically violent debates that seemed to pass for diplomacy between the kingdoms, made it little wonder that pilgrims found scant encouragement to venture across Tonogato.

So why, wondered Shiko, was Toshi-hito interested in knowing the details of such a pilgrimage? Unless...could the Kojuro possibly be planning a Hikari Pilgrimage?

Leaning back from the Index, in an excited rush of thoughts Shiko considered the possibilities. Toshi-hito was, after all, Kimeru's personal Spiritual Guide; if anyone would know of such plans, it would be the Master. And the Kojuro's policies always stressed the need for reconciliation and accommodation with Hajimeshi's neighbors.

But Shiko doubted that the Kojuro's health would allow him to undertake such a journey. He had heard rumors that on some days Kimeru could not rise from his bed. The other apprentices were always gossiping about such things, and it seemed to Shiko that there had been much speculation lately on the state of the Kojuro's health, and what would happen should he die.

When the Kojuro's elder brother, Fugawari, had passed away with no children, Kimeru had come to the throne. But Kimeru had a daughter, Princess Mikasama, and the inheritance would have to go through her. She had not yet married, though; and only a son, or son-in-law, could inherit the Kojuro's title. Some speculated that Kimeru's younger brother, Lord Itachi, would become regent and then hand over authority to Mikasama's husband once she married. However, Itachi was, by all accounts, not a pleasant man. Who knew what he might do, should he come to power?

Well, reasoned Shiko, he wouldn't find out the reason for Toshi-hito's query until he had located the information that the Master had requested of him. For now, it was time to stick his head into some scrolls and begin a few hours of musty hunting.

* * *

"But, Your Majesty, is such an expedition wise at this time?" The ingratiating voice of Takamaru curled out of his mouth much the way his words managed to wrap themselves around almost any argument. As the Omo Deshi, the most senior member of the order in Hajimeshi, Takamaru had the privilege of attending the Kojuro's Council Meetings. It was a privilege extended to him by the previous Kojuro and one which Kimeru, the present ruler, dearly wished he could revoke.

The half-dozen Council Ministers, arrayed across the floor of the Great Audience Hall of Hajimeshi Castle, knelt in a semi-circle before Kimeru. Although their ruler had once been muscular and solidly built, illness had clearly taken its toll. Now he struggled to remain sitting upright in that perfect ceremonial stillness required of a formal meeting of the Ministers. It was a measure of his determination that despite his discomfort Kimeru never let a hint of the pain he felt cross his cool visage. He displayed nothing but the stern face of a man used to having to deal with those of difficult mien. And those gathered now before him were certainly among the most difficult.

Each of the Ministers, representing powerful factions within Hajimeshi, commanded the personal loyalty of many retainers. They were therefore a force to be reckoned with; hence, their inclusion in the Council. Although none wore a sword while in the Kojuro's presence, they were no less dangerous for that. Kimeru smiled grimly to himself; he always preferred to keep the tigers together. In that way they spent as much of their time plotting against one another as they did against him.

The walls of the Audience Hall, faced with dark lustrous wood, made an appropriately somber setting for discussions of affairs of state. The floor on which the Ministers knelt was inlaid with oparu, a rare stone with small seams of gold running through it. The gold caught the light from the sconces set around the walls and tossed it back in diminutive sparkles. A spectacular room, thought Kimeru. Such a pity that so many of its occupants are not worthy of the mortar used to inlay the stones…

"Surely there is a proper time and place," continued Takamaru, his sharp nose bobbing up and down, "to undertake such a momentous journey as a Hikari Pilgrimage? Should we not, at this time, focus our efforts on the dangers the Hajimeshi people face from the kingdom of Shukyoshi?"

Inwardly Kimeru groaned. As the Kojuro of Hajimeshi all his subjects revered him. Yet few of them had any inkling that he had to spend most of his time dealing with fools such as the Omo Deshi. Quietly he replied, "Our people will have even greater difficulties if we ignore the prophecies of the Shizen." He sat upon an elevated dais in the center of the Hall, leaning with one elbow on a small stand in order to give himself some support. So long as he did not have to move, he could at least project a strong appearance.

His illness had begun nearly a year earlier. At first it had seemed nothing, a passing disability such as might afflict any man his age. But then it had grown progressively worse, the court healer at a loss to reverse the sickness that slowly devoured the Kojuro's health. Like vultures circling a wounded animal, over the last few months the political factions and their figureheads had begun maneuvering themselves for what they saw as the inevitable change in power. It would, Kimeru knew, take all of his influence and force of will to keep them from outright political warfare with one another. And that was absolutely vital, lest all of his plans come undone before the hardest trials, yet to come.

The meeting had already dragged on for several hours, taxing both the Kojuro's strength and his patience. But it was essential that he lay out his intentions for the pilgrimage now. Time, both his own and Hajimeshi's, did not allow him the luxury of a more subtle approach.

"The Shizen are our guides, of course, sire," Takamaru went on. "But the insidious infiltration of our people's minds by the Shukyoshi priests is—"

"—is nothing compared to being overrun by an army from Yutakashi!" interrupted Lord Itachi. The Kojuro's younger brother was as coarse and unrefined as the Omo Deshi was well-oiled. He was a soldier by both trade and temperament. Unlike Kimeru's stern countenance Itachi's was an unprepossessing face; some might even have called it delicate, although none would have been so foolish as to do so within his hearing. That face, however, was hidden behind a thick beard, which allowed Itachi to present the rather sterner image that he preferred. The beard had the added advantage for him of inspiring his men, as they thus felt that their commander identified with them rather than with the clean-shaven nobles of the Hajimeshi court.

While Itachi talked he jabbed the air with his tarka, his short ceremonial staff, as if it were the sword he normally wore at his side. "The Shukyoshi are nothing more than a band of crazed monks. They strut around with swords and call themselves 'warrior priests' but in a real battle their robes would tangle their legs before they ever had a chance to draw steel. The real danger lies in an army from Yutakashi, which is forming even as we speak." He turned to Kimeru, dismissing Takamaru from the discussion. "Your Majesty, I have reports that within a fortnight the Yutakashi will have gathered sufficient men to overrun our border battalions." He grasped the free end of his tarka with his other hand, casually bending the slender wooden staff as he spoke. "We must mobilize the Northern Army at once, lest we be caught unprepared."

Takamaru smoothly interjected, "Of course, my Lord Itachi is best qualified among all of us to assess military might. However, Your Majesty," he said, glancing toward Itachi, "not all attacks manifest themselves as something as simple as brute force. In far greater danger is the purity of Hajimeshi souls, which are threatened daily by the heretical thoughts of the Shukyoshi. I believe we should—"

"Enough!" said Kimeru sharply. "I did not summon you here for a debate on who is more fearsome than whom!" He was interrupted by a coughing fit, forcing both Takamaru and Itachi to subside into silence.

The Kojuro struggled to regain his composure, annoyed that he had allowed himself to lose his temper in front of the Ministers. He had expected their shock at his suggestion that a Hikari pilgrimage should be undertaken, and had anticipated their objections and their petty bickering. Even so, in the face of their continued obstinacy he found his own self-control sorely tested.

These men are not tigers, he decided, but wolves, howling at the moon. They are so blind; can they not see how narrow their concerns are? How meaningless, when compared to the Darkness? Already the Darkness is seeping across the land. There is famine in the south, and thieves and brigands control more of the roads between the kingdoms than even Itachi would care to admit. Slowly, insidiously; that is how the Darkness attacks. Not through a grand battle, at least not until the very end. When the forces of light have been worn down, divided into bickering camps of little men, like these...

He spoke firmly, wanting there to be no misunderstanding as to his intentions. "As I have said, I have received a prophecy from the Shizen. The Kotaishi must be located, or Tonogato will fall. All of Tonogato, not just Hajimeshi! So the Kotaishi *will* be found. Is that understood?"

As one, all of the ministers bowed. The crackling of the flames in the sconces was the only sound in the room. Kimeru kept them bowed over in silence to reinforce his point.

He understood, better than anyone, how tenuous was his hold over them, based on years of tradition and his own force of personality. No man among them would outwardly disobey the Kojuro, but he was only a man, and a none-too-healthy example of one, of which no one in the room was unaware. And just like those circling vultures, eventually one of them would be bold enough to strike. Not in public, not here, he knew; the blow, if it came, would be done quietly, whether it was a political uprising or a dagger in the dark. Thus Kimeru had to gauge carefully how far he could push, and when he must placate the quarrelsome egos arrayed before him. "Hajimeshi always faces dangers," he said, "from one quarter or another. I trust in each of you to deal with your own areas of responsibility." At these words, the ministers straightened. "I must consider *all* of the dangers, and lead us on the path that will save us from whichever is the greatest."

He shifted on his platform, the better to see each of the men in the room. Now, he thought; I must convince them now, or this interminable discussion will continue for more hours yet. "A thousand years ago the Darkness nearly overwhelmed Tonogato. Only the combined efforts of all the kingdoms prevented that catastrophe. Had not one man, the Kotaishi, brought the kingdoms together, then none of us would be sitting here having this debate!" He coughed again, mentally cursing once more the ailments that plagued his body. "The Shizen have foreseen that the Darkness is once more gathering, preparing to emerge from the depths of the earth. And only the Kotaishi can unite the kingdoms of Tonogato. Unless the kingdoms join together, as they did a millennium ago, we will all fall prey to the Darkness."

"Of course, Your Majesty," said Takamaru, bowing his head. "Your wisdom is inspiring to us all." The Omo Deshi betrayed no hint of his innermost thoughts to his sovereign; it was invariably an obsequious face that he presented to the Kojuro.

A thin, pallid man with a penchant for pursing his lips before he spoke, Takamaru was the titular head of the Deshi. In no way popular among his own brethren, the Omo Deshi's capacity for placation had, nonetheless, served his interests well in the past. Under Fugawari, Kimeru's impulsive late brother, Takamaru had extended his grasp and become one of the court favorites, providing political rather than spiritual advice. He was finding, however, that his position with the present Kojuro was not nearly as agreeable.

Inclining his head toward Kimeru, Takamaru said, "The Shizen are very wise. I am sure a journey throughout Tonogato, showing that

Hajimeshi leads the way in the search for cooperation, will provide us with considerable good will. And it will naturally allow us to promote the correctness of the Hajimeshi way of life to those beyond our borders."

The Omo Deshi's words caused a sudden stir among the men in the room. One, unable to restrain himself, issued a muffled snort.

Amidst the muttering, Itachi looked sharply over at Takamaru. Clearly put off balance by the Omo Deshi's sudden shift in position his eyes smoldered, but just as clearly he was determined not to let the initiative swing to his chief rival. Before Takamaru could follow up his advantage the Kojuro's brother spoke up loudly. "Your Majesty, such an expedition carries with it the pride of our entire land." He made a show of placing his tarka staff down on the floor before him, as if in supplication. "If it is the will of the Shizen that we undertake such a quest it should not be entrusted to any but your most loyal servants. I request," as he bowed to Kimeru, "that as your royal brother I be allowed to lead the Hikari Pilgrimage in the search for the Kotaishi."

Takamaru's expression was unchanged, yet Kimeru noted the bony fingers twisting furiously at one of the ties binding his Deshi robe. The Kojuro smiled, displaying his pleasure at his brother's proposition. Excellent, he thought; this saves me the trouble of having to find a reason for him to go. My poor brother, you are such a fool. Why was I cursed with such irksome siblings? "Thank you, Lord Itachi. I could desire none other than my own family to lead Hajimeshi on such an important journey."

A servant slid open the wooden shoji door leading into the Hall. He bowed from where he knelt upon the floor in the hallway outside. "Your Majesty, Master Toshi-hito has arrived, per your summons."

Kimeru knew that he had not summoned Toshi-hito. It was their personal signal; if Toshi-hito had himself announced in this way, Kimeru knew that his Spiritual Guide had something of greatest urgency to report. He nodded to the servant, who bowed and slid closed the rice paper-covered door. Appearing to wrap up the proceedings, Kimeru said offhandedly to Itachi, "I heard a report that one of the guards on the Border Bridge is missing."

Itachi, with barely the shortest pause, replied, "I am sure the man will turn up, Your Majesty. He has a poor record, and should have been punished some time ago. He will not be assigned to sentry duty again."

Kimeru grunted. "I see. Well, my lords, I must now extend the hospitality of Hajimeshi to the esteemed Lord Choshuka and his son. If, that is, my daughter will deign to speak with the young man in question." He was rewarded with a titter from the assembled ministers. "If she finds him agreeable, perhaps we may be able to avert future difficulties with Yutakashi." Kimeru knew this to be a hope without substance. He had heard enough about Choshuka's son to know that his daughter would reject him out of hand, as she had all the rest. But while Choshuka was here Kimeru could extend the 'negotiations,' and perhaps gain a little more time to defuse a crisis between the two kingdoms that was threatening to slip out of control. "We will adjourn until tomorrow. Thank you for your advice." The ministers bowed as Kimeru, with some difficulty, rose and shuffled slowly out to the adjoining balcony overlooking the Sacred Grove.

Takamaru was furious at not knowing about Itachi's plans. As he swept out of the room he did not even acknowledge the presence of his fellow Deshi, Toshi-hito, waiting in the hallway outside. All he could think of was the Kojuro. The man was a fool, he thought. Wasting resources on a pointless expedition. Darkness? The only Darkness was that clouding the Kojuro's mind!

Takamaru was nevertheless also angry with himself. He should have anticipated that Itachi would volunteer to lead this ridiculous quest. That cretin, he fumed; he must have already known about this expedition! Why else would he have tried to place himself at the head of it?

Takamaru's thoughts churned rapidly. He had worked long and hard to bring the Deshi to their current position of influence, and he was not about to let it all be swept away because *this* Kojuro could not appreciate what his order could accomplish. Under Takamaru's leadership the Deshi had been brought out of the backwoods and, via their knowledge, could become a power to be reckoned with in Hajimeshi. There were many among his brethren, he knew, who resented his changes as unwanted intrusions into their simple little lives of solitude. But for all their bookish knowledge not one of them understood the real world as he did. It was for that world that he was preparing the Deshi, whether they wanted it or not.

Pursing his lips as he strode down the palace hallway he pondered the pilgrimage and how to salvage something from such an exercise in futility.

Itachi, by contrast, felt immensely pleased with himself, as he too passed by the waiting Toshi-hito without even a glance. The Kojuro's brother didn't know what scheme the Omo Deshi might have concocted, but he felt certain that whatever it was he had now caused it severe disruption. At first, when Takamaru had suddenly supported the idea of the quest, he had wondered what the slime had been up to. The Omo Deshi must have already known about his brother's ridiculous idea, he had decided, and had then set him up to oppose it so that the Deshi could appear conciliatory. Well, Takamaru was mistaken if he had thought that only he could play political games; today, he had learned that he was not the only one with surprises!

Itachi was not worried about having to go on the expedition. He had needed an excuse to leave Hajimeshi, and now here was a ready made one. For he had plans of his own that involved a trip to Yutakashi. This foolish crusade of his brother's, he had realized, would provide an excellent cover.

Once he had concluded his 'business' in the neighboring kingdom he would slip away to the Northern Forest, where his men were even now secretly assembling. Then events would be set into motion that would change forever the face of Hajimeshi, and his brother's nonsensical whims would cease to be a concern.

As the last of the ministers took their leave, Toshi-hito passed through into the Great Audience Hall. The Kojuro's advisor was untroubled by the lack of notice the ministers paid him. Indeed, he mused, far better that none consider him anything other than a simple Deshi, here to help his sovereign mediate. It was an image that he, and Kimeru, had cultivated carefully over the years. If his Deshi training had provided him with anything, it was the capacity for patience.

He knew the Kojuro would be on the balcony; it was Kimeru's favorite viewpoint. Walking out into the sunlight he saw Kimeru sitting in his usual spot, leaning against the stone railing. Toshi-hito stood quietly behind him and took in the same view.

Stretching out in a large crescent from the base of the tower holding the Great Audience Hall, the vast sweep of the Grove was a miniature forest that reached right up to the castle walls. It was said that there were plants and trees growing there that grew nowhere else in Hajimeshi, or any place else in Tonogato. But no one could really say for sure, as entry to the Sacred Grove was forbidden to all but the Kojuro. Although, as Toshi-hito knew all too well, this was not strictly true...

"I wish you could have seen their faces, Toshi-hito," said Kimeru, aware of his advisor's presence even though he had not turned around. "I don't believe I have ever seen that room full of old women so speechless."

"I take it, sire, that they did not remain speechless for long?"

"No, no, there were plenty of speeches after that." Toshi-hito stepped forward and sat down as the Kojuro continued. "Itachi surprised me, however. He volunteered to lead the pilgrimage. I'm not sure what he was thinking. Perhaps he thought to head off some supposed scheme of Takamaru's."

Toshi-hito chuckled. "They are both so suspicious of one another, each would naturally assume that the other would have some hand in hindering his own plans."

Kimeru smiled. "Like two cats come across one another in a dark alley—the mere sight of each other causes their tails to rise. Mostly resulting in obnoxious wailing, ehhh?" His tone then became serious. "So, old friend, what news do you have?"

Toshi-hito, equally somber, said, "One of our friends has observed an unfortunate deed. The guard on the Border Bridge was murdered, sire, probably by an Anasatsu assassin from the description. The killer was observed heading off towards the castle during the storm last night."

Neither man spoke for some time, until Kimeru said, "Very curious, no?"

"Indeed, majesty."

"My brother appears unconcerned about the missing guard."

"He who sleeps with a sword, sire, has little to fear from the night."

*   *   *

The Sacred Grove was not the only woodland atop the hill. Elsewhere around Hajimeshi Castle other gardens and forested areas dotted the surroundings. One such verdant patch was the Royal Garden, where a young couple, sheltered from the eyes of casual passers-by, sat on a stone bench and enjoyed the shade from the sheltering branches of a joro tree.

The woman was coyly hiding her face behind a fan. But her concealment was mostly pretence, as the fan regularly fell away to reveal a laughing smile. Her companion, dressed in the uniform of a Captain of the Castle Guard, was telling her another story. This one caused her to let out a whoop of laughter, quickly stifled by her hand over her mouth.

The delighted eyes of the young woman, set well back over cheeks framing a buoyant smile, glittered in the morning light. Her long, silken black hair cascaded down, splashing across her shoulders and down the back of her kimono in vivid contrast to the garment's pure white silk. So subtle were the curves and lines of the kimono that its wearer appeared to have been wrapped softly in a passing cloud.

With a furtive glance around her as she struggled to control her giggling, Mikasama, Princess of Hajimeshi and daughter of the Kojuro, admonished her companion. "Nakama, you mustn't make me laugh so hard! What if Komori finds us here?"

"Let her," said Nakama. "That old mother hen keeps you cooped up like a chick who wanders too far from the brood." Nakama, like the Princess, was not quite twenty years of age, and possessed an open, friendly face and genial manner quite out of keeping with his occupation as a soldier. He had, nonetheless, already served for several years in the Castle Guard where his skill as an archer, and a natural gift for leading men, had gained him rapid promotion. Today, as he did every time he and the Princess met, he wore his finest tunic: the sleeves starched perfectly, every fold arranged in just the right place. His bow lay nearby; just as a swordsman would never stray far from his blade, so too did he keep his bow to hand at all times.

"Oh, I know, I know," said the Princess. "Nana-san means well. She just…worries about me, that's all."

"She worries about you too much. She doesn't see the Princess that I see."

Mikasama raised her chin in mock inquiry. "Oh? And what Princess do you see, Captain Nakama?"

"I see—" started Nakama in the same lighthearted vein, and then more seriously, "I see a hyason bird, soaring above the highest clouds, unrestrained by convention." Mikasama blushed, and Nakama continued. "I see a young lady who looks out at the world and sees it with her own eyes, not as what others tell her it is. And I see…." His own face reddened slightly. "I see a beautiful young woman, whose eyes light up whichever room she enters. And whose voice rings sweeter than all the bells heard throughout the land."

Flustered, her heart fluttering as much as the fan behind which she hid her gaze, Mikasama for once was speechless. Oh Nakama, she thought; you're the only one who can see inside my heart. Why oh why did you have to be a soldier? None of those courtiers my father keeps sending after me are worth a thimbleful of air compared to you.

It was, she knew, her duty to find among that constant parade of young men a suitable future husband. The Princess was the Kojuro's heir, but she herself could not assume that mantle. By ancient tradition only a male could become Kojuro, enter the Scared Grove, and seek the wisdom of the Shizen. Hence there was fierce competition for the Princess' hand, for whoever became her husband was destined to rule Hajimeshi after her father. And with the Kojuro's increasing illness of late, more suitors than usual were to be found loitering about the castle hallways.

Mikasama would have none of them. Not one single man among them was the least bit interested in her, or even felt compelled to speak with her before presenting his case to her father. To them she was nothing more than a means to an end. And an inconvenient means at that, if the gossip she had overheard from the servants bore any truth at all.

Had her father arranged her marriage when she had been younger, too young to understand, perhaps it would have been different. But now she was aware of what was going on, and she had no desire to simply be a stepping-stone for some ambitious courtier.

Nakama, she knew, was different. He was not of noble birth, and so could never marry her or become the Kojuro. In truth, she recalled, their paths would ordinarily never have crossed had it not been for that chance encounter in the spring, just as the blossoms were coming to life...

She had been out riding, enjoying one of her brief periods of freedom from the stuffy confines of the court. She always found it exhilarating to feel the wind in her hair, and to be able to roam at will throughout the plains that surrounded Hajimeshi. If she rode fast enough she could just about keep her escorting soldiers behind her, allowing her the decidedly uncommon sensation of feeling alone.

On that particular day she had recklessly attempted a jump that was far too high for her horse. Together they had fallen, and she had been thrown to the ground. She had not been hurt but her horse had injured a leg badly enough that Mikasama could not ride him back to the Castle. Nakama had been in charge of her escort on that trip, and had sent a rider back to the stables for assistance. Then the young Captain had hoisted her aboard his own horse, leading it on foot during the long trek back.

She had been distraught over the injury she had caused her horse, and in order to sooth her concerns Nakama had told her stories. She had been surprised at the extent of both his wit and his knowledge, and to this day he could still make her laugh with his seemingly endless store of tales, most of which Komori would be horrified to hear her listening to. She had asked for him to lead her escort again when next she rode, and he had done so ever since. Their differences in station, oddly enough, had permitted a degree of familiarity between soldier and Princess that Mikasama could not share with any of her peers. During their subsequent rides together they had continued to talk, endlessly it had seemed, and about everything.

Mikasama had found herself slowly being drawn to the handsome soldier, and more and more she had found ways to spend time in his company. As time had passed she had observed his honesty, and his compassion; he had a sense of honor that was all but completely lacking in the hapless suitors that pressed in upon her at court. And she had found herself all at sea as he had captivated her heart.

She knew that she was not supposed to become 'involved' with anyone outside the rarified confines of the nobility, let alone an archer from the Castle Guard. She had a role to play, and her life had been mapped out for her from the time she was barely out of the cradle. But those doing the planning had not factored in the spirit of the girl who had now grown into a strong-willed young woman. She had her father's temperament, and was used to having her own way. Any servants or underlings about the court who crossed her were quick to find themselves on the losing end of a serious tongue-lashing.

Now, Mikasama struggled with her emotions. All that separated her from a man who held her dear for who she was and not what she represented was a creased paper fan. That, and centuries of tradition and customs.

Well, customs be damned, she thought. I am not going to let them get in the way of this! I know, and my *heart* knows, that Nakama is whom I love. I may never find another like him. What right do traditions and customs have to keep us from being happy?

She reached out with her free hand, hesitating but a moment. Then she touched his cheek, gently stroking his face. "Nakama, my dear sweet Nakama...I—"

"Ah, there you be!" A loud commotion accompanied the bustling arrival of a small, elderly woman. So slight that she might blow away in a strong breeze, and old enough to be Mikasama's grandmother, she was dressed in the modest garments of a servant. Her grey hair was tied up in a tangled bun atop her head, loose strands falling this way and that. Her demeanor, however, was as purposeful as her appearance was chaotic. "Been looking all over for you, Mika."

With a sigh Mikasama dropped her hand once more to her lap. "Yes, Nana-san?"

"Juyama having a mighty big fit. 'Where's that girl?' he say. 'She no finishing her studies!'" Komori's accent marked her as a foreigner; in fact, she had come originally from Chigasa, one of the lands across the Southern Sea from Tonogato, which had been one of the few facts that Mikasama, or anyone else, had ever been able to pry out of the curmudgeonly caretaker.

Pointedly ignoring Nakama's unchaperoned presence with the Princess, Komori continued quietly, "Perhap best you go back to your books now, hey? Nana-san no want to have to explain to your Papa why school master falling over dead from one of his fits."

"All right, Nana-san," said Mikasama reluctantly, knowing that it was fruitless to argue with her caretaker. If there was anyone in the entire castle more stubborn than Mikasama, it was Komori. The Princess rose to go and Komori walked a few steps away down the garden path to wait for her. Nakama stood and bowed to the Princess, and Mikasama inclined her head in return. She was surprised when Nakama reached for her hand while still bent over, and briefly held it to his lips. Komori, ostensibly looking off toward the castle, cleared her throat loudly. Nakama quickly released Mikasama's hand as he straightened. "Until tomorrow, my Lady," he said.

Hiding her blush behind her fan, Mikasama turned and joined Komori. As the two began walking down the path, they suddenly heard Nakama shout. "Lady!"

As the two women turned around, Mikasama was startled to see that Nakama had taken up his bow, and had an arrow already notched. Before she could react, he had leveled the bow in her direction. Just as she felt Komori's hand grip her arm she realized that Nakama was aiming at something over her head, where a tree arched over the garden path. She saw Nakama release the bowstring, and watched as the arrow flew; looking up, she heard a rustle as the arrow passed through the branches overhead. Something small dropped down out of the tree right over her and instinctively she reached out her hands to catch it. With a gentle slap, a bright red apaya fruit landed in her fingers.

Her shock turned to delight as she marveled at both Nakama's skill and his daring. Komori, much less impressed, chose this action to finally acknowledge Nakama's presence. "Stupid!" she shouted at him. "Why you goin' around scarin' old women like that? Got nothin' better to do than shoot at trees?" Pulling on Mikasama's arm, she said to the Princess, "Come, Mika. Leave stupid soldier-boy to his tricks."

At Komori's insistent tug, Mikasama began walking with her, tucking the prized apaya into a fold of her kimono. With a final glance over her shoulder at Nakama, she saw him smile at her as he slung his bow over his shoulder. She chanced a quick wave before they rounded a corner and he was out of sight.

As they continued on the path back toward the castle Komori kept up a non-stop litany of complaints. "Idiot boy. Give Nana-san a bad heart, stupid tricks like that. Should be out doin' soldier-things, not scarin' harmless old women." Mikasama paid no attention as she walked alongside the 'harmless old woman.' The reassuring feel of Nakama's apaya against Mikasama's body reminded her of his laugh.

"What you smilin' at, hey?" said Komori. "Not worried Nana-san gonna fall over dead from fright? Just go right on, pay no mind, huh?"

"No, of course not, Nana-san," said Mikasama, as they reached the doorway to the castle. With one more glance back toward the garden, she said absently, "Where would I be without you?"

Noting her charge's preoccupation, Komori only grunted and ushered her inside. The heavy wooden door closed decisively behind them.

Nakama watched Mikasama's progress all the way back to the castle through a gap in the hedge that surrounded the garden. As she disappeared from view inside he sighed and sat down once more upon their bench. He brought his bow back around in front of him and unstrung it, the sudden loosening of the string mirroring his own state of mind.

From the very beginning, on that very first day with Mikasama's injured horse, Nakama had been more than happy to talk with such an engaging, and intelligent, young woman. He had recognized in her a mind equal to his own, and so enjoyed their challenging conversations. It had never occurred to him, due to the vast gulf between their social positions, that he had been anything other than a convenient companion for the Princess. That is until he had found himself, almost without realizing it, falling in love with her.

Mikasama affected him in ways he still didn't understand; she was quite unlike any other woman he had ever met. He did and said things with her that he wouldn't have dreamed of doing with anybody else, let alone a princess. He looked again at the spot where she had sat next to him and placed his hand down where she had been. With a start he realized how silly he must appear, and he quickly looked up to see if anyone was watching. Seeing no one, he gathered up his bow and walked out of the garden in the direction of the barracks.

For some time the garden was still, nothing but the rustling of leaves in the light breeze to disturb the quiet slumber of the flowerbeds. Then something else moved, something definitely not part of the natural setting.

From behind a large hedge, hidden from view from the stone bench on the garden's edge, a lone figure emerged. Dressed in gardener's clothes, he cleaned off the dirt from his hand tools and packed them away. With a glance in the direction to which Nakama had retired, and then over at the castle door that had swallowed up Mikasama, he leisurely made his way off in a third direction. His course did not include the groundskeeper's lodge; but it did happen to take him close by the quarters of Himitsu, the chamberlain.

✷   ✷   ✷

The lamplighter stopped along the parapet wall, transferring the flame from his taper to the lamp set along the wall's crenellated edge. The sun was just setting in the distance, and soon only his lamps would illuminate Hajimeshi castle.

As he made his rounds he passed the Banquet Hall. He stopped to listen to the loud and drunken voices of the Yutakashi troupe, who were still in high revel. With a snort of disgust, he continued on. Scandalous, he thought. No sense of decency or moderation, those Yutakashi.

His brother had gone there once, to Yutakashi, long ago. When he'd come back, he'd talked about the wonderful, grand streetlights in Yutakashi, all covered in glass. Well, thought the lamplighter, they'd certainly need plenty of light to find their way home if this sort of drunken carousing was typical.

He snorted again as he lit the last of the parapet lamps and started down the stone steps toward the Kojuro's chambers. Fine glass streetlights or no, they can keep them, he decided. Honest, hard-working men do just fine with simple lamps.

Sudori, the servant kneeling on duty before the doors of the Kojuro's Sleeping Chamber, observed the slow approach of the lamplighter. He could tell when the man was coming, even from around the corner of the passage, for when each lamp was lit there was a small burst of light. Once the lamplighter rounded the corner, Sudori watched him deftly transfer the flame from his taper into the lamps along the wall.

Sudori had always been impressed by the lamplighter's skill in handling the flame. Tonight, he thought, tonight I shall ask him how he learned to do it. But just as he worked up the courage to speak to the older man, he heard the sound of the court healer inside the Sleeping Chamber approaching the doors. Quickly Sudori slid them open and the healer passed into the hallway. As Sudori closed the doors softly, the healer turned toward him. "I have given your master some potions to help him rest. See that he is not disturbed tonight." With a curt nod to acknowledge Sudori's bow, the healer strode off down the now brightly lit hall.

Sudori saw that the lamplighter had already finished and moved on to another section of the castle. With a sigh he settled himself in for the long night.

Within the Sleeping Chamber the Kojuro lay upon a raised platform that formed the royal bed. The floor was covered with the softest and highest quality rugs, while the platform itself was draped with thick comforters. The Kojuro rested atop these, with several large pillows to support his head. The rest of the room was empty save for a small table to one side, holding a low candle that flickered uncertainly. Its wavering light cast eerie shadows across the room's walls, which were lined with carved openwork screens. The screens were ancient, having been created long before Hajimeshi became a kingdom. The small openings through the wood had been fashioned into minutely detailed hunting scenes, as it had been practiced in days long past, before the hunt had become nothing more than a harmless chase. Here, the screens showed wilder deeds: a boar being driven to ground, a lion being held at bay. The shadows, dancing across the screens, made the pictures almost seem alive: the hunters moving in pursuit, the prey dashing for freedom.

Several hours passed, marked only by Kimeru's labored breathing and the slow guttering of the candle. When finally it went out, the shadows slipped away and the room seemed to become even more silent. For a long time, nothing stirred.

Then, from above, a ceiling panel slowly slid back. Cautiously, a head emerged, looking long and hard at the sleeping form of the Kojuro. The head turned and scanned the room, looking for signs of anything amiss. Seeing nothing, the head momentarily disappeared. A pair of legs descended, as a figure dressed in black lowered himself through the opening. Hanging within a few feet of the floor, the intruder released his grip, touching down in a springing crouch to absorb both shock and sound. Poised, he listened for anything that might signal a trap. Hearing nothing, he moved forward silently on padded feet, toward the sleeping platform. Pausing but a moment, he reached over his shoulder to grasp the hilt of his sword. Just as the oiled blade began moving silently in its sheath, a sound like the sighing of the wind swept into the room. Followed by another, and another: arrows, flying from both sides of the room, began peppering the assassin.

With a grunt of pain the Anasatsu tried to move forward, struggling to get his blade out. The room was suddenly flooded with light, and shouting men, as the carved screens through which the arrows had been fired were pushed aside and hooded lanterns were uncovered. From narrow recesses behind the screens from either side, a half dozen Castle Guards emerged.

The assassin stumbled as more arrows filled his body. The last thing he saw before crumpling over in a heap was the Kojuro rising from his bed, sword in hand from where it had been hidden beneath the pillows.

Sudori, half-asleep outside in the hallway, was jarred awake by the sound of yelling men, followed by a loud commotion and banging noises from within the Kojuro's Sleeping Chamber. Quickly he leapt to his feet and threw open the doors, dumbfounded at the sight before him.

In what had been a dark room with a sleeping Kojuro there were now soldiers, all armed with swords or bows, the scene lit by half a dozen lanterns. Kimeru stood at the foot of the sleeping platform, holding a sword. Several of the men were turning over an arrow-festooned body at the Kojuro's feet. Standing dumbstruck, Sudori could do nothing but stare.

He was shaken from his trance by Himitsu, who seemed to appear as if from nowhere within the room. The chamberlain was speaking to him: "Please fetch Lord Itachi." For a moment Sudori wondered if this was all a bad dream, until Himitsu took hold of his arm and gave it a small shake. "Now, if you would, please," said the white-bearded man at his side. Snapping out of his reverie Sudori sped off at once to find the Kojuro's brother, wondering what sort of demons these were that could appear out of thin air inside closed rooms.

Himitsu returned to Kimeru's side and knelt by the body of the Anasatsu. Assuring himself that the man was indeed dead, he instructed the soldiers to remove the body and replace the screen walls that had covered their hiding places.

Sliding his sword back into its scabbard, Kimeru remarked casually, "He was very good. Had we not been forewarned, I fear our healer would have lost his best patient."

"Indeed, sire," said Himitsu, stretching aching limbs that had grown tired from crouching silently in the dark. "The Anasatsu are always most thorough."

"You sound almost admiring, Lord Chamberlain."

"One can always appreciate craftsmanship, sire, even if one deplores the end product."

Their conversation was interrupted as a loud voice from the hallway demanded, "Who was on watch at this door? Who let this assassin into the Kojuro's chamber?" Kimeru and Himitsu turned as Lord Itachi strode into the room, past the soldiers bearing the assassin's corpse from the Sleeping Chamber. "Your Majesty!" he called out, catching sight of Kimeru. "Are you all right?"

Coolly Kimeru replied, "I am short of a little sleep, my brother, but as you can see, otherwise unharmed."

Itachi glanced about him at the screens being replaced, and the soldiers cleaning up the mess. "Who was on watch tonight?" he shouted at the soldiers. "They will be executed! There is no excuse for this!" The soldiers paused uncertainly, and Sudori, who had followed Itachi back to the Sleeping Chamber, cowered on the floor by the doorway.

"No, brother!" Kimeru's voice echoed throughout the room. "No one is to be executed! I am alive because these men kept vigil. It is due to their diligence that I am standing here now. Where were you when this assassin stole into the castle and hid himself in the woodwork?"

Silence greeted this accusation, as all in the room held their breath in the midst of the threatening implication. Itachi glared at his brother, and in a strained voice shaking with anger, said, "You dare accuse me of complicity in this?"

"No, of course not," said Kimeru, softening his tone. "It would be unthinkable for any member of the royal family to wish harm upon another of his own blood. I merely point out that these men," all of who, he noted, had become very industrious once again at their tasks, "have served as required. They were here when they were needed. One cannot be all places at once, even you. An assassin slipped through our net, but did not achieve his objective. We must work a little harder at stopping them somewhat sooner, that is all."

Subtly, the tension lessened in the room. Itachi said stiffly, "Of course, Your Majesty. I shall double the sentries immediately."

"Good. Himitsu, please be so good as to assemble the Council. I believe we need to discuss the events of the evening."

"Certainly, sire," said the chamberlain. "Do you wish to convene in the Great Audience Hall?"

Kimeru thought for a moment. "No. Here. Let us meet here."

The Ministers were hurriedly gathered, and the Council convened right in the Kojuro's Sleeping Chamber. The room had finally been cleared of soldiers as well as the body of the Anasatsu, but his blood remained on the rugs as a graphic reminder of what had just transpired. A few of the more fainthearted of the Ministers tried with some difficulty to keep their eyes averted from the scarlet stain spread before them.

"The Yutakashi are most certainly responsible," said Itachi, as he settled back on his heels from where he knelt before the Kojuro.

Kimeru, the rush of energy from the failed attack having subsided, sat tiredly on a portable dais that had been brought into the room. Still in his sleeping robe, scabbard prominently in view where it protruded from the sash tied in front, he listened patiently as his brother carried on.

"They have been massing their troops for some time," said Itachi. "And now we ourselves have allowed more than two dozen of them within our castle walls!" He gestured angrily toward the dark stain that covered the chamber's rugs. "Clearly this was a pre-meditated attack, designed to launch their offensive. Again, sire, I request permission to mobilize the Northern Army, and to arrest 'Lord' Choshuka at once. I will see to it personally, if you so desire." He bowed to Kimeru, his tone clearly expecting agreement.

"We will wait," replied Kimeru. Stiffening, Itachi opened his mouth to speak, but the Omo Deshi spoke first.

"Your Majesty," said Takamaru, "before we worry about this army of shopkeepers of which Lord Itachi thinks so highly, perhaps we should investigate other possibilities. The Shukyoshi have, after all, been most forthright in their verbal assaults on your kingdom, and therefore by extension your person. It seems obvious to me that they would be the most likely perpetrators of such a sacrilege."

Itachi spoke before the Kojuro could answer. "The Shukyoshi are not gathering an army," he spat out, "nor do they have cohorts under our very noses! If you are so concerned about the words the Shukyoshi speak, I suggest you try meditating a little harder to exterminate them. Let others worry about the violence of the real world."

Casting Itachi a withering glance, Takamaru began a retort but was cut short by Kimeru. "Enough!" shouted the Kojuro. "I am tired of your constant arguing!" Kimeru turned to his chamberlain, who was almost invisible next to the other ministers. "Himitsu! You have not spoken. I wish for advice!"

The wizened old man paused and considered his words before speaking. "Your Majesty," he said, carefully avoiding the gaze of either Itachi or Takamaru, "whether or not the Yutakashi are ultimately answerable, I can state that Lord Choshuka and his retinue are not directly responsible. All members of his party have been accounted for, and most of them are at present sleeping off the effects of too much wine consumed at their welcoming feast today." He looked down, feigning embarrassment, and continued, "As there has been some—tension—with the Yutakashi of late, I took the precaution of having their baggage and palanquins examined as well. The assassin did not enter Hajimeshi with the Yutakashi party."

He paused, and Takamaru beamed. "Ah, there, you see, sire? Our esteemed chamberlain, well known for his excellent spy network, has said—"

"Not spies, Eminence," interrupted Himitsu. "Merely servants in the Kojuro's service, as are we all."

"—Yes, of course, my dear Himitsu. Mere servants. In any event, Himitsu's 'servants' have proven that Choshuka is not as stupid as he looks, and has not walked into a lion's den bearing a sharp stick. The Yutakashi would not send him to us unaware of an assassination attempt. Clearly, sire," as he glanced at Itachi, "we are dealing with a more subtle foe than may at first seem obvious." As Itachi glowered at him, Takamaru continued, "The Shukyoshi are well known for having no moral scruples whatsoever. It would be perfectly in keeping with their so-called beliefs to hire an assassin."

"Eminence, if I may?" said Himitsu. With a nod from a self-satisfied Takamaru, Himitsu went on. "Regarding the Shukyoshi, sire," as if

Takamaru had not even spoken, "I do not believe they are responsible for this attack." The Omo Deshi's smile faded as Himitsu continued. "Before it was removed, I examined the body of the assassin. He bore no identification, as is typical of the Anasatsu; but equally he did not wear a shasen pendant, as the Shukyoshi faithful must do. As I am sure the Omo Deshi would agree, the Shukyoshi are unlikely to have countenanced such an act as an attack on your person by any other than a confirmed member of their religion," as he glanced casually over at Takamaru.

With a venomous look at Himitsu, Takamaru began, "Sire, I—"

Kimeru raised his hand. "I have heard enough. We will not find the answer of who sent this assassin by continuing to argue." He broke into a spasm of coughing, while the Ministers waited patiently. Recovering, he said, "This is not the first sign of the coming instability we face from the Darkness. Nor will it be the last. We must heed the words of the Shizen and seek the Kotaishi."

Takamaru visibly ground his teeth in frustration. "As you say, Your Majesty. I have selected an appropriate Deshi Master for—"

"No."

"—the expedi—eh?"

"No," repeated Kimeru. "I have chosen the Deshi for this journey."

"Ah. As you wish, Your Majesty," said Takamaru, bowing in some discomfiture. "May I ask," he continued, straightening, "whom Your Majesty has selected?"

Kimeru replied, "My Spiritual Guide, Toshi-hito."

Takamaru tried to cover his shock and disappointment. "B-but, Your Majesty, who then will tend to your spiritual needs while Toshi-hito is away?"

Kimeru looked disdainfully at the Omo Deshi. "Is not the highest lord in the land worthy of spiritual advisement from the highest Deshi in the land? You shall be my Spiritual Guide."

A look of mortification briefly passed across Takamaru's face, before being quickly replaced by his more usual countenance of a fawning smile. The Omo Deshi bowed and replied, "Your will, Your Majesty."

Kimeru called to the servants kneeling outside the doors to fetch Toshi-hito. The Ministers could hear the quick acknowledgement as one of the servants leapt to his feet and ran to find the Kojuro's Spiritual Guide. In the Sleeping Chamber silence reigned while all waited for the appearance of Toshi-hito, each of the men waiting on the Kojuro thinking furiously about how to turn this chain of events to his own advantage.

The soft sound of the sliding doors announced the arrival of Toshi-hito, who entered and bowed down on the floor before the Kojuro. "Your will, Your Majesty?"

"Toshi-hito," replied Kimeru. "You are aware of the Shizen's prophecy concerning the coming of the Darkness?"

Toshi-hito nodded. "As guardian of your spiritual needs, you have seen fit to so inform me, Your Majesty." Takamaru visibly stiffened at this revelation.

"Toshi-hito," said Kimeru, "I have chosen you to be the Spiritual Leader of the journey to search for the Kotaishi. You must discover him, wherever he may be across the land, so that he may lead our people and unite Tonogato."

The Deshi Master cast his gaze down to the floor. "Your Majesty, the vessel you have chosen is inadequate for the task." Takamaru's eyes flickered back and forth between his underling and the Kojuro, as Toshi-hito added, "I am unworthy of such honor."

Kimeru shook his head. "No. I have seen it in my dreams. You are the one to find the Kotaishi. Onto you lies the responsibility, and no other." At this, Itachi shifted uncomfortably.

Humbly, Toshi-hito bowed. "By Your Majesty's command, this poor Deshi shall endeavor to fulfill the Shizen's prophecy."

"Your Majesty," interjected Itachi, "was I given to understand that you wished me, your royal brother, to attend this expedition? I would be most happy to accept the honor of leading the quest for the Kotaishi."

Kimeru cast an expressionless gaze upon his brother. "Certainly, brother, I expect you to be a part of this journey."

The response evidently not being exactly what he wished to hear, Itachi said quietly, "Surely Your Majesty does not intend for me to be subordinate to a simple Deshi?"

Ignoring the silent outrage emanating from Takamaru, Kimeru answered, "Of course not, brother. You are the leader of this journey. The men shall report to you." Satisfied, Itachi began to relax. "However," continued Kimeru, causing his brother to lean forward once more, "Toshi-hito is the one I have chosen to find the Kotaishi. In all things related to this end his word shall rule. All else, my brother, is within your purview."

Itachi, aware that for all intents and purposes his authority would be severely compromised, said stiffly, "As Your Majesty wills," and bowed. Upon straightening, he continued. "I have already arranged the troops for the expedition. The First and Seventh Battalions stand ready to—"

"No."

"—march—eh? Your Majesty?"

"I said, no! There will be no army on this journey. This is a journey of discovery, not a raiding party! You will take no more than ten soldiers, and the necessary servants."

Flustered, Itachi sputtered, "But—but—Your Majesty! This is—one cannot—we cannot simply walk into the kingdoms of our enemies like sheep being led to slaughter!"

"They are not our enemies!" replied Kimeru. "Not until you make them so! We do not know who sent the Anasatsu. Has Hajimeshi itself been attacked? Has any one of our farmers so much as lost a pig to our neighbors? No!" His breathing becoming labored with his exertions, Kimeru calmed himself then went on. "This is not just a pilgrimage to find the Kotaishi. It is a journey to show our neighbors that we are not a threat to them. That we can all live in harmony together."

Clearly astounded, and disgusted, Itachi paused just long enough to make it clear that he did not approve before bowing again. "As Your Majesty wills," he said once more.

Inwardly, Itachi silently screamed to himself. You fool! You've let that idiot brother of yours maneuver you into this!

Now, he realized, his honor was irreparably stained. He would be leading no more men than the lowest subaltern commanded, and under the direction of a Deshi at that! He remained bent over, afraid to rise lest his face betray the anger and shame he felt.

Takamaru, by contrast, secretly beamed inside. Wonderful, he thought. Splendid! What I thought at first to be a loss has now turned into a great victory. This expedition is no royal honor, it is a fool's errand! It is meaningless. Clearly it is a token excuse for the Kojuro to rid himself of his brother. Why hadn't I seen this coming?

Very glad now that he had not lost the services of a 'reliable' Deshi on such a ridiculous quest, he too bowed to the Kojuro. "I can supply Toshi-hito with three of my best Deshi to accompany him on this most difficult quest, Your Majesty."

Kimeru, watching them both, was not unaware of the emotions playing across their features, no matter how hard they attempted to conceal them. So busy with their little schemes, he pondered, that they fail to see that it is I who is using them, rather than the other way around.

To Takamaru he replied, "Toshi-hito will take whom he needs," turning to his Spiritual Guide.

Toshi-hito, who had sat impassive throughout the exchange, bowed once more. "Your Majesty, I have no need of anyone to assist me. One apprentice only, to help with my personal meditation."

"So be it," replied Kimeru. "Select anyone you want. Be ready to leave before sunset the day after tomorrow." With a wave of his hand, he dismissed Toshi-hito and the others. "Himitsu," he said, as the

Ministers dispersed, "I wish another word with you." The old man bowed and waited. Both Takamaru and Itachi pointedly ignored Toshi-hito as they left. Toshi-hito left last, closing the doors behind him, leaving Himitsu and the Kojuro alone together.

Kimeru's shoulders visibly slumped as the doors closed, his energy severely drained by the events of the last few hours.

Himitsu said quietly, "Shall I call for the healer, sire?"

"No...No, I'll be fine." Kimeru looked over at the chamberlain. "Once again, Himitsu, I owe you my gratitude."

Himitsu bowed. "I do only what is my duty, sire, no more. That my humble efforts might lessen your burden is all the thanks required."

"Humph. Do you never tire of being diplomatic? No, don't bother answering that; I know the answer already." Waving his hand in the direction of the departed Ministers, he added, "I only wish I possessed your patience when dealing with miscreants such as these."

"Patience, sire, is a virtue that has its place. As the ruler of Hajimeshi, who must lead his people down a difficult path, it is sometimes one that you must forgo when the times require it."

The Kojuro chuckled. "Leave it to Himitsu to turn absence of a quality into a positive trait." He turned aside as he was consumed with a coughing fit, while the chamberlain looked discreetly away. His voice thick, Kimeru went on. "Himitsu. This Hikari Pilgrimage is vital to the continued survival of Hajimeshi. I have my reasons for accepting my brother's presence on the expedition, but his involvement must not be allowed to hinder its success."

"I understand, Your Majesty. I believe I can assist in ensuring that Lord Itachi will not interfere with the goal you have established. However, the farther they travel from Hajimeshi, the less I can guarantee such guardianship. Does Your Majesty have any idea how far the expedition may have to travel before they find this Kotaishi?"

Kimeru looked off into the distance, his voice very soft. "Probably very far, Himitsu. Very far."

"I see," said the chamberlain. "Then I will have to ensure that someone I can trust accompanies the party directly. I will see to it, Your Majesty," as he bowed.

"Thank you, Himitsu."

As he rose to take his leave, Himitsu said, "There is one other thing, Your Majesty."

"Yes?"

"It has come to my attention that, of late, the Princess Mikasama has become rather—attentive—of a certain young man."

"Oh? And why should this be of your concern, Lord Chamberlain?"

"Ordinarily, sire, I would of course never pry into the personal affairs of the royal family. However," as he attempted to broach the subject delicately, "the young man in question happens to be a Captain of the Castle Guard."

Vexed, Kimeru said, "A commoner? But she knows she is to marry a noble! Why is she…?"

Himitsu sighed. "Your Majesty, she is young. Her position here does not permit her to associate freely with others of her own age, and her contacts with eligible young men have been—well, rather formal."

"But she is a royal princess, and my heir! She knows she cannot inherit, that whomever she marries will become Kojuro. Has her training been so lax that she misunderstands her obligations?"

Himitsu bowed his head. "Sire, please forgive this humble servant's impertinence, but while there are indeed times when you must be Kojuro above all else, there are times when you must also be a father. Mikasama is strong-willed and of her own mind; she is, after all, your daughter. She is at an age where she chafes at her role, and wishes to experience more than what the walls of Hajimeshi can offer."

Kimeru looked down at the dried scarlet reminder of danger so recently at hand. Quietly he said, "I used to think of this place as a safe haven for her, a shelter from the harsh world outside. Perhaps I was over cautious. I cannot prevent the cold wind from blowing; she must learn for herself, 'Time to bundle up warm, or to come in from the storm,' as the children's rhyme goes." He looked up at his chamberlain. "This relationship must not go any further, Himitsu."

"I understand, sire," said Himitsu sadly.

"Once the Hikari Pilgrimage is on its way, I will devote more of my time to Mikasama. I will help her spread her wings a little, teach her to glide before she attempts to take flight." He held his handkerchief close to his mouth as he stopped to cough, trying to hide from Himitsu the small trickle of blood that seeped into the cloth. "Good night, Himitsu," he croaked.

"Good night, Your Majesty," said Himitsu softly, bowing as he left.

The chamberlain stepped into the hallway outside as the servant closed the doors behind him. He noted approvingly, if somewhat regretfully, that there were now two Castle Guards stationed to either side of the door as well. A shame, he reflected, that things have come to this; that the Kojuro, leader of Hajimeshi, must resort to guards standing watch before his very bed.

Himitsu motioned to the servant; as the man stepped closer, Himitsu said quietly, "You are?"

"Sudori, my lord," said the servant with a bow.

"Sudori, you have done well this night. I have one more task for you. Please suggest to the royal healer that perhaps it is time he paid a casual visit on his Majesty."

"Yes, my Lord," said Sudori, who scurried off to find the court healer.

Himitsu watched him go, and turned to look at the closed doors once more before leaving. So little time, he thought. For the Kojuro, and for Hajimeshi.

Having lived many years and seen much of the frailties and cruelties of men, he had little faith in the utterings of forest spirits. Hikari Pilgrimage or no, Hajimeshi would need more than the promise of an elusive Kotaishi to keep the wolves at bay. Both from within and from without.

*   *   *

??? Alive? Am I alive?...No—not alive. But not dead, either.

The lance, it struck me, I saw it coming...saw my own death coming, felt the lance head as it pierced my chest...it hurt, gods did it hurt...and then I was so cold...

It seems...so long ago...

It is dark. I cannot see, cannot feel. Cannot smell. But I can think...

Where is this place? Deep. Yes, it is very deep. But I can hear them! Up there, people. I can hear all of them!—how strange...

There's a farmer, plowing somewhere in Hajimeshi. A moneylender, cheating someone in Yutakashi. All I need do is listen, and I can hear them all. Why?

??? Something—speaks—to me, in my head! What is it? Who are you? Where am I? What do you want of me?

Wait? Why? Why should I wait?

Revenge? Yes, of course I want revenge! But how—

Oh! Oh, yes! I see, I see it now...

Oh good, very good. Tell me more...No? Well, then I shall wait. Yes, yes, and I will listen...

It is gone now, out my mind. Which, it would appear, is all that has been left to me...

Revenge! Whatever it is, it says I am to have my revenge! That is why I still exist! It says it will tell me more, soon. For now, I am to listen. Very well, I will do so.

My revenge! Soon, soon...

2

The next morning the air was crisp and cool. The castle grounds were quiet, belying the frenzied activities of the previous night. As they would have on any other day, those charged with keeping the castle running rose with the dawn and commenced their daily tasks.

Over in the stables the usual routine of livery chores began. It was here that the horses for Hajimeshi Castle were serviced, whether those of the Castle Guard, those used by the Kojuro and the nobles, or the draft animals used for hauling wagons. The main building was old; having been built shortly after the castle itself, its stout wooden construction was still nearly as solid as the castle's stones. The building's long roof, supported on huge wooden beams, stretched over rows of stalls for the horses. At one end the stable was devoted to storage and maintenance of harness and tack. The smell of fresh hay, mingled with the strong scent of many horses, wafted through the air as the day's quotient of flies began their own routine. Just outside, a lark sat perched on a hitching post, his head darting this way and that.

A leatherworker was laboring on repairs to a saddle, while a stableman nearby rubbed down the horses. Word of the previous night's events had spread quickly, despite efforts by the senior servants to quell rumors. Anything that broke up the daily pattern was a welcome respite for those on the lower rungs of the social ladder.

The stableman, as he scrubbed one of the Castle Guard mounts, remarked, "Heard that old Himitsu sent that Anasatsu's sword over to the armory. Pretty cheeky, that. Wouldn't want no assassin's sword left lying 'round if I were Kojuro." The leatherworker merely grunted, carrying on with his task.

"'Course," continued the stableman, "guess it don't much matter, since Itachi's supposed to beef up the watch. Heard tell he's gonna double the number of guards 'round the Castle." He stopped and went to re-fill his bucket from the well at the entrance to the stable, saying over his shoulder, "Heard that the Princess already got her own personal bodyguard. 'Though I doubt that's what's on his mind." The leatherworker, while still appearing to concentrate on his work, said offhandedly, "Oh?"

"Sure," replied the stableman as he went back to patting down the horses. "One of the Guard captains, Nakama I think I heard his name was, he's been followin' the Princess 'round like a puppy dog for weeks. And I tell you what," he said, dropping his voice conspiratorially, "I got it on good authority that she been 'returning the favor,' if you know what I mean."

The leatherworker grunted again. "One hears all kind of talk."

"Oh, don't I know. But I heard this straight from Obasata, that fiery little linen maid. She heard that old bat, Komori, squawkin' at the Princess 'bout her 'soldier-boy' and how she had to be more, more 'descreet'-like. Talked 'bout those two meetin' in the Royal Garden, all alone." The stableman took out his large wire comb and untangled the knots in the horse's mane. "Can't tell me that no Guard Captain's goin' ta just meet a pretty little princess in a garden and talk 'bout flowers."

The leatherworker made no comment, continuing on until finished with his repair. He put away his tools and replaced the saddle along the wall shelving. "Well, that's all I got in here today. Guess I'll go over and check on the wagons; heard that some of the bed tie-downs were comin' apart." With that he walked out the far end of the stables.

With the leatherworker's departure, the stableman stopped combing the horse's mane. He went over to the doorway through which the man had exited and, staying just out of sight inside, looked around the edge of the door. The leatherworker, he saw, was walking quickly, not stopping at the wagon house but continuing on down the path toward the main castle. Nodding in satisfaction, the stableman returned and packed up his own tools. He stopped by the well, whistling as he washed up. He then made his way off in a direction that would take him to the chamberlain's quarters.

The horses in the stable neighed and snorted to one another. The lark launched himself up from his post and into the sky, flying toward the Deshi priory.

*   *   *

The long, low sound of the gong echoed throughout the priory, signaling the end of the morning meditation period.

Shiko, sitting on the floor of his room, opened his eyes and stretched. It was more from habit than from anything else. He had long since learned to work his muscles in tiny movements, allowing him to sit perfectly still while in mediation. Nevertheless he hadn't quite given up on stretching. Somehow, with the sunlight splashing through the open window at his back, it just seemed more relaxing.

His room was small, with just enough space to spread out scrolls and to roll out a bed mat. All of the apprentices' rooms were identical; as they were used only for sleeping, meditating, and individual study, no more space was needed. Each room had a large window to the outside, running almost from floor to ceiling. This provided abundant light, both for students to do their research and to enlighten their spirits. Opposite the window a door led to the main hallway of the dormitory building, and Shiko now rose and opened his, joining with his fellow students to attend the morning meal.

All of the Deshi had been up and about well before first light, working in silence at their morning chores, whether it was scrubbing hallways or preparing the morning meal. This was the quiet hour of dawn, during which the Deshi were encouraged both to reflect on whatever dreams had come to them the previous night, and to respect the dignity of nature's morning salutation. This was followed by the morning meditation period as each Deshi cleared his mind and set his course for the new day.

At the morning meal, by contrast, all was a constant babble as Shiko took his place in line to receive the food prepared by his fellow Deshi. The day was now fully begun and the Deshi encouraged their brethren to share their thoughts and feelings with one another while they ate. Shiko sat at the table set aside for the apprentices and listened with only half an ear to the conversations around him. He was still pondering the information he had uncovered about the Hikari Pilgrimage, and was more curious than ever about what Master Toshi-hito might want the information for. It was still with the impatience of youth that he hurried through his meal and returned to his room, there to collect the parchments on which he had transcribed his notes from the Archive scrolls. While the other apprentices went about their own daily routines, such as martial arts practice or tending the gardens, Shiko was ready to present his research to Toshi-hito. He turned down the hallway leading to the Master's room and gently knocked on the wood frame of the door. "Enter," came Toshi-hito's familiar voice.

Shiko slid open the door and stepped into a room only marginally larger than his own. A small cabinet of scrolls and a larger window were all that distinguished it from the room of the lowliest apprentice. Toshi-hito sat upon the floor, his back to the doorway as he gazed out the window. Shiko saw that there was a bird, a lark, perched on the sill. It turned and looked at the apprentice as he came into the room. Well, thought Shiko, the Master certainly seems to be popular with the birds these days.

He waited patiently for Toshi-hito to finish his meditation, which to Shiko's eyes appeared to be centered on the lark. At last the Master nodded and relaxed, and at the same time the bird took flight off into the trees outside. Toshi-hito turned to his student. "Ah, Shiko. Please," and he gestured that his student should sit.

Shiko sat before his teacher and placed the parchments on the floor with a bow. "Master, I have researched the Hikari Pilgrimage, as you requested. I believe all of the information you might need is here."

Toshi-hito made no move to look at the parchments but continued to look at Shiko. "And what is the essence of your findings?"

Anticipating such an oral questioning, Shiko had prepared. "The Hikari Pilgrimage was a spiritual journey, a journey of discovery not for a material thing but for knowledge or enlightenment. It is because of this that it was respected by all of the kingdoms in Tonogato, as the rulers knew that a Hikari pilgrim was not interested in the material things of their realms, and thus posed no threat. Also, since the pilgrim had usually given up his own life's work to undertake the journey, it showed a commitment of spirit. This devotion to enlightenment was treated with a great deal of respect."

"And you have researched all of the details of how such a pilgrimage is established, the ceremonies involved?"

"Yes, Master. Only a sovereign lord, such as the Kojuro, can ordain a Hikari Pilgrimage. He performs a ritual that includes lighting the Hikari lantern, which he then places in the hands of the pilgrim."

"And if it is the Kojuro himself who wishes to conduct a pilgrimage?"

"This has occurred on several occasions in our recorded history, Master. The Kojuro then retains the lantern after he lights it and carries it himself."

"Tell me then, Shiko. Based on your research, what would be done if the Kojuro wished to conduct a Hikari pilgrimage, but was unable to go himself?"

Shiko had been certain that somehow, through Toshi-hito, the Kojuro was involved; but he was equally certain that the sovereign would never be able to endure the arduous travel required. So, anticipating this possibility, he had researched the alternatives so as to be able to provide a reasoned answer. "Master, I found no records of a case where a pilgrim was unable to conduct his own pilgrimage. However, from reading about the ceremony and the accounts of other pilgrimages, I believe the Kojuro could send another in his place. He would still have to light the

Hikari here, but during the ceremony he could place it in the hands of another who would go on the journey in his stead. I believe this would still qualify as an authentic Hikari Pilgrimage, although some might question the interpretation."

Toshi-hito nodded in satisfaction, and finally looked down at the research material Shiko had brought. He idly picked up one of the scrolls. "That is the same conclusion I came to two months ago."

Shiko was confused. "Master? Then why—"

Toshi-hito held up his hand. "I wished you to understand the background of the journey we are about to take."

Shiko was surprised. "We, Master? Are we going on the Hikari Pilgrimage for His Majesty?"

Toshi-hito rose and stepped over to the window, from which he had a view of the Sacred Grove in the distance. His voice was quiet as he spoke. "About two months ago, Shiko, the Kojuro began receiving prophecies from the Shizen in the Sacred Grove. Terrible prophecies, such that would make a man, or a Kojuro, spend many a sleepless night worrying for his people. These prophecies warned of a terrible calamity that would befall Tonogato, destroying all of the kingdoms, including Hajimeshi. The danger was not described clearly, only that it was a great Darkness that would cross the land, taking the light from everything in its path." He sat down on the wide edge of the windowsill and abruptly changed the subject. "Do you know of the Tarkinsa scrolls?"

Shiko frowned, thinking quickly. "You mean the ones that Master Nobaka keeps under lock and key?"

"Yes," said Toshi-hito wryly, "those are the Tarkinsa scrolls. They are among the oldest documents in the Archive, which is why Nobaka is so protective of them. They are quite fragile." More somberly, he continued. "The language of the Tarkinsa scrolls is archaic and difficult to decipher. But it would appear, from reading them, that this is not the first time that Tonogato has been threatened by such a Darkness. Not quite a thousand years ago, according to the scrolls, a strange blackness, not unlike what the Shizen have described, descended over the land."

Shiko felt a sudden chill, even though the morning sun was still shining through the open window. What had seemed at first to be a bit of academic research for his Master was beginning to take on ominous overtones.

"The Darkness was preceded," Toshi-hito went on, "by a famine that had swept across Tonogato, and by periods of lawlessness and even outright war. Does this sound familiar?" he asked, giving Shiko a penetrating look.

The apprentice swallowed. "Yes, Master."

"Do you recall the stories of Sabakushi, the Desert Kingdom?"

Trying not to be rattled by yet another sudden shift in topics, Shiko answered, "Just—just that it is a legendary place, Master, probably thought up by the desert traders who sell their goods to Yutakashi."

Toshi-hito smiled gently. "Sabakushi is no legend. Not only did it exist, it was a flourishing kingdom that surpassed even the magical city of Tejinashi in its magnificence. In its prime it was not situated in the middle of a vast desert as it is now, but was the center of a land as verdant as that around Hajimeshi. If you look hard enough, you will find references to it in the scrolls." He sighed. "The clues are misleading. It is difficult to reconcile the descriptions of the oasis that was Sabakushi with the wasteland that now exists."

He looked wistfully out the window once more. "When the Darkness first spilled forth, the kingdoms argued among themselves, and none could agree on how to confront it. The citizens of Sabakushi were proud; disdainful of their southern neighbors, they chose to stand alone. They failed. Their city was overrun by the Darkness, and was lost. Every living thing, every human, every animal, every plant, withered and died. Whatever is left of Sabakushi lies buried beneath the deserts of the north. Since that time no one who has traveled there has ever returned. Even the desert traders avoid it, and their fearlessness is legendary."

Shiko sat very still. The morning light no longer seemed quite so bright as it did before. Master Toshi-hito continued to stare out the window, his gaze unfocused. What the Master was seeing in his mind's eye, the apprentice had no way of knowing. Shiko absently reached up and gently grasped the honsho around his neck.

"But," Toshi-hito went on, "the Darkness is not inevitable, nor is it invincible. After the destruction of Sabakushi, a man came forward who was able to unite the kingdoms. Together, the combined kingdoms were able to fight the Darkness, pushing it back into whatever had spawned it. The man who led the kingdoms, who convinced them to put aside their differences and work toward their common survival, was known only as the 'Kotaishi.' The prophecies the Kojuro has received speak of such a time again. They say that, once more, the Darkness is coming. And that there is only one person who can unite the kingdoms."

He paused, and looked at his apprentice. "We must find him, Shiko. None of the other kingdoms can see the danger. Somewhere there exists a man who can lead them, and Hajimeshi, to help defend Tonogato against the Darkness."

Shiko looked down at his parchments. His original curiosity regarding Toshi-hito's intentions seemed so shallow, so trivial, compared to the enormity of the task that lay before them. And then he realized what it meant to him personally: a pilgrimage would undoubtedly last for weeks, if not months. The Senior Masters would have conducted their Oral Questioning long before he returned, and he would have lost any chance at surpassing Utaka as the youngest Deshi…

Immediately he realized the insignificance of his goal, compared to the dilemma that faced Tonagato. And yet…he had spent so many days, hours upon hours, studying until he had fallen asleep over ancient, dusty scrolls. Before he could stop himself, he looked up questioningly at Toshi-hito. "But why do you wish to take me, Master? Surely there are other Deshi more knowledgeable than I…."

Only the merest flicker of emotion passed across Toshi-hito's face, so quick that Shiko almost missed it. Much too faint, Shiko was sure, to ascribe any meaning to, and yet he was certain that the Master was disappointed.

Toshi-hito replied, "I have told the Kojuro that I would need only an apprentice to help me on the pilgrimage. And, quite simply, Shiko, you are the best among all of the apprentices."

He said no more; but what more, thought Shiko, did he need to say? Toshi-hito would of course want a good apprentice to accompany him, and the Master was well aware, in fact more aware than anyone, of Shiko's progress. It would be a great honor to accompany an historic pilgrimage, and thus a reward for the fortunate apprentice chosen to join him.

But for Shiko it meant the loss of his goal, the thing that had kept him working so hard. His name would now be just one of many thousands inscribed on the rolls of the Deshi...

Toshi-hito waited, saying nothing. Shiko realized that the Master was waiting for him to decide. He must know, thought Shiko, how important the Oral Questioning is to me. Even though we have never spoken of it, the Master has been tailoring my lessons over the last few months toward the Questioning, helping me to be ready. Yet now he is asking me to leave it behind.

A sharp puff of wind blew in from the window, rustling past the seated form of Toshi-hito and upsetting the parchments Shiko had laid out on the floor. They scattered, and Shiko had to quickly grab at them to hold them in place, and then put them back into some meaningful order. It gave him another minute or two to think.

Tonogato, he thought; it is like these parchments. The kingdoms will scatter before the dark wind, unless the Kotaishi is found who can unite them. How could I possibly think that something as trivial as besting Utaka could be of any importance at all, compared to that?

Shiko looked up at Toshi-hito, then bowed his head to the floor. "I would be honored to accompany you on the pilgrimage, Master."

Toshi-hito nodded, giving no outward sign that he had perceived Shiko's dilemma. "There is much preparation to be done," he said matter-of-factly. "And important things to do once we depart. For one, I will need someone to watch, and to learn from what transpires. And to help with some of the chores involved, of course. Which brings me to the first item at hand: the Hikari." He stopped and looked meaningfully at Shiko.

The apprentice quickly bent over and retrieved one of his parchments. "This is the best description that I could find, Master; it comes from the diary of a pilgrimage conducted nearly one hundred years ago. It says 'The Hikari is a fairly large lantern, suspended from a pole carried by the pilgrim or by one of his party. It is held aloft so that its light shines over all, imbuing all who journey with the pilgrim with its protection and blessing.'" He looked up at Toshi-hito. "But where do we find a Hikari lantern, Master?"

"That is your first task, Shiko. You must find a Hikari."

* * *

The servants cowered on the floor, faces pressed down onto the stone as if they were trying to burrow into sand. Another wooden tray came sailing through the air to crash into splinters against the wall over their heads.

Lord Itachi had returned from his midnight meeting of the Council of Ministers in a towering rage, excessive even by his standards. His temperament had not improved by morning. The previous night he had ended up beating most of his domestic staff with his tarka until it had broken over the back of one hapless servant. This had served only to fuel Itachi's fury, and the poor unfortunate had suffered thereafter from multiple kicks while lying prostrate on the floor. While his compatriots had later helped remove him to an out-of-the-way room of Itachi's quarters in the castle, the rest of the staff continued to suffer under the noble lord's wrath.

"You are dung-hill scrappers, all of you!" shouted Itachi. "Even a mongrel dog would reject this food as unfit to touch!" He walked over and planted his foot squarely on the back of his cook, one of the servants who now cringed before him. "You say you are a cook? You are nothing but a preparer of dung-scraps! Since that is what you seem to make so well, you should at least get better at it. Shoden!" he yelled, turning toward the antechamber of his quarters. "Shoden! Come here!"

Shoden dutifully shuffled into the room. He was a huge man, his immense size contrasting markedly with the insignificance of his intellect. His face had the homely appearance of an ox, which, the rest of Itachi's staff had remarked among themselves, was in keeping with how he was generally employed. "Yes, my Lord?" Shoden said slowly. Some among the servants thought these the only words he knew, as it was all they had ever heard him speak.

"Shoden," said Itachi, gesturing at the trembling form beneath his boot, "this worthless carcass that dares to call himself a 'cook' needs to improve his skills. As he seems to prefer making dung that is where he will start. Take him down to the garbage pit and make sure he samples the fresh dung set out from last night's chamber pots." As Itachi released his foot from the poor cook's back the man started to rise only to receive a swift kick in the side. With a sneer of disgust Itachi then stormed from the room into his sleeping quarters.

Shoden tromped over to the cook, who was bent over double on the floor in pain, and with one hand effortlessly dragged the man to his feet. Without a word he shepherded the cook out the door to fulfill his master's order.

The remaining servants, still shaking in fear, rose and began cleaning up the mess from thrown trays and shattered crockery. The only person left in the room that had not been down on the floor was Chumo, Itachi's personal chamberlain. As Itachi had left the room, Chumo had finally let out his breath. He had stood as still as a statue throughout Itachi's tirade, unsure how far his master would go this time. His relief was palpable now that Itachi had chosen to unleash his wrath on a mere servant rather than on himself. Now that the immediate danger was past he vented his own anger and frustration at the fools who had caused Itachi's temper to overflow. "Hurry up!" he hissed at the servants as they cleaned. "I want this mess of yours removed before the next mark of the candle!"

With that he removed himself back to his usual post in the antechamber. He muttered to himself as he hunched down on the floor: "More room in here without that lump Shoden taking up so much air space."

Looking at where his own breakfast sat, cold and untouched, he realized sourly that with the cook now disposed of it was likely to remain cold. Irritated, his thoughts were interrupted by a knock on the door. He opened it with a scowl. "Yes?"

The leatherworker bowed nervously before him in the hallway.

"And you're sure of this?" demanded Itachi. He stomped his foot within inches of the leatherworker's head, which was face down on the floor of the Hajimeshi general's sleeping chamber. "If I find out your facts are wrong..."

The leatherworker's voice trembled. "I swear to what I heard! The Princess and her pet Captain, it's all the servants talk about—they never stop gossiping!"

Chumo, who had led the leatherworker in to Itachi, stood motionless against the wall as his master paced back and forth, fuming. Finally Itachi lashed out with his hand and swept the candlestand and other items from his side table, all of which crashed to the floor near the leatherworker. Chumo quickly stepped on the candles to douse their flames, then retreated again to press up against the wall.

"Damn that insolent fool!" yelled Itachi. "I should slit his throat for his pretension!" He turned to Chumo. "Bring him here, now!" His chamberlain slithered out of the room, grateful to be away from his master's wrath.

Itachi leaned against the side table, still shaking with anger. With but a sideways glance at the man on the floor, he said, "All right, get out. And say nothing about this to anyone, or you'll find your tongue on your dinner plate." The leatherworker rose shakily, and with a hurried bow nearly ran from the room.

The Hajimeshi lord punched the wall in frustration, the wooden paneling nearly cracking with the blow. Itachi had never been one to rein in his temper, even as a youth. As one of the royal princes, there had been little that anyone could do to restrain him. Indeed once he had reached his manhood it had only been the moderating influence of Fugawari that had kept his younger brother's anger in check. Whenever Itachi's temper threatened to get out of hand, Fugawari would take the young man with him on one of his frequent forays out into the town for endless nights of carousing. Then all animosities would be forgotten as those in the King's party treated themselves to the finest wines in Hajimeshi.

But those days had long since passed. Fugawari was dead, having drunk himself into insensibility before stepping off the castle ramparts on a dark, cold night. The serious-minded and scholarly Kimeru had replaced him as Kojuro, leaving the soldier Itachi to pick up what he, the youngest sibling, considered the scraps of the royal lineage. Forced to always ride behind his brother, to defer to what he considered Kimeru's ridiculous notions of military 'policy'…It was a situation that Itachi never forgot, or forgave.

Itachi bore many scars, both physical and mental; and he was never a man to forget a wound. He kept a mental list of all those who had wronged him. No matter that it might take years, he made sure that he exacted his vengeance. Over time his list had grown quite long.

Now Itachi's thoughts raged. How, he wondered, could that idiot Nakama think he would get away with this? Did the fool think that he could simply snub his nose at his betters? Or did he think he could whore-about with a royal Princess and that none would be the wiser?

Underscoring Itachi's concerns were his fears that the Princess might actually find a mate. Should she marry, and her husband thus become heir to the throne, it would seriously hinder Itachi's plans—plans that were intended to see the premature removal of his brother before Mikasama could marry. He had figured that the girl's intransigence with the suitors she had encountered to date would continue, thus giving him the time he needed to finalize his preparations.

But now, he fumed, this happens! A lowborn soldier, attempting to set himself up as a player among his betters. Well, I know how to resolve this. Killing him would be too easy. There are better ways to give a man pain. The little worm will find himself eating grubs, stripped of any honor. For a man without honor is nothing…

A short while later there was a knock on the door to Itachi's chamber. The door slid open, and Nakama was ushered, almost pushed, into the room, and the door closed behind him.

Nakama, unsure as to why he had been summoned, knelt and bowed to the Hajimeshi general. Sitting back up, he said, "You sent for me, my Lord?"

In a menacing whisper Itachi said, "Oh, yes, I sent for you." Staring down at Nakama, Itachi unleashed his wrath like a river smashing through a restraining dike. "You dog! How dare you? How dare you!" At the frightful sight of Itachi's rage, Nakama's eyes went wide, and immediately he bowed his head down the floor once more. "You son of a whore!" screamed Itachi. "Attempting to seduce the royal Princess. My niece! I should have you arrested and executed for such impertinence!"

"My Lord—" began Nakama, his eyes fixed firmly on the stone floor, but he got no further.

"No!" yelled Itachi. "No words! Nothing you could say could atone for this act of treason. You are a soldier. Do you hear me? A soldier! Not a nobleman. Not a member of the peerage. Or had you forgotten that? Perhaps you thought that you were better than the nobility? That you could take a royal Princess to bed as you would a common milking maid?"

"No, my Lord! I—"

"Silence! You have earned no right to speak." Itachi knelt down in front of Nakama, leaning over his head, and hissed, "I'll tell you what you've earned. As of now, you are no longer a Captain. You are a rank soldier. You will no longer have the honor of leading men; instead you will scrub the toilets of those who do the fighting!" He stood, and with disdain concluded, "I am setting out on an important journey tomorrow, and you will be going too, little man. You will be the squad's donkey. Not only will it remove you from your perverted attacks upon my niece, but I will have ample opportunity, as will the other men, of ensuring that you know your proper place." Without another word, he brushed past Nakama and left the room, slamming the door open with a crash as he strutted out.

Nakama remained on the floor, shaking and not daring to move. His own anger and shame nearly overwhelmed him. His confused mind shouted to himself, what have I done? What have I done? I am ruined…And Mikasama! I've put her in terrible danger! If Itachi dishonors her, it will be my fault…

It was some time before he felt able to rise. He quickly left Itachi's quarters, passing Chumo and Shoden in the antechamber on his way out. But he saw neither of them, his vision blurred with tears and his mind in utter turmoil.

Shoden, having completed his task with the unfortunate cook and leaving the poor man retching at the edge of the garbage pit, looked quizzically at the departing form of Nakama, and then at Chumo. He was answered with an indifferent shrug from Itachi's chamberlain.

"Wouldn't know," said Chumo, "but I'd say as that young fool has just about hung himself as good as if he'd tied the hangman's knot himself." He looked down at his stone-cold food. "Now, what are we going to do about getting some breakfast?"

* * *

Oh ho! There's one with a temper. See how he makes all the little people crawl beneath him! That's what makes a man—power, and the will to use it.

I could hear him, all the way down here...so much anger and hate in that one...he too seeks revenge. I can feel the fire burn in him, the way it does in me...

I remember now, I was the last to fall. We had been victorious until then, crushing all who had stood in our way. It was like leading lambs to slaughter. The Great Ones had told us it would be so, and we had followed them...

But then, something had gone wrong...the sheep had turned into wolves, and their armies, with their cursed banners of light, had fought back. We lost a battle, then another, and then were forced to retreat...back to where the Great Ones had come, their mountain of darkness...we stood our ground there, and fell because of it. All the glory, swept away...

But I was not swept away! The Great Ones, they kept me, here! So that I could wreak havoc on those who took from me what was rightfully mine...no, not the same ones, but their children's children's children...

No matter. They will all die! That thing that speaks to my head has shown me what will be. Soon...

*   *   *

Shiko walked out into the courtyard of the priory and stopped, completely at a loss. Find a Hikari, Toshi-hito had said. He knew better than to ask how he was supposed to do that. The Master's tone had made it clear that this was the apprentice's task to perform. Although it was true that, besides Toshi-hito himself, Shiko was probably more knowledgeable than anyone about Hikari lanterns based on the research he had just done, it did not make it any easier to figure out where a Hikari lantern could be found. Or even what one looked like.

Frustrated, he looked about at the other Deshi busily going about their affairs. Some were off-loading supplies from a cart; another Master and his students were sitting in a far corner engaged in a dialogue. Two other apprentices stood near him repairing the plaster on the walls. Everyone was going about their business as if nothing had changed. But things had changed, Shiko knew. And the rest of them just could not see it yet.

He realized he was still holding onto his honsho, and had been ever since walking out of Master Toshi-hito's room. Pulling it out from inside his robe, he gazed down at it.

The small bronze pendant, about three fingers wide, usually lay flat against his chest, its six edges worn smooth from the many years of Shiko holding on to it. On two of the honsho's edges, characters were inscribed that spelled out the syllables of Shiko's name. A third contained a star-shaped hole, through which was tied the leather cord. He remembered those days absently holding on to the honsho while writing with his free hand, transcribing scrolls for the Masters. Now, as he let go of the honsho and put it away inside his robe, the awful feeling that had prompted him to first reach for it back in the Master's room did not pass. Somehow, Shiko had a feeling that it wasn't going to pass anytime soon.

He reflected on what the Master had said. Now that Toshi-hito had laid it out for him, he was able to see the pattern in some of the terrible things that had occurred over the preceding months. What had seemed isolated incidents, even the attack on the Kojuro, he could now see as a progressive deterioration of the normal 'order.' No one could have failed to sense the increasing tensions and problems that seemed to have beset not just Hajimeshi, but all of Tonogato. He had even heard that the famine sweeping the south had been joined by a horrific plague. But everyone, it seemed, assumed that it was just 'one of those times,' that things would turn around and be better again soon.

They were wrong, Shiko now realized. Things would not be getting better soon, or for quite some time to come. If this Darkness was indeed returning, all of those around him, going about their daily routines, would find those routines shattered and destroyed. Just as his own routine, he reminded himself bitterly, the effort of years, could be swept away in an instant, by a decision to head off on a pilgrimage…

Stop it, he told himself. You're being a child! Of what possible importance could it be to best Utaka compared to what faced Tonagato? Indeed, it would be foolish to do so just to have the Darkness wipe away everything that the Deshi had ever done, as it ravaged the countryside.

Even knowing that, as he stood there in the courtyard, Shiko found it hard to convince himself. Everything seemed so normal. Those students over there, having to listen to old Dojuka's mathematics lecture; even these two fellows patching the wall—

His jaw dropped. One of the two apprentices was removing the night lantern from the wall where they were repairing the plaster. That's it, thought Shiko. The lamplighter! If anyone would know what a Hikari would look like, it would be him.

The quarters and workshops of the craftsmen were grouped together in the town of Hajimeshi, in a lane not far from the castle. The workshops were nondescript affairs, fashioned from utilitarian designs to each man's trade. The workshops proper, with their sleeping quarters above, were arranged along one side of the road, while opposite the shops a line of storehouses held each trade's supplies and raw materials.

Shiko walked down the dirt track between the two rows of buildings, feeling the heat as he passed the blacksmith's forge. As he walked by the leatherworker's shop, he saw the man unloading a saddle from his cart. Shiko waved, but the leatherworker didn't wave back. In fact the man scowled at him, then turned and dragged the heavy saddle off into his shop.

Shiko had not had occasion to visit the craftsmen's shops before, and so had never met the men who worked there. He noted with chagrin that, apparently, not all of them were inclined to welcome visitors.

At last he came to what he determined must be the lamplighter's shop; it would be hard to miss, what with the great light fixture hanging over the door. He knocked and waited.

He heard a shuffling from inside, and a voice said, "Wait, wait, just a minute…" Finally the door opened with a squeak, and the familiar face of the lamplighter peered out at him. Shiko had never talked to him, but had seen him lighting the lamps around the priory and the castle ever since he could remember. The man wore a sleeping gown, and Shiko suddenly realized with horror that the lamplighter would of course sleep late, having tended the castle's lamps much of the night.

"Your pardon, Master Lamplighter," said Shiko, with embarrassment. "I did not mean to wake you."

"'Tis all right boy, 'tis all right," replied the lamplighter, walking back inside and waving to Shiko to follow him. "'Twas time to be up and about anyways."

The apprentice followed the man into his workshop. At first glance, it was a room that was almost overwhelming to the senses. Everywhere he looked Shiko saw lamps and lanterns, brass frames, pieces of glass, cords of rope for wicks, and all manner of unfamiliar paraphernalia. The morning sunlight coming through the windows, striking the various bits of metal and glass, caused the entire room to sparkle.

Interrupting Shiko's reverie, the lamplighter said, "You be one of those Deshi boys, huh?"

"Yes, Master Lamplighter."

"Ah. Name's Tukeru, by the way. Be with you in a moment." He went over to a small wood stove. "Needs my hot kosha, get these old bones moving in the mornings." He poured out some boiling water from a well-dented pot into a tiny cup, one so small he could easily hold it in the palm of his hand. Placing some ground-up leaves in the cup, he swished the mixture around in his hand and then downed it in one draft. Putting the cup down with a satisfied "Ahhhhhh", he turned back to

Shiko. "Now then, boy, what be the problem at the priory this time? Still more candles needed for all that book readin'? Don't know how you Deshi-folk keep any of your eyesight," he muttered, as he shuffled over toward his workbench. "Just dropped off a whole case-full o' candles the other day. They makin' you study into the wee hours, boy?"

"No, Master Tukeru. Actually, I've come for something...well, something different."

"Ohhhh? Well, let me see," said Tukeru with feigned concentration. "Something 'different' he says," as he looked about. "Well, me boy, so sorry, but I be all out of 'different' today." He looked back at Shiko with a gentle grin. "'Less, of course, you can be a bit more specific?"

Smiling, Shiko said, "Well, somewhat, Master Tukeru. I'm looking for...that is, have you ever heard of a Hikari lantern?"

Tukeru gave Shiko a long considering look. Finally he said, "Nope. Never heard of one. But if you describe it, mayhaps I got something that would do the trick. What's it for?"

Deflated, Shiko thought about how much he should explain to the lamplighter. Deciding that discretion was perhaps in order he said, "It's for a special ceremony. It has to be lit during the ritual, and is then carried on the end of a pole until...well, until the ceremony is over," he finished lamely.

"I see," said Tukeru, who clearly did not. "Well, let's look at what sortsa lanterns I got over here that might fit your bill." He walked over to the far wall of the shop, where a bewildering variety of lamps and lanterns were arranged on pegs, from small table candle holders to large outdoor affairs used to light the pathways around the castles. "Be needin' somethin' fancy, I suspect. Most times people want lotsa pretty gee-gaws on their lights when they want one for weddin's and such."

Shiko listened without hearing as Tukeru rummaged through the lamps hanging on the wall. Large or small, they all looked more or less the same to Shiko. What, he wondered, was a Hikari supposed to look like? How was he ever going to find one?

As Tukeru pawed around down near the floor, trying to lift up a particularly ostentatious lamp, Shiko happened to glance over at the lamplighter's workbench. At that moment, a shaft of sunlight coming through the window fell upon a rather homely-looking lantern sitting in the middle of the table. Made of a dull metal, it was a working lamp of the type used for lighting hallways in the domestic staff quarters of the castle. A solid five hands high, its six sides contained plain un-etched glass, and the top had a ring for hanging the lamp from the ceiling. The sunlight reflected back and forth between the glass panes, creating a rainbow effect that belied the lamp's otherwise utilitarian appearance. As he watched, Shiko found himself mesmerized by the brilliant, shifting colors as they played about inside the lamp.

The Hikari, thought Shiko. This is the Hikari lantern! He walked over to the workbench, looking down in awe at the plain, simple lamp with the light cascading through it. Meanwhile, Tukeru finally hoisted up the lantern he was searching for, a gaudy affair covered with imitation gold paint and various beads and crystals.

"Ah, here we go," he said, turning to find Shiko no longer behind him. "Eh?" He looked over and saw Shiko standing at his workbench. Holding up the gilded affair, Tukeru said, "Boy? Is this here what your Hikari look like?"

Shiko, eyes fixed on the lamp on the workbench, said, "No, Master Tukeru. This is it."

Nonplussed, Tukeru set down the fancy lamp and walked over to the workbench. Looking in amazement at the lamp Shiko was staring at, he said, "This? This old thing? Boy, this's just a common hallway lamp. Brought it in for repairs a few days ago; finished it last night. You don't want something like this for no special ceremonies."

"Yes, Master Tukeru. I do." Gently Shiko reached out and lifted the grey lamp from the workbench. The sunlight continued to play on the glass, all the more resonant in contrast to the rough metal surfaces of the frame. "This is what a Hikari lantern looks like."

"Why use an old lamp like that, boy?"

"Because, Master Tukeru," replied Shiko, who now understood what he had been looking for. Holding the lantern up to eye level as he gazed into it, he said, "It is the light within the lamp that is important, not the lantern itself."

✳ ✳ ✳

A soft fizzle was the only sound to be heard from the sleeping chamber of the Omo Deshi. Takamaru was going about the room, slowly extinguishing the meditation candles. He had spent the last hour contemplating how best to take advantage of the circumstances that now presented themselves.

The game, he thought, must now be played with great delicacy. Fate has intervened to remove Itachi's overbearing interference; without the need to counteract that ruffian I can now employ a more serene approach in my dealings with the Kojuro. But first I must consider how best to utilize my new access as the sovereign's Spiritual Guide…

It had, he reflected, been so easy before. Fugawari, despite having been the eldest of the old Kojuro's boys, had never been anything more than a child, right up until his unfortunate demise. And like a child it had been so easy to get him to do what one wanted, once one knew how to provide the proper 'reward.' Thinking back on those days reminded Takamaru again of how far he himself had come. And how it had all been due solely to his own efforts, his own hard work, and his strength of character.

He had never been a 'model' Deshi; he had come late to the order, the third son of a cooper for whom there had been insufficient work to support a family. The cooper's son had become a Deshi apprentice at an age when most were already preparing to go before the Senior Masters. He had possessed, however, a great facility for memorizing facts, and this, plus his already somewhat 'worldly' maturity, had helped him to pass the Oral Questioning and don the Deshi sash.

But his interests had always lain less in learning from books than in learning the world around him. He had rapidly become bored with the bookish routine and had been more likely to be found exploring inns in the town than scrolls in the Archive. After all, he had reasoned, the Deshi were supposed to be guides for those less educated; how could they presume to provide advice if they remained cloistered inside the walls of their priory, never knowing what people out in the real world faced? If that experience had led him to the occasional gambling establishment, then what of it? That was how the common people lived, and as a result of his experiences he was far more knowledgeable about that real world than even the most scholarly of his Deshi brethren. At first he had been tolerated by the other Deshi, and then later ignored; they had always hoped that he would eventually change his ways. He smiled. But then he had found Fugawari!

He had introduced the Kojuro's heir to many of his 'friends' of somewhat dubious reputation, all of whom had been more than happy to provide the young prince with new experiences. Takamaru's gift for knowing just the people who could satisfy Fugawari's insatiable desires for the new and exciting had ensured him a favored place among the prince's retinue of courtiers.

Later, under Takamaru's influence, the heir to the Kojuro had put pressure on the Deshi order to raise Takamaru to the level of Master, against their wishes. When the young prince then acceded to the throne he had strongly 'suggested' that the order's then-Omo Deshi retire and that Takamaru be elevated in his place. The Deshi had acquiesced, not wishing to go counter to the desires of the new sovereign, and hoping that compromise would in the end restore a semblance of 'balance' to their order.

But Takamaru had not been interested in balance. He had no desire to accommodate what he considered to be the slow-thinking, slow-acting Masters who had always looked down on him. It had been clear to the new Omo Deshi that, under this young ruler, the Deshi could become a powerful influence. And he, Takamaru, would be able to become its most influential member. Fugawari, easily impressed by those who spoke with conviction, had readily agreed to Takamaru's proposals to enhance the prestige of the Deshi order. Over time, the new Omo Deshi had built up his own following of supporters, both within the order and without. His influence had seen him elevated to the Council of Ministers where he had gradually built up a power base of his own, independent of the Kojuro.

Yet now things had become more difficult. Kimeru was not as easily influenced as Fugawari, and these last few years had proven troublesome. The time had arrived to become a little more active in influencing the course of events in Hajimeshi...

A gentle knock interrupted his thoughts. "Come," he said, and the door to the room slid open.

A visitor stepped into the dim chamber and, after closing the door behind him, bowed to the Omo Deshi. The only light that illuminated them came from the few mediation candles that remained lit.

"Ah, good," said Takamaru. "I trust you were able to make the necessary arrangements?"

"Yes, Eminence," replied the man.

Takamaru continued around the room as he touched each candle with his ivory-inlaid snuffer, a puff of smoke curling up from where each flame was extinguished. "You understand, the sanctity and purity of the Deshi is paramount on a journey such as this. This is why such...unusual...methods must be employed. We must ensure that nothing occurs on this pilgrimage that might tarnish our image among the foreigners." The lazy streamers of smoke drifted up, twisting among the shadows in the rafters. "You may be called upon to undertake certain...actions...for the betterment of our brotherhood." Takamaru looked penetratingly at his visitor. "Do you understand?"

"Your will is my will, Eminence."

The Omo Deshi stopped before the last of the candles. "You will do nothing but observe unless you receive explicit instructions from me. I want to know anything and everything that happens on this expedition. I expect regular reports, whenever you are able to utilize our usual means." Speaking quietly, he added, "If more...active...measures are required, I will get word to you. Now go." With a bow in reply the man departed, leaving the Omo Deshi alone.

Takamaru gently quenched the last candle's light before setting aside the snuffer. Excellent, he thought. Everything is going quite well.

3

"Why?" cried an anguished Mikasama. "Why you? There are dozens of other soldiers who could go!"

Nakama sat ramrod straight, not daring to look at Mikasama. He kept his gaze focused on one of the well-tended rose bushes across the path from their bench in the Royal Garden, afraid that if he looked Mikasama in the eye he would lose his resolve. He must bear this burden alone, he had decided; he could not subject her to further jeopardy. As it was he was risking much by even seeing her again. Should Itachi find out about it…

But he couldn't leave without saying goodbye. At a loss for any better reason, at least one that he felt he could tell her, he forced out, "I'm…sure Lord Itachi needs a good archer for his journey."

"There are plenty of archers in the Castle Guard!" she rejoined. "Why would he suddenly decide he had to have you?" When Nakama didn't respond, she said, "It's because of me, isn't it? They want to take you away from me!"

Alarmed, Nakama spun toward her. "No, no, Lady! This is just…one of those things a soldier does. He goes where he is told. And…I've been told," he finished quietly.

He knew he wasn't sounding convincing. His mind had been in an uproar ever since his disastrous interview with Itachi. He was disgraced, his career in tatters. He had let his feelings for this young woman blind him to the impossibility of his situation. What had he been thinking? A soldier, a commoner, trying to impress a royal princess? And now his actions had nearly led her into disgrace as well.

He loved her. He loved her more than he had ever been able to tell her. And now he could not, must not let her know. He must be strong for both of them, and save her from further repercussions resulting from their illicit relationship.

Mikasama repeated, "Uncle Itachi could take any of the archers in the Guard. There can only be one reason he's insisted on you." She stood up. "I will go and speak to him, and ask him to choose another."

Nakama leapt to his feet, forgetting himself so much that he grabbed hold of her arm. "No! Mikasama, you must not do that!" His mind reeled at the thought of her trying to reason with the hot-tempered brother of the Kojuro.

The Princess glanced coolly down at his hand on her arm. Quickly he released her. "Lady, I beg you, do not pursue this. It will only lead to…to…"

"To what, Nakama?" When he did not reply, her tongue got the better of her. "I am not accustomed to being discarded like unwanted laundry. Have you decided you do not care for me? Is that it?"

Choking off a sob Nakama turned away from her, walking quickly over to the rose bush. His shoulders quivered as he tried to maintain his composure.

He felt her hand on his back. At her touch he stiffened like a board. He heard her say, "I'm sorry, my sweet Nakama. I didn't mean that. Of course I know how much you care for me." He did not turn to look at her, only bowed his head as she went on, "It's because I love you just as much that I don't want you to go. And I won't let them make you go."

Such agony, thought Nakama. This was much worse than he had imagined. To hear her say those words, the words he had always wanted to hear her say, now when it was all too late!

He realized that he shouldn't have tried to see her again. He had to go, now, before he lost all his willpower and succumbed to his heart's desire. She is a princess, he reminded himself, just as he was a soldier.

Like him, she must do what must be done for the good of the kingdom. He could not let her be hurt by those who would misuse their relationship to damage her reputation.

He reached out and caressed a rose bud that hung near his hand, afraid to turn around. With a final effort, he said, "Goodbye, Lady. I will...I will hope to see you...I shall write to you...upon my return." He pulled his hand away, dislodging several petals from the rose. Without looking at her, knowing that he could not possibly survive the anguished look in her eyes, he walked stiffly away.

Mikasama's voice trailed after him, shouting, "Nakama? Nakama! Please, don't go!" But he did not turn around, and marched out of the garden, each step piercing his heart like a dagger.

Mikasama watched him walking away, calling after him, "Nakama!"

But he was gone. She stood alone on the path, nothing but the muted echoes of her own voice for company, quietly repeating, "Nakama?" She grabbed and twisted at the long sleeves of her kimono, her thoughts spinning and confused.

When Nakama had sent word asking her to come quickly to their meeting place, she hadn't had a clue what had been so urgent. It had been difficult to slip away from Komori but she had managed it, brimming with anticipation at seeing Nakama once more.

She had known something was wrong as soon as she had seen him in the garden. She had noticed immediately that he was not wearing his usual dress tunic. More than that, however, had been the look on his face, a face that she had learned to read as easily as a scroll. And she had read nothing there but abject misery.

Then he had started talking about leaving, about marching off with Uncle Itachi on some sort of expedition. Suddenly she had seen how ephemeral had been their time together, how easily it could all be swept away. She had known that she had been breaking tradition by seeing Nakama but she hadn't really believed that anything would stop her either. But now this! She hadn't realized how insidious the supporters of convention and conservatism could be, especially when 'their' rules were being flouted.

Her emotions were in turmoil, and her anxiety had caused her to say things to him that she knew were not true. Why oh why, she thought, am I always opening my mouth before I think? I hurt him! I know he doesn't really want to go. So why did I say that to him?

Now he was gone, the garden empty but for her. Overwhelmed, she burst into tears and sat down upon the ground.

*   *   *

In the Great Audience Hall Himitsu knelt before the Kojuro. They were discussing the just-concluded interview with Choshuka, their Yutakashi visitor. Kimeru's eyes were closed, his energy drained from spending the previous hour in 'nuptial negotiations' with the slightly hung-over Choshuka. With neither man at his best the discussion had proven inconclusive, and by mutual agreement they had decided to resume tomorrow immediately after the Hikari Pilgrimage ceremony.

"I thought, sire," said Himitsu, "that Lord Choshuka showed a positive interest in the coming pilgrimage."

Kimeru replied with a grunt. "He was probably thinking of how to profit from the news." He shifted about on his dais, trying to find a comfortable position. While the healer's potions did much to assist his sleep they did little to enhance his ease once awake.

"Ah, Majesty, you are perhaps too harsh. Is not one of the reasons for sending the expedition, after all, to bridge differences in understanding?"

Sighing, Kimeru said, "Yes, of course you are right, Himitsu. As you usually are. However, after spending an hour face to face with Yutakashi's 'finest,' I am somewhat less than hopeful of the prospects." He coughed, trying to clear his ravaged lungs. "Well, at least I know not to invest our gold in tochuya farms." Choshuka, like many of his countrymen, never strayed far from mercantile concerns. During the meeting he had attempted to gain favor with Kimeru by passing on 'inside information' about the state of Yutakashi's crop yields.

"Very wise," smiled Himitsu. Rising from the floor he said with a bow, "Is there anything further I can do for you, Your Majesty?"

Kimeru thought for a moment. "I should speak with Toshi-hito before tomorrow's ceremony. Please send for him on your way out."

"Of course, sire—" At that moment, both men became aware of a commotion in the hallway outside the room. A raised female voice was shouting, smothering the sounds of a servant's quiet but insistent protests.

Kimeru frowned. "What is that noise?"

"I believe, sire, that it may be the Princess."

"Why is she shouting like that?"

"Perhaps it is related to the matter we spoke of yesterday, regarding the young Captain of the Guard."

"Ah."

At that moment Mikasama burst into the room, sliding the doors open in one violent movement. The door servant, his pleas ignored, fell to the floor, bowing in apology at his inability to prevent the intrusion on his sovereign. Mikasama crossed into the hall, her kimono fluttering behind her like the wings of an agitated butterfly. "Papa, I must speak to you at once!"

Kimeru leaned forward. "How dare you interrupt a State meeting! What manner of beast are you that barges in on official conferences to which you are not invited?"

Stunned, Mikasama stopped dead in the middle of the room. Her father had never spoken to her in such a manner, ever, in her entire life. A multitude of expressions crossed her face, from shock to anger to fear.

"Well?" shouted Kimeru.

Mikasama paused but a moment. Then she dropped to the floor like a stone, bowing her forehead to the ground like the lowliest of servants. In a small, strained voice she said, "Dearest Father, I beg an audience with you regarding a matter of utmost urgency to your unworthy daughter." Then she fell silent.

The Kojuro leaned back and glanced at Himitsu with a raised eyebrow. The chamberlain returned the look with a slight smile, both men knowing that not too long ago Mikasama would have continued to rant like a spoiled child. Kimeru was pleased that his daughter had progressed to the point of at least understanding when she had violated protocol. Of course, he thought, if Himitsu were to be believed (and he always was), his daughter had been doing all sorts of growing up without his awareness. He nodded to his chamberlain, who silently bowed his head and departed. As Himitsu exited the servant rose and quietly closed the doors behind them, leaving father and daughter alone in the Hall.

Mikasama had not moved. Kimeru let her stay there a moment longer to reinforce the point, much as he had done earlier with his ministers. What is wrong with people these days, he wondered, that I must continually end up doing this? Softly he said, "Yes, my daughter, now what is it that is of such urgency that you must interrupt your father's affairs?"

Like a spring suddenly released she leapt up and ran to him, only to fall once more at his feet, clinging to his knees. In a rush of frantic words mixed with sobs, she cried, "Papa, please don't let them take him away, please, I beg you…"

It was now Kimeru's turn to be stunned. He had not expected such fervent emotion, particularly after her show of restraint on the floor. This must be serious indeed, he realized. It was well that Himitsu had shown the forethought to take action. "Him? Take where? Little partridge, what are you talking about?"

"Papa," she blurted out, "Uncle Itachi wants to send Nakama away on a journey. Tomorrow! Please, have him take someone else."

"Who is this Nakama?" asked Kimeru with a frown. He sincerely hoped that word of Mikasama's transgressions had not percolated into any Yutakashi ears; should Choshuka think that his son, and by extension himself, had been spurned by Hajimeshi it would only exacerbate the tensions between the two kingdoms.

"He is a Captain of the Guard," she answered. She sat up straight and looked her father in the eye. "I love him, Papa. I love him, and I won't let anyone take him away from me."

Oh my, thought Kimeru. Yes, Himitsu, you were most certainly right. Poor little partridge, he reflected, looking down at her sadly. I know what it is like to lose a love. Oh yes. Even now, the pain cuts straight to my heart. If she only knew…

He spoke quietly. "Daughter, you know what is required of you as descendant of the Kojuro. We have less control over our destiny than even the humblest of our subjects. Our course is set for us, and we can but follow it as best we may." He took her chin in his hand. "I wish it were otherwise. Believe me, I wish sincerely that it were so. But it is not." He dropped his hand and sat back. "My brother is head of the Castle Guard. I cannot interfere with his authority; he would lose face in front of his men. If Itachi feels this young man must go, then go he must. If this Nakama is a soldier then he knows his duty. Just as you have a duty, to me and to your people."

"But Papa—"

"No," said Kimeru firmly, as he held up his hand. "There is no more to say. Go now, daughter, and let your father rest."

She sat looking up at him a moment longer, but when he did not relent she turned her head away. Woodenly she rose and bowed toward him. "Yes, Father." She slowly made her way to the doors, which the servant on the other side opened.

"Mikasama," said Kimeru. She stopped and turned in the doorway. "After the pilgrimage has departed tomorrow, we will talk some more. It is time I involved you more in State affairs. You have much to contribute, I know."

"Yes, Father," she replied listlessly. "Thank you." She turned and walked down the hall. The servant silently closed the doors once more.

Ah, little Mikasama, thought Kimeru. It hurt so much to see the light go out of your eyes. But sadness is merely the flip side of happiness, he reminded himself. One cannot have a complete life without both, only half a life. And one half cannot be appreciated without the other.

He closed his eyes and waited for the arrival of Toshi-hito. If ever his spirit needed guidance, it was now.

*   *   *

Mikasama walked down the hall, not seeing where her footsteps led her. She remembered hearing herself say, "Yes, Father," as if it had been someone else's voice, and walking out of the Audience Hall. Most of all she remembered that look in her Father's eyes. She had seen many conflicting emotions there but above it all she had seen that flinty hardness that she knew meant he would not be swayed.

Her mind felt empty, almost in shock. He had denied her! Had turned away an appeal that arose straight from her heart, all because duty had to be served. He must have known, she thought. Someone must have told him. Himitsu! That awful little man who always knows too much. He's probably the one who started the whole thing!

She wandered in a daze until she finally emerged outside the castle, through the door facing the Royal Garden. She didn't remember having set out to go that way. Like a moth drawn to the light she walked into the garden, past the tree where Nakama had felled the apaya, and over to their bench.

How cold the stone looked, she thought, suppressing a shiver despite the warm afternoon air. She sat down, looking around her, remembering her time here with Nakama: their laughter, their joy that seemed as if it would go on forever.

How foolish we were, she realized. All the while that we had basked in one another, here on this bench, others had been finding ways to draw us apart. And now they had succeeded.

She looked at the rose bush across the path. The flower that Nakama had held, when he wouldn't turn around to look at her, now hung limply, its remaining petals bent and twisted. She stood and walked over to it, looking down at what he had touched. Reaching out gently with her fingers, she straightened the petals.

She remembered the first time she had seen the Garden, as a little girl: it was with her father, who had carried her on his shoulders up and down the many winding paths. He had tilted her over so that she could smell all the flowers, like these roses, holding onto her legs with his big, strong hands. And she remembered the men, dutifully following along behind Papa, who had wanted to go on and on with their adult-talk. And finally Papa had put her down. She had wanted him to keep playing with her, and she had pulled on his arm; but he had told her to run along, and Komori had come to fetch her away, back to the castle and to her room…

She kicked at the pebbles strewn across the path. He was right, of course. She was the daughter of the Kojuro, and her choices began and ended with that simple fact. Like her father she had been given a garden to play in; but it was a garden bounded by the hedges that defined its borders, and nothing beyond those confines could be allowed to grow.

She knew she was spoiled, and had considerably more freedom than probably any other woman in Hajimeshi. In the end, though, her obligation was to her father, and to the kingdom. No matter her own feelings she must serve him, and the people. Even, she cringed, if that meant being a figurehead princess, or a stepping-stone for some ambitious lord.

She glanced down at her feet and saw a fat beetle waddling along the gravel path. His ugly feelers waving in front of him to no avail, he bumped into her foot, skittered about, and trudged off in another random direction.

Mikasama shuddered. What if Papa married her to someone awful, like that horrible boy from Yutakashi? For she had, indeed, heard about the visitors from the neighboring kingdom and the reason for their visit. Or some old man, who already had sons of his own? Then she would not even be allowed the privilege of bearing her own children, in order that there be no dispute over who might some day become the Kojuro…

These were not the things that she had dreamed of for herself when she had lain awake at night, staring at the stars through her window. She had dreamed of a dashing Prince, and many Ladies who would be her friends, and a family full of children that looked like her and her

Prince, and days and nights filled with fun and laughter.... The dreams of a child, washed up on the rocks of reality like so much driftwood. And as she watched her dreams being sucked away out to sea a burning anger grew inside her.

I am not somebody's 'prize', she proclaimed to herself. Or something to be set aside as a 'figure of State!' They think they've won. They think, all of them, even Papa, that I'll just meekly roll over and play the good little princess, and marry whomever they choose.

"But I have found what love is!" she shouted to the empty garden. It is a beautiful, wonderful thing that sends my heart soaring among the clouds! I will not let them pull me down out of the sky to grovel at the feet of some dung beetle, grasping courtier.

She reached down and snapped off the stem of the rose, held the bud to her nose, and drank deeply of its sweet scent. She tucked the rose inside her kimono, where once Nakama's apaya had rested. Determined now on what she had to do, she walked straight out of the garden without a backward glance.

*   *   *

Itachi's baleful glare held the men sitting before him as if each of them were fish transfixed upon a harpoon. "Does each of you understand? Any man who does not, speak now, for I will tolerate no misunderstandings later."

There was silence in the room. Itachi and the others sat inside a darkened hall, one of the Castle Guard barracks. It was locked tight against intrusion; dependable sentries, safely beyond earshot, were posted outside. Such precautions were necessary, for this was a treasonous meeting. Itachi and the half-dozen officers kneeling before him would face certain execution were word to leak out of the discussions taking place.

"Then we are ready," Itachi went on. "Once I have concluded the necessary business in Yutakashi, I will send word through my courier bird. That will be your signal to move; I will be right behind you with reinforcements." All the men bowed in acknowledgement. Just then a gentle knock was heard against the outside door.

Instantly the men before Itachi leapt to their feet, hands on sword hilts ready to draw as they formed a defensive arc before their leader. One officer, at a signal from Itachi, strode to the door, opening a small spyhole. Apparently satisfied with what he saw, he turned back to Itachi and nodded. The Hajimeshi general jerked his hand to indicate that the door should be opened.

The officer unlocked the door and swung it wide, hand still ready to draw his blade if need be. The sentry beyond dropped immediately to the ground, bowing his head.

Itachi shouted, "I said we were not to be disturbed! Perhaps I should cut off your ears, so that the sound of my voice can better penetrate into your thick skull!" At that moment, Chumo, Itachi's chamberlain, appeared around the doorframe, as he too knelt before the Hajimeshi general.

Irritably Itachi tapped his now-repaired tarka against his leg. "And what else did she say?"

He stood, along with Chumo, just outside the barracks hall. The Hajimeshi general's eyes were boring down on a kneeling servant, the same one who had recently served a shift before doors of the Great Audience Hall. The man groveled at Itachi's feet, anxious to impart his news and be on his way. In a quivering voice the servant said, "Th-that was all, my lord. She just agreed to what the Kojuro said."

Itachi frowned, and continued tapping his tarka against his leg impatiently. The sun was starting its descent below the castle walls, and his officers were still waiting for him inside the barracks hall. Soon he would have to release them from the meeting, as some of them had to leave tonight before the castle's gates were closed in order to rejoin their troops stationed in the woods to the north. And the more time he spent with this cretin trembling before him, the less time he had to deal with the more important business at hand.

At first angered that Chumo had brought the man here, considering the risks should his plans be discovered, his irritation had been mitigated somewhat by the report of what had transpired between his brother and his niece. And Chumo had been careful, keeping to the late-afternoon shadows and the lesser-traveled paths on his way to the barracks where he had known Itachi was meeting.

He decided that he had now extracted all he could from the quivering figure kneeling on the ground. "All right. Go." The man rose. Chumo, alert as always, tossed a couple of coins to land in the dirt before the man's feet. As the servant scooped them up, Itachi added menacingly, "You were never here, is that understood? And next time, do not approach my quarters directly! Send word to Chumo first, and he will meet you elsewhere." With abject apologies, the servant bowed rapidly, the coins disappearing quickly into the folds of his tunic as he departed.

Itachi laid the tip of his tarka against his cheek, thinking about the substance of Kimeru's interview with Mikasama. It was unlike that spoiled brat to give up so easily, he thought. She's cagey, just like her father. She's probably planning something. And what was Kimeru up to?

He didn't for a moment believe that his brother was in the least concerned with Itachi's standing with the Castle Guard; more likely, he thought, if the fool had any sense he would feel just the opposite. I would have expected my weakling brother to give in to the brat's demands. He always has in the past, coddling the little slut when she should have been dragged outside and given a strong whipping. So what was behind his feigned support? Does he seriously think his daughter will marry that fat little slug from Yutakashi? Only an imbecile would wager on that. And my brother may be a fool but he is far from stupid...

He turned to his chamberlain. "Chumo, I want someone to watch the Princess until we have left on the pilgrimage tomorrow. Report to me anything she does out of the ordinary." Chumo bowed without a word and left to perform his master's bidding.

A dependable man, thought Itachi as he watched his chamberlain depart. He hoped that his lieutenants were equally so, since they now had to put into motion some of his plans while he went off on this ridiculous quest. But, he reminded himself, the journey does make an excellent cover, and thus makes part of my objective all that much easier to obtain.

Satisfied, he turned and went back into the barracks to drill again into the men's heads where they had to be and when. They would only have one opportunity to do this right.

*   *   *

The shadows deepened and merged into the dark night that silently wrapped itself around the buildings of Hajimeshi.

Mikasama slipped quietly into the stable, holding her lamp tentatively before her. She had come in from the hay-feed barn so as not to attract notice. For the same reason she wore a simple cloak, such as any of the common folk might wear. The horses in their stalls stood silently, watching her as she entered. In the rafters overhead an owl quietly twisted its head and followed her progress.

The stable boys had all gone to bed but the night watchman, she knew, would be by soon. She continued on, the smell of leather and damp hay filling her nostrils as she looked over the livery equipment stored on pegs and racks about the walls. She had ridden horses as part of her 'training' but had never saddled one, nor paid any attention to how everything fit together on the animal. Now she was going to have to figure out how it was done. Staring at the bewildering array of equipment arranged on the wall, she was suddenly seized with doubts. Do I even know, she wondered, what it is that I'm doing? Is this really the right thing to do?

For perhaps the hundredth time, she went over her plan again. From the moment she had left the garden her course had seemed clear: she was going to leave Hajimeshi, and follow Nakama, wherever he was going. She would leave the following night, well after the Hikari party had left, hoping to catch up with the pilgrims on the road. How she was going to attract Nakama's attention without alerting Itachi or any of the others in the pilgrim party was a problem she had not yet worked out. But, she determined, she would cross that bridge when she reached it. It was enough for the moment to try and figure out how to deal with a horse.

All the rest of that day she had considered how she would proceed. In the afternoon she had watched the Guardsmen while they trained with their horses, observing what parts of the equipment went where. She knew that she would not have much time to do it herself, between the stable boy's departure and the rounds of the watchman. So she had come to the stables tonight to see where all of the pieces were kept and how she was going to get them on a horse, timing her nocturnal excursion for when Komori was asleep. But looking now at the daunting mass of unfamiliar equipment arrayed along the wall shook her resolve.

Plaintively she asked herself, what am I doing here? Why in the world am I trudging around in a dirty stable, wearing a smelly old cloak? Komori would skin me if she knew I was out here at night. And Papa, he would be so angry...

Papa. It kept coming back to him, she realized. How could she even think of leaving him, especially when he was so sick? Not only was it her duty to obey him, if she left and something happened to him how could she ever forgive herself?

Standing uncertainly, she gazed at the confusing mass of equipment. Guilt gnawed at her as she stepped back from the wall. Tugging on her hair and nervously chewing its loose ends, she had almost decided to give up and sneak back to her room within the castle when the owl overhead hooted.

She looked up but couldn't see the owl in the darkness; the lamp's light did not cast that far. Her eyes did, however, fall upon some of the equipment stored higher up along the wall, and these were items that she *did* recognize: they were the saddle-quivers used by mounted archers.

With a rush the image of Nakama's face, his smile, pushed to the forefront of her mind. She could almost hear his energetic laugh, as if he were standing right next to her; could almost smell his scent, the one she remembered so well from the times they had sat together in the garden, so close...

She slapped a hand against her leg. "Stop it," she said out loud. "Just stop it." If she kept this up, she told herself, she'd keep dithering away the whole night, and Nakama would have left on the pilgrimage before she'd done anything at all.

Papa will be all right until I return, she decided. After all, I'm not going for the entire pilgrimage; I'm only going so that I can show him how much Nakama means to me, and that I won't let him be taken away. Once he sees that, I'm sure he'll let Nakama return with me. After that...

After that, she realized, she had no idea what would happen. She couldn't predict the future that far. All she knew was that she could not let Nakama go. Something inside her was telling her not to let him go, that she must follow him. She had sworn to herself, back there in the garden, that she was not going to let her life be shunted down the narrow path that had been laid out for her. Whatever difficulties lay down this new road, she would deal with them as they came.

She walked up to the wall on which the saddles and other gear hung. Just as she started to finger parts of the harness she heard a sound from the far side of the room, where the main door led outside. Quickly she covered her lamp and crept back into the shadows.

The door opened, and Shiko walked into the stables. He was carrying loaded traveling packs in his arms, and a small hand lamp dangled from his fingers. He approached the horses that he and Toshi-hito would ride on the pilgrimage and put the packs down on the floor nearby. Having bundled up everything that he and Toshi-hito would need on the journey, all that would be left to do tomorrow after the Hikari ceremony would be to load the packs up on the horses. He had only ridden one once before and was looking forward to trying it again.

He reached up and patted one of the horses on the nose. Strangely, as his hand touched the animal's skin, he had the oddest feeling that the horse was somehow chuckling.

Smiling at the silliness of his thought, he turned back toward the door. Suddenly, though, he felt goose bumps on his skin. Someone was here, he realized, somewhere in the stable. He didn't know what it was that prompted him to feel that way; he couldn't hear or see anything unusual. Nevertheless, he was certain that someone *was* there, and close by.

Mikasama watched as Shiko turned and looked into the dark, directly to where she sat holding her breath. Even though she was certain he could not see her, he said, "Can I help you?"

Mikasama exhaled, and walked slowly out into the light cast by Shiko's lamp. "I was just...checking on my horse. I will be doing some riding tomorrow, and...I wanted to make sure he was all right."

Shiko looked at her oddly and started to speak, but before he could say anything there were sounds from the hay-barn through which Mikasama had entered earlier. Mikasama moved quickly back into the shadows, whispering urgently, "Don't tell anyone I was here!"

"But—"

"Please!" said Mikasama, poking her head back up into the light. "Promise me you won't tell anyone!" Shiko paused, and as the door to the hay-barn swung open Mikasama ducked down again out of sight.

A grim-faced man, who wheezed with each step he took, came through. Seeing the apprentice, the newcomer shuffled up to him. "Where'd the girl go?" he said gruffly.

Looking up and down at the man's unshaven face, rotted teeth, and filthy clothing, Shiko replied, "What girl?"

"The girl that came in 'ere, not five minutes ago! You would've had to seen 'er."

Calmly Shiko shook his head. "I saw no girl in here." With a brusque oath the man pushed past Shiko and hurried out the main door.

In the shadows Mikasama let out a sigh of relief. She hadn't any idea who the man was. He could have been one of Himitsu's 'spies,' or someone sent by her Uncle Itachi, or...or even her father, she realized. In any event, the man appeared to have lost her trail. She rose from her hiding place and walked back over to Shiko. She gave him a keen look. "Thank you for not telling him."

Shiko gazed back steadily. "I simply told him the truth. I saw no girl here." Bowing, he added, "Only the Princess Mikasama."

In some discomfiture at having been recognized, Mikasama quickly changed the subject. Looking at his brown robe she said, "You—you are a Deshi, are you not?"

"Only an apprentice, Lady; I have yet to pass the Oral Questioning before the Senior Masters. They, and Master Toshi-hito, will determine if I am ready to be a full Deshi."

Ah, thought Mikasama, Toshi-hito. He has always been kind to me. Yes, this would be one of his; so polite and honest. "Yes, well, thank you again, Shiko," she said. "I won't forget your kindness to me." Then she bowed to him.

Shiko, hesitantly and clearly embarrassed at the unexpected honor, returned the bow. Before he could say anything else the Princess turned and swept out the way she had come in, through the door to the hay-barn. Shiko watched her go in puzzlement, then turned and started out the main door.

The horses looked at one another, and several snorted, bobbing their heads almost as if in laughter. Up in the rafters, the owl continued to watch silently.

*   *   *

The next day dawned bright and clear, a slight breeze rippling the flags that flew above the castle ramparts. From there one could see for many miles, taking in the vast sweep of Hajimeshi in all directions.

The Kojuro walked alone along the walls, trying to enjoy the view. The day had finally come, he reflected; a day that filled him with both anticipation and dread all within the same moment. Before the rising sun had dropped once more into darkness on the far side of his kingdom, the pilgrimage would be set on its course. He would then have fulfilled the most important part of his destiny; the rest would fall upon the shoulders of others. From that moment forward he would face the much more difficult task of waiting. Waiting to see if the fruits of his endeavor should ripen, and in leaving the tree, thus save it.

He looked down from the walls, deep into the heart of the Sacred Grove below. Nothing could be seen, of course, for the vegetation grew so thick that all was a riot of natural greens and browns. But he knew. He knew what lay within the sheltering arms of those trees and shrubs. For all the times I have entered that place, he mused, never have I re-emerged as the same man who went in.

The Grove was not surrounded by any of the castle walls; there was no physical barrier to prevent anyone from walking directly into it. But a social taboo prohibiting anyone other than the Kojuro from setting foot inside it was so strong that only once in over five hundred years had anyone been known to try and enter the Grove. That man's headless body had been found outside the next morning, serving as an impressive reminder of the Grove's inviolability. At least that was the legend that had been passed down, which served admirably to preserve the sanctity of the Shizen's home.

For the reigning Kojuro, however, there was no concern about entering the Grove. It was his special place, and he was always welcome there. Fugawari, Kimeru's older brother, had entered the Grove only once, immediately after his coronation as Kojuro. He had never gone back. Kimeru suspected that his elder sibling had been unable to confront the truth that had undoubtedly been thrown into his face by the Shizen. Fugawari had been more interested in games and indulgence than governing, attracting a cadre of flatterers to cater to his whims. Standing before the Shizen, his pretences would have been stripped away, leaving nothing but the unadorned man underneath. It was not a revelation that Fugawari would have been predisposed to accept.

As he looked down into the lush expanse of the Grove, Kimeru repressed a shudder. No, he reflected, it is not a place for the weak of spirit.

He made his way down the narrow stairs that led to the entrance of the Grove, taking the many steps slowly, one at a time, to ease the strain on his beleaguered body. Finally arriving at the portal, almost directly below the balcony of the Great Audience Hall, he paused before its heavy wooden door.

The seal of Hajimeshi was crudely carved onto the door's otherwise unadorned surface. Kimeru ran his fingers over the rough-hewn wood, said by the Deshi to be the oldest door in the castle. Touching it always served to remind him of the history to which he was the guardian. The carving, functional rather than artistic, spoke of another age, a time when Hajimeshi was young and its leaders were bold men.

According to the history scrolls the First Kojuro of Hajimeshi, along with his army, had engaged in a bloody battle below the hill where the future castle would be built. They were fighting an invading army from the far south. By nightfall the Kojuro and his exhausted troops had fought the enemy to a standstill, but the next day would assuredly have brought about the demise of the small Hajimeshi force. The Kojuro, told by a local soothsayer about a copse of trees which supposedly held magical power at the top of the hill, had climbed up to seek it out. He had entered the wooded area alone to meditate for the souls of his men whom he knew would be lost on the morrow.

When the Kojuro had emerged, however, his demeanor had changed. He had begun issuing orders to his generals, who were astounded at the bold tactics that the Kojuro proposed. At first light the Hajimeshi host had swept down upon the invaders and driven them from the field.

The rumors had spread like wildfire about what the Kojuro had seen among the trees. All he would say was that he had spoken with mysterious beings, who he called the Shizen, and whom had shown him what had to be done. The Kojuro had made the hill containing what came to be called the Sacred Grove the center of his liberated kingdom. Eventually a small fortification had been built next to the Grove, and it was this humble structure that had been expanded and enhanced over the years into the present day's castle. And ever since that initial encounter, only the Kojuro had been permitted to enter the Grove and converse with the Shizen who dwelt there.

It was not, thought Kimeru, a responsibility to be taken lightly. He felt the resonance of many years, and many hands, through his own as he touched the wood. Taking a deep breath, he pushed open the ancient door and walked out into the Grove.

The first thing that struck him, as it always did, was how the very air itself within the Grove felt more vibrant and alive. It was as if the air, like the plants and trees, was a living thing, nurtured in this special place. Walking forward on the winding path that led from the door he felt as if he was a part of the Grove, one more living thing added to the rich mixture of life surrounding him. It made him feel both insignificant and indispensable at one and the same time: no greater or lesser than any of those things around him, but as vital to them as they were to him.

As he walked along the path, which the plants seemed to keep clear of their own volition, Kimeru had time to reflect on the occasion of his own first time entering the Grove. Contrary to the presumed inviolability of the Grove, he had not been the Kojuro when he had done so. Nor had he been alone.

Kimeru's father had already begun his long slide into senility, and had not gone into the Grove for a number of years. Hajimeshi too had begun to decline, and young Kimeru had been restless to do something, anything, to change what many considered to be the kingdom's inevitable descent into irrelevancy. He had been young and brash, full of a sense of self-importance and destiny. With the reckless abandon of youth he had been determined to find out if the Shizen could be persuaded to assist in reversing Hajimeshi's downward spiral. His accomplice had been a young Deshi apprentice, none other than Toshi-hito, a kindred spirit wishing to 'set the world right.' One clear night the two of them had brazenly entered the Grove from the outside, observed only by a full moon that had hung overhead like a great discerning eye.

They had not ended up headless on the path. But both had been forever changed by their experience.

They had seen the Shizen, yes; but it had not been what either of them had expected. In that meeting lay the seeds of much of what had transpired since, including the current Hikari Pilgrimage. The two of them had entered seeking a destiny and emerged having found it, albeit one which would take years, even decades, to reach fruition.

As Kimeru now neared the center of the Grove the trees to either side parted, leaving a small clearing. The foliage surrounding this spot was very dense, obscuring everything outside from view except straight up, forming a natural skylight of blue. Over the years many people had speculated on what was inside the Grove; perhaps a stone temple, they said, or a deep natural cave. There had always been rumors that the Kojuro kept a fortune in gold stored inside the Grove, or that he practiced black magic there in the middle of the night.

The reality, however, was more mundane, at least physically. In the center of the clearing, a large flat stone, as long and wide as a man was tall, lay embedded in the ground. Peeking up but a short way above the blades of grass, the rock appeared as if it were a stone carpet that had been thrown across the open space. Only its irregular outline and gently undulating surface hinted at its natural origins.

Kimeru walked to the stone's near edge, knelt down on the grass, and waited. He practiced no incantations, cast no magic spells. The Shizen would know he had entered the Grove the moment he came through the doorway. They would come in their own time.

This, he reflected, was always the most peaceful time. He could let the quiet joy of the Grove sooth his spirit, and be one with the other living things that dwelt here. The sound of birds flitting from tree to tree, singing to one another; the gentle rustle of leaves from the breeze, all served to calm his soul.

Slowly, almost imperceptibly, a pinpoint of light formed in the air in front of Kimeru, on the opposite side of the flat stone. With a soft rumbling sound, resembling the gentle burbling of a brook, the pinpoint of light began expanding, turning into a yellowish disk perpendicular to the ground. The birds became quiet; even the wind seeming to rest, and the swaying branches stilled themselves. It was as if the entire Grove stopped to pay homage.

The disk of light before Kimeru grew larger and larger, until it formed a circle nearly two shoulder-widths across. At the center of the disk the color began to dissipate, opening outwards toward the edges, leaving...what, it was hard to say. If he had ever had to describe it, Kimeru would have called it a window. Looking through the opening, he could not see the Grove on the other side. Through the window was...somewhere else.

That somewhere was lit by its own sun; or at least, the light that streamed through the window seemed to come from a different direction than the sun over Hajimeshi. Kimeru could not see much else through the window, for the view was dominated by the image of Shidosha, the supreme Shizen.

Shidosha appeared to Kimeru as a lioness, although he was never sure if she really was a lion or simply assumed that shape. She never roared or uttered any sound that one might think lions to make. Her way of speech was silent: the Shizen spoke directly to one's intellect without need of speech. As the familiar warm feeling that presaged Shidosha's 'voice' entered his mind, he focused all of his attention on the lioness's image before him and listened.

"*I have come,*" he heard in his head.

Speaking back in his mind, Kimeru thought, "*Greetings, Shidosha,*" as he bowed to the image. "*Are you well?*"

"*Yes. Today you send him away?*"

Always direct and to the point, thought Kimeru. He had found that Shidosha had little use for human small talk. "*Yes, Shidosha. We will have a ceremony later today, and then the Hikari Pilgrimage will begin.*"

"*And then he will return?*"

"*Yes, Shidosha, then he will return.*"

"*Good. Events transpire, of which he must be a part.*"

So easily put, thought Kimeru: 'events transpire.' Yet in that deceptively uncomplicated phrase lay the labors of years, now past, and the fate of Tonogato, yet to come.

But he did not doubt the import of those events. Shidosha, he had come to know, was the most powerful of the Shizen, and the one who most often came to 'speak' with him. With her the words formed easily in his head, and she was able to understand his thoughts with equal ease. With the other Shizen it took more effort, a careful mental discipline to actually 'hear' what they had to say and to reply in return. Shidosha had taught both Kimeru and Toshi-hito how to conduct these 'conversations,' and now both could carry on dialogs with nearly all of the Shizen, in or out of the Grove.

For that was one of the revelations of their initial encounter with the Shizen: while Shidosha and the other powerful Shizen lived 'somewhere' beyond Hajimeshi, the lesser Shizen lived in the 'real' world. In fact the Shizen were quite natural; they were embodied in all of the animals living throughout Tonogato.

This had been a great shock to Kimeru and Toshi-hito. Their knowledge of the Shizen had come from the same stories that everyone knew, that the Shizen were some sort of magical beings living only in the Grove. To learn that the Shizen were, in reality, the animals all around them, had taken a while to accept. However once the two men had left the Grove that first time, they had found that they were indeed able to talk with the birds and the forest creatures, albeit in only a rudimentary fashion at first. Where once they had taken for granted that animals were simply animals, with no more thoughts or cares than the trees and shrubs, they had come to find that there were entire societies and hierarchies of animals, rivaling in their complexity any of the human kingdoms.

Kimeru had never quite understood the relationship of Shidosha to the animals in Tonogato. He did not know if Shidosha, and the other Shizen that appeared to him through the 'window' in the Grove, were 'gods' to the animal Shizen in his world, or simply rulers who resided in some other 'place.' It was not a topic that the Shizen discussed with him.

What *was* clear was that the animals of Tonogato obeyed the Shizen that lived in that 'other' place in the Grove. Shidosha had commanded the animals to 'speak' with Kimeru and Toshi-hito, and so they had. Many, as Kimeru had come to find, apparently did not appreciate the contact, mirroring the lack of consideration that most humans showed to them.

The animals, Kimeru had learned, ranged far and wide all over Tonogato and beyond, bringing information to Shidosha and the other Shizen in the Sacred Grove. The Kojuro of the day was a beneficiary of this knowledge. In the past other Kojuros had used the knowledge shared by the Shizen to enhance the prosperity of Hajimeshi, or to avoid conflicts. If, however, the Kojuro chose not to hear what the Shizen had to say, as had happened in the later years of Kimeru's father's reign, and that of his elder brother, Hajimeshi tended toward decline. What the Shizen received as a benefit from this odd alliance with a human ruler of a Tonogato kingdom, Kimeru could not say. Such questions were never encouraged in his conversations with the Shizen.

Neither Kimeru nor Toshi-hito had ever revealed what they had discovered after their foray into the Grove. The nature of the Grove had always been the Kojuro's secret knowledge; even Fugawari, as irresponsible as he was, had never dared reveal the secret behind the Shizen. For in truth who would have believed him? The animals would not have spoken to any others, even had more humans known how to do so. The secret had remained with the Kojuro and the Shizen, in and out of the Grove, over the course of the centuries, at least until Kimeru and Toshi-hito's clandestine visit. To this day Kimeru had no idea why the Shizen had chosen to speak with him and his Deshi companion. Nor, he reflected, did it matter; it was enough that they had. And nothing had been the same since.

His musings were interrupted as Shidosha abruptly changed the subject. "*You are less well than before,*" she said.

Shifting uncomfortably, Kimeru tried to think of an appropriate response that would allay Shidosha's concern, before remembering that such subterfuge was wasted on a being who could speak directly to one's mind. Shidosha already knew his thoughts. "*Your time in this world grows short, Kimeru of Hajimeshi.*"

Kimeru felt himself grow cold and suppressed a shiver. He knew, of course, even if his court healer was unsure. He knew his frail body was choosing to leave the world of its own accord, whether he willed it to or no. For months now he had felt the sickness slowly eating away at his body. Still it was uncomfortable to hear another speak of it so definitively. There was always that small glimmer of unreasonable hope, that small shred of doubt, that just maybe he might turn a corner and become well once more.

But such self-deception was fruitless when one was able to see clearly beyond mere wishful thinking. Shidosha, moreover, had never been one to shrink away from unpleasant truths. Oddly though, after his initial spark of fear, with the erasure of hope Kimeru now felt more at peace with himself than he had in some time.

All along he had been formulating his plans, acting on the advice of Shidosha and the Shizen, but doing so in a detached manner. For the end result of their joint efforts had presupposed Kimeru's demise along the way. With confirmation of his fate, Kimeru could now achieve a focus that he had been lacking. Time, indeed, was growing short, he realized. But not just for him. If Hajimeshi, and the rest of Tonogato, were not united in time, they would all fall prey to the Darkness. Everything depended on the success of the Hikari Pilgrimage.

Kimeru looked unflinchingly at the lioness's image. "*Yes, Shidosha, my tenure is brief. But it will be enough. I will not fall until what needs to be done, is done.*"

Shidosha, not one to muse on human concepts of sentimentality, merely replied, "*Good.*"

The Kojuro bowed to the image of the lioness, whose head appeared to bow in return. Then the circle slowly faded, becoming paler. Finally it dissolved into a hundred small sparkles of light, each of which winked out like the stars fading with the coming of dawn.

Kimeru had come to the Grove that morning unsure of what he sought, feeling the need to converse with Shidosha before the Hikari ceremony upon which so many of their hopes were bound. Instead, he had found something unsought. As with his first journey into the Grove, all those years ago, he never seemed to find what he expected to find, but never was he left unchanged by the experience. Today had been no exception.

Prepared now to face whatever his future held, Kimeru sat for a moment, in the quiet of the Grove. Softly, the birds began singing once more. The sun had risen above the edge of the treetops, spilling light across the clearing and the surface of the large stone. Kimeru soaked up the sun's warmth, closing his eyes to listen to the other Shizen around him. Then he rose and left the Grove.

* * *

Ambassador Choshuka heaved himself down to the ground in a posture approximating the usual deferential kneeling position. Those kneeling next to him, including Himitsu and Takamaru, discreetly shuffled sideways to allow him more room. Due to his privileged status the visiting Yutakashi had been placed in the front rank of those who would watch the Hikari ceremony. His son was conspicuous by his absence.

Himitsu and the other observers sat facing the castle's Meditation chamber. This room, normally the private preserve of the Kojuro and his Spiritual Guide, featured one entire wall of sliding doors, now all opened onto the adjoining outdoor courtyard. It was in this courtyard that the various dignitaries had assembled to observe the lighting of the Hikari. The chamber itself was unadorned, containing nothing more than plain rugs lining the floor and a small low table in the center of the room. The table usually held the candles that were used as focus points for the meditations. Dominating the table today, however, was the rather larger shape of the Hikari lantern.

The plain hallway lamp that Shiko had found, the focus of a ceremony to which all the nobles and leaders of Hajimeshi had been invited, did not seem quite so out of place in the unadorned Mediation chamber as it might have in some other locale. As the rays of the sun crept over the walls of the castle and spilled into the courtyard, the lamp's glass reflected the light throughout both the courtyard and the room.

Kneeling inside the chamber, facing each other across the small table, were the two leaders of the pilgrimage. Lord Itachi was outfitted in his finest ceremonial armor, the gleaming black plates rippling as he moved, like the scales of the mythical dragons from old Tonagato legends. Expensive silk cords were draped ostentatiously across both shoulders and he held his ornate crested helmet lightly under one arm. Toshi-hito, hands folded in his lap, wore only the plain brown robe of the Deshi. Shiko knelt in a corner by the back wall, facing the courtyard. He was there to assist in the ceremony by handing the Kojuro the flints and other materials needed for lighting the Hikari.

Sitting arrayed facing this tableau, all in complete silence, were some two-dozen members of the Hajimeshi nobility. A door at the rear of the courtyard opened and all of the nobility, along with Itachi, Toshi-hito, and Shiko, bowed as Kimeru, dressed completely in white, walked stiffly between his assembled retainers in the path left open for him. Upon reaching the chamber, Kimeru bowed to the Hikari. As he straightened the others rose to a sitting position.

Kimeru turned to face the nobility. "Today marks the beginning of a quest, the outcome of which holds the fate of Hajimeshi, and all of Tonagato." He proceeded into the chamber and around to the opposite side of the Hikari and, with some difficulty, knelt facing the lantern and the open courtyard. This was the signal to begin the ceremony proper.

He recited the words that would mark his request for a pilgrimage. "I have received a vision, one that came to me unbidden, but which must be obeyed as being no less than the truth. I have been called to find that which will bind us; a healer of wounds; an assembler of bridges; a fashioner of doorways; one who will show us, and our neighbors, what must be done, together, to stand against the Darkness." With slightly sagging shoulders, he continued, "The husk upon which this burden has been placed is unable to carry out that to which the mind has agreed. I therefore request that I may nominate others to lead this pilgrimage for the salvation of our land." With that he bowed once more to the lantern, completing his portion of the ceremony as supplicant. The brief respite also permitted him to catch his breath.

He now assumed the mantle of Kojuro and granter of the privilege to conduct a Hikari pilgrimage. Slowly clapping his hands twice, he held them out as Shiko rose from his spot. The apprentice brought the flints over and placed them in the Kojuro's outstretched hands. As Shiko knelt down to one side and behind him, Kimeru struck the flints and lit a longmatch, which burned with a slow flame. Looking across the lantern to the assembled nobility, he said, "Our ancestors gave to us many gifts. These we cherish above all other material possessions, for they are the only true things we own. One such of these is the right to pilgrimage, to seek that which is greater than our mortal flesh, that which is larger than what our own minds can conceive. It is the right, and the duty, of the Kojuro to honor such pilgrimages and bestow upon them the sanctity of protection implicit in the Hikari lantern."

Kimeru opened the glass door on the side of the lantern and touched the longmatch to the wick inside. The dry fibers, freshly installed by the lamplighter when he had refurbished the lamp, caught with a rapid burst of flame. The sudden light sparkled across the panes of glass, casting a warm glow over the Kojuro's face. The brilliant incandescence seemed also to soak into Toshi-hito's robe, deepening its earth-tone colors. On the opposite side of the small table, the light reflected sharply off of Itachi's finely-polished armor.

All three men bowed to the lantern. Kimeru continued. "I decree that all who walk beneath this light shall enjoy the protection and honor of the Kojuro, as if they walked at my side; that all who encounter this light should protect and honor its bearers, and give to them all needed succor in achieving their goal; and that no one shall hinder or harm any member of this pilgrimage while shielded by its light." He bowed again, and this time his action was mirrored by everyone present as they acknowledged the Kojuro's will. Choshuka, too, as a representative of Yutakashi, by joining with the Hajimeshi nobility in bowing to the Hikari, bound his city and its people to respect the ancient rites.

Kimeru closed the glass door of the Hikari. Standing, he took hold of the ring at the top of the lantern and lifted it from the small table, holding it up for all to see. "As the pilgrim cannot personally undertake his journey, the Hikari will be placed in trust with those chosen to follow his path for him. Let he who accepts this lamp be the guide for all others, the beacon that lights the way for those who would follow."

Itachi squared his shoulders, having waited for this moment. With a quiet movement he set down the helmet he had been holding under his arm. Now, he thought, my brother must choose.

Whomever Kimeru handed the Hikari to would by default become the preeminent member of the pilgrimage. Either way would serve Itachi's purpose. If Kimeru handed him the Hikari, then it would show to all the assembled lords that Itachi was not only the leader of the expedition but recognized as the Kojuro's rightful successor should Mikasama never marry. For Kimeru would then be equating Itachi with the Kojuro in the eyes of the world by allowing his brother to conduct the pilgrimage in his stead.

If, on the other hand, Kimeru gave the Hikari to Toshi-hito, the insult to Itachi's honor would be obvious and blatant. There were many among the assembled nobility who would share Itachi's outrage at having a Deshi placed above him in such a public manner. It would fan the flames that Itachi had been carefully tending for some time.

If Toshi-hito experienced any such thoughts as coursed through Itachi's mind, he gave no sign of it as he sat calmly gazing at the lantern held by the Kojuro. Kimeru held the Hikari before him, making no move to hand it to either Itachi or Toshi-hito. The already-quiet assembly seemed to grow yet more silent as all waited to see what the Kojuro would do.

Abruptly Kimeru turned. He looked down at Shiko and said, "Stand."

Shiko's eyes widened in surprise. He looked up at the Kojuro, then to Toshi-hito, but the Master's gaze was expressionless. The apprentice looked back to his sovereign, then stood up uncertainly.

There was a rustle from the assembled lords. Itachi showed his consternation with a scowl. What, he wondered, was Kimeru doing?

The Kojuro turned back to look out over the courtyard. "This apprentice is the youngest of those who will journey on the pilgrimage. He is untainted by the politics, the temptations, which those of us of greater years have experienced. He symbolizes the innocence of Hajimeshi. As we walk out among our peers seeking honest brotherhood, he represents the next generation of our people, and thus the future of Hajimeshi. It is thus appropriate that the Hikari be placed in his care." Kimeru turned to Shiko and held the lantern out to him.

Shiko was stunned. The Kojuro, he realized, was giving *him* the lamp! He wanted Shiko to be the pilgrim in his place, to find the Kotaishi.

The apprentice looked at the Hikari. He had carried it here from the lamplighter's shop, when it had been nothing more than a common lamp. And here it was, being handed back to him again. Only now it was more than just an ordinary lamp. The light that shone from its center had been sanctified by the Kojuro, and was the symbol of their entire journey to come. Just a few days ago Shiko had been thinking of nothing but the Oral Questioning and gaining the Deshi sash. Then Toshihito had changed everything, by asking him to accompany him on the pilgrimage. Now the Kojuro wanted to make *him* the pilgrim! He wondered if it was all just a dream...

Mouth suddenly dry, Shiko hesitantly reached out to take the Hikari from Kimeru. For a moment, Kojuro and apprentice touched as each held the ring at the top of the lantern. Kimeru kept his hand in place, holding Shiko's eyes a moment longer. Quietly he said, "Walk well, young man." He then released the lantern, which seemed heavier than Shiko remembered it. The Kojuro turned away and sat once more before the small table.

Itachi bristled in silence. A clever trick, he thought. My brother has managed to avoid having to give the lantern either to me or to Toshi-hito. Typical of my spineless brother! Well, no matter. His little subterfuges won't save him.

Neither Itachi nor Toshi-hito had moved throughout the exchange between Kojuro and apprentice. From a side door, two servants appeared bearing a pole. They affixed it to the lantern's top ring, where it would be used to suspend the lamp above the pilgrimage party. In the audience, Choshuka chuckled softly. He leaned toward the Omo Deshi and whispered, "Very clever, your Kojuro. He plays his cards well. I will remember this when next we talk trade." Takamaru scowled, saying nothing.

The servants departed, and Shiko raised the lantern aloft on its pole. He knew, from having read about the Hikari ceremony, what was supposed to be said at this point. However he had never thought to be saying the words himself. He looked out into the courtyard, across a sea of unfamiliar faces. The lords of all the Hajimeshi domains, and the Kojuro himself, were waiting for him to speak. He felt a twinge of fear. What was he doing up here, before all of these leaders of Hajimeshi? He was just a Deshi apprentice…

He looked up at the lamp above him. The flame inside it reflected endlessly among the glass panes, the refraction casting a light even brighter than the morning sun. Perhaps it was the Hikari's steady glow, or maybe the years of Deshi training that had prepared him for dealing with the unexpected. But for whatever reason, looking up at the lamp, he felt a growing confidence, a feeling of certainty. Not only did he know what words had to be said; somehow he knew that they were the right words to say. The enormity of the task ahead, of which before he had thought himself but a small part, landed full upon him.

"My lords," he began somewhat shakily, "Your Majesty. Unworthy as I am, I...I accept this burden you have placed upon me." He tried to ignore the quiet muttering from the assembled nobles, and concentrated on reciting the words he had learned only the day before. "This light guides our way. It shines over all of us: those who walk with it on the pilgrimage, and upon those who stay behind. All here are witness to its light, and all are bound to honor it. Let no man block its light from another. Let no one, from highest lord to lowest servant, look upon this light and fail to be touched by it."

Those were the ritual words regarding the Hikari lantern; now he had to speak the words that would define the pilgrimage itself. He tried to keep his focus on the lantern, ignoring the steely gazes of the powerful lords sitting directly in front of him. What, he wondered, were they thinking? Some of them he knew by reputation: Baron Jakata, for instance, from the far north of Hajimeshi. He was an earthy man, one always at odds with the Kojuro, whoever held the throne. He was unlikely to be given toward feelings of 'brotherhood.' What would he make of a quest seeking to unite the kingdoms in common cause?

Shiko mentally shook himself. They were waiting for him to continue, and here he was daydreaming. He cleared his throat. "We...we face a great Darkness, which threatens to walk the land once more, as it did in the distant past. As then, we must unite our peoples or suffer utter destruction. The Darkness knows no mercy, and will sap the sun's own light, and that of every candle, of every lamp, leaving the world in perpetual night. Thus would perish every living thing: every person, every animal, every tree."

He glanced down at the lords arrayed before him. He saw frowns on some faces; on others, careful neutrality. Nowhere did he sense any feelings of wholehearted support. Quickly he looked away again, back to the Hikari. "We must seek the one who can bring the kingdoms together, who can show us the way past our differences, so that we may face our common danger as brothers, shoulder to shoulder." He swallowed. "We must find the Kotaishi."

As he finished, everyone present, from Kojuro to the most minor lord in the back row, dutifully, silently, bowed with forehead to the ground. Only Shiko remained standing, holding the Hikari.

4

"Hah! You stupid beast!"

A small man stood ranting at a mule in front of the castle's main kitchen, wildly waving his arms in agitation. The mule, grossly overloaded with saddlebags, pots and pans, water and wine bladders, and a host of other items, gave the appearance that the entire kitchen had been emptied onto its back. Not unreasonably the mule had refused to move, despite the entreaties of its would-be rider.

The little man was the cook assigned to the Hikari pilgrimage. Hardly taller than the mule's head, his rotund little body was perched on legs as thin as his pack animal's. Despite the seeming imbalance of his shape, the cook hopped and skipped around the mule with light-footed alacrity, fussing and re-arranging the load in an effort to get the animal moving. As he did not actually remove any items, however, the mule took no notice, and continued his stubborn stance before the kitchen door.

The cook had loaded the mule with all of the supplies he felt he could scavenge from the kitchens. The pilgrimage had been described to him as 'a journey whose end was not known,' and he had been told to pack 'accordingly.' Later he had simply thrown up his hands in disgust. Now what sort of fool thing was that to say? Would they be marching forever? All well and good for those in charge to make such crazy pronouncements, but somebody had to cook the food. How was he supposed to know what to bring?

As a result, he had tried to pack everything he could think of. But despite his outbursts, the mule remained unmoved. From the windows overlooking the kitchen courtyard, two servant girls watched and laughed. The cook swore up at them, telling them to go about their business, which advice they ignored completely.

A soldier approached, leading his horse into the courtyard. Dressed in the plain tunic uniform of a common soldier, Nakama still bore his bow and quiver of arrows, for every man on the pilgrimage who could do so might be required to fight. Despite his nondescript clothing, the young soldier still gave an appearance of competence and dignity. Such was evident by the appreciative stares of the servant girls, who fell silent as Nakama approached.

The cook, who had continued shouting at his mule, stopped to catch his breath. Nakama took advantage of the pause to inquire, "Excuse me? Are you the cook going on the pilgrimage?"

The little man turned toward the soldier, looking at Nakama as if the Guard was the stupidest ox he had ever seen. Then the man turned and looked back at his stationary mule, loaded to overflowing with kitchen and cooking items, and back once more to Nakama. With a flourish, the cook turned his head to the side and spit a large wad of...something...into a nearby slop bucket. "No! I'm the castle lamplighter! I just decided to come here and yell at mules today." With an irritated tug on the mule's reins, he continued, "Of course I'm the cook! Name's Ryori. And why else would I be arguing with this idiotic beast? But," he added, after a final unsuccessful pull, "he's probably got more sense than the rest of us—he knows a fool's errand when he sees one." He threw down the reins in a fit of pique.

Nakama looked dubiously at the obviously overloaded animal. "Lord Itachi sent me to find out why you're not ready to go. The pilgrimage is about to get underway."

"Well," replied Ryori, with exaggerated patience, "you can just go and tell his high and mightiness that when a simple cook is told to pack 'for the duration,' it takes a little while to get everything together. And even longer," he added, speaking directly to the mule's nose, "to convince certain others to cooperate!" The only response from the mule was an indignant flaring of nostrils.

Nakama raised an eyebrow. Looking from Ryori's overburdened mule to his own mount, he sighed. "We'd best put some of these things on my horse, then."

With reluctance Ryori agreed, and the two men began transferring items from mule to horse, the cook still grumbling about the unreliability of animals in general. From up above, the servant girls' adoration of the soldier was interrupted by a loud shout from somewhere inside the castle. Both women jumped back and quickly disappeared from view. The irritated face of an older woman appeared briefly at the window: the head servant, surveying what was causing the ruckus down below. After her own lingering, appraising glance at the soldier, she too turned back inside, her shrill voice audible even from down below as she scolded the servant girls for their idleness.

The two men finished their transfer, and Nakama led his horse out of the courtyard. Ryori's mule finally decided to get underway, and as the cook walked him toward the open gateway he spoke curtly into the animal's ear. "Hah! Maybe we both could have gotten out of this lunacy if you'd just stood your ground!" To this, the mule snorted. Ryori turned his head to the side and flung one last long spit, which landed on the flagstones some distance away.

* * *

Lord Itachi paced the length of his small troop: ten soldiers, including Nakama. To an observer the Kojuro's brother gave the appearance of reviewing an entire army. To salvage his dignity, he was conveying the impression that this expedition had as much weight and importance as if he were leading the complete Castle Guard out to battle. He stopped at every other man, tugging on a tunic to straighten it, or slapping a man over the head whose hair was not tied back in a neat enough queue. The men knew this was a commanding officer's ritual, and so accepted it stoically. When

Itachi reached Nakama, the Guard commander glowered, not deigning to speak at all. As for the servant Ryori, Itachi ignored him as if the diminutive cook were invisible.

Strutting back to the head of his small command, Itachi mounted his horse. This was the signal for the rest of the men to mount. Each man wore a special cassock over his tunic: dark grey on one side, white on the other. As part of the tradition of the Hikari pilgrimage, the tunics would be worn grey-side out until the pilgrimage had achieved its objective; then they would be flipped over to display the white side.

Toshi-hito and Shiko were similarly attired, having exchanged their usual Deshi robes for more practical traveling tunics to go along with the pilgrim cassocks. The two Deshi were already on their horses and waiting patiently for Itachi to signal their departure. The pilgrims were gathered just inside the main castle gate, and had been joined by Himitsu and several other court nobles who were present to see them off.

Itachi walked his horse over to Himitsu. "I would have thought," he said caustically, "that my brother would be here, considering the 'immense importance' to Hajimeshi of our journey."

Himitsu was unruffled. "Alas, Lord Itachi, the exertions of this morning's ceremony have left His Majesty severely depleted. It was his fervent desire to be here to wish his brother success with this most difficult endeavor. But the royal healer decreed that His Majesty must rest. The Kojuro knows, however, that you will carry on with as much faith and dedication as you have always shown."

Itachi narrowed his eyes at the chamberlain. Weasel, thought Itachi. One never knows what the old fart really means, or what he's thinking. His will be the second head to roll, after my brother's.

With a sharp tug on the reins, Itachi turned his horse to the gate, which was pulled open by the guards on duty. Himitsu and the other nobles bowed to the group, honoring the pilgrims' departure on a sanctified quest. Shiko, supporting the lit Hikari on its pole, moved his horse to the head of the line. Toshi-hito placed himself beside Itachi, who ignored the presence of the Deshi an arm's length from his side. The remaining soldiers formed up in pairs, with Ryori and his still rather overburdened mule bringing up the rear. All of the other guards, and the few other spectators in the courtyard, bowed as the pilgrims passed through the gate.

Up above in a castle window, the Kojuro watched the procession leave. It was true that the ceremony had left him somewhat drained, but not so much so that he could not have honored the departure of the pilgrimage. However, he had deemed it better to let Itachi leave thus, his brother's status left indeterminate to those who were watching the political winds. Kimeru wanted those winds to appear contrary, leaving it uncertain as to when, and if, a storm was in the offing. If thunder did strike, he wanted it to be at his own instigation.

As he looked down at the departing figures, he admitted to himself a more personal reason for his absence. His past, his future; these too were riding out of the gate down below. As resolute as he was to do what had to be done, he still did not entirely trust his feelings. He was afraid he would call the pilgrims back, try to save them from the dangers that awaited them. So he had removed himself from the field, to watch from a distance. It hurt no less for all that. He turned away and returned to his Sleeping Chamber.

Another watched as well, but from a different window in the castle. Oblivious to the machinations of Hajimeshi's leaders, either in the courtyard below or nearer to her in the castle, only one man held the focus of Mikasama's attention. He was seemingly just an ordinary soldier, but he still bore his bow and quiver of arrows, and he rode with back erect and face impassive. She knew that Nakama would fulfill his duties as faithfully as he had when he had been a Captain. And it was just that prospect which terrified her.

Mikasama knew that at Itachi's command, Nakama would ride single-handedly against an army, for honor would dictate that he must. Now, as she watched him ride out through the gate, she feared that in his reduced position, and with Itachi's wrath already incurred, at the earliest sign of danger her dearest Nakama would be the first to be sacrificed.

She had dreamed last night, after returning to her bed from the nocturnal excursion to the stable. She couldn't recall much of what the dreams had been about, but she remembered seeing herself outside the castle. She had been riding quickly, through the forest. There had been more, but when she had awoken in the morning most of the images were forgotten. The part she could remember, however, was clear enough.

As the rest of the party passed through the gate, she watched, eyes never leaving Nakama, as the group wound its way down the hill and through the town of Hajimeshi. She waited patiently for them to re-emerge into view whenever they passed between obscuring buildings. Eventually the pilgrims rode out onto the plain, where they were visible only as indistinguishable dots marching like ants; and yet still she watched. She did not leave her window lookout until they had finally passed out of sight and into the forest at the edge of the Hajimeshi valley. Then she rose, turning expressionless from the window to set about her final preparations.

*   *   *

In silence the Hikari group rode on, wending its way through the Hajimeshi forest. Itachi had not spoken since leaving the gate other than to give instructions to his men. The senior man among his soldiers, Bokusa, rode just behind his lord, ready to relay any instructions. And woe to any man who did not respond quickly enough, for Bokusa was rightly feared by all of the Castle Guards, and not a few of the officers as well. He was nearly as large as Shoden, but more quick witted; and whereas Itachi's servant exercised his strength only when ordered to do so, Bokusa took genuine pleasure in inflicting pain.

The rest of the soldiers were little better. In deliberate contrast to the Kojuro's aim of presenting a conciliatory face to the neighboring realms, the men Itachi had selected to accompany the pilgrimage were among the toughest and most violent among the Guards. When discreetly questioned on this point by Himitsu before the group had left, Itachi had shrugged off the chamberlain's concerns, saying he had delegated the responsibility for selecting the men to Bokusa. Himitsu had not pressed the point, recognizing the limitations of his influence insofar as military matters were concerned. But he had considered that it bode ill for the presumed peace initiative inherent in the mission.

The pilgrims emerged from the woods and approached the Border Bridge marking the boundary of Hajimeshi territory. Two guards now stood watch here, and they quickly stashed their dice game out of sight at the approach of the pilgrimage entourage. Standing stiffly at attention, holding their spears, they stared straight out beyond Hajimeshi's borders as if waiting for the approach of an enemy at any moment.

The Hikari group proceeded across the bridge, Shiko still in the lead. As they neared the end of the stone crossing, where the previous sentry had met his untimely demise only days before, Itachi's horse began to toss its head. The Hajimeshi general jerked the reins tight, which only caused the horse to become more agitated. The group slowed to a halt as Itachi fought to control his increasingly panicked animal, which sidestepped on the bridge as if not wanting to traverse the spot where blood had so recently been shed. Itachi cursed at the animal, smacking its side with his tarka.

Shiko had stopped at the end of the bridge, turning his horse to see what had happened. The two sentries, after looking briefly behind them as well, immediately turned back and resumed their unavailing vigil. At the back of the Hikari group, Ryori stood up in his stirrups, trying to see over the heads of the soldiers in front of him. "What's going on?" he asked Nakama.

The former officer, embarrassed at his commander's predicament, declined to answer. The cook finally got a glimpse of the war of wills between man and horse ahead of them. "Hah!" he said. "Looks like my mule's not the only one smarter'n the rest of us." This was accompanied by a long spit that sailed over the bridge railing and down to the river below with a plop. Nakama pretended not to notice.

Finally Toshi-hito rode up beside Itachi and, leaning over, laid hold of the aggravated horse's mane. While Itachi continued to struggle with the reins, the horse became more relaxed at the Deshi's touch. When at last the horse had stopped moving about on the bridge, Toshi-hito let go. With a final jab from his tarka Itachi got the animal moving forward once more. Furious, he did not acknowledge Toshi-hito's assistance but urged his mount across.

As the pilgrims rode off into the woods lining the far bank of the river, the two sentries finally relaxed. Setting down their spears, they retrieved the dice and resumed their delayed diversion.

* * *

They feed his anger...yes, I understand this one. They shame him, trying to put him in his place; but all they succeed in doing is fueling his hatred. As was once done to me...

Fools! One cannot tame a wild beast, once he has tasted the sweetness of his prey. The more they try to hold him back, the more he will strain against the leash until he turns on them, and brings them down.

What? Yes? You are back...

Watch these Hajimeshi? The ones leaving with the lantern? Why? What is so important about them?

...It is gone again. So strange, to be able to see everything above, yet nothing here. My mind is no longer my own; it is as if it were an open door, laid bare whenever 'it' wants to come calling...so unlike before, when I was just a soldier in its service, when the Great Ones crushed all before them...

Well, it wants me to watch this group in particular, but won't say why. No matter, I am intrigued by this one in any case. He seems so like me...how long until he slips those tenuous bonds that restrain him? How long until he lets free the anger that burns within him?

Yes, I will watch this one. It feels good to 'live' once more, even if only as a shadow to another...

*   *   *

The lamplighter had just begun his rounds, leaving glowing lights in his wake, when Himitsu returned to his quarters. The afternoon had been spent in another fruitless round of negotiations with Choshuka, an effort that would tax even a healthy man, let alone a man as ill as the Kojuro.

Or as old as the Kojuro's chamberlain, reflected Himitsu, as he slipped out of his ceremonial garb. He donned a light robe of fine silk and stretched his weary bones. He noted that he felt more fatigued than he had in times past. I must, he thought, indulge myself tomorrow, and challenge some of those young nobles to a brisk morning walk. Always a good thing for clearing the head.

Convinced that exhaustion was simply a state of mind, and that it could be excised by brisk and invigorating exercise, Himitsu always wondered why his companions on such excursions rarely seemed to agree...

The chamberlain moved over to his favorite spot, the wide stone sill of the window looking out across the castle grounds. From this vantage he had an excellent view of the sunset, which never ceased to please him with its warm glow. That it also allowed him to view the comings and goings of persons in and out of the castle's main gate was, naturally, purely incidental.

Before the sun sank beneath the level of the trees, he turned and reached for his quill to write out a quick letter by the fading light. He knew of a young man, one of the stable hands, who was an excellent rider; having grown up in the farmlands to the west, the boy was also familiar with the shortcuts through the woods. Himitsu calculated that his letter should arrive in Yutakashi before the Hikari pilgrimage, if the boy started tonight. With deft fingers the chamberlain wrote out his instructions.

* * *

In his chamber above the priory, the Omo Deshi sat back from his low desk near the floor. Takamaru had just finished his review of the order's finances, and was pleased; the sale of excess produce had turned a tidy profit for the Deshi treasury. If he were not mistaken, he would shortly have some excellent uses for the money. Rumors were swirling about the court, and it was the prudent man who prepared himself for any political eventuality.

His reverie was interrupted by a discreet knock, to which he replied, "Yes?"

The door slid open a short way, revealing the deferential form of Joto, his secretary. "They have crossed the bridge, Eminence."

"Excellent," said Takamaru, rising and closing his ledger book. "Come, Joto," he said, taking the man's arm companionably. "Do let us go and meditate upon the 'success' of our fellow Deshi's endeavor."

* * *

The owl swiveled its head around and watched the small point of light picking its way through the hay-barn. Finally the light reached the door to the stable, and the cloaked figure holding the lamp tentatively poked its head through. Mikasama entered the stable, carrying a travel pack, and went up to one of the horses.

"Well," she said softly, addressing the horse, "let's see if we can do this together, shall we? Any idea which piece goes on first?" The horse looked at her silently. "Humph," said Mikasama. "You're a big help." She set down the lamp and pack and walked over to the wall containing the riding gear and harness. Tentatively she grabbed hold of a saddle from one of the racks and tugged. It was heavier than she expected. She yanked harder, and the saddle came off the shelf and fell to the floor with a dull crash, narrowly missing her foot. She swore silently to herself, listening for a moment for any noises from outside the stable that might indicate the commotion had been overheard. Hearing nothing, she began pulling the saddle across the floor. It was so heavy she could barely lift its mass of oiled leather as she dragged it toward the horses. She was out of breath after maneuvering the saddle next to her chosen mount. How in the world, she wondered, am I ever going to get this thing up on the horse?

Panic set in as she realized that if she could not get the saddle on, her journey might be over before it even started. She tried bracing herself under the saddle and giving it a mighty push, but succeeded only in lifting it up against the side of the horse. Unfortunately, the animal took umbrage at being thus winded and promptly sidestepped away, causing both saddle and Princess to fall in a heap at its feet.

Cursing, Mikasama picked herself up and pulled the saddle back out of the way. Moving around to the horse's head, she whispered fiercely. "Now, look! I need some help here! Stop making things difficult!" The horse stared back at her. Trying to control her anxiety, Mikasama walked over and stood over the saddle again. "Think," she whispered aloud, "there must be a way." She grabbed hold of the pommel and tried lifting from that end.

"Why not let stable boy heave that on up there if you want to ride so much, hey?"

Mikasama almost jumped through the roof as she dropped the saddle. She spun around, whispering loudly, "Nana-san! What are you doing here? You're supposed to be in bed at this hour!"

Komori, in her usual loud voice, replied, "And you, Mika, you supposed to be washin' horses this hour? Pahhh," she said, as Mikasama tried to shush her. "Nobody here but you, me, and these horses. I don't doubt they be having as good a time as me watching you tryin' to put that thing on. Got a mind to be goin' somewhere, do ya? Wouldn't be after that solider boy of yours, now, Mika?"

Exasperated, Mikasama sat down on the saddle. After a moment she looked up at Komori. "They want to take Nakama away from me, Nana-san," she said quietly. "But I'm not going to let them. They don't need me here. I'm just some—some silly figurehead, somebody's footstool toward my father's throne." She kicked at the straw that covered the floor. "I'm not going to be anybody's footstool. And I'm not going to let them take Nakama away!"

Komori crossed her arms and looked down at the Princess. "Ohhh, and mighty fine words those be. They, they, they. Who they, huh? Your Papa, the Kojuro, maybe? The man who rules this-here kingdom, everybody bows to all the time? Not mentioning you be his daughter, and maybe owes some duty to, hey? What you want to go run away and make a big fuss? This just be first love—you get over it."

Mikasama stood abruptly. With quiet firmness she said, "Nana-san, I love Nakama more than anything else I ever have in this life. He makes me feel like a real person, not just some court decoration. And he—he treats me like a woman!" she added defiantly. "Everyone else thinks I'm just a child who can be ordered around!" She stared determinedly at Komori. "Don't try to stop me, Nana-san. If I don't get away tonight, I'll do it the next night, or the night after that. Neither you nor anybody else can stop me."

Komori looked sadly at her young charge. Softly she said, "Ah, Mika all grown up now. Not a child anymore, no, no, no." She looked down at the saddle, then back at Mikasama. "Can't go out on horse tonight, Mika."

Straightening her back, Mikasama said, "I will, Nana-san! If I have to work all night at getting this blasted saddle on!" She started to bend over to grab the saddle once more when she felt a whack against her shoulder.

"Silly Mika! Listen to Nana-san! You get that hunk of leather up there, how you gonna get horse out the gate, huh? Just gonna walk up and ask guards to oh if you please open gate so Princess can take midnight ride outside the walls?"

"Well, I—I don't know, I thought that I could—just—"

"Just what? Hadn't thought that far ahead, eh? So besotted with soldier-boy can't think straight. Be back here 'fore first light, under troop of guards. And Papa put you under lock and key and then where'd you be, eh?"

Mikasama sat down again on the saddle, shoulders slumping in defeat. Komori continued. "All grown up. Pahhh! Where'd you be without your old Nana-san, hey? Put stupid saddle-thing away. Nana-san take us out tomorrow; no one miss us."

Mikasama looked up. "What?"

"Nana-san talking to wall? Or maybe to horse? Put away saddle-thing, and tomorrow we go! No one know. Nana-san knows a thing or two about this place," she said, gesturing at the castle around them. "Now come on, 'fore that ass watchman finish his drinking and wander in."

"But Nana-san," said Mikasama, standing, "I can't take you with me! I don't know how long I'll be gone, or how far I have to go to catch up with them. Besides, the road's no place for—for—"

"For what? Old bitty like me? Pahhh! You need Nana-san to tell you where to go. You ever been out there, on your own? No, didn't think so. Nana-san has. I be more worried about you than me, were me you. Besides, no choice; you wanna go, you gotta take Nana-san with you. End of talk." Komori crossed her arms again, a gesture familiar to Mikasama from years of upbringing; she knew the argument was lost.

"All right, Nana-san," said the Princess, grinning. "You win!"

*   *   *

It was late the next afternoon when Mikasama and Komori set out together, ostensibly to take a walk in the Royal Garden. Mikasama had protested, complaining that they were already many hours behind the Hikari pilgrimage, but Komori had just shushed her. "Mika always in a hurry. Had some things to do first! We be on our way soon 'nough. Time yet to smell some flowers."

And so off they had gone, spending a casual hour wandering about while an increasingly agitated Mikasama fidgeted, oblivious to the floral attractions around her. As they reached the far end of the garden, Mikasama could finally take no more. "Nana-san, are you doing this on purpose to keep me from leaving?"

With a hurt expression, Komori looked up at her young charge. "No trust your old Nana-san, hey? You think I come alla way out here, standing in hot sun, just to keep you around? If I want that, I just tell your Papa and he make sure you stay. Eh?"

Mikasama could not argue with that logic; indeed, it seemed she usually found herself on the losing side of most arguments with Komori.

Her old caretaker went on. "There be a reason for little garden walk. Makes the man following us bored. He stop watchin' us so good."

"Man? What man?" Mikasama stopped and started to look around, but Komori hissed, "Stop that! Pretend to look at flowers!" Perplexed, Mikasama did as she was told.

Komori said, "He been watchin' us since we left the castle. He be good and tired now. See jaku bushes, at the end of the path?"

Mikasama looked ahead of them, and saw a line of jaku bushes running along the garden wall. Their tall, thick branches sprouted leaves as long as her arm, and two hand-spans across, all competing for the sunlight and overlapping one another in a dense tangle. "Yes, Nana-san, I see them."

"Good. When we get there, turn off path behind the bush. Then follow me, quick."

"But—" Further comment was forestalled as they were already alongside the first bush. Without missing a step, Komori turned aside and walked behind it. Mikasama lost sight of her, then quickly followed in the old woman's footsteps.

The Princess found herself standing between the jaku bush and the wall surrounding the side of the garden. The thick leaves of the bush blocked most of the sun, letting only small patches of light poke through. The effect was disorienting; Mikasama couldn't see Komori in the confusion of light and dark. "Nana-san? Where are you?"

"Right in front of you, Mika," replied Komori, as she suddenly moved, not two paces away from Mikasama. Startled, the Princess almost leapt back onto the path, but Komori took hold of her arm. "Stay close." Then the old woman turned and started moving between the wall and the jaku bushes, in a narrow gap just large enough for them to traverse. Mikasama followed. They had gone another twenty paces, making no sound other than the occasional rustle of jaku leaves, when Komori abruptly disappeared again from view.

Mikasama stopped in her tracks. "Nana-san, I can't see you." She felt a tap on her arm, and turned to see Komori standing between two of the bushes. Silently she signaled for Mikasama to follow her. The bushes here extended out into the garden away from the wall, and Mikasama had to push her way past the branches in order to keep up with Komori. In just a few paces they were standing at the back of a small shed, surrounded by the dense foliage.

An old window frame, long since missing its glass, stood open and overhung with spider webs on the back wall of the shed. Komori quickly brushed these aside and clambered through, surprising Mikasama with her agility. A hand emerged, motioning urgently at the Princess. She swallowed; pulling up the folds of her kimono with some difficulty, she managed to climb over the rotted windowsill and join Komori inside.

Dim light filtered through the cracks in the wooden walls as Mikasama looked around, trying to get her bearings. She realized that they must be in a gardener's shed of some sort: rakes and other tools were propped up along the walls, and flat wooden trays for transporting seedlings were stacked on the dirt floor. Over all lay a pervasive smell of fertilizer. Komori was kneeling by the window, looking out over the sill, and she waved at Mikasama to join her.

The Princess could see nothing for a while, but soon she could hear the sound of someone floundering through the jaku bushes along the wall. Almost without warning a man popped into view, looking around wildly. Unable to see the shed off to the side in the confused patterns of light and dark, he rushed on along the wall in the direction that Komori and Mikasama had first been heading.

Mikasama heard a low cackle next to her, and turned to see Komori grinning from ear to ear. "Just beginning, Mika. More fun to come!" Komori's joy was infectious, and Mikasama began grinning herself.

The old caretaker rose and went to the front door of the shed, cautiously opening it a crack to peer outside. The shaft of sunlight she let in removed the gloom from within, and transfixed Komori's body as it highlighted the unruly tangle of grey hair piled on top of her head. Satisfied, Komori turned to Mikasama. Raising her finger to her lips for quiet, she opened the door just enough to slip out, and the Princess quickly followed.

Trailing along after Komori, Mikasama discovered places she never knew existed, despite having grown up in and around the castle.

After sneaking out the front of the Royal Garden while their pursuer continued searching for them amongst the foliage, Komori led the Princess to the side door of a castle outbuilding. Beyond it was a steep wooden staircase, leading down into a cool, dark space. Komori hopped down the steps and was quickly lost in the dimness, and Mikasama had to hurry to catch up. It took a few minutes for her eyes to adjust to the dark. Eventually the Princess could see that they were in some sort of underground storage vaults. Komori was wending her way unerringly amidst a warren of shelving and racks holding items of the castle larder, building supplies, and linen stores.

Following behind her, Mikasama wondered when Komori had ever had the time to investigate all of these underground passageways, let alone remember where they all led. It had seemed Nana-san was always around wherever Mikasama was, and if not immediately to hand was always engaged in cooking or sewing for herself or for the Princess. Clearly, thought Mikasama, Komori had done some serious exploring at some point in her tenure in the castle...

Mikasama lost all sense of direction, relying on Komori to guide her as they turned this way and that. They had to move carefully from chamber to chamber in order to avoid the occasional servant passing through on some domestic errand. Finally the two women arrived before a door that Mikasama guessed led to the outside, judging from the tell-tale sliver of sunlight peaking out from beneath the door's bottom edge. Komori reached up to a shelf along a nearby wall and pulled down a large bundle. Intrigued, the Princess watched as Komori unwrapped the package to reveal a plain tunic and pair of trousers. Komori held them out to Mikasama. "Be quick, change now. Can't walk out lookin' like a Princess."

Mikasama took the clothes, amazed at the extent of Komori's preparations. Clearly the old woman had thought very carefully about what she was doing. It was so unlike the usual clucking mother hen Mikasama associated with her guardian that she wasn't quite sure what to make of it.

"No dawdling! Change now!" Hurriedly Mikasama changed into the plain brown clothing, stuffing her own colorful, and expensive, garments into the sack. Komori put the bundle back up on the shelf, then pressed an ear up against the wooden door and listened. She didn't move for a long time. Just when Mikasama was about to query her on what was happening Komori leaned back from the door.

"Time now, Mika. You stay right behind me. Pay no mind to what goin' on with the Guards; pretend you don' see it. Just walk right out behind me, hey?"

"Yes, Nana-san, I understand," said Mikasama restlessly, eager to go.

With a soft "Humph," Komori turned back to the door and listened briefly one more time. Mikasama could hear something from outside; people were shouting, and there was some sort of commotion. Suddenly Komori stepped back and swung open the door, walking straight out into the sunlight.

Quickly Mikasama followed her through, squinting in the bright sun. Komori marched up a set of steps from below ground level and walked away across the grass. Skipping to catch up, Mikasama attempted to look nonchalant while trying to figure out where they were.

They had emerged from underneath the castle, and were walking toward one of the side gates. Mikasama recognized it as the one used for deliveries from the town. In her younger days, playing around the kitchens, she had occasionally struck up games with children of the servants; the entry courtyard by this gate had frequently turned into a playing field for their antics. Once she was older, though, she had not been allowed to come here and play with them anymore.

A wagon was standing at the open gate, its driver watching something on the side opposite to Komori and Mikasama. A woman's high-pitched shrieking could be heard, and the thumping of something solid against flesh. The man on the wagon was laughing as Komori and Mikasama drew alongside. Despite Komori's admonition, the Princess chanced a look.

In the brief glance she had between the horse and the driver's feet, she saw one of the castle's maids haranguing a male servant, striking him over the head with a broomstick. Mikasama couldn't make out most of the words, but it sounded like she was accusing him of sleeping with another woman. The poor man was protesting his innocence as he tried, without much success, to fend off her blows. Out of the corner of her eye, Mikasama saw the two gate guards approaching the domestic squabble, presumably in an effort to separate the combatants.

Turning back, Mikasama saw that Komori was already some distance ahead of her, looking neither left nor right. The old woman had marched off through the gate as if she had every right to go where she pleased. Mikasama followed suit. The true extent of Komori's abilities finally dawned on the young Princess.

As the two women walked down to the river, having left the main road shortly after exiting the castle grounds, Komori started to chuckle. Mikasama smiled with her, then watched open mouthed as the old woman suddenly erupted with laughter. "Nana-san," said Mikasama, "why are you laughing so hard?"

Between cackles and gasping for breath, Komori just laughed some more. "''Cause…'cause…Haven't had so much fun in years! Oh, oh, oh…White Beard, that old fox, he just gonna die! 'Just a woman,' he always said. Oh, ho, oh ho!" Giggling like a schoolgirl, Komori hefted herself over a fallen tree along the riverbank.

Mikasama wondered briefly who 'White Beard' was, but then the sight on the far side of the fallen tree caused her to forget the question altogether.

Two horses stood quietly tied to a tree, each fully loaded with travel packs. Komori was patting one on its rump, smiling appreciatively. She said, "Look like we be done walkin' for a bit."

The Princess looked at the two horses. "We can't just take these horses, Nana-san. What if the owners come for them?"

"Oh, but the owners have, Mika!" With a glint in her eyes, Komori opened one of the packs and pulled out a lakana pie, one of her dessert specialties, its hard shell crust all wrapped up in a neat paper bundle.

Gazing in amazement first at Komori, then at the horses, Mikasama gasped, "Nana-san! Where did you get these horses? And how did they get here?"

Sobering, Komori laid her hand on Mikasama's arm. "Tell you all 'bout it. First, best we be on the road, 'fore certain snoopy people get smart and see we walk out right under their noses. Now, help your old Nana-san up on this thing."

Mikasama helped lift Komori up on one of the horses, then went around to untie them. Swinging herself atop the other one, she walked the horse away from the tree, getting a feel for the animal under her. Mikasama may not have known how to saddle a horse, but she had certainly had her share of practice riding one. She turned about, and observed that Komori's horse was still facing the tree.

"Nana-san, what's wrong?" she called over to her guardian.

"Stupid horse!" replied Komori. "He no wanna move!" She proceeded to kick her small feet against the side of the horse. The reins lay limp alongside the horse's neck as Komori poked at the back of its maned head.

Mikasama rode over to her and tried to keep the mirth from her voice. "Nana-san, you've never ridden a horse before, have you?"

"'Course not!" said Komori, surprised. "Why would old woman like me get up on stupid big animal like this?"

"Nana-san," said Mikasama patiently, "you have to turn the horse with the reins. Here, take these," as she put the reins in Komori's hands. "He's not moving forward when you kick because there's a tree in front of him. Now, watch me," she said, demonstrating the rudiments of horse control.

After a few false starts, Komori awkwardly got the horse to move away from the tree. Bouncing up and down uncomfortably, she said plaintively, "Why you fancy folk wanna ride these smelly things anyway? Stupid!" Then she had to hold on for dear life as the horse began to trot its way up to the road. Smiling, Mikasama turned her horse to follow, glad that for some things, at least, she was still a match for her old Nana-san.

5

Shiko tried to concentrate, forcing out the thoughts of discomfort he felt. Although he had been looking forward to riding a horse again, after a day and a half his body, and particularly his rear end, was still not sure it liked the idea. Master Toshi-hito always said, though, that a little discomfort was just the thing for proper meditation. It provided a focus for all those thoughts that needed to be set aside; the worldly feelings and sensations, all wrapped up together in one place, leaving the rest of the mind free for contemplation.

The Hikari group was riding through the Kurayami Wood, a thick forest that ran all across the eastern border of Yutakashi. The trees were close at hand on either side, with barely room for two men to ride abreast. The road stretched on for hours, with only the occasional clearing to provide a break from the monotony. Shiko and Toshi-hito rode side by side, following Lord Itachi and one of the Guards who had taken a spell at carrying the Hikari. For within the first few hours of their departure from Hajimeshi, Shiko had become acutely aware of the disadvantage of having a hallway lantern serve as the Hikari. Namely, it was quite heavy. In consultation with Itachi, Shiko and Toshi-hito had made arrangements for a rotating shift of lantern bearers. Today Donaku, riding at the head of the column beside Itachi, held the Hikari aloft.

Shiko stared at the lantern as it bobbed and weaved in the air. He used it as a point of concentration, working on the techniques that

Master Toshi-hito had taught him for extending his awareness beyond himself. Slowly, as if in small waves moving in rhythm with the movements of his horse, Shiko pushed his mind outwards. He stopped feeling the chafing of his legs against the saddle; ceased to hear the sound of creaking leather and the clopping of hooves. He could isolate the noises of the Hikari group as a whole, making them distinct from the sounds of the surrounding forest. Out there, he could hear the branches waving softly in the breeze; and the sound of water from a small brook, hidden somewhere back amongst the trees. Watching the Hikari move lazily up and down with the motion of its bearer, Shiko listened to the birds singing as the riders passed by. Strange, he thought, their tunes change as we walk past. Almost as if the birds are talking to each other about this odd group of humans, and passing on the word as we continue down the road.

Then Shiko heard something else, something that was out of place. At first he couldn't put his mental finger on it, but he cast about with his mind until he found it again. There, he thought; that's not a natural sound. It sounds like—like leather. Like leather moving against something...a horse! But not one of ours—I can still sense our group, all together in one place in my mind. There's another rider out there—no, several!

He drew his eyes back from the Hikari with a start, and turned to look at Toshi-hito. He could tell from the look on the Master's face that he had already sensed the same thing. Toshi-hito was looking around at where they were on the road, and at the path ahead. Slowly he stopped his horse, raising his hand to those behind. The group halted, while Itachi and Donaku rode on several more steps before realizing that the rest were no longer following.

Itachi turned on his horse. "Why are you stopping? We must keep up our pace if we are to get out of these woods before nightfall."

While Itachi spoke, Toshi-hito was turning his head slightly in different directions. "We have visitors, Lord Itachi. I thought it would be best to be prepared to greet them." At his words the men behind him stirred, hands going to sword hilts as they looked around, scanning the trees for signs of attack. Ryori, at the rear next to Nakama, nervously sidled his mule forward in amongst the Guards.

"Nonsense," said Itachi. "Who would attack a troop of Guards? You're hearing things; too much Deshi thinking, that's all." He turned back and urged his horse forward. "There should be a clearing not too far ahead—"

Before he could finish, men on horseback slowly, silently, appeared all around them from the forest. The intruders came so quietly that despite Toshi-hito's warning the Guards were startled. The Hajimeshi soldiers drew their swords, their horses becoming agitated as they sensed their riders' anxiety. The men from the forest wore no livery, nothing to say to whom they owed allegiance. All were armed, although their weapons remained sheathed. The Hikari party was surrounded, outnumbered at least two to one.

Itachi stopped, and Donaku looked to him for guidance. "My Lord," he whispered, "why do they not attack?" Indeed, the men from the forest remained silent, ringing the Hikari group on all sides but not moving out from the edge of the trees except on the trail before and behind the Guards.

Toshi-hito, followed by Shiko, rode slowly forward to where Itachi sat taking in their situation. The Deshi Master said nothing, only raising his eyebrows in acknowledgement that this was an area most definitely under Itachi's purview.

Itachi, frowning, walked his horse out in front of the Guards. He called out to the silent men before them. "I would speak with your leader!"

There was no response at first, but then the horsemen at the pilgrims' front parted and another rider came into view, nothing to distinguish him from the rest except a white band that ran diagonally across the face of his tunic. Itachi rode slowly forward to him, until he was just far enough away that Toshi-hito and the others could not overhear the conversation. As they spoke, Shiko edged his horse closer to Toshi-hito's.

"Master," whispered the apprentice, "this is not what I expected an attack by bandits would be like."

Toshi-hito was carefully watching Itachi as the Hajimeshi lord talked to the leader of the forest band. He noted a great deal of earnest discussion going on between the two men. "It is, indeed, not a typical approach," he replied.

Itachi turned back toward the Guards, calling out, "Matsugo!" One of the Guards peeled himself away from his compatriots, riding past Toshi-hito and the Hikari up to where Itachi and the leader of the marauders sat, still separated from the others. Matsugo gave Itachi a bag, and something appeared to change hands between the Hajimeshi lord and the bandit. Without a word the bandit leader turned and re-entered the forest. A soft whistle was heard, coming from another direction, and the other bandits all turned and disappeared into the woods as silently as they had appeared. Unnerved, the Guards remained alert, swords still in hand.

Once Itachi and Matsugo had ridden back to join the others, Toshi-hito gave the Hajimeshi general an inquiring look. "A most unusual attack, Lord Itachi. I was unaware that the bandits of the Kurayami Wood were of such a polite nature."

Itachi snorted. "Politeness had nothing to do with it. Look around you," he said, the sweep of his arm encompassing his troops. "These men are trained Guards. Bandits are cowards and rogues. They don't want to fight if they can help it. Why take on the best soldiers in all of Hajimeshi when there are easier alternatives?"

"Of course," said Toshi-hito delicately. "I presume you provided them with some coins, rather than force an encounter?"

With a look of contempt, Itachi grated, "In case you haven't noticed, we have few men on this little 'foraging party.' I'm not going to waste them on scum puked up by the forest. There may be need for serious fighting later."

"Very wise, of course. I trust you brought enough coins for the whole journey?"

Toshi-hito's irony lost on him, Itachi replied, "Forty gold pieces. Those vermin were content with ten." He spun his horse about. "Good thing *I* prepared for such eventualities. The *real* world can be a dangerous place." He waved to the Guards. "Let's move!"

As the men sheathed their swords and started off again down the road, Shiko chanced a look at Toshi-hito. The Master was looking ahead at Itachi but kept his thoughts his own. The apprentice couldn't help but notice, however, a definite sense of unease emanating from his mentor.

As the two Deshi fell in amongst the Guards, Ryori resumed his usual position next to Nakama. The cook said ebulliently, "Hah! Guess we showed 'em, huh?"

But Nakama did not reply. The former Captain simply rode on, his mouth set in a grim line.

* * *

The next morning the Hikari group neared the city of Yutakashi. They could gauge their progress by the number of fellow travelers on the road, with the amount of traffic increasing steadily as the pilgrims approached the great trading center.

Yutakashi had always been a crossroads of trade for all of Tonogato. To the east, on the road traveled by the Hikari group, lay Hajimeshi, which had been long renowned for the quality of its harvests. Off to the north were roads that led across the mountains, joining up with caravan routes that crossed the Sabakushi Desert. To the south was Kawashi, a river town and commercial port that was a vassal of Yutakashi and which provided it with a gateway to the sea. Goods, and people, flowed constantly in and out of Yutakashi, a fact that its citizens had long become adept at taking advantage of.

One result of such an emphasis on commerce was that a substantial portion of the ensuing wealth was siphoned off into the hands of a privileged few. As the power and influence of these men had grown, they had begun to shape Yutakashi foreign policy; on occasion, they had not been averse to using their military power when they felt it might be to their mercantile advantage. The port of Kawashi had learned this to its detriment when it had attempted to assert its independence from the financial oversight of its northern neighbor.

Yutakashi had thus grown both rich and powerful. It had become the meeting place of peoples from cities and towns far and wide, although such interaction often took the form of swindler schemes and political plotting rather than cultural exchanges. It was not a town for the faint of heart, or the faint of purse.

As the Hikari group passed through the outskirts of the city, the sides of the road began to fill with makeshift vendor stalls where entrepreneurial souls hawked their wares to road-weary travelers. The experienced knew that this was but the tip of the dragon's tongue and that far greater choices, and usually better prices, waited within the city proper.

The Hajimeshi pilgrims pressed on past the din of roadside buying and selling toward the main gate, the crush of people forcing them to slow the closer they approached. Shiko gazed up in wonder at the magnificent stonework of the gate, which towered above the city walls almost like a miniature castle of its own. It guarded the far end of a substantial bridge spanning a dry moat, built more for the purposes of controlling customs charges than for defense. All traffic in and out of the city was required to pay a toll at one of several gates like this one, and such was the cause of the congestion on the bridge.

Shiko saw a man near their entourage stop and stare as the Hikari, still borne by Donaku, went past. Taking in the lantern and the travelers' grey smocks, the man grabbed his companion's arm and pointed at the pilgrims. He was not the first bystander on their journey that the apprentice realized had recognized the lantern as a pilgrimage light. Others along their way had also stopped and watched, silently, while the Hajimeshi had passed. Tonogato thrived on traditions, and the story of the pilgrim and his lantern, Shiko presumed, had probably been passed down through many folk tales and family stories.

As the Hajimeshi, grey smocks standing out amongst the crowd, made their way up to the archway of the gate, Shiko recognized the colorful livery of Yutakashi soldiers as they inspected paperwork and collected tolls. He did note a difference, however, from those he had seen escorting Lord Choshuka back in Hajimeshi: here, each of the Yutakashi soldiers had either a blue or red band tied around his head, knotted behind with a long end trailing down the middle of the back. Quietly Shiko asked Toshi-hito about it as they approached the gate.

"Ah," replied Toshi-hito. "The Reds and the Blues. What else do you see about them?"

Shiko looked more closely at them for a moment. "There are the same number of Reds as there are Blues."

"Very good. Yes, you will always see them in equal numbers whenever official business is conducted. They represent the two ruling factions of Yutakashi, which bitterly oppose each other; they often resort to violence to resolve their disputes. In an attempt to maintain peace within the city, on which their trade depends, they are allotted equal representation at all official functions. Outside the city, they do not show their colors, but they are there nonetheless. Our visitor back in Hajimeshi, Lord Choshuka, is of the Blues, but one of the courtiers with him is Red and reports on everything Choshuka does."

The Hikari group reached the gateway, and the Red and Blue soldiers, obviously unversed in how to handle a pilgrimage, stood looking up at the group in confusion. Both sides sent runners to bring senior officers.

Lord Itachi, at the head of the line next to Donaku, demanded to know why they were being delayed. "This is a Hikari pilgrimage! No man may bar its path. Move aside!"

Yet his protestations went unheeded. Sitting bestride his horse next to Shiko, Toshi-hito, with a hint of amusement, said quietly to the apprentice, "I suspect that neither the Reds nor the Blues want to take the responsibility for letting us pass unchallenged, lest the other side accuse them of complicity in trade smuggling."

The Reds and the Blues both stood their ground silently, as Itachi continued his venomous verbal assaults. Traffic across the bridge backed up, causing angry shouts of impatience from those being delayed. At length, a pair of officials arrived, one Red, one Blue, sauntering up at a leisurely pace. The one wearing Blue looked up at Itachi, pointedly making no effort to bow. He said curtly, "Your business in Yutakashi?"

Itachi glowered down at the man. "We are on a Hikari pilgrimage. As any fool can see," he added, gesturing toward the lantern. "Now move these imbeciles aside and let us pass."

The Blue officer did not reply, but looked back over the entourage, taking in the armed soldiers in Hajimeshi livery.

The Red officer said, "You will pardon our concern. A pilgrimage of soldiers is...rather unusual." The Blue officer turned back to Itachi. "Your sovereign must have sanctioned your purpose, in order to be a legally consecrated pilgrimage." With that, he held out his hand.

Itachi swore and signaled sharply for Toshi-hito to come forward. The Deshi Master, as the spiritual leader of the expedition, had been entrusted with the parchment bearing the Kojuro's seal that authorized the pilgrimage.

Toshi-hito walked his horse forward and slipped the parchment out of his tunic. Shiko watched as the Blue officer took the parchment yet then barely glanced at it before handing it to the Red officer. The Red officer likewise gave it only cursory examination before giving it back to the Deshi Master. "You may pass. You may only conduct business relevant to your quest while in the city." He nodded to the Red soldiers, who moved aside, followed by the Blue soldiers at a wave of their officer's hand.

As Itachi kicked his horse into motion Shiko and the rest of the group moved forward once more, to the relief of the other travelers on the bridge. The apprentice overheard muttered comments from a few disgruntled onlookers about "Hajimeshi peasants" as the pilgrims cleared the gatehouse.

Once in the street beyond the gate, Itachi turned toward Toshi-hito. "Those bastards knew we were coming," the general growled through clenched teeth. "That fool Choshuka must have sent word ahead of us. They held us up as a deliberate insult." Toshi-hito did not reply, and Shiko, riding behind the two, had to suppress a smile. He knew that, to his Master, insults were nothing more than wasted words in the wind.

As the pilgrims entered the main boulevard of Yutakashi, Shiko found himself fascinated by everything he saw. He had read about the city, of course, but had never really imagined what it would be like to be in it. A hundred sights, and as many smells, assaulted his senses from all directions. He marveled at how people here could keep track of where they were; it was a veritable warren of streets and alleyways that went off in every direction. He imagined that someone from this city who visited Hajimeshi would think the birthplace of the Deshi to be nothing but a backwater hamlet.

As the group proceeded toward the district containing traveler's inns, Shiko noticed more people wearing the Red and Blue headbands. Not all of them were soldiers; quite a few were ordinary citizens. Amid all the hustle and bustle, people shouting, and furious bartering all around them, Shiko realized that none of the Blues seemed to be talking to any of the Reds, and vice versa. In fact the only interaction that he observed between them were scowls and the occasional rude gesture. Coming alongside Toshi-hito, Shiko asked, "Why does there seem to be such animosity between the Reds and the Blues?"

The Master only shook his head. "Why do the clouds come when they do? There is no answer that satisfies." He gestured back in the direction they had come. "Do you remember the ruins we passed, just after the mid-day meal?"

"Yes. I thought it odd there should be such a decrepit place so close to the city. The Yutakashi seem to utilize every square inch of space," he remarked, as he and Toshi-hito were squeezed together by a wagon passing in the opposite direction.

"They do indeed. The ruins are kept there as a symbol, although the lesson is largely forgotten. A long time ago, when the city first began to acquire its great wealth, the Yutakashi became famous for breeding horses, which they used in their great games. They staged these raucous pageants in their stadium, which is now that 'decrepit place' as you put it. Opposing teams of horsemen wore Red and Blue to distinguish one from the other; likewise, their supporters wore the team colors. The rivalries were great, so much so that violence was commonplace.

Eventually, the allegiances filtered beyond the games, and into the commercial life of the city."

Their group turned down a smaller lane, lined with buildings close up on the road on both sides. This was the Street of Inns, and in front of each establishment hung a sign with such colorful names as 'The Ribald Horseman' and 'Our Hearth, Your Home.' The smell of cooked foodstuffs wafted over the streets. "That spirit of competition," Toshi-hito continued, "is part of why Yutakashi has become so successful; but the price has been incessant civil strife. Everywhere the Reds and the Blues contest with one another. During a particularly bad riot many years ago, the stadium was burned down, and the games where then banned. The burned hulk of the stadium was left standing as a reminder of where violence can lead."

The group pulled up in front of one of the inns, whose sign was auspiciously labeled 'The House of Bright Light.' As Itachi led the Hikari group through an arched gateway into the inner courtyard of the inn, Toshi-hito added, "The Blues appear to be preeminent at the moment, but that can change rapidly. We must be careful not to do anything that appears to favor one side over the other."

Once the group had come to a halt within the courtyard and dismounted, the innkeeper rushed out, bowing profusely with every step. He solicitously ushered Itachi and Toshi-hito into his greeting chamber, where servants stood ready to ply the visitors with refreshments. While the pilgrimage leaders went to barter for the price of accommodation, Donaku and the Hikari remained just outside the greeting chamber as a subtle reminder to the innkeeper of their status as pilgrims.

Shiko took stock of his surroundings. The front of the inn, which formed the wall facing the street, contained the public rooms: a communal dining hall on one side of the main gate, with a kitchen forming the opposite wing. The remaining walls of the courtyard stretched up several floors, and held the traveler's rooms. A sturdy wooden staircase marched up the back wall to connect each level. At the rear of the courtyard, a ramp through a smaller arched gate led down to a stable area. Shiko saw that the Guards were leading their horses down to the stable, so he took his own and Toshi-hito's in hand and followed them.

Passing under the rear of the building through the small arch, Shiko saw that the stable fronted on a back alley running behind all the inns on this side of the street. He wondered why the alley was built at a lower level than the inns, until his nose answered the question for him. Apparently the sewage from the inns and the stables used the alley as a natural drainage course. Trying to ignore the smell, he tied up his horse and Toshi-hito's, then started unloading their travel packs.

Around him the soldiers had likewise begun unloading. The hulking Bokusa took the packs off his horse and turned to Shiko. "Here, squirt," he said, and he threw the packs at the young Deshi. Filled with gear and clothing for a large man, the heavy packs bowled Shiko over into the mud.

Several of the other Guards laughed, and Bokusa sneared, "Get my packs up to our room. And now that you've gone and made them all dirty, you can clean them up too." He turned to walk away, but found Nakama standing in his path.

The former officer, incensed at Bokusa's casual abuse, glared hard at the larger man. Quietly he said, "A Guard handles his own affairs. He doesn't demand service from others."

Bokusa straightened to his full imposing height, and the other men grew quiet. Shiko, still sprawled upon the muddy ground beneath the packs, watched as Bokusa, towering over Nakama, barked, "And what do you have to say about it, *soldier*? Do you have something to prove, *soldier*? 'Cause if so, I'm willing whenever you are." Bokusa kept both arms at his sides, but the tense set of his shoulders betrayed a willingness to set them swinging at the slightest provocation.

Nakama, however, did not rise to the bait. Instead he said, "The boy is not one of the Guards. If subservient work is to be done for a Guard, then another Guard should do it."

With a hearty laugh, Bokusa turned back to the other men. "You hear that? Sounds like a volunteer to me. All right, *soldier*," he added, turning back. "Since you—"

But Nakama had already walked away. He went over to Shiko and reached down to pick up Bokusa's packs, then helped Shiko to his feet. Slinging the muddy packs over his shoulder, Nakama then went over to

Itachi's horse and took those packs as well. Without another word he marched off through the archway, back into the inn's courtyard.

Bokusa glowered after him. Noticing that the other Guards were also sheepishly watching the former officer, he shouted, "Well, what are you all still standing around for? Get the rest of this gear inside!" He started off but noticed Shiko still standing nearby, half-coated in mud. He stopped and glared down at the Deshi. "As for you, squirt," he said menacingly, "just keep out of my way." Then he too stomped off through the archway.

Shiko stood trembling, watching the retreating form of Bokusa. He tried to apply his Deshi training to calm himself, but the nearness of potential violence left him shaken. Instinctively he reached for his honsho, trying to still his ragged nerves. The other Guards ignored him as they quietly finished unloading, which gave him time to review in his head what had just happened.

Among the Deshi, such bullying behavior was virtually non-existent, and so Shiko had not been prepared for how to react. Violence was common throughout Tonagato during these turbulent days; and he, like other apprentices, had practiced a number of martial arts. But he had never personally been threatened before. He found it very unsettling, particularly when he had thought that their group was united in the common cause of the pilgrimage.

It occurred to him then that, just because these men were from Hajimeshi, and in a strange city, it did not remove the possibility of conflict between them. Clearly, he realized, there was also some sort of friction that he did not understand between Bokusa and the other Guard, Nakama, who had helped him up out of the mud. He resolved to be more alert and aware of those around him, so as not to be surprised by their behavior. And to be more prepared for the unexpected.

Looking down at his soiled clothes, he decided he had best change before Master Toshi-hito wondered what he had been up to.

*   *   *

"When did you last see her?" Himitsu's voice, usually cloaked in diplomatic velvet, could also wear a suit of hardened armor when required. Such was this occasion, as a servant cowered on the floor before the chamberlain, who was himself kneeling before the Kojuro.

One by one, the entire household staff had been questioned relentlessly by Himitsu. He had called not a few of them back several times to the Great Audience Hall, where he cross checked their stories with new information from other servants. Throughout it all the Kojuro sat, watching and listening. With the departure of the Hikari pilgrimage he had grown weaker; much of his reserves of strength had gone into seeing the quest successfully off.

Now he faced this. His headstrong daughter had disobeyed him and run away. His anger and frustration at her transgression had further aggravated his condition. He had, with a supreme effort, controlled his emotions so as not to further damage the delicate physical strands that were keeping his body going. Above all else, he knew he must stay alive until the Kotaishi appeared.

Mikasama, he thought, you foolish girl! Now more than ever I needed you here, to show a face of stability to the vultures circling in Hajimeshi. Why did you choose this time to go off on some frivolous escapade?

He had sent every available Castle Guard unit out scouring the countryside. He shut off somewhere else in his mind what he would say to her when she was brought back; he was afraid his anger would just do his body more harm. It also allowed him to put off into the future thinking about her return. Because of course, she would be found...

Himitsu dismissed the last of the servants and turned to Kimeru. "It is difficult to say for certain, Majesty. From what the servants have told us, it would appear that your daughter and her guardian must have left sometime yesterday afternoon, although apparently no one can recall observing them depart. However, I am somewhat suspicious of the 'domestic dispute' that occurred at the kitchen gate. The man said that his wife began beating him for no apparent reason. His wife's story about his infidelity seems somewhat contrived. I suspect this incident was a ruse to allow your daughter to slip out during the confusion."

Kimeru frowned. "It is not like my daughter to resort to subterfuge. Many things about this incident trouble me, Lord Chamberlain."

"As they do me, sire. However, I do not believe that the Princess was the guiding hand behind the subterfuge."

"Oh?"

"Your daughter's guardian, Komori, is...well, an exceptional woman in many ways, sire. It was one of the reasons I recommended her to you as Mikasama's caretaker when the Princess was a child. I'm afraid I see the touch of her hand in this affair."

Kimeru scowled. "That this woman was your recommendation does not reflect well on you, Lord Chamberlain. I expect nothing but the utmost discretion and fealty in any attendant to the royal family. I have put my faith in you to recommend such individuals."

Himitsu bowed down to the floor. "Your Majesty, it pains me as much as yourself that this unfortunate turn of events has occurred. There is little I can do to alter that which has been done. However, rest assured that I have mobilized every resource within my purview to seek out your daughter and return her safely to you."

"I expect no less!" said Kimeru harshly. Himitsu remained bent over as the Kojuro rearranged himself upon the cushioned dais. Kimeru sighed. "My apologies, Himitsu. I know you are doing whatever needs be done." As the chamberlain straightened, the Kojuro closed his eyes and leaned back. "You cannot foresee every circumstance, or change of loyalty in another. It was enough that you saw in my daughter what I could not see; more the fool I then, for missing her heart so completely."

"You have had much on your shoulders, Majesty," he said. His gaze turned to something far away, in both time and place. "Often one must leave behind those closest to oneself when duty beckons."

"Yes," said the Kojuro, eyes still closed. He added wearily, "Inform me of any news."

Himitsu bowed again to the floor, then rose and left.

Making his way back to his quarters, Himitsu's mind was in turmoil. Ah, Komori, he thought. Why did you do this? Spite? Bravado? Probably both. And now where has it led?

She could not, he realized, have foreseen the consequences; how Mikasama's disappearance had weakened the kingdom right when it most needed stability. But that should have made her all the more cautious! If he had ever taught her anything, it was that one did not move until one knew, completely, what the results might be. Only then could one be prepared for any eventuality. His enemies over the years had never quite learned that lesson.

Yet here he had been outwitted at last, and by her, of all people! He had long since thought that he was past feelings of shame; that was for younger men, worried about their future. But now he found both shame and future very much on his mind. And, despite his anger, concern. Hopefully, he brooded, that cantankerous old battleaxe is all right…

* * *

"My arse is number than a farmer drunk on his last bottle, Mika." Komori slowed her horse down to a stop. "Can't we rest here a spell?"

Looking over at her caretaker, Mikasama felt sorry for her poor Nana-san. She remembered how sore she herself had been after her first time riding, how Komori had been the one to sooth her blistered behind with ointments.

But they had not made much progress since yesterday. After riding slowly southwards, away from the most likely route searchers might pursue, Komori had led them to a farmhouse. There a delightfully senile couple, clearly old friends of Komori's, had welcomed them for the night. Although rustic by her usual standards, Mikasama had enjoyed the visit as a novel experience. By first light, however, she had been eager to be on the road. She knew her father would send out men to look for her.

After leaving the farmhouse, the two women had taken an old cart path until they had joined up with the main Southern Road. Komori had said that this road paralleled the one that the Hikari group had taken. Soon, she had said, they should reach a crossroads and from there they would be able to turn north and eventually link up with the Northern Road. That would probably place them at least two days behind Nakama and the others.

Yet it had been slow going, for Komori was certainly never going to be a rider of any distinction. They had stopped many times, each pause accompanied by a series of Komori's complaints. With each stop, Mikasama found herself growing more and more anxious. She was feeling an overpowering need to press on. Nakama was out there, and she had to reach him.

However, she thought, looking over to where Komori had stopped yet again, at this rate...

Her caretaker had come to a halt by a copse of trees that lined the road, whose shade Mikasama had to admit looked very enticing. Just beyond the trees, the dirt road led up over the crest of a low hill, where there was certainly no shade to be seen. Acquiescing, Mikasama said, "All right, Nana-san. But just for a little while."

"Whew!" said Komori as she slid off her horse and down to the ground. With a string of assorted grunts, oaths, and groans, she stretched her limbs as she attempted to return circulation to her behind. She looked up at her young charge. "How 'bout some grub, hey? I be famished!"

With exasperation Mikasama said, "Nana-san! We just ate three hours ago! You said the crossroads were a day's ride from the farmhouse, and it's already afternoon!"

Komori looked hurt. "Old women need more food, if young fools gonna keep 'em up on smelly animals all day long." When Mikasama did not respond, Komori added enticingly, "Nana-san make some fruit maso...hey?"

The Princess smiled. Leave it to Komori, she thought, to somehow come up with her favorite dessert while out on the road. Giving in, she nodded. "All right, you win." She nudged her horse forward up the road. "I'm going to peek over the top of the hill while you make it up. Maybe I'll be able to see the crossroads from there."

"Well, don' be gone long. You know maso's no good, if gets left too long after mixin'!"

"Yes, Nana-san," said Mikasama's voice as it drifted back to Komori. "I'll be right back."

"Humph," said Komori, talking to herself. "Young people! Never got no patience. Always gotta be movin'." She looked at her horse, which seemed to be eyeing her as she spoke. "And what you gotta say about it, big fella? Huh? You who smell bad and make Nana-san's rump hurt?" She gave him a swat on the neck. He responded by swishing his tail at her. "Pahhh!" she said, opening the travel packs and digging for the food supplies.

Mikasama leisurely walked her horse up the hill. As much as she loved Komori, it was good to get away from her, even if just for a few moments. The excitement of sneaking away had long since worn off; the further they went from Hajimeshi the less interested Komori seemed to become in the journey. The old woman had kept up a steady stream of small complaints, and even when she didn't speak them out loud her groans from being saddle sore were sufficiently audible to be noticed. Which, Mikasama was sure, was exactly the intent.

She didn't know what Komori might have been thinking when they had set out from Hajimeshi. Perhaps she had thought Mikasama would 'get it out of her system' once they had successfully made their way out of the castle. Whatever the reason, Komori seemed less inclined to keep going on with each passing hour. But if they didn't keep up the pace they would soon be caught out after dark. Komori had said that there was an inn at the crossroads. Mikasama certainly hoped so; one night in a farmhouse was enough for a change of routine, but she certainly didn't want to make a habit of it.

Yet again Mikasama found herself wondering why she was out here in the first place. It had all seemed so clear to her, back in Hajimeshi. Leave the castle, find Nakama, and then...then what? Get him to run away too? She doubted he would abandon his duty, even after having been demoted to a common soldier. It had just seemed so compelling to her, the need to get away; and now that she was out here, it all seemed so much more...vast...than she had imagined. Endless miles of dry, dusty roads, all of which left her with too much time to think. *Papa must be so worried,* she thought. *Perhaps...perhaps I should go back and tell Nana-san that we can turn around, head back toward Hajimeshi...*

While she was musing, her horse had continued its slow pace up the hill. With each step, Mikasama could see a little further over the other side and into the distance. There were farm fields over there, what looked like a barn or two—

She gasped, and quickly dropped forward onto her horse's neck while at the same time pulling up sharply on the reins. The horse halted abruptly as Mikasama tried to stop the pounding in her chest.

Soldiers! A large troop of them, less than a league away on the other side of the hill. Cautiously Mikasama raised her head for a brief moment, just enough so that she could see over the top of the hill. There were about a dozen of them: Hajimeshi soldiers, talking to a man in a cart, probably a local farmer. Could her father's men already be looking for her all the way down here on the Southern Road?

Then it occurred to her that the men were ahead of them on the road. They must have already been out here, she thought. Nakama had told her that Uncle Itachi had been sending troops out to the borders. These men wouldn't know yet that she was gone. But then again, they might have heard something. They seemed to be talking to that farmer, asking questions. She risked one more look.

They were on the move, the troop moving up the opposite side of the hill toward her. In a panic she quickly ducked down and turned her horse about, kicking it into action back down their side of the hill. Her mind was consumed by a sudden, frantic feeling: I must not let them find me! We've got to hide!

Komori was startled as Mikasama rode up in a hurry, her horse skidding to a stop on the hard-packed dirt of the road. "Hey, what's the matter, Mika? You look like you been seein' ghosts! Maso's all ready."

"Never mind, Nana-san! Quick, we have to get off the road." Mikasama slid off her horse and hurriedly untied Komori's steed. "Gather up the foodstuff, hurry!"

"What? What's matter with you, anyway? Who gonna bother us on this road, all by ourselves?"

"Soldiers, Nana-san! They're coming this way. Now come on!"

Finally grasping the reason for haste, Komori scooped up her utensils and the uneaten maso and scurried after Mikasama, who was already leading the horses into the trees. They found a dense clump of bushes masked by several trees not too far in. While Mikasama tried to maneuver both of the horses into a position that would be the least visible from the road, Komori poked her head around one of the bushes to watch for the soldiers.

The jangle of their harnesses and the thumping of many hooves signaled the troop's arrival before either woman could see them. Mikasama stood between the noses of both horses, holding their reins and trying to exude a feeling of calm toward both of them that she didn't share herself. Their hiding spot might be adequate if no one looked their way, but even a casual observer was bound to see something amiss.

The sound of men talking and horses snorting filtered through the trees, and Mikasama could feel both of her own horses fidgeting. "Shhhh," she whispered to them. "I'm sure you'd like to go meet your friends, but we have to stay here right now." Komori gave her a look like she had been out too long in the sun, then resumed her vigil watching the road. The horses, though, to Mikasama's surprise, did indeed calm themselves.

Then she could see them, soldiers and horses passing by one by one: a flash of color, a creak of leather, as each crossed before the opening between the trees. The soldiers did not stop, but kept moving down the road. Once it seemed that they were almost all past, Komori began to settle back on her heels. Then both women heard a shout.

Tensely, Mikasama strained her neck for a better view. A wooden spoon! Komori had dropped a spoon; and there it sat, its dull brown contrasting sharply with the light-colored dirt of the road. Komori must have seen it too, for she whispered an expletive so foul that even Mikasama, having grown up hearing Komori say just about every word known to man, raised an eyebrow.

One of the soldiers had stopped, and was looking down at the spoon from atop his horse. Two more soldiers rode over and looked down at it too. The women could not hear what they said to one another, but it was clear from the way they pointed that they were looking at the fallen utensil. They looked up and down the road, but for some reason they had not yet thought to look into the woods. Mikasama was certain the men would look right at their hiding place at any moment. Her heart was pounding, and her hands holding the horses' reins began to tremble.

Just as she started wondering if she and Komori could mount their horses fast enough to flee, another shout was heard. It was deeper, and came from further away, probably near the head of the line. The men in view all looked up at the shouted command. One of them waved down at the forsaken spoon, but received only another guttural bellow in reply. With a shrug to his comrades, the first man turned his horse back to the road and rejoined the column, followed by the other two.

Neither of the two women in the woods moved for a long time. They waited until the sound of the riders had faded away completely, then waited a little more. Komori signaled silently to Mikasama that she was going to go out and look. Mikasama mouthed "Be careful!" to her; Komori mouthed back "Pahhhh!"

The old woman crept quietly out toward the road, stopping to listen every few yards. She reached the edge and cautiously stepped further and further out, looking down the road in the direction of the departed soldiers. Finally she straightened, walked over to pick up the spoon, and marched back in to where Mikasama stood with the horses.

"They be gone," she said. Waving the dusty tableware at Mikasama, she added, "Mika give Nana-san bad heart, all this sneakin' 'bout!" She gave the Princess a long, searching look. "Sure you wanna keep this up? I be willin' to go back, if you be tired."

Now that the soldiers were gone, Mikasama's heart had stopped racing. In its place, though, came a feeling of queasiness, along with a renewed feeling of urgency. Time was passing; they had to keep moving...

Mikasama walked over and put her hands on Komori's shoulders. "Nana-san, I'm sorry I dragged you out of Hajimeshi with me. I know you're tired and sore, and miss your old sewing chair back home. But," she said, looking into Komori's familiar old face, "I have to do this. I have to go on. I can't go back."

Komori gazed back into Mikasama's eyes. "I know, Mika, I know. Old Nana-san jus' feelin' her bones, is all." She patted Mikasama's arm. "We be all right. We find that soldier-boy of yours." Just then an odd expression crossed Mikasama's face. Komori, noticing, said with concern, "What, child? What be wrong?"

"Nothing, Nana-san." The Princess let go of Komori and turned away. "I'm fine." She nervously fidgeted with the straps of her travel pack.

But she was not fine. Just for a moment, she had forgotten that it was Nakama that had caused her to be here, running away from the life she had known. First there had been her fear of being found by the soldiers, and then after that the realization that they were safe, and that they could keep moving, keep going further west...but not, she realized now with a start, just because of Nakama. There was something else, something very far away, that she had to reach...

She shook her head; whatever the feeling was, it was gone now, although she found its lingering presence unsettling. "Come on, Nana-san," she said abruptly. "We need to be on our way. I think we have to find another road; those soldiers may talk to someone who's seen us."

"Well," said Komori, scratching her head, "I think there be another farm road, somewheres south of the crossroads. But, Mika, ain't no inns on that road."

Mikasama took a deep breath. "We'll just have to make do somehow. If we go to the inn at the crossroads, we'll be found out for sure. Do you have enough supplies to cook for us if we go on our own?"

"Oh, I be able to whip up somethin'. May not taste like maso," she said, picking up the bowl containing the congealed remains, "but be eatable."

Mikasama gave her a smile. Even so, her thoughts remained troubled as she led the horses back to the road.

6

Shiko stifled a yawn as he and Toshi-hito completed their morning meditation. The Guards were just beginning to stir from their sleeping mats as the two Deshi donned their grey pilgrim smocks.

The cramped room at the inn, although perhaps a fair size for a family, was severely strained by holding over a dozen men. Their first night out from Hajimeshi, sleeping by the road, had been a new experience for the young apprentice. Unfortunately, so was trying to sleep in a confined space with many snoring, sweating bodies. It had not been a good night for rest. At least, thought Shiko, today they were up and about early.

The previous day, after the pilgrims had established themselves at the inn, Toshi-hito had sent an official request for an audience with the Grand Council of Guild Merchants, the confederation of Red and Blue factions ruling Yutakashi. As the visitors were not only pilgrims but included a high-ranking member of the Hajimeshi royal court, it had been expected that the Grand Council would agree to see them promptly. However, as with most things in Yutakashi, political maneuvering had taken precedence over all else. For the remainder of that first day, no reply had come from the Grand Council to Toshi-hito's inquiry.

To Itachi the insult was blatant and infuriating, and he had refused to let any of the men out on leave into the city until their party was officially recognized. The tired, irritable soldiers had tried to keep out of each other's way in the cramped confines of their room for hour after hour. Their only diversion was to walk out onto their third floor landing, from which they had an excellent view out over the rooftops of the city.

It had been shortly before midnight, and only just in time to be considered a response on the same day, that two runners, one Blue and one Red, arrived from the Grand Council. Their message was that the Council wished to meet with the leaders of the pilgrimage immediately upon striking their bell for business the next day, which, the runners had explained, was shortly after first light.

Itachi, unused to being treated so cavalierly, had vented his considerable spleen upon the hapless messengers. The runners had nevertheless stood their ground and waited for either a yes or no response from the Hajimeshi lord. Once Itachi had expended his invective, he had waved the men away with a terse acknowledgement that the pilgrims would appear.

What with the day's hard riding, the tumult among the soldiers upon their arrival, and then Itachi's injured pride, it had been a quiet, and disquieting, evening.

Shiko now tried to sweep all of the previous day's events behind him. He had been taught that one remembered the past so that it could be studied and learned from, not so that it could be brooded over. As he took up the Hikari lantern to accompany Toshi-hito and Itachi to the Grand Council chamber, he concentrated on observing the turbulent city of Yutakashi through which they walked.

The three Hajimeshi, with two of the Guards as escort, made their way out of the Street of Inns and onto the High Road. Even at this early hour, Shiko saw that people were up and about and transacting business, commerce clearly already in full swing. Everywhere Shiko looked, people were either hawking wares from storefronts, haggling over prices, or arguing about the relative merits of products from neighboring shops. On both sides of the High Road, buildings rose up three and sometimes even four stories high, and in some cases arched out over the thoroughfare. A bewildering array of signs announced every establishment, each one attempting to outdo its neighbors. Shiko noted that the building facades were highly ornate and well constructed of stone and brick, but their attractiveness was almost entirely lost behind the gaudy expanse of signs. Yutakashi, he concluded, was clearly a city with but one thing on its mind.

The group's progress through the growing throng was scarcely noticed, despite the presence of the Hikari lantern suspended on its pole above them and the pilgrims' grey smocks. Arriving at the Grand Council's Guild Hall, the Guards remained outside while Toshi-hito, Itachi, and Shiko were ushered into a vast antechamber.

Inside, Shiko's breath was taken away by an impressive dome overhead, held aloft by slanting ribs that topped the circular room. The walls, though, were finished with dark, uninspiring wood, lacking any particular adornment. A few small torches were spaced evenly about the sides of the room.

The chamber was already nearly full of people waiting for their turn before the Council. The three Hajimeshi stood quietly amid the babble of voices, the Hikari's light dispelling some of the gloom from what was otherwise a dimly lit space. "Typical merchants," grumbled Itachi to no one in particular. "Won't even spend money on decent candles to light a room."

Just as Shiko's arms were beginning to tire from supporting the heavy lantern, a huge wooden door on the far side of the chamber swung ponderously open. Through an opening, large enough that a wagon could have been drawn beneath its arched frame marched an imperious official, scarcely taller than Shiko. He wore an elaborate uniform and bore a staff that reached more than a foot over his head. The crowd's chatter died away as many pairs of eyes watched the man stride haughtily over to the Hikari group.

Speaking to all three at once, in a tone dripping with disdain, the official said, "You are the pilgrims?"

Forestalling Itachi's expected retort, Toshi-hito spoke up. "Yes, we are on a quest, and would appreciate an audience with the esteemed Grand Council of Yutakashi."

The official looked them up and down as if they were something unpleasant brought in by a household cat. With a resigned air of irritation, he said, "Very well." Turning on his heel, he walked off toward the open door.

Shiko looked at Itachi and Toshi-hito, neither of whom had moved. The apprentice knew that, unlike Itachi, the Deshi Master did not suffer from sensitive pride. But given the opportunity to prick the pompousness of those who did, Shiko also knew that occasionally Toshi-hito could not resist the impulse…

As the official reached the doorway, he realized that he walked alone and turned about in consternation. Amidst general snickering from the assembled onlookers, he strode back over to the Hikari group.

Red faced, he said tightly, "If you will follow me…"

"Certainly," replied Toshi-hito, and the three accompanied the official as he re-traced his steps once more to the doorway. The great wooden door swung shut behind them.

"And you expect to find this so-called Kotaishi in our fair city?"

The speaker was one of the Grand Council, a man whose corpulence rivaled Lord Choshuka's. He sat, along with six others, atop a low platform that filled one side of the Council chamber.

The room itself was quite plain, barely a third the size of the Audience Hall in Hajimeshi. In contrast to the soaring dome of the antechamber, here the roof was low and flat. The room itself was also rather oddly shaped, much wider than it was long. As a result the Councilors sat quite close to their visitors. The effect, Toshi-hito noted, was to force one to continually turn one's head whenever a particular Councilor spoke. It was a subtle exercise of power; and quite typical, he mused, of Yutakashi thinking.

Three of the Council members wore Red, giving the Blues a one-vote majority. Off to one side, a phalanx of scribes, both Red and Blue, noted everything that was said. Toshi-hito knelt along with Itachi directly in front of the Council, with Shiko immediately behind, the Hikari on the floor before him.

As the Deshi Master answered the heavy-set member of the Council, he chose his words with care. "Esteemed Councilor, we do not know where the Kotaishi will be found. That is why we have undertaken a quest to find him. It would please us greatly, as I am sure it would you, were he to be found from among Yutakashi's noble citizenry."

One of the Reds spoke up. "If such a person were to come to light in our city, what…specific…benefits might Yutakashi derive from this?"

Toshi-hito knew that this would be the key question on the minds of most, if not all, of Yutakashi's ruling merchants. Similarly he knew his answer would not satisfy them. Which was why, he told himself, the Kotaishi was needed; in order to help these men, and those whom they ruled, to find the path for themselves…

With a nod of respect to the speaker, he said, "The one who is the Kotaishi will assume a burden beyond his birthplace. He will seek to lead the people of Tonogato to a common defense against the Darkness."

The Councilors stirred, and there was angry muttering among several of them. A Blue Councilor interjected, "What you are saying, then, is that not only will we get nothing out of this, but this so-called Kotaishi will seek to undermine us and take over Yutakashi, into some kingdom of his own?"

It was as Toshi-hito feared. The only threat the members of the 'Grand' Council could perceive was that coming from a human. The concept of what the Darkness represented, and the evil it presaged, was far beyond their comprehension. In their limited view, they could only see danger in the one man who might save them all.

"Councilor," answered Toshi-hito patiently, "a Kotaishi would not seek to overthrow, but to educate. He would show the people where they must go, together, in order to avoid their own destruction. In the end, their own desires would lead them to follow him."

Another of the Blue Councilors stood up. "This is seditious. These men should be arrested at once."

A Red Councilor interjected: "We in Yutakashi honor the pilgrimage of the Hikari." An old man, he spoke in a clipped voice; it was an economy of manner that seemed to match the pre-occupation of most Yutakashi. He pointedly ignored the suggestion of his Blue comrade, nor even looked at him. "We would never go against tradition and harm a pilgrim."

As the flustered Blue sat down, the others also became quiet and looked to the speaker. Although of the Red faction, he seemed by virtue of his age to hold the respect of the others. Gazing steadily at Toshi-hito he said, "You have come seeking something. You will not find it here."

"Perhaps not, Councilor," replied Toshi-hito, as he bowed to the older man. Their reaction to the pilgrimage was as he expected, even though he had held a slim hope that events might take a different course. But he reminded himself that men's characters are not so easily changed. "However, it is the nature of our quest that we must at least attempt to seek him out in each of the cities of Tonogato."

"And it is the nature of our city that no such person will be found here. Is that understood, pilgrim?"

"As you say, Councilor," replied Toshi-hito with another bow.

"Then your quest here is done." He folded his hands in his lap. "The Hikari is sacrosanct. But Hajimeshi is not popular among our people. Not all may understand traditions as we do. You would do well to leave our city by tomorrow."

"Of course, Councilor. May we have leave to replenish our supplies?"

"Hajimeshi gold is as good as any other. Purchase what things you need." Toshi-hito was interrupted in mid-bow as the man continued, "Be sure that a Kotaishi is not among them." Toshi-hito merely continued his bow to the floor.

Itachi, sitting next to the Deshi Master, gave a terse nod of the head to mimic Toshi-hito's bow, in acceptance of the Council's conditions. His nerves wound up like a tiger too long deprived of a meal, it took all his will power to keep from drawing his sword and removing a few heads from the smug merchants sitting opposite him. But he had plans that required a few of those heads in place, and so he kept his anger in check.

Pointedly, the Council members did not bow in return to Toshi-hito, nor did they acknowledge Itachi's nod. Unwilling to endure further insult, the Hajimeshi general promptly stood and turned toward the door to the Council chamber. Shiko quickly gathered up the Hikari, and as Toshi-hito rose to join them the door opened, revealing the short official who had escorted them in, smugly waiting.

Once the pilgrims had been silently deposited back in the domed antechamber, the official closed the great wooden door decisively behind him. The still-waiting crowd eyed the foreigners with hushed interest.

"Master—" began Shiko, but Toshi-hito held up his hand to forestall his apprentice's question. The group walked out past the curious eyes of the throng in the antechamber and returned to the bustle of Yutakashi's streets.

Itachi and the Deshi rejoined with their two Hajimeshi Guards, and the group headed off back toward the inn. Toshi-hito turned to his disciple. "Better to speak here, where the only words heard are those relating to coin."

Shiko struggled to keep the Hikari from swinging onto the head of anyone on the crowded street. "Master, they seemed quite certain we would not find the Kotaishi here."

Toshi-hito smiled apologetically. "I did not expect to find him here either." Seeing his apprentice's startled look, he continued. "The Grand Council would never acknowledge any leader as superior to them within their own city. If someone proclaiming to be the Kotaishi appeared from among their citizenry, I have no doubt that the individual would summarily...disappear. We will not find what we seek just yet."

The pilgrims had to stop abruptly as a man pushing a cart loaded with produce suddenly rolled across their path. "Then why," asked Shiko while they waited, "did we come to Yutakashi?"

"What I said to the Council is true," replied Toshi-hito. "We must visit all of the cities of Tonogato in our search." The path clear once more, he and the others, with the two escorting Guards behind, continued on. "However, the Kotaishi will appear when it is time. We have other reasons for our presence here. Among them is that word of our pilgrimage will circulate, so that when the Kotaishi does come he will be expected."

Nodding, Shiko added, "And the people will be more receptive to what he has to say than the Council."

"Precisely," agreed the Deshi Master. "If the people can be convinced, then their leaders will have no choice but to lead the populace where they want to go. There is no substitute for having a 'secret army' on one's side." Toshi-hito turned abruptly to the Hajimeshi general walking at his side, who had been unusually silent during their return walk. "Wouldn't you agree, Lord Itachi?"

"What?" said Itachi, startled. Toshi-hito noted the shock that briefly flitted across the man's face, before the more usual mask of superiority fell back into place. "Oh...yes," replied Itachi off-handedly. "Yes, that is a well-known principle of war. Subversion from within."

"Well," Toshi-hito went on, speaking to Shiko, "perhaps subversion is not what we seek in this case. Merely...enlightenment." His thoughts, however, were on Itachi, and the man's curious reaction to his question. As the group turned down the street toward the Inn of Bright Light, Toshi-hito found himself feeling very troubled.

Unbeknownst to Toshi-hito, one of the escorting Castle Guards had been paying rather closer attention to what was being said than had the Kojuro's brother. The Guard was one of two archers among the Hajimeshi pilgrims, Nakama being the other. Going by the name of Hisoka, this one's taciturn manner and tight-lipped visage had set him apart from the other Guards ever since the pilgrims had first set out from Hajimeshi. It was a fact that suited Hisoka perfectly well. He had no need for, nor any interest in, the other soldiers.

He noted carefully all that passed between the three men walking in front of him, all the while maintaining the empty expression expected of a Guard. His scrutiny of the conversation went unnoticed. Soon he would have much to report.

As the pilgrims reached the inn, Shiko lowered the Hikari to pass through the archway. The group climbed the stairs to their quarters and entered to find the remaining soldiers engaged in a vigorous game of dice.

A whoop of joy greeted the pilgrimage leaders as they came through the door, although it was quickly evident that it was not directed at their arrival.

"Hah! What did I tell you? When I got the luck, no man's gonna take my money!" With that, Ryori reached down to scoop up the coins piled up on the floor where the men were playing.

Nakama, who had been sitting by himself outside the circle of soldiers betting with Ryori, coughed loudly as Itachi came through the door. The other soldiers quickly shuffled away to sit on their sleeping mats, leaving Ryori in the middle of the floor with a mass of coins.

Unaware of why he was suddenly all alone, the cook looked about in confusion. Then he saw Itachi standing over him, the Hajimeshi lord tapping his tarka against his leg.

Looking down sheepishly at his horde, then back up to Itachi, Ryori said, "Ah…a…a good day, my Lord, don't you see…"

"I see," growled Itachi. Looking around at his men, he added, "You are all fools to play with a cheat such as this. Any money you've lost is due to your own stupidity." Ryori took on an injured expression, but was brought up short by Itachi's tarka poking his forehead. "As for you," said the Hajimeshi general, "concentrate on your cooking. I set high standards when it comes to food." Ryori bowed to the floor in reply.

Itachi looked around the room again. "Our business here is done. We leave at first light tomorrow. You are free of duties until then." Several of the men, including Ryori, grinned at the prospect of an evening of entertainment in cosmopolitan Yutakashi. "But," the Hajimeshi lord continued, "you will keep a low profile! No incidents—any man involved in an altercation will answer to me personally. Is that understood?" All nodded solemnly. Looking down, Itachi added, "You, Cook, will have no time for pleasure. I expect us to be fully re-provisioned for our departure." Ryori's crestfallen face betrayed his dismay. "The rest of you, remember we ride early. If you're too hung over to ride, Bokusa will tie you to your horse." As he turned toward the door he barked at Bokusa, "Post a guard on the Hikari. I will return later." As he swept out of the room, the men visibly relaxed. Wasting no time, they quickly gathered up what they wished to take with them out into the city.

Nakama was not surprised when Bokusa singled him out to remain behind and watch the Hikari. As the other Guards made their way outside, he made himself comfortable, sitting down near the lantern. Ryori had remained where he was, sitting in the middle of the floor, staring down at his pile of coins that were useless to him if he could not sample the pleasures of the city.

Toshi-hito attempted to lighten Ryori's mood. "I presume, Master Cook, that you will be heading toward the Market Place?" Ryori nodded glumly. "Shiko and I have business that will take us past there, so we would be happy to accompany you for a while if you wish." Ryori nodded mournfully as he scooped up his coins. "Perhaps at our next stop," added the Deshi Master, "you will be able to spend some of your new-found wealth."

"Hah!" replied the little man, as he stood and headed for the door. "In Shukyoshi? Not likely to be anything to buy in that nest of fanatics." He stopped on the balcony outside, and sent a long spit sailing over the railing to land in the courtyard below. As he started down the stairs, the two Deshi followed, Toshi-hito trying to suppress a smile.

As the three reached the High Road, Ryori looked up toward the north end of the street. Toshi-hito pointed toward the south. "I believe, Master Cook, that the Market Place lies in this direction."

Ryori appeared not to hear, continuing to scan the street to the north. Absentmindedly he said, "You two go on. Got plenty of time for vegetables." Then he seemed to catch sight of whatever it was that he had been looking for. "Thanks for the offer," he said determinedly. "I'll pick you two up something tasty." Without another word he strode off into the crowd, leaving the Deshi behind on the corner.

Shiko's puzzled look followed the cook up the street. "He seems a rather curious fellow, Master."

Toshi-hito was gazing in the direction that the cook had departed but lost sight of the small man in the crowd. Finally the Deshi Master caught sight of him again, as the cook stood rather nonchalantly gazing into a shop front full of woven baskets for sale. As he could not think of why Ryori would have any interest in decorative basketware, Toshi-hito looked about in the cook's vicinity. It somehow did not surprise him to see Itachi across the street, engaged in earnest conversation with a man wearing a Red headband. "Indeed," remarked Toshi-hito. "One can never quite tell what our mercurial cook has on his mind." With that he led Shiko off in the direction of the Market.

✳   ✳   ✳

The course taken by Toshi-hito led through streets that turned increasingly residential. Shop fronts gave way to high-walled compounds, each showing only a barred door to the street. Over the walls one could see multi-storied houses basking in a private sunshine of their own, their upper stories built of stout wood, with expensive paints decorating every visible surface. Delicate carved shutters kept out prying eyes from the street, while richly tiled roofs reached out to the very edges of each property. As to the appearance of the lower floors, behind the walls, only those who were well connected enough to be invited in would have been able to attest.

Toshi-hito turned without hesitation at the various intersections they encountered. Shiko began to suspect that the Deshi Master had been in Yutakashi before, and for quite some time, to be able to know his way around so well. But in response to Shiko's inquiry Toshi-hito was uncharacteristically non-committal: "I have traveled to a great many places. There is always much to see in the world."

Gradually the character of the surroundings changed as the two Deshi neared the Market. The dwellings became less ostentatious, and here and there a warehouse building or two cropped up. By the time Shiko's nose detected their imminent arrival at the Market, most of the surrounding buildings were devoted either to storage or shops selling foodstuffs. Suddenly, with one last turn of a corner, Toshi-hito ushered Shiko into the Market itself.

A vast square confronted them which, had it been empty, could have held the Deshi priory in Hajimeshi two or three times over. But the square was far from empty.

Shiko did not think that ever in his life had he seen more people in one place. A teeming throng of humanity packed the square, funneling between rows of stalls selling every kind of edible object possible. Each produce seller was attempting to out-shout his or her neighbors in the effort to attract buyers, and the buyers haggled over the prices of everything they picked up. The sounds, not to mention the smells, were nearly overwhelming.

Undaunted, Toshi-hito dove into their midst, Shiko desperately trying to keep up so as not to become lost in the sea of bodies. The Deshi Master ignored the entreaties of those who would tempt his purse as he passed. After a long time of what felt like swimming against a strong current in a wide river, Shiko noted the crowd beginning to thin. Then he realized they had crossed the entire square, and were exiting the other side. Almost as abruptly as they had entered it, they were out of the Market and back in the 'usual' crush of pedestrian traffic of a Yutakashi street.

The character on this side of the Market, however, was quite different from that of the side from which they had just come. Here there were no fine houses behind barred gates; most of the buildings appeared to be large and run-down apartment blocks, built of plain wood and lined with rows of anonymous windows. From nearly every one of those windows, clothing of various shades hung out on poles to dry from washing. To Shiko it looked as if the streets were festooned with multi-colored flags.

People filled the streets here as well, but their behavior was different. Buying and selling was noticeable by its absence; while a few people were carrying goods of one sort or another, they appeared intent on taking these elsewhere to sell. Many of the people Shiko saw were clearly less well off than those in the areas from which Toshi-hito and Shiko had just traveled. Their clothes in some cases were threadbare, and few if any wore jewelry or decoration. None were wearing the Red or Blue headbands. Most of the people seemed to simply be sitting or standing idly about, either alone or talking in small groups. He saw one old woman sorting through the remains from a tipped-over garbage pail, and was shocked to see her gnaw at the food scraps she had found. Whatever prosperity Yutakashi enjoyed elsewhere, it did not seem to have filtered down into this quarter.

Toshi-hito led them on deeper into the district until they finally stopped at an apartment block that, to Shiko, was indistinguishable from all the rest. Climbing the rickety stairs to the third level, they walked down the balcony landing to one of the doors, upon which Toshi-hito gently knocked.

A young boy answered the door, and was immediately joined by three other younger children crowding around. Toshi-hito looked down at them. "Good day. Would Master Kanyo be at home?" The children all giggled and laughed as if this was the funniest thing they had ever heard.

From inside, Shiko heard a man's voice say, "Is that Toshi-hito?" The next moment the door was swinging wide, with children cascading every which way in a laughing heap as they fell about the man's legs, and Toshi-hito's as well.

The man standing in the doorway was some years older than Toshi-hito, his grey hair framing a weather-beaten face and dark, penetrating eyes. The lines in his face all seemed to be the result of a perpetual smile. Looking at the children piled up at his feet, he laughingly told them, "All right, scat, all you little tona birds! You, Chushida, let go of our guest's foot! Go on, run along now, all of you!" He shooed them away inside.

Turning back to Toshi-hito, he said, "My apologies, sometimes they forget their manners completely." Toshi-hito smiled and waved his hand gently, dismissing it entirely. The older man then bowed, somewhat more formally saying, "Welcome to my home, Master Toshi-hito. You honor my house."

"The honor is mine, Kanyo," said Toshi-hito, returning the bow equally. "We can never repay what is owed to you."

Shiko found this a curious comment, but the old man waved it off in much the same way that Toshi-hito had done. "There are no debts owed to this house, old friend," he said. "But who is this?" as he turned to look at Shiko.

The Deshi master said, "This is Shiko. He is an apprentice Deshi, and has joined me on a journey across Tonogato."

At this introduction Shiko bowed to Kanyo. "I am honored to meet you, Master Kanyo."

Kanyo's permanent smile seemed to slip for just an instant, and in that brief moment Shiko thought he saw an entire range of emotions play across that craggy face. Astonishment, sadness, and joy all seemed to pass quickly by, but Kanyo had in fact not moved at all. Perhaps, thought Shiko, it was just the light.

Kanyo returned the bow to the apprentice. "Young Shiko. It is my house that is honored by your visit." As he straightened, his gaze seemed to linger once more before returning to Toshi-hito. "But please, come inside. Tanoshi will want to see you." With that he stood aside and bade the Deshi to enter.

The first impression that greeted Shiko as they stepped into the main room was one of utter chaos. There were more children here than had greeted them at the door; Shiko counted at least seven little heads all running about engaged in various games and activities. But the next thought that entered his mind was an odd sense of familiarity. He looked about, wondering what could have caused such a feeling. There was not much to see in the small room, devoid of any furniture save for a low table in one corner. The floor coverings were worn down almost to nonexistence, and the wooden walls were cracked and mildewed. Yet somehow the place seemed to exude a feeling of warmth. The odd sensation passed quickly, though, leaving him wondering at the tricks his mind seemed to be playing on him.

He had little time to ponder it, as a heavy-set woman came bustling through a doorway along the far wall. She spied Toshi-hito right away. Not standing upon any sort of formality as had Kanyo she immediately grasped the Deshi Master in a huge hug. "Toshi, Toshi, Toshi!" she cried, as Toshi-hito politely let himself be grappled. "Too many years!" she said. "When did you last come visit, hmmm? Oh, I know, it must have been—"

"Tanoshi," interrupted Kanyo, "there is another visitor as well."

Releasing Toshi-hito, she turned to Kanyo and Shiko. "My apologies. Sometimes, I just get all excited…" Her voice trailed off as she focused on Shiko. "Oh. Yes, we do have another visitor," she said quietly, looking back to Toshi-hito.

The Master Deshi said, "Tanoshi, this is Shiko, my apprentice. He is accompanying me."

Tanoshi's gaze returned to Shiko. "I'm sure he is, Toshi. I'm sure he is." Shiko felt slightly uncomfortable as she looked at him. He continued to feel odd flashes of emotion, but he could not put his finger on them. Before anyone could say more, another whirlwind erupted into the room.

"Papa, look, I finally got a—" The young woman's words stopped abruptly as she came through the still-open door from outside. About the same age as Shiko, her headlong rush ended a few feet inside the doorway, her outstretched hands holding a small brown bag. Wearing the same type of non-descript tunic as most of the residents of this quarter, her hair was cut short, unlike most girls her age; in fact, at first Shiko had thought she was a boy. Seeing the strangers, the girl quickly slipped the bag away inside her tunic and stood awkwardly, saying nothing.

Kanyo said, "Toshi-hito, Shiko; this is Nusumi. She is one of our brood."

Toshi-hito inclined his head to the girl, and Shiko did the same. She nodded in return, saying, "Welcome to our house. Ummm, Papa, I think I'll show this to you...later." Looking back at both of the visitors, somewhat self-consciously she said, "Well...goodbye." Then she slipped around the side of the room and out through the doorway through which Tanoshi had entered.

Kanyo chuckled. "She's quite a devil, that one."

Toshi-hito turned to Shiko with a smile. "Kanyo and Tanoshi have been foster parents to a great many children over the years. They never seem to tire of the pandemonium."

"Oh, never!" said Tanoshi. "We love them all. Got nine of 'em right now! Nusumi's the oldest. Bit of an imp, just like Kanyo said. Never can tell what she's going to get into next. Never goes hungry though," she added wistfully. "Helps keep all the other little ones going too." There was a moment of awkward silence before Tanoshi went on. "Well! Enough of that! You two most certainly need some food. Unless, of course, you've already gorged yourselves in the Market on the way here?" At the Deshi's joint denial, she continued. "That's settled, then! Lunch in just a skip!" And off she went, a bustle of energy as she scooped up a couple of stray children in the room to help her prepare the meal.

There was another moment of silence as the three men looked at one another, until Kanyo said, "Please, sit. You must tell me how your journey has gone so far."

* * *

Itachi squinted as he tried to make out the faces opposite him. The room was dark, with only two candles lit; and these had been placed behind the men whom he had come to meet. No names had been mentioned, on their side at least. Itachi's contact had assured him that he would be meeting 'influential men,' men with whom he might share 'common interests.'

Now three of them sat, their heads covered with cloaks, facing Itachi. No others were in the room, although Itachi felt certain that various eyes and ears were pressed closely to a variety of peepholes. He briefly considered how many of these Yutakashi scum he could kill before those watching burst in and cut him down. He decided that dying unseen in the dark would be an unworthy end.

For the hundredth time the head of the Hajimeshi Castle Guard cursed himself for trusting people who skulked about in shadows. But he needed their assistance if he was to be certain of gaining his objective. And darkness or no, he knew very well most of those who sat across from him in the dim room. Some of them he had encountered just that morning.

"Lord Itachi of Hajimeshi," said a clipped voice. "You have a proposal. State it."

Giving no sign that he had just listened to this same voice only a short while ago, Itachi responded, "The kingdom of Hajimeshi is led by an infirm and tired man. I have watched our kingdom lose its way, and am convinced that it can once more take up its pride of place among the cities of Tonogato. All it needs is firm leadership and a steady hand on the reins."

"Your hands?" inquired the older man's voice from the shadows opposite.

Pausing only briefly, Itachi replied, "What is required is a man who knows how to lead, and can turn out the deadwood that has cluttered up the Hajimeshi court for too long. It would be natural that another member of the royal family be considered, as honor and tradition dictate."

A snort of derision accompanied this comment from another of those opposite. "And what," said a similarly familiar voice, "does the city of Yutakashi stand to gain from such an…ordination?"

"A steadfast friend, an ally in whatever dangers might confront our two kingdoms. You would not want for lack of support from the Castle Guard." Itachi added as an afterthought, "I'm sure we could work out beneficial trade arrangements as well."

Silence greeted Itachi's comments, to the point where he wondered if they had understood what he said. Or, he wondered, was it that they expected more? If so, then they were fools.

Sooner or later, Itachi knew, the Yutakashi would march on Hajimeshi and attempt to bring it under their sphere. But that would result in a costly siege, and require a large army that would have to be paid. By loaning Itachi a few troops now in order to secure an ally, the money they could save would buy many fancy bolts of cloth, or precious stones. Surely, he thought, their mercenary hearts could see as much?

The older man spoke once more. "You tell us what Yutakashi might expect to gain. What do you expect from Yutakashi?"

The moment of revelation, thought Itachi; now he must commit himself. "I anticipate that some of the useless courtiers that hang about the palace might actually resist a threat to their complacent positions. In order to minimize the possibility of bloodshed, I seek the loan of a few of your troops to assist me in quickly establishing a new order. Then we can get back to business as soon as possible." Itachi thought that last was a clever bit of wording.

His comments were greeted by more silence. Do these men, he marveled, talk to each other without speaking? Or are they simply stupid?

Any such thoughts were quickly banished as another of the cloaked figures said, "And would these troops be deployed with your own men that you have established in the woods to the north and south of Hajimeshi?"

Itachi's blood ran cold. They knew! How could they have found out his troop dispositions? There must be a spy among his officers. Which one? No matter—no time to think about it now. He had to deal with the fact that the Yutakashi Reds had known about his plans, or could at least guess his intentions. "My men, of course, would bear the brunt of any potential fighting. I only seek the assistance of your soldiers to secure those areas that we have...cleared...of any potential resistance. There should be minimal risk to any of Yutakashi's troops."

"On the contrary," said the most recent speaker. "You seek a civil war, Itachi of Hajimeshi. Once Yutakashi has become involved, we are implicated in your struggle. We would have no choice but to continue to intervene, should your...preparations...prove inadequate."

Through gritted teeth Itachi replied, "My preparations are my own concern. I don't care how good your 'spies' are, they cannot know what I do about Hajimeshi defenses. I will be in control in a matter of days."

"No doubt," said the older man, asserting himself once more. "That is why we are here." He leaned forward, only his nose peeking out from beneath his hood to catch the light from the candles. "Soldiers are not a problem, Itachi of Hajimeshi. Should we be convinced of victory, as many as are needed can be supplied. But we expect more than 'trade agreements' and promises of friendship, in return for Yutakashi blood."

Shifting his seating position, Itachi asked, "What, then? Money?"

The hooded head opposite shook with a negative gesture. "You misunderstand us, Lord of Hajimeshi. If we are successful in 'improving' the condition of Hajimeshi, we must be assured of its future commitment to Yutakashi interests. We believe a Ruling Council, consisting of yourself and two members of the Yutakashi Red faction, would guarantee such a commitment."

Itachi's anger nearly consumed him. They expected to use him as a puppet! He, the brother of the Kojuro, to submit to a council of merchants! It took all his will power to keep from leaping across the room, sword in hand, to sever those cloaked tongues right out of their owner's faces. Fiercely he said, "Hajimeshi is not a vassal of Yutakashi, nor shall it ever be! I am not your lackey. I will be the next ruler of Hajimeshi, whether you are there to help or not. So you choose which it shall be."

"Then your business here is done." The robed figures opposite all stood. "Remember, brother of the Kojuro, that this city may not be safe for those of Hajimeshi. Do not expect any aid from us." A door behind them opened, and they filed out. As soon as the door was closed, a shaft of light spilled across Itachi's seated figure as another door behind him was opened.

Itachi stood and let himself be escorted out of the building, his hand gripping his tarka as if he intended to twist it apart.

∗ ∗ ∗

Out in the street the usual crowd of Yutakashi citizens bustled about, either hurrying to trade elsewhere or frequenting one of the many shops lining the road. One particularly boisterous, and popular, establishment was a serving house whose open front overflowed with small tables and stools. The passersby simply ignored the inconvenience of stepping around the loud patrons who protruded out into the roadway. Even the most obtuse observer could not fail to see that all of the serving house's customers wore Blue headbands. It would be a most unfortunate person who wandered in uninvited to a gathering spot of the Blues.

Further out from the shop front, halfway into the middle of the street, four Blues played a game of dice at a table. One, cursed with bad luck, nevertheless continued to throw one bad roll after another, swearing with each pass. Another, so far in drink as to be unconcerned whether he was winning or losing, kept bawling for more wine from the harassed serving maid. The other two Blues, facing the street, kept up with the game, but seemed to be paying it little attention.

Down the street a door opened and a darkly dressed man emerged, his face set in a hard scowl. The door slammed behind him, and with a look of disgust he marched off. His path took him past the serving house, and anyone who might have been looking could not have helped but notice the jewel-encrusted staff he continually slapped against his leg as he strode by, and the odd grey smock that he wore. From the look on his face it would have been a brave, or more likely foolhardy, vendor who attempted to make a sale to such as he.

His passage went unremarked by most of the denizens of the Blue serving house. However, the two disinterested gamers quickly tossed in their coins, leaving the Blue with bad luck to marvel at his sudden turn of fortune. One of the two who had left the game walked off in the direction of the scowling man, following him; the other went off on a path that led to the Main House of the Blues.

As the drunkard at the gaming table had recently passed out and was in no position to argue the case, his share of the purse was magically swept into the pocket of the bad luck Blue. Leaving a single coin behind on the table to pay for the wine, the suddenly well-off fellow left his companion snoring and made off to count his treasure.

For a brief time, the usual racket of the serving house continued as before. Then another Blue, one who had been sitting alone just inside the shop front, out of the sunlight, finished his wine and laid down a coin. Casually he got up and left the shop, turning down an alley a short way up the street. After a few turns he wound up on a narrow wagon path running between the high walls of two shops. With a quick movement he pulled his Blue headband off and pitched it into an empty barrel stacked along one of the shop's walls. As he rejoined another of Yutakashi's streets on the other side of the wagon path, he sent a long spit sailing into the gutter.

* * *

Interesting. This Lord of Hajimeshi fascinates me. His own brother! So much ambition, he would kill his own brother to gain what he desires...

That thing that speaks to me, I know what it wants: uncertainty and distrust, chaos, discord. Paving the way so that it can once again sweep across the land above and blot out the polluting light. This Hajimeshi nobleman, he would be a powerful tool for that purpose. Already, he is sowing the seeds of strife everywhere he goes...

I do not understand how I am able to 'see' what those like him above are doing and saying. It is frustrating. Watch, yes; that is all well and good. But watching is unsatisfying unless one can also do. Yet, I think there is more to this than that thing in my mind has let me know. If I could just reach out, and touch...

There! Yes, I touched his mind! The Hajimeshi lord stopped in the road and looked about, as if he felt something. It was me! Delicate, I must be delicate, not let him know that I am there. If I can walk inside his mind, as does that thing that speaks to me, perhaps I can move him faster in the direction of his own disposition. And thus bring closer the time that will see my own revenge...

7

Komori was singing. Truth be told, thought Mikasama, singing was perhaps a generous interpretation. However Komori felt that she was singing, and if it took her mind off of her raw and chafing behind then so much the better.

The two women had left the main Southern Road some hours before and were following a farm road. They occasionally saw peasants working in the fields, but they did not stop or talk to anyone. The threat of discovery, of being shepherded back ignominiously under guard to Hajimeshi, had led them to keep to themselves. The air grew cold as grey clouds began rolling across the sky. Mikasama shivered, and hoped that Komori had packed some warm clothes in their traveling gear.

"Hey," said Komori, interrupting her own chorus. "Mika, you remember when your Papa took you on hunting trip?"

Mikasama thought back, and remembered. She had been nine, and her father had arranged a hunt to honor visitors from Kawashi. The Hajimeshi hunts were far different than those of their forebears. The animals were stalked, but never killed or even shot at; the skill was in seeing how close one could approach the prey without being detected. It took great patience and expertise to outwit an animal in its natural habitat. The rush of exhilaration from a successful hunt, standing up within a few yards of an animal in the wild, seeing its startled expression as it bounded away into the woods, was an exciting event that could capture the imagination of a little girl.

The Kojuro's daughter had gotten wind of her father's plans, and had begged and begged to be allowed to go along. Ever indulgent, Kimeru had finally acquiesced. A great inconvenience to the whole hunting party, Mikasama had been oblivious to the concerns of the adults. She had chattered endlessly while she and her caretaker Komori were carried in a litter; everyone else had ridden on horseback. As they had neared the area of the hunt, she had been told to stay quiet, but she hadn't understood why. She had wanted to exclaim to Komori about everything she saw: the animals, the hunters creeping through the undergrowth. Finally her father had spoken sharply to her, reminding her that she was a guest on the hunt and that she must abide by its rules, otherwise she would be sent home. The day had lost some of its enchantment then.

"Yes, Nana-san, I remember it. Why?"

"You and me, we stay outside, in big tent? Got plenty cold?"

Mikasama shivered again just thinking about it. "Yes, Papa said we'd gone too far to get back before nightfall." It was not the cold, though, that she most recalled about that trip. At the end of the day, the sky had turned dark and menacing. Before their escort had been able to erect the royal tent, a peal of thunder had rumbled across the sky. Mikasama had never been outdoors in a thunderstorm, and the sharp crack of lightning, coupled with the wind-whipped rain, had frightened her more than anything before or since. She still made Komori close all the window shutters of her rooms whenever a bad storm was in the offing. "I remember that I snuggled against you in the blankets. I'd never slept outside before."

"Pahhh. 'Twasn't even really outside—inside big tent an' all. But tonight—tonight gonna really be outside. And be really cold. You warm up ol' Nana-san this time, hey?"

Mikasama smiled. "I'll keep you warm, Nana-san." Just then, her horse broke stride. He stopped, then started walking again, hesitantly. Mikasama leaned over and looked down at the side of his head, saying,

"What's wrong, boy?" Then she saw that he was favoring his left front leg. Each time he stepped, he set that leg down tenderly, then quickly picked it up again.

Komori's horse, which had been walking beside Mikasama's, continued on, causing Komori to pass ahead by a few yards. The old caretaker turned around in her saddle. "Hey! Why you slowin' down?"

"My horse; I think something's wrong with my horse." Mikasama pulled on the reins to bring him to a stop.

Komori, now even further along the road, shouted down at her own horse. "Stop, you! Your brother, he back there with Mika. Why you keep on going?"

Mikasama called out. "Nana-san! Use the reins, like I showed you!"

"Oh," said the caretaker, looking down in front of her. She pulled on the reins and got the horse to stop, then tugged him around in fits and starts until the two of them were facing Mikasama.

The Princess slid down to the ground and looked at her horse's leg. At first she didn't see anything, but then she realized that his left front shoe was missing.

"My horse has lost a shoe," she told Komori. She remembered seeing the stable hands walking horses that limped much the same way this one did now; they never rode them. "I think I'll have to walk him."

Stepping in front of the horse, she gently tugged on the reins. He didn't want to move at first, resisting her efforts. Finally he took a tentative step forward, still favoring his left front. Without her weight on his back, though, he seemed to walk easier, albeit rather slowly.

As Mikasama neared Komori the old woman said, "You gonna walk on foot? Get awful tired, Mika."

"I know, I know. But it's either that or stay here and wait for him to get better. And something tells me that might take a while." They set off again down the road, much slower, and sans singing.

As the day drew to a close, the sun peeked out weakly below the level of the clouds. It had no effect on the temperature, which had grown colder as the hours passed. Komori broke out heavy cloaks from their travel packs.

They had left the farm road some miles before, where it had turned toward a large village protected by a stockade. The sight of a village needing the protection of a wall did not fill either of them with pleasant thoughts regarding the area through which they traveled. But trying to gain entrance to the village, during the dinner hour when all the inhabitants would already be inside and the gates barred tight, would invite a host of questions that Mikasama would prefer not to answer.

So they had moved off onto an even smaller side road, more of a footpath, which led into a stand of trees. Komori had tried to piece together where they were in relation to the Northern Road but was unsure if they had already passed by where Yutakashi would be or not. What was certain was that somehow they had to connect with the Northern Road or they would never find the pilgrim group at all.

Mikasama had hoped that the footpath might take them around the village and they could rejoin the farm road, which at least was going in the general direction they needed to travel. But as the path went on deeper into the trees, and the light faded even more, she began to lose her sense of direction. While it seemed that the path turned, she couldn't be sure if she was really going the right way or not.

Her legs were tired, her feet were sore, and she desperately wanted a bath. Discomfort went hand in hand in making her irritable and moody. Komori, for her part, elected to keep her complaints to herself. She had been around Mikasama since the Princess had been a small child, and well understood her charge's moods.

The pair walked on in silence. Just as Mikasama was beginning to wonder how they were going to find someplace safe to sleep for the coming night, both women were startled by a small child running onto the path directly in front of them.

She was about six or seven years old, and the sight of the two women and the horses evidently shocked her as much as it did Mikasama and Komori. She let out a shriek and took off back down the path at a run.

Mikasama turned to Komori. "Well, she can't be from that village, to be this far in the woods when it'll be dark soon. Unless she's some sort of runaway." Like us, she thought to herself ruefully.

"Or maybe some forest spirit," said Komori with a shiver. She clutched her cloak around her more tightly. "Mika, maybe best go back to village. No tellin' what might be in these woods."

"Nana-san, I really don't think there are ghosts here in—" Her words were interrupted by the sound of breaking branches and disturbed undergrowth from the forest that surrounded them. Both women looked around in alarm, and Mikasama wished that Komori had thought to pack some sort of weapon. Although, she wondered, what good would a knife be against spirits?

But they were not spirits. They were horsemen, three of them, who burst out of the trees with swords in hand. Before Mikasama could react, the trio rode right up to the two women. One of them directed his blade straight toward the Princess, shouting, "What business do you have here?"

Mikasama froze. She had never actually been close to any danger in her life, and now here was a man pointing a sword at her throat. I am a princess, she thought, the daughter of the Kojuro of Hajimeshi; and now I'm going to die out on a dirt path in an unknown wood far from home...

She had been taught some rudiments of hand-to-hand fighting by some of her father's Guards, mostly from their indulgence and, she suspected, for their amusement. None of that helped her now, though, even had she been able to get her tired limbs to respond. All she could do was stare at the sharp tip of the sword pointing at her, her eyes transfixed by its glint in the all but extinguished sunlight.

"Hey, what you goin' around scarin' an old woman for?" Komori's voice broke the silence, and all three men turned their attention to her. "Put away those stupid swords. You got nothin' better to do than ambush women goin' about, mindin' their own business?" The sound interrupted Mikasama's trance, and she was able to focus beyond the end of the sword and look at the man who wielded it.

A creased, care-worn face was framed by graying temples and sagging, stubble-covered cheeks. The man's eyes, Mikasama noted, were bloodshot, yet also had a keen look about them. She glanced quickly at the other two riders and saw that they were younger, probably sons judging from their resemblance to each other and to the older man. All of them wore well-used clothes, and one, the youngest, rode a horse that was little more than a large pony.

The two younger ones looked to the older man for guidance. He in turn looked from Komori to Mikasama and back to the caretaker again, then slowly slid his sword back into its scabbard. The boys did the same.

"If you're out here alone," said the man gruffly, "then both of you are fools. These parts are full of thieves and brigands who would as soon slit your throat as steal your purse." He looked both of the women over carefully. "Where are you going? Come from the village?"

Mikasama, having recovered, decided it was time to assert herself. "We are travelers. We've been seeking a way to get to the Northern Road, and...took a wrong turn. Can you tell us how to get there?"

The three newcomers exchanged looks with one another. The older of the two boys said, "Best if you go back to the village. Take their road."

"We'd rather not," replied Mikasama. "Besides, they've already closed their gates for the night."

The young man cocked his head sideways. "They would let in two women." His unruly mop of hair tangled in front of his eyes, which even in the twilight glinted with a hint of mischief. He grinned slyly. "Unless you got something to hide..."

Mikasama bristled, her face turning red. She was unused to being questioned like this, by people who were clearly little better than peasants. Through clenched teeth she said, "Our business is our own. Kindly give us directions, or let us pass." She found time to be surprised at herself. One moment she was feeling panic and fear, the next she was making demands of three armed men. Somehow, Komori had sensed that the men were not themselves 'thieves and brigands.' She had been right; and now the two women just needed to find a way out of this unsought encounter.

The father appeared to consider what Mikasama had said. Instead of answering her request, though, he asked, "What's wrong with your horse?"

Mikasama looked down instinctively to her horse's leg. She decided that the man probably knew enough about horses that it would do no good to pretend that she simply enjoyed being on foot. "He's thrown a shoe. He's having a hard time walking."

The elder man pursed his lips. "You won't make it anywhere near the Northern Road with a horse in that shape. Best let us take a look." He moved his horse forward, closer toward her.

Mikasama stood her ground. "And you are?"

He pulled up, squinting down at her. After considering her for a moment, he appeared to come to a decision. "Name's Horoda." Gesturing toward the other two, he said, "My boys, Okami and Okazu." The two nodded their heads in greeting. Mikasama noted that the elder boy, Okami, was still grinning at her, as if enjoying some sort of private joke.

"I am...Mika," she said, thinking quickly. "And this is my mother, Komochi," indicating her caretaker. Komori just sniffed in the direction of the men.

"Well, then, Mika," said Horoda, "your horse needs to be looked at." He dismounted and walked up to the princess. Quietly he added, "I know a thing or two about horses. Mayhaps be best you let me take a look." She held his gaze for a moment, then stepped aside without further comment.

Horoda stepped past the horse's head and expertly lifted the animal's leg to examine the base of the hoof. He prodded with his fingers, at one point causing the horse to flinch. Then he gently let the leg down once more. "Horse's got a stone bruise," he said. "Going to be laid up for a good week, maybe two. You try to keep him on the road, he'll go bad lame for sure."

Mikasama visibly sagged at this news. Horoda walked back over to his own horse and re-mounted. "This wood's no place for two women alone. We're camped just off the path, about a hundred paces on. Best you stay there tonight. Figure out what you want to do in the morning."

The Princess looked over at Komori, who for once gave no sign of what she was thinking. Well, thought Mikasama, staying out here in the open certainly does not have much appeal. So far, other than when they thought she and Komori might be the 'thieves and brigands,' the men had not threatened them. The little girl must be from their camp, so more than likely there were other women around. "All right," she said. "We'll follow you."

*   *   *

After Toshi-hito had told Kanyo about the Kotaishi quest, Tanoshi called them in for the meal and the Deshi Master had to repeat everything again for her. It was a small price to pay, for the meal managed to be both sumptuous and simple at the same time. Large platters of food were set out before both Toshi-hito and Shiko, while Tanoshi set similar but smaller plates before herself and Kanyo. The four of them squeezed around a low eating table, the knees of their crossed legs all bumping one another in the tight confines of the dining space. A group of children watched silently from the doorway.

Shiko began eating some of the tochuya root that Tanoshi had boiled while he listened to Toshi-hito repeat the story of their journey. Neither Kanyo nor Tanoshi touched the food in front of them, which Shiko ascribed to politeness as they listened to Toshi-hito. Once the Deshi Master had finished talking, he picked up the smallest of the butano spuds on his plate and started to eat. However, while Shiko enjoyed his tochuya, still neither of his hosts made any move to eat anything from their plates. Once Toshi-hito finished his butano spud, he too ceased eating. He bowed his head to Kanyo and Tanoshi. "An excellent meal, Tanoshi. As always!"

She replied, "Please, Toshi, eat some more!" accompanied by vigorous nods from Kanyo. Toshi-hito shook his head. "No, really, I am quite content. What I have had is more than enough." And then Shiko realized why Kanyo and Tanoshi were not eating.

Finishing his own tochuya root, the apprentice bowed his head to his hosts. "Thank you for preparing such a wonderful meal." Then he turned to the children crouching in the doorway. "I am much too full to do justice to all of this excellent food. Would you care to share some with me?"

At a rush the children piled through the doorway and around Shiko, who dispensed food to eager little hands. Toshi-hito likewise handed out the remainder of his meal to the children, who then scampered off back to the main room.

Kanyo and Tanoshi both silently bowed their heads to Toshi-hito and Shiko. The two Deshi returned the bow equally. Tanoshi unobtrusively took away the two remaining plates; undoubtedly, thought Shiko, to be saved for the remaining children. He guessed that the old couple had probably offered all of the food they had to their two guests, while they themselves did without so that the children could eat.

"Well," said Kanyo, in the awkwardness that followed, "let's go back out front where we can stretch our legs a bit."

Ensconced in the slightly larger front room, Kanyo and Tanoshi plied Shiko with questions, wanting to know everything about him. The usual cacophony of sound from the other children was muted as they ate the remains of the meal.

Nusumi had slipped quietly back into the room, and was sitting in a corner watching. She had noted her foster parent's intense interest in the younger of the two Deshi, and she listened carefully to what everybody said. Her eyes and ears were sharp; those who got by on the strength of their wits alone could rarely afford to be otherwise.

As she watched Tanoshi's face, staring at the one called Shiko, Nusumi wondered what it was about this Deshi that they found so interesting. He seems fairly ordinary to me, she thought. Kind of nice looking, but ordinary. He doesn't look much older than I am. He did offer his food to the other brats; that was a nice thing to do.

"And your parents, Shiko? Did they send you to the Deshi?" Tanoshi had asked the question, and Nusumi could tell from the set of her face, and from the way Kanyo leaned forward slightly, that this was more than a casual question. She looked over at Shiko but detected no change in his demeanor.

"I don't know," he said. "I was only two or three years old when the Deshi took me in, so I never knew my parents. The Deshi have raised me. I assume that those who sired me must have desired that I be Deshi, or they would have left me someplace else."

Kanyo nodded. "Our children here come to us at all different ages. Some have known one or both of their parents; others came from aunts or uncles who could not afford to keep them. Tanoshi and I, we've never been able to have any of our own but, well, we both love children so much..." He waved his hand about the room to indicate the multitude of scruffy little heads. He paused, then pulled a small stick from out of a pocket and began picking at his fingernails with it. "Do you ever wonder, young Shiko, about your parents?"

"Of course," said Shiko, "but there is no way for me to find them. The Deshi found me on the threshold of their front gate, so no one knows who my parents were. Since they chose to leave me with the Deshi rather than just abandon me to nature, I assume they left me because they were forced to rather than by choice. At least, that is what I tell myself."

To Nusumi's observant eye, it seemed that both Kanyo and Tanoshi relaxed slightly. Tanoshi said, "I'm sure you're right, Shiko." As the conversation turned to other matters, Nusumi pondered what it all meant. This young Deshi meant something to her foster parents, but she didn't know what it was. They had never mentioned having anyone like him in their care, and besides he was from Hajimeshi. She knew for a fact that Kanyo and Tanoshi had never been outside the walls of Yutakashi. It didn't make a lot of sense. And she hated mysteries! While she was quick with her hands, which kept her from going hungry, she was also patient and methodical when she had to be. Sometimes the best 'catches' came from thinking carefully before acting. As a result she had learned to solve puzzles and figure things out that left others scratching their heads. It was what had kept her out of the clutches of the Yutakashi authorities so far. There was little sympathy in the courts for sloppy thieves.

"Kanyo, Tanoshi;" said Toshi-hito, "you have been most excellent hosts. But Shiko and I must be going. The Grand Council has requested that we leave by tomorrow, and I gather that after dark the streets may be…awkward…for those from Hajimeshi."

"Oh, those old windbags!" said Tanoshi. "Always scaring up trouble between Reds and Blues! Why don't you just stay here with us? Got plenty of room!" The area she swept with her arm barely contained all of the souls that were in it as they sat upright, let alone had they been prone on the floor.

Toshi-hito smiled. "Thank you, but we should rejoin our comrades." Turning to Shiko, he said, "I need to visit the Deshi priory here in Yutakashi, but before we leave we also need some meditation candles and more scroll paper from the Market. Do you think you can find your way through there well enough to get them?"

Shiko paused before answering, and into the conversational gap a different voice piped up.

"I'll take him," said Nusumi. All eyes turned to her, and inwardly she cursed herself for being so reckless. That was stupid, she thought. Why did I go and open my mouth like that?

She decided to put a cavalier attitude on it. "I'm going that way anyway; might as well be there to show him which of the vendors are the crooks to steer clear of."

"Thank you, Nusumi," said Kanyo warmly. The sincerity in his voice made Nusumi uncomfortable. What is it about this Deshi, she wondered, that's got everybody all riled up? Well, whatever it is, I'm going to find out.

She stood abruptly. "We should get going. You ready?" she said, turning to Shiko.

Shiko looked to Toshi-hito, who nodded, and the apprentice rose to face his hosts. "Thank you for your kindness, and for allowing me to share your home." He bowed to both Kanyo and Tanoshi. "I would be honored, should you ever visit Hajimeshi, to welcome you to the priory."

The old couple stood and bowed back to Shiko. Kanyo said, "The honor is ours, young Shiko, to serve you in our house. Hajimeshi may be a bit far for these old bones, but rest assured that were we a few years younger nothing would prevent us from coming to see your priory."

Nusumi, standing uncomfortably during this exchange, said, "OK, we're off. Be back later, Papa."

She strode between the old couple and the two Deshi and straight out the front door. Shiko, with a smile and a bit of a shrug at the others, turned and followed her.

Toshi-hito rose and looked out the door after them, joined shortly by Kanyo and Tanoshi. Watching the youngsters walk down the street, the older man said, "Lad's tall for his age."

Tanoshi said, "But too thin! Toshi, don't you ever feed him? He needs his strength!"

Toshi-hito did not reply for a moment, watching as Shiko, following Nusumi, turned the corner and was then lost to view. "He will be strong enough, my friends. Strong enough."

* * *

Shiko found the Market much less intimidating the second time through, although he was still glad to have the assistance of a guide. When Toshi-hito had asked him to go to the Market, he had been torn between admitting that he had been totally lost from the time they had left the Street of Inns, and not wanting to disappoint his Master. So he had been very grateful for the offer of assistance from Nusumi.

Not that she provided much help, he realized, as he struggled to keep up with her. Mostly she darted in and around the stalls so fast that he had a difficult time keeping her in sight. She didn't look to see if he was following or not.

The sounds and smells were still overwhelming, but at least Shiko could set them aside in his mind now and focus more on the surroundings. At first there had seemed to be little design to the Market's layout; everything appeared a chaotic jumble of open-air stalls and carts. Then Shiko started to see a pattern, albeit a fluid one.

The sellers of similar commodities were grouped together, each cluster of vendors separated by wide pathways that might hold four or five people abreast. Shiko had been unable to discern the pathways earlier, as they were full of people from edge to edge. Within each group, the seller's stalls crowded together more haphazardly, but always leaving a narrow path where buyers could at least squeeze past one another. The stalls ranged from elaborate wooden constructions with roofs and folding side panels, to produce spread out on a blanket on the ground.

Nusumi was leading Shiko through an area of spice sellers. One busy stall featured small, tightly bound bags of mixed herbs and spices tossed to buyers from behind a makeshift counter, with coins sailing back in return, all accompanied by ribald singing from the men behind the counter. Nusumi finally slowed her pace as they approached the small section of the Market devoted to non-foodstuffs. As he caught up to her, Shiko noted how Nusumi never stopped looking around, continually scanning the whole area. He got the sense that while she looked at the stalls nearby, she was also gazing beyond them, shutting out those things that distracted the eye and ear and taking in the neighboring area as well.

"What kind of candles do you want?" she asked. Even while talking to him, she was turning her head in all directions. Shiko described the type of candles used for Deshi meditation, and after pondering for a moment Nusumi made off toward one particular stall. Pointing to a rack of candles on display she said, "Something like that?"

The sound of her voice caused the proprietor, an old man with a beard, to turn away from the argument he was having with the vendor behind him. Seeing Shiko, his eyes lit up at the prospect of an easy sale. Then his gaze fell upon Nusumi, and his face was transformed by a dark expression. "What do you want, gutter urchin?"

Taken aback by the man's rudeness, Shiko was not sure of what to say. Nusumi, however, was not intimidated. "We came to buy candles. Are you selling or talking? If talking, your words are worthless and we can buy elsewhere." She tugged on Shiko's sleeve, turning him to go.

"Just a minute, just a minute," said the old man, unwilling to lose a sale but equally wary, it seemed, of dealing with them. Turning to Shiko, he said, "You have money?" Shiko nodded and raised his purse. He started to open it but Nusumi covered his hands with one of hers to forestall him.

"Price? For these?" she said, indicating the candles on the rack. The proprietor set hand to beard, stroking it. "Well, this kind of taper is hard to come by..." as he described in some detail the awful struggle it was to remain re-supplied with what to Shiko appeared to be fairly ordinary candles.

Nusumi rolled her eyes in exasperation, and interrupted the man's monologue. "Do they have a price or don't they? Or do you keep them there for your own after-hours amusement?"

Shocked at Nusumi's crudity, Shiko watched as the old man's face reddened. He practically spat out an amount, to which Nusumi laughed, offering a quarter of the figure. The old man waved his arms in the air as if he were being robbed, shouting to all within earshot that a simple gutter urchin was trying to cheat him of his life savings. Shiko, alarmed, looked around, but no one was paying them the slightest attention. In fact, similar tableaus were occurring at several other stalls. This was apparently the standard method of barter in Yutakashi.

Finally Nusumi and the old man grudgingly agreed on a price, a little over half of what the man had originally proposed. He held out his hand to Shiko, who filled it with the agreed amount of coins. As soon as the coins were pocketed the old man whipped down a set of candles. Then, Nusumi and Shiko forgotten, the man resumed his argument with the vendor behind him.

Nusumi turned away. "OK, let's find your scroll paper." She set off back onto the main pathway. Shaking his head, Shiko followed her once more.

She didn't dart ahead this time but kept pace with him as they cut across a corner of the tochuya root seller's area. She gave him an odd look. "Where'd you learn to buy? Open your purse like that and everything you ask for will cost whatever coins you have."

"I've never been anyplace exactly like this," replied Shiko. "We have a market in Hajimeshi, where the farmers sell produce, but I believe they just tell one how much it costs and people pay that amount."

"That's crazy!" exclaimed Nusumi. "Your farmers must be rich. They could charge whatever price they want!"

"No, I don't think so. I think they just charge what's a fair price, enough to keep their crops going. I've never heard of anyone who buys produce from them complaining about the price."

"What, don't you buy your own food? Or does one of the other Deshi do that for you?"

"No, we grow our food at the Deshi priory."

Nusumi stopped dead in her tracks. She looked at Shiko with an expression that was at once incredulous and envious. "You grow food? Yourselves?" At his nod, she continued. "You can eat whenever you want? Just go out to the fields and get food to eat?"

He laughed. "Well, not exactly like that, no. We have regular meal times, and the crops are harvested for use in the kitchens. We always make sure there is enough for each of the day's meals."

"Regular meal times." She shook her head in wonderment. "In Yutakashi, only the rich can own farmland. Most of what's sold here," she said, indicating the vast Market area with a wave, "ends up on the tables of the rich people, and the Reds and Blues. The rest of us, we get what's left. And not exactly 'regularly' either. There's more people than work, and the rich dole out the jobs to their friends, so it's hard for people from my side of the Market to—" All of a sudden she stopped, her eyes focused intently on something that was several stalls away. Quickly she looked around in all directions, causing Shiko to do the same. Seeing nothing other than the same bustle of buying and selling, he looked back at her once more.

Nusumi's gaze had returned to whatever had caught her attention in the first place. Without looking at him, she said quietly, "Look, wait here, okay? I'll be right back." Then she turned on her heel and walked in the opposite direction from where she had been looking.

Confused, Shiko watched her go and then lost sight of her as she ducked in between two stalls selling grain. With a sigh, he tucked the candles into the pouch tied about his waist and edged himself to the side of the path, trying to get out of the way of the crowd.

As he waited for her to return he took in some of the scenes of Market life. A drover was unloading cases of kosha from a horse-drawn cart into a stall, while next door to him two women argued over something that looked like a large tojonaka plant. Nearby a cat sniffed about the rear of one stall until it turned to look at Shiko.

The animal stopped moving and stared at him, and Shiko was struck by the incongruous image. Amid hundreds of moving bodies, only he and the cat stood stock still, looking at one another. I wonder, mused Shiko, what it's thinking...

Suddenly the cat twitched its head sideways. A broom-wielding matron from a nearby stall had spied the feline, and was advancing on the little intruder. Quickly the cat darted off, hiding among other stalls in the depths of the Market.

So absorbed was Shiko in taking in the sights around him that he was startled when Nusumi suddenly re-appeared beside him, saying, "Right, now let's go get your paper."

She had walked up, not from the direction in which she had gone just moments before, but from where she had earlier been staring so intently. He was just opening his mouth to ask her about it when he heard a shout. Nusumi grabbed his arm. "Time to go. Come on!" and she began tugging insistently at him.

Two men were pushing their way through the crowd, pointing toward Nusumi and Shiko. One of the men shouted again. "There she is!" Faces turned to look, first at the man shouting and then at what he pointed to. "Thief! Thief!" the man yelled. "She stole pajana fruit from my cart!"

The crowd parted for the two men, people distancing themselves from Nusumi and Shiko as if they had the plague. Nusumi yelled at Shiko, "Come on! We've gotta get out of here, fast!" Then she started running.

In an instant it all became clear to Shiko. Nusumi was a thief who stole food from the Market! That was what Tanoshi had meant when she said Nusumi kept the other children from going hungry. When he had first seen Nusumi, back at Kanyo and Tanoshi's, she had hidden something away, embarrassed. The candle seller's hostility toward her; she must have a well-known reputation already in the Market. The pieces all came together.

All of these things raced through Shiko's mind without full realization. What he did realize was that he had to make a decision, and quickly. It was the sort of decision that one could agonize over for days, but he didn't have days; he had about one heartbeat. The two men were nearly clear of the last area of stalls that bordered the rapidly emptying pathway.

From the reactions of those nearby, it was clear that thievery was a heinous crime among the Yutakashi. The two men would want justice, to which they were probably entitled if Nusumi was stealing their rightful property. Shiko was a foreigner, and should respect the laws of those lands he visited. Having a Hajimeshi involved in a crime here would cause all sorts of problems, and probably delay the Hikari pilgrimage.

On the other hand, he knew why Nusumi stole food. It was not for herself; it was to feed the other children who were going hungry. Shiko had seen the kind of people that Kanyo and Tanoshi were; in a city of unbridled greed and commerce, they gave what they had to those who needed it more. What they had was a little food, and a lot of love.

His one heartbeat was up; the men were on the path and running toward him. Without another thought Shiko turned away from them and sprinted after Nusumi.

8

The deep sound of the bell echoed up and down the small street in response to Toshi-hito's pull of the bell cord. He stood outside the door of the priory and waited patiently.

The Deshi priory in Yutakashi was well away from the commercial activities of the city, situated in an area of low rents and even lower prospects. Not surprisingly the activities of the contemplative Deshi were held in poor esteem by most of the citizens of the busy mercantile city, who found sitting around staring at candles to be a poor use of their time.

More specifically the other main Deshi preoccupation, that of disseminating knowledge, was viewed with great suspicion both by the city government and by private business interests. The Grand Council worried about subversive ideas, particularly those that might be introduced by foreigners. From a commercial standpoint information was a commodity to be bought and sold like any other. An organization that actually gave away knowledge was something to be viewed with great alarm; hence the low profile of the Deshi priory in Yutakashi.

Beyond locating them physically on the fringes of the city, the Grand Council tightly regulated the way the Deshi distributed information. Anything provided to a citizen of Yutakashi had to be recorded and filed with the Council where it was carefully reviewed for appropriateness; the identity of the requester was also recorded. As a result the Deshi tended to have few callers, and most of these came to satisfy their spiritual need for quiet contemplation. The Council, considering such to be a frivolous waste of time, didn't bother recording the names of those who came only to meditate.

Farming was also forbidden to the Deshi, as it was to all private citizens in the city. The farming conglomerates controlled all of the land beyond the city walls. The Yutakashi Deshi thus had to purchase all of their food from the Market, for which purpose the main priory in Hajimeshi sent a monthly stipend by courier. All in all it made a posting to Yutakashi a dreary assignment for most of the Deshi.

All of this Toshi-hito reviewed in his mind as he waited for the door to be opened. That was in itself, he reflected, another measure of the difference between Yutakashi and Hajimeshi: back home the gate to the priory was never closed. A seeker of knowledge was welcome at all hours, and a librarian was on duty even through the small hours of the morning. He remembered all too well his own hours of such duty when he had been an apprentice. Still, that the Deshi had a presence at all in a place such as Yutakashi was no small accomplishment.

The old wooden door swung open to reveal a small courtyard, obscured by a rotund little man with the merest fringe of hair circling his pate. From the crumbs dotting his tunic it was clear that he had just come from a meal, although the lunch hour was some time past. At the sight of Toshi-hito his eyes lit up.

"Toshi-hito! This is a surprise!"

"Not an unpleasant one, I hope, Kanrin?" replied Toshi-hito.

"Oh, heavens no," said Kanrin. "No, no, no, quite the contrary, it's good to see you again!" Realizing he was keeping Toshi-hito standing out in the street, he stepped aside. "Where are my manners? Please, come inside, come inside!"

At Toshi-hito's entrance, Kanrin swung the door closed and turned once more to take in his visitor from head to toe. "Well! I must say it is nice to see another Deshi face! Other than the three Deshi here, I only see a handful of Yutakashi faces at our door in any given month, and those are generally fairly pitiful ones, I'm afraid!" Looking down at

Toshi-hito's attire, he noted the grey smock. His voice dropped in volume. "But what's this? You're on a pilgrimage?"

"I am on a quest for the Kojuro, who is too ill to journey himself. We walk beneath a Hikari, which is with the rest of our party back at the inn. We leave in the morning."

"Well, then, I won't bore you with idle gossip!" In a slightly more formal tone, and accompanied by a bow, Kanrin said, "You are most welcome to our priory, Pilgrim. Our house is yours, and whatever we may provide to assist you in your quest, you need only ask." Toshi-hito returned the bow.

"Well!" Kanrin went on. "Come, come, come, let's go inside and have some kosha," as he ushered Toshi-hito toward the priory house across the courtyard. Over his shoulder he said, "You don't mind just a *little* gossip, do you? I so rarely get to talk with anyone new!"

*   *   *

Shiko's breath came in short quick gasps as he tried to keep up with Nusumi. She had the advantage of knowing where she was going, or at least having a greater familiarity with the terrain. All he could do was try to keep her in sight, heedless of where that was taking him. The two men were only a short way behind him, still intent on running to ground what to them must surely have appeared to be two thieves rather than one.

Nusumi ran like a cyclone through the market, scattering everything in her path as she leaped over baskets and darted between carts. Her arrival was so unexpected that most of the buyers and sellers had no time to react before she was gone, a trail of overturned goods in her wake. By the time Shiko passed through, however, the onlookers had recovered enough to shout imprecations at him, and in some cases hurl squashed produce at his retreating form.

It was clear that he was losing the battle. He kept losing track of Nusumi, only figuring out the right direction from the flustered reactions of those whom she had swept past. The men behind were getting closer; in another few paces they would be on him.

Just then a cat darted out from between two stalls, directly into the path of the pursuing men. Shiko looked behind at that instant and saw the brief flash of fur, which looked very much like the cat he had observed earlier being shooed away with a broomstick. The first man had to check up suddenly to avoid tripping over the darting feline form, causing his partner to crash headlong into him. Both men tumbled to the ground.

It was just the break Shiko needed. He turned down a side alley, into which he had seen Nusumi run. But it ended in a dead end, crates piled along the walls on all sides. Shiko stopped in his tracks. Where had she gone? As he looked around desperately, he heard the loud cawing of a crow. It was perched on top of the wall at the end of the cul-de-sac.

Shiko's danger-heightened senses noted that the crates piled against the end wall were bobbing slightly. Nusumi must have climbed up them, he decided, and over the wall. Quickly he ran to the crates and clambered up. He could hear the shouts of the men as they rounded the corner behind him. As he reached the top of the wall, he kicked with his foot to knock the crates down. The top one splintered into pieces as it hit the pavement, the other boxes falling in a heap.

Shiko dropped off the other side of the wall and found himself in a walled storage yard, with buildings forming the other three sides. There was no sign of Nusumi. A locked gate blocked a passageway leading through the building at the front, through which Shiko could see the street beyond.

Looking about, Shiko saw that there were more crates stacked against the walls of the buildings. He started toward them, figuring that Nusumi must have climbed up to the roofs on them, when somewhere in his mind a voice seemed to say, *No.*

He stopped, unsure of where the feeling came from. He looked again at the crates, and felt again, although he couldn't say why, that Nusumi had not gone that way. Frantically he looked for any other outlet. Then he spied a small opening, no more than a shoulder's-width across, along the base of the building to his right. It must lead to some sort of basement, thought Shiko. Would she have gone down there?

He could hear the men stacking crates up on the other side of the wall; he knew if he didn't do something quickly, he would be trapped here. He ran over and knelt down in front of the small opening. Inside it was completely dark. If Nusumi had gone in there, he thought, she must have known where to go. Who knows where I might end up?

His decision was made for him as he heard one of his pursuers encouraging the other as he climbed up the crates. The crow remained perched nearby, flapping its wings insistently. Shiko looked again into the darkness in front of him, then plunged headlong into it.

He didn't fall into a basement. In fact, he was still on the same ground level. It was apparently a crawl space of some sort underneath the building. He crawled forward a few feet, straining his eyes to see in the blackness. He thought he saw, off to the left, something that might have been light. He inched his way over in that direction, wiping away the cobwebs that flitted about his face. It was light, he realized; perhaps another opening?

He crawled energetically toward it, hoping that he would not become lost under the building and be trapped. He wondered what Toshi-hito would say. What would he think had happened to his apprentice?

His musings, and his exertions at moving forward, caused him to lose sight of the opening. Panicking, he moved faster. The dry dirt oozed between his fingers, and the musty smell of a place forever dark filled his nostrils.

Suddenly his forehead crashed into something solid. As he gasped in shock, his arms gave out and he collapsed down onto the dirt. Choking on the dust, he tried to mentally grab hold of the searing pain that swept through him, willing himself not to pass out. If he did, and he lost his way while alone in this dark warren...

Through the throbbing ache he looked up and saw, dimly, that he was beneath a large beam holding up the floor of the building above. He hadn't seen it in the dark as he had advanced, and had run headlong into it. His new vantage, though, lower to the ground, also allowed him to see something else: the light coming from the far opening. The beam had obscured his view of it as he had been crawling forward. More carefully now, he scrambled toward the tiny patch of brightness.

It was a similar opening to the one through which he had entered. Cautiously he stuck his head out. The bright sunlight made him squint. The only thing he could see clearly was the knife blade pointed directly at his nose.

* * *

"...And the poor woman was just beside herself; I mean really, can you blame her? With a husband like that?" Kanrin interrupted himself long enough to partake of more kosha, offering the small pot to Toshi-hito first. The visiting Deshi politely declined, and Kanrin poured himself another cup. "Well! Enough of my prattle. I'm sure you've heard more than enough about the comings and goings of Yutakashi folks. Tell me all about your pilgrimage! Where are you going, and what are you looking for?"

A metaphor for life if ever there was one, thought Toshi-hito. Those two questions drive us all before them, as the farmer forever goads on his plow-bound oxen. But Kanrin, unaware of any deeper implications to his inquiry, merely looked at his guest and waited expectantly.

The two of them sat in the priory's diminutive dining hall, which in a pinch could have seated the few resident Deshi but little more. One side of the hall opened onto a rock garden ("The only thing they'll let us grow!" Kanrin had joked). The long rectangular space of the garden containing a few strategically placed rocks brought from the Koyamaya mountains, far to the east; dark stone, with thin veins of pearlescent material running through it. The carefully graded sand ran in parallel rows down the length of the garden, except where it artfully flowed around the rocks. The garden was surrounded on three sides by a walkway, with the dining hall set on one of the short sides. The remaining sides containing the rooms where the Deshi studied and meditated. Each of the rooms had sliding doors opening onto the central garden.

Toshi-hito described the nature of their Hikari quest, including the prophecies of the Shizen, the coming Darkness that would cover the land, the need to unite behind a Kotaishi, and their pilgrimage to seek him out. When he finished, his host sat back.

"Well," Kanrin said breathlessly, "I don't suspect you'll have much luck finding him in Yutakashi! People here are much too busy, busy, busy to be bothered with what goes on in the rest of world." He picked up two of the sweet chona cookies that he had brought in for his guest. "Of course, most of them can't see beyond their own noses. This vast trading network of theirs is just that—all interconnected and interdependent. Take away one leg, and the stool upon which the giant sits will collapse. And what a prat fall that would be!" He smacked his lips as he popped the cookies into his mouth. With mouth full he continued, "They need someone like a Kotaishi to show them how their commercial interests really are tied to the well being of their environment, and those with whom they trade."

Toshi-hito was reminded by Kanrin's comments that the man was certainly no fool. He might like to indulge in passing along scandalous rumors, but he was both perceptive and observant. The Kotaishi, the Deshi Master thought, will need such assistance to win over the jaded self-interests of the Yutakashi.

Kanrin began to ask about the pilgrimage's next destination when he stopped in mid-sentence. "My word!" he exclaimed softly.

Looking down to the far end of the garden in the direction of Kanrin's gaze, Toshi-hito saw that one of the sliding doors to another room had been opened, and one of the Yutakashi Deshi was stepping out onto the wooden walkway. However, it was more likely the person behind the Deshi that had attracted Kanrin's notice, as indeed it had Toshi-hito's. For following the Deshi was one of the Hajimeshi Castle Guards, his grey smock showing him to be one of the Hikari pilgrims. Over his shoulder he sported a bow.

Neither man noticed Kanrin or Toshi-hito sitting inside the dining hall at the other end of the garden. They walked directly to the front of the compound and exited through the gate, out into the Yutakashi streets.

"My word!" repeated Kanrin. "It looks like Yosaburo has had one of your Guards here all along, before you even came! How odd...I'm usually the one to answer the bell. I wonder why he didn't tell me? He knows how much I like to talk to visitors."

Toshi-hito, too, wondered about the Guard. There were two archers in their group; this one, he remembered, was named Hisoka. Curious, thought Toshi-hito, that such a man should come to a Deshi priory; not many of the Castle Guard took any interest in Deshi learning. This one in particular, he recalled, had seemed most sour and sullen throughout the journey. Although he wasn't sure why, he found himself vaguely uneasy about such an incongruous meeting. However, he decided it would be best not to involve the gossipy Kanrin with his concerns. To his host he said, "Perhaps he is just a troubled soul, in search of some inner peace."

"Well," responded a frowning Kanrin, "you're probably right. Probably Yosaburo was simply helping him meditate." He nodded his head, the little curly fringes of hair bobbing this way and that. "Isn't that the way of things? Just when you think you'll die from sheer boredom, everything starts happening at once! Another cookie?"

* * *

Shiko tried to get his eyes to focus beyond the tip of the blade in front of him, but the knife quickly disappeared. Then he heard Nusumi's familiar voice as her hands grabbed hold of him. "Quick!" she said. "Get out here!"

She helped pull him through the hole, and as he lay gasping for air on the ground he watched as she slid a plank across the opening. She then secured it with another board so that it could only be opened from their side. The crawl space would now be a dark and exit-less cavern.

Shiko saw that they were in another storage yard, in a gap formed between the wall of the building and a broken-down wagon. The wheels on the far side of the wagon were missing, with that side lying on the ground, making the space they occupied a diminutive shelter beneath the wagon's bed. Weeds grew up all around the wagon, as well as among other broken equipment left out in the yard; somebody had apparently left everything outside to rust.

Although she had arrived earlier than Shiko, Nusumi was herself still somewhat out of breath after her wild run. "Sorry about the knife," she said. "I wasn't sure it was you."

Still trying to recover, Shiko breathlessly said, "How did—" He stopped, overtaken by a coughing fit as a result of inhaling the dirt and dust from under the building. The sudden movement also made his head spin. He fought to keep himself upright, steadying himself with both hands against the ground. Clearing his throat, he tried again. "How did you find this place?"

"This is one of my bolt holes," she said. "I scout out places where I can run, if I ever need too. Today, I needed too." She motioned to Shiko to follow her, and she crawled in further under the wagon's bed, away from any chance observation. As he situated himself in the small space she said, "You look like a mess."

He looked down at himself. His tunic sleeve was torn where it had caught on something as he had run. He could feel pain in his arm there too, so more than just his tunic had apparently been snagged. There were vegetable and fruit stains on him where angry sellers had found their mark; he was covered with dirt from scrabbling through the crawl space; and an angry red knot was forming on his forehead from where he had located the building's structural support. Yet all he could think to say was, "I'm glad I packed plenty of clothes."

Nusumi seemed to find this terribly funny, and started giggling. Shiko, too, now that the immediate danger was past, began laughing with released tension. Nusumi held up a finger to shush him, but the effect was negated by her own continued chortling. Soon both of them were holding their sides and laughing out loud.

Shiko, at least, finally had to stop, as laughing caused the pain in his head to worsen. Nusumi too was able to control herself, but in her case mirth was replaced almost immediately by a self-conscious silence. After an awkward few moments, she glanced at Shiko's forehead. "That bump's going to swell up bad. We need to find something to put on it." Yet she made no move to leave; instead, she remained sitting, pulling at the stems of the weeds that bordered their temporary shelter. Staring down at her pile of broken stalks, she said haltingly, "We should wait a while longer…make sure they've given up…" Then her voice trailed off again.

Shiko leaned back and closed his eyes. Although his head was beginning to throb, he certainly had no idea where to go to find something for it. He was content for the moment just to try and recover his wits and figure out what he was going to do now.

He had followed his instincts, but he was not sure they had led him down the right path this time. He had aided a Yutakashi lawbreaker, endangering his involvement with the Hikari pilgrimage. Considering how delicate relations were between the two kingdoms at this point, he might have endangered the entire expedition. He was tired, hurt, and filthy. He had no idea where he was, and the girl who had led him here had now grown silent and moody. It seemed highly unlikely that Toshihito would approve.

Finally Nusumi, in a quiet voice, said, "I'm sorry."

Shiko's natural politeness took rein. "It's all right. There is nothing to regret."

She replied sharply. "Yes, there is! I ran, and left you to follow. I didn't even wait to see if you were able to get away or not. I just…ran."

Shiko was not sure what to say. He didn't really blame her; she had been doing what she had to in order to get by, and for others to get by. If she hadn't had to come back to collect him in the Market, she might have been clean away before the men had ever seen her. He said as much to Nusumi, but it seemed to make little difference.

"I still shouldn't have left you behind!" she said. "You're from Hajimeshi; leaving you stranded in the middle of the Market to face charges on helping a thief...I don't know what they would have done to you, but it wouldn't have been good." She fell once more into silence.

Shiko leaned against one of the remaining wheels, trying to isolate the pain in his head and put it into a little compartment in his mind. After a while Nusumi spoke again.

"I was frightened," she said softly. "Not for me, particularly. I know what they'll do to me, I've lived it over and over in my mind often enough...But the kids, and Kanyo and Tanoshi...If I were caught, and they found out where I came from..."

She stopped again. Shiko could almost feel the turmoil within her. Every day, he surmised, she must risk not only herself, but those close to her as well; and all so that they could simply have enough to eat. A streak of fierce independence ran through her, he saw, but at the same time she was inescapably tied to her adoptive family. The two opposing emotions must lock her in a constant struggle with herself, he realized.

Shiko caught the faint glimmer of tears on her cheeks. Embarrassed, she quickly dashed them away. "I won't let anything happen to them," she said, and Shiko realized she was still thinking about Kanyo and Tanoshi and the children. It was as if his presence had been forgotten. He remained quiet and let her talk as much as she needed to; listening, after all, was one of the things Deshi were trained to do.

"They took me in when I was starving," she was saying. "Practically dead. They never ask about the food. I know it bothers them; but it's more important to them to keep the children fed than to worry about which rich folk's table is missing the tochuya roots from their silver bowl..."

She went on in a similar vein for a while. He tried to focus on her words, but he was almost too tired to think straight. He even tried to reflect on the inequities of the Yutakashi system, considering how it might be turned around and made fairer. But his reasoning became muddled, and it hurt to think. Then he realized that the pain was real; the pain had escaped its little compartment, and the lump on his head had turned into a searing headache.

Nusumi stopped her diatribe, realizing that Shiko was looking quite pale. "I'm sorry," she said again. She examined the growing knot on his head. "You should have just told me to shut up! Come on, we need to do something about that. It's probably safe for us to go now."

She crawled out from under the wagon. As Shiko started to follow, he said, "I hope the way out is different than the way in."

Nusumi's face popped back into view, its mischievous smile back in place. "Oh, it is. It's worse!"

She had been teasing him, of course; the way out consisted of no more than scaling a short fence at the back of the yard, which deposited them in an alley behind some warehouses. Nusumi kept them to back alleys for the most part as they worked their way west back toward the Street of Inns.

At one point she bade him wait for her, and off she went once more, out of sight. He worried at first that she was going to purloin something again, and wondered how he could manage another rapid flight in his current condition. Then he began to think that perhaps she had abandoned him. Maybe, he thought, she had decided that enough was enough; she had gotten him this far and he could find his own way. As he started thinking about how he would make it back from here, she suddenly re-appeared again, like a wraith in the night.

She stuck out her hand. "Give me your purse." Feeling sheepish at his lack of faith in her return, he untied the bag and handed it to her. If he felt somewhat awkward at handing over his moneybag to someone that was a known pilferer, it was tempered by the realization that she had not, in fact, left him to his own devices. He was beginning to feel that he could trust Nusumi's intentions.

Indeed she returned shortly, carrying a small pouch as well as his purse. She handed him back his moneybag. "I had to pay more than I wanted to, but you need this. Come on, there's a place near here where I can put this on you."

She led him down a sloping alley between two buildings, which ended in a half-flooded basin at the foot of an embankment. A large pipe, some five feet or so above the pool's surface, emerged from the embankment. Shiko saw that a constant flow of water was pouring from the pipe down into the basin. At the pool's deepest part, beneath the pipe, the water was about knee deep. Nusumi waded in over to the pipe, Shiko following.

"This water is clean," she said as she unwrapped something from the pouch. "On hot days, kids drink from this, and no one's ever gotten sick." The material from the pouch was some sort of gooey poultice, and she moistened it with water from the pipe. Gently she applied it to the bump on Shiko's forehead. He flinched at first. "It'll only hurt for a second," she said. "Then it'll feel better."

She was right, he concluded. After the first stab of pain, the knot on his head ceased to throb. Then the dull ache behind his forehead began to ease as well. The poultice had the odd effect of feeling cool on his forehead while at the same time suffusing his head with a feeling of gentle warmth. He asked her what it was.

"I don't know its real name," she replied. "I've always heard it called mayaku weed. Tanoshi used to put little bits of it on me whenever I had a cut or a scrape. The drug seller wasn't sure he wanted to deal with me, even though he knew what I wanted from how I described it. The sound of coins from your purse managed to convince him easily enough."

She finished spreading the compound across his forehead, and he indeed felt much better. She took hold of his left arm and looked through the tear in his sleeve. "You've been cut here. Take these off," she said, indicating his pilgrim smock and tunic, "or this stuff will get all over it, and it stains."

Although he felt somewhat self-conscious, never having undressed in front of a woman, he complied. He hung both smock and tunic on a nearby tree root that poked out from the side of the bank, leaving his upper half bare. She watered down some more of the mayaku weed, and applied it to a nasty gouge along his forearm. As she spread it on, she asked, "What does it mean?"

Shiko, having closed his eyes, enjoying the sensation of warmth traveling up his arm, was startled by the question. He opened his eyes and saw that Nusumi was looking at his chest, staring at the honsho that hung around his neck.

The honsho pendant glimmered in the reflected light from the water. Its edges bore ornate etchings of leaves and vines, painstakingly carved in such realistic detail that Shiko had been able to identify the various types of plants. They surrounded the characters of Shiko's name, now worn partially smooth from his fingers over the years. But the characters were still easily discernible.

Shiko realized then that Nusumi could not read. He reached down and held up the honsho. Pointing to one of the characters, he said, "This means *Shi*. The other one is *Ko*."

She reached up and held the honsho in her hand, staring hard at the characters. She rubbed her fingers over the raised symbols, as if trying to see the meaning behind the lines there. "Where did you get it?"

He shrugged. "I've had it all my life; the Deshi found it with me when I was left with them. No one knows where it came from."

Still holding the pendant she said quietly, "You could have turned me in. They might have even given you a reward. I'm just a gutter rat; you're off on some holy mission. Why did you follow me?"

While his head had stopped pounding, the effects of the mayaku weed had also made him slightly light-headed. He dimly realized that it must have had something to do with the aroma from the poultice, which had an odd sweet smell. He tried to concentrate on her question, and answered it with his own. "Why did you leave the crates along the wall, instead of knocking them down? Or leave the hatch under the building open? With the head start you had, you could easily have eluded those men if you had closed off the escape routes."

"I didn't...I didn't want to just abandon you," she said. "I wanted you to at least have a chance to get away."

"But I'm just an apprentice Deshi from Hajimeshi. I'll be gone tomorrow. You have to survive here. Why did you risk yourself to give me a chance?"

Nusumi let go of Shiko's honsho, but wouldn't meet his gaze. "I don't know. I just...well, I don't know," she ended awkwardly. Without thinking about it she had returned to rubbing the poultice on his arm, even though his arm now felt fine. In fact, the warm feeling had begun to spread outward from both his forehead and his arm, and he felt fine all over.

Nusumi, standing close in front of him, had stopped talking, her hands still moving slowly up and down his arm. Almost as if he was standing in a fog, he saw her stop, then finally look up, her gaze looking as confused as he was himself.

He stared into her eyes, and they seemed to him like the pool of water in which they stood. Seemingly transparent but in reality covering up much that lay just beneath the surface. He felt that if he just mentally reached out, he could swim beneath them, and could see what was there...

All of a sudden he *was* there, it seemed; he felt that he could feel her emotions, her conflicts, her anxieties, her desires...She was there too, inside his own head; he could feel her gazing about, gently touching his thoughts, knowing his feelings, his deepest fears; what made him happy, what made him sad...

A part of his mind wondered, how could two people do this? How do I know what she is feeling, and how can she be here within me? I've never known anyone this way...I know her now better than any other person I've ever met...

Slowly he leaned toward Nusumi, and she responded the same way. She closed her eyes, he did the same, and somehow their lips met in the middle. He felt her arms encircle him, and all he could hear was the pounding of his heart, the sound of his breath (or, he wondered, was that her breath, next to his ear?), and what sounded like a roaring river but could only have been the water running out of the pipe.

He felt his mind drifting, almost as if he had stepped outside his physical body and was watching himself standing next to Nusumi. There he was, shirtless, a long cut on his arm covered with mayaku. He had his arms around Nusumi's waist, and she had her arms around his neck. Their faces were touching, kissing. The two of them seemed to be having a pleasant time, his mind thought to itself; I should leave them to it.

His mental gaze wandered away, taking in the basin in which they both stood; the torn tunic; the water flowing from the pipe. The afternoon sun glittered in the standing water of the basin, casting little sparkles. Very pretty, Shiko's mind thought. Familiar, too; I wonder why?

His inner gaze looked again at the water spouting from the pipe, and the sunlight caused his mind to see it almost as if it were ablaze. That's odd, he thought; water looking like fire. Perhaps I could put some of it into a bottle and have my own little lantern…

Lantern…Hikari…With a rush, his mind swept back into his body. His senses all returned in an instant, and he was shocked to find he was holding Nusumi in his arms and kissing her. Startled, he released her and stepped back, splashing in the water.

Nusumi, unprepared for his sudden reaction, found herself holding nothing but air. The sudden shock jolted her senses back. She experienced a rush of conflicting emotions: confusion, embarrassment, anger.

Shiko was saying, "I'm…I'm sorry, I didn't…the poultice must have…have affected me…" His words stumbled out, a look of confusion in his eyes.

Nusumi stared at him with unbridled fury. She had no idea why she had reacted to Shiko the way she had. Some little part of her mind realized that maybe it had been the mayaku weed; Tanoshi had never used as much on her as she had on Shiko. But that sliver of rationalization was brushed away in her rage. All she knew at the moment was that Shiko had rejected her. She had reached out and had been figuratively slapped away.

Without a word she turned and stormed out of the basin, back up the sloping alley. Shiko retrieved his tunic and followed, trying unsuccessfully to apologize to her retreating form.

A crow sat perched along a nearby rooftop, watching. It cawed once then flew away.

*   *   *

Nusumi refused to speak as she guided Shiko back to the Street of Inns. About a block away from his destination she pointed him in the right direction with a terse wave of her arm, then turned on her heel and left.

Shiko had given up trying to talk to her on the walk from the basin. Now he tried once more as she walked away, thanking her for her help and even including a friendly goodbye. His words, however, went unheeded. He watched her retreating back until she was lost from view down the street.

Angry with himself, he trudged his way back to the House of Bright Light. He had risked potentially the entire pilgrimage by following Nusumi, and now he seemed to have alienated her completely. His head was beginning to hurt again, as was the cut on his arm. He felt filthy and worn out. To cap it off, although he had the candles that Toshi-hito had requested, he had not obtained the scroll paper. How was he going to explain to Toshi-hito what he had been up to all afternoon?

After dragging himself up the stairs and into their rented quarters, Shiko was relieved to find that the Deshi Master had not yet returned. Only Nakama and a few other Guards were there; everyone else was still out in the town. Nakama, sitting next to the Hikari, chose not to remark about Shiko's odd appearance, although the other Guards made a variety of ribald comments about his presumed activities. Ignoring them Shiko stripped off his mangled clothing and found another tunic from his pack. He stretched out on his mat and tried to think.

He felt confused, his mind in turmoil. The mayaku weed had stirred up all kinds of pent-up emotional and physical needs that his Deshi training had, if not suppressed, at least allowed him to compartmentalize. Now, even after most of the effects of the mayaku had worn off, he found himself still thinking about Nusumi, about the feel of her in his arms back in the basin.

It was not unheard of for Deshi to have companions, or even to marry; in fact, there were a number of Masters who maintained households of their own outside the priory. Usually, however, such situations came late in life for the Deshi. The members of the order spent most of their time divided between musty scrolls in the archives, or providing meditation services to the people of Tonogato; such activities made for poor companionship for most members of the opposite sex. Accordingly, most married Deshi were senior members of the order, who had encountered their mates during some long-term posting elsewhere and who had the time to develop a relationship.

So Shiko had never given the matter much thought, assuming that any such relationship for him was something to think about further down the road. Now, it seemed, he couldn't stop thinking about it.

The Hikari lantern sat on the floor of the room, its light suffusing the space like an overseer keeping an eye on a guilty conscience. Shiko turned to look at it, trying to focus his mind on the flame and shut out the clamorous racket that was going on inside his head. At length, his concentration asserted itself. The jagged nerve edges of raw emotions were calmed, and he worked on breathing slowly, calmly. He reached up and wrapped his fingers around his honsho, and steered his mind away from himself, away from Nusumi, and onto other topics.

She was right, of course, about the inequities of Yutakashi society, he told himself. Even though he had only been in Yutakashi not quite an entire day's span, what he had seen already confirmed her description of its inherent unfairness. As he had said to Nusumi, though, he was but an apprentice Deshi, back on the road come the morrow. He might think and ponder about better ways, but what difference would it make? More learned minds than his had undoubtedly already conceived of all the possibilities. A young Deshi was unlikely to make any impact on the Yutakashi way of life. Particularly one who couldn't concentrate on anything without continually seeing Nusumi's face passing across his inner vision...

As the afternoon drew to a close, Shiko sighed and shifted on his mat. The other Guards went out again, leaving only Nakama. The conscripted Hikari guardian sat by the lantern and kept himself busy by writing on a scrap of scroll paper, scratching out passages and starting over again several times. Sensing Shiko's mood, he kept his thoughts to himself as the shadows about the room lengthened.

A short time later Toshi-hito returned. He had given Kanrin some scrolls brought from Hajimeshi for the priory library, which had left his old acquaintance beaming at the prospect of a quiet evening reading new works, nourished along by a few choice fruits Toshi-hito had obtained from the Market. When Toshi-hito entered the pilgrim's common room, he immediately saw Shiko's change of clothes and the angry red knot on the young man's forehead. The elder Deshi looked to Nakama, who shrugged his shoulders before going back to his writing.

The Deshi Master sat next to Shiko's sleeping mat. "Were you able to find your way," he asked, "in the Market?"

Shiko would not meet his gaze but pulled out the meditation candles, somewhat the worse for wear from his escapades, and handed them to Toshi-hito. "I am sorry, Master. I was...unable to get the scroll paper. I will rise early tomorrow, and return to the Market. I will have the paper before we leave."

Looking down at the slightly mangled tapers, Toshi-hito heard more behind the words than what Shiko actually spoke. Sensing his young apprentice's disposition, however, he asked no further questions. "The scroll paper is not important. It can wait for another time." He did, however, insist on examining the swollen bruise on Shiko's head. The apprentice listlessly allowed the elder Deshi to poke and prod until satisfied. Deeming the young man fit, at least physically, Toshi-hito retreated to his own mat to meditate. For some wounds, he thought, only time, not words, would prove an adequate salve. Whatever the cause, it would appear such was the needed remedy for his young charge.

He himself had much to ponder. Many of the things Kanyo and Tanoshi had told him after Shiko had left had been disturbing: there were, his hosts had informed him, undercurrents of dissatisfaction rumbling just below the surface of Yutakashi society. While the Reds and the Blues played out their games of power, trying to intimidate Yutakashi's neighbors, they were ignoring the troubles in their own courtyard. Those citizens that did not enjoy the fruits of the city's prosperity were seething with discontent. Kanyo felt it was only a matter of time before there was a serious confrontation between the haves and the have-nots. At the priory Kanrin, too, had echoed much of what his friends had said. And a Yutakashi divided by civil war, Toshi-hito mused, would be in a poor position to support the Kotaishi when the time of crisis came…

Before long Ryori returned from the Market, hauling two large bundles of supplies. As he struggled through the door, Nakama rose to help him. "Hah! You Guards!" said Ryori, handing the archer one of the bundles. "All you do is eat. Should've brought a wagon to haul all this stuff!"

With an exaggerated groan the cook dumped his remaining bundle on the floor. He opened it and started taking things out, rattling off the contents to no one in particular. "Tochuya root, domi husks, butano spuds, yuka. Even rinashi tubers," he exclaimed, as he held up a thin pale green stalk. "This place sells everything. And good thing too," he added, gesturing toward Nakama. "You Guards will eat every bit of it before we're halfway to Shukyoshi. Hope you're good with that bow," he added, as he gestured toward Nakama's weapon propped along the wall. "You might be using it to procure your own dinner before this trip is over!" Nakama only grinned as he pulled out his piece of scroll paper to continue his writing.

As Ryori sorted the foodstuffs into the various pouches and pockets of all his travel packs, he commented to the room at large, "Quite a ruckus goin' on down in the Market." When this met with no response, he continued. "Heard that a coupla' thieves made off with half a cart's worth of pajana fruit. Big ol' chase right through the center of the Market."

Nakama looked up from his writing. Toshi-hito, eyes closed in meditation, might or might not have heard anything that Ryori was saying. Shiko was still sitting on his mat, arms hugging knees drawn up around his chest and staring at the Hikari, as he had been for some time. Out of politeness Nakama responded to Ryori's gossip. "Were they caught?"

With a quick glance at Shiko, Ryori said, "Nope. Got clean away." As the cook said no more, Nakama returned to his writing. Ryori continued shuttling items from bundle to packs, with an occasional glance at the silent young Deshi.

9

As evening approached, the Guards began returning. Having spent the day enjoying the city, their purses were running low and they had decided to take advantage of Ryori rather than waste their perfectly good coins on high-priced Yutakashi meals. The pilgrims' cook grudgingly obliged, making use of the inn's kitchen facilities to prepare a meal from his newly gathered supplies, muttering all the while about how there would be nothing left for the journey.

While Toshi-hito ate a little, Shiko had nothing at all. Nakama, having spent the entire day watching over the Hikari, gratefully accepted the portions handed out by Ryori. He had finished eating and returned to his writing, using the light of the lantern, when Itachi finally returned.

Toshi-hito, still sitting quietly on his sleeping mat, noticed that the Hajimeshi general's face was covered with scratches. He voiced polite concern. "Have you encountered some difficulty, Lord Itachi?"

Itachi's dark mood had lifted somewhat; having found a decent brothel, he had passed most of the afternoon there. It had been expensive, as he had nearly killed the girl and had then to pay the proprietor extra in order to compensate for the damage inflicted on the 'property.' But it had allowed him to work the anger out of his system. "No, no difficulties," he replied, offering no further elaboration. He was ravenously hungry, and so helped himself to food from Ryori's stock. He was quite pleased to find rinashi tubers. Perhaps, he thought, this idiot cook might yet be worth the effort of dragging his otherwise useless hulk along on the pilgrimage...

As Itachi settled down into a corner to eat, Bokusa, the last of the Guards to return, leveraged his big frame through the doorway. The man was roaring drunk. Swaying unsteadily, and oblivious to the presence of Itachi, he greeted his fellow Guardsmen heartily by trying to sing them a song. He only managed a single off-key verse before ending in a mighty belch.

Itachi was not amused. Out of all my men, he thought, it had to have been Bokusa to do this! "Hold your tongue, you imbecile. You two," he said, pointing to Guards who were nearest the unsteady Bokusa, "get him onto his mat."

The two men half-guided, half-pushed the big man over to his sleeping mat, where he laid his head down and within seconds was fast asleep. One of the Guards commented wryly, "Perhaps we'll need to tie *him* to his horse."

Itachi, already irritated at Bokusa's behavior, was in no mood for further breaches of discipline. "Silence! The next man who speaks out of turn will be tied *underneath* my horse!"

The men quickly averted their eyes. Spying Nakama still sitting by the Hikari, Itachi jerked a thumb in the direction of the landing outside their door. "You! Go stand guard outside. I don't trust these Yutakashi slum-dwellers not to slit our throats in the night."

Nakama, his face an impassive mask, put away his writing. Taking up his bow he went out to the balcony to stand watch.

The inn was quiet, all of its patrons having retired for the evening. The entrance gate was closed and barred, and even the proprietor had doused his lamps for the night. Leaning against the railing, Nakama looked out over the rooftops, watching as dusk faded into night. In ones and twos, then in larger numbers, the stars winked on in the dark canopy overhead, keeping the sky free from unbroken blackness. While he watched the evolving sky, Nakama fumed about the 'leader' of the Castle Guards.

What a despicable man Itachi is, he thought. Just like Bokusa. They both treat the men like dirt, but through sheer bravado they manage to evoke a sense of respect out of those hardened soldiers.

Both Itachi and Bokusa, he knew, were looking for any excuse to humiliate him. But it won't work, he told himself; my honor is lost already. And worse, I nearly brought shame and dishonor to the one person I care about. There is nothing more that either Itachi or his brutish sergeant can do that could be worse than that...

He tried to let his frustration waft away, like the cool night air blowing past. Better, he decided, that he should try to forget the conditions of his present hell. Unfortunately, there was only one other topic that continually beset him, much as he might try to avoid it.

Dearest Mikasama, he sighed silently to the evening sky. What are you doing right now? Curled up warm and snug in your sleeping chamber in Hajimeshi, Komori zealously guarding the door? Do you still think about me? Or have you forgotten me completely, nothing but a bad mistake to be excised from your memory? He sighed, outwardly this time.

"Am I intruding?"

Nakama was startled to see the young Deshi apprentice suddenly standing next to him. He had not heard the door open or Shiko approach. Fine watch he conducted, he admonished himself, standing here mooning over a lost love instead of attending to his duty! "No, not at all," Nakama replied.

Shiko leaned on the rail next to him, staring up at the sky. The wind was rising, blowing billowing masses of grey across the darkening sky. Nakama, following Shiko's gaze, said, "Some of the other Guards tell me that Yutakashi gets frequent rain showers at night. At least that's what they heard while they were out in the town. Something about clouds coming up from the sea, far away to the south, and once they reach here they release their burden before traveling over the mountains up north."

"Yes," replied Shiko, "I remember reading something like that. It has to do with the water from the sea rising, and somehow becoming a cloud. When the cloud gets old, it can no longer hold the weight of the water, and it falls."

Facts and figures, thought Nakama. How much easier is must be for the Deshi to deal with, than with emotions and feelings. If only the rest of life's questions could be answered simply by reading a book...

Both men fell silent, lost in their own thoughts. Nakama looked down to the city, out across the roof of the low wing of the inn that fronted the street. He watched as one of the city's lamplighters lit the ornate leaded-glass streetlights; the man's progress was visible by the periodic flash from each lamp as its wick was caught by the flame. Just like Hajimeshi, he thought.

Well, not quite. There was only one lamplighter in Hajimeshi, as far as he knew, and he only lit the castle; the streets of the town did not have fancy lights such as these. He found himself counting the lamps as the man came closer, and was puzzled when the flashes stopped some distance away. "That's odd," he said.

"What is?" replied Shiko, whose attention was still focused on the clouds overhead.

"The street lights," said Nakama. "The lamplighter stopped lighting them about two doors away."

"Mmmm," mused Shiko. "Maybe his taper went out." After another few moments of silence, Shiko, in a rather embarrassed tone, said, "Nakama, can I ask you...I mean, would you mind if..."

Nakama looked down at the apprentice. Even in the dim light he could see the young man's blush. "Yes, Shiko? What is it you want to know?"

In a rush Shiko blurted out, "What do you do when you've hurt someone that you...that you care about? A...a woman, I mean."

Such a question, thought Nakama. How could he possibly answer such a query? There was no way that he could tell this young Deshi apprentice how he felt about Princess Mikasama, how he would have fired arrows at the moon had she asked him to, how nothing could compare to the sweet sound of her laughter. And he had no words to describe the pain, the helplessness, once his world had been turned upside down. He could never redeem himself, or his honor, from the disgrace he had nearly brought on his Princess.

My Princess! Just listen to me, he angrily shouted to himself. I'm still acting as if I had some claim on her. No, I have removed myself from the field. She is free now to resume her life as it should have been, before I interfered with it.

So, he thought bitterly. Why am I still writing poems to her?

When Nakama didn't answer, Shiko said, "I didn't mean to pry. I—I shouldn't have bothered you." He turned to go back inside.

"No, wait, Shiko," said Nakama. The young Deshi stopped. "I didn't mean for you to go. It's just that there is no easy answer to your question." He paused, looking out across the city. As the moon popped in and out of view among the rolling clouds, it cast a pale glow across the endless sea of rooftops. Then, as the light was hidden behind one of the dark masses overhead, the sharply defined shapes merged into one incoherent mass.

Hundreds of people out there, he thought; some fighting, some making love, some simply existing. He spoke wistfully. "Every person, every woman, is different. What makes one laugh causes another to cry. When one grieves, what will make her world whole again is unique to her."

He fell silent, struggling with how to form what he felt into words. Shiko waited, and finally Nakama continued quietly, staring at something only he could see: "The secret is to know the road to her heart. Walk there, with her, hand in hand. If ever you let go…" But he didn't finish the thought.

"Have you done that, Nakama?" asked Shiko softly. "I mean, walked such a road?"

"Yes. Yes, I have." He pulled out the crumbled paper containing his poor attempts at love sonnets, looked at the words that could never adequately express his feelings. "In some ways, I guess I'm still on that road. But she's not here. She's far, far away."

Shiko noticed the tender way Nakama held the scroll paper, almost as if he could touch whomever it was through the paper that he held in his hands. "You must love her a lot. Have you been writing to her? Is that what you were doing all afternoon?"

"Writing to her, yes. But no words that she will ever see. More for myself, really."

"I'm sorry that the pilgrimage has taken you away from her. I'm sure she'll be waiting for you when you get back."

"No. No, I hope she won't be." Nakama roughly jammed the scroll paper back into the pocket of his tunic.

Shiko was perplexed. "But why? I don't underst—"

"Shhhhh!" said Nakama suddenly, holding his hand up to Shiko. He was peering intently down at the courtyard, over toward the gate leading to the street.

Confused, Shiko turned and looked toward the gate, trying to see whatever it was that had caught Nakama's attention. He strained his eyes in the semi-darkness.

There! Something moved, Shiko realized. In the space between the top of the gate and the archway, what looked like a head was moving slowly. There were no torch lamps in the courtyard, and without the streetlights being lit in front of their inn the avenue outside the gate was equally dark.

The two men on the balcony stood perfectly still, hidden in the shadows of the balcony roof. The gap between the top of the gate and the arch was very narrow; it hardly seemed possible that someone could squeeze through it. Nevertheless the head became a body as it managed to slip through the space under the arch and land feet first on the dirt of the courtyard.

Shiko could not make out any features, only that it was human and trying to be very quiet. The figure paused, cocking a head as if listening for something; then it began edging along the walls of the inn. When the lunar light was again eclipsed into shadow by the clouds, the figure started toward their stairs.

With the practice born of years of training, Nakama silently brought his bow around into position. As he notched an arrow, Shiko leaned over and whispered, "What if it's just somebody's husband sneaking back after a late night?"

Nakama shook his head and whispered back. "Too professional for that." He raised his bow. "Can't take the risk. I'll bring down whoever it is; we'll have to ask questions later." He took aim.

Shiko looked again at the figure moving in the courtyard. There was something about the way the person was moving...Quickly he raised a hand and pulled on Nakama's arm, preventing the Guard from loosing his shaft.

Nakama turned to him angrily, hissing, "What's got into you, boy?"

"Wait!" said Shiko urgently. "I don't think this is someone come to slit throats."

By this point the intruder had passed out of Nakama's field of fire, and was close by the wall of their wing of the inn. Whoever it was would now be able to come up the stairs toward them unimpeded. Nakama, bow ready, moved several yards closer to the stair landing and took up a kneeling position facing it. "You had better be right, Shiko," he whispered. "This will give me only one clear shot if you're not."

Both men waited. Either the intruder was not coming up their stairs, or was exceptionally good at being stealthy. Just when Shiko began to doubt himself, a head covered by a tight-fitting hood rose into view. The body following was halfway up in sight before stopping cold, evidently spying the two men waiting on the balcony. Nakama's bow was already raised; he had a bead on the intruder. Nobody spoke or moved for several heartbeats.

Then Shiko stepped out closer to the railing as the moon cast its light down through a break in the clouds. The intruder straightened upon seeing him, hands reaching up slowly to pull back the hood. Even in the dim light Shiko had no difficulty in recognizing Nusumi.

His heart felt as if it had stopped beating, and breathing was difficult. He recognized his emotional reactions for what they were, and tried to contain them. First, he had to find out why she was here. "Nusumi! What are you doing here? Why are you sneaking up on us?"

Nusumi had not moved, her eyes flitting back and forth from Shiko to Nakama's arrowhead pointed directly at her. "To warn you," she said steadily. "You, all of you, are in danger here. You must get away, before they come."

"Before who comes?" asked Shiko. "What danger? Are they coming to arrest me because of the Market?"

Nusumi came up the rest of the steps. "No, it's nothing to do with you. At least, not you personally. But the Blues are coming tonight, and they've been told to kill all of you. You have to leave before they get here."

Nakama, reassured that Shiko seemed to know whoever their intruder was, lowered his bow. "Why are the Blues going to kill us?" he asked. "And how do you know this?"

"I don't know why, other than that it has something to do with the man with the stick."

"Stick? You mean Lord Itachi, and his tarka?"

"I don't know his name. But he was seen dealing with the Reds. The Blues think that this Itachi, if that's his name, is trying to ally your Hajimeshi with the Reds. So they are going to kill him, and the rest of you as well."

"Nusumi," said Shiko. "How do you know all this?"

She didn't answer immediately, just bit her lip. Quietly she answered, "There are many people in Yutakashi who are fed up with both the Reds and the Blues. All those bastards do is hold on to their own positions, their own riches, and leave the rest of us to starve. Some of the people have...organized themselves, and are trying to change things." She looked down. "My foster father sent me. Kanyo is one of the reformers. Most of the rest, they could care less about a group of Hajimeshi. But your Toshi-hito is one of Papa's oldest friends. So Papa sent me to warn you. He knew I could get here and not be caught." Indicating her hood and dark outfit, she added, "The inn is being watched. I got the lamplighter to help by stopping early, so I could get in here without being seen."

Nakama turned to Shiko. "You obviously know this girl. Is she trustworthy?"

Shiko looked back at Nusumi, and their eyes met. Struggling to keep emotions under lock and key, he croaked, "Yes. Yes, I trust her." Nakama turned away and moved quickly in the direction of the door to the Hajimeshi quarters.

Shiko continued to look at Nusumi, who averted her gaze once more. Softly she said, "I told Tanoshi what happened, and she explained to me about the mayaku weed, about what happens if you use too much...She said...she said..." Her words petered out, losing their way. Looking up at him once more, she blurted out, "Well, I guess I'm trying to say I'm sorry, but I'm not doing a very good job at it."

Shiko started to reply, but by then Nakama had opened the door to their quarters and was shouting, "Alarm! Alarm!"

The Guards had already stretched out on their mats, wanting to get adequate sleep for the long day's ride ahead; but true to Itachi's boast of their fighting quality, all of them were on their feet and reaching for weapons before Nakama had finished uttering the second call.

Quickly Itachi started barking orders. Not knowing what the threat was or where it came from, he formed the men up ready to lead an immediate charge out the door. Nakama filled him in rapidly on what he had heard, and Itachi came storming out onto the balcony. "Where is this spy?" he shouted. "Let me see her!"

Nusumi stepped back, cringing. As Itachi marched down the length of the balcony, Shiko stepped into his path. Itachi drew up. "What is your involvement, Deshi? Speak or get out of my way!"

Shiko stood his ground, aware that Itachi could easily lift him bodily and pitch him over the railing to land in the courtyard below. He looked up into Itachi's furious expression. "Nusumi speaks the truth. We are in danger here, and must leave at once."

Itachi raised his fist before Shiko's face, and in a dangerously quiet voice said, "I know how to get the truth out of a woman. And I will have the truth before I risk fleeing through the streets!"

At that moment Toshi-hito appeared at Itachi's side. Seeing Nusumi, he turned to Itachi and said firmly, "Lord Itachi." The Hajimeshi turned to face the elder Deshi. "Nusumi would not be here unless what she speaks is true. We must go."

"Look!" It was Bokusa, surprisingly on his feet despite his earlier drunkenness, and now on the balcony with sword in hand. He was pointing down the street, over the roof of the front wing of the inn. A jumble of lights was moving steadily down the street: torches, being carried by many men.

Itachi swore, and turned away from the Deshi and Nusumi. He called out orders, and his men grabbed what gear they could before heading down to the stables. Toshi-hito asked, "Where is Ryori?" But the cook was nowhere to be seen.

The crowd in the street had reached the gate. Shouting and yelling, they pushed on the barrier, trying to force it open. Other guests of the inn, alarmed by the noise first from the Hajimeshi quarters and now from the clamor in the street, milled about the courtyard in confusion. As the Guards raced their gear down the steps to the stables, Toshi-hito turned to Shiko. "Take the Hikari," he said. "I will gather all the rest," and he scooped up their packs. Quickly Shiko grabbed the lantern, covering its light in a blanket, and leaving the pole behind. With Nusumi at his side he bounded down the stairs. Quickly they passed through the smaller archway at the back of the inn and down the ramp that led to the stables. Nusumi slipped on wet cobbles, and as Shiko steadied her he realized that it had begun to rain.

To his amazement, the Deshi apprentice saw that most of the horses were already out of the stable and were ready for mounting. The gate to the alley beyond stood open. Ryori was bringing the last of the horses and his mule out of the stable now, his usual irreverent manner notable by its absence. Had Ryori somehow known about the attack? Why else would he have been down here, preparing the horses for riding?

There was no time to stop and ponder, though. Toshi-hito had loaded his horse with the packs, and was already mounting his animal. Nusumi tugged urgently on Shiko's arm. "You won't be able to get out of the city by yourselves," she said to both of them. "That's the other reason Papa sent me; to guide you out. There's a gate where the watch standers are some of our people." She looked back toward the front of the inn. "Papa was hoping you could get out quietly, but it's too late for that now." As she finished, the front gate finally gave way under the press of the mob, and they poured into the courtyard brandishing swords, knives, and clubs. Innocent patrons of the inn who had the misfortune to be in the way were mercilessly cut down as the attackers piled in.

Several of the Guards, including Itachi and Bokusa, had yet to mount, but there was no time left. In seconds the mob would be pouring through the small archway from the courtyard and into the stable. Itachi turned and shouted at the rest of the Hajimeshi. "Ride! We will hold them!" He spun about and charged the opening, Bokusa a step behind yelling a battle cry. Two other Guards followed, and the four of them got to the archway just as the first of the mob discovered where their prey was. Several of the attackers tried to breach the archway but were felled by the slashing swords of the Hajimeshi Guards, their blades glittering first with raindrops, then with blood.

Despite the confusion, Shiko was able to see that none of the attackers wore Blues headbands. But this was no unruly mob, he realized; this was an organized attack. He was certain that Nusumi was correct, and that their attackers, for whatever reason, were in fact members of the Blues. Probably, he guessed, they were fighting without identification as a means to avoid censure for attacking pilgrims. No matter, he thought; the important thing now was to escape.

Toshi-hito, already atop his horse, was shouting down to Shiko. "Hand me the Hikari! Take Nusumi on your horse and lead the way." Quickly Shiko passed the Hikari up to the Deshi Master, then helped Nusumi up onto his own horse, climbing up behind her.

The handful of Guards, including Itachi and Bokusa, continued to hold the archway. Suddenly one of them fell; Shiko couldn't see who it was. Blood ran from where he had been wounded, running down the slope from the arch and pooling with the rain on the level ground of the stable yard. The other three Guards were still hacking and stabbing against the dark mass of bodies crowding into the small space of the archway.

To Shiko, everything seemed to be happening in slow motion. As he looked, another of the Hajimeshi defenders dropped his sword, then clutched his throat where it had been impaled by a knife thrown from somewhere in the mob. The Guard teetered and fell, his body rolling down the ramp into what was rapidly turning into a mud hole from the effects of many frightened, stomping horses. The sounds of battle caused the animals to dart about skittishly.

Nusumi, in front of Shiko, spoke urgently over her shoulder, "We have to get out to the alley behind the inn! Go west; I'll show you where we have to turn." He grabbed past her to take hold of the reins, and tried to get control of his horse and get it to move toward the alley. But he was not an expert horseman and with Nusumi blocking much of his view, he had difficulty maneuvering in the tight confines of the stable yard.

The weight of numbers was beginning to tell against the two remaining Guards holding the narrow space of the archway. One of them was hurt, favoring his left side, but still swinging his sword in deadly arcs around him. Suddenly three of the attackers managed to slip through, darting behind the two Guards to try and cut them down from the rear.

A swishing sound, and one of the attackers fell. Then another. In panic, the remaining attacker looked wildly about, turning just in time to see the arrow imbed itself in his chest. He too fell to the ground. Shiko saw Nakama, astride his horse, rapidly fit another shaft to his bow and take aim at the archway, waiting for another clear shot.

Shiko realized that if he didn't get moving soon, they would be overrun by the mob. Everyone was mounted now except for the Guards at the archway. And Ryori.

The cook was darting directly toward the fighting, brandishing a large kitchen blade. Shiko wondered if the cook had fatalistically decided that none of them were going to get away, and had chosen to die in some sort of misguided blaze of glory. But this was not, apparently, what Ryori had in mind.

The little man skirted the swinging blades and flailing cudgels at the arch. Belying his ungainly appearance, he scrambled up a large wooden drainpipe attached to the wall of the building. About ten feet up he began hacking at a rope that held a portion of the pipe, where it turned at an angle and went through the arch toward the main courtyard. As the rope parted, there was a sharp crack as something gave way.

With a howl the mob suddenly backed off. The large wooden pipe going through the arch, unsupported by the rope, had snapped. One end fell downwards onto the heads of the mob in front, knocking several of them to the ground. Out of the open end, raw sewage from the inn's upstairs plumbing flowed out in a putrid cascade into the faces of those behind.

Ryori jumped from his perch, yelling at the Guards at the archway to run. As they turned to race for their horses, Shiko finally got his own horse's head shoved around in the right direction and urged him forward. With a lurch they sped toward the alley, Toshi-hito close behind, while the other Guards covered for their comrades as they mounted.

The alley was slippery with wet sludge, and Shiko's horse almost skidded off his feet as he made the sudden turn out of the stable yard. Then they were pounding down the alley. Briefly Shiko wondered why the attackers had not blocked the rear of the inn as well. His question was answered for him, though, as they flashed past a group of confused men, just emerging from another stable yard from an inn several buildings down from theirs. Shiko's eye caught only a glimpse of a signboard on the wall facing the alley, but he was certain that it said "House of Bright Light." The men had been led to the wrong place! He had just the briefest moment to wonder about the extent of Nusumi's underground.

The Blues in the alley reacted quickly, however, after the first of the Hajimeshi horses had flashed past. Realizing that they had been tricked, they raised their weapons and attempted to strike at the riders that followed. Unfortunately for the attackers, these happened to be the

Hajimeshi Guards and not unarmed Deshi. Men on horseback having the advantage, the Yutakashi were quickly ridden down and scattered.

Shiko's horse burst out of the dark alley and onto a main street. The sudden brilliance of the glass streetlights cast an odd glow over everything, and reflected eerie images up from the wet streets. Nusumi pointed off to the right, unable to do more lest she slide off the half-out-of-control horse. Shiko managed to turn that way, as the rest of the Hikari group thundered behind him.

He had no idea which direction they were heading, trusting Nusumi to know where to lead them. They crisscrossed several districts of the city, startling the few passersby out on the streets as they galloped past. There was no pursuit; the Yutakashi mob had expected to surprise the men of Hajimeshi and overwhelm them at the inn.

Soon their ragged band entered a side street of warehouses, a deserted area at this hour. As there would be no curious onlookers to observe them here Nusumi told Shiko to slow down, and Shiko raised his arm as a signal to those following. Toshi-hito, awkwardly trying to balance the Hikari in front of him, rode up beside Shiko and Nusumi. The rest of the group bunched up behind them. As the horses snorted and wheezed from exertion, the riders took deep breaths and tried to calm racing hearts. The rain continued to fall, not a deluge but intermittent drizzle that left them all well soaked.

Itachi rode up from the rear, blood oozing from a wound. Shiko realized that the Hajimeshi general had been the Guard that he had seen hurt and bleeding from his side during the fight, but who had continued swinging his sword with deadly accuracy. Breathing hard, the Hajimeshi general looked at Nusumi. "Now…How do we get out?"

With the horses stopped, Nusumi could stop worrying about holding on for dear life. Things had not gone exactly as planned, she concluded breathlessly, but at least they had escaped from the Blues, if only for the moment. The city gate where her foster father's people were supposed to be was just ahead.

But things had happened so fast. What if the guards at the gate had not yet changed shifts? What if her father's people had been betrayed? It would not be the first time that some Red or Blue spy had wormed his way into their movement...If so, then Shiko's people would be walking into a trap, and most likely be killed on the spot. And she along with them.

Well, it was too late to worry about that now, she decided. They were ahead of any alarms for the moment; they had to get out of the city before the regular troops were summoned to quell the disturbance.

"Well?" the one called Itachi was asking again, the rain rolling off his black helmet.

Nusumi swallowed hard. "I have to give the sentry a signal. Then, when he's left the gate, we can go through. But we have to go out slowly, or one of the wall patrols might notice us."

"Then be quick about it! I don't want to die drowning in a gutter, with a Yutakashi arrow in my back."

She looked over her shoulder at Shiko, and the young Deshi turned his horse toward the end of the street and set the animal in motion. Gently they clopped out into a square, the soft rain making a gentle hissing sound as it struck the cobblestone paving.

Here there were shops surrounding the square, their fronts closed and locked up for the night. The upper floors sported rows of windows behind which, Nusumi knew, lived the shopkeepers and their families. The sound of the horse's hoofs rang loudly in her ears as she looked up anxiously at the dark windows. Like a string of blank, vacant eyes, the windows seemed to gaze down at the intruders, silently watching as the encroaching pair marched through their domain.

There was a gate in the city wall on the far side, opposite the street from which Shiko's horse had emerged. It was a much smaller gate than the one through which the pilgrims had originally entered. A guard was pacing back and forth before the closed and barred portal.

Nusumi felt quite exposed as they made their way slowly across the square; they were easy targets should anything go wrong. As they approached the gate, Shiko pulled up on the reins to stop his horse. The guard ceased his pacing and looked in their direction, lowering his spear in a defensive position. Nusumi raised her right arm over her head, then slowly lowered it until it stood out parallel with the ground, holding it for a count of three.

The guard raised his spear back to his shoulder. He turned and started to pace once more, but this time kept going until he reached a small door set into the wall. Propping his spear up outside, he went through the door and closed it behind him. Nusumi let out a long sigh of relief. "It's a privvy," she said over her shoulder. "Come on, we have to hurry."

Shiko turned his horse about, and slowly waved his arm back and forth. The Hikari party emerged from the alley, riding their horses slowly across the square. It was nerve-wracking; Shiko expected at any minute to hear a shout, men running, and the sound of swords being drawn.

As their group approached, Shiko counted heads. In the brief pause, other feelings rushed in, his heightened senses recalling in particular the feeling of Nusumi shivering in his arms as they had ridden out into the square. Quickly he pushed those thoughts out of this mind as he finished assessing their numbers. He realized that everyone was there except the two Guards he had seen killed at the archway. Incredibly even Ryori had made it, overloaded mule and all.

So had Bokusa, who had emerged without a scratch. The big man led the way over to the gate. Once there he quickly dismounted and shifted the huge timber that held the gate closed, then pulled open the heavy wooden door.

On the other side was a bridge across the dry moat. Looking through the gate opening Shiko could see another guard standing watch at the opposite end of the bridge, and the Deshi looked questioningly at Nusumi as the others gathered behind them.

"It's all right," she said. "He's one of ours." She repeated the same signal she had used earlier, and the guard leaned on his spear and turned away. She turned to address the others. "He won't 'see' us. Just ride quietly past as if he's not there." She nodded at Shiko, and he started his horse through the gate.

The surface of the bridge was made of wood, and the sound of the horse's hooves clopping on the planks made a frightfully loud noise. Toshi-hito followed Shiko out, clutching the covered Hikari close to his chest, and the others fell in line behind. Itachi was the last to follow, searching behind them for any signs of pursuit.

The rain had stopped, and the moon, having managed to push its way back through the clouds, reflected up from scattered pools of water in the moat. As Shiko's horse neared the end of the bridge, the guard stood perfectly still, leaning on his spear. Shiko could feel Nusumi stiffen in front of him, and he too held his breath. Now they were abreast of the guard; still the man did not move.

And then they were past. Shiko breathed again, and he felt Nusumi relax as well. Looking behind, Shiko saw that Toshi-hito had also passed by the guard. As the Hajimeshi soldiers started across, the scudding clouds blanketed the moon's pale light.

Itachi, bringing up the rear, had waited as his men crossed the bridge. He wanted to listen for anything that might indicate an alarm had been raised, and the stamping of so many horses on the bridge masked everything else. As the last of the Hajimeshi walked past the guard at the end of the bridge, he twisted about in his saddle, straining his ears for any sounds out of the ordinary.

Nothing. Turning back around, he started across the bridge, wincing in pain. The twisting movement had caused the wound in his side to open again, and he could feel the blood running down his leg once more.

He hoped that the Deshi had some healing skills. It had been a deep thrust from a sword, fortunately missing anything vital or he would now be rolling in the mud back in the stable. But it was deep enough to bleed like hell, and hurt even worse.

As he neared the end of the bridge, the guard still stood motionless, leaning on his spear. The moon slid out again from behind one of the dark, roiling masses above, silhouetting the guard against one of the pools in the moat. Despite the moon's reappearance, another of the clouds overhead chose that moment to loose its store of rain upon the fugitives below.

To Itachi, time seemed to slow down. It felt as if his horse was barely moving forward. The only sound was that of the rain on the bridge, which seemed to roar in his ears. He looked past the end of the bridge, and there was the Hikari party, waiting for him. They seemed so far away. He looked back at the guard. He couldn't see the man's face; the moon's reflected light from the pool was behind his head. But Itachi could swear the man was looking at him, turning his head and watching as Itachi rode slowly, so slowly past.

The Lord of Hajimeshi looked down, and saw blood on the bridge. His blood, running off his leg. Of course, he remembered now, he had been wounded. The blood was being washed away by the rain, off the edge of the bridge. He looked up again, and the faceless guard was still watching him. A shiver ran through Itachi, something that started deep inside and worked its way outwards until his whole frame was shaking.

Suddenly, he was across the bridge. The others were here, right in front of him, looking at him with concern. What was the matter with them, he thought. Why weren't they moving off down the road? That idiot Bokusa, what was he saying? His mouth is open, but no words are coming out. Well, that's typical; the fool rarely has anything intelligent to say.

Itachi twisted around again, and saw the guard on the bridge. Now the guard was the one that seemed far away. He had not moved, was still leaning on his spear. But he was watching Itachi. And still he had no face.

Itachi turned back once more to look at Bokusa, and felt another searing pain in his side. The last thing he saw before even the moon's light went dark was the sight of Bokusa's chest, racing toward his own face as he pitched sideways out of his saddle.

*   *   *

Himitsu sat on his favorite window seat and gazed out to the west. The morning sun was rising, and its first rays were tentatively exploring the landscape. He watched as first one beam of light, then another, poked out around the hills to the east and raced with one another across the Hajimeshi fields. These were joined by more rays, until like a beach washed with ocean waves the land was bathed in light.

The Kojuro's chamberlain tried to find solace in the spectacular dawn, but found his attention continually drifting to other concerns. Or rather, one concern. He twisted his fingers together in frustration. He knew that he was running out of both time and options.

Mikasama and Komori had not been found. The Castle Guards had scoured the countryside and found nothing. This did not surprise him; he expected that Komori would be talented enough to elude common soldiers. What worried him was that she had also outwitted all of his spies. He had alerted his entire network, even those in Shukyoshi. There had been no word of anyone matching the description of the Kojuro's daughter and her caretaker. Soon Himitsu would be forced to activate his one deep contact in Tejinashi, whom he had been keeping under cover for many years in the event of dire need. Little had he suspected that the need would take on the shape that it had.

Well, Komori, he thought, I clearly underestimated you. You always told me I never gave you enough credit, but I would not listen. I was always too busy with "stupid big affairs of state," as you called them; didn't pay enough attention to you. Well, perhaps you were right. The season is late, but perhaps amends can be made. I will find the time for things besides "affairs of state," once you and Mikasama have returned.

For Himitsu would not let himself think otherwise. It was much easier to think that Komori had simply been smarter than he had realized, and was keeping well hidden. The alternatives, that she and Mikasama had been killed by beasts in the forests, or ambushed by bandits, were just not acceptable. No, he thought, not acceptable at all.

He sat looking out to the west from his window ledge for some time.

10

The sun had stolen away, leaving only the fringes of dusk behind as Mikasama and Komori followed Horoda and his two sons into their encampment.

The camp was a short way off the trail, concealed in a forest clearing. Mikasama realized that they would have passed right by it unawares had Horoda not led them to it. In the dim light that still filtered through the trees, the Princess could see several wood-roofed, enclosed wagons arranged haphazardly around the open space, apparently the living quarters for the people of the camp. Each wagon contained a stout door at one end, with shuttered window openings along the sides; all were closed up tight. Around the edges of the clearing stood a number of two and four wheeled carts, along with a small corral containing a motley collection of horses.

A middle-aged woman was preparing a meal over a fire pit in the center of the clearing. Upon seeing the strangers entering their encampment, she called out sharply to Horoda in a tongue unfamiliar to Mikasama. It was clear, however, from the woman's manner that she was less than pleased about the sight of unexpected guests.

Horoda replied in his taciturn fashion, but not in the language used by the woman. "Two travelers. Gotta lame horse. We'll keep them here for the night." Mikasama couldn't help wondering if he meant the horses, or the travelers...

The woman, whom Mikasama guessed to be Horoda's wife, let loose a tirade of invective. This time, however, she spoke not in her strange language but in the common language that Mikasama understood. The Princess presumed the choice was intentional.

"You're crazy, a lunatic," the woman shouted. "There's not enough food even for us!" She banged her large stirring spoon repeatedly against the metal side of the pot. "How do you know these two won't kill us all in the night and steal our goods? How do you expect to trust strangers?"

Horoda completely ignored her imprecations. Pointing to the little corral and its ragged inhabitants, he indicated to the Princess that she should lead her limping horse and Komori's over to join them.

As Mikasama finished securing their horses, evening closed in around the campsite. The dark forest formed a dense, impenetrable wall, cutting off the outside world, leaving only the denizens of the camp clearly visible. Mikasama and Komori, distinctly uncomfortable, gravitated toward the fire burning at the center of the clearing. The two of them hovered at the edges of the light, unsure of their welcome.

Horoda's wife had not ceased her complaints, maintaining a one-sided dialogue with her silent husband, sometimes in her own, unfamiliar language, and occasionally with words that Mikasama could understand. Horoda, evidently finally tiring of her continuing harangue, shouted at her to hold her tongue and be about her business. Immediately she stopped; casting a look of anger and distrust at the two women trespassers, she sullenly resumed her chores.

Without a word Horoda waved to Mikasama and Komori to sit by the fire, where he and his sons, Okami and Okazu, had already started eating their evening meal. In fact no food was offered to the visitors, so Komori had to retrieve some supplies from their travel packs in order to make a quick meal. Everyone ate in silence, the men of the camp staring off vacantly into the night as they perfunctorily chewed their food.

"You two," said Horoda abruptly, pointing to the two women, "can sleep by the fire."

Mikasama started to protest, thinking that they should at least be allowed the comfort of one of the wagons. Komori, however, spoke up before she before she could voice her objection.

"Lookin' forward to a warm night by a fire. These old bones get brittle in the cold." With that she started unrolling blankets retrieved from their horses, leaving the Princess no choice but to follow suit.

The camp dwellers retreated to their dilapidated wagons, and Komori scuttled into her blankets. Mikasama tried to lie down and relax but she had never slept like this, outside by a fire. The ground was hard; when coupled with the strange surroundings and their bellicose reception in the camp, she soon found herself staring restlessly up at the night sky. As she watched the stars peek in and out behind the clouds drifting overhead, she turned this way and that, trying to find a spot where she could be at ease. It did not take her long to learn that she was unlikely ever to find such a place.

After a while she noticed the sounds of the forest: strange animal noises, or at least things she supposed were animals. And, she fervently hoped, if they were, then ones too timid to approach the light...

She shivered, and not only from the cold. The night felt eerie, strange; there was something in the air that just didn't seem...right, somehow. She rolled over, for what must have been the hundredth time, facing away from the fire so that her back might gain some warmth before she rolled back the other way again. She looked out into the darkness beyond the fire's light, staring at the strange, silent wagons. Who were these odd people, she wondered. Why were they out here?

No answer came to her, but a slight movement, out by one of the wagons, caught her eye. She squinted, trying to make out what it was. It moved again, and suddenly it came into focus for her.

It was Okami, the older of Horoda's two sons. He was outside one of the wagons, sitting on the ground, now motionless once again. Staring at her.

Startled, she tried not to move, or show that she had realized he was there. How long had he been sitting there? Had he been watching her all this time?

Now that she could make out his features, she could just see the light of the fire reflected back from his eyes. He never seemed to blink but just kept looking at her. She must have done something, or moved somehow, that made him realize that she knew he was there. For he began to smile, with that devilish grin he had displayed out on the trail. Mikasama could see clearly the line of his teeth. Yet other than that, still he did not move. Why was he doing that? What did he want?

At first frightened, slowly a sense of indignation grew within her. How dare he stare at her like that? Had he no sense of a person's privacy?

She thought of emerging from her blankets and walking over to him, to demand...what? That he stop sitting outside, in his own campsite?

She remembered that she was only a guest, and guests had to abide by their hosts' rules. If their hosts had no manners, there was little she could do about the situation. Well, she thought; he can just sit there all night, in the cold, if he wants too. I'm going to get some sleep.

She rolled back over, facing the fire. She watched the flames dancing, the slow fire working its way along the remaining logs placed in the pit. She tried to forget the young man behind her, but she could almost feel his eyes still staring at her, watching her back. Those eyes, she mused; those eyes were so clear, so focused. They had seemed to look straight through her, out there on the trail. What had he seen? What was he seeing inside her?

She shivered again. Her body felt odd, tingling, in a way she hadn't felt before. Must be the cold night, she told herself. He must be cold too, sitting back there by the wagon. He could come over by the fire, and warm himself. Why didn't he?

Her back felt strange, almost as if she could actually feel his eyes still focused on her. Or were they fingers, her drowsy mind wondered. Was he touching her?

Startled, she twisted her head around, but there was no one near by, only Komori snoring gently across the fire from her. If Okami still sat by the wagons, he made no sound; and she wasn't about to roll all the way over and look for him again. She closed her eyes, turning back to the fire, trying again to sleep. She had thought the attempt unsuccessful, just like all the others, but then she realized that she must have slept a little for she caught herself snoring and jerked her head awake.

Something was blocking the light of the fire, she noted dimly. An animal? No, she saw as her eyes focused.

It was Okami.

He was squatting down on both heels, between her and the fire. He was not warming his hands, but was facing her, still staring silently, not more than two feet away.

Her heart began to race, yet she felt completely unable to move. Her head, outside the blankets, was cold with the night, but her body was warm and sweating underneath. She was confused, still groggy with sleep, looking up at Okami as he continued to stare down at her.

Those eyes, close up, were just like she had seen before. His stare was fixed, relentless, almost as if his eyes could, by themselves, peel away the blankets that covered her. She felt naked beneath his gaze, her mind screaming at her to flee. Yet something held her back, some part of her wondering what he would do; and also wondering, she realized with surprise, what she would do. Slowly, ever so slowly it seemed, Okami grinned once more.

A sharp hissing sound pierced the darkness, over the crackling of the flames from the fire pit. Okami's grin froze in place, then receded. His head turned, looking across the fire. Mikasama glanced quickly over in the same direction.

Komori still lay under her blankets, but was wide-awake. Her steely gaze was targeted on Okami, her own teeth bared in a snarl unlike anything Mikasama had ever seen her do.

Okami hesitated, then abruptly stood and walked out of the fire's light, beyond Mikasama's field of view. A muffled creak told of his disappearance into the depths of one of the wagons.

Mikasama, still wrapped in her own blankets, felt dazed. She stared across at Komori, whose countenance had returned to normal with

Okami's disappearance. The old caretaker looked at the Princess in silence for a while before turning over and snuggling herself back down into her own blankets. After a while Mikasama could hear her snoring once again.

The Princess felt clammy and uncomfortable, and wished she were home, back in her own, soft bed. She thought of the playthings her father had given her, which she still kept piled on her bed, and the warm, familiar surroundings of Hajimeshi castle. She thought of Nakama, and longed to hear the sound of his voice.

She finally cried herself into a fitful, uncomfortable sleep.

* * *

Mikasama was being chased, like a wild animal. Deeper and deeper into the forest she ran, trying to escape—what? She wasn't sure, but she could tell that they were men. No, not just any men, she realized; some of them had on uniforms of her father's Castle Guard. Others wore strange blue robes that were unfamiliar to her. They wanted to catch her, to stop her, but she knew she had to keep running, keep hiding...

All of a sudden she was someplace else, and she understood, somehow, that she was dreaming. Only in dreams do people move around like this, her mind dimly realized. The Castle Guards; those had been my father's men, trying to find me and bring me home. They hadn't caught me, though. But who were the strange men in the blue robes? And where am I now? Who's that over there?

It was Komori. She was standing on a riverbank, tottering. Mikasama cried out to her, "Watch out!" but it was too late. Komori fell into the river.

Quickly Mikasama dashed over to the bank, only to see the old woman being swept away on the current. The Princess scrambled down to the water's edge, shouting after Komori. There was no one around to help her, so she jumped out into the river herself, trying to swim after her caretaker. But Komori kept floating further and further away, until finally she was gone altogether. Mikasama kept shouting, Nana-san! Nana-san! Where are you?

No answer came. The Princess, exhausted, stopped swimming, allowing herself to be swept along in the current. All of a sudden she found herself sailing over a waterfall. Surprisingly, it did not seem frightening at all. In that inexplicable way of dreams she landed, gently, on dry ground at the bottom. Looking around, Mikasama saw that Komori, all of their supplies and food, and even her clothes, all were gone.

Oddly, none of this seemed to matter. She was closer now, she realized. She was closer to what she had to find.

That part of her mind that was somehow detached, observing, knowing that it was a dream, asked 'What am I supposed to be finding?' The dream Mikasama did not answer, but just started walking, walking…where? That other part of her, the one watching, didn't know; only that it was toward the west. There were answers there. She was not even sure what the questions were, but she knew the answers lay there. And she had to know. It was almost a desperate, physical need. She *had* to know…

Mikasama felt eyes on her again. She managed to pry open one of her own, and saw that this time it was a little girl's face. Familiar, she thought. Where have I seen that face before? Oh, yes, she ran in front of our horses on the forest path, then screamed and dashed away. Then the men had come.

Her brain managed to get some focus and push away the cobwebs of sleep. She opened the other eye, and saw that the little girl was sitting in front of her. Mikasama lay uncomfortably on the ground, nestled between a pair of blankets by the remains of a campfire.

The Princess shuddered in the cold morning air, exhausted, as if she had not slept at all but had endured endless days in the wilderness. With a rush, the memories of the previous night returned.

Okami. Horoda's boy had sat there, staring at her, just where the little girl sat now. What had he wanted? And why had she felt so strange when he had looked at her?

And then there were the dreams, once she had fallen back asleep. Such bizarre dreams, haunted by terrible images. Wishing she could forget them, Mikasama closed her eyes again. She wondered what had they all meant. What had she been trying to find, there at the end? It had seemed so important, more important than anything she had ever done. Even now when she was awake, she could still feel that compulsion, an almost overwhelming need to push on. With a start, she realized it wasn't because of Nakama; he had been nowhere present in her dreams. There was something else...

The little girl still sat silently observing Mikasama, like an owl on a fence post watching for mice. She hadn't moved when Mikasama had first opened her eyes, but now as the Princess unraveled an arm from beneath the blankets to pull her hair back from her face, the girl ran off back to one of the wagons. Mikasama watched her go, and thought to herself, Am I running away too?

But the answer came back to her almost immediately, although from what part of her mind it arose she had no idea. It wasn't something she was running away from, but something that she was running *toward*. And it was something other than the man she had started out to pursue from Hajimeshi...

"Mika," came a quiet whisper from nearby.

Mikasama twisted her body so as to face Komori, her aching body rebelling at the movement. It was an agony of alternating stiffness and numbness. Her respect for soldiers who slept outdoors in all weather increased ten-fold.

"Yes, Nana-san?" she croaked. She finally managed to turn over enough to see her caretaker, who was still curled up in her blankets, her face framed by its usual border of ragged grey hair.

"Mika, you know who these people be?" Komori was still whispering, even though as yet no one else had emerged from the wagons.

"No, Nana-san. Just who they told us they were." She rubbed the sleep out of her eyes, and tried not to think how she must look. She could tell her hair was a matted mess, and her clothes were damp with sweat from her frightful dreams. And from the effect of Okami watching her. Or had he just been a dream too? "Why, what difference does it make?"

Komori pulled her blankets tighter around herself, as if they might somehow ward off danger. "They be Katanza!"

Katanza? Groggily Mikasama struggled to place the term. Her mind felt addled, struggling with the vivid memories of her dreams, and Okami, and Nakama...

Finally she tried to push all of the confused thoughts out of her head, and concentrated on Komori's question. Katanza...She seemed to remember being told once that they were wandering bands of families, not tied to any kingdom, living out of their wagons. Yes, that was it, she recalled; they traveled from place to place, all in their wagons, selling trinkets and doing the occasional odd job.

The Princess stretched, her joints making an uncomfortable popping sound. She remembered people saying that the Katanza were thieves, or practiced black magic. They rarely mingled with outsiders; once a year they held a large festival, in secret, to which no outsiders were permitted. Mikasama remembered hearing tales of what transpired at the festivals, and thinking that they were simply stories made up to frighten misbehaving little girls, like herself.

Well, thought Mikasama, so far she and Komori had not been robbed. And there was no sign of any black magic. "So?" she replied, her conversational interest at low ebb at this hour of the morning. "What if they are Katanza?"

"Wasn't sure, 'til I saw what their wagons looked like," said Komori. "Too dark last night." She struggled to sit up, managing to keep her blankets around her to ward off the morning chill. "Mika, we best go, soon. These people bad. Likely take horses, supplies, everything. Then they kill us, probably turn us into offerings to their strange gods."

Mikasama sighed. "Nana-san, if they were going to kill us, I think they would have done so while we slept." She tried not to think about Okami, and his wolfish grin. With an effort she sat up, then heaved herself into a standing position, trying without much success to re-arrange her clothing into some semblance of order. "I agree we should leave soon, but mostly because I suspect we're not entirely welcome here." That nagging feeling from her dream, the urgent need to press on, also popped back into her head; but she quickly pushed it away again. "There's the matter of my horse to attend to, though. We won't get far if we have to walk the whole way."

A male voice behind her said, "True enough."

She jumped, not having heard anyone approach. Turning, she saw that Horoda was silently walking up behind her. How much, she wondered, had he heard her say? And to what part was he referring to when he had said "True enough?"

If he had heard any of their comments, though, he kept that fact to himself. "Your horse take two, maybe three weeks to heal," he said gruffly. It was clear from his tone that she and Komori were not expected to stay with them for that length of time, even should they want to. Komori was uncommonly silent, apparently too distrustful of the Katanza to engage Horoda in a debate.

So, Mikasama realized, it was up to her to figure out what to do next. "Well..." she started. But she realized that she really didn't know what to say. They couldn't walk on foot all the way to the Northern Road. And even if they did, they would never catch the mounted Hikari group. In desperation she looked around, trying to think. Her eyes lit upon the corral, in which a number of horses besides hers and Komori's stood silently. She had a sudden inspiration. Turning back to Horoda, she said, "Will you sell us one of *your* horses?"

Horoda reached up and slowly scratched at his unshaven face as he turned and looked at the corral. At first he appeared to think about Mikasama's offer, but finally shook his head. "No. Can't afford to lose a working horse; we need all of 'em for the wagons and carts. And," he added, anticipating her next question, "we can't wait around here for that lame one to get well enough so's that it could pull."

Mikasama was crushed. She and Komori could not ride on one horse together along with all of their supplies, at least not for the distance they had to travel. And clearly Horoda's camp, for whatever reason, was about to move. She thought it best not to inquire why.

She had nearly exhausted every possibility until she heard a snort from Komori. Looking down at her caretaker, nestled back into her blankets as if they were a shield from the Katanza, she saw Komori silently jerk her head in the direction of one of the nearby carts. Mikasama looked over at the run-down apparatus, which held only a couple of bales of kobanya for feeding the horses. Then she realized what Komori was thinking. Of course! That would solve both their problems.

"All right," she said to the elder Katanza. "Will you let us buy one of your carts then, along with a horse? If you can find room for the kobanya in one of the other carts, then you wouldn't have to worry about the lame horse having to do any pulling." She knew it was a gamble, letting him know they had enough money to buy both a cart and a horse. The Katanza had not yet shown any inclination to rob them but she did not want to tease fate by providing them with too much temptation either. Even so, it was the only remaining option she could think of.

Horoda raised an eyebrow. He looked over at the cart, then at the corral; and without another word turned on his heel and returned to his wagon, climbing the small wooden steps to go inside.

Mikasama looked questioningly at Komori. "Did I say something to offend him?"

"Pahh!" Komori finally clambered out of her blankets, and sat by the smoldering embers of the fire. "Katanza! Take offence at everyone, everything." She looked off toward Horoda's wagon. "No, most like that dragon-woman runs this camp. He gone off to tell her 'bout offer, see if she says OK. Stupid."

Mikasama was not sure whether it was Horoda or his shrewish wife that was supposed to be stupid, but she didn't get a chance to ask. The little girl had wandered up again and was now standing tentatively near them. She coughed, making a somewhat wheezy and raspy sound, but otherwise didn't speak.

Komori looked at the little girl sternly. The girl stared back, not at all intimidated by Komori's unsmiling countenance. It was the old caretaker who finally blinked first in their tiny war of wills. Despite her distrust of adult Katanza, Komori just could not resist making a funny face at a little girl and seeing her giggle. The peal of childish laughter lightened the morning air in the camp. The girl ran up and sat herself down in a startled Komori's lap, but soon enough the two of them were busy trying to outdo one another in making truly lurid faces. Looking down at them, Mikasama had the oddest feeling that she was watching herself playing with Komori, a long time ago. Except for the girl's threadbare clothes, and her terrible cough, she could have been a younger version of the Princess, sticking her tongue out and pulling on the sides of her mouth...

Mikasama also detected the first signs of life from the other dwelling-wagon in the encampment. A haggard-looking, emaciated old man struggled down the steps, wandering over to the residue of the fire. He coughed even worse than the little girl, the guttural sound echoing harshly throughout the clearing. He dully picked out some cold remains from the previous night's meal, then without a word shuffled back to his wagon, hacking incessantly.

The creak of the other wagon's small wooden door caught her attention. Through the opening Mikasama could hear the shrill sound of arguing, and not just between Horoda and his wife. There was another woman shouting, an older one by its intonation. Horoda closed the door on both of them, and with a set look on his face walked over to the two visitors. Tersely he announced, "Cart's not for sale."

Crestfallen, Mikasama looked down at Komori. Her caretaker and the little girl had stopped their games when Horoda had walked up; both now were silent save for the girl's coughing. Mikasama turned back to Horoda, ready to try and persuade him otherwise, when she heard the wagon's door open once more.

An old woman, presumably the other arguing voice, climbed down slowly and painfully out of the wagon. Horoda's wife stuck her head out, yelling at the old woman. The old woman, once she was on firm ground, shook something that she held in her fist at the wife and shouted back up at her. Quickly the wife retreated and closed the door. The old woman shuffled over to the campfire.

Horoda had not moved during this exchange. In fact, his eyes wide, he seemed paralyzed by the old woman's appearance outside the wagon. The little girl, too, had opened her mouth in amazement. Mikasama, watching the old crone slowly making her way over to them, guessed that she did not come out into the daylight often.

Stopping in front of the Princess, the old woman peered up and looked into Mikasama's face. Despite the woman's cloudy eyes the Princess felt the unrelenting gaze boring into her, searching, penetrating. Unlike Okami's smooth, fox-like look, this woman's stare felt stern, and heartless. She held up the object in her hand; to Mikasama it appeared to be some sort of amulet, about the size of a man's fist. She put it up in front of Mikasama's face, where the morning sun's light caught on a red crystal embedded in its center. The light reflected back from the crystal's surface and darted into Mikasama's eyes, causing her to blink. Quickly the old woman lowered the amulet.

To Horoda she said sharply, "Sell the cart." Without another word she turned her back on them and retreated, slowly, back to the wagon, closing the door behind her after laboriously ascending the wooden steps. On the ground, Komori shivered, hugging the little girl closer to her.

Horoda, clearly aggrieved at being ordered about first by one then the other of the women in his camp, said brusquely, "Cart's been in my family for three generations. Built by my grandfather's own hand." He spat on the ground. "You want it, you leave both your horses behind along with coins for the cart. I give you the two cart horses."

Mikasama knew that the horses she and Komori rode were of exceptional quality, having been raised in the royal stables. Lame or not, trading them for cart horses used by itinerant laborers seemed a poor exchange. On the other hand, she knew her bargaining position was weak. She did not know why the old woman thought the cart should be sold, but figured that the offer was tenuous at best. "Agreed," she said. "We'll put our things in the cart as soon as it's ready." Without further comment, Horoda went off, shouting for his sons to come help prepare the cart.

The little girl stood up. Turning around, she looked closely at Komori's face. Reaching out tentatively, she traced her fingers around the creases lining the caretaker's cheeks. Then she leaned over and unexpectedly kissed Komori on the lips, before running off back into one of the wagons. Mikasama saw Komori's brief look of surprise, before the more usual disapproving frown folded itself back into place.

Okami and Okazu emerged to help their father with the cart. As the older boy passed by the Princess, their eyes met. Mikasama's breath caught momentarily, but the feeling passed immediately. All she saw now was a young man, still only a boy really, with a dull, vacant look in his eyes. She remembered the silence during the previous evening's meal, and how none of the men could so much as bring up a word to say. Looking at Okami now, she saw nothing behind his gaze but apathetic acceptance of his lot. Whatever she thought she had seen in his look yesterday, it had vanished with the dawn. If it had ever existed at all, except in her mind. As had the dreams, she told herself. Those terrifying dreams...

She stood watching the boys hitch the two draft horses to the cart. She wondered, not for the first time, what in the world she was doing there. It was insane! Here she was, buying an old cart from itinerant Katanza, trying to keep herself heading down the road, toward Nakama...or was it Nakama? He was not there, in the dreams; but something else was, something that she couldn't see, and that was what kept drawing her onward...

Irritably she stopped that line of thinking. Of course it was Nakama, she told herself harshly. What else could it possibly be? Those silly dreams were just her mind's way of keeping her moving. After all, Nakama was also heading west, so why shouldn't she?

She busied herself off-loading the packs from their horses, pushing out the confused thoughts her mind kept bringing up. Once the boys had finished with the cart, the Princess turned to Horoda and pulled out a number of coins from the purse she kept inside her tunic. No price had been discussed, but Horoda took what she offered without question. She had the strong sense that the amount was immaterial, as long as she and Komori were out of the camp as soon as possible.

Quickly the two women transferred their packs to the bed of the cart. As she did so, Mikasama patted her lame horse on the nose. "Thank you for bringing us this far," she said quietly. "I hope they treat you well." The horse, oddly enough, seemed to grasp her meaning, as he nuzzled her hand then turned to watch her as she walked away.

Mikasama climbed up onto the buckboard of the cart, Komori already seated beside her. After the appearance of the old Katanza woman, Komori had grown silent and withdrawn, clearly uneasy the longer the two of them remained in the camp. As soon as the boys had readied the cart she had clambered up, refusing to look at any of the Katanza, her gaze focused out among the trees.

Taking the unfamiliar reins in hand, Mikasama prompted the two cart horses into motion. With a jerk the cart began rolling forward. The Princess looked behind her once, to see Horoda standing in the clearing, his son Okami gazing after the departing visitors. The little girl was crouched beneath one of the wagons, peering from between the spokes of its wheels. And the old woman had stuck her head out of the wagon's door, clutching the strange amulet to her chest.

Mikasama suppressed a shudder. As the cart rolled out onto the path they had been on before encountering the Katanza, the forest swallowed up the clearing as if it had never existed. The Princess quickly turned around and urged the horses along a little faster.

Although she was greatly relieved to be leaving the Katanza camp behind, try as she might she couldn't shake a dismal sense of foreboding. The dreams from the night before kept coming back to her, running through her mind. Feelings of being chased, and of having to keep going, to find something...

They were just dreams, she kept reminding herself. Not enough sleep, and being outdoors in a strange place; that was all it was.

Then why, she wondered, did the dreams seem so terribly important?

The two women rode in silence, each lost in her own troubled thoughts, the only sound the harsh creaking of ancient wooden wheels rumbling along in the dirt.

*   *   *

Shiko and Nusumi sat looking down at Itachi, whose troubled body fidgeted and turned. The leader of the Castle Guard was still unconscious, recovering slowly from the wound in his side.

Once clear of the city, the Hikari group had picked up its pace in case the Blues had elected to follow. The pilgrims had been hampered by having to deal with Itachi, who had passed out shortly after crossing the bridge. Ironically, it had turned out to be the Hajimeshi lord who had to be tied to his horse.

Bokusa had led Itachi's animal as the pilgrims, guided by Nusumi, had fled deeper into the forests around Yutakashi, finally reaching an area of the woods that was relatively safe from Yutakashi patrols. It was one of the few places outside the city that Nusumi had traveled to, having used it, she said, as a temporary refuge when her activities in the Market necessitated a more distant hiding place. Shiko suspected that Kanyo's revolutionary friends also found it a useful sanctuary. Regardless, it served the Hikari group's purposes equally well.

The Guards had quickly prepared a small encampment, posting sentries to guard against both bandits and Blues. The unconscious Itachi had, with some difficulty, been maneuvered off of his horse and stretched out on the ground. Toshi-hito had carefully examined the wound and had applied a healing potion from the supply of medicinal herbs he always carried when traveling. The bleeding had stopped, and the wound had begun to close. It was now up to Itachi's body, Toshi-hito had said. The Kojuro's brother would have to mend himself. With that, the Deshi Master had made himself comfortable and had promptly fallen asleep, trusting that Bokusa could capably manage the martial affairs.

As the Guards had all been occupied in sentry duty, Shiko had volunteered to sit watch over the restless form of the Hajimeshi general. Nusumi, ignored by the soldiers once the safety of the forest hideout had been reached, had silently come to join him in his vigil.

But now, sitting with the young Yutakashi thief, the Deshi apprentice's thoughts were not about the Kojuro's brother who lay before them. In a short space of time, he and Nusumi had crossed an emotional bridge that neither of them had expected to cross. Almost as soon as it had been traversed, that bridge had unexpectedly collapsed, leaving a nearly insurmountable chasm between them. And then, equally unanticipated, a new bridge, a different one, had been presented to them. He wasn't certain, though, how to step out onto it, and was greatly relieved when Nusumi finally spoke first.

"He is brave," she said, looking at Itachi, "but I don't think I like him very much."

At least, thought Shiko, one of them had been able to start a conversation. "He can be very difficult. The Guards, though, seem eager to follow him. At least," he amended, thinking of Nakama, "most of them do."

Another period of silence ensued while each considered where to step next. With no mayaku weed to alter their thoughts, each maintained that reserve and self-possession that was their natural tendency. On the ride through the forest, as the immediate danger had lessened, Shiko had become acutely aware of Nusumi seated before him on his horse. The warmth of her body close against his, her hair billowing softly against his face, re-awakened feelings he had yet to master. However, without the effects of the mayaku clouding his mind, he had been able to bring somewhat more order to both emotions and desires. He had sensed the same in Nusumi, who had felt relaxed in his arms as he held the reins around her, but at the same time quietly distant.

Now Nusumi said abruptly, urgently, "Take me on your Hikari pilgrimage!" Before Shiko could answer, she went on in a rush. "I'm nothing in Yutakashi, just a gutter urchin. That's what the candle seller called me, and that's what I am. I have no future there." She pulled on the long grass that carpeted the clearing, twisting it around her fingers. "You're on a pilgrimage, a sacred pilgrimage with a lantern. Your life means something. You're going to go places and do things that I can't even dream about." She paused, looking down at the grass. "Probably be going to another city or two. And if you do," she added quietly, "you'll be hopeless without someone to show you how to keep all your coins in your purse."

Shiko had to stop from simply saying, yes, come, let's go, now; had to resist the urge to forget the pilgrimage and his role in it. Nusumi was unlike anyone he had ever known. He knew that he was experiencing a physical attraction to her, but he set that aside as best he could. There was more to her, a coarseness, a spontaneity, that contrasted with his own personality in an oddly complementary way. She managed to spark feelings in him that he'd never realized were there. And now that they had been unleashed, he found it increasingly difficult to keep them under control.

Even beyond those things, he knew that at her core Nusumi was a person of kindness, and charity. All of the things she did, her thievery in the Market, helping Kanyo and his associates, were for the benefit of others. It was her own fundamental nature that forced him to hold back his tongue on what he wished to say, and to say instead, "And what of Kanyo, and Tanoshi? How will the children get their food, if you are not there to help them?"

Nusumi snapped off the grass stems, and pulled them off her fingers one by one. "I can't be there forever! Tanoshi managed to feed everyone before they took me in; she'd be able to do it again."

"But things are different now, aren't they?" countered Shiko. "Things have been getting worse in Yutakashi; that's why Kanyo is risking himself, and Tanoshi and the children, by aiding a group of revolutionaries. Isn't it?"

"Yes," said Nusumi with irritation. "Yes, you're right." She pulled off the last of the grass stems and tossed them back down on the ground. "They probably need me now more than they did before. But,

I—I want—" Her voice quavered as she stopped, unsure of how to put into words what she did want. She tried to make brushing away a tear appear as if she were pushing back her hair. Only a telltale drop of moisture on the back of her hand gave her away.

Shiko reached over with a finger, and gently wiped the tear off her hand. Then he placed his hand over the back of hers. "I don't know how 'sacred' our pilgrimage is," he said. "All I know is…well, I think that I'm supposed to be here. Each of us has a place where we can best serve those in greater need than ourselves. Mine is with Toshi-hito, searching for the Kotaishi. Yours—" His voice caught, and he had to look away. "Yours is helping Kanyo, Tanoshi, and their children, and everybody else's children in Yutakashi."

Nusumi said nothing; she simply turned her hand over to face his, and their fingers interlaced. They sat that way for a long while, letting their coupled hands communicate what they could not say in words.

At length, as the midmorning sun arced up over the treetops and dappled the camp area with rays of light, Nusumi released Shiko's hand and stood. She walked a few paces away, then looked back over her shoulder with a smile both gentle and sad at the same time. "So…look for me next time you're in town."

Then she turned and walked away, retracing on foot her way back to Yutakashi.

The hours passed while Shiko sat, quiet and still, watching over the still-unconscious Itachi. All throughout that afternoon, and later that evening as he tried to find elusive sleep, he found himself reliving the moments with Nusumi over and over again in his mind.

When morning came at last, after an interminably long night, he looked down at the spot where she had sat next to him the day before. He could still see where she had pulled up the grass, but the stems had all blown away on the wind during the night.

*   *   *

How exhilarating, the fight in the inn's stable! It was just as I remember—the rush of energy, the feeling of invincibility and power! The blade like an extension of one's arm, reaching out and cutting down one's foes as easily as a scythe slashing stalks of kobanya...

And I was there, inside this Itachi's head, as he fought! I could feel his anger, the overwhelming urge to kill that took over his mind. He is good, a true fighter. Nothing clouded his thoughts but the need to extinguish his enemies.

I must try more. I must see if I can 'push' his thoughts, make him do something not of his own volition.

It is almost like being a god...

11

It was late afternoon on the second day when the Kojuro's brother finally stirred. Shiko had started to change the dressings on Itachi's wound when the head of the Castle Guard, struggling to open his eyes, croaked out, "Water!"

Quickly Shiko grabbed one of the water skins that the pilgrims had filled from the nearby stream. Holding Itachi's head up, the Deshi apprentice tried to pour some of the water between the man's parched and cracked lips.

"Where—" started Itachi, then he had to swallow some more water before continuing. "Where are we?" The effort of the few words exhausted him, and he let the weight of his head fall back onto Shiko's supporting hand. The slow-witted Donaku walked up and stood ineffectually behind Shiko, looking over the apprentice's shoulder. Most of the Guards were still keeping watch, out in the woods and well away from the center of the encampment. Only Donaku, who had been laboriously shaving down a tree branch to make a new pole for the Hikari, had remained behind with Shiko.

"Rest yourself, Lord Itachi," said the young Deshi. "You've had a terrible wound, quite deep, Master Toshi-hito said. He and Ryori have gone out looking for local flora; they hope to find something for making additional healing supplies."

As Shiko spoke, he was reminded of the rather enterprising skills demonstrated by the pilgrimage's cook. Beyond the man's facility with foodstuffs, he also possessed a thorough knowledge of healing. Upon realizing the extent of Ryori's knowledge, Toshi-hito had gladly accepted the cook's offer of assistance. Even so, Shiko recalled that while the two of them had tended to the unconscious Itachi the Deshi Master had felt compelled to inquire what had prompted Ryori to saddle the horses back at the House of Bright Light, well before the attack had occurred.

"Hah!" the cook had replied. "Heard enough in the Market while buying food to know we wasn't welcome. Was loading up my horse with supplies anyway, so's I thought to myself, 'Self, better safe than sorry,' so I saddled 'em all up. Just in case." Shiko remembered Toshi-hito's rather doubtful expression, but the Deshi Master had not pressed the point.

For his part, Shiko was certain that the Guards had been too busy at the time to pay much notice to Ryori's actions during the battle at the arch. He suspected, though, that even had any of the Guards observed what the cook had done, they would be disinclined to acknowledge the contributions of a mere servant in the fighting...

Itachi would certainly have been the last to acknowledge it, Shiko reflected, as he tried once more to help the Hajimeshi lord to drink. Most of the water he was pouring into Itachi's mouth spilled out, but enough was swallowed to moisten the general's tongue and allow him to speak.

"Enough, damn you!" sputtered the Hajimeshi general, pushing away the water skin. "I asked you a question. Where are we?" His forehead was wet with sweat, just from the exertion of drinking.

The young Deshi explained to Itachi about their hiding place in the woods, and that Bokusa and the others were standing watch. Itachi nodded then suddenly pulled his head up off of Shiko's hand. "How long?" he asked.

"This is our second day here since leaving Yutakashi, my Lord."

"Two days!" the Hajimeshi lord croaked. He immediately tried to get up, catching Shiko off guard, but with an oath he collapsed back onto the grass as he put weight on his injured side.

Shiko was alarmed. "Lord Itachi, you must lie still! If you try to get up now, your wound may split open again!"

Itachi waved the apprentice off, breathing hard and grimacing with pain. Ignoring the Deshi's remonstrations, he gestured at Donaku. "You! Help me up." When the Guard hesitated, looking at Shiko, Itachi said, "Didn't you hear me, soldier? *Help—me—up!*" Once again he tried to heave himself to his feet.

Needing no second prompting, Donaku shrugged and elbowed his way past Shiko. Placing his arms around Itachi, he just managed to help the man struggle upright. Itachi could not stand on his own, having to lean on Donaku in order to remain erect, but he gestured in the direction of the horses. As the two began a slow shuffle toward the tethered animals, Shiko grabbed up the remainder of Toshi-hito's medicinal herbs and followed. The man's probably still delirious, he told himself. What if he tears his wound open again? Toshi-hito will be extremely displeased...

Once Donaku had maneuvered Itachi to his horse, the Hajimeshi lord fumbled with the straps on one of the large travel packs strapped to the horse's side. He was too weak, however, to let go of Donaku, and could not manipulate the buckles one-handed. He swung his head in Shiko's direction. "Boy! Open this!"

As a Deshi, Shiko was not under Itachi's command, and he might have refused. Yet he was concerned that to do so would prompt further outbursts, which could worsen the condition of Itachi's wound. Reluctantly Shiko set down the healing supplies and undid the straps closing the pack. The Hajimeshi general commanded, "Take out the box."

Reaching into the open pack, the apprentice felt a wooden box. As he touched it, he felt an odd, uncomfortable sensation. He hesitated, but Itachi barked impatiently. "Hurry up!"

Shiko pulled the box out of the pack into the sunlight. It was not quite half-an-arm's length in each dimension, and made of a strangely colored wood. Mostly it was a dark, plain-textured brown, but there were strands of several different lighter woods embedded in the grain, as if it were composed of wood from a variety of trees somehow all melded together. A metal clasp held closed what looked like a lid, but Shiko could see no obvious means for opening the clasp.

"There is a pouch in the bag as well," commented Itachi. "Bring it, and the box." He gestured to Donaku that he wanted to move over toward a clearing, where some clear sky was visible between the treetops. As the two men slowly made their way, Shiko retrieved the additional bundle and followed them.

Something about the box he was carrying felt strange; it set his nerves on edge, although there was nothing visibly amiss about it other than its unusual composition. Somehow, though, it just felt…wrong.

By the time Itachi and Donaku reached the clearing, Itachi was dripping in sweat and breathing hard. He'll kill himself, thought Shiko; only his stubbornness is keeping him moving.

Donaku eased Itachi down to the ground and the Hajimeshi lord, too out of breath to speak, waved wearily to Shiko to bring him the items from his pack. Shiko set the box down on the ground and handed the pouch to Itachi, who unrolled it. Inside were writing implements, and various string ties and other small objects that Shiko could not identify. Breathless from exertion Itachi closed his eyes briefly; then he growled in a low voice, "Both of you…wait by the trees…until I am done." Donaku obediently walked away over toward the trees. Somewhat more hesitantly, Shiko followed. He was worried that Toshi-hito would return and find fault with his apprentice for allowing Itachi to get up too soon. I really should have insisted, he told himself, on Itachi letting me examine his dressings. Instead, he's got me ferrying his supplies around.

The apprentice looked over at Donaku. The Guard, a blank expression on his face, didn't appear worried about anything. He and Shiko had exchanged few words while the Deshi had been watching over

Itachi, and so they had little to say to each other now as they waited for the Hajimeshi lord to complete whatever it was he was trying to do.

Itachi was furious. Two days! All his plans were suddenly falling apart, and here he was, injured, lying in a forest clearing...

He fought back the pain of his injured body, trying to focus on what had to be done now. He had hoped to send back better news, telling his lieutenants that assistance from Yutakashi was on its way, himself not far behind; but he had miscalculated badly. Those fools in Yutakashi! They could have had an ally on the Hajimeshi throne; instead they threw it all away, hoping to take it all for themselves!

Now he had to re-structure his plans, and quickly. He had intended to be on the move toward Hajimeshi by now. The troop movements of the Guards he had started could be covered up for a short time but somebody, like Himitsu, was bound to find out sooner or later. And, he knew, he must be ready to strike once the men were in place; there would be no second chance.

Nevertheless simply turning back wasn't an option now. Those Yutakashi bastards, he thought again. How dare they! Driving me out of their city like a dog. No, taking the men back though Yutakashi lands was not going to work. It might be possible, but it would take too much time if they were to remain undetected, and the Deshi would certainly not go along with it.

He turned and looked at Shiko, standing at the edge of the clearing. Damn those Deshi, he fumed. I should just slit both their throats and be done with it, then make my way back to Hajimeshi as best I can. But that's too risky; even with these men, I can't trust that one of them might not talk.

And then he had the answer.

Shiko, waiting with Donaku nearby, observed that the Hajimeshi lord didn't seem to be doing anything at first; he just sat for a while, evidently thinking. When he looked over at the apprentice, however, the eyes that Shiko saw appeared cold, expressionless. It was at that moment that Itachi seemed to come to some sort of decision. He pulled something out of the pouch, and Shiko realized that the man was writing something but on an absurdly small piece of parchment. Itachi apparently made a mistake, or changed his mind, for he suddenly crumpled up the tiny piece of paper and tossed it aside to blow away on the gentle breeze. He started a new one, and when he finished writing he carefully rolled the fragment of paper onto a small cylinder of metal, tying it on with some string.

Shiko watched, still anxious to retrieve his 'patient' but equally curious about what Itachi was doing. The Hajimeshi general set the strange box down in front of him then touched a finger to the clasp, holding it there for several seconds. Nothing happened at first, but then the box began to move. Startled, Shiko realized that it was not the box moving but the wood that it was made of that was doing the moving. The different woods were shifting, sliding in various directions, their colors dissipating. Finally the movement stopped, and to the astonished Shiko what had appeared to be a box of wood now looked more like glass, its sides a weirdly unnatural, and disturbing, shade of blue.

The Hajimeshi lord removed his finger from the box, and the clasp opened of its own accord. Itachi carefully opened the lid and reached inside with his hand. Shiko gasped as the general slid his arm in deeper, with nothing coming out the other side. It was as if his arm were disappearing inside the box.

Itachi felt around inside the 'cage' with his hand. The birds were still there, of course; they could not escape the magical boundaries that held them captive. Even so, it was always with some trepidation that he reached in, for he did not understand what made the box work, or 'where' it was that he was reaching into. And he didn't trust things he didn't understand.

The cage had been purchased illicitly at great expense, smuggled out of the magic city of Tejinashi by an intrepid Yutakashi entrepreneur some months ago. It was widely known that in Yutakashi, virtually anything could be had, anywhere, if the price was right. Itachi had tested that theory to its limits in acquiring the cage and its occupants. The seller had profited handsomely, although he had sworn he would never attempt such a feat again, no matter what the reward. Deceiving the magicians of Tejinashi might work once; but only a fool would think he could pull off a repeat performance against the Zaitan. The man had returned to his more usual haunts in Yutakashi, making himself scarce until the knowledge of his deed had faded from memory.

The fruits of his excursion lay between Itachi's feet. It was, indeed, a cage, but one which existed, for the most part, in some invisible place. Only the box formed a connection with the 'real' world. What the inside was made of, neither Itachi nor the seller had seen fit to inquire about. It had been enough to receive assurances that, whatever it was, it was 'safe' for both humans and animals.

For it was animals that the cage was designed to hold. Birds specifically, and two special birds at that, which had been part of the 'deal' Itachi had transacted with the Yutakashi merchant. The inside of the cage never ran out of food or water; where it all came from, Itachi did not know. But the birds could not leave from wherever the box held them. They were trapped there, the only way out through the lid of the box. They were thus always within his reach.

The Hajimeshi general quickly grabbed one of the birds, plucking it out of the box and slamming the lid shut. Holding the bird in one hand, with quick movements he affixed the small cylinder to one of the bird's legs. The custom-fitted cylinders snapped on; they had been part of his deal for the birds, along with their 'cage.' Even so, getting it attached was a tricky operation, and one not made any easier by Itachi's current condition. Fortunately for him he had performed the maneuver many times before, and thus was well practiced.

Shiko, watching from nearby, was amazed to see Itachi holding a bird in his hand after the Hajimeshi lord had extracted his arm from the box. As the Hajimeshi general attached the cylinder to one of the bird's legs, the apprentice looked over at Donaku; but the Guard had long since lost interest in whatever his commander was doing and was staring off into the woods.

There was a burst of movement from the clearing as Itachi let go of the bird, which immediately took flight and winged its way to the nearest tree. It perched on a branch and looked back to where the box sat between Itachi's feet.

The Hajimeshi lord opened the lid and reached into the box, pulling out a second bird. He held it up, as if showing it to the bird in the tree, and made a show of slowly putting it back in the box and closing the lid once more. With finality he snapped the clasp shut, and the box changed once again back into its original multi-shaded wooden appearance. Looking back to the bird in the tree, Itachi scowled and waved his arm, as if in a gesture of dismissal.

The bird suddenly emitted a long, cooing cry. More than just the normal singing a bird might make, this had a haunting emotional quality, seeming at once both angry and sad. It hit Shiko forcibly, sounding for all the world like a lament of heart-wrenching despair and frustration. The sound reverberated all the way down into his bones, causing him to shiver.

The bird took flight, circling the clearing three times, emitting the same heart-piercing cry. Then it set off toward the east, back in the direction from which the Hikari pilgrims had come.

Shiko had never seen anything like Itachi's box, or heard a bird that could utter such a plaintive, sorrowful song. Nor did he understand why Itachi had attached the scrap of parchment to the bird, or why he had let it go while keeping the other one. Something about it, however, was unnatural, that much he could plainly tell. The sound of the bird's desperate cry was still with him, even after the bird had long since flown out of sight.

Itachi shouted to Donaku to come help him up. The Guard ran over and assisted his commander to his feet. Shiko, too, went over to see if Itachi's dressings had been dislodged and needed repair, but the Hajimeshi lord knocked Shiko's hands aside when the apprentice tried to examine the bindings.

"Keep your fingers off me, Deshi," he growled. He pointed to the box and the bundle of writing supplies. "Put these things back in my baggage. And," he added, looking at Donaku as well as Shiko, "neither of you speaks of this, to anyone." He stared directly at Shiko. "*Anyone*, Deshi." He motioned for Donaku to help him over to the stream, and the two slowly made their way out of the clearing.

Nusumi was right about him, thought Shiko, watching them shuffle slowly away. Brave, but thoroughly unlikable.

Looking down at the now-quiescent box on the ground, he decided Itachi was more than simply disagreeable, though. Something about the man struck a discordant note. The Yutakashi Blues had clearly thought Itachi to be involved in some sort of conspiracy. Toshi-hito, although he had never expressed it to Shiko, clearly distrusted the Hajimeshi lord. Shiko knew the Master well enough to sense the heightened caution, the carefully worded phrases, whenever Itachi was present. And now this strange episode with a magical box, and the birds. What could the man have possibly been doing?

Shiko's eye caught a flutter of movement in the grass. It was a zako, a small rodent that lived in woodlands. This one seemed to have wandered out into the clearing. Looking closer, Shiko saw that the zako had something in its mouth. The rodent approached hesitantly, a few steps at a time. Shiko remained still, not wanting to startle the little creature; he had never seen one up close, and was as curious about it as the zako apparently was about him. As the rodent came up near the box, it dropped whatever it was that was in its mouth and scurried away, darting among the tall grass until hidden from view.

Intrigued, Shiko knelt down to look closer at what the zako had dropped. He was quite surprised to see the crumpled piece of parchment that Itachi had discarded earlier, and which had fluttered away on the wind.

He glanced over toward Itachi and Donaku, but they were now some distance away, the Guard struggling to help his lord sit down near the stream. Shiko picked up the parchment and started to unfold it, then stopped himself.

Whatever it was, he realized, it was something Itachi had written, and he had always been taught that a person's privacy was not to be violated. Glancing down at the eerie magical box, however, he thought again about the bird that Itachi had forced back inside. The grievous cry of its companion as it had flown away still echoed through his mind. He decided.

Carefully he unfolded the small parchment, smoothing it out over his leg. He had learned several languages at the Deshi priory, but nothing on the scroll paper looked familiar. There were letters, but they appeared odd, and not in any pattern that he could recognize.

Frustrated, he refolded the paper and slipped it into his tunic. He would share it with Toshi-hito when the Master returned; perhaps the elder Deshi would understand the symbols. The Kojuro's brother had, it was true, 'ordered' the Deshi apprentice to remain silent, but Shiko had never actually agreed to Itachi's request. It was, perhaps, a fine line; but it was getting harder these days, Shiko considered, to maintain things in clear black and white patterns. In any event, he felt certain that Toshi-hito, as joint leader of the Hikari pilgrimage, should know about the magic box, and Itachi's strange actions with it.

Shiko picked up the box and walked back over to Itachi's horse. Before he returned it to the travel pack, he held the box up in front of his face in order to get a better look at it. The wood appeared quite solid, with no trace of the fluid movements it had exhibited earlier. With a quick glance over toward the stream, he tried placing his finger over the clasp.

Nothing happened. But he did feel something. Not anything physical, just a sensation at the back of his mind. An image, it was...

With a start, he realized it was an image of Nusumi. How odd, thought Shiko; why should touching the box cause me to think of her? Shaking his head, he replaced the magic box in the pack and re-fastened the buckles.

*   *   *

Mikasama used to love mornings. She would wake up snuggled in her comforters, stretching languorously. Komori would always be waiting just outside the door, a breakfast of warm ryocha already made. After Mikasama had called her caretaker in, the Princess would listen to Nana-san's recap of the previous day's gossip while leisurely enjoying the ryocha in bed.

It seems like some other life, thought Mikasama, a long time ago. Now she was cold, shivering in the bed of the cart where they had pulled off the trail the previous night. The morning had come, but it delivered none of the satisfaction the Princess used to associate with it.

The thin traveling blankets were no comforters, and trail food was no substitute for Komori's ryocha. The only thing the same was that Komori was up before her, bustling about. The Princess could hear her outside the cart, humming to herself. Mikasama rolled over and pulled the blankets over her head. If she could just shut out the sights and sounds of the forest, and the smell of the cart (what, she wondered, had they carried in this thing? It stank!), she would be able to recapture some of that wonderful feeling of long ago mornings.

Almost, she was able to do it. She remembered that Komori would always pick out something from the wardrobe suitable for the day, and help her dress. Then Nana-san would sit behind her and brush her long hair, always telling her how soft and pretty it was. And then they would...

What, thought Mikasama; what did we do? She tried to recall how she had spent her time as the daughter of the Kojuro, but now, thinking back, all the days seemed much the same. She had never done much of anything, she supposed. She had been a court lady, and court ladies had very few things to do.

And now...she sighed, the attempt to flee back to the past unraveling in disjointed memories. Now she was huddled under coarse blankets in a smelly cart, cold, hungry, and far from home. Komori called everything around her stupid, but had never used the word on the princess under her care. Mikasama wondered if it was not, however, the most apt description at the moment.

There had been more of the dreams last night. Some were the same images as before, of being chased by men intent on harm, and of Komori floating away down the river, out of reach. But there had been new ones too. Mikasama remembered standing in front of a wall made entirely of glass, with the sun shining through from the other side, and rays of light flowing past her, behind her...She had turned, and had watched the light passing through a doorway, and it seemed that she had to go through that door, even though it was dark on the other side...

It had been so intense, much more so than the earlier dreams. She could still recall every detail, every color, every feeling...a feeling of having to go on, to walk through that door...

She gripped the blankets still wound tightly around her. Why am I doing this, she asked herself. Why do I keep moving further and further away from Hajimeshi, from Father, from everything that I grew up with? Everything familiar, save Komori, is so many miles behind...so many miles...

"Wake up, Mika!" A sudden pounding on the side of the cart startled her, interrupting her train of thought. "Time for food!"

With a groan, the Princess threw off the blankets and sat up. Frightened and confused from her disturbing dreams, and feeling anything but rested, she climbed down to join Komori for breakfast. Her caretaker had managed to start a small fire using some flints. Mikasama was impressed with her skill, and told her so, but the compliment was brushed aside. "Pahhh. 'Tis an easy trick, just need ta 'know the technique,' as ol' White Beard used to say."

Mikasama remembered that Komori had mentioned that name once before. "Who's White Beard, Nana-san?"

But Komori would not answer her. "Never mind," she said. "T'aint important anyways." She would say no more, and concentrated simply on eating her food. Mikasama pondered again how much she did not know about this woman who had been part of her life since as far back as she could remember.

After eating the warm, if uninspiring breakfast, the two women set off once more. Lumbering down the trail in the cart, Mikasama missed the feel of her fine horse. Sitting on the buckboard, bounced about like an apple in a barrel as the Katanza horses slowly jerked the cart down the path, their progress was uncomfortable as well as excruciatingly slow. Komori, though, clearly was just as happy to see the riding horses gone. She had never come to terms with her mount, and found the comfort of a stable perch (if such a gyrating and pitching platform could be called stable, thought Mikasama) infinitely preferable to riding a 'big stupid animal.'

Mikasama, though, longed for the feeling of freedom the riding horses had given her. When she and Komori had started on their journey, she had felt as if she could ride on the wind. Being on her own horse, away from the boundaries of the Hajimeshi court, had sparked her sense of adventure. Even later, when her rear end had begun to complain about the length of time it had been required to chafe against the saddle, she had not lost her fascination with being out on the road, able to ride where she willed.

Now her backside was still sore, but in a different and far less pleasing way as it bounced against the hard wood of the buckboard. More to the point, she was tied to a slow-moving cart, sharing a small spot at the front with her caretaker. She was still out on her own, still deciding her own destiny. But somehow it had lost its allurement.

The sun had just passed its zenith, beginning its slow downward arc toward the west when Komori turned to Mikasama. "Hey, Mika, know what?"

"What, Nana-san?"

"You stink!" At Mikasama's puzzled look, Komori continued, "I stink too! Been too long on the road in these clothes."

They had emerged from the forest in the late morning to find that the path continued west, not north as they had hoped. Not wanting to backtrack, and fearing that the Hikari party would be too far ahead of them if they did, they had pushed on in the hopes of finding a crossroads. The land here was rocky, forming the foothills of a low mountain chain separating their path from the Northern Road. The trail followed the bank of a small river, and the cool water looked inviting as the two women slowly bounced along beside it in their cart.

Komori was pointing over to the river. "Best we use water now; no tellin' if there be anymore down the road. Pull off here. Let's see 'bout cleanin' up a bit—" She stopped, suddenly erupting into a harsh coughing fit.

Mikasama, alarmed, put her hand on Komori's arm. "Nana-san, are you all right?"

Komori just waved her off, croaking, "Fine, Mika, fine. Just caught bad air, is all." She pointed again to the river while trying to clear her throat, and Mikasama pulled the cart off the trail.

The Princess climbed down while Komori, still coughing, clambered into the back of the cart. Sorting through their packs, the old woman began pulling out clothes and tossing them over the side of the cart down to Mikasama. The Princess, her arms full, finally said, "Nana-san, I can't carry anymore."

Komori's head popped up over the side of the cart, as she held up another article of clothing. Holding her nose, she said, "Puuuhhh! Worst of the bunch," and tossed the offending item down on top of the heap in Mikasama's arms. Which placed it right under her young charge's nose.

"Last one anyway," continued Komori, climbing down off the cart. "Sleepin' back here sure don't help the smell." She looked at the Princess struggling to keep everything in her arms and not drop anything. "What you cryin' 'bout, huh? Wash women back home carry twice that, no complaints."

Speaking around the mound of laundry, Mikasama replied, "Nana-san, I am not a wash woman."

"Well, girl, I ain't neither. But's gotta be done, so let's see about doin' it together." She set off down to the riverbank, carefully followed by the Princess. Mikasama had to walk slowly, since she couldn't see her own feet and had no idea of what she was stepping into. Finally reaching a grassy area along the water's edge, she dumped the pile of clothes on the ground.

The river was about half-a-stone's throw across. Large rocks jutted up out of the water, disturbing the otherwise smooth surface with little whirlpools and miniature rapids. Komori picked up one of the Princess's tunics from the pile and waded out into the shallow portion of the river toward the nearest of the rocks.

Mikasama, watching her walk out into the water, felt a sudden chill despite the warm air. The water cascaded around Komori's ankles, then as she walked in deeper the caretaker lifted up the hem of her tunic. As the water swirled around her knees, it seemed to Mikasama to pull on Komori's legs, and the old woman tottered to regain her balance.

Visions of her dreams suddenly flooded into Mikasama's brain. She saw Komori swept away on a raging torrent, the Princess struggling to swim after her. The water roared in Mikasama's mind as she tried to call out after Komori, but already her caretaker was too far away; swept over the river boulders and out of sight. With an anguished cry Mikasama ran splashing out into the water, shouting, "Nana-san! Nana-san!"

Komori, still standing in the shallow water by the low rocks, turned around to look at Mikasama, puzzled. "What, Mika? What is it? Something wrong?"

And then all Mikasama could see was her caretaker standing in some low water, dirty clothes in hand. The river was quiet, gently flowing around the smooth rocks, a few fallen tree limbs, and the two women who had wandered out into its course. Sheepishly Mikasama called back, "No, Nana-san...it's...it's all right. Sorry."

"Well, good, then grab somethin' and come on over here. Water feels real good." With that she plunged Mikasama's dirty tunic into the water and started rinsing it out. The Princess walked back to pick up some clothes and follow her caretaker once more into the river. Yet the sense of foreboding she had would not go away.

They spent a good part of the afternoon washing out their clothes. Mikasama didn't have the first notion of how to go about it, but Komori, true to her amazing store of skills, dove right in. Dunk an article of clothing in the water, she said; beat it against the top of a rock to force the water through and the dirt (and the smell) out; rinse it off; wring it out. And repeat. Just as Mikasama had gained respect for soldiers who slept out in all weather, she now gained a healthy appreciation for the women who cleaned clothes as their daily lot in life. It was back-breaking, boring work, enlivened in this instance only by Komori's endless chatter.

"...So your Papa's Papa, he lines up his three boys, all inna row. There was Fugawari, rest his silly soul; boy could never keep his mind on nothin'. Probably just turn thirteen." Dunk. "Then there was your Papa, and then that brat Itachi." Smack against rock. "And your Papa's Papa, he says, 'Now boys, which one stole all the chokai fruit pies from kitchen? Write it down on scroll and give it here.'" Rinse, wring. "So they all write somethin' down and hand it to him." Dunk. "He looks at papers, calls in biggest Guard he got, and tells Guard, go thrash each boy, but good." Smack against rock. "But first, he tells 'em, 'Boys, here's why you gonna be beat. Fugawari, you said you weren't in the kitchen. Cook saw you there, so you lied.'" Rinse, wring. "Itachi, you said older brothers both took pies, an' you didn't. The Chamberlain saw you eat pie, so you lied." Dunk. "Kimeru, you said all three of you took pies. You spoke the truth, but," smack against rock, "man's gotta take responsibility for the men under him. Itachi, he be your little brother, so you gotta do right thing by him, and not show bad example." Rinse, wring.

Mikasama, much slower at the steps of clothes washing than Komori, just shook her head. Her caretaker always seemed to know all the funny stories about her father. He had never told her any of these things. She supposed she could see why; he probably didn't want his one and only daughter to know that he had stolen pies from the castle kitchen! She stopped to stretch her tired fingers. "Nana-san, how did you learn all these stories about Papa, anyway?"

"Oh, didn't learn 'em. Was there. Saw it all."

Mikasama looked at her with surprise. "I didn't realize you were in the castle that long ago. I thought Papa brought you in to look after me, when I was born."

Komori didn't answer at first. She twisted a tunic sleeve until all the water ran out. "No, girl, I be there already. Lookin' after somebody else, was all. Tried to, anyway. Hey, you gonna jus' hold that thing in your hand, or you gonna wash it?" as she pointed to the dripping tunic Mikasama held in her hands.

"Sorry," said Mikasama as she starting smacking the tunic against one of the rocks. There was so much about Komori that she really didn't know. She talked a lot about everybody else at court but rarely about herself. 'Nothin' to know 'bout me, just an ol' woman,' she would always say, then she would change the subject.

Mikasama tried to wring out some of the water. As they finished each piece they laid the clothes out on a long dead tree branch that hung low out from the bank, over the water. Mikasama set the tunic out to dry then had to stop and massage her aching hands. As she flexed her fingers to restore their circulation, she thought again about her frightening dreams. Komori's mention of the large Guard that Grand-Papa used on his boys had reminded her of them. The last time, when she was being chased, some of the men were Castle Guards, but it seemed they all had Uncle Itachi's face. She had no idea why, or what it meant. She'd never liked her uncle; he either spoke to her curtly or, more usually, simply ignored her as if she didn't exist. Looking over at Komori, ancient hands wringing out clothes without so much as a pause, she asked, "Nana-san, why is Uncle Itachi so rude? Has he always been that way?"

Komori's face screwed up, and she spat out, "Him. Pahhhh!" Smack against rock. "He be bad news since the day he was born."

"But why? He's always scowling all the time. How could Grand-Mama have had three boys who were all so different?"

"Well, they be not all that different when they little. Holy terrors, all three of 'em. Fugawari, he be the one took Itachi under his wing, taught him how to lie, steal. Your Papa, he do that too for a while, but pretty soon he figure out right from wrong. Fugawari, he never figure it out. Stayed that way his whole life. Poor boy," she said remorsefully. "Couldn't understand why kingdom go all to pot while he played."

In a sudden flash of clairvoyance, Mikasama pictured her father and her two uncles. She saw Itachi, in particular, and something connected subconsciously with her image of him in her dream. She couldn't quite put her finger on it, but the feeling was one of anger, bitterness. Wringing out another tunic, she said, "Uncle Itachi did figure out right from wrong, though, didn't he?"

Komori straightened up and looked at Mikasama. Quietly she said, "Yes, child, he did. And he knows darn well which path he's walkin' on." She bent back to her rinsing. "Your Papa, he knows his brother's mind. Been watchin' him. Your Mama knew it too."

Mikasama stopped her washing. "What do you mean, Nana-san? What did Mama know?" Having never seen her mother, Mikasama was always anxious to know anything about her. Usually nobody would talk about her, with the result that the Princess only knew bits and pieces about her, what she had been like. Nobody would even tell her if her mother were alive or dead. *If Komori had been there before I was born,* thought Mikasama, *she must have known my mother! Why hasn't she told me anything about her?*

But Komori would not answer. Instead, she placed the last of the washed clothes on the tree branch and startled Mikasama by suddenly pulling her tunic off over her head. Standing naked in the stream, Komori turned and said, "Well, c'mon girl, got's to clean that too," pointing at the tunic the Princess had on at that moment.

Instinctively Mikasama looked around to see if anyone was within view, even though they had not seen anyone at all since leaving the Katanza camp. She had never been undressed outdoors before, other than the brief seconds it had taken her to change tunics while they had been on this journey, and that had always been after dark. To stand out here, in the middle of a stream, in broad daylight...

As the Princess hesitated, Komori said, "Oh, don't be silly, Mika. Nobody 'round for miles. Get that off and let's wash it."

Self-consciously, Mikasama pulled off her tunic. Her skin tingled, the warm feel of the sun on her naked skin, along with the cool water still splashing about her legs, unlike any sensation she could recall. She looked at Komori, whose leathery skin showed all the folds and creases of one her age. Mikasama had not seen Komori unclothed since her caretaker had given her baths when she was a little girl. Back then, Mikasama had not paid any attention to how Komori looked. Now, as a young woman, more aware of the smoothness of her own body, she contrasted it with the rough texture presented by Komori's.

Wringing out her tunic, Komori noted Mikasama's attention. "What you lookin' at, hey? Same ol' body I had before." Mikasama guiltily began washing her own tunic, but Komori guessed what was on the Princess's mind. "You wonderin' if that pretty little body o' yours gonna end up a bag of bones, like mine? Huh! Tell you, girl, when I was your age, I had a body make men fall right over, pass straight out." At Mikasama's dubious look, Komori assumed an indignant expression. "Truth, Mika! Had them boys all tied in knots, wonderin' which one was gonna get me." Sensing a lack of belief behind Mikasama's barely suppressed smile, Komori decided that the smile just had to go. So she scooped up a big handful of water and splashed it all over her naked charge.

Mikasama let out a loud screech, leaping back as the water struck her. Komori whooped laughter at the Princess's discomfiture. Standing in the stream, water dripping off her, Mikasama's initial shock turned into a mischievous grin. Well, she thought, it's like that, is it? Two can play at that game!

Still doubled over with laughter, Komori never saw her charge's rapid recovery. Bending down, Mikasama had cupped both of her hands together and sent a wave of water surging over Komori.

Then it was Mikasama's turn to laugh, as Komori's cackles sputtered under the aqueous onslaught. Clothes washing suddenly forgotten, the two women started a vigorous splashing match until each was soaked from head to knee. Neither of them could stop laughing. The sun sparkled off the water drops on their bodies, the one smooth, pale, almost luminescent; the other creased and tanned like fine leather. As the final onslaught, Mikasama dipped her head in the water, soaking her long sable locks. Then she whipped her head up, throwing a massive sheet of water in Komori's direction. The water arched through the air, a rainbow of shimmering light, until it cascaded over Komori's head and shattered into a thousand droplets.

Komori's grey hair lay in sopping tangles as she cried out, "You win, hey! No more!" But her smile froze in place, then left altogether, and an odd look came into her eyes.

Mikasama, initially grinning from ear to ear, saw the subtle change in expression. Her own smile faded. "What is it, Nana-san? What's wrong?"

Komori didn't answer. She started to shiver then, suddenly, was shaken by a massive coughing fit, worse by far than the one she had experienced earlier in the cart. Coughing so violently that she doubled over, she lost her footing. She knelt straight down on the streambed as the Princess ran over to her side.

Mikasama, trying to hold Komori up, shouted, "Nana-san! Nana-san!" but was helpless to stop the hacking that shuddered through her poor old caretaker's body. All she could do was hold Komori as the old woman choked up bile, to be washed away down the river.

Finally the spasms ceased, and Komori leaned like a limp rag against Mikasama, both women heedless of the water coursing around them as if they were no more than rocks placed in the riverbed. Mikasama kept asking Komori if she was all right, holding on to her caretaker tightly. For a long time Komori could not speak, her breath coming in short, raspy, gasps. At last she croaked out, "Cold." Indeed, Mikasama could feel Komori's body shivering intensely in her arms.

"Come on," said Mikasama urgently, "let's get you out of the river." With an effort, she managed to help Komori get to her feet, and the two women slowly waded back to the river's edge. Mikasama eased her caretaker down on the grassy bank, the old woman's shivering unabated despite the hot sun overhead.

Kneeling down, Mikasama brushed the wet grey hair back out of Komori's eyes. "I'm going to get some blankets," she said. "I'll be right back!" Her own nakedness forgotten, she sprinted up the bank to the cart, grabbing every blanket she could find. When she returned to where she had left Komori, the caretaker had curled up into a ball and was hugging her legs to her chest. The sun had already dried out most of Komori's skin as Mikasama knelt down and wrapped blankets around her. The Princess tried to gently straighten Komori out so that the sun-warmed blankets could work on the shivering.

The old woman looked up at Mikasama and squeaked out in a small voice, "Pahhh! Quit fussin', Mika. Just got water down windpipe, s'all." Mikasama had felt Komori's skin, though, while wrapping her up. She was so hot as to nearly burn to the touch.

As her caretaker closed her eyes, Mikasama put her hand on Komori's forehead. It was definitely fever, she realized. At the feel of the Princess' hand, Komori opened her eyes. "Think shoe's on other foot, huh? Gonna take care of me, now? Silly girl." But she didn't object as Mikasama tucked in the blankets more tightly around her.

After a while, the shivering eased, and Komori slept. Her breathing never quite returned to normal, sounding raspy, almost as if she had breathed in water. But Mikasama knew its cause was not from inadvertently downing the river's lifeblood. She recalled the Katanza camp: the old man from the wagon, coughing horribly as he had claimed his food ration; and the little girl, playing with Komori, making funny faces as the two of them had rubbed noses together.

And the little girl's cough.

Mikasama looked down at Komori, laboring to breathe, and desperately tried to keep her fears in check.

12

The sun beat down on Shiko's bare head, and reflected into his eyes from the light-colored rock that lined either side of the narrow canyon.

For the last several hours, the pilgrims had been slowly making their way through the arid, treeless ravine. Only a few scrub bushes poked out from soil so dry it might have come straight from the Sabakushi desert. Large rock outcroppings marched up the steep walls bordering their path: silent sentinels gazing down dispassionately at this intrusion into their midst.

Toshi-hito had not commented to Shiko upon returning to the camp late the day before and finding Itachi up and limping slowly about. Although the Hajimeshi lord had not let Toshi-hito look at his wound either, the Deshi Master had simply shrugged and let the matter pass. Shiko had been desperate to talk to his mentor about what had transpired in the clearing, but Donaku had never been out of earshot. The apprentice knew he would have to bide his time until he could speak unnoticed by Itachi or the slow-thinking Guard.

Despite Itachi's condition, the group had set out shortly after first light. Bokusa had helped Itachi onto his horse, watched with concern by Toshi-hito. Both of the Deshi were astonished at how quickly Itachi was able to recover from his injury; after a further night's rest he had been able to walk unaided and had even started working at drawing his sword. The Guards, however, had taken it in stride as something a soldier was expected to do:

either stand and carry on, or be cut down; there were no alternatives in battle. Even so they had been impressed by Itachi's determination to resume the journey so quickly, despite his obvious weakness and pain. Silently, without any spoken agreement, they had all allowed Itachi to ride to the head of the column to lead them out of the makeshift camp. Ryori, bringing up his usual position at the rear, had consecrated the camp with one of his trademark expectorations.

Itachi and Toshi-hito had agreed that attempting to make their way back to the Northern Road while still in Yutakashi territory would probably lead to their arrest for being involved in a "disturbance," or even worse, result in another confrontation with members of the Blue faction. Since Shukyoshi was, as Toshi-hito had pointed out, the pilgrims' next intended destination, the group had set out due west, away from the mercantile city, and toward the lands of the religious warriors.

Now it was past midday, and the sun beat down unmercifully. Not a breath of wind stirred to relieve damp skin; sweat flowed in rivulets and soaked through clothing. Shiko tried to focus and meditate but found that his mind just would not cooperate when his body was so uncomfortable. He pulled rapidly on the front of his tunic, trying to generate his own breeze. The dust kicked up by the horses stuck to his skin where the sweat had not rolled off, and what didn't stick made him sneeze and itch. He wondered if the canyon would ever end, or if they would have to march on like this for days, single file through a narrow burning cauldron.

Just as he was mulling over such unpleasant thoughts, he noticed Toshi-hito ahead of him straighten in his saddle. Shiko listened but heard nothing, only the sounds of creaking harnesses and tired men. He dug down a little deeper, forcing his mind to concentrate; and to move out beyond his own weary body, beyond the trudging horses, and down the canyon ahead of them.

It was hard, but finally he sensed something. Up ahead, where the gorge twisted about—yes, he could feel it! There was water! And it was moving—not just a well, then, or a pond. It was a river.

Exhausted by the effort, Shiko's mind snapped back to his fatigued frame. Soon, he told himself; soon, we will all be able to take a break.

When at last the Hikari group reached the end of the gorge, a light breeze swept up the canyon, heralding their arrival at the river. Sighs of relief were heard up and down the line. The men knew that soon they would be able to escape from the warm, clinging air that surrounded them.

Toshi-hito saw that the canyon's mouth widened where it sloped down into the river, indicating that the ravine must once have been a tributary of the river but had long since dried up. Out in the river itself a few large rocks shouldered their way up into the sunlight, the water flowing smoothly around them. Good, he thought; the water is not too deep. We should be able to ford here without too much difficulty.

He saw that Itachi, though, was still sitting atop his horse at the river's edge, staring across to the far bank. There was nothing on the other side save a few trees, which stood watch over low rolling hills covered with wild grass. Most odd, he pondered. Why does Itachi not start across? It was as if the man were waiting for something, or someone…

At that instant a shrill cry echoed down from above them. Toshi-hito looked up and saw a hawk, circling high above the canyon. A few of the Guards looked up as well but most were focused on Itachi, waiting for his signal to begin crossing the river.

Something was wrong, Toshi-hito realized. The bird was far away, but it was trying to warn him. About what?

He turned his horse around, facing back down the canyon. Shiko was close by, one of the Guards beside him. Bokusa was moving up toward Itachi, who had finally begun walking his horse down to the river.

The hawk dropped straight down, right into the gorge's opening, with an ear-splitting screech that tore right through Toshi-hito: *Act, now! No time!*

Quickly Toshi-hito kicked his horse with both heels, charging straight at Shiko. The apprentice sat open mouthed as the Deshi Master rode toward him at full speed and was totally unprepared as Toshi-hito's hand came up and planted itself solidly against Shiko's chest. The apprentice's upper body was knocked backwards flat onto his horse's rear quarters, only his feet in the stirrups keeping him from being thrown completely to the ground.

A split second later an arrow sliced through the air that Shiko had occupied before being knocked asunder and buried itself in the side of the Guard next to the apprentice. The man screamed in pain and fell from his horse. The sudden movement spooked both his and Shiko's mounts, and they bolted.

The rest of the Hikari group had little time to react as the air all around them was suddenly filled with arrows. In the space where Toshi-hito had been immediately before spurring his horse, two more arrows rent the air. One impacted into the loose dirt with a slight *whump*; the other, let fly perhaps by someone with quicker reflexes, managed to nick Toshi-hito's tunic just as the Deshi had begun to move.

Several horses reared up in fright as men yelled and swords were drawn. Other arrows rained down on the group, but by some miracle no one else was hit. Toshi-hito's charge caused him to barrel through most of the line of pilgrims but he managed to pull up by the time he reached Ryori. The little cook's demeanor had once again shifted from bantering servant to something more akin to a soldier, as he squinted up the cliff side and pointed, yelling, "There!" A shaft swished out from the canyon bottom as Nakama, directly in front of Ryori, let fly at the small movement high up the canyon wall. They were rewarded with a cry of pain as a figure toppled out from behind a large boulder with Nakama's arrow deep in his chest. The man's body rolled down the steep cliff as Ryori and Nakama searched for more targets.

At the head of the column Itachi spun his horse, splashing in the shallow reaches of the river. By the time he had turned around, the rider-less horse of the Guard hit by the first arrow had entered the river. In a panic the horse surged across to the far bank. Right behind was Shiko's horse, the Deshi apprentice desperately struggling to pull himself forward and re-grab the reins before he could be thrown off. But he was repeatedly tossed back against the horse's rump and then pitched forward again as the horse lurched about. Reaching the river's edge his mount continued on after its compatriot and forded the current, the mass of its body creating a wave of water that drenched Itachi just as he was heading back to shore. The sudden slowing as Shiko's horse began swimming through the river allowed the apprentice to pull himself up, but as the horse lunged forward he could do little more than hold on.

Back in the ravine Bokusa was organizing the Guards. As the attackers withdrew up the cliff Nakama winged one more man, who nevertheless managed to keep climbing out of the canyon along with his fellows. The other archer, Hisoka, who had been near the head of the column had now ridden back, bow in hand; but by the time he arrived the attackers had climbed up out of range. Just as Bokusa was detailing four of the Guards to go up after them, Itachi arrived, dripping, on the scene. The Hajimeshi lord yelled out, "Wait!" The Guards had already dismounted and were preparing to scale the cliff, but now turned around in confusion at Itachi's shout.

"They have gone!" Itachi called out. "All we accomplish by pursuing them is to divide our forces, making it easier for them to take us down. Re-mount, all of you!"

Perplexed, the men hastily returned to their horses. Itachi turned to Bokusa. "Get everyone across the river, quickly. We don't know if they might return." Bokusa, never one to question his leader's orders, nodded and directed the Guards toward the river and out of the canyon.

Toshi-hito, once he had slowed his horse, had turned and ridden back toward the canyon's mouth, looking for Shiko. Gazing across the expanse of the river he saw that Shiko's horse was just emerging atop the far bank, the young man still gripping the horse's mane tightly. Judging the apprentice to be safe for the moment, the Deshi Master dismounted to examine the fallen Guard, struck by the arrow that had been meant for Shiko.

His examination did not take long. Itachi, riding back toward the river, stopped next to them. Toshi-hito remarked somberly, "He is dead, Lord Itachi."

"Pity," said the Hajimeshi general. "We are down to seven Guards, then." He looked toward the back of the column, where Nakama and Ryori had dismounted to look at the fallen attacker from the cliff above. "You two!" he shouted. "Didn't you hear my orders? Get across the river, now!"

"Lord Itachi," called Nakama, pointing down at the dead man. "Ryori says this man is wearing clothes much like those of the bandits we encountered in the forest, before we reached Yutakashi. I believe we should search him further; if he is from the same group, then it could well be that their bribe did not last very long."

"I don't care what you believe!" yelled Itachi. "All bandits look alike. I will not lose more men to be shot down in a ravine because you think you have an idea! Now remount and get across the river, before I put an arrow in you myself!" He spun his horse about and trotted swiftly back to the river's edge. Nakama and Ryori looked at each other, and with a shrug Nakama returned to his mount to follow Itachi. Ryori glanced once more at the attacker's corpse before walking his mule up to where Toshi-hito was settling himself back atop his horse.

The Deshi, looking down at the fallen Guard, remarked sadly, "Most unfortunate, Master Ryori."

"Hah!" answered the little cook as he swung his short legs up over his saddle, still encumbered with various kitchen utensils. He looked over his shoulder back down the canyon. "Pretty poor for bandits who're supposed to make their living off of killing others. Fellas shootin' at you and the boy were pretty good shots; they only missed 'cause you moved so quick. The others, they didn't seem like they could hit a thing." He gestured toward the shafts that lay on the ground or embedded in the dirt. "There was a Guard right in front of you, holdin' a great big lantern. Seems to me like that'd be a pretty good target, don't you think? Not a scratch, though." He turned and looked over at the Deshi Master. "Watch your back, were I you." Then he prompted his mule down and into the river.

Toshi-hito watched him go, before turning to look again at the body of the fallen Guard. The arrow that had felled him pointed up toward the cliff like an accusing finger. This one, too, thought Toshi-hito, is to be left behind unburied, like the two in Yutakashi. But unlike the fight at the inn, here there seems little likelihood of further attack, despite Itachi's fears.

The Deshi Master looked up to the sky, where the hawk still circled above. It is fortunate, he concluded, that I have friends to help me watch my back.

Shiko's horse had exhausted itself by the time it had crossed the river, and it had come to a stop of its own accord once upon dry ground. When Shiko had finally slid off, shaking, he had nearly fallen down as his knees threatened to give out.

By that time the fighting had already stopped across the river. Shiko had seen the Guards milling about, but at first there had been no sign of Toshi-hito. He had hoped that the Deshi Master was all right, that he was simply further back up the canyon. Unarmed, there was little Shiko could have done if he had returned to the far bank, other than to get in the way. That was even supposing he could have convinced his horse to go back.

Now the Guards were beginning to cross the river. Of the attackers Shiko could see nothing; they were long gone. Just as the first of the men began splashing ashore, Shiko saw the familiar form of Toshi-hito waving to him from the far side of the river. The apprentice waved back, then turned to ask the arriving men what had happened.

The Guards, however, were reluctant to talk about their abortive fight. One man complained about having lost one of their number in a cowardly ambush as opposed to an honorable fight. But when he wondered out loud why their leader had pulled them back from pursuit, he was quickly told to keep his mouth shut by Bokusa. Thus the Guards, wet, irritable and close-mouthed, sat atop their horses until Itachi finally arrived from the other side of the river.

"All right, all of you dismount and rest," he said sharply. "I want you all ready to fight, and not falling asleep in the saddle as you obviously were back there in the canyon." With a grunt of pain he lowered himself to the ground, tossing his reins to Bokusa.

As the Guards sullenly tied up their mounts, Toshi-hito and Ryori finally sloshed their way up the bank and out of the river. After tying up his own horse Toshi-hito immediately went over to Shiko and bowed to the surprised apprentice. "My apologies," he said, "for striking you. It was…necessary."

Embarrassed, looking around to see if the Guards had noticed, Shiko gave a quick bow in return. "Please, Master, no apologies are required. You saved my life." He reached up and felt for his honsho, which had left a mark were Toshi-hito had hit him. "Better a bruise than an arrowhead. But how did—"

Toshi-hito held up his hand. "How did I know? I will tell you, soon. But now is not the time," he said quietly, eyeing the Guards lying about nearby.

With a loud groan, Ryori perched himself on a rock overlooking the river, near where Nakama sat apart from the other Guards. Gazing back across the water at the canyon opposite, now deserted save for dead men, the cook said offhandedly, "Good shot with that bow."

Nakama had grown used to having Ryori around as a result of their usual positions at the tail end of the column. Most of the time the cook had an extended conversation with himself, commenting acerbically on one topic or another while Nakama lent a polite ear and scant attention. As a result, their actual talks had been few and far between. Which suited Nakama just fine; he would as soon have been left alone to his own brooding thoughts. He answered Ryori's statement with a succinct "Thanks."

Ryori, however, was not to be denied a conversation. "Kinda strange, a fella like you, just a ranker like these other dullards." When this did not elicit a reaction, he persisted. "Would've seen you more the officer type. Gotta smart head, quick witted; good archer. So why—"

"*Yes*, Ryori, I used to be an officer," interrupted Nakama. "That was then. Today is a different day."

There was a pause, which Ryori finally filled with "Oh?"

Nakama sighed quietly. He looked out across the gently flowing river. "I ran afoul of Lord Itachi. And nearly brought shame upon a woman of far greater dignity than myself." He picked up a stone and threw it into the river, where with a small splash it quickly dropped out of sight. "Serving as a common soldier is little enough censure for the damage I might have caused to such a lady."

"I see," nodded Ryori, who asked no more questions. He simply watched, in silence, as the river coursed by. Nakama briefly wondered why the little cook cared so much about his past, but decided that the man was just an insatiable gossip. He picked up another stone and skipped it across the river, getting it a little closer to the far bank this time before it dropped from view beneath the water.

After a brief consultation, Itachi and Toshi-hito determined that if the pilgrims followed the river south they would re-join the Northern Road by late afternoon, and thus be able to continue on to Shukyoshi. As the river, in fact, defined the border between Yutakashi and Shukyoshi lands, technically they were already visitors to the kingdom of the religious warriors. Given that the river crossing from Yutakashi had been eventful, to say the least, everyone was alert and watching for potential trouble.

The Shukyoshi had long professed nothing but fierce enmity for what they considered the 'unclean' peoples beyond their borders. Only the citizens of Yutakashi had been unconcerned about the heated religious rhetoric, as a thriving black market exchange existed between the two kingdoms. For those willing to undertake it, the underground trade provided a much higher margin of profit than any 'normal' trade relations would have allowed.

However, with the recent rise to power of the militant warrior priests, Shukyoshi's enmity had turned to persecution, making even the black market a problematic venture. To the new breed of Shukyoshi religious leaders, there was no room for tolerance among the fundamental tenants of their canon. Upon gaining power, they had unleashed a wave of religious ferocity that had swept the kingdom 'clean' of unbelievers, as the leaders had attempted to 'purify' their homeland. Most particularly, the Deshi were considered heretics, spreading blasphemy about false knowledge. As a result there were no Deshi, nor Deshi priories, in Shukyoshi.

All of which was well known to Toshi-hito, having had experience in the past with the zealously devout Shukyoshi. For Shiko, however, it had all been theoretical, cloaked in scroll-bound stories that had been a part of his studies. Until now, riding next to the Deshi Master on the Shukyoshi side of the border...

The group was riding, two by two, along a raised bank edging the river. They had seen no one since their crossing but Itachi was taking no chances and had dispatched scouts out ahead of their group, watching for signs of any Shukyoshi. Toshi-hito, sensing his apprentice's apprehension, said quietly, "You are worried about our reception among the Shukyoshi."

Shiko turned to looked at his mentor, his brow furrowed. "I can't say that the things I have read of them seem very positive, Master."

Toshi-hito nodded. "I am certainly under no illusion that we will be welcome in the kingdom of the warrior priests. It had, however, been my intention that we should arrive at the border while on the Northern Road, as proper pilgrims, and from there seek a formal audience with the Anasaki. You recall the role of the Anasaki?" he asked, knowing that Shiko would have the answer close to hand.

And indeed Shiko answered immediately: "The Anasaki is the ruler of Shukyoshi, both their military leader and their supreme religious authority. He interprets the word of their Goddess."

Toshi-hito smiled inwardly. He suspected Shiko had been reviewing in his head every single thing he had ever been taught about the Shukyoshi. Which, he surmised, was a wise thing to do, for an informed man was better prepared to handle unforeseen eventualities. Like this one..."Yes," he replied, "and that makes him a dangerous combination, particularly when either a powerful or highly orthodox individual occupies the position. Of which the current Anasaki is both." He gestured ahead, to where Donaku carried the lantern. "My hope was that the Anasaki would acknowledge the tradition of the Hikari and, despite his religious views, permit us entry into his lands, if only to allow us to deliver our message regarding the Kotaishi. But our task has been made that much harder for having entered Shukyoshi territory through a 'back door,' as it were, however unintentional; it makes a receptive contact much more unlikely."

The late afternoon sun glinted on the surface of the nearby river, and Toshi-hito could see kamura fish pushing their way against the current, pacing the pilgrims. A brief splash and their heads popped up, breaking the surface, before they dove back down out of sight. To most people it was a mystery why they felt compelled to struggle up river when it would have been so much easier to glide along with the current. But Toshi-hito knew that for the kamura the struggle was their way of life, and they knew no other way. Their destiny lay up stream, not down, and thus they swam against the flow. Like our own journey, he reflected; there was no way for it to succeed except to confront the difficulties head on, and to hope that all concerned were stronger than the river...

Shiko interrupted Toshi-hito's reverie. "Master, even if we are able to see the Anasaki, do you think that he will listen to us?"

Toshi-hito pursed his lips. "I do not expect that we will meet with any greater success with the Anasaki than we had with the Grand Council in Yutakashi. The Shukyoshi are rigidly orthodox and communally minded; it would be highly improbable that there exists here a rebellious underground willing to spread the word, such as existed in Yutakashi. Nevertheless, it is essential that we at least attempt to deliver our message." He did not elaborate further, but his apprentice nodded his acceptance of Toshi-hito's explanation and asked no more questions. They rode on in silence alongside the river and their kamura fish companions.

Toshi-hito knew that Shiko trusted his judgment as to what was required for the pilgrimage. Such honest faith, he mused; it is not something to make use of lightly. I hope, for all our sakes, that it has not been misplaced…

Almost without forethought the group had been riding closer together, forming a tighter circle around Donaku carrying the Hikari. Toshi-hito concluded that its light, and the ancient tradition that it represented, might be the only protection they would have. What will come, will come, he reminded himself. If we cannot even trust ourselves to our neighbors, then the Darkness will have already won.

After several hours of riding, the trees grew thicker as the group entered a small forest. Bokusa spotted a herder's track through the woods, and the group strung out single file as it made its way through the trees. Although the path stayed near the riverbank, the ground rose up, leaving a steep drop down to the water.

The sun was low in the sky when the group entered a small clearing, where Itachi called a halt. After conferring with Bokusa the Hajimeshi general decided that camping here rather than near the main road would be preferable until the tone of their welcome, or otherwise, could be assessed. It was while the group was pitching camp, and Shiko was removing his travel packs from his horse, that the Deshi apprentice felt an odd sensation; something familiar, but not anything he could immediately remember. He resumed his unloading, but the feeling would not go away.

He looked about. Bokusa was detailing soldiers for sentry duty; Toshi-hito was talking with Itachi; Ryori was preparing a cooking ring. Nothing unusual seemed to be happening. Then, very softly, came a sound. It was so quiet that he doubted anyone else could have heard it.

But it was not a sound he was likely to forget. The last time he had heard it, it had been as an anguished cry from a bird separated from its companion. Now, it was the same tone, but uttered softly, almost an imitation of the former sound. He looked up at the trees surrounding the clearing, scanning the branches. Then he saw it.

The bird was perched high up, near the crown of one of the trees. All Shiko could see from this distance was a small patch of white, but somehow he felt that this was the same bird whose plaintive cry had echoed throughout that clearing in the Yutakashi forest, and which had lodged deep inside his soul. Once his eyes had alighted on it the bird took wing and flew off, away from the clearing and deeper into the forest.

Shiko looked around once more, and decided he would not be missed for a few moments. He walked out of the clearing in the direction the bird had gone and quickly found himself in dense underbrush. He pushed on until the sounds of the camp behind him were lost, all the while looking at the trees overhead for some sign of the bird. He shoved at a large bush, and its branches snapped back and scratched his face. This is silly, he thought. My imagination is running away with me. How could it have been the same bird? We are many, many miles from where it had flown away.

Just as he was about to give up and turn back, Shiko heard it again: the same, low call. He stopped and looked up. There! On a tree limb not ten feet over his head. It *was* the same bird, he realized.

The apprentice stood and watched the bird, which seemed to be looking back at him. Not knowing why, he decided to try and extend his mind, using his Deshi meditation training. He focused his concentration on the bird, which gently fluttered its wings. He felt something—something there—

Abruptly a hand gripped tightly down on his shoulder, nearly knocking him to the ground. The hand spun him around, the fingers digging hard into his shoulder. Shiko gasped as Itachi planted his face inches from Shiko's own.

"What are you doing out here in the woods, Deshi? Trying to get yourself killed?"

Shiko stammered back, "N-no, I was—I was—looking for a place to relieve myself, that's all."

Itachi continued to stare into Shiko's eyes, but relaxed his grip slightly. "What, are Deshi so prudish they cannot shit in front of other men?" Shiko did not answer, and Itachi released the apprentice with a slight shove. "Get back to the camp. Or would you prefer that Bokusa enlist you for sentry duty?"

"No, my Lord," said Shiko, as he hurriedly started back toward the clearing. Although his knees shook, he noted that Itachi did not follow but stayed behind where he had found Shiko. And the bird.

Itachi watched the apprentice go. He was still in pain from his wound, but able to walk and ride unaided. Tomorrow he would start exercising with Bokusa, finding ways to draw steel and fight while working around the injury. So angry was he, however, over the botched ambush at the gorge that he wished he could draw his blade right now and finish the job himself. Those fools, he thought; they hadn't even been able to take down two unarmed men! Instead he had lost one of his own, and he was still saddled with the two Deshi...

He despised having to rely on such brigand trash in place of professionally trained soldiers. Soon, though, he would be able to dispense with their 'services.' Once he had placed himself at the head of Hajimeshi his first order of business would be to squash Yutakashi like a rotten fruit. Then he would take his troops, sweep the brigands out of the forest, and hunt them down like the wild animals they were.

Turning back to the bird, which had remained in the tree above, Itachi raised his hand. The bird did not move, and Itachi clenched his fist and waved it insistently. Obstinately the bird still would not fly down. The Hajimeshi lord pulled out something from a burlap sack that he had carried into the woods with him: the small box that was the 'cage'. Raising the box, he shook it violently in the direction of the tree.

Now, he thought, you had better get your scrawny little neck down here, and quickly.

The tree-bound bird immediately fluttered its way down to a low branch close to Itachi's head. The Hajimeshi lord placed the box on the ground and grabbed the now-acquiescent bird from its perch, snatching the small cylinder off the bird's leg. With a grunt he knelt on the ground by the box, using the clasp as before to change the box into its strange blue form. Opening the top he roughly shoved the bird inside before slamming the lid closed once more. He could hear the two birds beginning a soft, cooing song. Impatiently Itachi pushed the clasp shut, and the sound died away as the box changed back into its wooden appearance.

He removed the small parchment scrap from the cylinder. Reading the code symbols, his face darkened. The first part of the message acknowledged his request for the ambush and assured him the bandits would strike as planned (hah!). But it was the second part that caught his attention.

His confederates within Hajimeshi had reported that Princess Mikasama was missing, and was presumed to be chasing after the Hikari group. The Kojuro had sent out every available man to search for her, to no avail. The rest of the message simply said that Itachi's troops would be kept out on maneuvers as long as possible, awaiting his return.

Itachi crumpled up the piece of paper and tossed it away. He didn't want all of Hajimeshi's soldiers out in the countryside; some of them might stumble upon his secret cache of weapons and supplies, or worse yet get into a premature fight with the loyal Castle Guard troops he had stationed in the forests. Stupid girl, he thought. She's as half-witted as that brother of mine. Well, if they haven't found her by now, she's probably already dead. Outside the safe walls of the castle, a young girl on her own would be easy prey. For animals or humans.

And then he had an idea.

Mikasama must be dead, he realized, or soon would be. With her out of the way, Kimeru truly had no hope of an heir. But the fool wouldn't conveniently roll over and die tomorrow, leaving the kingdom to his brother. In fact Itachi wouldn't put it past his brother's minions like

Himitsu to see that the Kojuro's younger brother met with some unfortunate 'accident' before Kimeru passed on to the next world.

But what if Itachi could lay a greater claim on Hajimeshi than Kimeru himself? Something that his brother had already decreed would be "the future of their kingdom?"

His mind started racing. The Kotaishi, he thought. *I need to become the Kotaishi! Then Hajimeshi will fall to my feet, without a drop of blood! Not that blood matters but the more soldiers I can keep in one piece, the easier it will be to deal with the likes of Yutakashi, and irritants like forest brigands.*

Yes, he mused, warming up to his plan. *I'll use my brother's own stupid fantasies about a supposed mythical leader to work against him! The Deshi; they will somehow have to be convinced, or forced, to acknowledge me as the Kotaishi. That will be the key; they have to come back with me, showing the others that not only was the Kotaishi found but that he had been right amongst them all along. That could make all the difference. But how to make that happen?*

He puzzled over how to 'turn' the two Deshi, but could reach no firm conclusions. He realized, however, that he needed to keep the two Deshi with him, alive, until he figured it out. Perversely glad now that the brigands had failed in their task, he picked up the birds in their 'cage' and started back to the clearing. His mind was busy devising the plans he would send back to his lieutenants; they would need to begin laying the groundwork in Hajimeshi for the miraculous 'discovery' of the Kotaishi.

              *   *   *

Yes! How easy! All it took was the merest suggestion and now this Itachi thinks he has brilliantly solved his problem. He has no idea that I planted that seed, that he should simply proclaim himself this Kotaishi, and return in triumph to Hajimeshi. So simple, but he could not see it...

I know what he will do when he returns there—the blood will run in rivers! Brother against brother, such always makes for the fiercest battles...when it is done, Hajimeshi will be weak, and easy prey for—
Yes? You are back. I—
What? No, I—wait, wait! I'm sorry, I didn't mean to interfere, I only—
Arrrrrrgh! Ahgggghhhhhhhhhhhhhhhh..............

Such pain. I have never felt...such pain before. Even when the lance struck me...
It has left again. It was angry, enraged that I had interfered with those above. It had told me to watch, not to intervene. But I was only trying to help! I saw the chance to escalate the tensions above, to weaken it's enemies...
It wants to find out who this Kotaishi is that they seek; it wants to destroy him. It fears that my 'meddling' has jeopardized its learning who the true Kotaishi is. So it punished me, so that I would not forget my place...
No, I will not forget my place. My place is as a slave to that thing! I have no body, I cannot walk away...I am a prisoner here, in the dark...
So I must watch...for now...

✱　　　✱　　　✱

When Shiko returned to the camp he found that Donaku had been sent off on sentry duty. With Itachi still gone, Shiko realized that this might be his only chance to talk to Toshi-hito about what had happened back in the clearing in Yutakashi. The Deshi Master was sitting with his back against a tree, meditating with eyes closed. Shiko walked over and sat down next to him.

"Yes, Shiko, what is it?" asked Toshi-hito, still with his eyes closed. His awareness was such that he had known precisely who had sat by him, and that his apprentice was eager to tell him something.

Shiko, trying to appear nonchalant, also assumed a meditation position. Quietly, so that his voice only carried as far as Toshi-hito beside him, he recounted everything that had happened at the Yutakashi clearing and his most recent encounter with the bird just beyond their present camp.

Toshi-hito did not speak until Shiko had finished. Then he asked about the message that Shiko had retrieved. The apprentice described the lettering, to which Toshi-hito commented softly, "I will examine it later. Tell me more about the birds."

Shiko tried to describe them in some detail, particularly the piercing cry that had seemed to stay with him. Toshi-hito nodded his head and frowned. To Shiko, it was clear that the Master was upset, although most others would not have noticed.

"Shiko," said Toshi-hito, "I believe Itachi has corrupted for his own ends that which does not belong to him. I do not know how he has managed this but it is a dangerous precedent. I must know what the birds know." Which, to Shiko, seemed an odd thing to say, but he knew better than to question the Master when he had set his mind to something. So he listened carefully to the instructions Toshi-hito now gave him.

Not quite an hour after Itachi had returned to the camp with his small burlap bundle and returned it to his travel pack, Shiko screwed up his courage and walked up to Bokusa. The big man scowled as Shiko approached him.

The apprentice said, "If—if you think it would be helpful, I will walk the horses down to the river to drink."

Bokusa just stared at Shiko, then over at Itachi, who was sleeping on the ground across the clearing. The other men were all out in the woods, watching for brigands or Shukyoshi. Shiko could almost see the thoughts churning slowly through the man's mind as he tried to decide what to do. With a sneer he finally said, "Go ahead." As the apprentice turned away toward the tethered mounts Bokusa couldn't resist adding, "And make sure you bring 'em all back. I'm real good at breaking bones without leavin' a mark." Shiko didn't look back; he simply nodded and carried on.

After roping the horses together he walked them out of the clearing and gingerly down the bank toward the river. It was tricky footing, and it was only due to their being tied together that the reluctant horses kept moving. Once they had cleared the trees the way became easier, as Shiko found a fairly even slope down to the water's edge, out of sight of their camp. As the horses walked out and dipped their heads in the shallow water by the bank, Toshi-hito silently appeared, having slipped out of the clearing to 'relieve himself,' or so he had told Bokusa.

Quickly the Deshi Master walked over to Itachi's horse and flipped open the travel pack containing the box. Pulling it out, he placed his fingers against the clasp, and to Shiko's utter astonishment the box transformed itself, just as it had with Itachi.

"Master!" began Shiko. "How—"

Toshi-hito held up his free hand. "In time, Shiko, I will explain. But time now is short. I must use it wisely." He lifted the lid to the box, staring down into whatever was inside.

Shiko could hear the birds begin a furious exchange. Even though their way was now clear to escape, they seemed to be making no effort to fly out from wherever they were. Toshi-hito stared down at them intently, almost, thought Shiko, as if he were listening to a conversation. Finally, the Deshi Master nodded his head and closed the lid, allowing the box to revert to its wooden state and returning it to Itachi's pack.

"It is as I feared," he said to Shiko. "These are chodaka birds. They are very rare. They live in pairs, one male and one female. They are inseparable, and have the ability to find each other no matter how much distance there is between them. I have heard of one locating its mate from over 400 leagues away." He shook his head sadly. "Itachi has found a way to use them as messenger birds. He is keeping them prisoner in a magical cage, which he must have obtained in some fashion from Tejinashi. I can only speculate on how Itachi came to possess it. It would seem he is keeping the female captive and using the male to send notes back to his associates in Hajimeshi. May I see the note that you retrieved from the camp in Yutakashi?"

Shiko fished out the scrap of paper and handed it to Toshi-hito. The Deshi Master studied it for a moment then said, "It is as you described. This language is not familiar to me either. I believe it is some sort of code that Itachi is using to keep his communications from falling into the wrong hands."

"But Master," asked Shiko, "why is Lord Itachi sending secret messages back to Hajimeshi?"

Toshi-hito looked at his apprentice gravely. "I do not wish to speak without proof. I will only say that the Kojuro has expressed...concerns...about his brother's intentions. Itachi's behavior on this journey has, unfortunately, tended to confirm those suspicions."

Shiko pondered this information slowly. "You believe Itachi to be plotting against the Kojuro?"

"I have not said what I believe. But I am of the opinion that Itachi's behavior bears close watching."

Shiko began rounding up the horses to return them to the camp. "Nusumi said that the Blues believed Itachi was meeting secretly with the Reds. Do you think he really was?"

Toshi-hito looked out thoughtfully across the river before answering. "After you left for the market with Nusumi, Kanyo and I discussed the situation in Yutakashi. I knew of Kanyo's involvement with the underground movement in their city. It was one of the reasons I went to visit with them; I hoped that his people would circulate knowledge about our quest for the Kotaishi. I am sure Kanyo's associates are reliable, and would be well informed of what the Red and Blue factions are doing. Thus I think it entirely possible that Itachi was, indeed, in secret discussions with the Red faction of the city. So Nusumi's tale rang true when she appeared at our inn that night."

"But why? From the things he's said, I would think that Itachi would want as little as possible to do with the Yutakashi."

"Who can know what thoughts course through our Lord Itachi's mind? Desire can sometimes make odd companions."

"What will you do, then?" asked Shiko.

"I don't know," said Toshi-hito simply. At his apprentice's shocked expression, he went on. "One cannot plan for every contingency, Shiko. There are too many influences that can affect one's course, as has happened to us now." He gestured toward the river. "It is far better to learn how to navigate the stream than to expend all your energy trying to divert its flow to your will. However," he added, changing the subject, "on another matter of interest, I believe I know at least some of what was in the most recent message that Lord Itachi received via the chodaka birds."

Puzzled, Shiko looked back to the travel pack on Itachi's horse containing the box. "But how is that possible, Master?"

Toshi-hito put his hand on Shiko's shoulder. "There are things that I must teach you, but they will take some time. For now, trust that what I tell you is true." Helping Shiko line up the last of the horses before they started back up the steep bank, he continued, "It would appear that Princess Mikasama has run away from Hajimeshi. It is rumored that she is trying to catch up with us."

Shiko's curiosity about how Toshi-hito could know what message the bird had carried was interrupted by this revelation. The Princess—he remembered he had seen her the night before they left Hajimeshi, in the stables. It occurred to him that she must have been making preparations to flee even then. He related this encounter to Toshi-hito, who said, "Interesting. And who was this man asking after the Princess?"

"I don't know, Master. I had not seen him before." As he led the horses back up to the clearing, he said over his shoulder, "If the Princess is trying to follow us, should we not turn back and try to find her?"

Toshi-hito's voice was tinged with remorse. "She has chosen her own path. Now she must walk upon it." Just before they reached the encampment, Toshi-hito casually asked, "When you saw the chodaka bird, Shiko, and heard its cry, did you...feel anything?"

Shiko tilted his head. "Now that you mention it, I did feel a little strange. For some reason it kept reminding me of Nusumi." Behind him, Toshi-hito silently nodded, as the two of them brought the horses back into the makeshift camp to be welcomed by the smell of Ryori's cooking.

* * *

"Just a little while longer, Nana-san; I can see the top of the hill now." Mikasama urged the horses along as they struggled up the hill, hauling the cart carrying her and Komori. The old woman leaned against her young charge, her customary petulance absent. Whatever was the illness that she had contracted, her usual ebullience had been an early casualty. Mikasama worried as she felt Komori's overly hot skin pressed against hers as they were jostled in the cart.

They had been travelling for hours, through forests and then out among fields. The land they were traversing now was rocky, with low ridges of hills running north and south. In each low valley between the ridges there were small farms, the houses tucked away well back from the road. Occasionally they would see people out working in the fields, but there seemed to be far fewer people about than there should have been. No one seemed to pay any attention to the lone cart rolling slowly down the road.

As the afternoon wore on Komori's condition worsened, the cough developing a harsh, hacking sound. Mikasama tried to get her caretaker to drink more water to soothe her throat but the old woman could not keep it down. As the Princess urged the horses up yet another ridge, Komori wheezed, "Mika, you got—" She was interrupted by a bout of coughing. When she stopped, she tried again. "You got more blankets back there?"

Komori already had one blanket wrapped around her, Mikasama noted, and yet still she shivered as if in the grip of an icy stream.

"Nana-san," she said, "I think you should lie down in the back. Then I can tuck you in all warm and cozy."

"Pahhhh—" Cough. Wheeze. "Nana-san sit here with Mika. Mika need Nana-san to show her the way." Mikasama knew that Komori had lost track of their whereabouts since shortly after leaving the road that led north, past the fortified village. But she said nothing, having no better idea of where they were. The Katanza had told them that this road eventually connected with the Northern Road, but did not say where. Mikasama began to think that Katanza ideas of 'eventually' and hers were considerably different in terms of scale.

She pushed such thoughts out of her head quickly as Komori started another round of violent coughing. Mikasama halted the cart. "Come on, Nana-san, you need to lie down." She gently guided a no-longer-protesting Komori to the back of the cart and covered her with another blanket.

Komori said weakly, "Pretty soon, hey, we sleep in real bed. Nana-san like that...Nana-san tired of road now." She burrowed down into the blankets.

Pretty soon, Nana-san, thought Mikasama, pretty soon. I sure hope so too.

She climbed back up onto the buckboard and started the horses moving again. She was getting tired herself, but thoughts of giving up and going back, or asking anyone at the farms they had passed to send word back to Hajimeshi for help, were dismissed as soon as they were realized.

For the dreams had returned. Some of them were becoming familiar to Mikasama now, as they repeated in her mind with only slight variations. Each time the details were sharp and clear, as if she were seeing things with her own eyes and not simply in a dream. The men chasing her, the waterfall, all of it almost exactly the same.

But something else was occurring along with their repetition. She could now anticipate the fear that seemed to drive her on through each part of the dream. With that anticipation, she was able to step aside within her mind and watch herself fleeing from the imagined terrors.

There was a purpose, she realized, some reason behind the dreams. They were trying to show her something. She still could not understand what it was; but it was important, much more important than Nakama, or her, or Komori, or anything else she knew. And whatever it was, it lay before her. To the west.

As the cart bounced along the dirt track she wondered again whether all it really meant was that she was going crazy, whether all this thinking about dreams was just her mind's way of saying, "See? You're really all right. You can think clearly about these dreams, can't you? So, you must be sane." But what if she were not?

If not, she realized, then she was endangering Komori by pushing onwards. She should find some place to stop, where they could stay until Komori got better.

As soon as she considered such thoughts, though, a sudden vision would flash across her eyes, as if she were asleep and the dreams had returned; a quick glimpse of the light from the wall of glass...

It was, she determined, too late to go back.

The cart crested the top of the hill, opening up to a long vista on the far side. Mikasama halted the horses and Komori, from her place in the back, croaked out, "Hey, Mika, see nice big inn? Big fire, big beds?"

Mikasama looked down into a valley that seemed to stretch for miles and miles; the next ridge was almost out of sight, nothing but trees and fields in between. There was a wisp of smoke from the far edge. There might be a village there but it would take hours to reach it. Grey clouds had begun forming overhead, blotting out the sun. As the air began to chill, Mikasama said, "Pretty soon, Nana-san. Pretty soon."

The sun was beginning to set as the wagon rumbled slowly into the village. It had begun to rain about an hour before. Komori, her breathing raspy and labored, still lay prone in the back, having fallen into a fitful sleep before the rain had come. Mikasama had hurried the horses as much as she could but they were draft animals and were unused to any sense of urgency. All she could do was cover Komori with another blanket as they had plodded on in the rain.

Now as they trundled into the village, Mikasama could see that it was small, little more than a hamlet of ramshackle wooden houses. Like grave markers, the decrepit buildings stretched down either side of the road in soundless, perpetual proximity.

As the cart reached the first of the houses the Princess pulled up on the reins and quickly climbed down. Running up to the door, she knocked loudly.

"Come on, come on!" she whispered urgently, impatient for someone to respond. Finally the door creaked opened to reveal a middle-aged woman gone prematurely grey, a small child wrapped around her leg. She didn't say a word, so Mikasama spoke first. "We need a healer, and some shelter. My companion is very sick." Used to rapid obedience to her requests, the Princess frowned as the woman continued to stare at her. She seemed to be looking for something on Mikasama, who, misunderstanding, said, "If you want payment, I have money."

The woman looked up at Mikasama's face, and a look first of fear, then of loathing crossed her worn features. She clutched a large hexagonal ornament that hung about her neck, and, dragging the child back out of the way, slammed the door in Mikasama's face.

The Princess was stunned. She stood there in the rain, water pouring off her once neatly coifed hair, and pounded on the door once more. "I said we need a healer! Don't you understand?" When it became apparent that no amount of pounding would elicit further response Mikasama returned to the cart, cursing. Komori was tossing restlessly in her sleep in the back. "Don't worry, Nana-san," said Mikasama to the sleeping form, "I'll get you some help, if I have to pound on every door in this place," as she looked determinedly down the road toward the next house.

But the response there was the same. This time a young man looked immediately about Mikasama's person, did not find what he was seeking, and without a word clutched a hexagonal pendant like the one worn by the first woman and closed the door on a protesting Princess. After trying another house across the road with similar results, Mikasama figured out that the people were looking for the same pendant on her. When they didn't find it they apparently wouldn't have anything to do with her.

Why are they doing this, she wondered. What's so special about wearing a pendant that they should refuse someone needing help?

She looked back at the door of the last house and noticed that there was a similar hexagonal marker bolted onto the doorframe. Something from her mostly forgotten hours of tedious schooling poked its way up into her consciousness. Those door markers, she realized, I've heard of them before. Old Juyama tried to teach me something about them—no, not about them, about the people who put them on their doors. They were—

With a start, a flood of memory from Juyama's lectures came back to her. *"The Shukyoshi are rabid about their shasen symbol. They put the hexagonal marker on their doors, on their tools, they wear them—they are obsessed with the importance of such things. How you look, what you wear, these are the measures of 'faith' in their minds. It is adherence to a rigid code of behavior that for them provides their sense of salvation. 'He who thinks for himself serves but himself; he who thinks for the community serves the community' is one of their parables. Princess, are you paying attention?"*

Shukyoshi, she realized. We've left Yutakashi territory and crossed into Shukyoshi!

Mikasama shivered, as she comprehended the predicament they were in. Other remembrances of Juyama's lectures came to her. She didn't realize how much of what the old man had said she had retained; it had seemed at the time that she was thinking of anything but his dry, boring teaching. But she did remember: she remembered that the Shukyoshi were fanatics who considered all others to be heretics, vermin to be scourged or burned at the stake.

Standing in the rain by the cart, Komori coughing in her sleep, Mikasama felt very alone, and very frightened.

13

"Cook! Extinguish your flame, now!"

Ryori, in the midst of cooking the evening meal, didn't hesitate at Itachi's shouted command. He had served soldiers all his life, and knew that a warm meal was one of the few enjoyments they had when in the field. Therefore an order to put out the fire signaled a serious situation. Using his fire-tending stick he quickly knocked the logs apart, then shoveled dirt onto the wood to smother the flames and minimize the smoke.

Toshi-hito, having returned to his meditation by the tree, immediately realized that something was wrong. As Itachi ordered Bokusa to recall the remaining sentries the Deshi Master rose and approached the Hajimeshi general. Before Toshi-hito could inquire, Itachi turned to him. "Hisoka has spotted a Shukyoshi patrol, just to the south of us. They're working their way back and forth, moving this way; they'll almost certainly come across us if we remain here."

Toshi-hito glanced up to where the late afternoon sun had settled well below the treetops. "Their stumbling unexpectedly upon a group of Hajimeshi soldiers in the woods at dusk might lead to an unfortunate confrontation."

"Exactly. It appears to be a routine patrol, according to Hisoka. As yet, they do not know we are here. I want to keep it that way." Itachi too looked to the west, as the long shadows cast by the trees marched across their clearing. "We have perhaps an hour before dark. If we ride now, we may be able to reach the Northern Road just before sunset. We should be able to get past the patrol once they are on their furthest leg away from us."

"And when we reach the road?" asked Toshi-hito. "What are your intentions then?"

Itachi scowled. "Then, Deshi," he grated, "it's up to you and your lamp to keep us all from getting killed." The Hajimeshi lord turned on his heel and marched off toward the horses. Toshi-hito, watching him go, hoped that being Deshi did not bring down exactly the opposite result upon their group.

The Hikari pilgrims made their way silently through the woods to the south, taking care to avoid the Shukyoshi patrol. Bokusa had warned that the first man to make a noise louder than his own breathing would find even that sound stilled forever, but the men needed no encouragement. All were familiar with the stories told about the fanatical Shukyoshi: the burnings, the inquisitions. What were tales used to frighten young children now seemed to be all too real a possibility.

Just as the sun slid behind the distant western mountains, the forest track emerged onto gently rolling hills. The pilgrims could see the Northern Road a short distance away, the river that demarcated the Shukyoshi border still visible off to their left. Toshi-hito and Itachi rode in the lead, followed by Shiko and Donaku. By tacit agreement the other Guards had granted to Donaku 'ownership' of the lantern's portage. Not quite grasping their desire to avoid being burdened with hauling the lantern about, Donaku took his newfound responsibility seriously, holding the Hikari prominently aloft. The rest of the Guards trailed behind.

As Itachi's horse set foot on the hard-packed dirt of the road, he looked east toward the border. A low stone building stood to one side of a bridge crossing the river. A barricade was erected across the near end of the bridge; presumably, thought Itachi, to allow for suitable inquiries into a man's personal affairs before being allowed entry into the 'cleansed' land of the Shukyoshi. Disgusting hypocrites, all of them, he fumed silently. He seriously doubted that even one of them had the unblemished character they so espoused as their ideal. He, better than most, knew what was in most men's hearts. That was what allowed him to control others so easily.

As he watched he saw movement near the building: sentries, running out into the road, and pointing at the Hikari group. Probably, he surmised, taken aback to see riders on the wrong side of their barricade, 'defiling' their precious land.

Now he saw more men, running toward a stable at the back of the stone building. Ah, cavalrymen, he thought. One, three, six—no, at least a dozen. More. Well, now we shall see.

The Shukyoshi wore black armor that was polished to an almost mirror-reflective sheen. The only color came from the surcoat they wore over the armor: made of a bright blue cloth, it was emblazoned with the hexagonal shasen symbol front and back. Their holy sign, the symbol that opened the doors of their heaven should they fall in battle fighting the heathens. To a Shukyoshi there could be no greater glory than dying in such a cause.

Itachi turned to face the men behind him. "All right, listen, all of you! No man draws a sword. Do you understand? We are pilgrims, following the Deshi on their quest. Our job is to protect them from forest brigands, no more. If any one of you so much as twitches an eyebrow out of place, that's all the excuse these vermin need to cut us down. You are soldiers of Hajimeshi. You are the Castle Guards. Show your discipline now." He turned back just as the mounted Shukyoshi thundered up in a cloud of dirt and stamping hooves, quickly surrounding the pilgrims. Each rider carried a long pike, and every lance head was pointed at one of the intruders. True to their orders, not a man among the Hajimeshi so much as shifted in the saddle. The only movement was the flickering flame of the Hikari lantern suspended above the group, eerily illuminating the polished armor of the Shukyoshi.

Shiko, holding his breath, wondered if they would all be impaled where they stood before being allowed to utter so much as a word. Everywhere he looked, all around them, was nothing but a ring of pikes. Slowly the Shukyoshi lancers advanced, tightening their circle, and Shiko's hand trembled as he gripped the pommel of his saddle tightly. The pilgrims' horses, nervous, began shifting and snorting, and the apprentice could hear the creaking of leather and armor from the men around him.

Suddenly there was a shout. The surrounding horsemen hesitated; then they stopped their aggressive advance. The array of pikes, however, remained fixed in the direction of the Hajimeshi.

Another rider, apparently an officer and the owner of the shout, walked his horse through the ring of cavalry around the intruders. He looked up at the Hikari lantern, its light rapidly becoming the only source of illumination in the all but extinguished sunlight, and then to Itachi and Toshi-hito at the head of the group. He screwed up his face in distaste at the sight of the Deshi, and addressed his comments only to Itachi.

"You are violators of our land! Were it not for the presence of a pilgrim lantern among you, you would all be dead as of this moment." He cast an angry look across the group. "Who among you is the pilgrim? Have him step forward." Left unspoken was the obvious inference that the rest of them would be killed as soon as the lantern was out of their midst. As the man spoke, foot soldiers arrived at the run from the barracks down the road, some carrying torches. They quickly took up positions backing up their horsemen.

Although the officer had looked to Itachi it was Toshi-hito who answered. "We are *all* pilgrims, who journey beneath the light of the Hikari. We seek audience with his Excellency, the Anasaki."

The officer ignored Toshi-hito, staring only at Itachi. "Soldiers as pilgrims? Sneaking across our borders?"

Itachi jerked his head in Toshi-hito's direction. "We follow the Deshi as fellow pilgrims, to guard against thieves and brigands. We were attacked not far from Yutakashi, and lost our way in attempting to escape. We crossed the river and headed south, hoping we were on the proper path that would lead us to the road."

"You may have found the road, Hajimeshi heathen, but I seriously doubt you have found the proper path," replied the officer. He leaned forward in his saddle. "I know of these pilgrimages involving lanterns. You must have a seal from your heretic sovereign. Otherwise you are little better than spies, masquerading as legitimate pilgrims."

Toshi-hito wordlessly pulled out the scroll signed by the Kojuro and held it out to the Shukyoshi officer. The man hesitated, as if taking something from an 'unclean' person might irreparably soil his hands. Then he took the scroll and unrolled it. He read it through carefully; then a second time, finally re-rolling it and handling it back quickly. Tapping his fist against his saddle in indecision, he stared hard at the band of pilgrims.

Shiko held his breath. All the fine words he had spoken during the Hikari lighting ceremony rushed back into his mind; but out here, facing these men, the words seemed no more substantial than a sheet of parchment held up against the wind. It was the Hikari, its faint glow highlighting the pilgrims' grey smocks against the sea of black armor, which had to speak for them now.

As if the man were reading his thoughts, Shiko saw the officer glance up at the lantern, the light reflecting eerily across the metal seams of his helmet as he moved his head. He stared at it for some while, as both pilgrims and warrior priests waited in perfect stillness. Finally he looked back down at the group of Hajimeshi. "You will be taken to the Fortress," he said with finality.

Inwardly Shiko breathed a sigh of relief, although he tried hard to keep his face from betraying any emotion. The immediate danger was probably past, he decided; he guessed that the officer must not have the authority to deal with the pilgrims himself, especially as the Hajimeshi had produced an official sanction from the Kojuro.

Shiko had heard of the Fortress: it was the Anasaki's great castle, located in the capital of Shukyoshi. In all the scrolls he could remember that dealt with the Shukyoshi, he could recall none with any mention of a non-Shukyoshi ever venturing inside the Fortress. It would appear that they were going to be the first. Hopefully, he thought, they would also be the first to be able to leave it...

The officer continued, "My men will escort you. You would do well to hold your tongues; anyone who speaks blasphemy will be killed immediately, pilgrim or no pilgrim. Our land is sacred, and it is the duty of every Shukyoshi to lay down his life to maintain that sacredness. If you force them to choose between that duty and honoring the pilgrim tradition—" He left the remainder unsaid, as from down the road to the west came a small commotion.

A band of Shukyoshi horsemen, eight in all, had emerged from the woods, apparently the patrol that the Hajimeshi group had eluded earlier. Having spied their compatriots in battle formation on the road, the horsemen had spurred on their mounts and were now rushing to the scene.

The officer in front of Itachi and Toshi-hito turned his horse away from the men of Hajimeshi and walked his mount out through the ring of men. The approaching riders pulled up sharply, the patrol leader calling out, "What has happened?"

The officer answered quietly. "You have failed in your duty. These vermin," indicating the Hajimeshi group, "walked right past you and into our land. You have allowed Shukyoshi to be contaminated."

The patrol leader's eyes opened wide as he surveyed the scene in front of him. "Impossible! We would have seen so large a group!"

"Not impossible," replied the officer. "They are here. You have failed. There is only one punishment for allowing desecration."

The patrol leader glanced behind him at his fellows. All of them looked fearfully at him and then at one another, but none had anything to say. The other Shukyoshi soldiers on the road all stared impassively forward, either watching the intruders or their officer. None looked at the patrol leader or at any of his men.

Hesitating but a moment the patrol leader, eyes downcast, slowly dismounted, as did his men behind him. Foot soldiers from the barracks walked up and led away their horses. The patrol leader straightened his shoulders and spoke, quietly, his eyes focused on something far away. "If we have brought pollution to our land...then we are...unfit...to be Shukyoshi." Then he knelt down in the road and leaned forward.

The officer did not reply. Leaning over from his horse in one swift motion he drew his sword from its scabbard and sliced the man's head off.

As the head rolled down the road toward the other men of the patrol, they too quickly knelt down. They waited patiently as the officer dismounted and ritually cleaned the blood from his sword with the hem of his blue habit.

Shiko was stunned and shocked. Throughout their journey death and danger had seemed to stalk them, but what had transpired so far paled beside the cold-blooded brutality of this officer toward his own men. He remembered what one of the Masters had taught him about the Shukyoshi, back at the priory: *"For the Shukyoshi, blood spilled on a consecrated blade may only be removed by something similarly consecrated. Thus the warrior priest will use his habit to wipe his blade. He will then wear the habit with pride, for it will have been 'bloodied' in the name of the Goddess."* A lesson that had seemed so abstract and remote at the time now was all so horrifyingly real. As the officer finished wiping the blood from his sword, Shiko saw the shasen symbol engraved up and down the length of the blade reflecting back from the light of the torches held by the nearby soldiers.

The officer walked over to the row of men from the patrol, and one by one he dropped his sword, severing each head. After each he stopped and carefully wiped the blood from the blade, only to splash the crimson flood up and down its length once more with each stroke. Itachi and the others watched impassively from their places within the Hajimeshi ranks. Shiko, sick to his stomach, thought that such men were probably hardened to the sight of brutal death. All he could think of, though, were the families whom these unfortunate patrol members were leaving behind...

When the last man had been felled the Shukyoshi officer spoke to the foot soldiers near him, pointing to the severed heads and the bodies that had until recently owned them. "Throw these into the woods for the carrion eaters." He returned to his horse and rode calmly back over to the surrounded Hajimeshi pilgrims. He stared resolutely at Itachi and Toshi-hito. "We will leave. Now."

Toshi-hito simply nodded his head. Itachi, however, looked toward where the sun had long since dropped out of sight below the hills. "We ride at night?" he asked.

"In the land of the Shukyoshi," said the officer, "there is no need to fear the dark. Unless you are damned." He turned his horse about, saying over his shoulder, "Do not doubt my earlier warning."

To Shiko, the bile rising in his mouth at the sight of the decapitated corpses being dragged away, it seemed inconceivable that any man among the pilgrims could possibly doubt the Shukyoshi's intentions. One hand gripping the honsho about his neck, with the other he held the reins of his horse as tightly as he could.

The officer set off to the west, toward the Fortress at the center of Shukyoshi. The Hikari pilgrims formed up on the road behind, a detachment of the cavalrymen to either side. As they advanced, the horses stamped the pools of blood into the dirt.

* * *

Far to the south, the rain that swept up from the Great Sea continued to fall. It was growing dark, and Mikasama knew that a night out in the open, cold and wet, would be dangerous for Komori. She had to find them shelter, and a healer.

Looking up toward the end of the village, she saw a large stone structure. Probably the home of some minor noble, she thought; perhaps he might be persuaded to aid two distressed travelers. Although, considering where they were, it was more likely that he would be the first to arrest them, or worse, for being heretics…

A bright flash caused her to jump, and a massive, rumbling peal of thunder assaulted her senses. It was so loud that she had to cover her ears.

Instantly the vivid memory of her father's hunt flooded back into her mind: she was frightened, shivering, burrowing against Komori who was holding her tight, safe against the storm. But now Komori was sick, and Mikasama stood alone, out in the open. In a blind panic, she grabbed the horses' halter and dragged on it, urging the slow animals to move. She had no idea where she was going, only that she had to get out of the open, now! Another crack of lighting startled her, and even the draft horses became agitated.

"Come on, you stupid beasts!" she shouted at them. Her cries, though, had about as much affect on the animals as it had on the resident Shukyoshi. The horses lumbered forward with what to Mikasama was an agonizing slowness. She tried to think clearly, but every thought was quickly dashed out of her mind with each booming crash from the skies overhead. She struggled to lead the horses up the road toward the stone building, the cart's wheels squishing through what was rapidly congealing into a muddy broth.

As she drew nearer she saw that the stone building was actually a high wall, with a range of small buildings beyond it. There was a wide wooden gate set in its center with a bell pull mounted to the side. Just as she stopped the cart before the gate there was another flash and another booming roll of thunder almost directly over her head. Desperately she pulled on the bell cord.

There was no response at first, and the Princess waited with nerves set on edge, wringing her hands. Komori groaned from the back of the cart, and just as Mikasama reached to pull the bell again a small shutter in the wooden gate opened. A pair of eyes peaked out wordlessly.

Before the inquisitor could slam the shutter closed, Mikasama quickly blurted out, "Please! Can you help us? We are travelers, and my companion is very sick. We need shelter, and a healer!" The owner of the eyes still did not speak, glancing past the Princess who stood with hair dripping and plastered to the sides of her head, toward the cart where Komori groaned once more. Mikasama too looked over her shoulder with concern, then back to the silent eyes beyond the gate. "Please!" she said again, earnestly. "I beg for your help."

The eyes looked Mikasama over once more, then the little shutter slid closed. For a brief moment Mikasama felt lost, sure that she had been locked out just as she had been at each of the village houses. Then she heard the creak as the large gate moved, swinging inwards. Momentarily she was overjoyed, until she saw who had opened the gate.

She was a young woman, perhaps a few years older than Mikasama and somewhat taller, but it was not these things that caught Mikasama's attention. Partially obscured by a cloak to keep out the rain, the woman wore beneath it a blue habit, covering her from shoulder to foot. A blue headdress completely covered her hair, and also looped across under her chin, framing her face. The blue was the same shade Mikasama had seen in her dreams, being worn by the men chasing her. Something connected between her dreams and old Juyama's lectures, and she knew that the woman standing in front of her must be a Sister of the Shukyoshi religious order. Mikasama had rung the bell on a Shukyoshi monastery.

The woman spoke. "Bring the cart inside."

Shocked into immobility at the sight of the Sister, it took Mikasama a moment to respond. It was too late to turn back now, she told herself, as she walked the horses into the courtyard.

The Sister, however, ignored Mikasama and climbed up into the back of the cart. The Princess followed, and watched as the Sister gently pulled the blankets away from Komori. The woman placed a hand over Komori's forehead while at the same time gently pressing two fingers into the side of the old woman's neck.

In the close confines of the cart, Mikasama had an opportunity to get a closer look at the Sister while she worked. Other than the blue of her habit, the only other color to be seen was that in the woman's eyes. Mikasama was surprised to see that they, too, were blue, a very unusual eye color for anyone of Tonogato. Their intensity rivaled the bright shade of her clothes.

The odd blue eyes swiveled up and met Mikasama's. "How long has she been like this?" the Sister asked dispassionately.

"She's been sleeping like this, moaning, for the last several hours. She first started to be sick two days ago."

The Sister removed her hands and tucked the blankets back in around the old woman. "She is your mother?"

Mikasama hesitated just a fraction of second. "Yes. Yes, she is my mother."

The Sister looked up sharply, then glanced down, searching for Mikasama's shasen symbol. Not finding it, she slowly raised her eyes again until the two women's gaze met.

Mikasama's breath seemed to desert her as she sat transfixed by that icy blue stare. Neither woman spoke; there was no sound but that of the rain pelting down on the wood frame of the cart. Suddenly Mikasama heard voices. Another female voice, from outside the cart: "Shudojo? What is it?" And another woman: "Is everything all right?"

Mikasama waited, heart pounding. She and the Sister continued to look at one another, the raspy breathing of Komori between them. Mikasama bit her lip, afraid to look away, to break the spell, certain that the Sister would surely denounce her and Komori. From outside the cart came another query. "Shudojo?"

Finally, the blue eyes never leaving Mikasama's, Shudojo said, "It's all right. Two travelers; one is ill." She sat erect and looked over the side of the cart. "Bring a litter. We will need to carry this one to the sick ward." She glanced back only once at Mikasama, then busied herself with preparing Komori to be moved.

The Princess slowly breathed out again. She had no idea why Shudojo had chosen to help her, but she silently thanked all the gods she had ever heard of. Quickly she vacated the cart to allow the other Sisters room, as several of them climbed up to help move Komori. All were dressed similarly to Shudojo, with heavy cloaks to repel the rain covering their long blue habits. Mikasama could only stand and watch, her exhaustion nearly overcoming her, as Komori was maneuvered to the ground and onto a litter. Shudojo removed the blankets that covered the old woman, which were sweat-soaked and clammy as well as sodden from the rain. The Sister removed her own rain cloak and covered Komori with it, for while the cloak's outside was wet from rain it was warm and dry on the inside.

At that moment another Sister strode up, this one walking beneath a parasol. "What is this?" she demanded imperiously. "What are you doing?" She was older than the other Sisters, with a narrow, hawkish face, her voice edged with aggravation. The other Sisters stopped tending to Komori and stood about uncertainly.

Shudojo turned to the older Sister. "Travelers at our gate, Sister Choda. One is ill with the plague; I am having her taken to the sick ward."

Mikasama felt the word stab right through her as if it were a knife. The plague! Was it possible? All of those empty fields, and the abandoned farms Nana-san and I passed; could that all have been as a result of the plague?

Then her heart was gripped with a sudden fear, as the image came back to her of the emaciated man from the Katanza camp, and the little coughing girl who had played with Komori. Nana-san, she shouted silently to herself; what have I led you into?

Sister Choda strode over to Shudojo. "Who gave you authority to admit visitors?" she demanded. "You were assigned to watch the gate; nothing more. It is not your place to open it without seeking guidance from your superiors." She turned her disdainful gaze to the soaked and dripping form of Mikasama. "Who are these people?" Turning to the other nearby Sisters she said, "One of you go bring torches; it is too dark to see."

So they all waited, Mikasama dripping, Shudojo becoming equally soaked, Choda impatiently beneath her parasol. Once the requested light was brought, Choda strode over to Mikasama and looked her up and down. "Who are you? Where are you from?" she demanded.

Too tired to think of a better answer, the Princess replied, "My name is Mika. We are from Hajimeshi."

There was a gasp of surprise from the other Sisters as they looked at Mikasama and then down at Komori. They all backed away from the prone figure of the old woman, while Choda spun to face Shudojo. "You foolish girl! You have admitted heathens into our sanctuary! You have gone too far this time, Shudojo. I will scourge you personally for permitting this sacrilege!"

"Choda." A new voice arrived out of the dark. As its owner stepped into the pool of light from the torches, Mikasama could see that she too was an older woman, although shorter and more stout than Choda. While she spoke quietly, it was with an air of authority that was clearly used to being obeyed. "I will authorize scourging, no other." She walked forward into the midst of the women, looking down at the figure of Komori, whose labored breathing was the only sound to be heard beyond the patter of raindrops. She wore a rain cloak like the younger Sisters, eschewing the use of a parasol. "Perhaps," she said, turning to face Choda, "you would be so good as to explain."

Choda gestured impatiently at Shudojo. "This witless girl was assigned to watch the gate, Mother Narisa. She opened it," she spat out disdainfully, "and has admitted heathens into our midst."

Narisa looked at Mikasama, then down at Komori on the ground. "This one is ill with the plague, I presume?"

Shudojo was the one who answered. "Yes, Mother Narisa. They are from Hajimeshi."

The older woman looked up sharply at Shudojo, then returned her gaze again to Mikasama. She walked over to the Princess, on whose face the raindrops glistened in hundreds of little sparkles from the light of the torches. Silently she looked into Mikasama's eyes. Under the older woman's scrutiny the Princess felt as if her pretenses were suddenly all stripped away. Narisa spoke calmly, holding Mikasama's gaze. "Take the ill one to the ward, and tend to her."

Choda exhaled in a shocked gasp. "Mother Narisa!"

Ignoring her, Narisa nodded her head toward Mikasama. "Give this one some dry clothes and some food. When she is ready, bring her to my study." She turned away and walked out of the light from the torches, leaving a flustered Choda to organize the other Sisters.

"Well, then," said Choda, with barely constrained irritation, "stop standing about and gawking!" She directed the Sisters to lift the litter and carry Komori to the sick ward. She cast a withering look at

Shudojo. "As the presence of this heathen is your doing, she is now your responsibility." Shudojo, expressionless, bowed her head in acknowledgement.

Mikasama watched, feeling helpless, as Shudojo and several of the Sisters lifted Komori's litter. The Princess felt numb, exhausted; and was worried sick about her caretaker. She knew there was little more she could do, particularly if Komori had indeed contracted the plague. As a vast building on the far side of the courtyard swallowed up the litter, and the Sisters carrying it, Mikasama felt terribly alone.

Choda turned to the remaining Sisters in the courtyard, and pointed toward Mikasama as if she were refuse from the kitchen. "Do as Mother Narisa requested; clothe and feed this other one. And," she added, waving an agitated hand, "get that front gate closed!"

The young Sister detailed to assist Mikasama silently led the Princess inside one of the buildings surrounding the courtyard. They walked down a long, cold hallway, lined with wooden doors and illuminated by a few torches set at irregular intervals. The Sister stopped in front of one door, which appeared just like all the others to Mikasama, and opened it. She gestured for the Princess to go inside.

Mikasama stepped in and found she was standing in a small room with nothing but a pallet of straw and a single coarse blanket on the floor. Wondering if she had been consigned to some sort of jail, she turned toward the Sister, but the woman was gone. Well, thought Mikasama, the door is still open, so it can't be too much of a prison...

Her dripping clothes began to form a puddle of water on the stone floor as she considered what to do now. Her exhausted brain had not made much headway before the young Sister returned bearing an armful of clothes. The girl held them out, then quickly drew her hands back once Mikasama accepted the bundle. Mikasama said, "Thank you," but the young girl seemed at a loss for any reply. Finally in a shaky voice the girl blurted out, "They were left behind by—by one of those taken by the plague." Then she turned and hurried off down the hallway.

Mikasama looked down at the clothes in her arms, and suppressed a shiver. Clothes from the dead. Well, she imagined, the Sisters probably didn't have anything other than blue habits, and she certainly couldn't wear that. The clothes seemed freshly laundered, so she decided to put their origin out of her mind and take advantage of the opportunity to get dry.

As she stripped off her sopping clothes, she thought about the young Sister. The girl had seemed genuinely terrified. It was as if the Princess were some sort of monster, something completely outside the world that the girl understood. Much like what I've experienced, she thought ruefully, nearly every day since leaving Hajimeshi...

She finished dressing in the clothes, which were several sizes too large, and tried to untangle her long black hair. It was a hopeless task without a comb, besides which it had always been Komori who had combed her hair. Mikasama had never tried to do it herself and certainly not in the condition her hair was in now. She gave up, undoing a leather tie-strip from the clothes brought in by the Sister and using it to gather her hair back in a long queue. She gave the ebony tail a good twist to try and wring out some water onto the already-wet floor, then sat down on the pallet and waited. It gave her a chance to think.

Despite what Juyama had taught her, these Shukyoshi had not killed them outright; although some, especially Choda, had seemed quite hostile. But first Shudojo, and then the head Sister, Mother Narisa, had given them a reprieve. It was little enough luck, but how long would even it last?

She put her head in her hands, fervently hoping that the healing skills of the Sisters were sufficient to combat the plague. Hopefully, she thought, Komori's illness was recent enough that her caretaker would be well again soon, and they could continue their journey.

All at once a tremendous wave of guilt swept over her as she realized what was going through her mind. How can I even be thinking that, she wondered. Komori is gravely ill, and here I am talking about pushing on! What's the matter with me? Are these dreams really making me lose my mind?

She sat, brooding, trying to keep the images from her dreams out of her head. It wasn't until the young Sister returned, tentatively knocking on the still-open door, that Mikasama realized how hungry she was. The Sister had brought a tray with a couple of small bowls of unidentifiable food, but it was warm and would have tasted good regardless of what it was. The Princess ate busily, pushing the images of waterfalls and glass walls out of her head. When she had finished, the Sister, watching from the hallway, called in, "Mother Narisa wishes to see you, when you are done."

Mikasama stood and tried to straighten her misshapen clothing as best she could, then she joined the Sister. "I'm ready." Wordlessly the Sister led her off down the hall.

Mother Narisa's study was awash with light, causing Mikasama to blink after being ushered in from the dim hallway. There were numerous torches around the room, their smoke curling up and lingering around the beams supporting the roof.

The room was not much larger, Mikasama realized, than the bath chamber she used in the castle at Hajimeshi. The walls were bare, as was the floor. The minimal furniture in the room was clearly intended strictly for working use: a rack holding various scrolls, and a small cupboard. Opposite the door was a short table, behind which sat Mother Narisa, busily inscribing on a piece of parchment. A brace of candles to either side of her cast their glow over the woman's deep blue habit.

As Mikasama was led into the room the older woman acknowledged their presence without looking up. "Thank you, Tishuno, you may go." The young Sister quickly departed, closing the door behind her. The Princess stood alone with Mother Narisa.

For a while the older woman simply continued with her writing. Finally, still without looking up, she said, "You may sit, child."

Hesitantly Mikasama walked further into the room, and knelt a respectful distance from the low table. The only sound was that of the pen's nib scratching across the parchment. The Princess glanced about the room, wondering why it was so much better lit than all the others. Almost as if Mother Narisa had read her thoughts, the Sister said, "I find I get much more work done at night. But these tired old eyes need plenty of light in order to see well." She dipped her pen in the ink, then continued her writing. "You say you are from Hajimeshi?"

Mikasama swallowed, and managed a small, "Yes, Ma'am." She was still uncertain of her status, and decided she had better tread carefully. Having survived this far she didn't want to risk Komori, or herself, by saying the wrong thing.

"And you are travelling...?" It was left as a question, clearly intended to be answered. Mikasama had run many potential questions, and possible answers, through her head while on the road, in case anyone inquired too closely. But this was one question she had not considered.

By custom, it was usually considered rude to ask travelers where they were bound. Juyama, her old teacher, had explained to her that at one time people had considered that to be asked such a question implied the traveler was not sure of his or her destination. So Mikasama did not immediately have an answer to Mother Narisa's question, which had been so cleverly worded that it could pass as a statement rather than a question, and thus not cause offense.

"I—that is, we are going—" Mikasama realized that she could not say they were still on their way to Yutakashi, that having been left far behind them; nor was it likely that they had been intending to travel to Shukyoshi. "to—to Tejinashi." She couldn't very well tell this Sister of the Shukyoshi that she was trying to track down a party of Hikari pilgrims, in order to re-unite herself with Nakama. So the only place left to say was the city of magic far to the west.

Mother Narisa's pen stopped, and she raised her discerning eyes to look at Mikasama. "I see." She looked back down at her parchment, and said casually, "Remote as we may seem, we do occasionally receive news from other parts of Tonogato. Even from places as distant, in more ways than one, as Hajimeshi." She resumed her writing, leaving Mikasama to squirm inside.

She knows, thought the Princess. My father's people have reached even this far! What will Mother Narisa do? Is she writing to my father even as we speak? Will I be bundled back to Hajimeshi like a sack of grain, shamed, everything I have gone through for nothing?

And what about Komori? What will happen to her? She can't travel back to Hajimeshi in her condition. I can't leave her behind!

While the Princess fidgeted, her mind spinning with possible outcomes, each worse than the last, Mother Narisa finished her writing. She sanded the parchment, blew off the grains, and set it aside. Her eyes came to rest once more on the young woman kneeling before her.

"Your—mother—is very ill," said the Sister. "We have been afflicted by the plague for many months. Some have survived, once having been taken with the sickness. But very few." She leaned back from the table. "She will have to stay in the ward for quite some time. You may stay here, in the monastery, until…well, until there is a change." She collected her writing materials, wrapping them into a bundle. "You will observe our meal times, although, being heathen, you will not be required to attend our prayer gatherings. I trust," she said, looking at Mikasama, "that such an arrangement is acceptable?"

Mikasama was taken aback. Of the all the possible outcomes, this had seemed the least likely, although in a tiny part of her heart she had hoped. Fighting to hold back tears, she bowed down to the floor. "Yes. Yes, thank you, Mother Narisa."

Mother Narisa ignored the bow, and stood up. "You may use the cell which Sister Tishuno took you to. I will instruct the other Sisters to leave you in peace." She looked away, adding quietly, "We are not quite as strict, or as ready to persecute, as our Brothers to the north; but there are some among us who would see you as an abomination. May the Goddess preserve them, and show them the way of mercy." She looked down again at Mikasama. "I would suggest you get some sleep. You may visit the sick ward tomorrow." She walked past the still bowed-over form of the

Princess and left the study. Mikasama, tired, emotionally exhausted, stayed bent over for a long while, letting the tears quietly flow.

14

The atmosphere in the Hajimeshi Council chamber was turbulent. All of the nobles of the kingdom, even those from far away holdings, had been summoned to meet with the Kojuro. They had been gathering in the chamber over the last hour, each bringing rumors, complaints, and concerns that found an increasingly receptive audience among those already present. Arguments broke out, voices were raised, and it was only with some difficulty that a servant was able to shout loud enough to be heard.

"My Lords, the Kojuro!" He had to repeat the announcement three times before the room stilled sufficiently that all heard. As the assembled peers turned toward the door, the Kojuro slowly shuffled into the room. As one, all of the nobles knelt on the floor and bowed to their sovereign. Policy might be disputed but honor and tradition would be upheld.

The Kojuro moved over to the backless chair that served as the royal throne and carefully lowered himself onto it. Directly behind came the chamberlain Himitsu. Once seated, the Kojuro nodded his head in acknowledgement of the lords before him. They all rose to a sitting position, and waited for their sovereign to speak.

In this, however, they were disappointed. Kimeru simply waved at Himitsu, who moved forward from his position behind the Kojuro's throne to address the assembled peers. "My Lords," he began, "as many of you are no doubt aware, Lord Choshuka of the Yutakashi took his leave of us this morning. Due to…events…in Yutakashi, relations with our neighbors have taken an unfortunate turn."

"I have heard," interrupted Takamaru, the Omo Deshi, "that our Hikari pilgrims were attacked by the Yutakashi." In the absence of Itachi he was now the most influential of the leaders, and he was determined to reinforce this position by being the first of the lords to speak. "Is this true?" His allegation prompted muted sounds of indignation from several of those gathered.

Himitsu spoke carefully. "Our pilgrims were attacked, yes. But the Reds and the Blues were not officially involved; it appears to have been a spontaneous gathering of Yutakashi citizens."

This was greeted with sounds of derision and disbelief. Another voice spoke out: "Were this true, why did not the Reds and Blues defend the sanctity of the pilgrims, as was their obligation?" More shouts of agreement accompanied this statement. As the Kojuro had chosen not to speak, the lords felt free to debate the chamberlain. He was, after all, no more than one of them.

Himitsu held out his hands, palms downward, as if to calm a seething storm. "My Lords, I only tell you what the Yutakashi have officially told us."

"I am given to understand," said the Omo Deshi smoothly, "that his Majesty's personal representative for the pilgrimage, my colleague Toshi-hito, never had any intention of finding the Kotaishi in this city of merchants. Is this true? And if so, why were our people led there, to a place of potential danger? Was there some other purpose to this expedition?" Further grumbles of unrest greeted this revelation.

How does he find out these things, wondered Himitsu. Sometimes I question which of us should really be in charge of the Kojuro's spies…

Ignoring the gist of Takamaru's question, the chamberlain provided an oblique answer. "The Grand Council expressed their opinion about the search for the Kotaishi. It appears that a faction of them believe that our pilgrims intended to foment revolution in their city. We, of course," throwing back a barb, "are not so naïve as to accept this accusation at face value; however, the Grand Council appears to be using this as a pretext for severing relations with Hajimeshi."

"Preposterous!" shouted one of the senior lords near the front. "Pilgrims seek personal growth and enlightenment. They would never take part in a rebellion." He pounded his fist against his thigh. "This outrage must be avenged!" Several other lords cried out their agreement to this proposal, while some of the younger lords started slapping the floor with their open palms. Their combined pounding began to spread, making an insistent call for action. Himitsu tried to speak again but was drowned out by the pounding and the voices of many lords all trying to declare their positions, for or against. Finally the Kojuro, with a visible effort, rose from his chair and walked forward to where the lords sat.

Quickly the voices stilled and the pounding died away. One impetuous noble, the youngest of those assembled, did not stop soon enough; those to either side of him grabbed his arms and held his hands to the floor. The Kojuro would speak, and honor decreed that all must listen.

Kimeru looked out over the sea of faces and knew that events were swiftly moving beyond his control. Those who sat before him looked at the Kojuro and assumed that he held the reins of power that could shape Hajimeshi's destiny. Many longed for such power, even his own brother. But none of them understood that such power did not exist. At best, as he was all too aware, a Kojuro influenced events, nudging the tiller on a ship so vast that no one man could ever sail it where he desired. Most of the time it resembled bobbing along on a small raft atop a raging river, trying desperately to steer a desired course while keeping the raft from being swamped. These men, he reminded himself, would never understand the limits of 'power' until they had tried it on for themselves. He tried to remember their desires, and dreams, as he spoke.

"My Lords, you have heard the words of my chamberlain. Our pilgrims arrived as messengers of peace, but the Yutakashi chose to return to us a different reply. Clearly they are on the ascendancy, and feel that violence against their neighbors is in their interest. I would remind you that a careful man does not challenge another unless he feels reasonably certain that he will win. Whatever you may feel about the Yutakashi, it is not disputed that their business acumen has made them well able to evaluate risk, as well as return." He scanned the faces sitting before him, seeing a nod here and there, but many still flushed with anger or with eyes and ears blind to anything put before them. "Hajimeshi cannot allow itself to become a vassal of the Yutakashi; but similarly we must not allow ourselves to enter into a war for which we are not prepared. I ask only that you consider this. If it becomes necessary we will fight, and every soldier of Hajimeshi blood will defend its honor until there is no more blood left in him. But it would be foolish to throw away what we have over misunderstandings. It is my hope that we may still find common ground with the Yutakashi." Silence greeted his remarks, and he returned to his throne and sat once more. The weariness of his voice had clearly shown his exhaustion at the effort of speech making.

One of the senior lords in the front rank bowed, speaking respectfully. "Your Majesty, what then of our pilgrims?"

Kimeru nodded to Himitsu, who responded to the query. "I have heard, from reliable sources, that the Hikari pilgrims have now entered Shukyoshi territory, albeit from an unconventional direction due to their…precipitate…departure from Yutakashi."

"Well," commented the Omo Deshi archly. "Now we are unlikely to hear more." As he looked at those around him, he added somberly, "We may never hear more of them again."

The Council meeting adjourned with nothing more decided than that a formal protest be issued to the Yutakashi Grand Council, chiding them for their failure to protect the sanctity of pilgrims. Privately, however, many of the lords were vehemently opposed to any sort of appeasement and felt that honor required a military response. It was immaterial that Hajimeshi was unprepared for conflict or that she might lose; better to die with honor than to live shamefully. The cauldron, thought Himitsu, had been brought to a high boil. He was unsure whether the Kojuro would be able to keep the lid in place.

Kimeru had retired to his vantage overlooking the Sacred Grove. Once Himitsu had seen the assembled lords off, he joined the Kojuro on the balcony. Both men sat in silence for a time, trying to replace in their minds the stress of human conflict with the peaceful sights and sounds of the Grove. At length Kimeru spoke.

"Have you news of the others?" Himitsu knew of whom the Kojuro spoke; while worried about the pilgrims, the fate of his daughter had never been far from the forefront of Kimeru's thoughts.

"No, your Majesty," said Himitsu with difficulty. "I regret to say that their trail has grown cold. I received a report that a band of Katanza had encountered two travelers matching the descriptions of the Princess and Komori, but…"

Kimeru turned his increasingly cloudy eyes onto his chamberlain. "But?"

Himitsu, unable to meet his sovereign's gaze, looked out over the Grove. "The Katanza said they last saw the two women heading toward Shukyoshi lands."

The Kojuro closed his eyes, bowing his head. "I knew there was danger in sending the Hikari pilgrims. I had prepared myself for the worst, and am content that the fates will do as they will. I can do no more for them. But my daughter…"

It was clear that he struggled to hold back tears; but a Kojuro, even in front of his closest advisor, could not show weakness of will. He breathed deep, then continued. "It was unkind for the fates to land such a blow, when all hinges on the success of the pilgrims. I must remain Kojuro long enough to see them returned. Nothing must imperil that." He turned away from Himitsu and stared down into the Grove at something only he could see, somewhere in his own mind. "I will trust my daughter to the fates as well. I will trust that they will not harm her simply to spite a dying man. She will return when the time is right." He turned slightly, saying over his shoulder, "Thank you, Himitsu."

The chamberlain bowed, accepting the dismissal. As he exited through the Council chamber he paused by the outer door. The room was quiet now, the tension having dissipated like an ill wind with the departure of the lords of the realm. Yet while the room itself may have become quiescent once more, Himitsu doubted that the same could be said for the nobles' relations with the Kojuro. He feared that the cauldron would soon be tipped, whether by accident or by design, and the boiling waters overflow. In so doing, they might very well quench the light of the fire that fueled them.

And, thought Himitsu, what of Komori? Relying on the fates may be adequate, and perhaps necessary, for a Kojuro, but he would prefer not to depend on such fickle gods. He was consumed with worry as, head down, he strode back to his quarters and his own window of solitude.

* * *

Dawn was lightening the sky as the Hikari pilgrims neared the Fortress. Riders had been sent ahead by the Shukyoshi officer and the way cleared of all traffic. It was in eerie quiet that the pilgrims, surrounded by the Shukyoshi soldiers, made their way through the outskirts of the city. Above the rooftops the dark spires of the Fortress citadel rose to pierce the clouds overhead.

The Hajimeshi and their escorts had been on the move all night since the pilgrims' appearance at the Shukyoshi border crossing. Having had only a couple of short rest periods since the ambush at the gorge and crossing the river, the Hajimeshi were tired and suffering from lack of food and water. The Shukyoshi had not permitted them to stop or to retrieve anything from their travel packs. Shiko noted that their captors shared this same deprivation, but that they had made no word of complaint.

The hours of journeying had been undertaken in nearly complete silence. Once, early on, Toshi-hito had attempted to converse with the Shukyoshi officer, commenting that many of the fields that they had passed seemed fallow. The officer had rejoined that they had suffered from the plague for the last several months, sown by vermin from the east like Toshi-hito. He had added that he and his men would most likely be quarantined for having come in contact with Toshi-hito and his band. The disgust with which the man's comments had been tinged had rather effectively ended the conversation. No one else had deemed it advisable to make any further attempts at discourse.

The empty streets echoed hollowly with the clatter of the horses' hooves. To Shiko it seemed almost as if the city were dead, merely a skeleton of houses and buildings with its lifeblood, the people, having been drained away. The structures were dull and nondescript, devoid of ornament save for the ubiquitous shasen symbol. There were no taverns, no traveler's inns; only houses and workshops lined the roads. Nor were there any street lanterns. It was a city, he noted, that must shut down at night, devoid of anything but the mechanics of daily existence; focused not on this life but on a promised afterlife, as foretold in the Shukyoshi holy books.

Evidence was abundant, however, that the city was indeed not deserted. Carts stood alongside the streets, still loaded with goods. The structures were well maintained and neat, the pathways weed-less. As the group wended its way up the sloping streets toward the Fortress, Shiko occasionally caught a glimpse of a shutter moving, or a door opening a crack. *They are afraid of us*, Shiko realized. *Frightened, perhaps, that we bring more plague among them. Or simply of things that they do not understand...*

Recalling his lectures about the Shukyoshi, Shiko mused that perhaps having an escort of soldiers was not such a bad idea while traversing their capital city. To the Shukyoshi priests, non-believers were anathema, a scourge on the world, as they perceived it. Their holy books spoke of the need to cleanse the land; indeed, no greater 'salvation' could be obtained than by 'purifying' their world. Since the rise of Shukyoshi military power, only the superior strength of the Yutakashi, and the magical abilities of the Tejinashi, had kept the Shukyoshi in check and within their own borders. Here, however, inside their most sacred city, their fanaticism was sure to know few boundaries.

Toshi-hito and the other Masters at the priory had taught him about the kingdoms, and he knew that in the past Shukyoshi had been less zealous in its pursuit of religious purity. They had always held deep convictions, many of which ran counter to the beliefs of others in Tonogato; but in earlier times the Shukyoshi had been content to leave non-believers to follow different paths. Somewhere along the way that tolerance had apparently evaporated, and been replaced by a burning desire to stamp the Shukyoshi view of reality upon all of Tonogato.

A shutter opened high up on one of the houses that lined the avenue, and a woman's head appeared just long enough to spit down on the Hajimeshi walking below. It missed, hitting the cobbles of the streets between the horses, but the woman did not see the results as she quickly slammed the shutter closed again.

Ryori, closest to the spewed missile, looked up contemptuously. "Could've nailed her from down here, given half a chance," he muttered. The nearest Shukyoshi soldier leveled his lance in the cook's direction, and Ryori quickly turned away.

The street that the pilgrims and their escort were on ended a short distance away, opening up on to a vista of clear land at the base of the Fortress. The group of horses walked out of the street and into the clearing before the hill. It was certainly an impressive sight that unfolded before them: for a distance of two hundred paces around the base of the steep hill, all trees and vegetation had been cleared. A ditch had been dug completely around the hill, separating the flat cleared portion from the precipitous crags marking the hill proper. Lines of pointed stakes had been placed within this dry moat as a first line of defense; hardly needed, thought Shiko, considering the impregnable look of the castle itself that lay beyond the moat.

The walls of the Fortress proper emerged as if growing straight out of the hillside, merging seamlessly with the natural rocks. The early-morning sun struck the dull ochre of the stone blocks making up the walls, causing the entire Fortress to look as if it were an angry fire burning atop a mountain.

Turrets had been placed all along the wall's length, with even taller towers placed within the Fortress overlooking the cleared ground outside. There was no approach to the castle that was not within the line of fire of at least two towers, Shiko noted. A single massive gatehouse, itself bounded by towers on each of its corners, stood along the wall facing the city. Its drawbridge was raised, the castle sealed from within. No soldiers were visible on the ramparts as the Shukyoshi cavalrymen herded their charges over to a small stone stable and guardhouse, situated just beyond the edge of the city. The Shukyoshi officer turned to Toshi-hito and Itachi. "You will leave your horses and baggage here. All who enter the holy Fortress do so on foot, in supplication to the Goddess."

Itachi scowled, looking back along his line of men. "We will leave the cook here. We won't need him with us."

The officer smirked. "You need not fear theft of your ill-gotten property, heathen. No one here would soil their hands with it. Leave the servant behind if you want. It will make no difference."

With those decidedly discouraging words, the Hikari pilgrims dismounted. Each of the Guards walked his mount over to Ryori, who tied them to a hitching rail in front of the stable. As Toshi-hito delivered his horse Ryori said quietly, "Moat covered with stakes. Fortified gatehouse. Crenellated towers. Arrow-loops. We're in the center of their kingdom and they look set for a siege. Can't quite see what they got to be so afraid of."

Toshi-hito looked back at the Fortress. "Perhaps it is not physical might that worries them, Master Cook. I suspect it has more to do with things that no manner of wall, despite its thickness, can withstand." At Ryori's puzzled look, Toshi-hito smiled sadly. "Ideas, Master Cook. The most dangerous of weapons." He left his horse and re-joined Shiko and the others.

Itachi was forming his men into ranks, their depleted numbers making for a small formation. Toshi-hito turned to the general. "I would like Shiko to carry the Hikari into the castle." Itachi nodded his agreement. Presumably, Toshi-hito surmised, the Hajimeshi lord was glad to relieve one of his fighting men of the burden. Not that they stood any chance should it come to that, he realized. But he understood that a soldier would prefer to be unencumbered if he had to make a fight of it.

The Deshi Master, on the other hand, had quite a different motive in mind. He had grave doubts that, once having entered the Fortress, they might walk out again. If any of them had the slightest chance it would be he who physically carried the Hikari. There was the slight possibility that the bearer might be spared, the Shukyoshi honoring the ancient tradition enough that they would not strike down one who held aloft the light. If so, he had decided, then Shiko must be that one. He watched as Donaku handed the lantern to the apprentice, the Guard resuming his place among the ranks.

It had been some time, thought Shiko, since he had felt the weight of the Hikari, but its very heaviness felt reassuring. He was apprehensive; while having less knowledge than Toshi-hito about the Shukyoshi, it was evident to all of the Hajimeshi that their situation was perilous. They might be doing no more than marching to their own execution. Oddly, though, frightened as he was, something about holding the Hikari again somehow felt…right. His mind and his body were alternating between agitation and exhaustion; but somewhere deep inside he found a quiet peace, totally separate from the events swirling outside his physical space. He tried to focus on that feeling, and use it to help him keep steady the light that hung above them all.

Once every man was ready, Itachi nodded at Toshi-hito. The Deshi Master led the way, Shiko at his side bearing the lantern. The Guards fell in behind, led by Itachi. Ryori watched as they marched, alone, out on the path toward the castle. He drew in to spit, but spied a Shukyoshi soldier eyeing him with a frown. Very carefully, he swallowed.

As the pilgrims walked toward the raised drawbridge, Shiko suddenly felt an urge to talk. After all the hours of unnatural silence, if this was to be their last sunrise he wanted to make the most of it. The Deshi order believed that the only true possession a person owned was knowledge, and so Shiko reverted to his training and initiated a dialogue with Toshi-hito. "I used to think, Master," he said, forcing his voice to sound calm, "that we in Hajimeshi lived more coarsely than others, particularly the Yutakashi. But seeing *these* people makes our home seem gentle and refined by comparison."

Toshi-hito smiled, seemingly as serene as if he were strolling into the castle at Hajimeshi rather than the Fortress. "The Shukyoshi value simplicity above all else. If it does not serve the Goddess, then it is superfluous."

"Their faith must be very strong, then, for them to live like this."

"The difficulty of believing does not in itself make faith well-placed. As we passed through the city, did you see any public paintings? Any theaters? Art and culture only flourish where there is freedom of thought. Here there is none. A people without culture live behind a closed door, and can but see the world through the keyhole."

The group walked up to the edge of the moat, coming to a halt before the vast drawbridge. Still there was no sign of life from within the castle, no acknowledgement of their approach. They waited, the sun having now reached up to its mid-morning height and bringing with it sweat to the already apprehensive pilgrims. At last, even though there had been no sign to indicate that they had been observed, a deep rumble heralded the movement of the drawbridge. Slowly, its chains clattering in a teeth-jarring cacophony, the drawbridge tilted down toward them, so close that to Shiko it seemed as if it would land atop them and squash them like troublesome insects. Finally it dropped level with the clearing, seating itself in a stone shelf along the moat's edge.

The gaping mouth of the gatehouse stood open, the inner portcullis already raised. No Shukyoshi emerged to usher them in. Once the rattling noise of the drawbridge chains had stopped, there was no other sound but that of the low wind whispering among the stakes in the moat, their sharpened points angled up like rows of colossal teeth.

Toshi-hito looked straight ahead through the castle gate. "Let us deliver the message of the Kojuro." He strode forward across the drawbridge, and the rest of the pilgrims followed, until all were swallowed up by the darkness of the gatehouse passage.

The stone passageway was dark, but Shiko could see enough in the dim light to identify drop-holes in the arched ceiling where boiling pitch could be dropped on the heads of attackers, as well as arrow-loops in the walls to either side. The air was cool but musty, almost fetid. He supposed that the gates must normally be kept closed, only opened when people were allowed to pass through: a transitory space where no one dwelt, only hurried through while crossing from one side to the other. An open arch marked the end of the passageway. Toshi-hito did not hesitate but led the Hajimeshi directly out and into the open.

The sun had not yet risen high enough to spill over the castle walls, the space the pilgrims entered still in partial darkness. The shadowy light available, however, was enough for the Hajimeshi to see that they had marched forward into a small inner ward. It was completely enclosed by its own small wall, surrounded in turn by the higher walls of the rest of the castle.

Stationed around the perimeter, atop the wall, were Shukyoshi archers, each standing a few paces from the next. Their black armor and helmets blended in with their faces in the dim light, making each man indistinguishable from his neighbor. They looked down on the courtyard on all four sides, bows in hand and arrows notched at the ready.

Along the far wall opposite the arch was a short raised platform, surmounted by a canopy to provide shade from a sun that could not yet reach it. Atop the platform were half a dozen men, one of whom was seated on a backless chair in the center, the others kneeling around him. The large man sitting on the chair, Shiko realized, must be the Anasaki, and those around him his senior warrior priests. The Shukyoshi leader was a large, barrel-chested man, with strong, muscular arms. Shiko recalled that the Anasaki was rumored to have killed an even-dozen 'heathens,' two of them in hand-to-hand combat.

The Anasaki's hair was silver but from the looks of him Shiko had no doubt that the man could still hold his own against a warrior half his age. The man's face was set in a grim mask, his armor a mirror copy of the other Shukyoshi save for its color. In place of the lustrous black of the common warrior priest, the Anasaki's armor was of iridescent blue, accented with a shawl draped around his neck that trailed down to the level of his knees. Made of heavy cloth, the shawl was emblazoned with the shasen symbol down its entire length. The other senior warrior priests on the platform sported similar shawls, and were armed with swords at their sides.

All were keeping their eyes forward, focused on the approaching pilgrims. No other Shukyoshi were on the ground inside the compound; all the rest were ranged along the walls above. As he made his observations Shiko found time to be surprised at himself. Here he was, marching into a hostile castle, where death might fly down from the walls at any moment. Yet still he was observing, and remembering, in true Deshi fashion. Even so, were both his hands not gripped about the Hikari's supporting pole, he knew he would be holding his honsho even tighter...

The Deshi Master strode unhesitatingly toward the platform along with his fellow pilgrims. No one among the Shukyoshi spoke or moved. The Shukyoshi archers were well disciplined; no arrows were loosed upon the 'heretics,' or even so much as an arm raised. When Toshi-hito had walked halfway across the courtyard, the Anasaki raised a hand slightly from the arm of his chair. At this subtle signal, one of his senior warrior priests rose from his kneeling position. Eyes never leaving the approaching Hajimeshi, the man walked forward and stepped off the platform. He strode forward and planted himself, feet spread wide, directly in Toshi-hito's path. His right hand rested on the pommel of his sword, the traditional warning to others that a man was prepared to fight. From underneath the brow of his helmet a face peered out that was devoid of fear, confidant in the righteousness of his beliefs.

Toshi-hito calmly came to a halt a few paces away from the priest, Shiko and the others stopping behind him. Slowly the Deshi Master drew his arms out away from his body; then, with careful and deliberate movements, designed to show that he carried no weapon, he reached with his right hand inside his tunic. He withdrew the parchment scroll from the Kojuro authorizing their pilgrimage. Holding on to one end, he held the tightly rolled scroll aloft. He spoke quietly, his voice echoing in the open space. "I come as a pilgrim beneath the Hikari, to deliver a message to the Anasaki."

The priest standing before him glowered and declared in a strident voice, "Only those who revere the Goddess may have audience with his Excellency, the Anasaki. Are you a believer in the Goddess?"

"If," answered Toshi-hito, "by your question you mean, do I interpret the world only by what the holy books of Shukyoshi proclaim, ignoring all evidence that my own eyes and ears perceive, then the answer would be no." A few paces behind Toshi-hito, Shiko tensed. The Hajimeshi Guards all stood perfectly still, their rock-hard discipline rivaling that of the Shukyoshi.

The priest spat out, "Then you are an abomination; you despoil the land of the Goddess!" In a precise movement, he pulled his sword out several inches from its scabbard, revealing a portion of the steel blade. To a warrior this was a direct challenge to combat.

"Nevertheless," countered Toshi-hito, stepping forward, "I walk under the Hikari, the sanctity of which pre-dates even the Shukyoshi. I come to speak to the Anasaki."

"You shall speak to the Goddess first!" cried the priest.

What occurred next took but an instant, and it took Shiko some time to realize exactly what happened. The priest, in one fluid motion, drew his sword, slicing up and to the right in a move calculated to remove the Deshi Master's head with a single blow.

But Toshi-hito's head was not there. At the first hint that the blade was being drawn Toshi-hito relaxed his knees, while keeping his upper body rigid. He thus dropped nearly straight down while remaining upright. The priest, unable to change his direction quickly enough, slashed his sword through empty air where Toshi-hito's head had been, missing by less than a hair's breadth. The stroke left his sword arm stretched out from his body and his front unprotected. Without having made the expected impact, he was now also off balance and had pitched forward slightly.

In that precisely timed instant Toshi-hito, having hit the ground with his knees, lunged upward with his right arm, holding the parchment. It had been rolled so tightly that when combined with the heavy thickness of the scroll paper it had the resiliency almost of a wooden stick. The end opposite to that held in Toshi-hito's hand impacted hard against the priest's throat, just below his helmet strap, collapsing the man's windpipe with a sickening sound like that of a rotten fruit crushed underfoot.

All of which had happened in almost the blink of an eye. Shiko had been shocked to first see Toshi-hito drop, then the glint of light as the sword flashed through the air, followed by the priest staggering as he was hit by the Deshi Master.

The swordsman instinctively turned his arm, ready to deliver a downward deathblow to his opponent on the ground, then found he could not breathe. His left hand reached up to his throat as he stepped back, then he dropped the sword and clutched madly at his neck. The falling sword nicked Toshi-hito's left arm as it fell, cutting into the flesh before dropping to the dirt. The priest staggered backward, eyes bulging. Toshi-hito never moved after striking the priest, even when the sword blade drew blood as it fell.

Itachi, never an easy man to impress, was nevertheless surprised. Grudgingly he took a fleeting moment to admire the Deshi's skill in defeating an armed opponent. Well, he thought, it's done. Now we are certainly dead men; I wonder where the first arrow will strike?

He resolved to reach for his blade as soon as he felt the first blow, even though he doubted that he would be able to draw it before he was brought down. But he would die ready to fight, as a warrior should.

The arrows, however, did not come. No one on either side made a sound, except for the warrior priest who had attacked Toshi-hito. He gurgled and gasped, a horrific sound, as he tried to force air into his shattered throat. Staggering back several paces, he collapsed to his knees. The watching Shukyoshi remained immobile as the priest's face turned blue, then white, and he collapsed sideways to the dirt. The ward was blanketed in silence, the twitching of the dying man's body the only movement. Only when that at last had stopped, and the body relaxed in death, did Toshi-hito stand.

Shiko's arms had begun shaking, and it was only with difficulty that he managed to keep the Hikari aloft. Like the others around him, once he realized what Toshi-hito had done, he had expected that they would all be killed instantly. Instead they had all watched a macabre scene as the warrior priest had noisily died. Why were they waiting, he wondered. Why had the Anasaki not signaled to those on the walls to shoot them all down?

Toshi-hito looked back over his shoulder to the Hajimeshi behind him, a signal to follow. He walked forward, the blood unleashed from the falling sword running down his arm unheeded. Shiko, struggling to keep the contents of his stomach from rising, forced his legs to unlock and moved forward as well. Itachi and the others followed behind.

Toshi-hito stepped directly over the dead warrior priest who had tried to block his path, his own blood dripping on the man as he passed. He walked another few paces then stopped. Shiko stopped just short of the dead priest, the body practically at his feet. He kept his eyes averted, concentrating on Toshi-hito. He could not, however, remove the smell of death from beneath his nose. Toshi-hito looked to the platform, and with deliberation once more repeated, "I come to speak to the Anasaki."

To Shiko it was clear that the Deshi Master intended to fight as many of the Shukyoshi warrior priests sent against him as needed until he was allowed to deliver his message, or until he was killed. The apprentice had many times observed Toshi-hito practicing his martial arts skills, but had never seen him perform a move anything like the one he had used against the warrior priest. Even so Shiko very much doubted that his Master would be able to pull off such a feat a second time. Despite a trembling panic that threatened to overwhelm him, he still found himself able to fear for Toshi-hito.

No one among the Shukyoshi moved. At length, the Anasaki himself spoke, in a deep, gravelly voice. "Hutagano's faith was clearly wanting. He was bested by a heathen, and an unarmed one at that. A poor showing for one of Shukyoshi's senior warriors." He kept his gaze fixed on Toshi-hito, as if no one else were present.

Toshi-hito replied, "I regret the necessity, your Excellency, that led to your follower's death. However, I am on a holy pilgrimage, and cannot betray the Hikari for any man of Tonogato."

"Do not grieve for the fallen, heretic," replied the Anasaki icily. "Were he virtuous enough Hutagano would be standing before me now, and your head lying in the dust. That it is not is due solely to the insufficiency of his faith." He looked past Toshi-hito at Shiko and the Hikari, and the small contingent of soldiers behind. "I would not have expected such an appropriately modest procession from a heathen such as your Kojuro. It is some small credit toward his eventual redemption by the Goddess." When Toshi-hito did not respond to this, the Anasaki's voice took on a harder edge. "The Hikari lantern is all that stands between you and the damnation of your souls. It was well that a man of your standing was sent, as you are but a messenger of ill-conceived thoughts. Were you the Omo Deshi, even the Hikari would be insufficient to save you."

"I journey under the guidance of the light, your Excellency," answered Toshi-hito, "not that of the Omo Deshi. He is but a man, and all men are vain." Throughout Toshi-hito's exchange with the Anasaki, no man among the Hajimeshi had moved. Unnoticed, however, one of the Castle Guards behind Toshi-hito narrowed his eyes at this derogation of the senior Deshi leader.

Toshi-hito continued: "What any man may consider the right path in one age, and writes down as the truth, may be considered wrong and excoriated in another. Who decides? Only he who follows the light in his own heart can truly understand the world."

The Anasaki frowned at Toshi-hito. "I will not debate theology with you, heretic. Any words you speak are perforce blasphemous." He leaned forward. "I am not unaware of your Hikari pilgrimage. Your search for a Kotaishi to unite Tonogato is correct in principle, merely misguided in its execution." He paused, spreading his thick arms to either side. "Does it surprise you to know that I too believe in the Kotaishi? It is true; I do not doubt that a Kotaishi will be found. But contrary to what you misled souls from the east believe, he will be a follower of the Goddess, for it is clear that the Shukyoshi are the chosen ones." He stood up and walked to the edge of the platform. He gazed over at the Hikari that Shiko held aloft, then back down to Toshi-hito. "The Hikari is an ancient tradition. It is even spoken of in our holy books. When those words were written, pilgrims from our land journeyed forth to spread the word of the Goddess, but they were ridiculed, ignored. Soon our message will be ignored no longer. A Kotaishi will reveal himself, and he will be a true believer. He will lead us in uniting Tonogato under the banners of the Goddess."

Shiko, even from a distance, could see the intense fervor in the man's eyes as he spoke. There was no doubting the Anasaki's absolute conviction in his principles. He was a man, the apprentice realized, who would follow his principles into death, believing in the will of his Goddess.

The Anasaki turned his back on Toshi-hito, returning to his chair. He took several moments to resettle himself, letting the tension hang in the air as if it were a palpable thing. Finally he cast his gaze back onto the Deshi Master.

"You will leave our lands," he said offhandedly. "I spare you not only for the honor of the Hikari, but because you walk for a cause that in the end will see Shukyoshi preeminent in Tonogato, bringing the glory of the Goddess to all the heathens of this earth. It matters not that you are too ignorant to see this end; it is the inevitable outcome. If your deluded journey assists the other heathens of Tonogato in accepting the inevitability of a Kotaishi, then it serves some small purpose of the Goddess." He waved his hand in a gesture of dismissal.

Toshi-hito bowed to the Anasaki, then turned and stepped once more over the form of the dead warrior priest. Arm sticky with congealing blood, he looked down at Shiko. "Come," he said quietly.

Itachi and the Hajimeshi soldiers parted ranks, allowing Toshi-hito and Shiko to walk between them, the Hikari lantern suspended above. As the two Deshi marched out through the gatehouse, the Hajimeshi soldiers followed behind, Itachi bringing up the rear.

No one was more astonished than Ryori to see the two Deshi emerge from the castle, the Guards right behind. He dashed out into the clearing and let out a whoop, the scowling Shukyoshi lancers notwithstanding. He waited until Toshi-hito was within speaking distance, then called out, "Figurin' it'd be the last I'd see of any of you. Thought I might have to take up Shukyoshi cookin'." Then the cook noticed Toshi-hito's wound. "Well, wasn't all fun and games, I see. Best I get out the healing herbs again." Before he could turn away, Itachi strode up.

"Where are the horses?" demanded the Hajimeshi general.

Ryori turned to where the horses had been. The hitching rail was empty, the pilgrims' packs thrown upon the ground. The Shukyoshi lancers sat atop their own horses near the stable, otherwise ignoring the Hajimeshi. There was no sign of the pilgrims' horses. "Well," said the little man, "these here horse soldiers, they said they figured that all animals belong to this Goddess of theirs. Seems they feel that heathens like us ought not to be keeping any animal of hers, and so, well," he gestured helplessly, "they took 'em. Guess they don't consider horses to be 'ill-gotten' property."

Itachi grabbed the cook by the front of his tunic, twisting it in his fist. In a low, menacing voice, he said, "You let these Shukyoshi take all of our horses?"

Ryori looked up into Itachi's blazing eyes. "Wern't too much I could say 'bout it, don't you think, my Lord? I'm just a cook."

Itachi glowered into the cook's face then released him with a shove. He turned and looked back up toward the castle. "Thieving hypocrites," he said bitterly. "If I had been allowed to bring the number of men I had wanted on this journey I would have taken this pathetic rock pile and reduced it to pebbles."

Bokusa was staring stupidly at the empty hitching rail and at their packs and gear. "How can we go on now? How do we carry all of this?"

Toshi-hito stepped forward. "On our backs," he said softly. He hefted his travel pack with his good arm. "The Shukyoshi have faith in their Goddess, and this lends them strength when other men would fail. We are no less strong for the things that we believe in. Horses are convenient; but before we tasked them to become our servants, man walked his own burdens." He settled the pack over his shoulder and set off down the hill, pausing only long enough for Ryori to quickly bind up his wound.

Nakama quickly separated himself from the group of soldiers and lifted his own pack, and Shiko's. He and the apprentice, who was still carrying the Hikari, set off to follow the Deshi Master.

The other Guards stared at Itachi, whose expression grew even darker. "Well?" he demanded. "What are you waiting for? A Shukyoshi lancer to carry your pack? Make like horses!" The men gathered up their belongings from the ground and followed the Deshi in a ragged line down the hill. The last was Ryori, his pots and pans clanging from every side as he staggered under his overstuffed pack.

15

Singing, thought Mikasama. It sounds like birds singing.

The soft sounds echoed in her mind as she passed in and out of sleep. Her thoughts tumbled about, disconnected in that way of dreams. It must be morning, some part of her thought, for the birds to be singing. How odd; they're all singing the same tune.

She rolled over on her pallet and came abruptly awake as a strand of straw scratched against her face. Groggily she tried to focus her eyes, but it was too dark. The singing was still there; it was not birds, she realized, but people. The Sisters were all singing. She could make out, faintly, some of the words: it was their morning prayer.

With a groan she rolled over again and tried to sleep, but sleep would not return. It was just as well, she thought; I'm so tired of the dreams...

She was startled into full wakefulness, however, by a knock on the door to her diminutive sleeping cell and the sound of a woman's voice from the other side. It was one of the Sisters, waiting to conduct her to the common eating hall. The Princess had never awoken before to the sound of anyone but Komori. As far back as she could remember Nana-san had been a part of her mornings. She felt a profound emptiness as, dressing quickly, she slipped out into the cold, dark hallway to follow the silent Sister.

The monastery was called Fumosa. Some two-dozen Shukyoshi Sisters, both young and old, called it home, serving their Goddess with prayers and simple labor; and now, nursing as well. For since the plague had come, more and more people from the surrounding countryside had fallen ill. Having no other healers the farmers brought their sick to Fumosa, where the Sisters did what they could. They had a few rudimentary healing skills and a variety of medicinal herbs; but these were largely ineffectual against the plague. For the most part all they could provide was prayer and, at the last, burial rites.

The Sisters had been no more immune to the plague than the farmers, and their ranks had suffered as well. At one time Fumosa had been a major religious house of the Shukyoshi, a center for religious instruction and direction for all of the southern Shukyoshi lands. A chapter of male priests had also been in residence, with a senior priest leading both the Brothers and the Sisters. Those in the south, however, had always held slightly different views than their brethren to the north: more open to ideas, a little less rigid in following orthodox precepts. As the warrior priests had gained the ascendancy in the north, these views had become significant points of disagreement. Fumosa's senior priest was recalled and never replaced. The chapter of Brothers was disbanded, most of its members traveling north to swell the ranks of the emerging warrior-priest culture centered in the Fortress.

The monastery had declined into a rural religious house; where once it could boast of attracting the daughters of well-bred and refined families among its members, now most of the Sisters came from farms or working families. A few had no past at all, or at least none that was inquired about. No volunteers to the service of the Goddess were turned away at Fumosa.

Then the plague had come, further reducing the number of Sisters at Fumosa. The common eating hall, built to hold nearly a hundred souls, was now usually cavernously empty; less than a quarter of that number were in attendance at any one time. The emptiness was a constant reminder to the monastery's residents of both their own past and their perilous present. Prayers to the Goddess were plentiful in these turbulent times.

True to her word, Mother Narisa had instructed the other Sisters to leave Mikasama alone, and thus she sat apart in the dining hall at a table that had been built to seat ten or more. Compounding her isolation was the fact that Shukyoshi meal times were conducted in absolute silence, as the Sister who had escorted her to the hall had cautioned her. Conversation was never encouraged at any time during the day, she had been told, except as necessary to conduct one's work. Meal times, however, were considered a time to nourish the body and the soul together, and the soul's nourishment came from prayer and contemplation, not from idle chatter. Looking at the meager food provided, Mikasama hoped that the nourishment the Sisters received from their prayers was more filling than that provided by their diet.

After she had finished eating, the Princess watched with a moment of fleeting panic as all the Sisters rose to leave. She didn't know where to go or how to find the sick ward where Komori had been taken. In their identical blue habits all of the Sisters looked alike to her; she didn't recognize any of the faces she had seen the previous night.

Then one face stood out, clear and sharp in her memory: a pair of blue eyes, intensely reflecting the color of her habit. Shudojo!

The blue-eyed Sister was exiting the eating hall with two others. Mikasama quickly rose and followed the trio outside, catching up with them as they walked across the courtyard in which Mikasama and Komori had arrived the previous evening.

"Shudojo! Wait, please!"

The three Sisters stopped and looked at the Princess as she ran up breathlessly. "Please, can you take me to the sick ward? I have to see Ko—my mother."

The other two Sisters looked briefly at Shudojo, then silently turned and drifted away. Shudojo glanced after them as they departed then turned back with a frown. "I am on my way there now," she said impassively. "Sister Choda has detailed me to care for your mother. You may accompany me if you wish." She turned and continued across the courtyard, leaving the Princess to follow behind her.

Mikasama, unused to such coldness, bit back a retort. This Sister, she reminded herself, had taken them in when nobody in the village would. Had it not been for her, Nana-san might still be shivering outside in a cart.

With Mikasama a few steps behind, the Sister crossed to the far side of the courtyard toward a large building, which the Princess now recognized as the one she had seen the Sisters take Komori to the night before. It was taller than the other buildings but had no windows into the courtyard, only a single stout-looking wooden door. Its roof, like those of the other buildings of Fumosa, was covered with rust-colored tiles, in between which grass and weeds had long since taken root along with several bird nests. Indeed, a couple of birds now sat perched atop one corner of the building, looking down at the people going about their affairs down below.

Shudojo walked up to a large wooden door and grasped the iron bar that served as its handle. The heavy door slid sideways in its frame as she pulled. The shrieking sound it made as it moved startled the birds; they took wing together, and flew off beyond the walls of the monastery. The Sister looked over her shoulder briefly at the Princess then stepped through the open doorway. As Mikasama stepped over the threshold to follow her, the sounds and smells of sickness assaulted her senses. She stopped just inside, instinctively raising her hand to cover her nose and mouth.

She stood in a long open room, the roof supported by a row of large pillars down the center. She guessed, from the room's shape, that at one time it must have been used as a barn; but now it was lined with sleeping pallets down its entire length. There were ranks of them along the wall, and several more rows crowding the floor space in between. Nearly every pallet appeared occupied.

An old man was coughing violently, and just inside the doorway a young girl was crying, curled up into a ball. The Princess kept her hand up to her face as Shudojo led her through the warren of pallets, Mikasama trying to keep from stepping on stray arms or legs hanging out in the ragged pathway between the rows. Several large copper kettles had been set up in the center of the room as makeshift washbasins. Along one wall, a line of short, wide windows was set high up near the roof. The glass was dirty, and the weak light that made it through to illuminate the hall caused eerie shadows to play among the roof beams.

Komori had been placed along the wall with the windows, covered with a blanket now rather than Shudojo's rain cloak. She was asleep, her breathing as hard and labored as it had been the day before. Mikasama, trying to keep the stench of so many sickly bodies from overcoming her, looked down at her caretaker.

Shudojo's voice still bore no trace of emotion. "She has not woken since you arrived." She leaned over and straightened one end of the blanket that Komori had kicked off in her sleep. "Her body is concentrating on fighting the plague. Only the Goddess knows if she will win."

* * *

By the dawn of Mikasama's third day at Fumosa the sound of the Sisters' morning prayer singing had started to become familiar to the Princess, less alien than it had seemed at first.

Komori had not regained consciousness on the first day, nor on the second. Mikasama had watched, and waited, feeling helpless while Komori had groaned and tossed in her enforced sleep. Shudojo had applied wet cloths to Komori's sweating brow and had attended to the old woman's bodily functions, which occurred on their own schedule. All of which had left Mikasama very uncomfortable. Having been raised as a princess, proximity to nursing tasks had not been a part of her life; she had never taken care of anyone. As a result she had sat by helplessly while Shudojo attended to the needs of Komori's body.

What will I do, Mikasama now wondered as she lay on her pallet, if Nana-san stays this way and never wakes up? Will my days always be like this, waiting to see if she will? Waking to the sound of prayers sung to a Goddess I know nothing about? Or will I end up like one of them, wearing a blue habit and tilling a field with a hoe? It's so far removed from Hajimeshi court life, from being a princess, it almost seems like some other world. Oh, Nana-san, why won't you wake up?

A knock on the wooden door interrupted her reverie. Before she could answer, the door opened just a crack. The light of a candle spilled through the opening, held in the hand of one the Sisters. Before she spoke, Mikasama recognized who it was, the blue eyes reflecting the candle like twin sapphires.

"Your mother is awake. She is asking for you."

In the meager light provided by the candles, set to either side of Komori's pallet, the pallor of her skin was less noticeable. When Mikasama knelt by her side, the tired old eyes fluttered open, then closed, while the old woman forced a weak smile through parched lips. Shudojo gently lifted Komori's head and poured a small amount of liquid down it. Most of it was coughed back up, but enough went down to ease Komori's speech.

"Hey, Mika..." the old woman croaked. "Thought I'd gone off to land o' the dead," as she gestured feebly at the blue-clad Shudojo. "Thought I'd missed sayin' goodbye." She reached out with a weak hand to grab hold of Mikasama's arm. "Good to see your pretty face again." Looking up at the Princess's head, she mumbled, "What you done t'yer hair, girl? Look awful. Get Nana-san a comb; she make it right." But her eyes closed, and she fell back into sleep.

Mikasama struggled to keep her tears in check. All around them the sounds of coughing and sickness filled the air, as others afflicted with the plague fought their own private struggles. Shudojo rose, clearly uncomfortable. Mikasama looked up. "What is it? What's wrong?"

The Sister looked first at Komori, then to Mikasama. "I'm sorry. Sister Choda has order—has asked that I assist the other Sisters. We have many sick from the plague, some of whom are less afflicted than your mother…" She turned her head away. "You have watched what I have done. The things you need are here, to make her more comfortable." She started to go.

"Wait, please!" said Mikasama in a panic. "I—I don't know how to do any of this. How can I care for her?"

Coldly Shudojo replied, "She is your mother. It should not be too difficult for you to figure out what to do. One simply does what one must, to ease the other's pain." She turned and walked away, leaving Mikasama alone with the sleeping Komori. As the Princess looked down at her, feeling helpless, the tears came again.

Komori drifted in and out of sleep. Mikasama stayed in the ward, propping herself up against the wall to rest while Komori slept, kneeling by the old woman's side whenever she stirred. Once-pampered hands tentatively tried to change a soiled sheet, but Mikasama's efforts to minimize untidiness in the end only made things worse. The resulting mess forced her to have to wash herself at the common washbasin. After that, she resigned herself to the necessary routine of care and tried to set her squeamishness aside.

Well, she reminded herself, there's no one else to do it; and maybe, just maybe, if I take care of her well enough, Komori will get better sooner. Because she has to. She just has to.

In the evening, Komori began shivering again with fever. She awoke from a fitful sleep to see a tired Mikasama staring down at her. The old eyes opened wide for a moment, then closed. "Humph," she said weakly. "Thought you was your Mama, for a minute…Startin' to look jus' like her."

Despite her tiredness the Princess was shocked by Komori's words. "Nana-san! You never told me you knew my mother!"

"Oh, yes...she was pretty one...Headstrong, too, just like you." She coughed harshly, and Mikasama lifted Komori's head to help her to drink a little water.

After she had laid Komori's head back on the pillow, and brushed some of the tangled grey hair out of the old woman's eyes, Mikasama leaned against the edge of the pallet. "But Nana-san, Papa said my mother died."

"Did he now?" replied Komori feebly, eyes closed. "Is that what he said?"

"Well, he—" Mikasama thought back. She hadn't actually spoken to Papa about her mother in years. It had always seemed to make him so sad, so she had learned not to bring it up. From the way her father had acted, though, Mikasama had always just assumed that her mother was dead. "I'm not sure—all he said, I think, the last time I asked was something like, 'She left us, a long time ago.' "

"Oh, she did, she did...But she didn't die, no, no, no..." Komori's eyes closed, and her voice grew faint. "She had to go away, is all."

"Had to go away? What do you mean? Where? Why did she have to go?"

"Oh, too many questions!" said Komori tiredly. "Not supposed to talk about, anyway...Never mind..." She turned her head away.

"But Nana-san, wait, please! How did you know my mother? Is she still alive?"

"Nana-san tired now, need to sleep..." She opened an eye, and squeezed Mikasama's hand feebly. "Talk more later..." Then she dozed off, leaving Mikasama in turmoil.

The Princess sat by the sleeping form of Komori for a long while, her eyes focused elsewhere. *Why*, she wondered, *had my mother been sent away? Why wouldn't Papa talk about her?*

As she looked down at the sleeping form of Komori, her brow furrowed. *And why hadn't Nana-san told me about her during all these years?*

Mikasama spent a restless night curled up on the floor at Komori's bedside, amid the coughing of the other patients in the ward. She had almost grown used to the smell of sickness but the sounds of those in pain at times was almost too much for her. She tried to keep her hearing focused on Komori, listening for any sign that she might stir, but the old woman's labored breathing never varied.

Sleep for the Princess finally came late, and was troubled again by the dreams, so familiar to her now but still unsettling. She awoke in a cold sweat and waited for the dawn while listening to the groans of the ill around her. As the faint light of morning fell from the windows overhead Shudojo arrived, bringing the Princess some food from the eating hall. The Sister then helped to shift Komori about on her pallet to a cleaner spot, although still the old woman did not wake. Komori's fever came and went, and for the moment had broken once again, leaving her brow glistening with sweat. While Shudojo cleaned Komori's face with a damp cloth, Mikasama sat on the opposite side of the bed and watched the Sister.

"Shudojo?" she asked suddenly. "Why didn't I get sick?" She put her hand on Komori's arm. "We were together on the road the whole time."

Shudojo shrugged as she finished cleaning Komori's face. "We have seen large families where only one person fell ill; another where a dozen were laid to rest, the only survivor being a great grandfather, condemned to see his entire progeny die before him." She wrung out the cloth into a bucket by the bed then turned her gaze back to Mikasama. "Who can say? The ways of the Goddess are not apparent to us."

Those odd blue eyes, thought the Princess; I wonder if they see the same way ours do? Or does she see the world differently?

"Why did you let us in," she asked, "that night that we came? Why didn't you throw us out for being heathens?"

Shudojo stood as she pulled Komori's blanket up under the old woman's chin. "Your mother was ill. I thought she might not be too far along with the plague."

"Yes, but doesn't most of your order think the fewer heathens the better?" Shudojo turned away, and Mikasama immediately chastised herself, thinking she had let her tongue get the better of her once again.

But at length the Sister spoke, quietly. "Life is a gift from the Goddess. She gave it to all things that live." Her radiant blue eyes touched on Mikasama's briefly before looking away again. "She told me what I must do." Then Shudojo walked away, down to the far end of the ward to where a young boy had been brought in late the night before. The Princess watched her go, reaching out absently and gently stroking Komori's clammy forehead.

She could see a castle. It glittered with light, and strange things that she had never seen before. No one was chasing her, for a change; that was good. She was tired of being chased.

And up ahead, that castle. It was not Hajimeshi; it was not home. But somehow, it felt like home. She wasn't sure why, but she knew she wanted to go there. Had to go there.

"Mikasama?"

Yes? Who is it? Who's calling my name?

In her dream, Mikasama turned back again to gaze at the castle of light.

"Mikasama?"

There it was again. Someone's calling me.

Abruptly she was awake. It was Komori! Nana-san had called her name. She never called Mikasama by her name. In all her life, she could never remember Komori ever referring to her as anything but Mika, or 'the Princess' when talking about her to others.

Mikasama opened her eyes and realized she was sitting on the floor, leaning over Komori's pallet. She must have fallen asleep. As she raised her head, still gathering her wits about her, she saw Komori looking up at her.

"'Bout time," said the old woman feebly. "Girl, you sleep the sleep 'o the dead."

"I'm sorry, Nana-san." Mikasama reached clumsily for the water pitcher. "I didn't realize I had fallen asleep."

Komori waved the water away. "Listen, Mikasama…Have to talk." Hearing Komori's voice say her name sent shivers down Mikasama's spine. The old woman reached out and clutched the Princess's hand in a weak grip. "Need to explain…and…want you to forgive."

Bewildered, Mikasama took Komori's hand in both of her own. The fever had returned and the old woman's skin was hot to the touch. "Explain what, Nana-san? Why should you want me to forgive anything? It's my fault you've gotten sick!" Mikasama's mind started spinning; looking down at Komori's sunken, glassy eyes, she finally realized that her caretaker was slipping away. She desperately wanted to hold on to every minute of Nana-san's life. All of the sounds, and her awareness of the ward around them, melded into a meaningless jumble of noise as Mikasama focused all of her senses on the frail old woman that lay before her.

"Hush," replied Komori. "Just listen…" She rolled painfully to face Mikasama. "When you get back home…want you to deliver message. Want you…to go to White Beard, tell 'im…tell 'im that Komori loved 'im, then…and now." She coughed weakly, choking, and Mikasama managed to get her to take a little water.

"Nana-san," she said once Komori had leaned back again, "I don't understand. Who's White Beard?"

"You really never knew, hey?…Well…that the forgive part." Komori turned her rheumy eyes onto the Princess. "Himitsu. White Beard…he be Himitsu."

Himitsu? Mikasama was bewildered. *Why is she talking about Himitsu? She's dying! We may only have a short while left together. There's so much I still want to talk about! What could Himitsu have to do with anything?*

"Himitsu, child," Komori repeated. "He…he be my husband."

In shock, Mikasama sat back. Husband? "You never told me you were married, Nana-san! And...Himitsu...but...how can that be?" Her mind was confused, her emotions falling to pieces all over themselves. But Komori had yet more to say.

"It was a long, long time ago, child...long before you be born. White Beard...he see me in marketplace, down in Kawashi." She coughed again. "Ship I was on, just docked. And White Beard, he...he decide I look pretty good. I told you," she said with a weak smile, "I made the boy's head's spin, back then...So he buys me."

"Buys you? Nana-san, what are you saying?"

Komori closed her eyes, speaking softly. "Jus' that, girl...He buys me...I was slave girl."

Mikasama was stunned. Nana-san had been a slave? Himitsu had *bought* her?

Komori continued on. "The boy's heads I turned, they be slaves too...White Beard, he puts down money for me...but I don't think he ever knew just what he was buyin'!" She tried to chuckle, but it just made her cough even worse. Some spittle drooled from her mouth, which Mikasama quickly dabbed away. "Made life pretty interestin' for 'im," the old woman went on. "I weren't very good as a slave..."

There was much behind that which Mikasama longed to hear, but she didn't want to stop Komori now that she was talking. She continued wiping the sweat from her caretaker's forehead as she listened.

"Somewheres along the way...old fool decided he loved me...and, I guess, I loved 'im too...He sets me free, then damn if he don't...just tie me up again by taking me to wife." She took a raspy breath and looked up at the Princess. "You know what he do, girl. He be spymaster for the Kojuro...Your Papa, his elder brother, *his* Papa...White Beard never talked 'bout his slave-girl wife...'dangerous,' he said...Enemies, they use that kind of thing against you...So, we love in secret. So many years..."

Her voice trailed off, and Mikasama was afraid she would drift off into sleep again; gently she nudged her caretaker, unwilling to let her go.

Komori's eyes fluttered back open, and she went on as if she had never stopped. "When you was born, White Beard, he say, 'this girl, she very important...Need to make sure nothin' ever happen to her.' So...so...he has me watch over you, and...and tell 'im everything that you do..." She turned her head, eyes filling with tears, and looked at Mikasama. "I watch you grow up...become so pretty." Her hands clutched at Mikasama's. "Please, Mika. Forgive your old Nana-san."

Mikasama could only sit there, shocked into insensibility. What was Nana-san telling her? She was married, to Himitsu of all people. And it was he who had arranged for Komori to be Mikasama's caretaker. Disbelief written across her face, she looked down at Komori, clutching her arm. This frail woman, who had nurtured her since she had learned to walk; who had cared for her, every day of her life; this woman had been *spying* on her, for Himitsu!

Mikasama felt as if the floor had suddenly been swept out from under her feet. Her mind was spinning out of control, all the familiar things to grab onto suddenly out of reach. Komori had been one of her last foundations, and now that too seemed as ephemeral as all the rest. Nana-san and Himitsu. What about Papa? Had he known? He must have known! But why would he have let someone be set up to spy on his own daughter?

"Mikasama!"

The urgent, raspy whisper caught her attention once more. With a start, she focused her eyes back onto Komori. The old woman, tears flowing down her craggy cheeks, was staring up at her, and talking. What was it?

"Please, Mikasama, Mika...forgive silly old woman...Did it for him, I loved him...Then did it for you...Never had my own child; couldn't, with 'im...Had to always hide away...You were my girl. I wanted so bad, be your Nana-san..." She choked, coughed. Instinctively, Mikasama grabbed for the water jug and got Komori to drink. The old woman lay back, exhausted. Her plaintive eyes looked up at Mikasama.

The Princess laid her hand on Komori's forehead. Quietly she said, "Hush, Nana-san. It's all right. Everything's all right." Komori closed her eyes with a sigh. Shortly thereafter she fell back into sleep.

Mikasama sat staring at her for a long time.

*   *   *

As evening came one of the Sisters summoned Shudojo, asking her to go to the sick ward. When she arrived, the feeble light that spilled through the narrow windows of the ward had already dimmed and fled for the night.

She made her way to where she knew the stricken heretic lay, along with the young woman who had said she was her daughter. It was clear to Shudojo that the mother had taken a turn for the worse; her head was turning back and forth, and drool was running down her chin. The girl called Mika was holding one of her mother's hands, watching wordlessly.

Shudojo knelt down on the opposite side of the pallet. She pressed two fingers against the old woman's neck, as she had done the night of the two women's arrival. After a moment she removed her fingers, then reached over and took hold of the mother's other hand as she looked up toward Mika. Blue eyes met black; neither woman needed to speak to know that the mother's time was ending soon. Shudojo inclined her head and closed her eyes, moving her lips in soundless prayer for the old woman's soul.

Later, when the candles at their pallet were the only ones still burning, the old woman died. Shudojo felt the fingers she held grow cold, and she knew that the soul had gone. She prayed that the Goddess had been merciful.

When she opened her eyes, it was to see Mika still sitting silently across from her, staring down at her mother. Shudojo gently placed the old woman's hand across the now-still chest, then reached over and took the other hand from an unresisting Mika and laid it atop its mate. The Sister stood and blew out the candles around the pallet, save one. She looked at the young heretic girl, still staring down at her lost companion.

She is one of the Goddess' children, thought Shudojo, *even though she may not know it, even though the other Sisters may refuse to believe it. But it was the Goddess who spoke to me, back in that cart, when these two arrived; I know it! I don't know why she would want to help unbelievers, but it doesn't matter. If it truly was the Goddess, then perhaps she has finally heard my prayers, and now she will speak to me, and show me that I am indeed on the right path...*

She saw the girl Mika lay her head down on the edge of the pallet. There was something strange about this one, she was certain about it. What such a young woman, obviously from a well-off family, was doing out in the dangerous countryside, was as mysterious as were the ways of the Goddess.

She turned away to join the other Sisters gathering for their before-dawn prayers, leaving Mika alone.

Mikasama, too, hoped in her own way that Komori's soul had found peace, somewhere. For her own soul was a swirling cauldron of turmoil.

She had brought Komori to this, she kept reminding herself over and over. She had been the one to be so obstinate in not turning back, and because of it Komori was now dead. Her Nana-san was dead. That bantering voice, cajoling, clucking, always there—and now, there no more.

And right before the end, those terrible secrets, things she wished she had never heard, and things she wished she knew more about. Himitsu and Komori? She found the thought repellant. All those years…everything she did, every confidence she had with Nana-san, betrayed…

And her mother. What about her mother? Where was she, why had she been forced to go? Komori had been there, had known…but now Mikasama would never know.

She wanted to cry, but she had shed so many tears over the last few days there were no more to be found. And she wasn't sure who she was crying for, Komori or herself…

16

As the light of morning slipped over the sills of the high windows, spilling gently over the sick ward, the Sisters came. Several of them carefully wrapped up Komori's body in the blankets in which she had died, and then they took it away.

Looking down at the pallet, bereft of its recent occupant, Mikasama felt a similar void within her. That place where Nana-san had dwelt within her was now barren, deprived not only of Komori's physical presence but empty as well as a result of knowing Komori's secret.

Nothing being left for her there, the Princess rose and left the ward. With nowhere else to go she wandered back to the tiny room in which she had spent the first few days after her arrival. She curled up on the pallet there, hugging her knees tightly to her chest. In an effort to avoid the painful emptiness left in her heart, her mind cast about until it found something else to latch onto: guilt. She used that to first occupy her mind, and then to flagellate her soul.

Stupid! The word rolled around and around inside Mikasama's head, over and over.

That's the word Nana-san always used, she thought. Never more so than me, now. What lunacy has driven me to this? Yes, maybe that's it; I've really lost my mind. What else could explain my obsession with leaving home, enduring all these deprivations on the road, pushing on when any sane person would have turned back? I know Papa must be worried sick about me and with his health already so bad, that can't have done him any good. How could I have been so callous as to ignore the effect on him of my gallivanting off about the countryside?

And now, now I've really gone too far. I kept pushing, pushing, and loyal Komori would never abandon me. She tried to keep up. But she was old, and I pushed her too hard. She was my caretaker but in turn I was her mistress; I was responsible for her, as I would be for anyone who served me. I abandoned that responsibility, just as assuredly as I abandoned my responsibility to my father.

Why? What is this compulsion that keeps pushing me further and further away from home? Is it pride? Is it Nakama?

She stopped and thought hard about Nakama. After all, it had been to follow him that she had left Hajimeshi in the first place. But somewhere along the way, after encountering her father's soldiers while out on the road, she had come to realize that there was more to her leaving than that. She truly loved Nakama, and right now in particular she would give anything to be with him again. In her heart, though, she could see that there was more to her compulsion than just her pursuit of happiness with Nakama. For whatever it was that was drawing her on, she knew that happiness was not at the end of that road.

Her churning thoughts turned again to the dreams and visions. What are they? she wondered again. Where are they coming from, and why do they have such a hold on me? Are they so strong that they could force me to give up everything? Give up—she had to stop and think for a moment—give up being a princess?

"Is that why I'm doing this?" she asked out loud, her voice a hollow echo in the small chamber. "Am I running away from being what I am? And if I were not Princess Mikasama, then what would I become?"

She thought about the Sisters; their blue habits, their garden implements, their prayers morning, noon, and night. Theirs was a hard life, spent in service to others, corporeal or not. Would that life suit her? she wondered. Was it her destiny to end up here, serving their Goddess?

Mikasama uncurled herself from her pallet and walked hesitantly to the door of her room. She could hear the Sisters singing in their mid-morning prayer gathering. She opened the door a crack and the melodious sound slipped in and filled the tiny space, echoing around the stone walls. Without conscious thought she walked through the doorway and followed the sound of the hymns, the notes that floated down the hallways her trail. She followed them until she came to a large wooden door, embossed with iron studs fashioned after the shasen symbol. Its heavy mass was swung closed, but was no barrier to the joined voices beyond. Mikasama remembered being told that this was the chapel of the Sisters but of course she had never been inside. All she knew was that this was where the Sisters came to commune with their Goddess, and was certainly no place for an outsider.

Now she stood uncertainly. A part of her wanted to just hide from everything, like a small animal fleeing the dangers lurking in the dark. Another part of her, though, knew that she could not escape her life by running away. She had to confront her own demons and discover if her dreams truly had any meaning, or if she were simply going mad. The singing had drawn her here to this door, and as she listened to the gentle voices beyond she found herself intrigued by what drew the Sisters together in this hard life of theirs. A rational voice in her mind cautioned against barging in on the Sister's sacred service, but it was overwhelmed by the sound of the so many more voices that flooded her mind from the other side of the portal. She placed her hands against the door and pushed.

Surprisingly its well-balanced weight swung easily and without a hint of a squeak. Mikasama opened it just enough to slip inside. The room she stepped into was large, with a high ceiling held up by massive beams. The stone walls were bare, enhancing the sound of the Sisters' signing. From her position just inside the doorway she was greeted with a view of the entire congregation of Sisters of Fumosa. They were facing away from her, toward a large, gilded altar along the opposite wall. It was not the altar, though, that caught the Princess's attention; it was the alcove in which it sat.

The huge recess was ablaze with natural light, in complete contrast to all of the other rooms Mikasama had seen in the monastery. From floor to ceiling, stretching up nearly two stories, the alcove's walls were virtually all glass. There were hundreds of tiny panes, each either opaquely frosted or decorated in colorful dyes with scenes from the Shukyoshi holy books. The morning sun filled the room to overflowing with light, reflecting the bright gold of the altar onto the blue habits of the Sisters, which in turn shimmered in the reflected brilliance.

In a rush, images from her dreams flooded Mikasama's mind. She remembered standing in front of a wall made entirely of glass. This wall, she realized with a start. As in her disturbing visions, the sun was shining from the other side, with rays of light flowing past her, behind her...

Instinctively she turned, looking for the doorway she had seen in her dream. But all that was behind her was the great door to the hallway outside, from where she had come.

She turned back to face the brightly-lit wall, awe-struck by its beauty. The feelings of terror and dread that the rest of her dreams had foreshadowed were absent here. All she could feel was a sensation of warmth that matched the touch of the sun's light as it fell upon her face.

None of the Sisters noticed her; Mikasama saw that all had their eyes closed as they sang. The singing was the perfect complement to this perfect light, she thought. Who could know that the Sisters kept this treasure here, behind a heavy wooden door, when all the rest of their world was so drab?

The Sisters sat on rows of benches facing the altar. The Princess started walking forward and at the last moment stopped herself from going straight down the center aisle. Turning aside, she edged along one side of the room. Most of the benches were empty, as there were so few Sisters left at Fumosa. Some three rows from the front, one of the benches was unoccupied and Mikasama silently sat down. She closed her eyes and let the sunlight and the singing wash over her. The peacefulness of the combined sensations made her mind feel as if a tight spring were being gently unwound inside her head.

So relaxed had she become that she barely noticed when the singing had ended. It was only the muffled sound of exclamations and whispered voices that caused her to realize that something had changed. She opened her eyes and saw all of the Sisters staring at her. Sister Choda had risen to stand facing them, prayer book in hand; evidently she had been about to deliver a sermon. The look on her face was a combination of shock and fury. Mother Narisa also rose from where she sat on the far side of the room, in the first row. Turning, she saw the Princess.

Mikasama looked around with embarrassment. "I'm—I'm sorry, I didn't—I didn't mean to intrude. The singing..."

Sister Choda opened her mouth to speak, but Mother Narisa placed a restraining hand on her arm. "It's all right, child," she said to Mikasama. "When the Goddess calls, one can but respond." She glanced at Choda. "Continue with your instruction, Sister." Then she sat, but on a chair against the wall where she could view both the Sisters and the Princess.

Choda, with an angry glance in Mikasama's direction, began slapping pages open in her prayer book. Finally she started to recite.

Mikasama tried to listen, but the woman's selected soliloquy delved into the holy nature of the Shukyoshi and the evil of the world around them. Her mind gradually ceased to hear the words and her eyes drifted back to the magnificent window behind the altar. As the sun's rays passed through the huge glazed wall, the myriad angles of the many panes caused the shafts of light to bend in random directions. It was, thought the Princess, like some giant kaleidoscope of color, wheeling its way about the room. Why, she wondered, had she been seeing this window in her dreams?

The visions had repeated so often that by now she could grasp what at least some of the images in her dreams represented, even if she was no closer to understanding why they occurred at all. She assumed that the soldiers chasing her were supposed to be her father's men, sent out to search for her. The people in blue, she now figured, must be the Shukyoshi, among whom she now sat.

But then there was always this vast wall of light, with which the dreams now ended. She had never understood what the wall was supposed to mean...

From her position at the side of the room, Mother Narisa watched her charges as they listened to Choda's sermon. Inwardly she sighed; a typically tactless choice of subject matter, she thought. Well, Choda is set in her ways. Her views will not change no matter what evidence the Goddess places before her. That such evidence was at hand was plain to see, to anyone who would stop to notice.

Her gaze traveled over to linger on Mikasama, sitting on the far side of the room. The young woman was ignoring Choda's sermon, as Narisa was sure many of the Sisters were, despite their apparent attentiveness. They, however, were looking dutifully at Choda, whereas this young woman's gaze was instead focused on the altar. No, not the altar, she realized; it was the window. What was the girl seeing? she wondered. What was the Goddess showing her?

The object of Mother Narisa's scrutiny sat oblivious to the attention. As Choda's words droned on, she became increasingly mesmerized by the shifting patterns of color and light before her. Just when a certain pattern seemed to be set, it changed unpredictably. The light moved, and where one color had been bright it now dimmed and another flared into brilliance. All revolving, never staying the same, but always finding some way to re-cast the light into another shade, another color.

Quite suddenly, understanding came to her. At least, some understanding, for if she were at all correct, she could never understand fully. Her life, she realized; it was like the shifting patterns of light. What had seemed stable and never changing had only been an illusion. All things change, she saw, including her. But the light itself was not transformed; that was the constant. Just as looking through the window from a different angle presented a different picture of the same light, so did changes in one's life present merely a different view of the same person.

My life, thought Mikasama, has changed irrevocably. Komori is gone, and with her my confidant, my caretaker. I am alone, and have no one to help me. I am still me, just a 'different' me. And what is it that this different me is seeking now? Is this it, here? To be a Shukyoshi Sister, serving their Goddess?

She knew even as she asked herself the question that the answer was no. Her destiny was not here; it was still out there, further west. She had to go on. The need was still there, and she had no better idea of why than before. But now it bothered her less than it once did. She understood now that her life would always be a series of changing patterns, many of them unpredictable. All she could do was accept them, and try to see the new patterns in the light rather than searching for old ones, now lost.

Sitting before the brightly-colored light in Fumosa, she felt more confident than at any point since she had set out on her journey. She knew it was just a matter of time before she would reach her goal. Whatever it might turn out to be.

Sister Choda continued to excoriate the congregation of Sisters, pointedly ignoring the heathen seated within their sacred chapel. However, her composure became somewhat strained when she glanced over at Mother Narisa and observed that her superior was not listening to her words, but was instead staring at the heretic creature in their midst. Her tenor became more strident as she neared the end of her sermon.

Mother Narisa, meanwhile, continued her observation of Mikasama. She knew who the girl was, and had realized the risks she had taken in not immediately sending her back to her homeland. Yet a lifetime of service to the Goddess had taught her to trust her instincts. There was something about this girl that was special. She didn't know what, or how it affected the Sisters, or Fumosa; but she trusted that the Goddess would tell her when the time was right.

She, too, knew that Mikasama was not for the Goddess. One could see it in her eyes, even from here, she thought. It is not the Goddess's altar, but the light from the sky that has animated her soul. It was evident to any observer that the girl was experiencing a revelation; or at least, it was evident to anyone whose mind was not forever closed, she conceded, with a stray thought toward Choda. She suspected that their young visitor would not remain long at Fumosa.

As Choda finished her sermon she slammed her book closed, the sound jerking their visitor's attention back to the present. The girl looked briefly at Choda before casting her gaze down to the floor.

Mother Narisa rose and led a short final prayer, after which the Sisters left their benches and silently filed out of the large hall. Their visitor rose as well, but hesitated, looking over toward Mother Narisa.

The head of the monastery was listening patiently to a furiously whispering Choda, who stood by her side. Sensing the young girl's scrutiny, though, Mother Narisa gestured for her to approach. Choda stopped talking abruptly as the girl walked over to them. Their visitor bowed her head, speaking tentatively. "I—I don't wish to intrude…"

"Not at all child," replied Mother Narisa, ignoring Choda's scowl, "not at all. What is it?"

The girl swallowed. "I think…well, I think it's time for me to go, Mother Narisa."

The old woman nodded her head. "Come to my study after the midday meal. We will talk some more."

"Yes, Ma'am," and she followed the last of the Sisters out of the hall.

Choda whirled on Mother Narisa. "How can you tolerate that heretic here?" she hissed. "Or even speak with her?"

Mother Narisa looked coldly at Choda. "The Goddess is not found only in pious sermons, Choda. You would do well to have your charges memorize less dogma and spend more time seeing the Goddess in her natural state. As should you; it might be a revelation to you." With that Mother Narisa swept out of the room to join the Sisters in the fields, performing her own daily labor, leaving a seething Choda behind.

*　　　　*　　　　*

Mikasama knocked lightly on the door to Mother Narisa's study. In response to the older woman's, "Come," she entered the room she had only seen once, that first anguished night of her arrival. It was as she remembered: simple and unadorned, a room for working in.

Mother Narisa, she had learned, certainly worked in it, often for hours after the last of the communal wall lamps had been extinguished in the hallways. The older woman was hard at work still, bent over yet another scroll. She was carefully reading the text with squinting eyes, candles placed to either side of her table.

Mother Narisa didn't look up as she said, "Close the door, child, and sit." Mikasama complied, then knelt before the table while waiting for Mother Narisa to finish her reading.

When the old woman at last set aside the scroll, she looked up. Direct and to the point, she said, "You say it is time for you to go, Princess Mikasama. Do you know where you are going to?"

Although she had suspected that Mother Narisa had known who she was all along, it still surprised Mikasama to hear her name and title spoken out loud. It had been so long since she had heard anyone call her Princess...

She took a deep breath. "No, Mother Narisa, I—I'm not sure where I'm going. It's not here, no disrespect intended," she said, casting her eyes down.

"None taken, child. The life of a Sister is not for everyone. Some adapt quite well, others...well," she continued, "let us just say that others find the transition to monastic life a trial in itself. Yours is a spirit that would be hard put to withstand the discipline of life in a monastery; that much is clear to me. What is not clear to me, Princess," she said, her voice edged with deliberation, "is why you do not return to your rightful station in life? Why are you venturing out on the road, putting yourself, and those around you, at risk?"

Why indeed, wondered Mikasama. I've been asking myself that question for days and haven't yet come up with an answer that satisfies even me, let alone someone as astute as Mother Narisa. How can I possibly answer that? How can I justify the fact that, by my actions, Komori is now dead?

So she responded the only way she knew how, with honesty. "I don't know," she said. "I really don't. There is something inside of me, something I don't understand, that is telling me I have to go on, that I can't go back. I've tried to understand it, believe me; but what the reason behind it is, I still have no idea."

The older woman narrowed her eyes. "Could it perhaps be that the Goddess is speaking to you, advising you of what you must do?"

Mikasama shrugged. "Perhaps, Mother Narisa. I really cannot say. If it is, she is not making that fact plain. All I am certain of is that I must continue."

Mother Narisa nodded slowly. "There have been times in my own life when my path was clear, even if the reasons were not. I found that the Goddess, in the end, provided all the explanation that I required." When Mikasama did not respond, she went on. "Your recent loss has troubled you greatly, I know. I assume she was not, in fact, your mother?"

Mikasama grimaced. "No. Her name was Komori. She was my caretaker. She may as well have been my mother; she raised me from as far back as I could remember." She put out of her mind Komori's final confession, that she had been Himitsu's secret companion during all that time. "She was the most loyal servant a person could ever have. I miss the sound of her voice terribly; it had become almost a second voice to my own."

"It is never easy to lose one so close." Mother Narisa paused before saying delicately, "Knowing your position in Hajimeshi, I have to ask if you feel prepared to journey on the road alone? It is no less dangerous than before; perhaps even more so, as you journey further west. The ravages of the plague have contributed to a rash of lawlessness, and the usual considerations meted out to travelers may be lacking."

Mikasama had considered the question while sitting in her room after the morning prayer service. How would she get by? Could she go on, alone, with no one to talk to, no Komori to turn to for advice? It was her own impetuousness that had landed her in this predicament in the first place. Without an experienced companion to help guide her, would she have met a tragic end somewhere well before now? Would she have been the one who was now dead, her body moldering in a thicket of woods somewhere? As with the question of what drove her onwards, the answer to this one, too, had eluded her. The thought of pushing on alone terrified her almost more than she could stand.

But only almost. The need to go on was stronger, and so she would do it, no matter what the consequences.

"I know it is dangerous," she said with finality. "But I have no choice. I must go."

Mother Narisa looked at her keenly, holding her gaze, as if judging her spirit by the reflection of the candles' light in her eyes. "Nevertheless," the older woman said, "it is a perilous undertaking. I would feel that I had done the Goddess a disservice if she has indeed touched you, and I did nothing to assist in safeguarding your passage. Therefore I have decided to ask one of the Sisters if she would be willing to companion you on the remainder of your journey, wherever that may lead. Two are safer than one and, while our martial skills are quite rudimentary compared to our northern cousins, they might provide some small measure of added security."

Mikasama was taken completely aback. She had not expected such an offer at all. A companion? Someone else to talk to, to share her concerns with, to confide in…Komori had known her, had been able to anticipate what she might do based on a lifetime's exposure to Mikasama's whims and ways. But a mature Shukyoshi Sister, someone to whom she could turn to assuage her doubts, to ease her fears, might be just what she needed in order to forge ahead. Vigorously she nodded. "Yes, Mother Narisa, that would be wonderful! And very generous…thank you!"

Mother Narisa tried to hide a smile. She reached over and tapped a small gong on the table with a miniature hammer. "I have taken the liberty of already speaking with the Sister I thought most appropriate to accompany you. I have not told her who you are, only that your true name is Mikasama, and that you are a noble lady from a great house. I leave it to you to tell her more as you see fit. I believe you will find her a fitting companion."

"Yes," replied the Princess, "I'm sure whomever you've—" At that moment the door to the study opened, and Mikasama's mouth fell open. Rather than the older, experienced woman that the Princess had expected, a pair of cool blue eyes regarded her dispassionately from the doorway.

"Sister Shudojo," said Mother Narisa, "please come in. I believe the two of you are already acquainted."

Shudojo came into the room. "Yes, Mother Narisa." She turned to Mikasama, who had stood up as the Sister entered the study. "Lady," she said coolly, tilting her head in the Princess's direction. "I am prepared to journey with you. When do you wish to go?"

Mikasama stood nonplused. This was not what she had imagined at all! Shudojo? Yes, the Sister had let them in to the monastery, and had cared for Komori. But the woman was so young! Barely older than Mikasama herself. How could she be of any help in easing a tortured soul? She was not exactly talkative. In fact, her whole demeanor was one of standoffishness. A journey on the road with her would be…well, thought Mikasama, would be worse than being alone.

She turned away from Shudojo. "I'm—I'm sorry, Mother Narisa, I thought…well, you really shouldn't take one of the Sisters out of the monastery just for me; I'm sure you need all the help here you can get. I'll be alright, really."

There was a moment of awkward silence. Mother Narisa's eyes took on a flinty aspect. Finally, in a voice devoid of overt expression, she spoke. "As you wish. You will find your cart in the stable behind the main building."

Clumsily Mikasama said, "Thank you. I—I appreciate everything you've done." When this met with no response, she quickly nodded to Shudojo and left. The blue-eyed Sister watched her go, then turned back to Mother Narisa with a raised eyebrow.

Mikasama returned to her room and began packing her things. Her mind was spinning again, the clarity she had found earlier seeming to dissipate like a dandelion in the wind. She had already been resolved to carry on by herself, and it had not been until Mother Narisa had suggested the possibility of a companion that Mikasama had realized how terrified she actually was at being alone on the road. Not just physically alone, but secluded within her own mind, with no one to talk to her but her own inner voice. She no longer trusted that inner voice; afraid that without someone else to reflect back her perceptions she would push blindly on into things, and that might lead to fatal consequences.

But Shudojo! That was not at all what she had in mind. How would she be able to share her feelings with such a cold and unapproachable person? How could someone so young possibly have any wisdom to share with a Princess? No, thought Mikasama, I'm better off with my own demons.

She recalled Shudojo's belittling look when Mikasama had flinched at caring for Komori's physical needs. The last thing I need, she brooded, is a Sister rebuking me for failing to meet some presumed set of Shukyoshi standards.

She grabbed up her pack and walked with resolution toward the stable area. In her mind she kept repeating words of encouragement to herself, forcing her thoughts to be positive. Outside, a chill wind whipped through the courtyard; it set her long hair adrift, and she had to use one hand to hold it back from her face while hefting the pack with the other. None of the Sisters were about, this being the hour when they were at work in the fields. Mikasama reached the gate of the stable and shoved it open. Even with the stiff breeze the strong smell of many animals in a closely packed space surrounded her as she stepped inside and searched for the cart.

She found it near the back of the stable, with its two attendant horses already hitched up for her by the Sisters. The horses stood dully, patiently, as Mikasama threw her bag over the side of the cart. Her disappointment over having to use the cart rather than ride the fine mount she had begun the journey with resurfaced, but she pushed that thought out of her mind. Soon, she thought, I'll be on the road once more.

Climbing up onto the buckboard, she looked back into the bed of the cart. It was just as she had left it the night she and Komori had arrived. Those things she had not taken inside were still there, among them Komori's travel packs. Seeing them sent a sharp, wrenching pain through her heart. These things, these inanimate objects, were all that was left to her of Komori. On an impulse she climbed back into the bed of the cart and opened one of Komori's packs.

Inside were many of the items she had already seen on the journey: supplies, utensils, grooming tools. There was also something she had not seen before—a small packet, wrapped in leather. Pulling it out from between a travel pot and a bag of sweet herbs, Mikasama saw that it was held closed with a cord, the ends of which were tied together through a small amulet. The amulet was carved in the shape of a tiny liana bird. Made of fine ivory, only about the width of two fingers, the amulet had a small hole in it for passing the cord through. Gently Mikasama untied the cord and set aside the amulet, whereupon the packet fell open easily.

It contained a bundle of small parchments, which she had to grab hold of quickly to keep from blowing away in the wind. Peering at them more closely, she saw that they were letters. Carefully she pulled one out and began to read.

With a start Mikasama realized that it was a love letter, between Komori and Himitsu. Komori could barely write, and her words were a mix of vocal spellings of words she clearly did not know well, and fairly sophisticated terms, presumably taught to her by Himitsu.

The words brought back to Mikasama's mind her days at her father's court. She had never spoken much with Himitsu, his presence always making her uneasy. What she had seen of him had usually made her skin crawl, although in truth he had never actually said or done anything to warrant such a reaction. He just seemed to her to be a person not to be trusted, someone always involved in the power struggles at court.

As she read more of the letters, she saw aspects of Komori's life unfolding that she had never suspected existed. Here was a different side of Himitsu. The man written to in Komori's letters was admired, loved, chided. It was clear that he had been desired by the woman Mikasama had known only as Nana-san, but who in reality had been much more.

Komori's letters to Himitsu were evidently first drafts and copies; there were many cross-outs and scribbles as she had tried, Mikasama imagined, to write letters that he would approve of. There was a response to most of the letters, although not all. The letters he wrote to Komori were witty, and full of amazing gossip that only one in his position would know. Clearly he trusted Komori's discretion completely. He talked of his work, of the strain, of his concerns for Hajimeshi and the Kojuro. And of his fondness for 'Liana,' which Mikasama gathered must have been his pet name for Komori, just as 'White Beard' had been his own. She looked down again at the amulet, and longed to hear the story behind it and Komori's nickname, but doubted now that she ever would.

She had to admit that most of her negative feelings about Himitsu centered on his attitude toward her when she had been a little girl. She just remembered him as someone who had never been any fun. He had always been taking Papa away on "business," and never had time to play with a little girl; while Papa's other retainers had always made a show of entertaining her. Now, she realized, that was exactly what it had been: a show, designed to impress the Kojuro by humoring his daughter. It had nothing to do with her. Himitsu, who never bothered to play such games, had simply been carrying on with the work of the court.

She looked up, squinting in the sunlight. All these letters, she thought; Komori and Himitsu were writing all these letters while I was growing up. While Komori was combing my hair and fussing over my clothes, she was sending missives full of love to my father's councilor. And he, in turn, took time from aiding my father in running Hajimeshi to send her back notes of the affection that he could never show her in public.

Mikasama brushed away tears, trying to convince herself that it was just from the wind rattling through the cart. Struggling to keep her hair back out of her face, she shoved the packet between her knees and used the cord that had bound them to tie back her flailing locks. She carefully wedged the bundle inside her pack.

She picked up the liana bird amulet and rubbed the fine lines carved onto its surface, as if by doing so she could find a way to touch its missing owner. Then a thought came to her. She undid the cord she had used to hold back her hair and threaded it back through the hole in the amulet, then tied it around her neck, carefully tucking the liana bird away inside her tunic. It would be her reminder, that small piece of ivory. Her reminder of Komori; and her reminder that not everything was as it first appeared, even those things one felt certain about 'knowing.' How odd, and sad, she reflected, that it was only now, with Komori gone, that she was beginning to understand what had made Nana-san the person that she was.

She looked at the empty buckboard in front of her, the two horses still waiting patiently beyond. Suddenly the thought of journeying on alone again filled her with dread. She couldn't force her arms and legs into action, to get up and grab the reins and make the horses move. She thought of long days and cold nights, alone, wandering on into the unknown lands to the west. Her hand reached up and felt the small bump under her tunic where lay the ivory bird, nestled between her breasts. Perhaps, she thought, I just need to change my view and see the light differently.

* * *

Mother Narisa had hitched up her blue habit, leaving her legs bare from mid-thigh downwards. She was bent over, carefully planting the small stalks of rice in the wet paddy field; around her more Sisters were planting, stretching in a line across the field. The water of the paddy came up over her ankles, and was warmed by the mid-afternoon sun. Although the labor was back breaking, she enjoyed the feel of touching living things, planting the shoots that would grow, and in turn feed other living things. It was so much more satisfying, she thought, than ledger books and scrolls, and dealing with obstinate people, whether Shukyoshi Sisters or otherwise. There was something very pleasing about getting good, clean dirt under one's fingernails.

She straightened up to stretch an aching back and saw the girl coming, wending her way carefully along the narrow dry ridge between the rice paddies. The other Sisters paid her no heed, continuing on with their planting. Knowing why she had come, Mother Narisa waited.

The Princess stopped a few feet away. Balancing herself on the narrow ridge, Mikasama slowly bowed to the older woman. "I ask for your forgiveness, Mother Narisa," she said quietly, still bowed over. "I spoke rashly, and with conceit. It was very generous of you to suggest Shudojo as a companion for my journey, and imprudent, and impudent, of me to refuse. I humbly ask if you might reconsider."

Mother Narisa said nothing at first. She wiped her hands on the cloth she had tied to her rope belt, then sloshed her way over to where Mikasama still stood bowing to her. She placed her hands on the Princess's shoulders to gently raise her upright.

"It is not my place, child, to grant forgiveness," she said. "Only the Goddess may do that." She looked into Mikasama's eyes a moment longer, then nodded. "Meet Shudojo in the stable in two hours."

The Princess bowed her head. "Thank you, Mother Narisa," she said softly. Then she turned and made her way back to the monastery compound.

Mother Narisa watched, feeling a mixture of sorrow, good will, and perhaps a touch of envy, as the Princess walked away. Yes, she thought, I was once like that. Proud, full in the knowledge that I could tackle any challenge. And tormented by guilt, as this one is. Mikasama, too, needs to find her rightful place, as I have found mine.

She turned back to her rice paddy and resumed her planting.

When Mikasama arrived in the stable at the appointed time she found Shudojo already there, but was nonplused to see, instead of the cart with its attendant draft horses, two much finer riding horses. Mikasama blurted out, "Whose are these? And what about the cart?"

Shudojo shrugged. "When Mother Narisa asked me if I would accompany you, I suggested that we would travel more expeditiously, as well as more safely, were we mounted rather than tied to a cart. She agreed." She patted the horse on the neck. "Many of the ill who have come here brought their animals and horses with them. In some cases the entire family died, and thus Fumosa inherited animals for which we have little use. However carts are always in short supply. Mother Narisa readily agreed to a trade."

Mikasama was taken aback. On the one hand, she was annoyed by Shudojo's presumption in making such arrangements without talking to her first. Yet the thought of leaving the cart behind and once more riding her own horse tempered her irritation.

She lifted her pack on to one of the horses. As she looked around for Komori's packs Shudojo said, "I split the things from the others between yours and mine. There seemed little sense in having to handle more baggage." The Sister turned and walked her horse out of the stable, leaving Mikasama to stare after her.

How dare she, thought Mikasama. How dare she simply go and rearrange Komori's things, without so much as a by-your-leave!

Angrily, the Princess snatched up the reins of her horse, glad at least that she had already put Komori's letters inside her own pack, safe from the fingers of strangers. Despite her change of heart in having Shudojo accompany her, when confronted now with the reality of dealing with this cool, impersonal stranger Mikasama's doubts came rushing back to her. Am I making a terrible mistake, she wondered, to be journeying with this woman?

As she walked her horse out into the main courtyard, she spoke sharply, "Did Mother Narisa tell you where I'm going? How long you might be gone?"

The Sister turned her blue eyes onto the Princess. "She told me you travel to the west, Lady. As for how long..." Her gaze drifted out past the open gate of Fumosa. "As long as it takes, I imagine, for you to find whatever it us you are looking for. I believe Mother Narisa feels it more likely to be extended rather than brief. Which," she added, looking back, "suits me as well." At that moment two Sisters emerged from the residence hall and hurried over to where Shudojo and Mikasama stood. The Princess recognized them as the two who were with Shudojo the morning after Mikasama's arrival. They came to see Shudojo off, hugging her and giving her small parcels of food that they had prepared.

Shudojo looked embarrassed, but clearly touched as well. The Sisters' affection for their departing comrade made Mikasama envious. The Princess had never had the opportunity to make many friends, and a part of her begrudged Shudojo even that small familiarity she shared with her fellow Sisters. As Mikasama mounted her horse, she spoke curtly. "We should go before it gets too late in the day."

Shudojo, frowning, mounted her own horse; then waved as her friends called out their good-byes before returning to their chores. When she turned back around she saw that Mikasama had already walked her horse out of the gate and into the road outside. The Sister gazed briefly around her at the walls of Fumosa then urged her horse on to follow. As she came alongside the Princess, the pair rode in silence.

From inside Fumosa's chapel, Mother Narisa, having returned from the fields, looked out through the multi-paned pieces of glass that made up the wall behind the altar. It was something she saw every day, and so tended to take for granted; but Mikasama's scrutiny of it had caused her to realize that it was in need of a serious cleaning. So she was now carefully wiping dust and dirt away from the individual panes of glass. Sister Choda stood nearby, leaning on the altar, interminably discussing some problem about overdue accounts from a local farmer. Oh why, thought Mother Narisa, did the Goddess bless me with such a thick-headed woman as my senior Sister?

From here, Mother Narisa had a view of the path taken by Mikasama and Shudojo. As the two women rode slowly past she stopped her cleaning to peer at them through one of the clear panes. Sister Choda, noticing her superior's look of concentration, walked over and pressed her long bony nose up to the glass, a portion, noted Mother Narisa, that had just recently been cleaned.

The senior Sister of Fumosa snorted in disgust. "Goddess preserve me, Mother Narisa, I don't understand how you could possibly have tolerated that heretic within our midst."

Mother Narisa resumed her cleaning, as she had many more panes to go before it was done. "Sometimes, Choda, the light of the Goddess shines in ways we do not understand. It shines in that one, Shukyoshi or no."

"Well, I for one am glad to see her gone. As for Shudojo, she was always useless, if you ask me. She will never make a good Sister of Shukyoshi."

"Oh, but I think you're wrong," answered Mother Narisa, continuing to watch Mikasama and Shudojo. "I think this is just the experience Shudojo needs. Don't forget where she came from before she arrived on our doorstep. She knows how to survive, yes; but her faith will be sorely tested by what she finds out there, beyond Fumosa. I, for one, believe she will endure, as will her faith."

She stopped cleaning as the two young women were finally lost to view. "In fact, it may very well be that the two of them will see more of the Goddess than any of us will ever know…"

17

The weary line of Hikari pilgrims halted at the river's edge, sliding packs off of aching shoulders. Most of the Guards promptly sat down to rest their feet. Marching was something they did for a living, and one of the first things they learned about soldiering was how to care for their feet.

Three days had passed since the Hajimeshi had left the Fortress at Shukyoshi; three days of endless marching, carrying everything on their backs that once their horses had conveyed for them. They had walked from sunup until they could no longer see the track before them, eager to quit themselves of the hostile Shukyoshi. Everywhere they had been shunned, the populace ignoring them at best, shouting and spitting at worst. Only the small troop of mounted Shukyoshi soldiers, shadowing them some thirty yards behind as escorts, had restrained the more demonstrative of the citizenry.

Intellectually Shiko had known that the people of Shukyoshi had been indoctrinated to distrust, if not outright loathe anyone who was not a believer in their Goddess. The people's beliefs, coupled with the fear that strangers might bring more plague to their towns, had gone some way toward explaining their behavior. None of which, he had thought, had made it any easier to be the target of such vehement hatred.

By the morning of the third day the pilgrims had finally left the last of the towns behind. Their escort had wheeled and departed without a word. As the horsemen had ridden back the way they had come, Ryori had shouted after them, "Have a pleasant day!" They had ignored him, and the Hajimeshi pilgrims had turned away and continued with their march.

Now, having reached the banks of the river marking the border with Tejinashi, they took a moment to rest and get their bearings. Across the river Shiko could see a large, flat raft, beached on the far bank. Attached to it were heavy ropes that stretched completely across the swiftly flowing river. He remembered seeing rafts like these before in Hajimeshi, where teams of horses on either bank were used to pull the raft back and forth across rivers. Only here, there were no horses anywhere to be seen.

Instead on the opposite bank stood a perplexing assemblage of wheels: some small, a few quite large, all mounted in a complicated structure made out of heavy timbers. Large ropes connected to the raft wound in and among the wheels. On the pilgrims' side of the river the ropes came up out of the water and encircled a single, large wheel, mounted between a pair of heavy posts driven deep into the soil of the riverbank. Shiko could see no sign of horses on their side either; and on the opposite bank all that was in view besides the great wheel assembly was a small stone hut. A thin streamer of smoke issuing from its chimney was the only evidence that anyone manned the river crossing.

As he gazed across the river the apprentice became aware of Toshi-hito walking up beside him. The Deshi Master had spent most of the march since leaving the Fortress walking at the rear of the column, next to Ryori. The cook had cut away the sleeve of Toshi-hito's tunic to aid in changing the dressing on the wound, but the cut on the Deshi's arm from the Shukyoshi blade was not healing well. It continued to ooze blood, although the Deshi Master stoically ignored the pain. Shiko, however, because of his close bond with Toshi-hito, was able to see the strain beneath his Master's usual calm expression.

He had also observed what was, for Toshi-hito, fairly uncharacteristic behavior: ever since the morning meal, the Deshi Master had grown quiet and had refused to let Ryori change the bandage on his arm. A Deshi, Shiko knew, learned to bear his discomforts without burdening others; nonetheless, he was becoming worried. During the last few miles of walking, he had been pondering how to suggest that Toshi-hito should allow Ryori to change his dressing, without appearing to contradict his Master's wishes. He had just decided what to say when Toshi-hito unexpectedly strode right past him. The Deshi Master walked up to a large metal gong mounted on one of the pilings that supported the wheel. Without hesitation Toshi-hito raised his good arm and with the edge of his fist struck the gong in its center.

A deep, low tone, sounding like the moaning of some anguished spirit, sailed out across the river. Its eerie note sent shivers up Shiko's spine. It seemed, somehow, to be a fitting entrance to the land of the Tejinashi.

Tejinashi...For Shiko, the thought of seeing the fabled city of magicians filled him with both awe and dread at the same time. He had read much about the Tejinashi: they had wondrous devices that could raise water straight up, and allow voices to be heard from one end of the city to the other. They could, via their magic, provide food for the entire city, not relying on the output of farms and the whims of nature. As Toshi-hito had explained to him, since the Tejinashi had no need for any of the goods or services of their neighbors, they had decided to cut themselves off from the rest of Tonogato. Thus it was only occasional travelers who managed to gain admittance to the city, and then only for short periods of time. The stories that came back with them were ascribed by most Hajimeshi to be fanciful creations of some storyteller's imagination. Shiko, though, had seen the scrolls in the Deshi archives that described in great detail many of the amazing Tejinashi accomplishments. They had provided many hours of fascinating reading for a young Deshi novice.

Those same scrolls had also taught him that the magicians were organized into a hereditary council, the Zaitan. All of them were female; no man was allowed to practice magic in Tejinashi. Each member of the Zaitan had a specialized skill, handed down to a designated successor, usually a member of her own family. In this way they kept the secrets of their craft from all outsiders, even from among their own people. The most powerful of the magicians, the Kordaijan, presided over all of the other Zaitan, but was less a ruler than first among equals.

Equal, however, only among their own kind, for the Zaitans' control over the common people and the city of Tejinashi was absolute. Toshi-hito had told Shiko that the penalty for anyone else attempting to perform spellcraft was death. The Zaitan were quite jealous of their monopoly of power and were ruthless in their safeguarding of it. This could extend, Toshi-hito had emphasized, to seemingly innocent information, such as that usually provided by the Deshi to whomever asked for it. The Deshi Master had cautioned him to be discreet should anyone in Tejinashi stop him to seek knowledge. So while his curiosity was intrigued by the chance to see the magical city, Shiko was also aware that Tejinashi could be a dangerous place for the unwary.

From across the river the apprentice spied a short, rotund form emerging from the hut in response to the sounding of the gong. The figure gazed across the river at them then turned back to yell at someone inside the hut; the words were indistinct but Shiko could deduce from its pitch that the rotund form was female. She walked out onto the raft, and waited. Shortly thereafter another figure, tall and thin, hurried out of the hut and over toward the great assemblage of wheels. Despite his height he was still less than half the size of the largest wheel. He grabbed hold of a lever protruding from the wheel's face and heaved.

Startlingly all of the wheels began moving at once, some in one direction while others moved the opposite way. The rope connected to the raft started to move and the raft slid off the far bank and glided across the river toward them. The slender person, having started the motion of the wheels with but that one movement, gazed after the departing raft, waiting patiently.

Shiko watched in amazement as the raft moved silently across the water, seeming to race along with the shadows that dotted the river's surface from the clouds overhead. Toshi-hito walked slowly back over to where Shiko stood. Softly the Deshi Master said, "The first of many interesting Tejinashi 'machines,' as they call them." His voice, Shiko thought, sounded strained; his wound must be hurting him terribly.

Injury or no, it did not stop Toshi-hito from instructing his apprentice. "I do not know what makes the wheels work, but see how they slow their rotation, just as the raft approaches this shore." The raft was visibly slowing down, now only a stone's throw from where they stood. "The wheels appear to be designed to push the raft just far enough to reach the other side. Then they must be started again." As he spoke the raft grounded on the bank and the great wheels opposite slowed to a halt.

The stout old woman stood leaning against a decrepit wooden railing that ran along one side of the raft. She said nothing as Toshi-hito approached her and removed two coins from his purse, but quickly snatched them out of his hand, and they disappeared somewhere into the many folds of her ragged clothing. She stepped aside and motioned the pilgrims onto the creaking conveyance.

Had the Hajimeshi had their horses with them it would have taken at least two, and possibly three trips, to get them all across. As it was they were able to shuffle all their weary bodies onto the raft together, prompting Ryori to comment with some concern about the state of the raft's buoyancy. The woman pointedly ignored him. Once all were on board, she raised her arm and the slim figure on the opposite bank set the wheels in motion once more. With a groan of strained timbers the raft was dragged off the bank and wobbled uncertainly across the river.

They floated in silence for a time. Most of the Guards were fascinated by the action of the many moving wheels on the other bank, which looked even more complex the closer the raft approached. As the sun reappeared from behind a passing cloud, the light of the Hikari lantern hanging above them on its pole glittered off the river water.

Toshi-hito, leaning against the railing, turned to the old woman. "There were once many Raftmen, here on the river Sutashan, were there not?" She eyed him with a wary, weary, look, but nodded in agreement. Toshi-hito continued, "Surely there is still enough trade through the south of Shukyoshi to maintain travel across the river? What has become of the other Rafters?"

The old woman took her time in answering. When she did, it was in a quiet, raspy voice full of bitterness. "Gone. Magicians don't care. Never did." She rubbed a hand along the railing, her skin worn with age like the timbers of the raft. "They set up the Rafts long time back, 'fore they could make their own food, an' all them other things. Then they figured they didn't need food from 'cross the river no more. Let the Rafts all go, fall apart. Who cares if folk livin' out here starve, can't afford fancy foods made in the city?" She turned her head to the side, and spit with such force out into the river that she raised a considerable splash. Ryori's eyes opened wide in appreciative approval.

Itachi, standing at the front of the raft, ignored the discussion behind him, his mind elsewhere. In fact he wished his mind were indeed elsewhere, along with rest of his body. Everything, he fumed, was falling apart! All of his plans, the months of preparation, disintegrating like parchment left lying in the rain...

A more thoughtful man might have taken such setbacks as a sign of disfavor, either from the gods or just luck in general, but the Hajimeshi lord was not a man for self-reflection. Should his mind stray toward self-criticism, it always seemed to be easily deflected by the existence of someone or something else to blame. Once again events had moved beyond his control, and he was not a man to accept loss of control lightly. Once he had settled on his plan to become the Kotaishi as a means to overthrow his brother, all it had needed was a way to get the Deshi turned, one way or the other, to his support. But he had not been able to think of a solution to that problem before the Shukyoshi patrol had forced their hand, resulting in their foray to the Fortress. There had been no choice then but to follow events through, either until he was dead on the ground or once more free from the threat of superior forces.

And now, he realized bitterly, that lunatic Anasaki had decided that the Hikari pilgrims were actually benefiting his *own* grandiose prophecy and had thus set them free. On the wrong side of Shukyoshi...

He realized that his troops could remain in hiding no longer. To do so they increasingly risked discovery, and without him there to lead them they could not succeed. His lieutenants were competent but no more than that. It needed a leader of men to bring a new order to Hajimeshi, and he was the one to do it. The only one who could do it. He resolved that, sooner rather than later, he would force it to happen. No matter who fell before his sword.

The raft bumped lazily up against the far bank. The pilgrims had arrived in Tejinashi.

The Guards picked up their packs and moved off the raft, forming up again in marching order on dry land. From here Shiko could see that the thin one who had started the wheels was a young man, his unusually long hair tied in a queue down his back. He appeared nervous, and stayed near the wheels while the Hajimeshi disembarked from the raft. Last to come ashore were the two Deshi and Ryori. As Toshi-hito stepped down off the raft he stumbled, falling to his knees on the sandy bank. Quickly Shiko and Ryori leaned down to help him up, but to their dismay Toshi-hito did not move.

Alarmed, Shiko knelt down beside the Deshi Master. Toshi-hito sat on his knees, eyes closed. Ryori quickly swung off his heavily laden pack and began fishing for his medicinal herbs.

"Master," said Shiko urgently, "are you all right?" Toshi-hito, breathing heavily, nodded his head but made no effort to move. Ryori unwrapped the bandage on Toshi-hito's arm. Once the wound was revealed, he let out his breath in a low hiss.

"What?" asked Shiko. "What is it, Master Cook?"

Before he could answer, Itachi, having seen the commotion, strode over and looked down at Toshi-hito. "What is the matter with him?" the Hajimeshi lord demanded.

Ryori sat back on his heals, making no move to apply any of the herbs from his kit. Without looking up, in a flat voice he said, "Poison. The wound be poisoned."

"Poisoned?" exclaimed Shiko. "How?"

It was Toshi-hito who answered, his eyelids fluttering. "The Shukyoshi...The blade was tainted. Probably...a toxic extract of some kind..." He screwed his eyes back shut, wincing with some internal pain.

"But why?" said Shiko, bewildered. "Why should they poison their blades?"

"Perhaps...perhaps their faith is not strong enough...for steel alone..."

Impatiently Itachi asked, "Can he walk? If we have to carry him, it will slow us down."

Ryori looked up at Itachi with an angry glare that Shiko had never seen in the cook before, but with which he felt much empathy. The Hajimeshi lord's callousness was typical of the man but even so, after enduring it for so many days Shiko was finding himself hard put to restrain his own anger. Before either he or Ryori could answer, however, Toshi-hito abruptly stood. Through gritted teeth he said, "I can walk."

Itachi looked keenly at the Deshi Master, then glanced at the others. "All right. We will wait a few minutes for him to catch his breath. Then we march." He turned and made his way back to the Guards waiting nearby.

Ryori watched him walk away, fury still plainly visible across his face. He turned to the slightly unsteady Deshi Master and spoke in a harsh whisper. "You knew! You knew you be poisoned, yet you said nothin'!"

Toshi-hito smiled slightly. "And what difference...would it have made, Master Cook? The poison would have proceeded regardless. I had hoped...that perhaps the wound was slight enough...that I would be able to fend off whatever it was that had invaded me, but..." His voice trailed off as he struggled to remain upright.

"Do not strain yourself, Master," said Shiko anxiously. "Please, sit, until we are ready to go." But Toshi-hito stubbornly would not sit, saying that a man who could not stand would most certainly not be able to walk.

Shiko was confronted with a rush of emotions. He was furious, at the Shukyoshi for hurting his Master, and at Toshi-hito for abusing himself in order not to impede the pilgrimage. And he was worried, for he had never seen Toshi-hito so ill. Even severe winter illnesses had never stopped the Deshi Master from his usual work, such was the internal control he exerted over his body. The poison must be strong indeed for such a small amount as what might have been on a sword blade to reduce Toshi-hito to such infirmity. Might it kill him? wondered Shiko. No! It can't! It just can't!

Toshi-hito was like a father to him, having tutored the apprentice since the earliest day Shiko could remember at the Deshi priory. He couldn't even think of life without Toshi-hito's guiding hand.

Apparently sensing his young charge's anxiety, Toshi-hito reached out with his good hand and placed it on Shiko's arm. "I will be...all right, Shiko," he said. "Do not worry just yet...for your old Master."

Ryori, however, was undeterred. "You may well think that, but we be taking your pack anyway," as he eased Toshi-hito's pack off of the Deshi's shoulders. The fact that Toshi-hito did not complain only added to Shiko's anxiety.

As Ryori shifted the Deshi Master's pack items among his own and Shiko's, Toshi-hito turned to his apprentice. "Is the Raftwoman...still close by?"

Shiko looked about and saw that the woman was still standing on her raft. She was watching the tableau before her with an air of apparent disinterest, but Shiko saw that her eyes missed nothing. "Yes, Master, she is still there."

"Ask her to come here."

Shiko beckoned to the woman, and she slowly shuffled over toward them. She stopped a few yards away, however, apparently unwilling to venture any closer to someone who was so apparently ill.

Toshi-hito took a deep breath before speaking. "Good woman...the Raftmen used to sell...supplies...to those crossing. Do you still do so?"

She shrugged. "Got some things, could sell. Not much. Not many travelers, these days."

Toshi-hito nodded to Ryori. "Purchase what you can, Master Cook…we may not find many farmers…to buy from on the road to Tejinashi."

Ryori looked at the old woman, who jerked her head toward the hut. She set off at a slow shuffle, Ryori close behind. She gestured at the young man who had tended the great wheels, still standing near the massive pilings supporting the structure. "Ja'yan! Get inside. Pull out some o' the traveler's goods."

As she and Ryori, quickly followed by the young man, disappeared inside the hut Shiko resumed distributing Toshi-hito's belongings among the packs. Itachi was pacing nearby, clearly impatient to get underway. The Deshi apprentice fought down his irritation. Doesn't he realize, thought Shiko, that the whole purpose of this expedition is for Toshi-hito to find the Kotaishi? Forcing the Deshi Master to march when he is unwell jeopardizes our whole undertaking.

As if in deliberate refutation of Shiko's line of reasoning, Itachi strode over to where the two Deshi stood. Ignoring Shiko he said brusquely to Toshi-hito, "It is time to move. Where is the cook?"

On impulse, before Toshi-hito could answer, Shiko stepped in between the Deshi Master and Itachi. His mouth went dry as he stared up at the Hajimeshi general, who seemed to look down at him as if noticing him for the first time. Itachi's brow furrowed and he opened his mouth to speak, but just at that moment Ryori emerged from the hut bearing a large bag stuffed to overflowing. The cook walked right up to Itachi. "Toshi-hito said we'd need our own supplies from here on in. If we carry his load, I can't haul this stuff too."

Itachi transferred his angry glare from apprentice to cook. Over his shoulder he shouted, "Nakama! Come take some of this servant's supplies." Stoically Nakama broke ranks and took the sack from Ryori, wordlessly hoisting it over his shoulder. The Hajimeshi general cast a dismissive glance at Shiko before turning away and striding back to the head of the line. "All right, let's move!"

Shiko, watching Itachi walk away, found himself breathing hard. He didn't know what had prompted him to step in between the Hajimeshi lord and Toshi-hito; perhaps it had simply been a desire to protect his Master. The burning fury in Itachi's eyes had been frightening, but then his casual dismissal of Shiko at the end had upset the apprentice even more. *I can see,* thought Shiko, *why the Master is uneasy around that man...*

Toshi-hito had remained silent during Shiko's quiet confrontation. As he tentatively stepped forward Shiko raised a hand to his elbow to help steady him, but the Deshi Master shook his head. "It is all right. The rest was all that I required. I can walk without aid." Slowly, then with a more positive step, Toshi-hito set off after the soldiers. Ryori and Shiko glanced at one another then took up position behind him, ready to aid the Deshi Master should he require assistance.

From the doorway of the hut the old woman and Ja'yan watched them go. The woman, wiping her hands on her already-dirtied smock, turned and went back inside, the excitement of strangers now over. Ja'yan, however, remained in the doorway, watching until the last of the Hajimeshi disappeared from view over a hill in the distance.

✶   ✶   ✶

The pilgrims walked on until late afternoon, mostly in silence as the men conserved their strength. The way took them through small woods and past open fields, the latter obviously cleared at some time in the past for farming but now mostly overgrown with weeds. The few farmhouses they passed were empty, their tenants long removed, judging from the general state of disrepair.

Only Ryori felt the need to converse, as he walked with the two Deshi at the tail of the group. "Strange birds, those Rafters," said the cook. Neither Toshi-hito, focused on walking, nor Shiko, watching the Deshi Master, responded; but this was scant inhibition for Ryori. "Talked a mite with the ol' woman while the boy got the stuff together. Real holdouts, they are. Seems that their's the only raft still crossin' the river. The boy's got a gift, she says, for keepin' the wheels runnin'. So it's just the two of them, holdin' out there waitin' for the odd traveler to come by." He smirked. "That'd be us, all right. Odd travelers." With a grunt he shifted the load on his shoulder, even heavier now than when they began their journey. "Guess the boy won't leave his wheels, least 'cording to her. He didn't say a peep. Strange, like I said." His audience less than enthralled, Ryori finally lost enthusiasm. He contented himself with his usual muttered refrains about fool's errands, particularly whenever they starting climbing a hill.

As the day's light waned, the pilgrims approached a range of steep foothills, seeming to rise up to catch the falling sun. Bokusa, scouting just inside one of the sheltering woods through which the road traversed, found a spot for an encampment situated near a stream. Deciding that an early halt was appropriate, Itachi instructed the men to make camp. Only a token sentry watch was set. There had been no sign of danger once they had crossed the border into Tejinashi, much to the relief of the weary soldiers.

Toshi-hito gingerly let himself down to the ground, leaning his back against a tree. The walk had been excruciating, taking all of his mental discipline to hold the pain at bay and force first one foot forward, then the other. Once he had set a rhythm it had become easier to disengage his active mind and let his body carry on, while letting his brain busy itself with thinking. Now, however, at the end of the day, with his rhythm interrupted, his physical condition reasserted itself. He leaned his back against the coarse bark of the tree and let his aching frame relax, willing it to rejuvenate itself. They were still a long way from their ultimate destination, and his task was not yet done. Just as the Kojuro compelled his declining body to press on, so too must he force his own to persevere.

"Master?"

Shiko's quiet inquiry interrupted his thoughts. Toshi-hito opened his eyes to see his worried apprentice kneeling before him. The young man's face, not yet adept at that shield of imperturbability presented by more senior Deshi, displayed all of his anxieties. It would not do, thought Toshi-hito, for Shiko to become overly fixated on worrying about my health; he must maintain his focus on our pilgrimage. I was not yet prepared to teach him those things he must know, but fortune has not abided my wishes. Perhaps now is the time, for it will serve to re-direct Shiko's thoughts. Then, too, there is always the possibility that I might worsen, perhaps even die, before I am able to teach what has to be taught. An unpleasant prospect to contemplate.

He looked at Shiko and smiled. Summoning up his reserves of strength, he spoke in as normal a voice as he could manage. "I believe there is a stream nearby, is there not?"

Shiko nodded. "Yes, Master, just behind this stand of trees, I think."

"I feel like a brisk washing would do my tired old limbs some good." Toshi-hito steeled himself, then pushed himself up to his feet. "Perhaps you would care to join me?"

While Ryori put the finishing touches on the evening's dinner fire, and the smell of cooking wafted about the camp, the two Deshi made their way through the trees to the nearby watercourse.

While the marching had been difficult, trying to present a normal appearance to Shiko was far harder for Toshi-hito. He could not separate his mind from his body as he had with rhythmic walking; now he had to move and talk as if he were not in constant agony. He wrapped his mental fingers around the pain, squeezed it in a mental grasp, and held it at bay off to one side of his mind. He knew that he would most likely pay for the effort later but he had one lesson, at least, that he needed to impart to Shiko while he was still able to do so.

As they reached the edge of the stream the two Deshi found a wide, flat rock that lay half on the bank, making a shelf that jutted out over the water. Toshi-hito thought this would make a convenient excuse for delaying the physical exertion of bathing in the stream. He needed all his strength in order to look, and sound, healthier than he was. "I think, before we bathe, that I might like to rest my feet in the stream. It has been a long time since I have had to walk so far." He settled himself down on the rock, Shiko beside him, and the two of them dipped their tired feet into the cool running water.

For Shiko, it was a fairly unusual experience to be sitting so casually with his Master. Usually his time with Toshi-hito was spent either meditating or in instruction. As worried as he was for his Master's health, he still found it enjoyable to simply sit and relax in the older man's company. Neither spoke for a time, until Toshi-hito asked him suddenly, "Shiko, what do you know about the Shizen?"

The apprentice pondered for a moment before replying. "Beyond what everyone knows, Master, that they dwell in the Sacred Grove and speak only to the Kojuro, just that which is in the Izumay scroll back in the Deshi archives." The Izumay scroll was one of the oldest documents at the Deshi priory; it was a treatise by one of the original Deshi, who first wrote down what the Kojuro and his immediate successors had said about the Shizen and their intervention in the Great War. All subsequent analysis of the nature of the Shizen started with Izumay's work, for no Kojuro since his day had spoken of what transpired in the Grove.

Toshi-hito nodded. "What Master Izumay wrote is, for the most part, quite accurate. There are, however, some details of which he was unaware."

Shiko found this most interesting; he had never heard of any other source of information, so Toshi-hito could only know of things told to him by Kimeru, in his role as Spiritual Guide to the Kojuro. Such things were held in strictest confidence, of course, so naturally Toshi-hito would never be able to tell the apprentice about them. "It must be difficult," Shiko said, kicking his feet gently in the water, "to have knowledge from such a reliable source, yet not be able to share it."

Toshi-hito smiled. "Well, I like to think of myself as a reliable source. But yes, it has been difficult not to share what I have seen with others."

It took Shiko a moment to realize what Toshi-hito was saying. Then as the realization hit him he looked at the older man. "Master! Are you saying you have been *inside* the Grove?"

Solemnly Toshi-hito replied, "Yes."

Seeing the amazement written all over the young man's face, the Deshi Master noted that Shiko's lack of control over outward facial expressions also extended to incredulity. However, he was pleased that at least for the moment his apprentice's worries had been diverted. Now, he determined, those thoughts must be channeled into seeing a new vista. It was time to throw open the door to the richer world that existed all around them, but which most people never saw. It would have been hard enough, reflected the Deshi Master, to teach the necessary techniques in the quiet confines of the Deshi priory. To attempt to do so while on the open road, in a foreign land, and with a physically suspect teacher, was going to be decidedly difficult; but it must be done.

He proceeded with a quiet deliberateness, forcing his voice and manner to sound even and relaxed. "There are things I must show you, Shiko. As I am, perhaps, not at my best, you will forgive me if I instruct at a rapid pace. There is much to be learned."

Toshi-hito thereupon related the story of two young men, heads brimming with ideas, who had set out on a foolhardy expedition into the forbidden Grove. He glossed over the details of their preparations, relegating it to the misguided arrogance of youth; but described with succinct clarity what the two trespassers had seen once they had crossed beyond the Grove's perimeter.

To Shiko, who had never conceived of anyone violating the sanctity of the Sacred Grove, let alone his own Deshi Master, the tale was as astonishing as it was unexpected. As described by Toshi-hito, deep within the Grove were plants and trees that grew nowhere else in all of Tonogato. He described small rodents, even a strange type of lizard, which had no equivalents anywhere. The most interesting revelation, however, was the great stone and its mysterious portal. When Toshi-hito described the lioness, Shidosha, chief among the Shizen, Shiko could no longer restrain himself.

"But Master," interrupted the apprentice, "how could you possibly know that this image of a lioness was the leader of the Shizen?"

Toshi-hito said simply, "She told us." Before Shiko could voice the inevitable question, he added, "That is the real secret of the Grove, Shiko. Not the unique plants and animals, not even the magical portal to some other place. The Shizen can 'talk' to people, inside their minds. Shidosha is the most powerful of the Shizen, but she dwells only within the portal, inside the Sacred Grove, along with others of her type. But there are other Shizen, here in Tonogato, with whom we can also 'speak.' They are the animals all around us."

Startled, Shiko looked around quickly, as if suspecting to see an audience of animals watching. Then he glanced back at Toshi-hito with a hint of suspicion. "Master, are you telling me all this so that I will not worry about your health? This tale seems so unlike you, and so far removed from reality, it is very hard to credit." He added quickly, "I'm sorry, I didn't mean to imply—that is—"

"It is all right, Shiko," replied Toshi-hito. "I understand your skepticism. And I applaud your discrimination. One should never accept at face value any given set of 'facts,' regardless of the trustworthiness of the source, unless it meets your own test of credibility." He paused, peering down into the stream as if looking for something. "While it would be reasonable to question information provided by one suffering from such an injury, my physical condition is not such that it has impaired my mental faculties. At least, not yet!" The Deshi Master put his hand on Shiko's arm. "Do not let my health be of undue concern to you. I have greater reasons than that for sharing my knowledge with you. And I have yet more of greater value to tell."

Pointing into the stream, Toshi-hito said, "Do you see that frog? Over there, sitting in the shallows?" Shiko nodded, seeing the small frog where it sat resting on a nearby rock. Toshi-hito stared at the frog for a moment, then spoke quietly. "He is hungry. He is waiting for the fish beneath us to move upstream before entering the water to begin his evening feeding. He doesn't like fish."

Shiko looked skeptically at his Master. "But how could you tell that? How could the frog speak to you?"

"It is less the frog speaking to me, than me listening to what is on his mind. All of the animals' thoughts are there to be heard; it is just that most of them do not have much to say. Their thoughts are generally confined to their daily needs, such as with our little friend here. And what I hear from most of them are not words but more a sense, an understanding, of what the animal is feeling." Toshi-hito gestured toward the trees across the stream. "Many of the larger animals can be more articulate, when they wish. Most do not feel a need to 'talk' to people, particularly since most never have an opportunity to do so. To my knowledge, only the Kojuro, and at present myself, know how to converse with them."

He turned and looked at Shiko. "That, however, will now change. It is time, my young apprentice, for you to learn as well."

*   *   *

Shiko tried to concentrate. There was a door, Toshi-hito had said, and behind that door lay the world of the Shizen; one had but to search until it was found. He was trying to find the path that Toshi-hito had described, but it was elusive. For the last ten minutes he had done nothing but stare at the frog across from them, who had hopped around a few times but was still in view.

The Deshi frequently used the imagery of pathways and doors when describing their approach to meditation. Although Shiko knew one's mind was not really built that way, the mental picture it provided aided the soul in findings its bearings. Toshi-hito had explained to him how he could find the path that lead to the Shizen, so he had entered a meditative state and set off to locate it.

It was certainly not easy to find. He turned down many mental alleyways, only to find himself backtracking and trying a different route. How vast was the mind, he thought. He usually contented himself with meditating in a relatively small mental area, seeing no need to venture beyond that 'known' space within his head. He 'walked' now in unknown territory, dusting off metaphorical cobwebs as he went. He was vaguely aware of Toshi-hito sitting patiently next to him, probably grateful for the respite. Well, the Master was right, he thought; this certainly has taken my mind off of him. But I'm going to have to find a way to get him to rest more; I can see his strength visibly waning. Wait, wait; there! Is that it?

He used his Deshi training to try and make a visual image in his head of where he was, forming the picture of a door in front of him to represent what he felt. He let the image form naturally, so that the door took a shape that symbolized what it was. Gradually he made out a heavy wooden door, with great iron hinges. It was very old, sealed with the dust and dirt of countless ages. Probably, he thought, because it has never been opened! There was a great ring mounted on the door as a handle.

He could hear a voice, but not from within his mind. It was Ryori; he was asking if the two Deshi wanted their dinner cold, or not at all, as hot was no longer an option.

Shiko didn't hear Toshi-hito's reply because he was already focused on grabbing hold of the ring with his mental hands. He tugged; it would not move. He pulled harder, and felt it move slightly. Putting all his weight behind it he dug in his heels and strained, willing the huge door to open.

With a startling suddenness, it sprang open, dumping him off his feet. In an instant, his mind was filled with noise. *"HUNGRY. HUNGRY. HUNGRY. FISH, GO. FISH, GO. HATE FISH. FISH GO. HUNGRY."*

It was the voice of the frog, booming inside Shiko's head. He tried to pull back, overwhelmed by the intensity of the contact. It was, as

Toshi-hito had said, less words than mental thoughts cascading out of the frog and into his own mind. But it was so loud! "*HUNGRY. FISH GO,*" its simple mantra kept repeating. It was mentally deafening, and Shiko could not find his way back out through the door.

In desperation he tried to swing his external focus away from the frog. That, however, was a mistake, for although he and Toshi-hito had not noticed any other animals nearby they were of course there, hiding in the trees, perched on branches, asleep waiting for the night. And all of them had thoughts.

A raging torrent of mental voices cascaded through Shiko's mind, from lucid to succinct: "*Need more nest stuffing.*" "*EAT. EAT.*" "*Strange, large animals, by water. Wait. Wait.*" "*RUN, HIDE, BIRD COME.*" Shiko held his mental hands over his ears, but to no avail. The sudden assault on his internal senses overwhelmed him, and he felt his consciousness slip away.

He heard voices again, but human voices this time:

"...The boy's passed out. Be he all right?..."

"...I believe so. He seems to be stirring now. I do not believe it is serious..."

"...Hah! What is with you Deshi? You all just walk around ailing until you up and keel over?..."

Carefully, Shiko opened his eyes to see Toshi-hito and Ryori bending over him. He was apparently flat on his back, as he was looking up at them. The hard surface pushing against his spine told him he must still be on the large rock by the stream.

He saw Ryori sit back. "Well, you two obviously need more food than the miserly portions you've been eatin'. I'll go bring you some, an' I don't want no arguments about it." He left Shiko's field of view, leaving only Toshi-hito, looking down at him with concern. Such a short time ago, thought Shiko, it was I worrying about him.

He struggled to sit up, and Toshi-hito placed an arm about his shoulders to help him. Tenderly the Deshi Master said, "I am sorry. I did not expect that it would be so overwhelming for you. Perhaps, when Kimeru and I were in the Grove, the power of the Shizen controlled what we heard, allowing us to hear gradually."

Shiko nodded, still feeling slightly woozy from the experience. He stopped, mentally checking to see if he could still find his way back to the door. Yes, there it was, shut up tight again. Well, he would approach it more cautiously next time. "Thank you, Master," he said. "I am...fine. It was, as you said, unlike any other experience."

"You will find, as I did, that in time you will be able to control better what you hear. You will be able to make it quieter, or shut it off altogether. And, at the same time, control what you 'speak.' For," Toshi-hito concluded quietly as Ryori returned with food in hand, "the animals can hear you as well."

After the two Deshi had finished their meal, watched over diligently by Ryori, they elected to remain by the stream while the cook returned to the camp. The daylight was fading rapidly, but Toshi-hito said he wanted to make sure Shiko had his newly found skill under control before they rejoined the others.

"I have learned," said the Deshi Master, "that some animals are better at communicating than others. The birds, for instance, are the most vocal. Their singing is of course their way of speaking with one another; but they seem to delight in expressing themselves, even if just for their own amusement." He pointed to where Shiko's initial friend, the frog, had sat before leaping away into the long grass nearby. "Many of the smaller animals, such as the frog, do not seem able to think about much beyond their immediate needs. Typically they have not responded to my inquiries. Even with the birds, in general I am only able to understand a few 'words,' with which they express their thoughts; and then, only when they are nearby where I can see them. Only with Shidosha, in the Sacred

Grove, have I ever been able to actually have a 'conversation,' as such." He noted that Shiko's attention seemed to be drifting. "Are you sure you're feeling better?" he said sharply.

The mental sounds from beyond the door had begun to intrude on Shiko's consciousness, even without his being aware of it. He caught himself being mesmerized by their murmuring, and the question caused him to jerk his attention back to Toshi-hito. "Yes, Master, I'm sorry. There are just so many…sounds out there, it is hard to keep them all back."

Toshi-hito nodded. "Yes, it is as if you are forever in a crowded room. You must learn to shut them out or you will not find peace. Nor," he added dryly, "be able to sleep, as I know from experience."

"Master, what about the horses? We rode all the way to Shukyoshi on them, burdening them with our supplies. Do they know what they do? Why should they want to carry us, or our things?"

Toshi-hito answered the question with another. "Why does a farmer leave his fields to come to the city and do piecework in a craftsman's workshop? There are those who trade their freedom for the certainty of a plate of food upon their table, and are the happier for it. So it is with the Shizen. For most of the animals, life is hard, a constant search for food and shelter. Some, like the horses, find it less burdensome to serve people than to fend for themselves."

"Did you talk to your horse, while we rode?"

Toshi-hito smiled. "Horses don't appear to have much need to 'talk' to people, or even each other," he replied. "They are actually rather dull company."

"*Here, here!*"

Startled, both Deshi turned to look around them. Shiko saw it first, pointing across the stream. "There! In that tree! It's one of the chodaka birds!" Indeed, a pair of odd blue eyes stared down from a branch, not ten feet above their heads.

"Yes," agreed Toshi-hito. "He must be returning to Lord Itachi from one of his courier runs."

Shiko heard what sounded like a rude noise, then, *"Itachi, man is fool."* The bird fluttered down to the ground, perching near them. He cocked his head sideways, peering up at Shiko. *"Can hear now?"*

"Yes," said Shiko.

Toshi-hito put his hand on Shiko's arm. "They can 'hear' better if you think what it is you want to say."

Shiko looked down again at the bird, and found once more the door in his mind. He saw that it was open just a crack, so he pulled it open gently and concentrated on forming words in his mind. *"Yes,"* he thought. *"Thank you."*

The bird flapped its wings. *"Speak good!"* He hopped closer to where Shiko sat. *"No need, thank me. Feed me, yes. Thank me, no."*

Shiko smiled. To Toshi-hito he said, "He's hungry!"

The Deshi Master nodded. "Little wonder, if he has flown all the way from Hajimeshi. Here," he said, offering the bird the remains of his evening meal. The bird eagerly pecked at the remnants of Toshi-hito's food. To Shiko the Deshi Master said quietly, "We should try to find out what he may know regarding Itachi's plans. He may have overheard something of value while waiting for a reply to be prepared."

Shiko frowned. "You think Lord Itachi is still trying to take the throne? Is that possible, from so far away?"

"I have learned," said Toshi-hito sadly, "never to underestimate the ambition of unprincipled men."

Just at that moment the sound of brush being shoved aside interrupted them. Into the open space by the stream stepped none other than Itachi. Shiko's breath caught in his throat, as he remembered his last sudden encounter with Itachi in the woods. The chodaka bird had been present then too. Itachi scowled as he caught sight of the chodaka bird eating from the Deshi food bowls. "It is getting dark," he snapped, a fact quite obvious to Shiko already. "I want everyone inside the camp." At the sound of Itachi's voice, the bird had jumped back, perching on a nearby rock.

Toshi-hito looked coolly up at the Hajimeshi lord. "Are you expecting an attack? We have not been molested thus far while in Tejinashi."

"True," replied Itachi, "and I want to make sure we are prepared should that change." Meaningfully, he did not move, but stood and waited.

Reluctantly Shiko helped his Master to his feet, and the two made their way back to the camp. The apprentice noticed that Itachi did not immediately follow, nor did the chodaka bird move from his spot.

18

Darkness had already overtaken Mikasama and Shudojo by the time they reached the foothills leading out of the valley. The Princess had assumed that, due to the Sister's presence, they would be able to board during the nights with local farmers along their route. She was quickly disabused of that notion once she broached it to Shudojo.

"Lady," said the Sister, "no farmer in Shukyoshi will allow you on their land, let alone under their roof. Nor would I presume to take advantage of the monastery's good will with the people by imposing on them. There are not likely to be many farms in these hills, in any case." She gestured toward an open space among the trees that lined the road. "We should sleep here, as it will be colder the higher we climb."

"Fine," said a disappointed Mikasama, dismounting her horse. She had already spent a night in the open, at the Katanza camp; she could do it again, she told herself. She led her horse over to a nearby tree and sat down on a log. Shudojo did likewise and rummaged around in her pack. Pulling out a small packet of food, the Sister began chewing on the end of something that, to the Princess, looked like shoe leather. Mikasama pointedly cleared her throat.

Shudojo turned to look at her, raising an eyebrow. "Yes, Lady?"

"Aren't you going to make a fire?"

Perplexed, Shudojo replied, "No. I have no need of a fire." She bit off another piece of the 'shoe leather,' and shrugged. "If you wish to make one, I suppose you could. Although I suspect we are better off without one; it might attract the wrong sort of attention. However, this close to Fumosa we are unlikely to be bothered."

"But," sputtered Mikasama, "what about dinner? How will we eat?"

The Sister looked down at her own food, then back to the Princess. "I *am* eating. I assumed you weren't hungry." Her expression changed slowly from one of surprise to anger. "You expect me to cook for you, don't you? You think I'm some sort of servant?" Angrily, she stood up. "I serve no one but the Goddess, Lady. If you weren't prepared for this journey, then you should have stayed in Fumosa, or returned to where you came from!"

Shudojo roughly stuffed the remains of her food back into its pouch and stomped over to her horse. In the dim light remaining, the Princess watched as the Sister removed a sleeping blanket from its leather bag and rolled it out on the ground. Shudojo placed her travel pack as a pillow at one end and without another word lay down with her back turned to Mikasama.

The Princess sat dumbfounded. I don't know how to build a fire, she thought. I don't know how to prepare any kind of food at all. I have what the Sisters gave me before we left, but once that's gone, I don't know how to make anything from the supplies that Komori brought.

The Princess realized then an unpleasant truth. Despite her feelings of independence, despite her longing to run her own life and find her own way, she was ill-equipped to manage even her own affairs. She saw just how much she had always depended on Komori for the needs of her day-to-day existence. It had been a harsh adjustment at Fumosa, once Nana-san was gone, but its impact had been masked by the presence of the Sisters, and their fraternity, to take care of Mikasama's needs. Only now did she begin to understand what it really meant to be without Komori.

In a panic Mikasama hurriedly opened her travel pack, staring in the fading light at the packets of foodstuffs that Shudojo had salvaged from Komori's pack. A couple of them she recognized; as for the rest, she only knew the prepared foods that Komori had made from them. She didn't have the slightest idea how to make them herself.

Stupid, she thought. Here I am, being stupid again! Why hadn't I thought of this? All I wanted to do was get moving again, to get back out on the road. Now that I'm here, I don't even know the first thing about how to survive.

Her stomach growled as if in reproach. She grabbed at one of the few items she recognized in the pack and hastily ate a few bites. Then she retrieved her own blanket and stretched out uncomfortably on the ground, staring at the uncompromising shape that was Shudojo lying nearby. Darkness slowly settled over their impromptu campsite. Mikasama felt the vast emptiness of Komori's absence once again, like an enormous black void within her soul, barren of even a shred of light. She closed eyes that were filled with tears, and turned away.

It proved to be a long and largely sleepless night.

The following morning, with barely a word spoken between them, the two women set off once more. The air was crisp, the women's breath visibly floating away in the slight breeze. As Mikasama forced her aching limbs up onto her horse she decided that sleeping outdoors, particularly without a fire, was now fairly high on her list of least-favored activities.

As the morning slowly passed into afternoon, the Princess found she missed the easy companionship of Komori, even recalling with fondness the old woman's fussing and complaining. Shudojo, on the other hand, was an enigma to her. Why, she wondered, was the Sister doing this? What was *she* running away from?

Mikasama assumed that Shudojo must have been running away from something, for why else would she leave the simple routines and structured regimens of Fumosa? Surely it was not just to escape the repulsive Choda; horrid as the woman was, Mikasama could not conceive of self-exile on the road just to flee her. So what was it that drove this silent Sister to set out with a near total-stranger, and one who did not share her religious beliefs at that? The Princess could deduce no answer.

Suspecting that any query on the topic would be rebuffed, she kept her thoughts to herself.

The long silence between the two women also gave Mikasama time to think about her own motivations for being out on the road. In the brief periods of sleep she had managed to snatch from the night, she found that her dreams had changed. The images of soldiers, and the prophetic vision of Komori being swept away, had ceased. The glass wall, though, remained. Why? she wondered. Was it supposed to be a reminder?

And then there was the dark doorway, always open and waiting for her, and which she knew she must pass through…

*   *   *

Unbeknownst to Mikasama, Shudojo was no less confused about her own reasons for being on the road, although she would never have admitted it. She barely even acknowledged it to herself.

The two women were riding side by side on a mountain trail, bordered closely on either side by dense stands of trees. The track was not so narrow that the women had to ride in single file; but they might as well have been for the lack of conversation that passed between them. As Shudojo noticed her companion shifting in the saddle for what must have been the hundredth time in the last hour, she looked away. If the lady wants to stop, she thought, I'll let her be the one to tell me.

The Shukyoshi Sister's gaze wandered off into the trees, helping to keep her mind busy by watching for forest animals. Any misgivings she had about being on the road with a pampered and confused noblewoman were secondary to the fact that she was outside. She was finally free of the four walls of Fumosa monastery, and of the rigid conventions of a community of women. Although she loved the Goddess with all her heart, becoming a Sister of the Goddess had, perhaps, not been wise.

Shudojo smiled sadly to herself. That, she thought, was probably putting it rather mildly. At the time it had appeared to be her last refuge, the only option left to her in a world where options had been in short supply.

The memories of those dark days swept back into her head, stamped indelibly in her mind no matter how much she might want to forget...

In the months before she had arrived at Fumosa, she had been wandering, lost, a woman without home or family. She had walked from her village, the fishing town of Hochan in the far west, and had kept on walking until no one knew who she was or had ever heard of her family name. She had found food where she could along the way, begging when she could not. She had prayed to the Goddess for salvation, and forgiveness for the awful sin that she had committed...

Finally she had stumbled upon Fumosa. Hungry, shivering in the cold, she had reached the end of her stamina. Not knowing where she was, she had knocked on the great wooden gate. It had been simple fortune, or perhaps the hand of the Goddess, that Mother Narisa had been talking to the Sister tending the gate that night. The small shutter had opened, and Shudojo had pleaded for food. A compassionate Mother Narisa had ushered her inside, asking no questions. It was an act of kindness of a sort that Shudojo had never experienced before, having grown up in the tough, seaport environment of Hochan where charity had been considered the lot of fools. Nor, she mused, had that lesson been forgotten, as she glanced over at the young woman riding next to her. Another of the Goddess' children, arriving at Her gate in a time of need...

When Mother Narisa had taken in Shudojo the Sisters had clothed and fed her, and finally given her a place within their world. Shudojo had thought then that perhaps Fumosa was where she belonged, that she could begin again in a new home.

Inwardly she sighed. Things never seemed to quite work out that simply for her.

She had chafed under the mindless routines of the monastery, the ceaseless carping over minor details of theology. She remembered thinking, 'The Goddess is just *here*, right in front of us; why do idiots like Choda have to go on and on debating fine shades of meaning in the holy books?'

As a result Shudojo had become increasingly estranged from her fellow Sisters; only a handful of them had remained willing to talk to her or befriend her. She was ashamed to think that, at the time, she had wondered whether those who had been nice to her had been put up to it by Mother Narisa. But the sincerity of their warm words and gifts when Shudojo was leaving was proof of just how jaded her thoughts had become.

And now? Now, she thought, I am wandering the land again. Only this time I am not alone.

It was the only way, she knew, that she could have left the monastery. Simply leaving on her own was not something she would have done, regardless of Choda's irritating behavior. She had walked the land alone once before, and no matter how poor the present company it was still preferable to those long, lonely nights, when she had feared to lose her own mind. So she had leapt at Mother Narisa's suggestion that she accompany their 'guest' on her journey to the west. It didn't really matter to Shudojo where the woman was bound; it was out there, somewhere. And so she had agreed, secretly overjoyed at the prospect.

Even so, now she began to have doubts. This woman was increasingly turning into a royal pain in the behind. How, wondered Shudojo, could this lady have set out on the road and not know the first thing about how to travel? She must have come from a very wealthy family, where she could be sheltered from the harsh reality of actually living. Well, I am not about to take care of her. I promised Mother Narisa to look after her, and keep her from harm on the road, but I'm not going to make up for her ignorance! If she asks, I will show her how to cook, or how to find food out of the forest. If she'd rather ride in silence, that's fine too; then the growling of her belly can be her companion.

The silent pair rode on, finally emerging near dusk on the far side of the hills. As the sun's light faded, to be replaced by that from the stars,

Mikasama and Shudojo made another quiet, cold camp. They had crossed the unmarked border into Tejinashi.

*   *   *

The Hikari lantern bobbed and weaved on its pole as Donaku, once again its bearer, marched along with the other Guards. Trailing behind, Shiko and Ryori struggled to keep up while helping an increasingly ailing Toshi-hito.

The effort the Deshi Master had expended in teaching Shiko about the Shizen had clearly exacted a steep toll. Toshi-hito had once again withdrawn into himself. Eyes focused straight ahead, he relied on Shiko and Ryori to guide him as they walked; the two spoke softly to let him know when there was a stream to ford, or a detour required due to a fallen tree. Without comment he accepted their aid, further heightening Shiko's worries for him.

For the last hour the pilgrims had been following the ill-maintained road that led deeper into Tejinashi. It was clear to Shiko that few travelers came this way, which was unsurprising given the indifference of the Tejinashi and the religious isolation of the Shukyoshi. The pilgrims had seen no one at all since leaving the river far behind.

Walking beside Toshi-hito, the apprentice looked ahead to where the Hikari continually moved further away from them. Itachi was setting a deliberately fast pace, making no allowance for Toshi-hito's condition. It was, thought Shiko angrily, almost as if the man delighted in seeing how far he could push Toshi-hito's endurance. Whenever the Guards left the Deshi and Ryori behind and out of sight, after a time Itachi would call a halt until they caught up. Yet the Deshi were never allowed to rest; as soon as they reached the end of the column, the Guards started walking again.

Toshi-hito was in no condition to confront Itachi about it, and Shiko and Ryori, as Deshi apprentice and cook, were certainly in no position to argue. So they marched on, Shiko fuming, and Ryori doing whatever he could to ease Toshi-hito's discomfort. Whenever the pilgrims encountered difficult terrain Shiko's efforts were concentrated on helping his Master; but on level ground Toshi-hito was able to walk unaided, leaving Shiko with more time to think.

Thinking, though, was making him angry and frustrated, as he felt helpless to do anything about Itachi. He sought to control his thoughts, though, for such was the Deshi way. He used the techniques taught to him at the priory: find a topic; explore it; analyze it. Do not squelch the emotions, said the Deshi Masters, but hold them in check by giving the mind productive things to do. Then channel those emotions, use the control you have established to make the emotions work for you to achieve your goal.

Shiko repeated the teachings to himself, then applied them. As the group of Hajimeshi bunched up once more while traversing a shallow ravine, he thought again about what he had learned regarding the Shizen. His encounter with the frog seemed so long ago, although it was less than two days past. Had it really happened? he wondered. Maybe I just dreamed the whole thing up. It seems so fanciful, talking to animals. But since we started walking again, I've haven't had time to think about it. Perhaps I should—

"*Hel*-lo? *Can you hear me?*"

Startled, the apprentice stopped in mid-stride, causing Ryori to glance over in his direction. Shiko quickly started walking again, looking up ahead where he could see Itachi and Bokusa marching beside Donaku and the Hikari. He realized, as he stared at the pack slung over Itachi's shoulders, that he was hearing the voice of the chodaka bird. In his mind, Shiko ran over to the mental 'door' he had found earlier. From the other side he could hear the bird call out again: "*Are you listening?*"

Shiko carefully pulled the 'door' open once more, and tried to form the words to express himself. "*Yes,*" he thought, "*I'm here.*"

"*Humph. About time,*" came the reply. "*I've only been shouting at you for the last few hours.*"

"*I'm sorry,*" answered Shiko, as he glanced over at Ryori and Toshi-hito. Neither gave any indication that they heard or noticed anything, as the three followed along after the Guards. *"I've been....kind of busy, I suppose."*

"Well," answered the bird, *"just be glad you have something to be busy with. Bouncing along in the dark here is excruciatingly dull, to put it mildly."*

Shiko thought about the box, and how Itachi had shoved the birds down inside it. He was amazed that he could hear the bird from there. He said, *"Are you all right in there, wherever—I guess, wherever there is?"*

"Oh, fine, just fine. Food, drink, what more could we want?" said the bird caustically. Shiko felt, rather than heard, the bird's tone change to one of curiosity. *"You seem to be able to hear much better now. It's easier to talk with you than with the other one."* Instinctively Shiko knew that the bird meant Toshi-hito.

The apprentice realized that the bird was right. He could now understand the words much more clearly than when he had first opened the 'door.' Even now, when the birds were tucked away in their 'cage' inside Itachi's pack, fairly distant and out of sight, the 'words' formed in his mind with great clarity. Toshi-hito had said that he could only 'hear' the animals when he could see them, but Shiko seemed to be able to hear the chodaka bird's thoughts as if the bird were perched on his shoulder. *"Yes,"* he answered, *"although I don't understand why."* He paused for a moment, still coming to grips with the fact that he was actually talking with a bird. Then he asked, *"Do you—do you have a name?"*

"Yes, of course. Let me see, I guess you would say it—" Shiko felt, rather than heard, a sound that formed in his mind: 'Ton.

"'Ton. Well," replied the Deshi, *"my name is Shiko. I'm—I am pleased to meet you."*

Shiko felt something akin to laughter. *"Your kind are so funny,"* said 'Ton. *"I 'met' you days and days ago, when you helped this oaf up here send one of his silly scraps of paper. But still we have to be introduced!"* Again Shiko experienced the odd sensation of mental laughter, which felt like the touch of spray from a mountain waterfall. *"All right. 'Glad to meet you too.' There, how's that? Is that how your kind does it?"*

Sheepishly, Shiko said, *"Yes, ah...I suppose that's right."*

"And this is my mate, whom you might call—" Shiko felt another name form in his head: 'Cha.

"Stop teasing him, 'Ton," said a new 'voice.' Shiko realized it must be 'Cha; somehow, the 'voice' sounded more feminine than 'Ton. *"Give the young creature a chance. It's not as if you've talked to a lot of them yourself, you know."*

Shiko pulled his attention away from the conversation briefly to focus on where his body was walking. Seeing that the pilgrims would be walking along a fairly level stretch for a time, he tried dividing his attention between keeping his feet from tripping over each other and talking with the birds.

"Hello, 'Cha," he said. *"My name is—"*

"Shiko, yes, I heard. But we already knew that, anyway."

"You did?" said Shiko with surprise. *"But how—"*

"Never mind," answered 'Ton. *"We can talk about that later. How's the other one?"*

Shiko realized that they, too, were worried about Toshi-hito. Not only did he hear their words but he could sense their emotions behind them as well. Why, he wondered, should they be concerned with the Deshi Master? Up until a week ago Toshi-hito had not even been aware of their existence. What could 'Ton and 'Cha possibly know about him? He wanted to ask so many questions, but decided that he had best answer their query first.

"He is...not well. He was poisoned by a sword blade in Shukyoshi. I hope we stop marching soon, otherwise..."

"Typical," said 'Ton. *"You creatures are always arguing about something or other, and then getting hurt. You should learn from the bears, who make a big show of things but rarely actually fight. Biggest bluffers I ever saw."*

Shiko, looking up again to the head of the line, thought about their cage and about being cooped up in the dark of Itachi's pack. How awful for birds! Trapped where they cannot fly, cannot even see.

"Yes," replied 'Cha, who seemed to have heard every thought Shiko uttered. *"These accommodations are certainly—well, less than ideal."*

He was a bit shocked that 'Cha seemed to be able to read his mind, even when he hadn't tried to form words out of his thoughts, but he put his curiosity aside for the moment. *"I should try to set you both free! You don't belong in there. I just need to find a way to do it without getting caught. Perhaps when—"*

"No—that's all right," interrupted 'Ton. In response to Shiko's mental question mark, he went on. *"Well, it's not that we don't want out; believe me, we want nothing more. Its just that…well, since I came back from my last trip, I've been…advised…about what all of you creatures are up to so far from home. And…well, we need to be here. For now."*

"I don't understand," said a confused Shiko. *"Why would you have to stay in there? And who advised you? Other birds from Hajimeshi?"*

His query was greeted with mental silence. Finally 'Ton said, *"I can't say right now. Later, perhaps…"*

And then Shiko's attention was diverted. The Hikari up ahead was stationary, the Guards milling about. As Shiko approached he saw that they had stopped at the edge of a cliff. *"I'll talk to you so more later,"* he said hurriedly to the birds. *"I think I have to see what's happening up ahead."*

"Just leave that 'door' of yours open a bit more, OK?" came the rejoinder from 'Ton.

Shiko left Ryori standing by Toshi-hito and approached the knot of Guards ranged along the edge of the steep cliff. They were all looking over the side into a deep ravine. When the apprentice peered over the edge, he could see a mass of timbers far below. From this distance they looked like a pile of children's play sticks that had been dropped onto the boulders carpeting the bottom of the ravine.

The timbers had clearly been shaped by human hands, and Shiko realized that he was looking at the remains of a bridge which must have collapsed some time in the past. All that remained now was a single huge rope, suspended across the open space of the ravine. It was tied to stout trees on either side, which had evidently once supported the failed bridge. Looking across to the other side of the ravine, Shiko saw a tall basket perched atop the opposite cliff. It hung below the remaining rope on two grooved wheels, one placed in front of the basket and the other behind.

Shiko grasped right away that someone must have set up the basket as a means to get across the ravine as a replacement for the bridge. It was similar, he recalled, to the baskets on pulleys he had seen in Hajimeshi; builders used them to haul stones up to the top of walls they were constructing. Only here, the basket went across a canyon instead of up a wall, and was much larger, appearing big enough to hold, he guessed, perhaps two people.

Shiko knew that for the basket to work there would have to be another rope for pulling it back and forth. He looked around, but the only rope he could see was the one from which the basket was suspended. Then he saw it: there *was* another rope, but it hung down limply from the basket, swaying in the light breeze and bouncing against the outcroppings of the opposite cliff. It had broken, or had come untied, from their end; and thus there was now no means to haul the basket back over to their side.

Itachi and Bokusa were conferring, evidently trying to determine what to do. Deciding that he had best act as Toshi-hito's emissary, Shiko screwed up his courage. He walked up to the two men, whose backs were turned to him as they surveyed the ravine. He cleared his throat, and hoped that his voice sounded more confident than he felt. "Excuse me, Lord Itachi; what do you intend to do?"

Slowly Itachi turned around to look at him. "We are going to cross," he said patronizingly. "In the basket," gesturing toward the far cliff. At Shiko's perplexed look he went on, speaking as if to a dim-witted child. "Bokusa is going to go across on the rope. Then he's going to come back over, in the basket, pulling himself here holding on to the rope. Then we'll go two at a time, each man in the basket pulling on the rope to get across. So," he added, jerking a thumb in the direction of Toshi-hito, "you had best get him ready. It will be hand-over-hand for whoever is going."

Shiko's face flushed as he realized what Itachi intended. Striving to keep his anger in check, Shiko said quietly, "You know Toshi-hito cannot pull himself across."

Bokusa, standing with arms crossed, sneered at the apprentice. "Then you'd best work up some muscle, squirt. You're gonna need it to pull the two of you across." He laughed, a sound resembling pebbles flailing around inside a metal pail. Itachi grinned, and the two men turned away.

Determined not to give in, and desperate to ensure his Master's well being, Shiko reached up and grabbed Itachi's arm. Faster than he thought possible, the apprentice's hand was knocked away and the front of his tunic crumbled up inside Itachi's fist as the Hajimeshi lord jerked him up off his feet. Looking into Itachi's eyes, scant inches from Shiko's own, the Deshi saw nothing but blind fury and unthinking cruelty.

* * *

Oh, yes, the rage has returned. I can feel it! It flows though him, like blood. It is the one thing that drives him, like a wildfire rushing out of control through dry grass...

It is tempting...watch, yes; I am only supposed to watch. But surely it could not hurt to experiment just a little...to see if...

* * *

The voice, when it spoke, was low, and thereby all the more menacing. "Do not lay a hand on me again, Deshi," said Itachi, "or you will find you have no hands left with which to do so."

Shiko, senses heightened by fear, felt Itachi's strong breath against his face. He nodded, painfully aware that Itachi's fist had gathered up some of the skin off his chest as well as his clothing. Even with his nod, however, the Hajimeshi lord did not release the apprentice. The man's expression screwed up in a feral snarl, and with fatalistic certainty Shiko sensed that Itachi was about to toss him off the edge of the cliff.

Then another voice spoke. "I will pull Toshi-hito over, Lord Itachi." It was Nakama, who had walked over from the cluster of Guards, all the rest of whom pointedly ignored the discussion.

Suddenly, to Shiko's astonishment, Itachi's eyes grew vacant, almost as if the man were no longer seeing the apprentice that he clutched in front of him. He did not at first respond to Nakama; then suddenly, the spell broken, he released Shiko, who dropped back to the ground clumsily. Itachi turned his vacant stare onto Nakama, and spoke in the same low voice. "So be it, *soldier*." He looked at Bokusa. "Go ahead, show these worms how a Guard gets across a piddling crack in the ground like this." Bokusa grinned. He walked over to where the rope spanning the ravine was tied around the tree on their side, a few yards back from the cliff edge.

Shiko, still breathing hard, scarcely heard Itachi's words, or noticed that the man had turned away. It took him a moment to realize that he was still there, atop the cliff; he had been so certain, seeing the rage in Itachi's eyes, that he was going to be lying at the bottom of the ravine, a broken collection of bones.

Control, he reminded himself; the essence of Deshi thinking is control. Once lost, then passion rules the mind, rather than the mind ruling the passion.

Slowly Shiko calmed his breathing, and the pounding of his heart. As he did so he watched Bokusa, facing the tree, swing his feet up to wrap them around the rope. The big man edged himself along the stout cordage until he was clear of the cliff edge, looking down only once to the long drop that ended among huge rocks and the heap of smashed timbers. Then he began sliding himself along, a foot at a time. His fellow Guards, Nakama excepted, crowded around the cliff, cheering him on.

Shiko turned away, rejoining Ryori who stood with one hand lightly holding Toshi-hito's elbow. His thoughts were quickly diverted from his recent confrontation. "How is he?" he asked.

Ryori glanced at the silent Toshi-hito, whose eyes were closed and whose breathing, even allowing for the rest, sounded labored. The cook shrugged. "Who can say? No clue what's goin' on inside him. Outside sure looks like hell, though." A shout came up from the Guards. Ryori quietly spit in the direction of their turned backs. "Sounds like the big ape made it." He gestured toward Toshi-hito. "Guess we'd best get him ready to go."

The two of them guided Toshi-hito closer to the others, ready to help get him into the basket when their turn came. As they neared the group Shiko could see Bokusa, face beaming and dripping with sweat, inside the basket now and pulling it back along the rope. His great arms reaching up overhead, he heaved himself and the basket along; when he was within reach of the other Guards, they grabbed hold of the basket and swung it up onto the ground. Bokusa climbed out, turned to Itachi, and bowed. In an out-of-breath voice he said, "Your carriage, sire." The object of his attention laughed, as did the other Guards. Shiko, however, couldn't help noticing Bokusa's casual use of the word 'sire' in reference to Itachi...

The Hajimeshi general directed two of the Guards to go across, and the chosen pair climbed into the basket and rapidly pulled themselves over to the other side. Itachi had worked out that one man would exit on the far side, and the second would pull the basket back for another man. When those two had crossed, the first man over would spell the return puller, until eventually everyone was across.

Itachi himself went over next, taking his own turn as a return puller as well. Once settled on the far side, he sent word back to interrupt the flow of men and to send across all of the packs. This set off a flurry of activity as some of the Guards began redistributing the weight from some of the heavier packs to make it easier on the pullers.

Shiko, waiting with Ryori and Toshi-hito for their turn to cross, glanced over to where Itachi's pack waited with the others. The apprentice sent an image of the ravine to 'Ton and 'Cha, along with a mental note of reassurance not to worry, that the basket looked quite safe.

'Cha replied, *"It's all right, heights don't bother us very much."*

"We are birds, you know," added 'Ton.

"Ton..." said an admonishing 'Cha.

"Sorry..."

"Don't like this," said Ryori quietly, interrupting Shiko's dialogue with the birds.

As the apprentice shifted his attention back, the little cook nodded in the direction of Itachi on the far bank. "Man's gettin' nastier by the day."

Shiko, rubbing the raw area of his chest where Itachi's fist had grabbed, started to reply but noticed that Toshi-hito's eyes had opened. "Master?" he said. "How are you feeling?" Toshi-hito did not respond, his gaze fixed on something else. Suddenly the Deshi Master started moving, walking quickly toward the Guards. "Master?" said Shiko after him. "Where are you going? It's not our time yet." Toshi-hito did not stop but kept right on walking. Alarmed, Shiko and Ryori looked at each other then set off after him.

Matsugo, one of the Guards sorting out the pack contents, was holding a small bag in one hand. With his other hand he was rummaging around in the depths of a pack. Just before Shiko and Ryori caught up with Toshi-hito, the Deshi Master walked full-tilt into the Guard. Both men went sprawling to the ground. Matsugo dropped the bag, where it broke open, spilling a fair quantity of gold pieces across the dirt.

"Master!" shouted Shiko as he knelt down. "Are you all right?"

Toshi-hito waved him away, leaning on Ryori who had also bent over to help. In a weak voice Toshi-hito forced out, "I am...fine. Help...gather the coins..." Then he let Ryori help him back to his feet.

Matsugo dusted himself off as he got up. "What the hell's the matter with 'im?" the man growled, gesturing at Toshi-hito. "He blind, or what?"

The Deshi apprentice shrugged, as Ryori led Toshi-hito back out of the way. "I—I don't know. I'm sorry, I—I think he was just—confused, that's all." But Matsugo had stopped listening once he had realized what had been spilled on the ground. The Guard quickly bent down to collect the coins. Shiko, remembering his Master's admonition, said, "Here, let me help you." The two of them scooped up all of the coins and put them back in the pack.

Itachi's voice could be heard, shouting across the ravine to find out what the holdup was. In a disgusted voice, Bokusa called back that "the old geezer had a fit" but that he was out of the way now. Once Shiko had finished helping Matsugo he returned to where Ryori stood with Toshi-hito. As the first of the packs was sent across, Shiko asked, "Master, why did you go over there? We would have told you when it was time to go."

Wearily, Toshi-hito shook his head. "...Not that," he said. "How many?"

Shiko was puzzled. "How many what, Master? How many trips until we cross?"

"No...How many...coins?"

Coins? He isn't making any sense, thought Shiko. Why does he want to know how many coins there were? "I don't understand, Master. I didn't count them; there seemed to be quite a few."

Toshi-hito tiredly waved his hand. "Deshi are trained...to count rapidly. Did you not...learn this?"

One of the Deshi training exercises was to display a varying number of objects, and force the viewer to reconstruct from memory how many things were seen and what they were. It helped to sharpen the powers of recollection. Shiko, taking a moment to remember, tried to re-assemble a mental picture of the coins on the ground, combining it with updated 'views' as he and Matsugo had re-loaded the bag.

"I would say between thirty-eight and forty coins, Master," he said, once he had calculated it out. "I can't be certain, as he picked up at least one or two before I started. But why does it matter?"

"He's losin' it, lad," said Ryori sadly. "That's all there is to it."

"Not...lost yet, Master Cook," croaked Toshi-hito.

Nakama walked up at that moment. "It's time for us to go over," he announced quietly. "I will help you get him into the basket."

"Thank you," said Shiko, "we will be right there. Give us just a moment. Please." Nakama pursed his lips, but nodded and returned to wait by the basket, where an impatient Bokusa stood tapping the basket's side with his fingers.

"Master," repeated Shiko urgently, "why does the number of coins matter?" He sensed that for Toshi-hito to have made such an effort to find out, it must be important. Ryori, he knew, was wrong; regardless of what ailed the Deshi Master, Shiko was certain that Toshi-hito would have a reason for his actions.

In a harsh, quiet whisper, such that both apprentice and cook had to strain to hear it, Toshi-hito said, "Brigands...in Yutakashi. Itachi said...paid ten of his forty gold pieces...to 'buy them off.' But...you see, the coins...are still here."

Ryori, quick to see the implications, straightened up. "Meaning they were his men. And the ones who ambushed us in the gorge—"

"His too...perhaps," said Toshi-hito. "If so..."

"If so," nodded Ryori, looking across the ravine, "then we be haulin' ourselves into a heap o' trouble over there."

A shout from Bokusa interrupted them. "Let's go!" he yelled. "Either plant him as a tree or load him into the basket!" With a meaningful glance between them, Shiko and Ryori helped walk Toshi-hito over to the basket and the waiting Nakama.

*   *   *

Yes! It was easier than I thought. He was ready to throw the boy off the cliff, heedless of any other consequences. And he would have done it! I could feel the anger, the frustration...he is not a man who takes frustration easily. He would have pitched the boy into the ravine to smash against the rocks, to satiate the thirst of his rage.

But I stopped him! I made him override his most basic urge to kill! If I can do that, I can make him do anything. I could probably even make him kill himself!

'It' would not be pleased with that, though. It would be angry, and I have no wish to endure its wrath again. I was careful this time; I moved quietly, slowly, with just enough touch to bend this Itachi's will to my own. So, one fragile life was spared which otherwise might have been extinguished. Little matter; that one's life has no more worth than the rest. Soon, all of them will be ground into dust...

19

"Shudojo, the light is fading." Mikasama, tired, saddle sore, and missing the guiding hand of Komori, pestered Shudojo with complaints. "It's cold. And I don't want to have to spend another night outside."

The two were riding slowly down a forest lane as the lowering sun cast dim beams of light through the branches overhead. Once they had crested the hills surrounding the valley holding Fumosa, their way had been generally level. The many hours of riding had left women and horses alike tired and longing for a rest.

Shudojo had grown weary of Mikasama's continuing petulance, which had been going on nearly non-stop since daybreak. "Lady, the sun will set whether you will it or not. Nothing is gained by wishing for what is not here. We should find a place to make camp for the night."

"I will *not* sleep another night in the cold and damp." Mikasama's horse, sensing her mood, began fidgeting, causing her in turn to become more distressed. "I'm sick and tired of waking up with bugs making their breakfast out of me. We will go on until we find some place civilized to spend the night!"

"Lady," grated Shudojo, "we have passed no inns along this road. There is no reason to think—"

"Wait!" said Mikasama. She pulled up sharply on her reins, her horse tossing his head in irritation at the abrupt move.

Shudojo, fearing trouble, stopped also. "What?" she said. "What do you hear?"

"Not hear. Smell. Can't you smell it?"

Shudojo turned her head about until a faint whiff of something registered. It took her a moment to realize that it was something being smoked, probably over a cooking fire.

Mikasama turned to the Sister eagerly. "If we can smell cooking, perhaps it means an inn."

"Or other travelers on the road, already camped," was Shudojo's rejoinder.

Mikasama ignored the Sister's response. "It can't be too far off. Come on—perhaps tonight we'll have warm sheets and comfortable beds!" She nudged her horse on down the road.

Shudojo reluctantly followed.

The light was all but gone as the two women entered a clearing. To Shudojo's surprise it did indeed contain an inn, if such it could be called; to her, even in the half-darkness, the building looked more like a converted barn. The roof sagged, an apparent victim of uncounted years of weathered storms and shabby maintenance. The stones making up its walls were poorly mortared, and many of the spaces between them were stuffed with straw where the mortar had decayed. The courtyard was littered with decrepit livery and agricultural implements, none of which appeared to have moved for years judging by the growth of weeds around them. Had it not been for the wisp of smoke emanating lethargically from the chimney, and the presence of horses tied up outside, the building would have appeared utterly abandoned.

The women looked at each other. Finally Shudojo said, "I do not think that this is a place where we should look for lodging."

Mikasama hesitated. The obvious seediness of the place would not meet anyone's expectations of a comfortable inn. Nevertheless she shook her head obstinately. "Nonsense. We are travelers, and this is a public road. I am sure they will have some sort of guest quarters." She urged her horse up to where the others were tethered, a doubtful Shudojo following behind.

Taking their packs with them the two women moved toward the entrance of the 'inn.' The windows were all covered; no light was visible from outside the building. Just before they reached the heavy wooden door, loud voices could be heard. There was shouting, but neither woman could understand what was being said. Suddenly the door sprang open, crashing back on its hinges against the wall. A figure stumbled out and before he said a word Mikasama and Shudojo could smell the strong odor of liquor. The man wobbled a few steps before coming up short before the two women. He tried to focus on them, failed, then mumbled almost incoherently, "Thattt...wine musta been...strongern' I thought..." The last word found him falling face down in the dirt between the two startled women.

From the open door, Shudojo could hear the raucous laughter of drunken revelry, and the stink of too much sweat and too much wine confined in an enclosed space. Earnestly she said to Mikasama, "This place is not for us. We should leave, now."

The Princess answered stubbornly, "No. I want to sleep in a bed. We'll insist on their best room, and hope that it is on the far side of wherever the..." She looked down at the unconscious figure on the ground. "...the dining room is. Come on."

"Lady!" said Shudojo, but Mikasama was already striding forward through the door before the Sister could stop her. Quickly she followed the headstrong Princess in. As she entered, she noted that the bawdy laughter had died away to silence. The room was small, only big enough for two tables. A low-beamed ceiling pressed down overhead, making the space seem even more oppressive. The air was stale and the smell of wine even more pronounced here inside. There were men at the tables, but Shudojo could not tell how many since the only light in the room was from the feeble flame of a fire on the far side. As much of its smoke was drifting about the room as was going up the chimney.

Mikasama stood several feet in from the door, apparently trying to adjust her eyes to the gloom. While Shudojo tried to adjust her own, she heard Mikasama say imperiously, "We are travelers, and seek accommodation. Please show us your best room."

Shudojo heard several snickers from the group of drunken men. One said, "I'll show you *my* room, Sister. It's the best one in the house!" The others laughed, and started making catcalls at the two women.

Mikasama was not dressed as a Shukyoshi Sister, but the men, Shudojo realized, having seen her own habit, must have thought them both from the religious order. Eyes stinging from the smoke Shudojo was finally able to see well enough to make out a fat man with a filthy apron, presumably the owner of the 'establishment,' standing in front of Mikasama. He said, "We ain't got no finery here, lady. All sleep in a common hall."

The Princess was taken aback. "That—that is not acceptable. We need to have our own room." This pronouncement elicited another round of jeers from the appreciative audience. Foolishly, Mikasama continued, "We have plenty of money, if price is the problem."

As Shudojo inwardly groaned, she could hear the men's response to this revelation. "Ohhh, plenty of money, has she?" said one. "Needs to *pay* to take on men, ehh? That's a nice twist!" as the others roared their approval.

The unkempt proprietor gazed at Mikasama irritably, but kept eyeing her moneybag. Finally he grabbed a candle-lamp and motioned her to follow him. He set off through a curtained doorway at the back. As the two women followed Shudojo could hear the ribald talk continuing behind her.

The tavern owner led them through a dark, smelly hallway. Coming up to a door he shoved it open with his foot, went inside, and hung the candle-lamp from a hook on the wall. Mikasama stepped inside and looked about indignantly.

"This is horrid!" the Princess complained as Shudojo entered. "You expect us to sleep in here?"

Shudojo saw a room little larger than an oversize closet, which the light from the guttering candle revealed less of than they probably wanted to see. There was nothing in the room but straw mats on the floor and a chamber pot, which judging from the odor had not been emptied anytime that day. A small window was set into the wall opposite the door.

"I don't expect you to sleep anywhere, Miss High and Mighty," replied the tavern owner crossly. "You want to pay me for a room, this is the room you get. It's the only one with a door. And if you take my advice," he said, looking back toward the dining room, "you'll be wantin' a door." With that, he held out his hand. Reluctantly Mikasama opened her moneybag and gave him a silver coin. He looked at it in the feeble light, then sneered, "Pleasant dreams." He turned and left, closing the door behind him.

Shudojo, expressionless, looked at Mikasama. Halfheartedly the Princess said, "Well, it's a room. At least we won't have insects crawling on us all night."

The Sister, looking down at the straw mats, saw what appeared to be movement. "I'm not so sure about that." She knelt down and turned the mat over. Even in the dim light both women could see the rapid movement of many insects scampering away.

Mikasama swore, which was a revelation to Shudojo—she didn't think a pampered lady capable of such language. The Princess started for the door. "That swine! He can get some of those drunken louts out there to clean up this room!"

Shudojo grabbed her arm. "Lady! Don't be a fool! We shouldn't be here in the first place!" Mikasama glared at the Shukyoshi Sister but Shudojo went on, heedless of the Princess's indignation. "Those men out there don't care who you are, whether you're high born or low. To them you're nothing but something to spend their passion on!"

Mikasama jerked her arm out of Shudojo's grasp. In a cold voice she replied, "What does a Shukyoshi Sister know about such things? What makes you so wise in the ways of men's loins?"

Shudojo's eyes grew large, a range of emotions flitting rapidly across her face. She turned away as if slapped, and leaned against the wall. Her body began to shake.

Mikasama realized immediately that she had said something terribly wrong.

The long hours of riding, with effectively nothing but her own thoughts to keep her company, had left the Princess feeling ever more isolated and despondent. Her desire to be out on the road, her delight at being free to search for the answers to the visions in her dreams, had suffered in the face of afternoon heat and buzzing flies. All of her anxieties about what she was doing so far from home had resurfaced and gnawed at her mind.

And now, she thought, I've really done it. I've been pushing Shudojo at every step since we started out together, taking out on her all of my frustration. I wanted someone to talk to, someone to help me; and when I ended up instead with a moody, judgmental Sister, I focused all of my disappointment on her.

She realized, though, that it didn't matter what she might have wanted. Shudojo was the person here now, not Komori, not some other older, wiser Sister. She had been taking advantage of Shudojo, making the Sister a lightning rod for all of her own troubles.

Mikasama knew that the Sister had not done or said anything to deserve the way she had been treated; she had simply been trying to give advice, and to keep them both out of trouble. It was not Shudojo's fault that her manner was brusque and standoffish. However, thought Mikasama, it will be *my* fault if I let that brusque manner blind me to Shudojo's good intentions. Particularly, she admitted, if I overrule her judgement and land us in uncomfortable circumstances. Like these, she reflected, screwing up her face in disgust as she looked around the dingy room.

She stepped toward Shudojo, unsure of what to say. Thinking to comfort the Sister she reached out a hand, but uncomfortably let it drop again. Instead, with a shrug, she said, "Look, I'm sorry. I didn't mean to hurt your feelings."

She was unprepared as Shudojo whipped around on her, the Sister's eyes burning in the dim glow from the candle. "You're sorry?" said Shudojo. "Sorry? Never so sorry, Lady, as I!" Mikasama was shocked to see Shudojo shaking with barely suppressed fury. "Sorry that I'm such a fool to have volunteered for this journey! I thought to redeem my faith, and that maybe converting a heathen would allow the Goddess to redeem me for my sin. But, oh, she has seen fit to test my faith to the limit!" She pointed a finger at Mikasama. "I've endured your mindless complaints for too many miles, Lady! I am finished trying to be your watchdog." She sat down abruptly on the floor and started pulling things out of her pack. "Tomorrow, I go my own way. I will leave you the things you need to continue your journey."

Stunned, Mikasama could only stand and watch as Shudojo tossed things out of the pack and into a corner of the room. Her own cheeks flushed with anger. At first this was directed at Shudojo, but even before the Sister had finished talking Mikasama realized that she herself had been to blame for Shudojo's outburst. I caused this confrontation, she realized. My temper, and my mouth, spoke too fast. At home, in Hajimeshi, it had never mattered; I was the Kojuro's daughter, after all.

Even as that thought coursed through her head she understood how shallow it was, and how selfish she had been during her life as a Princess. Back then, other than her father and Komori, she had been required to hold her tongue for no one, and as a result she had never learned to curb it. Things were different now, she saw. The stakes were much higher, and her will was no more important that those of the people around her.

Juyama had always been saying something like that, she recollected. What was it? Oh, yes: *"As a princess, it is your duty to care for those who trust their welfare to you. You must set the examples for them; of competency, of compassion, and of cooperation. You must always think of others before yourself..."* She remembered him saying that it was the single most important lesson he could teach.

Ashamedly she thought about how poorly she had absorbed that lesson. It was only now, standing in a filthy hovel of a room with a woman she barely knew, somewhere deep within a foreign land, that she understood finally what he had meant, and how self-centered she had always been. When the time had come for her to be tested, not in Juyama's classroom but out in the real world, she had failed. Miserably...

Worse, with a sinking feeling in her stomach she realized that she was about to lose, yet again, her companion on the road, with nobody to blame but herself. The prospect of traveling onward, alone and friendless, was unbearable.

Yet she sensed that there was more to it than that. She had an almost overwhelming feeling that Shudojo must stay with her. Like the darkened doorway in her dreams, opposite the wall of glass, the feeling made itself felt without explanation, yet it was a need almost as strong as the urge to press on to the west. The Sister's presence on her quest was important. She couldn't let her go.

Mikasama sat down in front of the Sister, who was still sorting out the belongings. "Shudojo?" she said quietly.

"What?" replied the Sister, not looking up.

"Shudojo," repeated Mikasama. "Please look at me." The Sister stopped her work and looked up at the Princess. The steely blue of those eyes almost unnerved Mikasama but she forged ahead. "Shudojo, you are right. I have done nothing but complain while on this journey. You have tried to suggest what was best for both of us, but I cast your advice aside."

"Your point, Lady?" said Shudojo stonily.

Mikasama took a deep breath. "I started this quest thinking that I knew what I was searching for." She sighed inwardly. It had seemed so simple back then; rejoining Nakama had seemed like the only thing of importance. It was like a dream from some long ago time...

She sniffed, and the stink of the room brought her forcefully back to the present. She gazed steadily at the Sister. "I'm not sure what it is I'm heading toward now, Shudojo. But I think...I think I've been *led* to take this journey. Something is telling me to go on, but I have no idea what it is. All I'm sure about is that it is more important than my reasons for leaving home. Or me." She looked down at the stained floorboards. "I cannot undo the things I've done, or the words I've spoken. I cannot even promise that my tongue will not get the better of me in the future. But I want you to know that I understand, and appreciate, what you have tried to provide, and…and that I still want to have you with me on this journey. Besides," she said, looking up with a slight smile, "I don't want to be the only one providing a breakfast feast for these bugs."

Shudojo stared back at Mikasama. She cocked her head to one side, examining the Princess as if trying to see her in a new light. What was it about this woman, she wondered, that made one want to be around her?

She had felt it ever since Mikasama had arrived at the gate in Fumosa. For some reason she had felt drawn to this young woman from that moment. And for the life of her she could not understand why. The Goddess knew, the young noblewoman could be insufferable. Yet there was something about Mikasama that rang true beneath that impetuous countenance. Despite her annoyance, even as she had been throwing things out of the pack Shudojo had found it hard to actually contemplate abandoning the woman, and her quest. Was it, she wondered, the hand of the Goddess? Was the Goddess directing this Lady in what she must do?

She looked carefully at Mikasama, staring into the girl's eyes, trying to see what thoughts really coursed through her mind. "Lady," she asked, "Mother Narisa said she thought you'd been touched by the Goddess. What—"

A loud pounding on the door interrupted her. Startled, both women leapt to their feet. A drunken voice bellowed from the other side. "Hey! We want some singing'. Come out here and sing for us!"

Mikasama and Shudojo looked at each other, and Mikasama realized that the door was not barred. Quickly she jumped up and dropped the wooden slat in place. Shudojo shouted through the door to the unseen reveler. "We are tired and wish to sleep. Go away."

This only irritated the voice on the other side, as he shouted again his demand. Another voice was heard, too: "And when you're done singin', we'll give you both a nice reward!" Much hollering and laughter followed, as the men on the other side shoved ineffectually against the door.

Shudojo turned to Mikasama and whispered. "There are at least three men on the other side of this door, maybe four. We have to do something to calm them down, or they won't stop until they get in here. Can you sing?"

"What?" said Mikasama incredulously. "Surely you don't expect me to go out there—"

"No, of course not," replied Shudojo. "Start singing from in here. Maybe it will calm them down a bit."

Mikasama had been the bane of choirmaster Luzo in Hajimeshi, and the thought of trying to sing under these circumstances seemed ludicrous in the extreme. Shudojo, though, had turned away and was now scrambling around among the packs. The Princess earnestly hoped that she had a knife or some other weapon hidden away.

Even though her present state of mind lent little to her efforts, the Princess tentatively began singing. The only song she could remember was a hymn taught to children to honor their parents.

"Oh, Good Father," she quavered, "we give to thee our hearts. Oh, Good Mother, we bring to thee our love." At her first verse, the men outside fell quiet, and so she continued. "Our hands, our souls, are yours to teach; our thoughts go out to you, while we sleep..."

She paused, and one of the unseen voices spoke. "What the hell kind of singing is that? We don't want no damned church choir!" As the door pounding started up again, another said, "Open up the door, wenches, or you'll be getting a hell of a lot more than your Good Father gave you!" The door began creaking on its old hinges; it was only a matter of time before the weight of bodies on the other side carried it off its deteriorated frame.

Mikasama looked to Shudojo in alarm. The Sister motioned toward the window. "Lady, we had best flee," she said, as she moved quickly over to the small window and tried to pull it open. It was stuck fast. "Help me!" she whispered urgently, as the door visibly started to bend inwards.

Mikasama rushed to Shudojo's side, and the two women strained against the rotted wood. Finally their combined efforts broke the frame right out of the sill, shattering the glass and dumping both women backwards onto the floor.

There was a pause in the commotion from the other side of the door. Mikasama could hear one of the men mutter, "What the hell was that?" The two women picked themselves up, and Shudojo squeezed gingerly through the broken window frame, trying to avoid the glass. They heard one of the men shout, "They must be goin' out the damned window. Come on!"

The sound beyond the door receded as Shudojo stuck her head back through the window opening. "Hurry! They'll be around the back quickly!" Then her head disappeared once more. Mikasama, with a last look at their packs, the contents still strewn about the floor, pushed herself out through the small opening and into the dark.

She landed in a pile of something soft, which probably did not bear thinking about. The night had come in earnest, and she couldn't see a thing. She felt Shudojo's hand on her arm. The Sister said, "Quick! This way. We must get away from the building."

The Sister dragged her along, as the shouts of drunken men could be heard approaching. The full moon overhead slid out of the clouds, casting its bright, ghostly light over the rear yard of the inn. Eerie shadows jumped out in stark relief from the discarded agricultural apparatus littering the yard.

Mikasama's eyes focused enough to see that Shudojo was leading them toward the woods behind the inn, where a path was visible between the trees. As they passed a dilapidated wagon, Mikasama tripped and fell over something in the overgrown weeds. Just as the Sister reached down to help her up, the men burst around the corner of the building.

Shudojo realized they would never make it to the woods if they tried to run. There were four men, and even in their inebriated state she knew that two unarmed women would not be able to put up much of a struggle. Quickly she started casting about amongst the abandoned farm implements near them even as she heard Mikasama say, "Didn't you find your knife?"

Without thinking Shudojo replied, "I left my knife behind a long time ago...in another man's belly."

The four men slowed down, spreading out as they approached the two women. One of them said coyly, "Come on, little pretties. We won't hurt you. We just want some singin', is all."

Shudojo found a badly rusted scythe blade amongst the weeds, which broke in two as she picked it up. Immediately she hurled the pieces at the approaching men. One of them struck home, and as the man who had spoken howled in pain at the jagged metal now stuck in his arm, the others stopped in their tracks.

Shudojo grabbed up a long rake handle and shouted, "Run, Lady! I will hold them here." Mikasama hesitated, and Shudojo shouted again. "Run, damn you!" Mikasama took off toward the trees.

The men quickly recovered from their shock at being attacked. "You damned bitch," the wounded man said. "You'll pay for that. Yazaka, go get the rope off my horse. I'm gonna tie this one up to a tree and find out what makes *her* squeal." As Yazaka went off towards the front of the inn, the other three advanced on Shudojo. Slowly she backed away, keeping the wagon behind her so as to prevent them from completely encircling her. As they got closer, the men approached more warily. One of them clumsily tried to lunge for the Sister, and she easily sidestepped and brought the rake handle down across his head. Crying out an oath, he stumbled back, dazed. The other two moved in, and Shudojo raised her rake handle again.

The Sister heard, before she saw, a screaming banshee run past from behind the wagon. It was Mikasama, rushing out of the dark, the head of a rusted pickaxe held in front of her. Yelling at the top of her lungs, the Princess used the axe head like a battering ram, crashing directly into the chest of one of the men. Both Mikasama and her target fell heavily to the ground.

The remaining man, the one Shudojo had hit with the broken scythe blade, reacted more quickly now, and came at the Sister. Deftly she brought the rake handle down on his arm where the jagged cut was still bleeding. Yelling in pain, he backed off. By then Mikasama had staggered to her feet, and Shudojo shouted, "Come on!" The two women set off at a run toward the woods while the drunken men re-grouped.

Shudojo, still grasping the rake handle, led the way down the path through the trees, both women running as fast as they could. The Sister could hear the men behind them; they were not going to give up so easily. Out of the gloom ahead, she spied a small bridge. "Lady," she said breathlessly. "We will...have to stop them...on the bridge."

"Why..." gasped Mikasama, "why...there?"

"If they catch us...in the open...we stand no chance. On the bridge...they can only attack...one or two at a time." They were on the bridge now, and Shudojo stopped in the middle. Leaning on the rake handle she pushed Mikasama toward the other end. "Go on...I will hold the bridge."

"No...I'll help you."

"I have been trained...by the Sisters to fight," answered Shudojo. "You will just get yourself killed...Go."

"I will not." Shudojo did not press the issue further, as the first of the men were now approaching the bridge. It was a narrow wooden structure, with room for only two to walk side by side between its railings. Below was a river; Shudojo could hear the rush of water but could not see it in the dark. All she could see were faceless men, coming for her and for Mikasama; men who wanted to take them, and use them. She would not let it happen, she resolved. She had paid the price for that once before. She would die before she let it happen again.

Yazaka, the man who had gone for the rope, was the first to reach the bridge. As he neared, Shudojo neatly parried him away with the rake handle. Another of the men succeeded in grabbing an end of the Sister's staff. Shudojo struggled, trying to pull the handle back, but she had little room in which to maneuver. Suddenly the man let go as his face swung back, a foot planted firmly in it.

Mikasama had climbed up on the bridge railing and had kicked out at the man. Shudojo brought the end of the rake up and stabbed forward into the dark mass of bodies, and was rewarded with a grunt of pain. Mikasama tried to kick again, but a hand grabbed her leg, trying to pull her down. She kicked wildly, and finally the man released her. The Princess, unbalanced on the railing, fell backwards over the edge of the bridge.

With a sickening feeling in her stomach, Shudojo heard a splash. Mikasama was gone, probably swept away and soon to drown. Alone now on the bridge with the men, Shudojo heard the sound of steel, and realized that a blade had been drawn amongst the men opposite her. She would go down fighting, she told herself, gripping the rake handle tightly. She prepared for a last stand.

Through the red mist of her anger, she heard another sound. It was someone yelling. Who would be yelling like that? she wondered. It doesn't matter...I have to focus on these men...Have to stop them, any way I can...Dear Goddess...There's that yelling again! What's it saying?

The Sister realized it was Mikasama. "Shudojo!" she was shouting. She sounded far away, thought Shudojo. Not up here on the bridge. That's right, she fell off. She's in the river. "Shudojo! Jump!"

The Sister shook herself, and realized that Mikasama was calling to her, from the river. Abruptly she ran back several steps, catching the still-drunken men off guard, and climbed up on the side of the bridge.

"Shudojo!"

Shudojo looked down, but could not see anything. She was terrified; heights had always scared her. She froze, looking down into a black nothingness. "Shudojo!" shouted Mikasama again.

Looking back, Shudojo saw the men rushing at her, although in her mind it seemed as if they moved in slow motion. No, she said to herself. Never again.

She pitched herself forward, off the bridge, into the dark.

*   *   *

It was during the morning's march that Toshi-hito collapsed.

After crossing the ravine the day before in the wheeled basket, the pilgrims had found the tree-lined road in reasonably good condition, if increasingly steep. Tejinashi lay at a higher elevation than the other kingdoms of Tonogato, and once the group had begun to climb the air had become colder. The Deshi Master had continued to push himself, walking with the others until a camp was set for the night.

The next day, with a grey sky overhead and a hint of drizzle dampening every exposed surface, the group had set off again. Less than an hour had passed before the group had found itself unexpectedly halted by the Deshi Master's collapse.

Toshi-hito's body apparently could no longer be persuaded to ignore the ravages of the Shukyoshi poison. His iron-hard control had become brittle under the strain, and when it finally shattered it was sudden and without warning. One moment Shiko and Ryori were walking slowly beside the Deshi Master; the next, Toshi-hito was face down in the dirt of the road.

So startled were the apprentice and cook that it took them a moment to realize what had happened. They had each grown used to the silent form walking between them and had begun to take for granted his slow, ambling gait. But their response was rapid once they comprehended what had occurred.

Quickly Shiko knelt and rolled Toshi-hito over, clearing the dust and dirt away from his nose and mouth. Ryori ran up the road, shouting after the Guards, who had once again marched almost out of sight around a bend in the road. Fortunately Toshi-hito had not fallen directly forward; he had crumpled sideways, cushioning some of the blow. Even so, the apprentice could feel a massive lump on the side of his Master's head when he gingerly explored it with his fingers.

As soon as Ryori had gained the attention of the Guards, the cook rushed back. Kneeling beside the stricken Deshi he checked Toshi-hito's limbs and face for any broken bones. Finding none, he unwrapped the Deshi's bandage to assess the state of the wound.

Itachi and Bokusa came back down the road, the other Guards stopping a short distance away. Nakama had taken a shift carrying the Hikari, and its light was the only brightness to be seen; the clouds had rolled in thicker with the advance of the day, and rain was in the offing. Itachi looked down at the eerily still form of the Deshi. "Can you revive him?"

At that moment Ryori undid the last of the bandage, and none of those nearby could escape the sudden putrid odor that permeated the air. Screwing up his face, Bokusa said, "He's finished." At Shiko's startled look, the big man added callously, "Never seen a man live when a wound's gone that bad. Best end it for him now." He put his hand to his sword hilt.

Shiko rose from his position beside the prone Toshi-hito as he realized what Bokusa intended to do. Staring first with disbelief, then with anger that quickly boiled over into rage, he stepped forward to stand before his stricken Master. Face flushed, throat constricted, he couldn't even find words to express his fury.

Barbaric! That's what these two are, he shouted to himself. I will not let Toshi-hito die! They will have to cut me down first!

His mind fought back his fear even as his stomach struggled to hold down its contents. He clenched his hands into fists, digging the nails into the flesh of his palms. He stared up at the two men defiantly, ready to sacrifice his own life in defense of his Master's. He almost didn't hear the words when Itachi said quietly, "No. We will take him with us." As if in some sort of dream, he watched Itachi turn to the Guards behind him. "You, you, and you," he said, pointing to several of them. "Go gather wood to make a litter. Be quick; I don't want to wait all day to get moving again."

Surprised, the men looked at one other briefly then rapidly set off to do the Hajimeshi lord's bidding. Itachi looked down once more at Toshi-hito, then with a final dismissive glance at Shiko turned on his heel and walked off. Bokusa, dismayed, cast a menacing scowl at the apprentice before setting off after Itachi.

Shiko had not moved; his breath still coming in short spurts. A gentle hand was laid on his arm. He turned to see that it was Ryori.

"It's all right, lad," said the cook quietly. He watched as Ryori pointed down at Toshi-hito. As if through a tunnel he heard the cook say, "Here, help me move the old boy, will you?" He watched as Ryori knelt down beside the fallen Deshi; Toshi-hito's legs had bent partially underneath him when he had fallen, and Ryori was trying to straighten them out.

Slowly, as if descending from a mountaintop shrouded in fog, Shiko's world fell back into place. Uncurling his fists, a drop of blood lingered in one palm where his nails had cut the skin. He knelt to help Ryori get Toshi-hito ready for his new conveyance.

     ✶   ✶   ✶

Interesting...All that was required was for me to say "No" when this Itachi was ready to let the one lying in the road be killed. The rest of it, carrying the man in a litter, was something his own mind conceived of. Once he had accepted my direction, his mind concluded that he had to do something else with the broken body on the ground, and so decided that it had to be taken with him. He still thinks to use that one, if the body survives...

I will have to be more careful...I must be explicit enough to prevent surprises like this, without exerting too much control; I must not arouse the interest of that thing which keeps me here.

I want this one, this Itachi; I want to make him the glove that fits my hand...

*   *   *

It was still dark as Shudojo and Mikasama staggered out of the river, holding each other up. As soon as they were on dry ground they fell to their hands and knees, having no energy left for anything but gasping air. Finally their arms too gave out, and they lay on their backs staring up at the black wall of the sky, unrelieved by even the tiniest star behind the thick blanket of clouds. It was as if they were marooned in a land far from everywhere, two women alone with the river and the blackness. After a time Shudojo tried to speak, but ended up coughing from swallowed river water instead. Finally she got out, "Lady...is anything broken?"

"Only my head...from where it hit that log," replied the Princess, shivering.

"Lucky for you...your head is thick enough...to be stopped by a log without knocking you out...You would have certainly drowned."

Mikasama only groaned in reply. Neither woman spoke for a while, waiting until they were able to breathe again. A break in the clouds appeared and an edge of the moon peeked through, revealing little more than a few hardscrabble trees growing out of the desolate soil on the riverbank around them. Mikasama sat up, dripping water. "I heard you hit the water, after you jumped, but I didn't see you until you had almost floated by..."

Shudojo sat up as well, a rain of water cascading from her own hair. The two of them looked like drowned cats; the same thought must have occurred to both of them at the same time for they started giggling like schoolgirls. Soon this became outright belly laughs, as they finally realized that they had survived.

But Mikasama's laughter would not stop. Soon she was crying hysterically. "Lady," said Shudojo with alarm. "Stop it! We are all right. We're alive!" She grabbed Mikasama and shook her, and when this did not stop Mikasama's crying fit she took hold of the Princess's chin roughly and forced her to look into Shudojo's face. She shouted, "Lady! Stop! Everything is all right now!"

Mikasama managed to focus on Shudojo's face, and slowly her crying ceased. As the Sister released her, the Princess said dazedly, "Everything's all right? Is that what you said?" At Shudojo's nod, Mikasama retorted, "How can you say that? We've *lost* everything!" She stood up unsteadily, looking down at the river that had brought them there. "Our horses, our supplies, everything is *gone*!" She gestured around them. "We're lost! We don't know where to go, and we have no food. And *you* say everything is fine!" With a whimper she sat down again on the muddy bank.

The Shukyoshi Sister sat for a moment without speaking, looking at Mikasama. She could see that what had once undoubtedly been a fine head of hair had now become a bedraggled mass; a dripping and knotted frame around a face shiny with a mixture of river water and tears. She's still such a young girl, Shudojo reminded herself; and daughters of noble houses are not generally permitted the luxury of learning how to survive in the wilderness.

Speaking calmly, Shudojo said, "Listen to me, Lady. The Goddess has seen fit to spare us. I don't know why, since probably neither of us deserves it." Mikasama turned to look at her, and she went on. "She has taken from us our possessions, but left us with our lives. Back at the inn, you said that you believed your quest had become something more than what you first thought it to be. Well, I too believe there is more to our being together than just your needing a guide. I can't pretend to know what it is either, but the Goddess clearly has a plan. She would not have left us alive, and together, if she did not. I will put my faith in that."

"And will your Goddess find us food?" Mikasama said crossly. "Or show us the way to the road?"

Shudojo stood up. "We are alive." She looked down at the Princess. "That is enough for me. The rest we must do for ourselves."

She turned and walked to the top of the bank, and looked around. The pale moon slipped further out into the open, reflecting off her wet skin. She wrung out the drenched clothing that clung to her. "I can see a hill a little ways off. From there we should be able to see enough to get our bearings, once the sun comes up." Without another word she set off in that direction.

Mikasama looked back up the river, back the way they had come, but the moonlight did not shine brightly enough to let her see anything that way. Stiffly she hoisted herself up and followed Shudojo.

20

The Hikari pilgrims progressed more slowly on their path toward Tejinashi, once again as a single group. Two of the Guards now carried Toshi-hito in a make-shift litter, with Shiko and Ryori walking behind them. Ryori had re-wrapped Toshi-hito's wound and bound his arm against his side; the Deshi had not regained consciousness but his breathing had become more relaxed than when he had been trying to walk and keep up with the others.

The hours that followed were long and difficult for the apprentice. At first he was sick with worry for Toshi-hito, and then later sick to his stomach in reaction to his near-encounter with Itachi. After the mid-day stop, when he had checked on Toshi-hito again for what Ryori assured him was at least the fifteenth time, Shiko realized that he was exhausting himself.

He knew Toshi-hito would have chastised him had the Deshi Master been able to observe his apprentice. Was it not the Deshi way, the Master would have asked, to search for the calm at the center of every storm? Should one not find the quiet path in one's mind amid the clamor of the outside world?

Shiko knew those words were true. He had to find the quiet path, lest he let his worries surround and overwhelm him. If ever there was a time, he decided, for peaceful meditation, it was certainly now.

Although he knew the group would not be halted for long, he needed to spend some time alone. Assured by Ryori that he would keep Toshihito under his watchful eye, Shiko walked out among the trees, far enough away from the Hikari group that he was just out of sight.

Wandering amid the undergrowth of the forest the apprentice took deep breaths, taking in the sweet smell of living things. He stopped in a little clearing and let his eyes gaze around him. It was good, he realized, to actually stop and see the plants and trees; so often they were just fleeting images in the background of his senses. If one really stopped to look there were so many colors, and so many patterns, to be seen, and all of them were a delight to the eye.

How easy it is, he thought regretfully, to lose all of one's training. He had been trained in the Deshi way all his life, learning how to channel his emotions and control his physical body. Until now all of it had been theoretical; nothing dangerous ever happened in the priory at Hajimeshi. That is if, he remembered, one discounted Master Koyana's falling off the roof last summer and breaking his leg, but that certainly hadn't required much in the way of emotional control for Shiko. In fact it had mostly required strong discipline to keep from laughing, since Koyana was famous for berating apprentices for their clumsiness.

Shiko walked on for a while, until he came upon a massive tree that stretched up so high he could not see its crown even when he arched his back as far as he could. What a marvelous tree, he thought; it must have been here for ages.

He placed his hands on the tree's venerable bark, tracing the deep lines that pitted its surface. In his mind he pictured the cracks and lines and ridges as if they were canyons and valleys and mountains. It was a Deshi technique for regaining control over one's own self; the tree became a world of its own, and one focused on seeing, and feeling, all that one could about that world.

Concentrating on the feel of the bark beneath his fingers, Shiko tuned his mind to grasp everything about the tree. He breathed in deeply, letting the rich smell of the wood and the soil in which it stood fill his senses. Gradually the rest of the world slipped away, one worry at a time, as he concentrated on the tree. He saw a small round hole in the bark and realized that some creature must be living within. He probed gently with his mind, but no one was home. He tried wrapping his arms around the tree but it was so large he didn't think his hands made it even a quarter of the way around. It was sturdy, and solid, and felt good. The tree had stood for a very long time, perhaps even before the kingdoms in Tonogato, and had seen many cares come and go. What were his small worries compared to what it had seen? His world was but a brief interval of time in the life of something as majestic as this tree. Even after he had grown old and died, and all his lifetime's concerns with him, this tree would still be here.

Shiko knew the Deshi were wise, and understood how ephemeral were the affairs of men. They recognized that people should never make more of themselves than what they were. And so, he thought, he would do what he could, and trust that whatever it was would be enough.

After a time he realized that he should be starting back toward the Hikari party; they would be ready to resume marching soon, and it would not do for him to be the one to delay it. Yet he was reluctant to let go of the peace of this place. He took another moment and sat down at the base of the great tree, leaning his back against it. Closing his eyes, he let himself think about Toshi-hito.

Yes, that's better, he thought. I can think about him now more rationally. Toshi-hito is doing what he must, and there is little more I can do for him now. I will let his body fight its battle, while I deal with the world outside that he cannot see.

He reached up and felt for the honsho around his neck. Its touch reminded him of Nusumi, back in Yutakashi, when she had held it in her hands and had tried to read the symbols. All of that seemed so long ago now, he mused. He wondered what she was doing, and if she was still running rings around the vendors in the Market...

Shiko tried to keep his thoughts about Nusumi under the same control as his other feelings, but it was difficult. He realized that the bond that had formed between the two of them, the closeness allowing them to know one another as well as two who had been companions for years, was a result of the mayaku poultice. Even knowing that, he still felt as if she had touched him in some way that he did not fully understand. She had a wild streak, unrestrained and uninhibited, that was completely at odds with everything he had learned growing up with the Deshi. As such she intrigued and fascinated him.

He could see how being around Nusumi could bring excitement, and challenge, into his life. Over the years at the priory he had been taught to suppress such feelings, to bury them behind walls of control; yet here was someone who had reached right in past those walls as if they did not exist. She had plucked his heart strings as easily as if she had held the keys to his soul.

And yet...and yet he knew that Nusumi was not the path for him. However stimulating she was, however much the thought of being with her appealed to him, he knew that the two of them simply did not belong together. He was a Deshi; that was what he had trained for all his life, and it was a path he must follow. Nusumi, he was sure, had her own destiny, and it was unlikely to be as companion to a scholar. He suspected that, had they attempted to stay together, in fairly short order she would have become hopelessly bored...

A zako rodent skittered across the clearing, darting under some bushes along the far edge. Seeing the little creature reminded Shiko of Itachi, and brought the apprentice's mind back to the present and the problems that he had to deal with now.

One of those problems, he realized, *was* Itachi. He seemed always set on a course of conflict with the Hajimeshi lord, but he didn't know how to prevent it. He wondered how Toshi-hito did it. No matter what the provocation, the Deshi Master was always able to turn any argument around, or somehow defuse the tension. Toshi-hito must have been born with some natural skill that allowed him to avoid conflicts so neatly...

"Except for the one that he's dying from," said a voice inside his head.

'Ton. He looked back toward where the Hikari group had stopped, but he could not see anyone from where he sat. Despite that, he could sense that the two chodaka birds where there, still hidden in their cage in Itachi's pack. *"Hello, 'Ton,"* he said. *"You're right,"* he added sadly, replaying again in his mind the fight in the Fortress courtyard. *"I guess some battles cannot be avoided."*

The mental voice of 'Cha chimed in. *"We were listening to you earlier. When you thought the cruel ones would end the other creature's life, the one you call Toshi-hito. You were ready to give your life for his."*

Stated so plainly, it made Shiko break out into a cold sweat, made all the clammier by the chill mountain air. Only partly, he realized, was it a reaction from remembered fear. The stronger part of it was fear of a different sort. Had he really meant to do it? To stand up to Itachi and Bokusa, and put himself in harm's way to save Toshi-hito? Or was he just replaying the memory in his head differently? Was it his mind's way of convincing himself that he was better than he really was?

"No," said 'Ton. *"What you felt was true. We know."*

Shiko had forgotten that the birds could hear even things he did not speak. Exasperated, he said, *"But* how *can you understand my feelings? Toshi-hito said that he could only pick up simple words and images, and yet the two of you seem to be able to see everything that's inside my head."*

There was silence from the avian pair. At length 'Cha said, *"We do not know. We do not understand what it is that allows us to hear you at all."*

'Ton added, *"It doesn't really matter, does it?"*

"What do you mean?" replied Shiko.

"Well, your kind always seems to want an answer for something. It's almost as if you think that by explaining it, you have control of it; and if you control it, then you can repeat it whenever you want to. But the world's not like that. Some things just are. *And those things, we just don't worry about. We can talk to you, you can talk to us. Fine. So let's chat."*

Smiling in spite of himself, Shiko thought of all the questions he wanted to ask. What was it like to be a bird? No, silly question, he thought; they would say, compared to what? What about—his growling stomach interrupted his thinking. Ah, well, that's probably more important anyway.

"*Are you two getting enough to eat? Should I try to sneak you some food?*"

Another silence ensued, which stretched long enough to make Shiko worried that the birds had stopped listening. But then 'Ton answered once more. "*We are hungry, yes. Although this place where we are kept provides food, of a sort, it is tasteless. Revolting, actually. When I am allowed out to fly, I bring back some things for 'Cha, which I regurgi—*"

'Cha interrupted. "*You can skip the details, 'Ton.*"

"*Right. Well, to answer your question, yes, we're hungry. But please don't try to get food to us; it's too dangerous.*"

Contritely, Shiko said, "*What's a little more danger? I almost stuck my head in front of Bokusa's sword not too long ago.*"

"*Listen to me, Shiko creature,*" said 'Cha earnestly. "*You must not put yourself in danger. For us, or even for the Toshi-hito one.*"

Shiko was puzzled by the intensity of feeling he felt behind 'Cha's mental words. "*I don't seek danger, 'Cha, but I must help those in need, or those who can't help themselves, like Toshi-hito.*"

"*You don't understand,*" said 'Ton patiently. "*It's you who are important. You must carry on. We, and the Toshi-hito one, we are not important. Well,*" he added, "*we're important to ourselves, of course. No one wants to die, especially in a dark cage within some other creature's smelly leather bag. But we do not matter. You do.*"

"*What's so important about me?*" queried Shiko. "*Toshi-hito is the one leading the quest for the Kotaishi. He's the important one.*"

Just then Shiko heard Ryori shouting for him, telling him that it was time to move on. The apprentice tried to extend his awareness again toward the chodaka birds, but they did not, or would not, answer.

Reluctantly Shiko left the comforting solace of the great tree and made his way back to the clearing and the Hikari group. As the pilgrims prepared to set off he took up his place behind the Guards carrying Toshi-hito's litter, looking up to where Itachi carried the pack of faded leather holding the chodaka birds. The group marched out of the clearing and began ascending ever higher into the mountains, while the enigmatic words of 'Ton and

'Cha kept rolling around inside Shiko's head, an odd answer in search of a question.

*   *   *

As night fell the pilgrims made camp beside a long, narrow lake. The road curved and twisted as it followed the undulations of the shore, the land to either side of the lake steeply pitched and blanketed with forest.

Shiko decided that the lake must have been the aftermath of one of the great ice migrations. He remembered that Master Mochiya at the priory had lectured once about steep-sided lakes just like this one, where a massive flow of ice had swept through the mountains as if the hills had been no more than butter. The ice would have moved on such a giant scale as to make the great tree that Shiko had touched earlier seem like nothing but a piece of kindling wood.

The prospect of having water nearby was one reason the pilgrims had stopped where they did. Everyone in the group was weary from marching, and both water and food rations were becoming decidedly thin. Ryori did his best, but tochuya root could only be cooked so many ways, especially when there was very little of it.

The area selected for the camp was in a natural hollow that sheltered the pilgrims from the cold wind slicing across the surface of the lake. As Ryori massaged his tired feet, trying to restore circulation before making his preparations for the evening meal, Itachi strode up. Without preamble he demanded, "How long will the food last?"

Ryori, his normal audacity increasingly bordering on the insolent over the last few days, shrugged in reply. "Hard to tell." No further comment was apparently forthcoming, and the cook suddenly found a boot planted in his chest as he was roughly pushed to the ground.

Standing over him, Itachi, in the low voice that presaged a violent explosion of temper, hissed, "What did you say?"

Finding it difficult to speak with someone half standing on him, Ryori croaked out, "'Twas only trying to count it up in my head, Lord Itachi. Don't think so fast, the older I gets."

Itachi continued to glare down at the cook, his eyes leaving no doubt that he would stomp his boot into Ryori's face should the cook press him further. Finally lifting his foot off of the man's chest, he stepped back. "And now? Seeing," he added sarcastically, "that you've had more time to think it over."

Ryori straightened his tunic as he sat up. Avoiding Itachi's gaze he said, "We'll be out of food inside two days, at the rate we're goin'. After that, we'll have to start huntin' for food."

Itachi said nothing for a moment, then shouted over his shoulder. "Bokusa! Half rations for everyone, starting now." He looked back at Ryori. "Soldiers make poor hunters, cook. You had better make it last." He turned on his heel and walked off. Ryori fought the urge to spit after the man, concluding that the momentary satisfaction it would afford would not be worth the price of losing his head.

The soldiers placed Toshi-hito's litter at the base of a large tree, whose huge roots rose up out of the ground and curved about until they almost touched. The tree's foundation thus served to keep the wind off the Deshi as he lay, arm still strapped to his side.

As Shiko sat next to him, waiting for the evening meal, he studied his Master's face. The apprentice had received instruction from many of the Masters at the priory in Hajimeshi, but Toshi-hito had been the one he had known the longest. It was curious, Shiko thought; Toshi-hito's was the earliest face he could remember, when he was but a child at the priory. Yet when he brought a picture to mind of what Toshi-hito looked like, it didn't match the actual face lying before him. This face was different. It had lines and ridges across its surface, not unlike the bark of the great tree back down the trail. Despite seeing this face every day, he had never actually stopped and looked closely at it. Now he could observe the differences between it and his mental image. Toshi-hito was older, he realized, and the face before him showed the lines of a life spent in service to others.

Ryori came over from the fire with food for the Deshi, while the soldiers helped themselves from the communal pots. As the cook handed Shiko his portion the apprentice said, "Thank you, Master Cook, but I will save mine for Toshi-hito."

Ryori raised an eyebrow. "Best you keep yourself fed, boy." He gestured toward the Deshi Master. "Won't be any help to him if you starve."

Shiko opened his mouth to reply but was stilled by a hand suddenly grasping his arm. Startled, he looked down to see that Toshi-hito had reached out with his good hand and was holding on to him. Quickly he knelt over the Deshi Master, who still lay with eyes closed. "Master!" Shiko whispered. "Don't strain yourself. We have food for you—"

"Not...yet," croaked Toshi-hito through parched lips. Ryori was already kneeling beside him, water skin in hand. As Shiko tilted Toshi-hito's head up, the cook managed to pour some of the liquid into the Deshi Master's mouth. He lay quiet for a moment, then spoke softly to Shiko. "Where...?"

"We have camped near a long lake, Master. It appears to be the remains of a great ice flow."

The faint trace of a smile touched Toshi-hito's features. "Ah, Mochiya's lecture..." He was silent for a moment, then resumed. "Close, then...Are we...at the eastern end?"

"I think so, Master," replied Shiko. "I—I'm sorry I can't be more specific. Without a map, I can't tell for certain."

"I have no need...of a map...I know the way." It was eerie, thought Shiko, listening to Toshi-hito speaking with his eyes closed; he must be channeling whatever energy he has in to speaking. "At the far end...of the lake, there is a tree...growing from three rocks. A trail...goes north. You must...follow it."

Shiko looked up at Ryori, but the cook had no better idea of what Toshi-hito had in mind than the apprentice did. "Is it some sort of shortcut to Tejinashi, Master?" asked Shiko.

There was no answer for a moment, and Shiko cast Ryori an anxious glance. Then they both heard softly: "Sekai Monastery...you must go...to Sekai Monastery."

Shiko, confused, said, "A monastery? But why must we go there? Do you think the Kotaishi might be there?"

Toshi-hito shook his head weakly, but Shiko wasn't sure that it was in response to his question. The Deshi Master went on as if the apprentice had not spoken. "When you are there...you must speak with the Abbot..." Suddenly Toshi-hito's grip on Shiko's arm intensified, surprisingly strong for one in his condition. "You must go, Shiko..."

The apprentice glanced again at Ryori, but the cook shrugged his shoulders as if to say he thought the older man delirious. Shiko looked back to Toshi-hito. "But—but what should I say to the Abbot, Master? Does he have knowledge of the Kotaishi? Or does he have healing medicines that will help you? Lord Itachi will want to know why we should go that way."

Toshi-hito did not answer; he had lost consciousness once more, his grip relaxing on Shiko's arm as unexpectedly as it had appeared. Shiko waited to see if Toshi-hito would re-awaken, but when he did not, the apprentice tucked the Deshi Master's good arm back against his side for warmth. Reluctantly, Ryori left to attend to his clean-up chores by the fire, leaving the apprentice alone and more bewildered than ever.

As Shiko lay down and stared once more at his Master's face, he pondered. Why did Toshi-hito want to go to this Sekai Monastery? What was there, and who was the Abbot he was supposed to talk to? He didn't even know what he was supposed to say to him.

As he watched the light from the fire play across the lines of Toshi-hito's face, Shiko hoped that his Master would re-awaken enough later to tell him what he was supposed to do. Suddenly a shadow flitted across Toshi-hito's features. With a start Shiko looked over toward the fire, and saw someone passing between the flames and the root-walled enclosure sheltering the two Deshi. It was Itachi, walking by as he headed toward Bokusa on the opposite side of the camp. The apprentice felt a stab of anxiety. How would Itachi react toward taking a side trip to Sekai Monastery? Shiko didn't know, but he thought it likely that enthusiasm would be distinctly lacking. And it would fall on him to tell the Hajimeshi Lord that they must go there...

The following morning was frigid, the mountain air chilled further by its passage across the glassy surface of the lake. Despite the cold, Shiko could feel the sweat inside his clothes as he walked behind Toshi-hito's litter.

He had slept very little, his mind struggling all night. He still did not know what he was going to say to Itachi. Their last confrontation had come within a hair's breadth of violence. Whatever he did, he would have to think of it soon; he could tell that the western end of the lake was not far off.

The road that snaked along the shore twisted and turned, sometimes in amongst the trees, other times going right down to where they could reach out and touch the water. The mountain peaks on the far side of the lake drew closer. Shiko knew that when those peaks reached around to touch those on his side, the time for decision would arrive.

He could hear the sounds of the men in front; they had stopped. As he rounded a bend in the trail, Shiko saw that the Guards had paused in a natural clearing. The walk from the camp had taken nearly two hours. Although the distance was not far as 'Ton and 'Cha might have flown, on the ground the winding road had taken quite some time to traverse. The men were taking advantage of the rest stop to drink.

And there it was, Shiko realized.

On the far side of the clearing stood three huge rocks, each nearly as tall as he was. From the center one, in a great crack, rose a stunted tree, its gnarled roots growing down into the gap and across the surface of the rock until they found soil. Several of the roots had crossed the gaps to the neighboring rocks, and had laboriously made their way across them to tip their ends into the ground below.

It was most certainly a tree growing from three rocks. And there beside it, almost hidden by the shrubs to one side, he saw the unmistakable signs of a trail.

Shiko took a deep breath and walked over to look at the path. He passed by Ryori, who was redistributing the load of his pack. The cook watched the apprentice go by before silently resuming his sorting.

Shiko gazed down the trail, but could not see beyond a few yards as the path turned and was lost among the trees, heading toward the western edge of the lake. Was Toshi-hito right? he wondered. Was there really a monastery somewhere at the end of this trail?

He nearly jumped sideways when Ryori suddenly appeared at his side. The cook spoke quietly. "The water skins need refillin', before we leave the lake. You can take 'em, if you want…"

The apprentice glanced down at the slew of empty leather bags draped over the man's arm, then up into Ryori's eyes. He could see nothing there but an earnest regard. The cook had heard Toshi-hito speak of the monastery, on this same trail that led from the tree with three rocks. Ryori had voiced skepticism then, but now it was as if he knew what Shiko was thinking, and Shiko sensed that he had come to offer the apprentice a way to see for himself, at least for a short way, what might lie down this path…

Silently Shiko nodded, taking the empty water skins and draping them over his own arm. With a final glance behind at Toshi-hito, he stepped out of the clearing and onto the trail. Within moments the forest had cut off his view of the clearing and he was alone among the trees.

The path meandered steeply downwards, the undergrowth so thick to either side that it completely obscured his view of the lake. At last the trees thinned, and almost before he knew it he had walked out onto the shoreline, almost stepping into the shallows of the lake.

His breath caught as he stopped short at the sight before him. Standing just off shore in the lake, hidden from view from the clearing above, was what looked at first to be some sort of temple, or shrine.

Was this it? Shiko wondered. Was this the monastery that Tohsi-hito had spoken of?

But he realized almost immediately that this small structure could not be a monastery. Its square, open-sided platform was only a few paces across. A low, peaked roof, supported by four heavy columns at each corner, afforded a small measure of protection from the elements. From the center of the structure's roof hung the most massive bell that Shiko had ever seen: a dull bronze color, showing the effects of the harsh winter weather by the high mountain lake. Several large rocks formed a natural bridge from the shore out toward the bell. There was a large gap separating the last of the rocks from the platform, spanned by a small wooden bridge.

Shiko had the most incredible feeling as he looked at this incongruous bell, situated in the middle of nowhere. He felt as if the bell was waiting just for him, quietly, patiently, here with the high snowy peaks, watching the seasons slowly pass…

He pulled himself out of his reverie. It must be the air up here, he told himself. He had heard that mountain travelers sometimes became lightheaded if they stayed too long in the company of the high peaks. The weight on his arm reminded him of his task, and he stepped toward the water's edge and knelt to re-fill the bags. Even as he did so, however, he found that he could not keep his eyes off the massive bell, hanging silently in its small structure. Why was it here? he wondered. Who had built it? And for what reason?

When he had filled the last of the water skins and hung the now-bloated bags over his shoulders, he started to turn away to retrace his steps up the path. Yet he found he could not pull himself away from the mystifying bell. Although he heard nothing, not even wind amid the trees in the still morning air, it seemed that the bell was calling to him, to the apprentice from Hajimeshi…

He just had to take a closer look. Setting down the water skins, he walked down the trail where it skirted the edge of the lake, right by the first of the rocks that led away from the shore toward the bell. Gingerly he stepped out onto the rock and then hopped his way over to the wooden bridge. Standing atop the bridge's rough-hewn planks, the little shrine no longer looked so small. Up close he could see that the bell was truly impressive, nearly as tall as he was. He walked forward slowly until he stepped onto the platform, the great bell directly in front of him.

So quiet, he thought. It's so quiet out here, over the lake...

He reached out and touched the side of the bell. The metal was cool, his fingertips tingling as he traced his fingers over its smooth surface. He placed both hands on it, and then without thinking simply pushed on the side of the bell. So well balanced was it that it moved easily at his urging, swinging a good arm's length away from him.

He stepped back quickly, aghast. What did I do that for? he asked himself. But before he could even formulate an answer, the bell swung back and the metal clapper inside it struck the bell's side. Instantly a deep, sonorous chime rang out, cascading across the surface of the lake. The bell swung back again, once more the metal bar struck, and another chime burst forth. It echoed among the surrounding mountain peaks, the sound multiplied a hundred-fold.

Shiko was shocked at what he had done. By what right, he asked himself feverishly, did I ring this bell? It's probably something holy, or at least extremely important, to somebody; and here I have just come along and casually caused it to ring. Toshi-hito would be furious if he knew what I had done.

Yet even as the bell slowed its swing, Shiko could sense something else. It was the echoes of the bell's sound, he realized. They were not just coming back across the water; they were coming up from *beneath* the water...

Stupefied, he walked to the edge of the platform, staring down into the lake. The surface was still glassy-smooth, no ripples marring its surface. He could see his own reflection staring back up at him. And yet it still seemed as if the sound was not just coming from the bell behind him, or from the echoes off the surrounding land. It seemed to reach up from the depths of this lake, from someplace far below, where it had waited for a very long time...

Shiko felt the echoes traveling up through the platform, through his feet, through his whole body, until they reached his head. He could almost feel the sound rumbling around throughout his mind. And with it, mysterious and unbidden, came an almost calming certainty.

The path from the clearing, he realized; it *is* the way. I don't know why, but I can *feel* that it is the path we must take. Toshi-hito was right. The Hikari quest goes in this direction, up into the mountains.

After the first two peals of the bell it had slowly ceased its swinging, and with it the sound, and its echo, quietly died away. Shiko turned and once more touched the bell gently with his fingers. He could feel the resonance still there, that same feeling of certainty coursing through his body. Even when at last the bell had stilled, the feeling remained.

He stayed a while longer, gazing down into the far depths of the lake that sheltered the bell.

As the apprentice returned to the clearing he could hear Bokusa calling the men together. Ryori came over to relieve Shiko of the water skins, and the young Deshi nodded in the direction of the Guards. "What did they make of the bell?"

The cook looked at him quizzically. "What bell?"

Shiko frowned. "The bell. Did you not hear the sound of a deep bell, just a few moments ago?"

Ryori hoisted the water skins over his shoulder. "Boy," he replied, shaking his head, "I'm beginning to think you Deshi are all a little soft in the head. If you're hearin' bells way out here," as he tapped his finger against his forehead, "then the ringing's gotta be all upstairs." He turned away and made his way back toward his pack.

Shiko was puzzled. Surely, he told himself, I could not have imagined the bell?

The apprentice turned and saw Itachi lifting the pack containing 'Ton and 'Cha from the ground and swinging it over his shoulder. No, he decided. That bell and the sound it had made were real enough. As was the feeling that it had left with him. He knew what must be done.

"Lord Itachi," Shiko called out, more calmly than he had any right to expect himself to be. "We must go this way." He pointed to the trail beside the three-rock tree.

Itachi, securing his pack, looked only briefly in Shiko's direction. "Your opinion was not asked, Deshi," he said contemptuously. He walked off to take his place at the head of his men.

"Nevertheless," said Shiko loudly, "this is the path the Hikari Pilgrimage will take."

Suddenly the sounds of men preparing to march were stilled, and heads turned to look at the young apprentice. Itachi slowly turned and looked back at Shiko, eyes narrowed. "You had better take your place in line, boy. Before you find yourself in worse shape than that one," as he gestured toward Toshi-hito lying in his litter.

Shiko did not move. He ignored all of the others, keeping his gaze focused on Itachi's face. Equally quietly, he answered the Hajimeshi general. "Lord Itachi, the Deshi were commanded by the Kojuro to search for the Kotaishi. You are the leader of the men that accompany us on the quest, but the Deshi decide where the quest shall lead."

Not a sound was uttered by anyone as they waited to see what would happen. Itachi undid his pack and let it fall off his shoulder. In his mind Shiko heard what sounded like the mental equivalent of an oath as the pack and its occupants hit the ground. He quickly shut off his mental 'hearing,' not wanting any distractions just at that moment, although not before he caught the traces of a warning from 'Cha. But his course was now set; there was no turning back.

Itachi walked slowly over to him. The voice was quiet, but the eyes blazed with fury as he spoke. "What did you say to me?"

Shiko could see the man visibly trembling with rage, a wild animal barely held in check; another moment would see him unleash his wrath completely. Shiko nearly faltered, a part of his mind screaming at him to run, to hide.

Then the same feeling returned as before, when he had first heard the deep echo from beneath the lake: brief, but unmistakably the same. He felt it as if it were spreading across his back from the trail behind him, filling him with a warm feeling of calm. He held Itachi's gaze. "The Hikari quest must take this trail. We must go to the Sekai Monastery."

The Guards shuffled their feet, exchanging glances. No one stood up to Lord Itachi and walked away from the encounter; they expected their leader would snuff out the Deshi apprentice's life with one quick sword blow. Ryori, standing by Toshi-hito's litter, silently moved his hand down to his belt, where he kept a dagger for self-defense. But he was too far away, and knew it.

Shiko's eyes never left Itachi's. The Hajimeshi lord's face clearly betrayed his emotions: shock that anyone would continue to defy him, a resurgent anger that caused his face to flush to a deep crimson. His mouth curled into a snarl, and his hand moved toward his sword hilt.

*   *   *

I can feel him burning; yes, the anger, the hate...He thought to keep this boy, and the injured one that they have been dragging along. But his mind forgets all that now, in the heat of his rage. He will draw his blade and with a single movement dispatch this one who dares to confront him.

But wait...drawing a blade and snuffing out this upstart boy is far too easy. Before, when I let his own mind decide, it became creative and decided to drag the lame one along in a litter. What can it do to be creative in killing? If I were to prevent him from killing now, but told him that he must kill the boy later, what would he do?

I must see how far I can control him, this puppet of mine...Gently, I must touch him ever so gently, and force his will, thus...

*   *   *

Oddly, Itachi's hand stopped moving, his fingers inches from the hilt of his sword. The snarl fell away from his face, to be replaced by a calculating look as his eyes narrowed once again. "I don't care what you do, Deshi," he hissed. "*We* are going to Tejinashi. Go to this monastery, if that's what you want. My men are coming with me." Jabbing a finger in the direction where Toshi-hito lay, he added, "If you want to take him along, you're going to have to drag that litter yourself."

Before the astonished Shiko could speak, the sound of Ryori's voice came between them. "Lord Itachi, I will carry one end of the litter." As Itachi turned his angry gaze toward the cook, Ryori continued. "I'm not a soldier, General. I'm the most expendable. If the boy is going, he'll need someone to carry the other end of the litter. I'll leave the food and supplies with your men."

Once again Itachi appeared to visibly struggle with his anger. Several of the Guards exchanged perplexed glances; this was quite unlike the Itachi they knew. Instead of the expected violent outburst, they watched as the Hajimeshi lord merely turned back to Shiko. "And if you go, boy," he said, "then what of that?" He pointed to the Hikari, still held aloft by Donaku.

Shiko felt his breath desert him, as if he were caught in some sort of invisible vice. The Hikari! If the Guards did not go with him, how could he carry it? He couldn't possibly hold it and the litter both. As his mind raced, trying to find an answer, yet another voice broke the stillness.

"I will go with them, Lord Itachi." It was Nakama. "I will carry the other end of the litter while Shiko carries the Hikari." He started to step out of line, toward Itachi and Shiko.

Bokusa, directly in front of Nakama in the marching order, grabbed the former officer's shoulder and spun him around. "Get back in line, *soldier*," he shouted. "No one authorized you to volunteer for anything."

"It's all right, Bokusa," said Itachi softly, as he walked slowly over to where Nakama stood. The other Guards shuffled nervously. They had never seen Itachi behave this way; but they did know that usually the quieter he became, the more violent was his temper.

The Hajimeshi lord walked to within a few inches of Nakama's face, staring into it. Nakama did not flinch, standing his ground. Bokusa's hand drifted to his sword hilt, ready to draw at a word from his superior.

Abruptly, though, Itachi turned away. He strode back over to Shiko. "You can have these two, and that one," as he pointed to Toshi-hito's litter, "but the Hikari stays with me."

Shiko looked into Itachi's steely eyes and could sense the man's cunning, a determination to manipulate things his way. For whatever reason, he had chosen to allow Shiko to go, along with Ryori and Nakama. Behind the Hajimeshi lord Shiko heard Bokusa speak: "But—Lord Itachi—"

"Silence!" shouted Itachi, his eyes never leaving Shiko's. To the apprentice he continued quietly, "Which is it to be, Deshi?"

Shiko felt the tremendous pressure increase, squeezing not only his body now but his head as well. The Hikari! How could he leave it behind? It had been placed in his hands by the Kojuro himself; he had sworn to follow it and never leave it. It was the symbol of the pilgrimage. What would they be without it?

He looked over to where Toshi-hito lay, so still on the litter. He thought about what Toshi-hito meant to him, how much a part of his life the Deshi Master had been. Toshi-hito had told him he must go to the Sekai Monastery. And he knew, he just knew, that it was what they had to do.

He felt himself torn apart, caught between two paths, both of which had to be taken. If he only took one, he would fail in the other. His road forked here, literally and figuratively. He could not take both of them. He must choose.

"I will go to the Sekai Monastery, Lord Itachi." He held his breath, unsure if Itachi was leading him on. Perhaps Itachi had only been giving him a final chance to recant. If so, then in the next instant he would probably be dead, Itachi's sword wet with his blood. He waited.

But no sword blow came. "So be it," said Itachi, and he turned away from the Deshi apprentice without another word. To Nakama he said, "Help the cook redistribute his load among the men."

The tension suddenly evaporated, like water dried up by the sun. Only a lingering confusion among the Guards signaled that anything untoward had occurred, as they accepted portions of Ryori's gear. Shiko realized that he had tensed nearly every muscle in his body. He tried to slow his racing heart, and forced himself to breathe slowly, calmly. He walked over to where Toshi-hito lay, and knelt down by his Master. Gently he put a hand on Toshi-hito's shoulder. "We are going to the monastery, Master," he whispered quietly to the silent form. "I hope they have something there that will help cure you." Ryori and Nakama joined him, the two men each taking an end of the litter and raising it up slowly. They settled their grip, ready to walk. Both looked to Shiko.

The apprentice stared at the Hikari. It's light flickered as brilliantly as ever, even in the daylight casting a glow over the uniforms of the Guards nearest it. Itachi gestured silently to Bokusa, who turned to the Guards and called out, "All right, let's move!" The soldiers headed off down the road, the Hikari moving at their head, soon visible only as a weaving light above them. Itachi stood staring at Shiko a moment more, then turned and followed his men.

Ryori and Nakama watched the others depart but now looked back to the Deshi apprentice. Shiko misread their expectant looks. "It's not too late; you can still rejoin the others. You shouldn't put yourselves at risk for me. I—I—" He looked away awkwardly. "I don't even know why I'm going to the monastery."

A wad of spit hit a nearby tree. "Doesn't matter, boy," said Ryori. "If I had to spend one more day with that lout," gesturing with his head in the direction that Itachi had gone, "one or t'other of us would've been dead."

"But we have no food," countered Shiko. "And we don't even know for certain that there is a monastery on this trail. Toshi-hito might be confused, or not really be remembering it right."

"Doesn't matter," repeated Ryori. "I'm a cook. I can find us things to eat. Soldiers might be too proud to hunt, but a hungry man does what he must. Got plenty of water," he added, nodding his head toward the lake.

Shiko looked at Nakama. The archer shrugged. "I agree with the cook. I, too, have had enough of our esteemed Lord Itachi. I have marched thus far to satisfy honor; but when in service to a man who has none, it is wasted. I am willing to try another road."

A gentle cough came from Ryori. The cook said plaintively, "Can we go now? This load ain't exactly light," as he shifted his grip on the litter.

Embarrassed, Shiko replied, "Yes, of course, I'm sorry." He quickly turned and stepped onto the trail beside the three-rock tree. He hoped to experience again that momentary feeling of correctness, a reassurance that this was indeed the correct path to follow, but there was nothing. All he felt was a great emptiness. It was at that moment that he realized just what he had done.

The Hikari was gone. He had sworn to the Kojuro that he would follow it, and he had failed. And more, he had *chosen* to let it go. No matter how right it might be to go to the Sekai Monastery, it could not absolve him from abandoning the Hikari. He had found it in the lamplighter's workshop, and had watched it be consecrated by his sovereign. And now he had watched it be taken away.

Was Toshi-hito right about going to the monastery? *Was* there even a monastery? Toshi-hito was so ill, who could say if his thoughts were really lucid? Shiko thought he had felt something when he had heard the bell. Had he only imagined it? Had he only hoped to feel something special, and so his mind had obliged?

It was too late now for second thoughts. He sensed the impatience of the men at his back, carrying the burden of Toshi-hito. He forced his legs to move, hoping desperately that he was not leading them all down a dead end path to starvation, or worse. He started along the trail, Ryori and Nakama following behind.

* * *

The Guards trudged on, Bokusa and Donaku at the front. They had marched only a short way, however, when Itachi, still walking at the rear, shouted for a halt. Puzzled, Bokusa held up his hand and the men ceased marching. Itachi walked to the front then faced his small troop. "You men, wait here." He gestured at Bokusa to follow him off the road into the trees. As the big man, looking puzzled, followed the Hajimeshi leader, the Guards exchanged confused looks and anxious mutters. A rest again so soon? What was it all about?

Bokusa and Itachi went far enough into the woods to be out of easy earshot of the men. When Itachi stopped and turned toward him, Bokusa opened his mouth to form a question but the Hajimeshi lord raised a hand to forestall him. "Just be quiet and listen," he said. "I've decided what I need to do." He lowered his voice, looking around conspiratorially as if someone might overhear them still. "I'm going to become the Kotaishi."

Bokusa's homely face would have been hard put to look any more astonished than at that moment. Itachi ignored his adjutant's expression and continued. "The magicians in Tejinashi are powerful. If I can convince them that I'm this chosen one, then I'll be able to get their support. We can return in triumph to Hajimeshi, and my brother will step aside. He's already admitted that he'll follow this Kotaishi." He looked off to the north, in the direction that Shiko and the others had gone. "Those Deshi have been a stone around my neck for this entire journey. I had thought that bringing a wounded one with me might have strengthened my hand, showing the magicians that I was 'compassionate,' dragging him around with me. But that brat apprentice is making things difficult. So I've decided I'm better off without them."

"And—and Nakama?" asked Bokusa, trying to wrap his slow thoughts around Itachi's plan.

"Him! He's unreliable. I need to make sure that everyone is with me on this. Better to get rid of him." Itachi peered up at his large adjutant. "How are the others?"

Bokusa looked thoughtful, which mostly made his homely face look even uglier. "Well, confused, mostly. They don't know what to do, or what's going on."

A flash of annoyance crossed Itachi's face. "They're soldiers, damn it! They aren't supposed to think. They're supposed to follow orders. Are there some of them that aren't going to follow my orders?"

Bokusa quickly backed off. "No, no, my lord, it's just—well, we've a lost a few of the boys, and—and, well, the men fight better if they know what's up, that's all."

"They'll find out when I need them to know. So keep them in line until then. Understood?" Itachi received a silent nod in return. "Now, I need one of them for a special task."

The waiting Guards stood uncertainly, looking anxiously up the road ahead of them. Leaderless, standing in the light of a bright lantern on a strange road in a foreign land, made them all tense. It was with some relief that they saw Bokusa emerge from the trees, but he stopped just off the edge of the road, shouting, "Hisoka!" The pilgrim group's remaining archer stepped out of line. Bokusa gestured at him. "Come here."

Itachi's adjutant turned and re-entered the woods, Hisoka following. The remaining men fidgeted, feeling even more confused. At last Itachi and Bokusa returned, taking their usual places at the head of the line. Bokusa shouted, "Let's move!"

Donaku, standing next to him with the Hikari, said uncertainly, "What—what about Hisoka?"

Itachi turned to him. "Hisoka is not your concern, soldier! Your concern is to make sure you keep that lamp up over your head! If you can't do that, I'll find another of the men who can! Do I need to do that?"

"N-no, Lord Itachi," sputtered Donaku.

"All right, then, march!" Itachi strode off down the road, Bokusa a step behind. The other Guards, instinct taking precedence over thinking, immediately followed; but more than one man looked back over his shoulder to where Hisoka had followed Bokusa into the woods, and had not re-emerged.

Oblivious to the concerns of the men behind him, Itachi walked ahead of the Hikari as the much-reduced group of pilgrims made its way toward Tejinashi. The lantern, he was sure, would be enough to convince the magicians of the legitimacy of his claim. Who better than the brother of one of Tonogato's rulers to be the Kotaishi? He knew that the Tejinashi had cut themselves off from the other kingdoms. How would they know that the other lands had not already proclaimed him as the Kotaishi? Arriving under a sanctified Hikari, with an 'honor guard' of men, he would appear as the epitome of the pre-ordained leader. Then it should be a simple matter to get them to lend their support to a glorious march back across Tonogato. Yes, once he had the Tejinashi on his side, everything else would fall into place.

And Hisoka! How fortunate that Bokusa had been paying attention to the men's casual conversations. He had no idea that one of his Guards had taken such a dislike to that old fool Toshi-hito, until Bokusa had told him. And a man who keeps to himself at that; no bragging or loose talk. Which made him an excellent choice.

It was with a lighter step than he had felt in some time that the Hajimeshi lord paced the road toward Tejinashi, his uncertain troop marching behind.

21

Once in the mountains, as the trail climbed upwards, the air grew increasingly cold. Ryori and Nakama struggled with Toshi-hito's litter, negotiating tight corners around rocks and trees that would have been narrow even for the passage of a single man. Shiko helped where he could, holding on to Toshi-hito when they had to tilt the litter, adding another blanket to the Deshi Master as the air chilled still further. An hour's steady ascent found them all exhausted.

After leaving the clearing where they had separated from Itachi and the Guards, Shiko and his small band had passed close by the platform along the edge of the lake, its bell now silent and unmoving. Ryori had glanced at the apprentice oddly as they had walked past the small enclosure, but had otherwise made no comment. Shiko, though, had been hard put to suppress an urge to dash out and ring the bell once more, if simply to experience its sound again and the feeling of certainty that it had presaged. But neither he nor his companions had felt inclined to stop so near to where they had left Itachi, lest the Hajimeshi general have a change of heart and try to recall them. For Shiko the stillness and the quiet as they left the bell behind had left him feeling unnerved, and questioning his resolve once again.

Now, higher up in the mountains, they found a small space among the trees that lined the trail. Ryori and Nakama gingerly placed the litter on the ground; then both men collapsed, their heaving breath surrounding their heads in self-produced clouds. They loosened their packs, shrugging them off aching shoulders while Shiko broke out the water skin and passed it to both men.

"Thought Deshi life...supposed ta' make a man lean," said a winded Ryori, inclining his head toward Toshi-hito's silent form. "Not this one." Still out of breath, he added, "Passed some...good lookin' hochala plants...back a bit. Think I'll collect some...never know what kinda food'll come in handy." He stood up and reached for his pack but froze in mid-movement as an ear-splitting howl rent the air, followed seconds later by a second, then a third.

Nakama and Shiko both leapt to their feet. The sounds came from all around them, somewhere unseen amongst the trees lining the trail close by on either side. It was an eerie, keening tone, both mournful and rapacious at the same time. Nakama quickly grabbed his bow and notched a shaft. "Wolves," he said urgently, scanning the trees. "A pack, close by."

Ryori and Shiko moved closer to Toshi-hito's litter, the cook pulling out his dagger. They were in a poor spot to defend themselves against wolves; there was little room to maneuver, but plenty of opportunity for a predator to emerge from the dark woods and be on them before they knew it. After the first howls, silence had fallen once more. Three pairs of eyes swiveled tensely this way and that, searching for any sign of movement.

Then, off to one side, something moved. Ryori spotted it first. "There!" he shouted, and Nakama spun quickly in that direction. A dark, grey shape slowly emerged from the surrounding trees. Another appeared nearby, then a third. "Look!" cried Shiko, pointing to the opposite side of the trail, where more grey forms were becoming visible. Soon there were over a dozen, their panting breath also filling the cold air with tiny clouds.

At the first sound of the wolves' howling, Shiko had experienced an overwhelming sensation inside his head: *"HUNGER!"* It was the sound of many mental voices, all combined into one, and with but a single overriding objective. Even as he heard them Shiko knew that he and his companions *were* that objective. Then, as the many grey forms took shape among the trees, he sensed something else.

There! That one, felt Shiko, as he picked out one of the grey shapes from among the others. The one moving out in front. He's the leader!

While Ryori gripped his knife, and picked up a nearby rock to fling at an attacker, Shiko stared at the leader of the wolf pack. Dark, malevolent eyes peered back; behind them, all Shiko could hear was the same refrain: *"Food. Hunger."*

Then the leader stopped. He lifted his head, turning it sideways. The other wolves, in some confusion, followed his lead and stopped as well. They shifted about, and those in the rear dashed from side to side, apparently intent on getting into a better position for the kill.

Shiko held the gaze of the wolf leader. He didn't know what to 'say,' so he just opened his mind up and let the wolf see it. The wolf sat there, mouth open, panting. It seemed to Shiko almost as if he were considering.

At that moment Nakama, sensing an opportunity, raised his bow. Shiko saw the movement as the Guard sighted along the shaft, aiming directly for the wolf leader. Quickly Shiko leapt toward him. "Stop, Nakama! Don't kill him!" But the Guard had already released his grip, and the arrow had begun to move. In what seemed like slow motion Shiko saw his own hand reach out; saw it grab Nakama's arm that supported the bow. Knocked askew, the arrow spun up well clear of the wolf, landing amongst the trees.

Nakama, furious, spun on Shiko. "What are you doing?" He grabbed madly for another shaft. "Are you trying to get us all killed?" Before Shiko could answer, Ryori yelled out.

Deshi and Guard followed the direction of Ryori's pointed hand. The lead wolf had turned away and was walking back into the woods. The other wolves, in slow, shuffling groups and with low growls, were also blending back into the trees. The leader stopped then turned and looked again at Shiko. Eyes met one more time, and Shiko felt a peculiar sensation, almost as if it were some sort of acknowledgement, or recognition. Then the wolf turned and vanished with his fellows.

The three men, and their ailing companion, were alone once more. They sat, tense, for some time, unsure of the reprieve. When at last they felt it was safe to move, they gathered up their things quickly. As Ryori rapidly slung on his pack, he said quietly, "Think perhaps I'll just skip those hochala's...Sure there'll be more later..."

Shiko looked at Nakama. "I'm sorry. But I—I was hoping that he would call off the attack."

It was Ryori, however, who responded. "He?" said the cook, as he finished gathering up his things. "You mean he, as in the wolf that Nakama almost took down? Hah!" He waved a dismissive hand. "No tellin' what changed their minds. Best not to stick 'round and bother findin' out, though."

Nakama said nothing, although he looked keenly at Shiko as he slung his bow back over his shoulder and hefted his pack. The Guard and Ryori lifted up Toshi-hito's litter and fell in behind the Deshi apprentice as Shiko once more led them up the trail. As they walked, Nakama continued to look at Shiko, and wonder.

The sky became a solid grey, ever darker as the day advanced. The three men were silent, only expending energy on making progress toward the hoped-for monastery.

Shiko, with less to burden him physically, used the time to try to understand what had happened with the wolves. He wasn't even sure what he had been trying to do. He had sensed, though, that their only hope had been to try to communicate, to make the wolves see them not as food but as individuals, like themselves...

It had not been the same type of experience as with 'Ton and 'Cha. He had not 'spoken' with the wolf, but the animal had somehow understood him. There had been an element of surprise, then of recognition, in the feelings he had sensed. But how could the wolf have known who he was?

Shiko thought of his conversation with 'Ton, when he had tried to introduce himself and the chodaka bird had laughingly told him that they had already met. That had been true enough, in a sense, although they had not actually 'spoken' with one another. What he did remember of that first encounter was how the haunting cry of the bird had stayed with him, reminding him of Nusumi. And later, when he had seen 'Ton in the woods after they had crossed into Shukyoshi, it had been the echo of that same cry that had prompted him to leave their encampment and search for the chodaka bird. That had caused him to think of Nusumi too...

Nusumi...of course! he realized. The bird's cries always reminded him of Nusumi! Now that he made the connection, he was almost certain that the association of the two was no accident. The birds must have used his feelings about Nusumi to make sure that he had noticed them. Yet how could they have known about her, or have understood his feelings about her?

He wished that the ability to mentally 'converse' worked between people, and that he could have 'talked' with Toshi-hito and asked the Deshi Master all of the questions that filled his head, before the Master had grown so ill. He certainly couldn't discuss the chodaka birds with Ryori or Nakama; they would undoubtedly decide that they had elected to follow a madman. And he still felt too uncertain about his own abilities to try conversing with other animals. It was only with 'Ton and 'Cha that he felt comfortable enough to be understood. They were a long way away, but he had to try. *"'Ton?"* he thought as loudly as he could. *"'TON? CAN YOU HEAR ME?"*

Silence. Shiko figured that he was just too far away. Then a faint scratching noise rubbed at the edges of his mind. He tried to find it; lost it; then finally regained it once more.

"...Shiko?..."

"YES, 'TON! I CAN HEAR YOU!" shouted Shiko back.

"...I can hear you...but not too well. You must be far away..."

"I AM. ARE YOU ALL RIGHT?"

"...Yes. They stopped again not long after you left..."

That's odd, thought Shiko. I wonder why? Itachi seemed to be in such a hurry. No matter…*"WE RAN INTO SOME WOLVES…"*

"*…It's alright.*" Shiko heard 'Cha's familiar 'voice.' "*You don't have to shout. We can hear you, you're just a little faint, is all…*"

"Sorry. We ran into some wolves. But they didn't attack us. It seemed like…well, as if the leader knew me somehow."

There was no reply, and Shiko was worried that he had lost them. "*'Ton?*" he called out. He heard 'Ton's familiar snort in reply.

"*…Wolves. Nothing but a bunch of thieves. No manners whatsoever…*"

"But do you think he could have known me?" asked Shiko. "I opened my mind to him, and he seemed to see something; something that made him stop."

There was another long pause from the birds, and then 'Cha answered. "*…Don't worry about it, Shiko. Who can say why animals do what they do?…*"

"I just wonder," said the apprentice, "*what he saw when he looked inside my head? I mean, it was you who put the image of Nusumi in my head back in Yutakashi, wasn't it? How did you know what to look for inside me that would get my attention?*"

"*…Actually, that was 'Ton. I thought it was very clever of him to do that…*"

"*…Why, thank you, dear…*"

"*…You're welcome…*"

Shiko found himself smiling; 'Ton and 'Cha seemed to have a more pleasant relationship than any two humans he knew. "*But 'Ton,*" he asked, "*how did you know to use Nusumi?*"

"*…What was that? Sorry, you're getting harder to hear…*"

"How did you know to use Nusumi to get my attention?"

"*…Oh, that. That was easy. You were broadcasting feelings for her like a bonfire. Just figured I'd catch a little of the light and reflect it back until you noticed…*"

"Was it that obvious?"

"*…Sorry, didn't hear that…think we're just about…'bye…*"

"*...careful, Shiko...*" he heard 'Cha add. Then all was silent.

"'Ton? 'Cha?" he called out. But there was no reply.

The birds had answered his question, though, at least in part. If his thoughts and emotions were that plainly evident, the wolf leader must have been able to see something that had resulted in his calling off the pack's attack. Shiko seriously doubted that it had been his thoughts about Nusumi. So what, he wondered, was in his head that the wolf had seen to cause that flash of recognition?

Troubled by his inability to understand what was going on inside his own mind, Shiko trudged on, wrapping his arms about himself to keep the cold air at bay. Knowing that 'Ton and 'Cha were too far away to talk with made him feel very alone. How odd, he thought, that he could miss something that until a few days ago he had never even known he had.

A bonfire, mused Shiko. That's how 'Ton described my feelings for Nusumi. I guess he was right, even though my time with her was so brief.

He reached up and felt his forehead. The external bruise had healed, but he could still 'feel' where it had been. What, he wondered, had really happened? The physical contact between him and Nusumi, he realized, had been nothing more than the key to a locked door, behind which had lain...what? Emotions, longing...love?

No, it wasn't love, he concluded. It was clear to him now that what he had felt for Nusumi, what he still felt for her, was only a pale imitation of what the birds, 'Ton and 'Cha, felt for each other. He chided himself for questioning whether the birds could have grasped his feelings for the Yutakashi market thief. It was obvious the chodaka birds had a bond between them that demonstrated true love.

It wasn't just the easy conversation the two birds exchanged. He could sense, in both of them, that everything they did was in reference to one another in some way. Whether 'Ton was flying Itachi's messages while 'Cha remained hostage behind, or they were simply sharing the same 'smelly leather bag' together, the two of them were inseparable. Life for them consisted of the two of them, and then everything else.

Shiko tugged on the straps of his pack, pulling it in tighter to prevent it from swinging as the trio clambered over a rough section of the trail. What then, he wondered, of Nusumi? Why had he been so attracted to her?

Made easier by distance, he tried to consider Nusumi objectively. He tallied up how she looked, her actions, her opinions, and came to realize that the most important thing he felt for her was…respect.

There had been other feelings at the time, of course. He had been physically attracted to her, even though some of that had been as a result of the mayaku weed. Her unconventional nature had appealed to him also, helping him to see how life could be lived in a world not constrained by Deshi thought. Yet those things were largely side benefits. More important, he felt, by far was the way they had each reacted to one another, and how they responded to the events in their lives. In many ways he and Nusumi were complete opposites; but through their feelings of compassion for others they had more in common than was at first apparent.

She had wanted to come with him, he knew, because she had thought he was on some kind of noble quest, while she had considered herself to be nothing more than a street urchin. The truth was that she was living a far nobler life than he was, every day, right there in Yutakashi. She was sacrificing herself, her own goals and dreams, for those around her. What had he done that could compare to that? Ironically, while Nusumi had been hoping to escape her life on the street he had been hoping that, by being close to her, he could have been able to become more like her…

Shiko smiled wryly to himself. He doubted that she would have believed him had he figured all of that out at the time and had tried to tell her. Now, with many miles and days between them, he could see that his feelings had flared brilliantly for a time, and had then slowly begun to cool. All that was left of the bonfire now were peacefully glowing embers, his memories of her.

His self-absorbed introspection was interrupted by a curse from behind him as Ryori slipped in some mud on the trail. Quickly Shiko placed his thoughts up on a mental shelf as he hurried back to help.

* * *

"Nothing."

Mikasama stood next to Shudojo, staring out at the desolate landscape.

"Nothing," repeated the Princess irritably. "Only rocks and trees." She turned to the Sister beside her. "If we can't find any food, we'll starve!"

Shudojo ignored the absurdity of Mikasama's patently obvious statement. "We will find what we need," she shrugged.

Under the previous night's occasional moon, the two women had managed to find their way toward the high ground above the riverbank. In silence they had awaited the coming of dawn and the chance to get their bearings. In the pale light of day that now pushed through the grey clouds, they were greeted with a sight that did little to inspire them. As far as they could see in all directions, there were only low hills composed of dry, rocky soil, and a few trees, hardly more than shrubs, determinedly hanging on close by the river.

The Sister looked out over the rolling hills, searching for a trail or some other evidence that might lead them toward a farm or village. She saw nothing; they were alone in the wilderness.

"So," asked the Princess, after a few moments of sullen silence, "which way do we go? Do you have any idea where we are?" She had been trying, without success, to unsnarl her disorderly mass of hair; in frustration, she gave up and tossed the tangled mess back over her shoulder.

"No," said Shudojo simply. At the Princess's irritated glance, she added, "It really doesn't matter which way we go, Lady. Our chances of finding something in any one particular direction are as good as any other."

In the end they decided to set out walking west, away from the river, in the hope of regaining the road. As the hours passed though, the desire for a road was supplanted by the wish to simply see anything that hinted of people living somewhere, anywhere. The desolate, unchanging landscape offered little respite from either sun or thirst.

Shudojo found herself slipping back, beginning to think again like that poor wretched girl who had once been shunned out of her village: always searching for something to eat, watching out for danger, wandering the land like a wild animal.

No, she told herself forcefully. I am *not* that same person. I am not the same guilt-driven, homeless, girl who scraped the dew off of leaves in order to slack her thirst. I may end up having to do that again, but I will never *be* that person again.

As she walked, silently, she kept her eyes focused forward, always scanning the next hill, or the next valley.

It was later, as the day began slipping slowly into afternoon, that the Princess first realized how dependent on Shudojo she had become. They were walking past a stand of wild trees, whose twisted limbs bore misshapen, roundish fruit. Her stomach growling, sending her sharp reminders of its need, Mikasama decided that enough was enough. She walked over to one of the trees and tugged on one of the odd fruits until it snapped off the branch. She wiped off the morning dew that still clung to the slight fuzz that coated the skin and prepared to take a bite. Just as she raised the fruit to her mouth she was startled to find it suddenly knocked from her hand, falling to the ground with a squishy thud.

She spun to face Shudojo. "How dare you!"

Shudojo, unperturbed, stared back at the Princess. "Lady, had you eaten of that fruit, your bowels would have emptied themselves uncontrollably." Blanching at the crude imagery conjured up by the Sister, Mikasama opened her mouth to argue but Shudojo went on: "The michya fruit can only be eaten cooked, and then only in small amounts. It's not usually used for food, only as a medicine to relieve stomach cramps." She turned and pointed to a low hill not too far away. "We should head for that area over there. I think I can see rokayna trees; if so, that will be something we can fill our bellies with."

The Sister walked away, and Mikasama looked down to where the michya fruit had fallen. Already ants were swarming on it, delighted by their newly found feast. Queasy, and now not at all hungry, she followed Shudojo.

And so the day had gone on, as they saw no one and spoke little. They had indeed found rokayna trees, and once they had stripped off the tough outer skin of the fruit Mikasama found them to be quite tasty. Later, in the evening before the light had gone, they stumbled into a patch of daka berries, giving them something to hold them over until morning.

They had no blankets, only the clothes they wore, which were dirty and frayed from a trip through the river and a day's long marching. The night promised to be cold, and it wasn't until the sun slipped behind the hills that Mikasama actually wondered about how they would sleep. Fortunately Shudojo had given it some thought. The area near the daka bushes sprouted tall grasses; the Sister grabbed large armfuls of the grass and matted it down, layering them crisscross to one another. She ended up with a passably soft bed, the surrounding wild grass serving to block some of the night breeze.

Impressed by Shudojo's knowledge of outdoor survival, Mikasama followed suit, trying to arrange herself around whatever lumps in the ground were not smoothed out by the makeshift 'bed.' She was startled when she felt Shudojo slide up against her, back to back.

Feeling the Princess's body tense up, the Sister said, "It will be cold tonight, Lady. The only warmth we will have is that which we make ourselves. We will be the warmer for sharing it."

Mikasama saw the truth in the statement; nevertheless, it took her some time until she felt able to relax. She had never lain so close to anyone, even Komori. It wasn't until she heard the gentle breathing of the Sister lying next to her, as Shudojo slipped off into sleep, that she was able to loosen her muscles and try to rest herself. It was a long night, spent mostly listening to crickets.

The Princess was surprised when she awoke to find the sun already beginning to slide up over the eastern hills. Shudojo was nowhere to be seen.

Alarmed, Mikasama sat up, instinctively reaching out her hand to where the Sister had lain. The grass there was still matted, she noted; and more than that, it was slightly warm to the touch. Shudojo had not been gone very long then. She stood up, looking out over the grass. She spotted Shudojo almost immediately, as the Sister waded her way back through the grass to their sleeping spot. As she neared Mikasama asked, "Where did you go?"

"To relieve myself," answered Shudojo without pretension. "Over there." She pointed to a clump of bushes some distance away. "I'll pick some more berries for later, while you go."

The Sister turned aside toward the daka bushes and Mikasama realized how badly that she, too, needed to take care of nature's calling. Setting off toward the area from which Shudojo had come, she thought about how she had yet to get used to the idea of relieving herself outside. She reflected on how ironic it was that she was still so uncomfortable performing such a natural function outdoors, even in such a natural setting.

Habit and artificial custom, she realized; that's all it was. Once the trappings of custom were no longer available, one eventually reverted back to the realities of existing.

She sighed. I'm starting to sound more like Juyama every day, she mused.

More nights were spent out in the open, most of them less comfortably than their first night and its improvised bed of grass. Despite the accumulation of grime from hours of traveling the two women now readily sought warmth from each other as night fell. Mikasama quickly left her inhibitions behind, and morning generally found one or the other of them entangled about the other as each sought to maximize both comfort and warmth at the same time. Nothing was said, however, when the morning woke first one of them and then, by default, the other; they simply slipped apart and resumed their routine. After a few bites of the berries, carefully hoarded from that first day's find, they set out once more. Shudojo was always on the lookout for anything else edible along the way, while both women kept alert to any signs of streambeds where they could slack their never-ending thirst.

It was on the fourth night, after the two had lain down as darkness fell, that the Princess felt compelled to break their self-imposed silence. She had been walking with Shudojo now for days and yet knew no more about her than when they had first started out. Stubborn; that's what they both were, Mikasama realized; it was pointless to go on, dragging themselves through the wilderness, if they could not even be civil to one another. Huddled together, arms around one another, Mikasama looked at the Sister, their faces but a few inches apart.

"Shudojo?" she said tentatively.

"Mmmm?" answered the Sister, already drifting off.

"Shudojo, how did you learn all these things? What to eat, how to make a bed out of grass?"

The Sister didn't answer at first, causing Mikasama to think that perhaps she had fallen asleep. The reply, when it came, was quiet. "It was a long time ago, Lady...another life; one that I've left behind."

"But," Mikasama went on, heedless of the strain in Shudojo's voice, "who taught you? Is it the custom where you come from to train women in living out of doors?"

Shudojo answered by abruptly turning away from Mikasama, leaving nothing but a back for the Princess to converse with. At first Mikasama was insulted; then she stopped to reconsider. *I'm doing it again*, she thought; *I'm trampling all over someone. I'm so intent on my own needs, what I want to know, that I'm not paying attention.* What was it

Shudojo had said? Something about it being left behind? Well, of course; then there I go trying to force the issue when she doesn't want to talk about it.

"Shudojo?" Silence. "Shudojo? I'm—I'm sorry. It was rude of me to pry. It's just—well, what I was trying to get at, actually, was that I admire your skills. Nobody has ever taught me things like this. I can perform five different court dances but I don't know one kind of tree from another."

When she got no response, Mikasama quietly turned away and lay on her back. The clouds were coming in again, but every now and then there was a hole through which she could see stars. For some reason, they made her think of Nakama. How strange, she thought; I haven't thought about him in so long. I wonder where he is right now? Probably snug and warm in some inn along the road, he and the others with the Hikari. How I wish I could hear his sweet voice, saying my name…

It was not Nakama's voice she heard, however, but Shudojo's. When the Sister at last spoke, her words were quiet, and she was facing the other way. Mikasama had to roll back over in order to hear her clearly.

"Nobody taught me how to survive," said the Sister. "I had to learn that on my own. When I…had to leave my village, I had nowhere to go. I walked and walked and walked, alone. I had no money. I slept on the ground. I learned what I could eat, what I couldn't. Believe me," she said ruefully, "once you learn the hard way what not to eat, you don't forget. After I starting studying plants at Fumosa, I was amazed that I hadn't killed myself with some of the things I had eaten."

She fell quiet, and Mikasama thought she was done. After a time, though, the Sister continued. "I must have walked for months. It *felt* like years. After a while it seemed that everything I had done before had happened to someone else. That *other* person had lived in the village; I was someone different. All that I had was the Goddess inside me. I had thought that was all I needed; that she would provide the strength for me to keep on walking." Her voice quivered slightly. "It—it was hard to keep faith, for so many days…By the time I had reached Fumosa, and the Sisters took me in, I must have looked like an animal to them…They gave me a home, a new family. Now—" But she didn't finish the thought.

Mikasama, in the dim moonlight that peeked through the clouds, felt Shudojo move, and thought she heard what might have been a sob. She wasn't sure, but she acted regardless. Wordlessly she wrapped her arms around Shudojo and held her. The Sister did not protest, and so the night passed.

*   *   *

When morning came, nothing more was said about the previous night's discussion. The two women set off again, walking in silence. Everywhere the way was wild; thick forests that they tried to skirt, or rolling hills populated only by rocks and shrubs. It was during another long afternoon that Shudojo suddenly stopped. Holding up a hand to shield her eyes, she stood gazing off to one side of their track as Mikasama said, "What? What is it?"

The Sister uttered an excited, "Yes!" She took off at the run toward a grove of trees in the distance, leaving a perplexed Mikasama behind.

When the Princess finally caught up to her, the Sister was climbing up one of the trees. "What are you doing?" Mikasama shouted up at her.

Shudojo didn't stop climbing as she looked back down at the Princess. "Bisato trees! These are bisato trees! Their seed pods are wonderful!" The Princess had to arch her back to see where Shudojo was going as the Sister moved around amongst the branches, snapping off several smaller ones. "Great traveling food!" Shudojo continued. "They keep for weeks, and fill you with energy to boot. Here, catch!" Mikasama just had time to reach out her arms before a bundle of the snapped-off branches landed on top of her. Clumsily she caught the bulk of them, some sliding off onto the ground.

"Careful," shouted Shudojo from the tree above. "They're no good if they get squashed."

Once Shudojo had sent down what she considered a sufficient quantity, she climbed nimbly back to ground level to rejoin the Princess. Mikasama was struck once again by the Sister's curious appearance. The blue eyes were still her most arresting feature, but nearly as remarkable was Shudojo's hair.

During their inadvertent trip down the river, the hood of the Sister's habit had been swept away. Once the two women had made their way inland from the river bank where they had landed, Shudojo had loosened the wet, tangled mass of her hair, by then half-wrapped around her neck, and had let it fall free. As the sun had risen and the Sister's hair had dried Mikasama had been startled to see that rather than the normal black, Shudojo's hair was actually an odd shade of brown. Everything else about the woman spoke of her being native to Tonogato, but the hair and eyes set her apart. Mikasama had not asked about it at the time, figuring that if Shudojo wanted her to know she would have offered an explanation. Someday, thought Mikasama, I must ask her what it feels like to have brown hair.

Shudojo brushed off the stray leaves and twigs she had picked up on her way through the upper reaches of the tree. Mikasama was also astonished to see that the Sister was—smiling! It was the first time she could ever recall seeing the usually reserved Sister smile.

"Well?" asked Shudojo, still grinning. "Want to see how to peel one of these?"

With a broad smile in return, Mikasama nodded, and the two women knelt together to tackle their harvest.

*   *   *

Hisoka moved up the trail swiftly, but quietly. At intervals he stopped, turning his head slightly to listen. Occasionally he stooped down and examined the surface of the trail, touching the indentations in the dirt and leaves. He found a churned area of mud, and the unmistakable indications of human feet. Good, he thought to himself. They are not too far ahead.

When Bokusa had summoned him off the road, shortly after the Deshi and the others had departed, Hisoka had been as perplexed as his fellow Guardsmen. His confusion had turned to elation, however, once he had learned what it was that Lord Itachi wished him to do. The Hajimeshi lord's reasons for the request were immaterial; in fact, Hisoka had paid them scant attention once Itachi had explained what was required. Hisoka had merely bowed, answering in the affirmative when asked if he would undertake the assignment. Inwardly, he had rejoiced.

Over the course of the pilgrimage, his resentment at the Deshi Master Toshi-hito had festered and grown. Now, he would be able to exact retribution.

Hisoka had chafed at the Deshi's arrogance and attitude ever since the beginning of the pilgrimage. Always so smug, always so superior, he thought. Never expecting that some lowly soldier was listening carefully when he had openly said, after they had left the Yutakashi Grand Council, that he did not expect to find the Kotaishi there. Hisoka had reported with disgust the Deshi's comments back through their contact in the Yutakashi priory. Then, later, while in Shukyoshi, Hisoka recalled his horror at the things that Toshi-hito had said before the Anasaki. Slandering the Omo Deshi! That had tipped the balance, as far as he had been concerned.

The Omo Deshi had tasked Hisoka with reporting everything that happened on this journey; this he had done, while he had been able to use their contacts in Yutakashi and elsewhere. After the pilgrims had entered Shukyoshi he had been on his own, with nothing but the Omo Deshi's earlier instructions to guide him. He remembered those instructions clearly.

"You may be called upon to undertake certain...actions...for the betterment of our brotherhood. Do you understand?" Yes, he had understood. At the time he had thought that his patron's edict was directed at Lord Itachi, never a supporter of the Omo Deshi. But he had been dismayed to observe the behavior of the supposed Deshi Master, Toshi-hito. He had shifted his attention to the traitorous Deshi Master, listening, observing. And so, when Lord Itachi had Bokusa summon him away from the others, he had found it an easy decision to accept the proffered assignment.

His plan was to catch up to the Deshi and the others while they stopped to rest. He paused once more, examining the trail. Leaning his face down close to the ground, he checked again for signs of recent footfalls. Not very far ahead, now. They had stopped in a clearing almost an hour ago, so they ought to be tiring again soon.

Deshi Masters, he thought disgustedly, as he rose and continued stealthily on his way. May they all rot, their bones bleached by the sun. None of them amount to one finger's worth of the Omo Deshi. That such a great man has had to put up with them all these years is intolerable. The Omo Deshi should simply crucify the lot of them and be done with it.

Inevitably, whenever he thought about the Deshi Masters, Hisoka recalled his own attempt to enter the Deshi order. He had been but a boy, just turned seven, orphaned by a destitute father who had killed himself when the family farm had failed. His mother had died giving birth to him. He had never known the softness of a woman's touch, and had learned to be tough, and to endure. Once his father was gone he had become just another mouth to feed in a family of too many mouths, and not one of his relatives had wanted him. He had made his way to the Deshi priory, seeking a roof to put over his head. A Deshi Master had interviewed him. He didn't even know the man's name, but he would never forget the contempt evident in the man's face, nor the scorn in his voice. "We don't accept vagrants," the man had said. "Come here if you are seeking knowledge. If it's handouts you want, you must try elsewhere." So he had been turned away, to rummage through the streets and scrape out his own survival. Until the Omo Deshi, then a Master himself, had chanced upon him.

The great man had been leaving a brothel, one where Hisoka had occasionally received leftover remains of clients' meals from the sympathetic girls who worked there. The future Omo Deshi had taken pity on

Hisoka, had taken him home and fed him properly. He had taught his young charge about the Deshi, about how corrupt the other Masters had become; how he, alone of the Masters, knew the way to guide the order back to the right path. Youthful ears had listened eagerly, and believed. From that day forward he had served the Omo Deshi loyally.

He had been sent to enlist in the Castle Guard, to be his benefactor's eyes and ears in places where Deshi did not go. He had learned how to fight, how to use the bow; and always reporting back to the Omo Deshi what he heard, whom he had seen.

And now he had an opportunity to repay his patron's trust.

Ryori and Nakama, exhausted from carrying the litter along the narrow trail, gently set down their load before dropping to the ground themselves to rest. While the two men caught their breath Shiko explored the small clearing where they had stopped.

There were only a few small bushes in the open space of the vale, which was bordered on the west by a steep slope covered with immense rocks. The eastern side fell away gently into woods, so Shiko rummaged there amongst the trees attempting to find something suitable for them to eat. Eventually he came across several trees where a leafy vine, growing upwards, had wrapped itself around the trunks; tucked up underneath each of the leaves was a long bean pod.

Shiko pulled one of the beans off and held it up to his nose for a sniff. He didn't recognize either it or its odor. There didn't appear to be anything else suitable in the vicinity, so he went back to show the bean to Ryori, hoping that perhaps the cook would know what it was.

When he returned Ryori was just passing the water skin to Nakama. Shiko walked over and showed Ryori his find, which the cook fingered with professional interest. He broke it open, rolling the seeds inside between thumb and forefinger. "These'll do; I can make us somethin' out of these. Be bland, but it'll be enough. But," he said to Nakama, "a little spicin' up would make it tastier. You remember that overgrown bush we passed, just 'afore we reached here?"

"Ohhhh yes," replied Nakama. The bush in question had been overhanging the trail, slapping its sharp-edged leaves against their faces as they had tried to pass. Shiko had ended up having to hold it out of their way while they passed beneath it.

"Well," Ryori went on, "those leaves, ground up real fine, gotta a nice little bite to 'em. Make this a better meal. How 'bout you go grab a handful, while I get some of Shiko's beans here?" Nakama nodded in reply and set off back down the trail. With a nod of his own at Shiko, Ryori went off in the direction of the bean plants.

Shiko tried to get some more water into Toshi-hito but the Master's body would take no more. As the apprentice sat and watched the regular rise and fall of Toshi-hito's breathing, he wondered what was going on inside the Master's mind. Was he dreaming? Or did his thoughts mirror the battle his body was waging, making up symbolic images of the struggle for survival? Perhaps, Shiko thought, there was nothing at all, and Toshi-hito's mind was simply quiet while his body struggled.

He reached out a hand and put it on Toshi-hito's chest. He could feel the heart beating, feel the air going in and out of the lungs. Sitting alone on the trail with his silent mentor, Shiko felt once again the sharp pang of loneliness. Don't die, he silently urged the figure under his hand. Don't die; I still have so much to learn! I've lost the Hikari; I don't want to lose you too…

His reverie was interrupted as Ryori noisily returned with several handfuls of beans. Shiko rose and began gathering the packs together. As soon as Nakama returned, they could resume their journey.

"Not a bad patch at all," said Ryori as he approached. "Should be enough for—"

Shiko looked up as Ryori stopped talking. The cook was looking at something behind Shiko, up toward the rocks that covered the nearby slope.

"What is it, Master Cook? What's—"

He never had a chance to finish the thought as Ryori suddenly lunged at him, shouting, "Down! Get dow—" The rest of the comment was lost, for as the cook pushed him to the ground an arrow imbedded itself in Ryori's side.

Shiko fell half across Toshi-hito's legs, and Ryori, after teetering and looking in shocked disbelief at the arrowhead protruding from him, collapsed on top of both of them.

* * *

Up on the cliff side, Hisoka swore. Damn! That idiot cook had spotted him before he could get in a clean shot.

He had arrived moments earlier, working his way around to the other side of the clearing, until he saw that the cliff side offered an excellent vantage point from which to fire down upon the Deshi below. He had wanted to take out Nakama first but the Guard was nowhere to be seen. So he had waited, hoping to catch first the soldier, and then the other two. It would have been a simple matter to dispatch them once Nakama was out of the way. He had toyed with the idea of then leaving the Deshi Master to the mercies of the animals of the forest, but had decided he would have to be sure. What was the expenditure of one more arrow, versus certainty?

But then it had looked as if they were preparing to leave; the apprentice had started to gather up the packs when the cook returned from the woods. Fearing he might not get a better opportunity for such a clear shot, he had prepared to bring them down.

Then that fool of a cook had seen him. At least he was down, even if it was not a very clean strike. The boy was underneath him; time enough to deal with him later. Now, where was Nakama? That shout probably alerted him—

The snapping of a twig was the only thing that saved Hisoka. Acting on instinct he dived sideways just as an arrow sliced through the air and into the pocket of rocks where he had been hiding. Instead of landing square in his back the arrow impacted his right arm just above the elbow, shattering the bone. With a yell of pain, he rolled onto his left side, making sure even so to hold on to his bow. Grimacing in pain, he crawled out of the line of sight of the arrow's flight, leaving a trail of blood behind. As soon as he cleared the boulders that clustered about his vantage point, he stood with difficulty and shuffled as quickly as he could into the trees north of the vale.

* * *

Nakama hopped over the rocks, trying to get into position to shoot another shaft at their attacker. He found the trail of blood and tried to follow it, but the trail ran cold after entering the woods. He guessed that the man must have been clever and had wrapped up his arm to stop the bleeding. Not sure of how badly wounded the attacker was, and fearing to leave Toshi-hito and the others unprotected in case he should double back, Nakama retraced his steps back to the vale.

Approaching his companions on the trail, he feared the worst. He saw Ryori, face down with an arrow protruding from him, lying on top of Shiko and Toshi-hito. Seeing no sign of their attacker, Nakama quickly ran over and knelt down by the litter.

Shiko looked up at him, winded, but apparently alive. "Ryori...he's been hurt. I—I can't lift him up—my legs are turned the wrong way." The angle at which Shiko had fallen and had been pinned by Ryori made it such that the apprentice could not lift the cook's weight off.

Nakama leaned over and looked at Ryori's face. A trickle of blood ran out of his mouth, and his eyes were glassy, but he was alive. Looking at the arrow, he saw that it had come out Ryori's abdomen, blood running down the shaft toward the barbed head. The head itself had stopped up against Shiko's chest, the point just cutting the skin but not going in any deeper. Carefully, Nakama lifted Ryori up, trying not to disturb the arrow too much, and gingerly avoiding having it go any further into Shiko. The movement caused the cook's head to snap up, and he howled in pain.

Shiko quickly crawled out from underneath the cook, and the two of them gently set Ryori down next to Toshi-hito. The cook lay on his side, while Nakama examined the arrow wound more closely to see if anything could be done. Shiko went over to feel Toshi-hito, making sure that he had not been injured. Once he was satisfied that the Deshi Master was unharmed, he quickly moved back over to where Ryori lay and leaned down by the cook's face. "Ryori?" he said. "Ryori? Can you hear me?"

The cook's eyes opened briefly then shut again. More blood dribbled out of his mouth, and his face contorted in pain. When he spoke, the blood flecked against his lips.

"Knew the bastard...would do me in..." he muttered softly. "Said so, didn't I? Him or me..."

"Lie still, Master Cook," said Shiko worriedly. "Perhaps Nakama can remove the arrow." Even as he said so, a glance at the Guard was returned with a slow shake of the head; there was nothing to be done. Ryori knew it too, for he said, "Tell 'im...not ta' bother. Ain't gonna get up from this one." He coughed up more blood, then looked at the apprentice. The eyes were already starting to fade, Shiko could see; how odd that one could observe death approaching.

Ryori held his gaze with what little light was left in his eyes. "Round my neck...a signet..."

Shiko paused but a moment, then gently reached down inside the man's tunic. He pulled out a small round medallion, held on a string around Ryori's neck. It was smaller than Shiko's honsho, and devoid of writing; but it did have a picture engraved on it. A peacock, its tail feathers in full spread.

"Family..." croaked Ryori. "Take it back...to my family..."

Holding the medallion in his hand, Shiko replied, "I will, Master Cook. I promise."

"Tell—" He had to stop, as more blood clogged his throat. In a choking voice, he said, "Tell the ol' man...Ryori done a good job..." Then, quite suddenly, he stopped. The eyes were still.

Shiko, eyes filled with tears, looked up at Nakama.

Nakama sat impassive, although he shared the boy's grief. He had seen too much death as a soldier to allow emotion to overtake him at yet one more. Even so, to be hunted down like a wild beast, shot from afar...It made him sick, and angry.

He had seen the movement, up above them on the cliff, shortly after he had left to collect the leaves. Not knowing if there were one or many of them, he had thought to circle behind and surprise them before they were able to attack. Expecting to find brigands, he had been shocked to see Hisoka taking aim at his companions on the trail below. Before he could get close enough, he had heard Ryori's shout and seen Hisoka loose his shaft. He had leapt across the rocks and brought up his own bow, but the man must have heard him approaching and had slipped sideways so that Nakama's arrow only struck his arm. And then the villain had fled.

Shiko was still sitting, in shock, holding Ryori's medallion. In silence Nakama pulled his dagger from its sheath and severed the cord around the cook's neck. Shiko stared down at the medallion in his hand, as the blood from Ryori's body slowly congealed among the beans, lying where they had dropped when Ryori fell.

"Shiko," said Nakama softly. The Guard had to repeat himself several times before the apprentice, whose eyes were locked onto the medallion, tore his gaze away and looked once again at Nakama. The soldier said, "We have to go on. Hisoka may come back; we have to start moving again in case he does."

"Hisoka?" said Shiko in a daze. "You mean Hisoka, the Guard?"

"Yes," said Nakama bitterly. "A Hajimeshi soldier, acting like the lowest of brigands." He glanced down at Ryori. "We can't even stay to bury him. It will be dark soon. We must go while we can, and trust that nature will be kind to his remains." He rose and began assembling their packs.

Shiko reached out and closed the sightless eyes of the cook; it was the least he could do for him, he thought. He saved my life, at the cost of his own. Now all that was left was his medallion.

The apprentice removed the honsho from around his neck. Untying the knot, he carefully threaded Ryori's medallion onto the string, where it slid up against the honsho with a gentle click. Retying the knot, he slipped the string back over his head and tucked the two together inside his tunic as he rose to help Nakama.

* * *

Pain searing through him, Hisoka made his way through the undergrowth. His breath was ragged, and sweat pored off his forehead and stung his eyes.

As soon as he had cleared the rocks back by the trail, he had pulled the sash off of his tunic. Working quickly, lest he pass out from loss of blood, he had used his good hand to awkwardly wrap the strip of cloth about his shattered arm. Once he had entered the woods, he had stopped and pulled out the remains of the arrow. He had yanked once, hard, while biting down on one of his own arrow shafts to still the scream that would have otherwise revealed his position.

Now, trying to keep ahead of any pursuit, he struggled through the dense thicket of trees, one arm still clutching his bow despite the useless arm hanging limply on the other side.

Son of a whore! he screamed inside his head. Where had that bastard Nakama come from?...All the time I was lining up my shot...he was sneaking up on me...and I missed hearing him completely!...Now I don't stand a chance of taking him out...not with this arm. What to do?...What now?

He realized he was getting dizzy. He eased himself onto a fallen log to catch his breath. Best to stop a moment, he thought; Nakama certainly wouldn't have pursued him this far. He would have gone back to check on his traitorous friends. Well, there should be one less traitor now for him to cavort with.

The bleeding from his arm, held in check for a while by his makeshift bandage, had resumed, and was now dripping down the length of the damaged limb. His thoughts started to become disjointed.

If I can't attack...perhaps I should go back...go back to Itachi, tell him what happened...no, can't admit failure; better to die...all right, then...can I get close enough to Nakama to use a dagger?...maybe...probably not. But at least I'd go down a warrior...yes, that's the way to do it...take out as many as I can...

He stood shakily. Not good enough for the Deshi, they said...good enough to be a soldier, though—

His rambling thoughts were interrupted by a piercing wail. He straightened, seeking the source of the ghastly noise, when he heard it repeated from another direction. And again, from somewhere else. All around him.

He saw the grey shapes loping into view from the trees surrounding him. Their howling reached a fever pitch, and he tried to draw his dagger, but it was too late. Razor sharp teeth tore into flesh as he went down, the animals of the forest showing no mercy this day.

22

Shiko's arms felt as if they were pulling out of their sockets. Although he was carrying the lighter end of the litter, supporting Toshi-hito's feet, it was still almost more than he could manage.

He and Nakama had set off quickly, as much from worry over being caught out in the open overnight as from concern that Hisoka would strike again. As they walked, both tried to keep an eye out for any sign of their pursuer. The constant tension wore on them, and no words were spoken other than what was necessary for maneuvering the litter.

At first Shiko did not notice the weight. Driven by a combination of anger and fear, he pushed himself to cover ground as quickly as could. As time passed, however, the surge of energy dissipated and the cold started to seep in once more. The strain on his arms went from discomfort, to pain, to searing agony. When Nakama first suggested that they rest, the apprentice shook his head, determined to push on. Later, however, at the Guard's second suggestion, Shiko acknowledged his own flagging strength. As they lowered Toshi-hito's litter the apprentice sank wearily to the ground.

Nakama briefly scouted the periphery of their resting spot but found no sign of immediate danger. He dropped tiredly next to Shiko, gratefully accepting a water skin from the apprentice. As the soldier took a deep draught, Shiko flexed cramped fingers. Just lifting the water skin hurt his arms; even so, the pain his body endured was nothing compared to the ache he felt within himself.

There had been little time for grieving after they had first left Ryori's remains behind. The overriding need to keep moving, alert to danger, while trying to man-handle the litter, had kept Shiko's mind occupied. Now, though, weary and spent, he began to doubt himself once more.

What if there is no monastery at the end of the trail? he wondered. What if the path simply ends, petering out in the hills, leaving us stranded and alone? Then Ryori's death will have been for nothing.

And, he wondered angrily, why had Hisoka attacked them in the first place? Had Itachi really sent him? He must have, Shiko decided; other than Nakama, the Guards had always obeyed every order their general had dictated. But why would Itachi send someone after them? If he had planned to kill them, why hadn't he done it there on the road, before they had separated? None of it seemed to make any sense.

Wordlessly Nakama leaned over and pressed Shiko's shoulder. Nodding, the apprentice resignedly picked himself up and shuffled over to the litter, lifting his end with a grunt. As he and Nakama slowly set off on the path once more, Shiko concluded that there was simply no telling what Itachi was thinking, or might do. All that he could be sure of was that the man was planning something, and that whatever it was it probably bode ill for those things, and people, that Shiko held dear.

By the time the sun dipped below the mountain peaks to the west, the air had chilled even more. The two litter bearers' heads were swathed in clouds of their own breath as they struggled over the uneven terrain. They had crossed above the tree line some way back, the rocky ground now supporting only the stubby growth of a few hardy shrubs.

So tired had Shiko become that it took some little while before he realized that it had begun to snow. When he did it was only the small white flakes sticking to his eyelashes that alerted him to the change. Baffled, he glanced at the bushes lining the trail. Sure enough, as he and

Nakama struggled onwards, these became gradually coated in a fine layer of white.

Inwardly Shiko almost laughed. What more, he wondered; now, not only can we starve to death but we can freeze in the snow at the same time! Oh Master, he reproached himself, directing his thoughts to the silent shape on the litter behind his back; is this what you trained me for? To take you, and others, on a fool's errand? To end up as nothing more than a snow-covered heap on some unknown mountainside?

His face set in a grim mask, Shiko forced his feet to keep moving. An hour passed, then perhaps another, before he first heard the sound. To begin with he thought his mind was playing tricks on him, or that it was the first signs of mountain sickness. Perhaps that was how it started, he thought, when one's mind became too cold to work properly.

Yet the sound did not stop. It seemed to be random notes, just at the edge of his hearing; they were melodic, peaceful. One part of him wanted to stop, to just sit down right where he was and listen to the restful notes. Another part, though, kept him moving, aided by the continuing pressure of Nakama walking with the other end of the litter and pushing him on. Slowly the sound grew louder. Nakama slowed, then both men stopped. Shiko looked over his shoulder. "You hear it too?" he croaked. At the soldier's nod, Shiko turned his head to try to better focus on the sound.

It was definitely real, and not very far away. As one, the two men began walking again, picking up the pace as much as their worn-out bodies allowed.

Nakama saw it first. As they rounded a bend in the trail he let out a hoarse shout. Shiko pulled his head up from where he was watching the ground, trying to avoid tripping over rocks, and gasped in amazement.

Not far ahead of them the trail angled down, right up to the edge of a steep cliff. A rope bridge was suspended over a deep, narrow ravine, reaching out from the cliff edge to end against a grey wall on the far side. The wall was built of huge irregular stones, and formed a substantial square on a large promontory jutting out from the opposite side of the ravine. Within the walled compound Shiko could see several buildings made of similar stones, each capped with a steeply angled roof. Mounted along the top of the surrounding wall were wind chimes; hundreds of them, their gentle notes filling the air and cascading off the edges of the ravine like a musical waterfall.

Sekai Monastery. What else could it be? thought Shiko. Toshi-hito had not been delusional then, it was here after all...

The Deshi part of his mind wondered who could have built such a complex on the far side of an impassable ravine, and why. But the part of him that was concerned with survival cast such questions aside, seeing only salvation from a cold and miserable death. The two men hurried their burden down to the rope bridge.

Two pillars supported the near end of the bridge, each a single massive piece of stone planted firmly in the ground. Shiko stepped out on the planks of the bridge, which curved out across the open space of the ravine. As the two men walked across, the bridge swayed gently.

Shiko looked down, but the bottom of the ravine was hidden in mist. It was clear, though, that it stretched a long way below them. The sound of the chimes echoed all around them as they crossed.

Set into the wall of the compound on the far side was a stout wooden gate. Upon reaching it the two men set Toshi-hito down and Shiko tried to lift an arm to pound on the gate but his arm refused to rise up, and all he could do was lean against the coarse wood. Looking behind him he saw Nakama, equally spent, holding on to the ropes of the bridge, trying to stay upright. With a determined effort Shiko pushed himself back off the door, his clouded mind seeing a pull-cord extending from the stone frame of the gate. Ignoring the stabbing pain of his muscles, he reached for the cord and pulled it. The sound of a deep gong cut through the lighter notes of the chimes. Even the small effort of pulling the cord sapped what little reserves Shiko had left, and he leaned once more against the gate.

Above his head a small window in the door slid open. An old pair of eyes looked out, startled to see the Guard leaning against the side of the bridge, and a figure lying on a litter on the ground. Then his eyes traveled further down and saw a head covered with snowflakes just beneath his little window. Quickly the window closed, and the great gate began to swing open.

Shiko, too tired to move, swung with it, falling forward onto hands and knees as the gate opened. Worn out arms could not hold him up, and he passed out in the snow.

He must have been unconscious for only a few moments, for his next impressions were of many hands helping to carry him. He could tell he was indoors, presumably in one of the buildings they had seen from across the ravine. He heard voices, but they were quiet, muted; he wasn't able to pick up more than a few isolated words: "...nearly frozen...Deshi...bring Abbot Akiya..." Some of the voices were male, others female. The hallway they traversed seemed dim, although he could make out torches placed along the walls at regular intervals.

Finally Shiko felt himself being lowered onto something soft. He looked about, and saw them setting down an apparently senseless Nakama next to him. Trying to speak, Shiko croaked out, "Toshi—Toshi-hito. Is he—?"

Hands were placed on his face, fingers on his lips. Their touch was warm, and calming. A gentle female voice said, "Quiet, now. All will be well." And then he passed out again.

When he woke, it was to find several robed figures standing near his feet. All were looking at him and his companions with worry and concern.

Turning his head first to one side then the other, Shiko saw Nakama lying to his left and Toshi-hito, still on the litter, to his right. The robed men were talking softly to one another; if there had been any women there, Shiko did not see them now. As he watched, an older man, wearing the same dark brown habit as the rest, entered the room. The apprentice heard someone say, "We brought them inside immediately, Abbot. Brother Numa is already on his way from the sick ward."

While the first man spoke, the older one knelt down next to the still-unconscious Nakama. Putting a hand on Nakama's head, he looked the Guard over. "From Hajimeshi," he said. Turning to look at Shiko, he noted that the apprentice was awake. "And a Deshi."

Shiko heard another voice say, "The other is also Deshi, Abbot. He has been wounded."

The Abbot moved quickly past the apprentice to Toshi-hito's litter. Shiko's mind was still murky, but it seemed to him that as the man leaned down to look at Toshi-hito's face his eyes widened in surprise. Turning to those waiting the Abbot said quietly, "Go and hurry Brother Numa along, will you? Tell him this is not just another broken bone from a slip on icy steps."

One of the men left, and Shiko could see an open doorway beyond, where the man had stood. An even older man hovered nervously just outside in the hallway, leaning on a staff. He was not dressed in a robe like the others. He said, "Don't know how long they was out there, Abbot. Not sure if they'd done seen the bell pull. I opened the gate soon's I saw 'em."

The Abbot continued to examine Toshi-hito, carefully unwrapping the bandaged arm. Without turning away from his task he said, "It's all right, Tusoda. You did well." Shiko saw the old man, Tusoda, nod, and with a final worried look at Shiko and his companions move out of the apprentice's line of sight.

Tusoda was evidently making room for Brother Numa, who was of rather more substantial girth than any of the others Shiko had seen. At Abbot Akiya's urgent gesture the large man moved quickly over to Toshi-hito. Shiko tried to raise himself up, to tell them about the poison, but his head began to swim and he passed out again.

* * *

The sound of scribbling filtered into Shiko's mind. The steady scritch, scritch, scritch became a point of focus, and he tried to discern its source. Ah, he realized, it's not inside my head; it's out there somewhere...

Slowly he managed to pry open one of his eyes. He saw one of the robed figures sitting next to him, busily inscribing on a sheet of parchment. Turning his head slowly Shiko saw that he still lay where they had brought him, with Toshi-hito to his right. Nakama, however, was gone.

Shiko started to lift himself up, and the movement caught the eye of the scribbler. "Oh," said the young man, quickly setting aside his writing, "wait, let me help you." He reached behind Shiko's shoulders and helped him to sit upright. The apprentice felt a weight dangling around his neck and realized that his honsho, along with Ryori's medallion, had slid out of his tunic. He tucked them back inside as he sat upright.

This time his head remained clear, but his mouth felt as if it were full of cotton when he tried to speak. Handed a wooden cup of water, the apprentice downed it eagerly while the young Brother anticipated his first questions. "You have been asleep for some time. I imagine you must be quite hungry."

"Yes," answered Shiko, as he looked over at Toshi-hito. "But, my—my companion, is he all right?"

The robed man, not much older than Shiko himself, said softly, "He is still very ill, I'm afraid. Brother Numa has done what he can. We must trust in the Fates for his recovery."

"The Fates?" asked Shiko, as he struggled to stand.

The young man lent a hand in support. "Yes, the Fates. We cannot predict which paths they will offer to him, or which he shall choose to follow." As Shiko gained his balance, he added, "I am Brother Konya. Do you feel well enough to walk?"

Feeling weak but at least able to hold his own, Shiko said, "Yes, I think so." He tried to bow but found it made his head woozy again. As Konya reached out a hand to steady him once more, the apprentice said sheepishly, "Sorry. My name is Shiko."

"Yes, I know," replied Konya, nodding toward where Nakama had lain. "Your other companion told us your name." Peering into Shiko's face, Konya said, "If you're still unwell, I can have some food brought to you here."

"No, no, I'll be fine, thank you. Where is Nakama? Is he—?"

"He is fine. He is being attended to. If you feel up to it, please follow me," said Konya as he edged toward the door. "Abbot Akiya has asked that you be fed, and then, after a bath, that you be brought to him."

Abbot Akiya. Shiko remembered now; he was the older man who had looked at them when they had first been carried in. Toshi-hito had said, "...you must speak with the Abbot..." This must be the same one. But what was Shiko supposed to tell him? He still didn't know.

The apprentice looked down at the Deshi Master, and thought of Brother Konya's words: trusting the Fates. Well, he reflected, that is pretty much what I have done ever since the Master fell ill. If this Brother Numa could not do more for him, there is little else I can do to help. I *am* starving; there is no point in trying to stay and maintain a vigil if I pass out again from lack of food. And I must speak with this Abbot Akiya.

Nevertheless it was a reluctant Deshi apprentice who nodded to Konya and followed the Brother out into the hall.

As the two turned down the passage neither man saw, at the opposite end of the hallway, a figure watching quietly from the shadows.

The watcher, dressed in the same robes as all the Brothers, save that the robe's hood was pulled forward over the head, observed Konya and Shiko until they had passed out of sight. Moving silently, the hooded figure emerged from the shadows and moved directly for the door to the room where Toshi-hito still lay.

Once inside the watcher stopped. A pair of hands reached up and pulled back the hood, revealing a woman of middle years. Her lined face was framed by shoulder-length hair streaked with shades of grey.

She stood for some time, staring down at the quiescent figure before her. Finally she knelt down beside Toshi-hito and studied his face. No emotion played across her features, but the eyes spoke of great deliberation within. She looked away and held up both of her hands, staring at them as if she were seeing them for the first time. Turning them first this way, then that, she took a deep breath. Then she reached out with both hands toward the unconscious Toshi-hito.

As Shiko and Konya walked the stone hallways, the apprentice noticed that he was actually warm. If he hadn't known better he would have sworn that he was in the priory at Hajimeshi rather than up among snow-bound mountains. Looking down toward the floor of the corridor, he saw bamboo pipes running along the base of the walls on either side, with what sounded like water running through them. Once, as his foot brushed near one, he could feel heat radiating from it.

It was heated water, he realized; they must run heated water through the bamboo pipes, and it kept the inside of the monastery warm! He wanted to ask Konya about it, but the young Brother was walking briskly and the still-weak apprentice needed all his breath just to keep up. In the hallways they passed a number of other Brothers, and a few women as well, all dressed in the same robes. Konya greeted them all as "Brother." Each bowed in greeting to Shiko and the apprentice, somewhat unsteadily, tried to bow politely in return.

Konya led Shiko to a windowless, low-ceilinged room, unfurnished save for floor mats and a few torches mounted along the walls. A handful of figures sat upon the mats throughout the room, eating from bowls. The smell of food came wafting through an adjoining doorway.

Able to catch his breath at last, Shiko turned to Konya. "Do you all come from Tejinashi?" he asked. "Do you use magic to keep the water in the pipes hot?"

Konya, looking uncomfortable, turned away. With a slight hesitation he said, "Abbot Akiya will answer your questions. Please, sit, I will bring you something to eat."

But Shiko did not sit immediately; he was looking around at the others within the room, searching for Nakama. Konya evidently noticed, for he said, "If you are looking for your other friend, he is not here. Come, make yourself comfortable while I bring food."

"But where *is* Nakama?" asked Shiko with some anxiety. "Has he already eaten? I would like to see him."

His expression unchanged, Konya stared back. "Your friend is not here," he repeated. "Do not fear; he is well." With that Konya left for the kitchen, leaving Shiko in the dimly lit room.

The apprentice felt his skin crawl. There was something about this place, he thought. Something…odd. A feeling of some kind pricked at the back of his neck. He wasn't sure what it was, or what it meant. He wasn't even sure that it was a bad feeling; it was just…odd. As Konya returned with some hot stew, he finally sat down on one of the mats.

"Are you sure you're all right?" asked Konya, handing Shiko the bowl.

"Yes," answered Shiko, not really sure at all, "yes, I'm fine."

After he had eaten Shiko was escorted to the monastery's small bathhouse. To the apprentice the bath was a wondrous affair, containing a large wooden barrel filled from a stream of hot water. The water flowed from one end of a pipe like those Shiko had seen in the hallways. Once he had washed away the dirt and grime of many days on the road, he donned a Brother's robe that was a size too large and rejoined Konya.

The Brother looked the apprentice up and down, observing the poor fit of the robe on Shiko's frame. "Well, it will suffice until your own clothes have been washed. Come, let me take you to the Abbot. He is waiting for you in the garden."

Thinking of the snow outside, Shiko wondered how a garden could grow in such an inhospitable climate. He was somewhat taken aback when, instead of heading outdoors, Konya led him into yet another large walled-in chamber. This one, however, did not have a roof of stone. Amazingly, the entire ceiling appeared made of glass.

Great clear panes, angled so that the snow outside slipped off, had been laid atop substantial wooden beams. As bright as the dining hall was dark, this room was suffused with light everywhere. Rows of plants, mostly vegetables, were growing in the soil that formed the room's only flooring. Large barrels full of water stood around the edges of the room, with more of the bamboo pipes draining into their open tops. From the surface of the water in each barrel steam rose in gentle clouds, thus raising the temperature in the room considerably over that of the rest of the monastery. Softly, the sound muffled by the glass ceiling, Shiko could hear the many wind chimes from the walls outside. The light, and the sound, made the whole room seem a serene and peaceful place.

The bright noonday sunlight streaming down from overhead was the first daylight Shiko had seen since awakening, and he realized then that he must have slept through the night. It had been near dusk when he and Nakama had staggered up to the monastery's gate. It was no wonder that he had awoken so hungry.

Absorbing the wonders of the remarkable garden room, Shiko didn't even see Akiya until Konya said, "I have brought the Deshi to see you, Abbot." Shiko looked down toward the far end of the room and recognized the older man whom he had seen shortly after his arrival. The man was sitting on the ground, digging in the soil just off a path that led between the rows of plants. Looking up as Konya spoke, Akiya waved a small hand hoe in their direction.

"Thank you, Konya. Come here, young man," he said to Shiko, "sit with me while I tend my little flock."

Konya nodded to Shiko and left. The Deshi apprentice advanced hesitantly to where Akiya sat working the soil, and knelt respectfully a short distance away. Upon closer inspection, Abbot Akiya appeared little older than Toshi-hito, although his hair was a silvery-grey. His hands and robe were covered with dirt from working with the garden soil. The Abbot tilled the small plot in the garden with a slow, confident manner, continuing his work as he spoke. "I see Brother Konya has provided for you. I trust you are feeling somewhat better than when you first arrived?"

Reminded of how desperate had been his and Nakama's situation before they had reached the monastery, Shiko bowed low, forehead to the dirt floor. "I offer you our sincerest thanks, Abbot Akiya, for the hospitality you have shown us. We would not have survived a night in the open. I and my companions are forever in your debt."

Akiya waved his hand. "Posh on that, my boy. Sit yourself up." As Shiko rose, he went on. "Our doors are never closed here. Well," he amended, "not figuratively, anyway. The gate, as you saw, was shut; but that is to keep every animal in the mountains from wandering in to join us." He carefully drew small furrows in the soil with his hand hoe. "I see you are appreciative of our garden." Shiko realized then that the Abbot must have been watching him as he came in, even while tilling his soil. "It is, beyond a doubt, our favorite accomplishment here at Sekai. And all without aid or benefit of magic." He said this without any hint of rancor, only a sense of pride. It made Shiko wonder who these people really were who had exiled themselves into the cold hills. The mention of magic had made Konya very uncomfortable; were the Brothers outcasts from Tejinashi? Rebels of some sort?

Akiya ran his fingers through the loamy soil. "I come here every day, to do a little gardening. I like to keep in touch with the ground from which we all sprout." He looked at Shiko keenly. "But I don't believe you traveled this far just to admire our garden. Tell me, young man, what brings you here, you and your Hajimeshi Guard companion, bearing an ailing Deshi Master?"

Reminded of Toshi-hito's entreaty to speak to the Abbot, but still with no idea of what he was supposed to say, Shiko blurted out, "Master Toshi-hito—that is his name—he was wounded by a poisoned sword. He has been very ill. Can your healer—that is, does your healer know if he will live?"

The Abbot reached into a pouch on the ground beside him. Pulling out a handful of seeds he began laying them in the furrows. "That is a question that only the Fates can decide." At that moment a door on the far side of the garden opened, and another Brother entered. Walking silently toward them, the Brother stopped and sat a discreet distance away from Akiya.

Shiko noted that the newcomer was a woman, with streaks of grey in her hair. She said nothing nor did Akiya speak to her. He merely looked in her direction as she sat down, and she returned the look with a silent, unreadable expression. She folded her hands in her lap and cast her eyes down, as if studying the nature of the soil floor of the garden. Akiya turned away from her and paid her no more attention. Shiko assumed her to be Akiya's assistant, or a scribe.

The Abbot continued. "Sometimes the Fates can be influenced, and a soul may take an unintended path. When that happens, who can say where the path will eventually lead?" He patted the soil over the top of some of his seeds. "Your concern for your Deshi Master is most commendable. But, my young friend, you have not yet answered my question. Why have *you* come to Sekai Monastery?"

Shiko felt once again that odd sensation on the back of his neck. Was it the heat of this room, he wondered, making him uncomfortable? Or was it the arrival of the female Brother that made him feel strange? He stole a glance at her, and was startled to see her staring intently at him. There was no expression on her face, but her eyes never blinked. They seemed locked onto his own eyes, as if he were the only focus of her attention. Glancing down, he saw her hands lying limply in her lap, as if they were not even a part of her.

Unsettled, Shiko returned his gaze to the Abbot. "I—we were looking for shelter, of course, and help, for Toshi-hito. We—we were also part of a pilgrimage."

"Oh? And what are you seeking?"

Shiko looked down at the ground. All of a sudden he found it difficult to admit to the failure of the quest that he had been a part of. How could he describe his own inability to see the pilgrimage through? There was no answer he could give that would do anything but highlight his own failure to keep the pilgrimage alive when Toshi-hito had fallen ill. But the Deshi creed was one of honesty before all else, so only the truth would suffice.

"I—that is, my companions and I—are, or rather we were, on a quest to seek the Kotaishi. The Shizen have prophesied that only the Kotaishi can unite Tonogato against a great Darkness that is coming."

Akiya sat back and regarded Shiko with a penetrating stare. "I see. And did you find the Kotaishi?"

"No. No, we have not found him. And—I'm afraid that now we never will." Shiko told Akiya about their journey: the Kojuro's mandate for the Hikari pilgrimage; the difficulties they had encountered in Yutakashi; the tense confrontation in Shukyoshi; and the struggle since then to maintain the group's purpose once Toshi-hito had fallen ill.

Akiya listened silently, save to ask for an occasional clarification. He finished tamping down his seeds, and reached for a small watering can sitting nearby. "I am very sorry to hear about the death of your companion, the cook. I will send some of the Brothers down the trail to attend to his body." He started watering each of his furrows. "And so you believe this Lord Itachi will not be pursuing the pilgrimage's goal of seeking the Kotaishi?"

"I'm not sure, Abbot. I don't believe he will, but I'm not really sure what he intends at all." Shiko chanced a look back at the other Brother sitting nearby. She was still staring at him. "I—I am not sure what he will try to do in Tejinashi, now that he has taken the Hikari." He tried to keep his voice calm and even, but found it hard to keep a slight bitterness from creeping in.

Akiya was too astute to overlook it. "You feel responsibility for letting go of the Hikari." It was a statement, rather than a question.

Shiko nodded sadly. "The Kojuro himself placed it into my hands. I was entrusted with it; even though I didn't always carry it myself, I always knew where it was." Softly he said, "Now I've let it be taken away."

The Abbot finished watering, and set aside the can. "Do not worry about the lamp, Shiko. It is but a symbol of the light that guides your pilgrimage. If you have the light within you, then you have no need of the symbol. The symbol only exists to lead others whose clarity of purpose may not be as strong." He stood up, brushing the loose soil from his robe. Both Shiko and the nearby Brother rose as well. "You speak as if the pilgrimage is over, since this Itachi has made off with the Hikari. I submit that your true search has only just begun. You must now find your own way, follow your own inner light, to locate the object of your quest."

The odd feeling that Shiko had felt in the dining hall came back to him very strongly at that instant, at the same moment that a spark of hope flared within him. Continue the pilgrimage? Search for the Kotaishi without the Hikari?

He felt as if his mind had somehow turned a page in a book, and that now a whole new set of words confronted him, each with new possibilities. Could he do it, he wondered. Could he continue the pilgrimage anyway?

He thought back to the Hikari lighting ceremony, when the Kojuro had suddenly turned to him and placed the Hikari into his hands. Despite his shock, the Kojuro's words had stuck in his mind: "Let he who accepts this lamp be the guide for all others, the beacon that lights the way for those who would follow." The *person* was the beacon, he realized, not the lamp. Only now did the words make sense to him. The Kojuro had entrusted him with the responsibility to be the guide; the lamp was only a representation of his role.

But was he worthy of that responsibility? If the person was supposed to be the guide, why had the Kojuro not given the Hikari to Toshi-hito? The Deshi Master would have been a far better choice to be a guide for others.

Then he realized why the Hikari had not been given to the Deshi Master. Shiko remembered the look on Itachi's face during the ceremony, how out of place it had seemed. At the time it had not meant anything to him, other than to make him feel uncomfortable. Now he understood. Even then Itachi must have been plotting against his brother; he had lusted after the lamp, for the prestige of being the pilgrimage leader, to use it for his own ends.

What was it the Kojuro had said about me? 'He is untainted by the politics, the temptations, that those of us of greater years have experienced.' Giving me the lamp, he concluded, was a way to avoid the conflict that would have ensued with Itachi, had he given the Hikari to Toshi-hito. I was just convenient, a way to avoid a problem. I was not chosen for any special reason. So what makes me think I can be a guide now, and lead the pilgrimage on my own?

He thought about Nusumi and Kanyo, leading a daily life of subterfuge and rebellion in Yutakashi. Every day of their lives they risked themselves for something they believed in. He thought about Toshi-hito, standing alone in Shukyoshi, surrounded by enemies. Standing his ground for the pilgrimage.

And what have I done, he thought. I stood up to Itachi, and followed Toshi-hito's wishes to come here. But how can that compare with the sacrifices that others have made? How can I presume to conduct the pilgrimage by myself? How would I even begin?

Then, quite suddenly, it came to him.

It doesn't matter, he realized. It doesn't matter if I don't know *how* to do it. If I knew, then it wouldn't be a pilgrimage. The whole point of it being a pilgrimage is that it is a search for something that cannot be easily found. Toshi-hito had not been sure of how to find the Kotaishi either, he simply had a plan that he had hoped would reveal the Kotaishi to him in the end.

That is what I must do, Shiko decided. I must search now, and let my heart lead me where it needs to go.

Then he stopped himself. What about Toshi-hito? I cannot leave until I know his fate. Pilgrimage or no, I cannot abandon him now. I helped bring him here. I will stay with him until—until I know which of the Fates' paths he has taken.

All of these thoughts flashed through Shiko's mind in an instant, like the sudden flaring of a torch coming alight in a dark room. He bowed deeply to Akiya. "Your words are both wise and true, Abbot Akiya."

Unconsciously he squared his shoulders. "I must, and I will, carry on the quest, even if by myself alone. That is the only honorable path, and the path that is right. However," he added, "I must stay until I know if Toshi-hito—if Toshi-hito—"

He paused in mid-sentence as the door at the far end of the room opened again. Through it strode the last person Shiko expected to see up and about. His jaw dropped as he watched Toshi-hito walk up to them. The Deshi Master bowed to the Abbot.

"Greetings, old friend," said Toshi-hito as he straightened. "I apologize for arriving in so inconvenient a manner."

The Abbot waved his hand again as he returned the bow. "No need for apologies between us; never has been." He turned toward Shiko. "Your apprentice was just speaking of you, I believe."

Shiko was astounded at Toshi-hito's appearance. The Deshi Master looked perfectly healthy. He still wore his worn traveling clothes, his tunic missing the sleeve that Ryori had removed to tend to his injury. Yet his arm was no longer bandaged; the apprentice could see only a slight red line to mark where the poisoned wound had been.

How could this be, he wondered. Could this Brother Numa be so well versed in medicines and herbs? Even so, how could the wound on Toshi-hito's arm have almost completely disappeared?

His amazement turned to embarrassment as Toshi-hito turned toward him and bowed deeply. "The Brothers have told me of your resolution in carrying me to Sekai. I owe you my life."

Conscious of the others watching, Shiko returned the bow. "Master," he said, "I am—I am—astonished. Pleased, too, of course. How—?"

"Perhaps," interrupted Akiya, "we should rejoin your other companion, the Hajimeshi Guard. We may then all hear of your journey so far. As I understand it," he added with a look at Toshi-hito, "you have missed a great deal of…recent events."

"That is true," answered Toshi-hito. "And I would like to express my thanks to Nakama as well." He turned to look at the female Brother standing nearby. No words were exchanged; to an observer, they merely caught each other's glance for a moment. Then Akiya spoke again.

"Come," he said, taking Toshi-hito by the arm. "I also want to hear more of what you've been up to these many years." As the two apparent acquaintances walked together from the room, Shiko, still stunned, followed. He noted, though, that the other Brother remained behind, her eyes staying on him until he had turned the corner.

* * *

They came upon Nakama in another part of the monastery. Shiko determined that it must have been a library of some sort, judging by the many scrolls that lined the walls in pigeon-holed frameworks. Nakama, however, was not reading, nor were the Brothers who were keeping him company. The Hajimeshi soldier and three of the Brothers sat together, on four sides of a large mat, their heads bowed over in deep concentration. At first Shiko thought that perhaps they were studying something of great interest that lay between them. That is, until he heard the unmistakable sound of dice.

As Akiya, Toshi-hito, and Shiko approached Nakama looked up briefly from his game. Seeing Shiko first, he waved his hand distractedly. "Shiko! Good to see you're up and about. You won't believe this game they have taught me. Amazing! With only three throws you can—" At that moment, Nakama's gaze strayed to the other newcomers in the room and his eyes opened wide. "Toshi-hito!"

Quickly he stood up, almost knocking over the Brothers with whom he had so recently been engrossed. He looked the Deshi Master up and down as if disbelieving what his eyes were showing him. "Toshi-hito! But how—?" He looked questioningly first at Shiko, then at Akiya. The Abbot did not answer his question, though, only replying with a statement of his own.

"I am glad that our brethren have been able to share some of our pastimes with you." He nodded at the three Brothers, who in turn bowed respectfully and withdrew. "As you can see," he added with a chuckle, "we require more than books to keep our minds busy during long winter nights."

Nakama, however, was still looking in awe at Toshi-hito. The Deshi Master, as he had done with Shiko, bowed to the startled Hajimeshi Guard. "You endured much in the effort to carry me, when I was unable to help myself. My thanks to you, Nakama."

Quite embarrassed, Nakama returned the bow quickly. He turned toward Akiya. "Whatever healing abilities you have here, they are unlike anything I have ever seen. Poor Ryori; he would have been amazed to see it!"

"Ryori?" asked Toshi-hito with a frown. "Has something befallen him?"

In the awkward silence that ensued, Shiko realized that he had not yet had an opportunity to explain to Toshi-hito everything that had transpired. Slowly he drew the honsho out from around his neck, Ryori's medallion still clinking against his own. Holding the medallion up for Toshi-hito to see he said quietly, "Ryori gave his life for mine, while we were on the trail coming here. He asked me to return this to his family."

Toshi-hito took the medallion in his hand, peering at it carefully. With a sigh, he handed it back to the apprentice. "It was as I suspected." He shook his head in sorrow. "Poor recompense for such a good man. His 'family,' as you say, will be greatly saddened to have lost him. But I believe he, and his 'family,' were aware of the special risks when he joined us."

Shiko frowned. "What do you mean, Master? What special risks?"

The Deshi Master looked at his apprentice with eyes full of sadness. "I had suspected that cooking was not Ryori's only skill, although he was quite good at that as well." He pointed to the medallion Shiko still held in his hand. "That is the symbol for the House of Himitsu. It means, in all probability, that our friend Ryori was one of Himitsu's 'associates,' placed among us to be the chamberlain's, and the Kojuro's, eyes and ears."

Shiko and Nakama looked at each other in surprise. To Shiko it explained some of the cook's odd behavior during the journey. As he remembered Ryori's resourcefulness during the fight at the inn in Yutakashi, he almost missed Toshi-hito's quiet comment, "I doubt he would have known how important was the sacrifice he made."

"Master?" queried Shiko, but the Deshi Master did not explain.

Instead Toshi-hito said, "When we return to Hajimeshi, Shiko, you must keep your promise. Take Ryori's remembrance to Himitsu, and let his memory be honored."

The apprentice nodded solemnly in reply, placing his honsho and the medallion back inside his tunic.

"Well," said Akiya gently, "it would appear that you have some catching up to do, Toshi-hito. Perhaps we should take advantage of this meeting spot," as he pointed to the erstwhile gaming location, "so that you may all discuss what has transpired, and what will be done."

And so Shiko and Nakama recounted what had befallen them since Toshi-hito had dislodged the money bag from one of Itachi's men, which was the last thing the Deshi Master recalled. Toshi-hito listened, saying little other than to inquire about specific things Itachi said or did. When Nakama recounted the attack by Hisoka, Toshi-hito's only comment was, "So bold? Itachi either has a plan he feels is without fault, or he has slipped past the bounds of rational thought." It was clear the Deshi Master was worried about the Hajimeshi lord, and what the man planned to do.

As Shiko described their approach to Sekai, Akiya took up the thread of the tale. "When Tusoda, our watchman, opened the gate and sounded the alarm, we were quite surprised to find two Deshi and a Hajimeshi Castle Guard collapsed on our threshold. The Brothers took you all to the warmest part of the monastery, and they called me from my study." He cast an apologetic glance at Toshi-hito. "Having fallen asleep atop the parchment scroll I was reading at my desk, I had not heeded the alarm. It is an occupational hazard of age, I am told." He sat back and looked into his friend's face. "I recognized you right away, of course, despite," he added with a pointing finger, "all those lines that were not there when last we...well, never mind," he amended. "And now, you have all had a chance to rest, and to eat. Sekai can provide you with horses, so you need not travel on foot. But you must tell me, where do you plan to go from here?"

"To Tejinashi," said Shiko suddenly. All heads turned to look at him. He flushed in embarrassment, unsure of why he had spoken up so forcefully. He cast his gaze downward. "I'm sorry, I didn't mean to sound so presumptuous."

Akiya drew his lips into a thin line. Toshi-hito, however, cocked his head at the apprentice. "Not at all," said the Deshi Master. "You have every right to speak your mind. Tell us why we must go on to Tejinashi."

Shiko swallowed hard, trying to overcome his awkwardness at discussing strategy with his elders. "The Kotaishi must unite all of Tonogato. Itachi may go to Tejinashi to find him, but more than likely he will simply try to find allies in his cause for overthrowing his brother, the Kojuro." As he spoke, the thoughts fell into place inside his head, almost without effort. It became so clear, what they had to do. "If Itachi tries to use the Hikari for that purpose, the Tejinashi will not be very receptive to another band of pilgrims from Hajimeshi trying to spread the word about the Kotaishi. Therefore we must go to the city and speak directly to the Zaitan council and their leader, the Kordaijan, and tell them what has happened. Once they understand, surely they will support us rather than Itachi."

The other men looked at each other, and Shiko noted their silence. Concerned that he had sounded foolish, Shiko looked down once more. "I'm—I'm sorry, I shouldn't have spoken," thinking how naïve his plan must seem to them.

Akiya, who had visibly tensed when Shiko had mentioned the Zaitan, said stiffly, "Those who rule Tejinashi are unlikely to be swayed by sentiment. What appears fair or honorable to you or I has little bearing on what course of action they choose to pursue."

Toshi-hito reached out and put a hand on Akiya's arm. Shiko noted that he used what had been his injured arm, now completely back to normal. "Old friend," the Deshi Master said, "do not let your prejudices toward the Zaitan blind you. As your Fates would tell you, many times the simple, the direct, proves in the end to be superior to the complex and involved." He turned to his apprentice. "Your path contains many potential dangers, Shiko, for the behavior of the Zaitan cannot, as Akiya has said, be judged as others can be judged. But our purpose is clear: we must find the Kotaishi. I believe," he added with a nod toward Shiko, "that our instincts may well indeed be our best guide."

The following morning the three Hajimeshi prepared once more for the road. As they mounted the horses provided by the Abbot, Akiya spoke as he held Toshi-hito's reins. "The Brothers I sent out to tend to your companion Ryori found one more as well. Another Hajimeshi Guard, from the description. It would appear he ran afoul of the wolves that frequent these mountains."

Toshi-hito nodded sadly. "The hunter ending as prey. An unfortunate end."

"Well," said Akiya, "at least you will not have to worry about him on your way to Tejinashi." The Abbot shifted his grip to Toshi-hito's leg, saying earnestly, "Be careful, my friend. I have few remaining supporters in that place, but you will not have even that. Go carefully."

Toshi-hito patted his friend's hand. "I will, Akiya. Trust your Fates. All will be well." The Deshi Master spurred his horse toward the gate.

Shiko, once more reunited with his own tunic, rode up to the Abbot, and the older man looked up to him. "Travel well, young man," Akiya said. "Bear your light with confidence."

Shiko half-bowed back from the saddle. "Thank you, Abbot Akiya. And good fortune with your garden!" Akiya waved him on, and Shiko passed through the gate held open by Tusoda. The old man raised his staff in a farewell gesture, doing the same for Nakama as the Guard followed Shiko out.

The morning air was cold, but the sky as yet was clear. The sun was just peaking over the eastern hilltops, casting shadows in sharp relief around them. Far to the south, though, Shiko could see masses of dark clouds, and knew that rain was falling heavily there.

The horses walked easily through the shallow snow once the now-reduced pilgrim party had cleared the bridge. Shiko noticed Toshi-hito looking intently back toward the monastery. Turning in his saddle, Shiko strained to see what his Master was looking at.

He could make out a solitary figure, standing atop the wall watching the pilgrims depart. It was hard to make out for sure but it appeared to Shiko that it was the same female Brother he had seen earlier sitting beside Abbot Akiya in the garden. Although she was too far away to see clearly, he could almost sense her short, greying hair, blowing in the breeze, her hands held before her. It caused that odd sensation he had felt inside the monastery to flood back through him, a feeling of...what? He still wasn't sure.

He caught a glimmer out of the corner of his eye, causing him to look down into the canyon below the monastery. He tried to find what had attracted his attention, but saw nothing. Looking back toward the monastery, he saw that the Brother was gone. He turned back in the saddle and settled himself in for the long ride.

The Deshi Master, too, had seen the glimmer from the canyon, but he had known what it was. He had recognized the well-camouflaged shape of a horse and rider as it threaded the precipitous, almost invisible path he knew existed on the far side of the ravine. Only the chance glint of sunlight reflecting off a bit of harness had revealed the rider to him. He knew that the rider had emerged from the monastery's postern gate, opening on the far side of the canyon. Inwardly he nodded to himself, knowing that the messenger would reach Tejinashi before them.

Then, knowing too that she would have already left the wall, he took one last look at Sekai before returning his attention to the trail ahead.

23

The letter had traveled a long way, and a slow way at that. It had to, for it was the first of its nature. Getting it into Tejinashi, and into the right hands, had required careful planning on the part of the sender, along with the patience not to cut corners. Any small slip along the way and the seeds planted decades ago might be turned up out of the ground and laid bare, withering before ever having had a chance to grow.

The letter's recipient fingered the small leather pouch. It had arrived without warning, left by a tradesman making a routine delivery. Opening the pouch revealed a letter written on fine parchment, sealed with wax. The insignia impressed on the wax was a special one, known only to the sender and to the one who should read it. By such did the reader first know that what had arrived was of great import.

Breaking the seal, the reader scanned a page covered in nonsensical characters. At least that would be the impression that anyone else might have had. The greatest codes, however, are those that have a key known only to those who correspond. In this case the two had created their own code years ago, and had committed it fully to memory. Thus the lines of seemingly meaningless characters came alive under the scrutiny of the reader.

"Dear Friend," began the letter. "I trust you are well. There are some events of which I feel you should be aware." The letter recounted the prophecy of the Shizen regarding the impending Darkness, and the

Kojuro's pilgrimage to seek the Kotaishi. "It is to this latter issue," wrote the letter's author, "that I find I must, at last, seek your aid. I suspect neither of us, in those days well past, knew where our association might lead. Most certainly, this was not the circumstance I expected would be the catalyst. But all other avenues available to me have run dry. Yours is my only recourse."

Curiosity piqued, the reader continued on. "Shortly after the pilgrimage left Hajimeshi, the Kojuro's daughter, Princess Mikasama, foolishly ran away in pursuit of a soldier sent along with them. She was aided in this endeavor by her guardian, Komori..." Ah, thought the reader, the reason for the letter becomes clearer... "The Kojuro is, of course, consumed with worry, for he loves his daughter dearly..."

The reader stopped, and stared at the flame of the brazier set into the floor a few feet away. Love, of course, was of great significance, whether it should be for a daughter, or for another; but it paled in comparison to the consequences should the Kojuro's daughter be lost. Yes, without Mikasama, things will be bad, very bad indeed...

The flames flicked this way and that, casting dancing shadows all about the room. The shadows popped up, swirled menacingly, then just as rapidly disappeared, only to reappear elsewhere.

"I have not been able," continued the letter, "despite all my resources, to locate the Kojuro's daughter, or her guardian. They may have fallen prey to one of the many dangers on the road, although even in that event my sources should have been able to tell me their fate. Had they become a meal for some creature of the forest, I believe that news too would have come to us..."

Ah, thought the reader, so you too know the truth about the nature of the Shizen. Well, it should not surprise me what you know. Which makes the fact that even you cannot find two women, wandering alone in the countryside, most surprising...

"I beg your indulgence, that you do whatever you can to seek out the Princess. You know what is at risk. I leave it to you how to deal with it should you find her."

The letter was signed, "Your Tired Friend."

The letter was re-read once, to ensure no nuance was overlooked, then carefully fed as fuel into the brazier until nothing remained. The leather pouch would be discarded tomorrow.

The reader sat back, thinking. Certainly a matter of grave import. And undoubtedly worthy of breaking years of silence, given the stakes. But it was also clear that, behind the words that were written, there was the plea of a heart-broken man for a woman believed lost.

*   *   *

The rain left Mikasama and Shudojo drenched. At first they had waited out the worst of it underneath the dense foliage of a wild jaku bush, the huge sponge-like leaves intercepting the heaviest of the rain. But eventually hunger drove them onward once more, rain or no.

They soon found a patch of lakata plants, the roots of which Shudojo said were edible if unappealing. The upper stalk of the plant sprouted razor-sharp leaves. "Be careful when you pull the plant out of the ground," said the Sister. "Grab it like this." She knelt down and wrapped her hand tightly around the base, tugging upwards until she had worked the plant out of the ground. The wet soil allowed the plant to come free fairly easily. The roots were fattened tubes, covered now with mud and looking quite unappetizing. Shudojo held them in the rain to clean them after snapping off the upper plant, and then began casually nibbling the whitish roots.

Mikasama screwed up her face in distaste. As the rain rolled across her face, she debated the merits of staying hungry versus tackling the lakata roots. She felt tired, so very tired. It seemed to her as if she had spent her whole life on the road; or rather, wandering across a road-less countryside. What was it Shudojo had said? Something about it feeling like everything had happened to someone else? She decided that's how she felt right now. That Princess who woke to warm baths, her hair tended lovingly by Komori; that person must have been someone else. Or else it was a dream, of some life she had never really lived.

She reached up and fingered the tangled mass of black hair that hung in dripping tendrils from her head. It had been so pretty once. Hadn't it? Hadn't Komori combed it, brushed it, until it lay like a silken blanket across her shoulders? Hadn't Nakama run his fingers through it lovingly?

Nakama...

"Lady?" Shudojo interrupted her daydreaming. "Are you going to eat?"

Brought back to the present, Mikasama's hunger cried out for relief. With a sigh of resignation she knelt down in the mud and tugged on one of the lakata plants. Immediately she drew back with a cry of pain.

"I told you to be careful," said Shudojo. "The leaves are sharp as a knife. Pull it like I showed you."

Sucking on her injured finger, Mikasama fought back a flash of resentment. It does no good to be angry with Shudojo, she reminded herself. I'm here because I chose to be here. If there's anyone to blame, it's me.

As she pulled up the lakata plant, this time taking greater care to avoid the leaves, Shudojo's mention of a knife caused her to think about the fight with the men back at the inn. She remembered that Shudojo had told her to sing while the Sister had grabbed for something in her pack. Mikasama had thought at the time that it was for a knife to defend them with. Out in the yard behind the inn, though, just before the men attacked, Shudojo had said she had lost her knife a long time ago. No, not lost, she remembered; had used it against someone else...

"Shudojo?" asked Mikasama.

The Sister, with mouth full of root, looked toward her.

"If you weren't looking for a knife in your pack back at the inn, what were you trying to get while I sang to those...those..."

"Beasts," answered Shudojo as she swallowed the last of the root. She wiped her hands on her tunic, now as grimy as Mikasama's from many days spent out in the open. "I was looking for my shasen."

"What?" said an astonished Mikasama.

"My shasen," said Shudojo again, misunderstanding Mikasama's look of shock. She reached inside her tunic and pulled it out from where it hung about her neck on its small chain. "I had taken it off after we left Fumosa. I—I hadn't been sure that I was still worthy to wear it. It wasn't until that moment, at the inn, that I realized I could not leave without it."

Mikasama's face flushed with anger. "Do you mean to tell me," she said with barely controlled fury, "that you made me sing to...to those barbarians, just so that you could get that stupid necklace? When they were about to break down the door and rape us?"

The Sister turned her steely gaze full upon Mikasama. Those strange blue eyes never looked so foreign as they did then. Whatever door had been opened between the two women in their shared deprivations now slammed shut with a startling suddenness. Icily Shudojo said, "To a Shukyoshi, it is one's most important possession. Without it, life means nothing. It is the repository for our soul." She tucked the shasen back inside her tunic. "If I had left it behind for those savages to desecrate, I might as well have left my body there for them as well." She stood, staring down at the Princess with a withering look. "It is not something the likes of you would understand." She walked off, leaving Mikasama kneeling in the rain by the remains of the uprooted plants.

When they resumed their journey, it was shrouded in a silence heavier than the grey clouds rumbling overhead. The way became more rugged, and the women had to struggle over a broken landscape dotted with large rocks. Soon they faced a series of steep hills, and their feet slipped constantly in the mud as their course led them further upwards. There was no other way around, for the hills before them stretched north and south as far as they could see. The wind had picked up as well, driving the rain directly into their faces.

Lifting a foot up out of the clinging mud Mikasama cursed herself as a fool, directing Komori's favored imprecation at herself. Stupid! Why am I always so stupid? Why can't I learn to think first, before I let my anger speak for me?

She pushed her tangled hair out of her face yet again. The wind was whipping it around and, combined with the rain, was making it difficult to see where she was going. Beside her, Shudojo also clambered awkwardly up the slope of the hill. The old gulf loomed between them once more; and, thought Mikasama, once more it was her own big mouth that had put it there...

As the hours had dragged wearily past, Mikasama's own annoyance had dissipated as she had replayed in her head their argument. It had been her injured pride, having had to sing to a bunch of drunkards, which had caused her to lash out at Shudojo. She hadn't even stopped to think about the importance to the Sister of the shasen. She reminded herself that just because something was not a part of her world it didn't mean that it was unimportant to others.

She recalled how pleased she had felt when she and Shudojo had been feeding from the fruits of the bisato tree. For a brief time they had overcome their mutual stubbornness and had worked together, even laughed together. Now Mikasama saw that she had thrown it all away again. The Sister had shut Mikasama out completely.

The women emerged onto the top of a ridge. The wind was fiercer up here, making even standing difficult. Between the dark clouds overhead, and the heavy rain pelting them, neither woman could see more than a few yards in any direction. Even so, it was not hard to see that the way down on the opposite side of the ridge was considerably steeper than the way they had come. The only way down that slope would be by tumbling like a rock.

They looked around but there was no obvious direction to go. For no apparent reason that Mikasama could see, Shudojo pointed to the north. "This way." She trudged along the crest of the ridge, not bothering to see if Mikasama followed. Irritated, but not having any good reason for going in the other direction, the Princess set off after her.

The two women followed the ridge for the better part of an hour as it began twisting, rising, and falling; finally merging into a larger, and steeper, set of hills. Mikasama was beginning to worry if they would ever find their way down when, quite suddenly, their available options were narrowed considerably.

As they squeezed between a series of tall rock outcroppings, both women stopped abruptly. A torrent of water was rushing past directly in front of them. On their right, the rocky ground pitched up steeply, feeding the river via a series of steep cascades stretching up into the misty gloom above them. To their left, only a handful of paces away, the water flowed over the edge of a precipice in a dramatic waterfall, throwing billowing clouds of spray up to be instantly snatched away by the wind.

Mikasama realized that the hills, and the wind, must have masked the sound of the waterfall. Only here, standing right in front of it, could they hear the roar of the falls, as the water plunged down, down, somewhere well below them, until it crashed in a larger spray, barely seen in the gloom.

While they were surveying this disheartening scene, Mikasama suddenly shouted. "Look!" She pointed downstream, toward the falls. "Do you see that?"

Shudojo, wiping the rain out of her eyes, spotted what had attracted Mikasama's notice. It was a pair of ropes, spanning the gap from their side of the stream to the opposite bank. On the far side they were secured to a stout wooden post mounted atop a stone platform, jutting out into the river. She recognized it instantly. Sucking in her breath she said, "It is a washer woman's line." Bitter memories that she had hoped were long dead and buried rushed back into her mind. No, she thought; I will not think about that again. Anything but that!

Trying to distract herself, she explained to Mikasama. "There is just one rope, wrapped around this sheave." She pointed to where the two halves of the rope came together on their side and wrapped around a wheel. "The washer women affix the clothes to the rope, then pull them out into the stream from the platform. It is safer than trying to wade into fast-moving water. My village did much the same." Inevitably her eyes were drawn back across the stream, back to the stone platform on the other side. Try as she might, she could not exorcise her own memory. It was so long ago, but now it seemed as if it were yesterday...

The Princess was looking beyond the platform, toward the rocks that rose up on the other side. "Do you see that?" she said. The Sister turned her gaze to where Mikasama was pointing and saw a small stone building set back from the far bank of the river. It stood beside a trail leading down into the trees. The hut's crude door was askew, but the roof appeared intact. Mikasama asked, "Do you think anyone is there?"

Shudojo shook her head. "No. That would be the drying room, where the washer women hang clothes to dry, away from the rain and, probably, in this place, from the spray," as she gestured toward the waterfall. "Their village is probably down on the lowlands somewhere. I suspect the hut also serves as shelter from storms, if they are caught up here during one."

"Like we are," said Mikasama.

The two women looked despondently at the surging water. So close to the falls, it would be foolhardy to attempt to wade across; one slip, and they would be carried over the edge. There was no other path on their side but the way they had come, retracing their steps until they had returned to where they had first ascended the ridge. They knew there was nothing in the way of food along that path, and both women were once again feeling the pangs of hunger.

Shudojo stood unmoving, staring at the platform on the far side, where one end of the rope was anchored. Mikasama carefully edged her way along the bank to where the rope and its sheave where attached on their side. The rocks bordering the stream were slick with moisture, and the rope was only a few feet from the edge of the falls.

The wheel that held the rope seemed sturdy enough when Mikasama tugged on it. She supposed that the turbulent water near the edge must have somehow aided the women in their cleaning, accounting for the rope's proximity to the precipice of the falls. But her heart sank as she looked out across the fast-moving water. It was a good thirty paces across, and even holding on to the rope would be dangerous, that close to the falls. Assuming, she realized, that the rope did not come undone from the other side.

"Shudojo," she asked over her shoulder, "what do you think? This looks awfully risky to me..." Receiving no answer, she turned to look at the Sister.

Shudojo was still standing in the same place, oblivious, it seemed to Mikasama, of what was around her. She just kept staring across the river at the washer woman's platform. "Shudojo!" Mikasama shouted. "Come here and look at this!" The Sister looked dully in Mikasama's direction then moved with leaden steps toward her.

Mikasama pointed down at the rope. "Do you think it would hold us? Would it be tied tight enough on the other side?"

Shudojo did not reply. When Mikasama looked at her again the Princess saw a look of abject terror on the Sister's face. Shudojo was staring wide-eyed at the sheer drop over the edge of the falls, only a couple of feet away. Slowly she started backing up in small steps.

Puzzled, Mikasama said, "What's wrong? Where are you going?" The Sister, however, did not respond; instead she shuffled backwards until she bumped up against the nearby rocks.

Confounded by Shudojo's odd behavior, the Princess walked over to her and put a hand gently on the Sister's shoulder. She could feel Shudojo trembling. "Are you alright?" Mikasama asked gently. "What's wrong?"

Shudojo just shook her head, once, then several times violently. She stared past Mikasama, toward the falls. In a tiny voice she croaked, "...Can't...too high..."

Mikasama frowned, turning to look in the direction that held Shudojo's gaze. She couldn't see anything unusual, until she finally realized what it must be. Heights! Shudojo must be afraid of heights!

Frustrated, the Princess dropped her hand. Wonderful, she thought; we get this far, and now Shudojo can't cross the river because she's scared of heights.

At that moment, a bright flash sparked across the sky, causing both women to raise their hands toward their eyes. A moment later a massive rumble rent the air around them, building up louder upon itself, once, twice, then with a final deafening peal. Startled, both women quickly grabbed one another.

Lightning! thought Mikasama. We're in a thunderstorm, out here in the open!

Now she was the one suddenly seized with panic, as another crackle of light momentarily blinded them, followed by another bellow from the sky as if a hundred drummers had gone berserk. Mikasama's mind snapped back to the hunt with her father, standing outside, the thunder booming overhead...she was crying, holding on to Nana-san, begging her to make the noise stop...

With a wild look in her eyes, Mikasama shouted at Shudojo. "We have to get across! We can't stay here!" She tugged on Shudojo's arm. "We have to get across, over to the hut. We have to get inside!"

Shudojo jerked her arm back. "No...no, you go...I'll...stay here!"

Frustrated, Mikasama yelled back, "If you stay here, you'll die!" When Shudojo still made no move, the Princess reached up and put her arm around the Sister's shoulders. "Come on," she said urgently. "We'll do it together! I'll be right next to you!" Still Shudojo resisted, trying to edge back against the safety, the solidity, of the rocks. Mikasama kept on, guiding her forward, toward the falls.

The rocks were slippery, and Mikasama knelt carefully as she neared the edge of the river. Shudojo stopped moving but did not retreat. Gingerly Mikasama stuck out a leg, dipping her foot into the water. With a gasp she drew back. It felt like ice against her skin. Most likely, she figured, it *had* been ice up there on the mountain until a short time ago.

She reconsidered, wondering if they would be able to make it across without becoming so numb that they lost their grip on the rope. Then the lightning flashed again, and panic once more overruled her thoughts. Boldly she shoved her leg back in again, felt the water splashing around her, the agony of the searing cold. But she kept it there.

She reached out and grabbed the rope, and felt it sway wildly in her grasp. She pulled, and the rope stayed in place; it was still tied securely to the other side. She shuffled out into the course of the stream, keeping the rope between her and the edge of the falls. If she slipped she figured she might at least have a chance to wrap an arm around the rope before she was swept away. The bitingly cold water came up to her hips as she edged further out.

Turning to Shudojo, she lifted out a hand. "Come on," she said. Shudojo did not move. "Come on!" repeated Mikasama earnestly. "You can do this! Take my hand!"

The Sister looked down at Mikasama's hand. She couldn't think straight; all her instincts were shouting at her to run! To get away from the edge of the falls! Nothing that Mikasama was saying to her made any sense. Go out there? Into the river?

She looked down and saw Mikasama's outstretched hand. Mikasama was shouting something at her, but she couldn't hear the words. She remembered that Mikasama said they would go together. It would be all right, if they went together. Wouldn't it?

She focused on the hand. She tried to block out everything else around her; all sight, all sound, just that hand and nothing else. That seemed to help. She saw another hand reaching out, grabbing Mikasama's. With a start she realized it was her own. Then she was being pulled, insistently, down into the water.

As soon as the cold hit her, the Sister panicked once more, flailing about and splashing. "Stop it!" she heard Mikasama shouting. "Calm down, or we won't make it at all!" Holding onto the rope with one hand, Mikasama grabbed one of Shudojo's wrists with the other. Forcefully she set the Sister's hand on the rope. Once her fingers touched it, Shudojo gripped the rope tightly, the cold forgotten against the reassuring feel of something solid in her hand.

When Shudojo finally put her other hand onto the rope, Mikasama breathed a sigh of relief that quickly turned into a violent chattering. She told herself that they had better get moving or they'd turn into blocks of ice themselves.

In slow movements she edged herself sideways, her back to the racing water that coursed around her in a bubbling froth. Directly in front of them, the stream plunged off into darkness, only the spray and the sound giving any indication of its ultimate fate. At first Shudojo did not move, but Mikasama reached over and gave her a tug and the Sister began awkwardly emulating Mikasama's movements.

They had passed halfway when another brilliant flash of lightning shattered the gloom. The sky was lit up brighter than the noonday sun, revealing everything around and in front of them.

For both women, the effect was terrifying. There was nothing but air before them as far as they could see, while below a furious cauldron frothed, as if in anger at being denied its due. For the Princess, it simply spurred her on to get to the other side as quickly as possible. For Shudojo, it almost spelled the end.

The Sister had been careful to avoid looking down; indeed, had been careful to look at nothing at all, thinking only about the rough surface of the rope under her hands, and of moving next to Mikasama: moving when she moved, stopping as she did. The sudden light startled her, and instinctively she looked down.

Her heart froze colder than her icy hands and legs. Whatever vestige of control she had suddenly snapped and, overcome with fear, she found her feet swept out from under her as she slipped.

She threw her arms across the rope, which probably was the only thing that saved her. She could feel her feet being dragged beneath the rope, towards the edge, soon to go over the falls…

She could hear shouting, who was it? Was it Mikasama? Why was she still here?

She felt someone pulling on her. Hard. Her arms, her legs, though, felt locked into position. Safer that way, she told herself. Don't move. Like a river stone. That's what I am, a river stone, moored to the solid bottom of the river, immovable. Safe.

What was that? Oh, Mikasama, shouting again. Close your eyes, she said. Close my eyes? Why? Well, if it makes her happy…

She closed her eyes, and rather suddenly she felt herself snapped back into the present moment. She almost let go of the rope, and would have followed the water on its plunge to the depths, but Mikasama grabbed hold of her arm sharply. It was just enough to let her manage to wrap first one hand, then the other back around the rope, while still keeping her eyes screwed tightly shut. Awkwardly she regained her footing in the fast-flowing water, and let Mikasama guide her on to the other side.

Finally she struck a hard rock, and could feel Mikasama dragging her up out of the water. Heaving from exertion and fear, she tried to open her eyes, but it made her head swim and so she shut them once more.

Mikasama was shouting again. Why was she always shouting? She wants me to move. All right, if we must…

She managed to get her eyes open again, and stumbled as Mikasama tried to support her as they walked. Walked…We must be on dry ground, realized Shudojo…Yes, on a trail…And what's this? A hut?

Mikasama pushed open the fallen door of the washer woman's hut and managed to drag the nearly unconscious Shudojo inside.

The Princess gently helped the Sister down to the earthen floor. Wearily, shivering from the cold, she collapsed next to her. She was startled when Shudojo suddenly reached for her. Before she realized what was happening, the Sister had wrapped her arms around Mikasama and was sobbing uncontrollably. The Princess was taken completely aback.

After a moment Mikasama put her own arms around Shudojo and held her. "It's all right," she said softy, rocking the Sister back and forth. "Everything's all right…"

24

Perfect; he behaved perfectly! This Itachi sent another to do the killing! I told him not to kill himself, to find another way to snuff out the weaklings' lives, and so he found another to do it for him.

His mind is so easy to manipulate; scant wonder all those petty little figures up there live in such fear of the Great Ones. To think of what can be done, when one can force their minds to—

Ah...you—you've returned...W-wait! Wait, I'm sorry! Yes, I know what—No, I didn't mean to cause interference. Wait! Hear me out!

You brought me here! It was you that gave me the power; what fault can it be of mine if I try to use it, for your greater glory? I seek only what you promised. You promised revenge, and I—

What? A test? What others? There are more like me? Why didn't you tell me?

Failed? How could I fail, when I didn't even know what you wanted? Well, yes, you told me you wanted me to watch, but—

Banish me? To where? What could be more banishment than this dark hole, this 'nothing,' to which you've already consigned my mind? Where—

AAARRRGH! Agh! ...No, too much pressure...Squeezing, like...being stuffed inside a bottle...

*   *   *

The city of Tejinashi soared up from the narrow plain upon which it sat like a veritable fountain of buildings, all rushing up to the sky. The delicate spires and towers caught the morning light that slipped over the eastern hills, displaying a vast profusion of structures that seemed as if they might launch themselves away had they not been constrained by the huge wall that surrounded them. It bespoke of incredible industry to raise such lofty edifices; the average stone building in Tonogato was no more than two or three stories tall. Here, even the lowliest of buildings rose up higher than the Great Tower of the castle in Hajimeshi.

Even more remarkable was the color. Virtually every surface in the city, from the buildings to the outer wall, was faced with green stone, causing Tejinashi to shimmer in the sunlight spilling over it. Its brilliant color was just one of the many stories about the city that had been passed on by travelers, even those who had only seen it from afar. For few were admitted within the city walls to see the splendor first hand. The Zaitan were highly selective in whom they allowed to enter their fabled metropolis.

The dawn's light also revealed the mountains that framed the city, with low hills in the east rising to majestic snow-covered peaks across the remaining arc of the compass. When the sun had finished bathing the city in its morning glow the daylight spread out along the floor of the plain, reflecting brilliantly off another of the Tejinashi wonders. Entirely circling the city was a vast moat, sweeping completely around the walls at their base. Inexplicably it flowed with a strong current, propelled by some unseen force as if it were a river fed from the peaks that bordered the plain. But it was a river to nowhere, effectively sealing off Tejinashi from anyone wishing to invade its self-proclaimed isolation.

All of which, by this time, Itachi and his soldiers knew all too well. They had arrived two days ago to find the great moat too wide, and the current too strong, for anyone to swim. There was no bridge, nor sign of any type of boat. They had shouted themselves hoarse, trying to attract the attention of those in the city, but to no avail. If anyone there paid them any heed it was not apparent to any of the Hajimeshi.

The only thing on their side of the moat was a tall thin pole, made from an odd sort of metal, imbedded in the ground near the water's edge. There were no markings on it, or anything to indicate its purpose. Bokusa had pulled on it, and had struck it with the hilt of his sword, but beyond a dull clang it had produced no response.

Strangely, once the Guards had arrived before the city, Itachi had seemed to withdraw into himself. To Bokusa, who had served with him longer than any of the others, it seemed that when it was clear they could not get across the moat the Hajimeshi general had become confused, unwilling to decide on another course of action. It was a side of his leader that he had never seen before. Consequently, he didn't know what to do either. He knew that mentioning anything about it was certainly not among his options, so the big Guard sat silently brooding along with his leader by the remains of the previous evening's fire. All that was left now were cold, charred bits of wood, the night's rain having doused the flame. Only the Hikari remained lit, unaffected by the rainfall.

The Guards, wet and chilled, had occupied their time camped before the city foraging for food. At night they had huddled close together, both to escape the rain and in dread of the strange blue glow that, at night, emanated from the city across the water. And they complained, although only amongst themselves.

The men's natural inclination to follow had been severely tested over the preceding weeks; now they were tired and wanted to go home. Sitting in front of this strange place, unable to move forward, their leader refusing to retreat, and some wondering about what had happened to Hisoka, made for an uncertain mood. Bokusa, sitting across from Itachi, had noticed the disaffection among the men, but was not fool enough to risk the general's wrath by bringing it up.

Itachi picked up a half-burned branch from the fire pit and threw it into the nearby moat. As he watched it carried swiftly away on the current, he said to Bokusa, "How long to build a raft?"

Bokusa screwed up his face, looking around at the sparse woods nearby. "A while. These trees are pretty small. And we don't have anything easy to tie it together with. Have to search for some kinda vines somewhere."

Itachi picked up another stick, snapping it in frustration. "These damned Tejinashi know we're here; they're just playing games with us!" He jabbed the end of the stick into the dirt, churning it up into a muddy goo. "Well, they won't be playing for long. Magic or no, I'll make them crawl on their hands and knees, along with those Shukyoshi and Yutakashi dogs."

Bokusa was careful to keep any hint of doubt out of his face. Whatever he thought of his leader's schemes, he was just smart enough to keep it to himself. Instead he opened his mouth to utter a word of support, but before he could speak a word his jaw dropped open, as if the muscles supporting it had become unhinged.

Itachi glanced up to see Bokusa staring past him, over his shoulder, back in the direction of the road that led down to the moat. Turning to see what Bokusa was gaping at, he stood abruptly, knocking the dying embers of the fire pit askew.

No, he shouted silently to himself. No! How could this be?

Riding toward them were three horsemen. Instantly Itachi recognized the two Deshi, as well as Nakama.

*   *   *

The trio had made their way from Sekai Monastery, descending from the hills that flowed out into the plain surrounding the magicians' city. It was Nakama who had spotted Itachi's party almost as soon as Tejinashi had come into view. To Shiko, they had still been so far away all he could see were small figures, insignificant in the distance. He was, however, able to discern the bright glow of the Hikari, where it had sat amongst Itachi's men.

The three travelers from Sekai had stopped to decide what to do. Toshi-hito had not seemed surprised that Itachi had been denied entrance to the city. What was a surprise to his companions, however, was that the Deshi Master recommended that they re-unite with Itachi's men before trying to enter the city.

Nakama had objected strenuously. He had pointed out that Itachi's behavior had become both dangerous and erratic. There was no way to predict what he might do; he might try to kill them all, right then and there, in front of the city. Even Shiko had quailed at the thought of being in close quarters with the lord from Hajimeshi, having now seen how far the man could go.

Toshi-hito, however, had patiently explained his logic. A divided pilgrimage, he had said, stood little chance of convincing the Zaitan of the pressing need to seek the Kotaishi. If they tried to enter separately, their cause would be over before they ever had an opportunity to present their case.

If Itachi had not yet been able to gain entrance into the city, Toshi-hito had said, he was even less likely to do so should he attack his fellow countrymen on the very threshold of Tejinashi. For the Deshi Master was sure that the Zaitan would have been watching every movement of the unwelcome visitors camped on their doorstep. Toshi-hito had argued that, even should Itachi's behavior be suspect, the Hajimeshi lord still desired something he had not yet obtained: his brother's throne. The Deshi Master did not doubt that Itachi would do whatever was necessary in order to further that goal, and for now, the Zaitan were his only hope for proceeding. The Hajimeshi lord's behavior once they were all inside the city would most certainly bear careful watching; but they must trust in the integrity of their own quest to convince the Zaitan of the worth of their pilgrimage, and thereby counteract anything Itachi might try to achieve.

Even then his two companions had not been entirely convinced, and Toshi-hito had heard them both out. In the end, though, neither Shiko nor Nakama had been able to refute the basic soundness of the Deshi Master's reasoning, and so they had reluctantly agreed to his plan. The archer, however, swore that he would keep his hand close to his bow anytime he was within an arrow's flight of Itachi. The three had then made their way down toward Itachi's makeshift camp, Toshi-hito leading the way,

Now, as Shiko looked down from his horse at Itachi, he had to exert considerable effort to mask the wave of revulsion that coursed through him.

The apprentice was perversely reminded of Itachi's comment to Ryori that soldiers make poor hunters. On their way from the monastery, he and his companions had found the cook's burial site. The Brothers had created a mound of rocks around Ryori's remains, placing him off to one side of the trail. At his feet they had planted a long, straight branch, with a small pennant tied to it that had been flapping softly in the breeze. Toshi-hito had told Shiko and Nakama that it was a guidepost; its purpose to lead the Fates to where the dead lay, to offer a choice of further paths to follow. The three men had conducted a brief, silent vigil for their fallen comrade, and Shiko had reached inside his tunic to hold the cool metal of Ryori's medallion in his hand.

And now here he was before the man who had undoubtedly been the instigator of Ryori's death. Shiko felt the weight of Ryori's medallion around his neck, even though it was lighter than his own honsho. He wanted to reach for it, to hold it up in front of Itachi's face, to force the man to see that a part of Ryori still lived. Instead he held back, sensing that the situation was already on the thin edge of a blade that might turn and cut them at any moment.

Damnation, screamed Itachi inside his head. Hisoka should have killed them all! And even if he hadn't, the Deshi Master should have been dead by now; that wound would have killed any man. But here he is, riding! Like some sort of demon, risen from the dead...

[He is such a fool! Without me to guide him, he is helpless...
Banishment...this is what it meant! No longer a prisoner in the dark, but a prisoner here, in this little man's mind! I cannot touch him, he cannot feel me; all I can do is watch, and see what he sees. I must live in his life...so small, so insignificant...a living hell, after what I had been able to do...
He could decide nothing, not even whether to go forward or retreat, without me there to touch his mind! He had become used to my influence, had grown to depend on it. Now he is little more than a child, lost in the woods. And I am trapped inside, and can do nothing...]

"Greetings, Lord Itachi. I see you have waited for us before proceeding to Tejinashi; that was quite thoughtful."

The fury in Itachi's gaze was clear for all to see as Toshi-hito called out to him. The Hajimeshi lord's eyes narrowed. So, he thought, this Deshi thinks to play games with me. I should take his head right off his shoulders and see what he thinks of that. Only Bokusa and I know for certain what Hisoka had been sent to do. The worthless cook was not with these three; had Hisoka managed to kill one of them at least? No matter, the man had failed in his primary task, that of killing the Deshi. Either these three had killed Hisoka, or the man had never reached them at all. They must have found the monastery the brat had been so insistent upon reaching; where else could they have found horses in those mountains?

He could not know for certain what the Deshi might have figured out. It might be safest to kill them all now, but a cunning warrior, Itachi reminded himself, never tips his hand unless forced to. Besides, a melee on the shore, in full view of the Tejinashi, would jeopardize any hope he might have of getting the magicians on his side.

Thinking quickly, he gave a mock bow to Toshi-hito. "Of course, we have waited for you. What would the pilgrimage be without the Deshi to guide us?" He ignored Bokusa's queer look at him. "We have been merely…thinking…about ways to get across, so that the pilgrimage would not be delayed once you arrived." Bokusa next to him still had a stupid look plastered across his face, but Itachi trusted that the big oaf would simply keep his mouth shut and let Itachi pull the strings.

The soldiers had sensed the increased tension that surrounded the return of the remaining pilgrims, despite the apparent courtesies between Deshi and Hajimeshi lord. They fidgeted nervously, waiting for a sign from their leader as to what to do. The air was flat with unspoken thoughts.

Then, silently, Toshi-hito spurred his horse forward toward the tall metal rod embedded near the moat. The Deshi apprentice followed, along with Nakama. Itachi watched them, unmoving, waiting.

As he came abreast of the pole Toshi-hito reached out and grasped it with his hand. At first nothing happened, but then all of those gathered on the shore perceived a low hum, almost felt rather than heard. It seemed to come up out of the ground directly through their bones, becoming stronger as the seconds passed. The Guards shifted on their feet uneasily. Then all eyes turned toward the sweeping waters of the moat, as directly in front of Toshi-hito the water began surging upwards.

The horses stepped back nervously. Just as quickly as it had begun the rush of water subsided. It was not the water of the moat that was rising, but a massive stone platform, some ten steps across, which was pushing its way up above the surface of the water. The flat-topped column rose up nearly half-an-arm's length out of the waters of the moat before it stopped. As the current bubbled around it, the water coursed off its six-sided top, leaving the platform itself relatively dry.

Another surge of water heralded the ascension of another column, just beyond the first, rising up to almost touch its partner. It was as a third column rose up beyond the second that it became apparent what was happening. Toshi-hito had somehow activated a bridge!

Bokusa, perplexed, said, "I had my hands all over that pole. It didn't do nothin' for me."

Sitting calmly atop his horse at the water's edge, Toshi-hito overhead. Without looking over his shoulder, he said, "It is keyed to those who have once been guests of the Tejinashi. Without their leave, none may enter."

One by one, the stone columns rose up out of the waters of the moat, stretching across toward the city of Tejinashi. Even before the last had fully risen from the depths Toshi-hito urged his horse forward onto the first platform, the hooves clacking against the damp stone. The Deshi apprentice immediately followed, as did Nakama, their horses carefully stepping over the narrow gaps between each column.

The Hajimeshi general scowled in disgust as he watched the horsemen begin to cross over toward the city. What, he wondered, was to prevent the Tejinashi from leading them all out over the water, then having the columns conveniently drop away below?

He had heard all about the stories of Tejinashi. He knew about the Zaitan, a council of women magicians who supposedly ran the city. Rubbish, he thought to himself. I'll lay my sword to the table that somewhere behind them are men who do the dictating, and men who are not afraid to use a knife in the dark. Those are the men I must find, and win to my side. That can only be done quietly, by making inquiries in dim alleyways.

To do that he must first gain entrance into Tejinashi. Whether the Deshi suspected his hand in Hisoka's actions or not, they were unwittingly playing into his hands now by helping them all gain access to the city. Such an opportunity could not be wasted.

He turned impatiently to his Guards. "Are you all going to stand and watch until the bridge sinks back beneath the water? Move!" He reached down and grabbed his pack, hoisting it roughly onto his shoulders. The soldiers, looking at each other with trepidation, prepared to follow him out onto the magical bridge.

Shiko, looking back over his shoulder, saw Itachi heft his pack. 'Ton and 'Cha! In the tension of the moment he had forgotten about them. Quickly he sent out a thought: *"'Ton? Are you there?"*

"This is 'Cha. I am here." Shiko sensed an undercurrent of tension in her thoughts. *"'Ton was sent out by this one with another message."*

"Are you all right?"

She paused before answering. *"Yes, although 'Ton has been gone a long time. It—it always seems much darker in here when he is away."*

Shiko looked ahead as the walls of Tejinashi loomed up before them. *"We're entering a large city. 'Ton might have trouble finding us in there."*

"'Ton will find me. He will not stop until he does." Her quiet, confident faith underscored for Shiko the unique bond between the two birds. He certainly hoped, for her sake, that 'Ton was indeed able to find them once they were swallowed up inside the walls of Tejinashi.

Toshi-hito's horse walked off the last column and stepped onto the flagstones of a large forecourt. The huge empty space was surrounded on three sides by the walls of the city, with the moat forming its remaining edge. Directly in front of the pilgrims, a pair of massive doors filled an archway that soared some three stories high. The city walls extended up even higher, topped by purposeful-looking crenellations. With not even a tree to break up the solid expanse of green stone in the forecourt, the effect was imposing and not a little unnerving; which, Shiko supposed, was most likely the intent.

Even from this angle the Deshi apprentice could see the majestic buildings of Tejinashi rising up above the walls. Unlike the somber, militaristic Fortress of the Shukyoshi, or the glittering facades of Yutakashi, the buildings of Tejinashi stood with an elegance that appeared to Shiko more refined than anything else in Tonogato he had seen.

Toshi-hito rode directly up to the great doors, and waited. Shiko and Nakama walked their horses up beside him. As Itachi and his men finished crossing the moat, the apprentice turned to watch them. He saw that Donaku was carrying the Hikari, and his heart was warmed to be once again near the lamp, however symbolic it might be. It reminded him of his commitment to see the pilgrimage through, with or without a light to guide his way.

He looked back at the great doors in front of them. Peering at them more closely, he gasped with astonishment. "They're stone!" he exclaimed. "The doors are made of stone!" He tilted his head back to take in the size of their massive, three-story height then looked over at Toshi-hito. "How could they possibly move such giant doors?"

"There are many things about this city that defy simple explanation," said Toshi-hito. He added quietly, "You may find it best to observe, and accept, rather than force your mind to try and explain."

At that moment, Itachi, with all his men safely across the bridge, walked up between the mounted Deshi. "What does it say?" he asked gruffly. He was pointing to a short inscription carved on the face of the stone. It was in a script that Shiko had never seen before.

"It says," replied Toshi-hito, "'I am the door.'"

"'I am the door?'" said an incredulous Itachi. "Of course it's a door! Are these Tejinashi so short of wit they can think of nothing more intelligent to say?"

The Deshi Master kept his eyes forward. "A door can open onto many things, Lord Itachi. You cannot know what is on the far side of a door that is closed. Once you open it and pass through, you can never again return to the ignorance that you enjoyed before you opened it." He gestured toward the inscription. "This is a warning, that what one may find on the other side may reveal more than what one sought."

Itachi opened his mouth to reply but was forestalled by the sound of stone rumbling against stone, heralding the opening of the great doors of Tejinashi.

* * *

Mikasama thought, 'If ever I had contemplated turning back, it is surely not an option now. There was no way either of us could ever face trying to return across that waterfall...'

The muted light of dawn was beginning to filter in through the doorway of the hut. Wearily the Princess turned over to try to ease the aching that came from nearly every part of her body. It had only been her utter exhaustion that had permitted a few fitful minutes of sleep during the night. The remainder of the long hours had been spent shivering, or being jolted awake by the sound of thunder from the storm outside. She reflected that it was not a night that she was likely to forget, however much she might wish to.

After the two women had collapsed inside the hut Shudojo, crying inconsolably, had clutched the Princess for a long time. Mikasama's own fears, meanwhile, had diminished, no matter that the shelter had been minimal at best. Out there, on the far side of the waterfall, each of them had reacted instinctively, their actions driven by panic. They were both lucky to have survived the crossing without having been washed over the falls to their deaths.

During the night the intermittent flashes of lightning had briefly illuminated the interior of the crude hut. Mikasama had seen what looked to be a pile of fabric lying in a corner. Once Shudojo had stopped crying the Princess had crawled over to the pile, hoping it might be a blanket. It was not: it had turned out to be a mass of cast-off clothes, covered with dust and dirt. Shaking out the stiff, musty garments, Mikasama unearthed some ragged tunics. She had managed to pull off her own clammy tunic with difficulty, as it had clung to her wet skin. When the cold night air struck her, she had wondered briefly if it might not have been better just to keep the wet clothes on. But she had forced herself into the dry garment, its creased and flattened form expanding with reluctance.

Shudojo had responded listlessly as Mikasama had cajoled her into sitting up and exchanging her own sopping habit for one of the unearthed tunics. Afterwards the Sister had retreated into herself once more, pulling her legs up and wrapping her arms around them. Mikasama had thrown the remaining clothes haphazardly over Shudojo and herself in a sort of makeshift blanket; then had lain down, exhausted, next to the Sister. Putting her arms back around Shudojo for warmth, she had hoped to find sleep, but for the most part it had not come.

Now, as daybreak brought light but no added warmth, Mikasama was reluctant to stir from beneath their makeshift bed, despite her discomfort. All that awaited them, it seemed, was a cold morning; how much better to simply lie still, to close one's eyes, and wish the whole thing away as a dream.

Thinking of dreams reminded her of one of her visions, that of being swept over a waterfall and landing, softly, at the bottom. Well, she thought, that would have been quite unlikely had she slipped, or had the rope come untied from its post while they had been trying to cross. Although, in truth, she had to admit she *was* safely past the falls now, and the trail they had seen outside the hut gave evidence that they should be able to make their way out of the hills...

The Princess felt movement, and she rolled back over to see Shudojo sit up. The Sister was staring down with a perplexed expression at the strange clothes she wore. Then she took in Mikasama's ragged tunic, and then finally their original clothes, lying where Mikasama had dropped them. Without a word Shudojo rose up and collected their still-damp garments, taking them outside. Wondering what the Sister had in mind, but too tired to care, Mikasama simply rolled back over again and closed her eyes.

The Princess had her back to the door, but soon she felt as if someone was watching her. She turned over to find Shudojo standing in the doorway, staring down at her. As their eyes met the Sister looked away.

"What?" croaked Mikasama, mouth parched. "What is it?"

Shudojo would not meet Mikasama's gaze. "The sun is out," the Sister said awkwardly. "It should dry our clothes in a little while."

The Princess nodded, still too groggy to worry about why Shudojo seemed so ill at ease. Nature was calling in any case, so Mikasama shed the remaining cast-off clothes and stood. As she walked to the door, the Sister stepped aside but still would not look at her.

What is wrong with her now? wondered the Princess. We're alive, when we so easily could have been smashed against the rocks below the falls, or drowned.

As she emerged outside the hut, she saw that the sun was, indeed, already beginning to warm the air. The growling of her stomach also told her that they had better find food this day.

Strangely enough, the prospect did not worry her. At first this surprised her, but she concluded that it must have been as a result of what they had gone through the previous night. How could they make it through that, she surmised, having crossed an icy waterfall during a thunderstorm, only to die from starvation? Somehow that just wouldn't make sense. She couldn't explain the feeling, even to herself, so she knew better than to try and talk to Shudojo about it. Yet now she felt certain, more than ever, that it was more a matter of when, rather than if, she would be able to find what it was that she sought.

"We need to get out of these hills," Mikasama said to Shudojo when she returned to the hut. "We haven't found anything up here that we can eat, and my stomach's doing nothing but cramping up from lack of food. If this is some sort of washer woman's hut, then their village must be nearby."

Shudojo did not respond other than to nod her head, and still she would not meet Mikasama's gaze, which began to worry the Princess. Had something happened to Shudojo last night? she wondered. Has her mind gone?

Once the sun had dried most of the dampness from their clothes, the two women changed back into them. Shudojo stood, apparently waiting for Mikasama to decide where to go. The Princess found this unnerving;

heretofore it had always been Shudojo who had led the way, deciding which path to follow. Now, for whatever reason, she seemed willing to relinquish that responsibility. Well, thought Mikasama, I'm hungry and I'm not going to stand around here all day waiting for her to shake off whatever's bothering her.

The trail that led from the hut continued down a slope, and Mikasama set off on it without another word. She could hear Shudojo shuffling along behind her, but the two women did not speak.

The path became steeper as it dropped down. As the trail switchbacked down the hill, Mikasama found she could see for miles. The storm had blown itself out, and the morning's clear blue sky was lightly populated with cottony clouds. The land, too, appeared lightly populated, for she could see no large clearings, or areas where a village might be. Certainly she saw no smoke, which meant no cooking fires. Which meant any food to be had would likely be wild berries or some other kind of edible plant. She had hoped that they would have more luck finding something on this side of the hills.

Looking back at her companion, she saw that Shudojo walked with her head down, staring at her feet as they headed downhill. She hoped, too, that the Sister might come out of her reverie long enough to identify anything poisonous before Mikasama stuck it in her mouth.

Once the trail hit level ground it skirted the bank of a river, the same one, Mikasama realized, fed by the falls that they had so precariously crossed. Finding a clear spot on the bank she scrambled down to the river's edge and lifted handfuls of water to her mouth, bringing welcome relief to her parched tongue. She had considered going back to the falls for a drink before they had left, but had been worried about what Shudojo might do. The whole area had seemed to cause the Sister such distress she had thought it prudent to leave the vicinity as quickly as possible, although her cracked lips and dry mouth had caused her to regret that choice more than once as they had started down the trail.

Now the feeling of cool clear water refreshed her enormously. Once she had drunk her fill she splashed it over her face, already warmed from a combination of the bright sun and the long walk. She turned to look for Shudojo.

The Sister stood above her on the bank. She made no sign that she was going to join Mikasama down by the water. The Princess called up. "Aren't you going to get some water? You've got to be as thirsty as I am." Shudojo shook her head silently, vigorously. Her eyes seemed to grow wide with alarm. Quickly Mikasama looked around, seeking whatever sign of danger had caught Shudojo's attention.

But there was nothing: just the river placidly gliding along, with rushes growing in the shallows and bowing gently in the puffs of a light breeze. The only sound was that of a few birds singing nearby.

Mikasama turned back to Shudojo and saw that the Sister's expression had returned to normal. Frowning, the Princess hauled herself back up the bank to stand in front of her traveling companion. "Shudojo," she said quietly, "what's the matter? Why are you acting so strangely?"

The Sister would not look at her, however; she just continued to stare at the ground. The Princess reached out to touch her shoulder, and the response was as swift as it was unexpected. Shudojo snapped her arm up and knocked away Mikasama's hand, taking a step back and raising her face in anger to glare at the Princess.

Shocked, Mikasama took a step back herself, wondering what she could have done to provoke such a reaction. The burning look in those odd blue eyes was at once both disturbing and comforting; the former because of the sheer unexpectedness of it, the latter because it was, at least, some of the old familiar Shudojo back in form. Whatever the cause, it seemed to bring Shudojo back to herself. In her abrupt manner, she turned away from Mikasama. "I am all right. You need not concern yourself with me."

All at once Mikasama felt tired of dealing with this moody traveler that she had become saddled with. With a heavy sigh she turned and went back down the bank, intending to get some more water before setting off again on the trail. If there were no villagers wherever they were headed, then the chances of finding fresh water further along were slim.

After a few moments, as the Princess was cupping her hands and taking in more of the river's sustenance, she heard Shudojo coming down the bank at her back. Ignoring her, Mikasama continued to stand in the shallows. It was hard to imagine, thought the Princess, watching the water bubbling softly around her legs, that this was the same rushing torrent that had surrounded them during the crossing of the falls.

"I'm sorry." Shudojo's voice was quiet, but Mikasama heard it over the sound of the flowing river. She straightened in surprise, for it was rare that she had ever heard Shudojo apologize for anything. Turning to face her, the Princess saw the Sister sitting down on the grassy slope of the bank. She was looking at Mikasama now, but the anger was gone from her eyes. In its place was something that, to Mikasama, appeared more like weariness. Sensing that Shudojo needed to talk, the Princess silently waded out of the river and found her own spot upon the bank.

"I—I apologize," said the Sister quietly, once Mikasama had sat down, "for my behavior at the falls. I jeopardized both of us. I reacted foolishly. I have always tried to be…stronger…than that. I am…not used to having to rely on others," she ended, with some embarrassment.

Mikasama, keenly aware of how difficult it must be for Shudojo to talk about it, tried to console her. "It's all right," she said. "I behaved just as badly, dragging us across the falls in the middle of a thunderstorm." She shrugged. "We each seem to have our own fears."

The Sister shook her head. "There was more to it than my reaction to heights," she said tonelessly. A long silence ensued, and Mikasama was uncertain whether Shudojo would elaborate. Finally though, the Sister went on, speaking softly. "The local lord over our village," she said, "cared nothing about us. As long as we paid him his taxes, and supplied men for his little wars with his neighbors, he ignored us. We were beneath his notice." She stared down into the water, rushing past at their feet. "I was a washer woman in my village. All the young girls were; it was part of our responsibilities. The men went off to fight; we stayed behind to maintain hearth and home. We had a washing platform, much like that one back there," tilting her head in the direction of the waterfall.

Quietly, eyes staring vacantly at the river, she said, "I was alone; I had been late getting the wash started that day. All the other women had left. That was when he came." She shuddered. "I had never seen him before, had no idea who he was. Obviously a nobleman, from his dress. He—" She stopped, choked. "He didn't even say anything, just ...assumed...that I was his for the taking. I called out, shouting for help. No one heard, or if they did, they chose to ignore it. He slapped me to the ground, then—"

Her eyes closed. "I had taken with me one of the blades used in the kitchen. Somebody had not cleaned it properly after using it on juko beets, and the stuff had dried on it like stone. I was going to try to scrub it clean in the river."

Her voice became leaden, as if she were reciting lines from a book, about a story of somebody else. She opened her eyes, but they no longer saw the same river that was in front of her. "He had managed to rip off most of my clothes, despite my scratching and kicking at him. The knife blade was lying in the pile of wash next to me; he hadn't noticed it. When he tried to get between my legs, in desperation I reached for it." Her eyes closed again. "I never knew how quickly blood could flow, had never seen so much blood in my life. It ran all over me, all over the washing platform, the washed clothes. It even stained the river water. Imagine, a river of red..." Her voice trailed off as she stared down at the flowing river.

Mikasama sat stunned. She couldn't even begin to imagine what Shudojo's experience must have been like. To be attacked like that, in a place familiar and so close to home...

The Sister had not finished. "I left him there, and I ran, screaming, back to the village. They went and found him, where he had bled to death on the platform. He was the local lord's son," she said flatly.

Mikasama drew a sharp breath, knowing then what must have happened even before Shudojo spoke it. "Everyone began to panic," the Sister went on. "They thought we would all be executed. Then someone suggested that they cover it up, pretend some bandits had killed him." She laughed bitterly. "They were such fools. They knew nothing of bandits.

Why would bandits have killed a nobleman, instead of holding him for ransom?" She shook her head. "They threw his body into the river. It washed up somewhere downstream, where some of the lord's men found it. There was a great hue and cry. Before the soldiers came, searching, I had to help the others scrub the blood out of the stones of the platform."

She turned and looked at Mikasama. "Do you know what it is like, Lady, to have those around you, those you trusted, people with whom you had spent your whole life, suddenly become strangers to you?"

Mikasama nodded, as a vision of Komori passed fleetingly across her mind. Nursemaid, later guardian and caretaker; and all the while, wife of Himitsu the spymaster. Someone that the Princess had spent her whole life with, and now, as a result of knowing about Komori's secret life, had in some ways become a stranger too...

But Shudojo went on, not even noticing. "The village elders decreed that I had dishonored them. No matter," she said acidly, "that I had been trying to defend myself, and that *they* were the ones who had decided to cover it up. I was to blame. So they shunned me, and turned me out of the village. Even my family. No one would speak to me, even offer me a loaf of bread to take with me. I was cast out." She picked up a stone and tossed it across the surface of the river, watching it skip in little splashing hops before it sank below the water. "And so I have been, ever since. Cast out and adrift."

Mikasama didn't know what to say. What could be said? It explained so much of the Sister's behavior: her moodiness, her unwillingness to trust or befriend others. Who could one trust after that?

At the same time, it underscored for the Princess how trivial her own life had been. Nothing she had ever done had been of any consequence. She had never had to deal with the sort of trauma that Shudojo had experienced.

It was not, she acknowledged, as if she had been driven out from Hajimeshi. She had chosen to walk this path, first in pursuit of Nakama and then in response to the strange images in her head. Yet still she did not know what those images portended. She had wondered, during all their long walking, whether those sensations might have been nothing more than delusions. And yet something inside her still burned, still told her that her destiny was ahead of her, to the west.

Shudojo interrupted her reverie. "I don't know why I'm telling you all this, Lady. You couldn't possibly know what it's like, to be of less consequence than the lowest insect." She pitched another stone across the water. "What does it matter anyway? I can't go back, and I have nowhere else to go."

The Princess sat and watched the ripples fanning out from where the stone had hit the water. The little waves started boldly, a solid ring, then gradually smoothed out, merging back in with the run of the water, becoming once more part of the same river. "You're right," she answered the Sister. "I can't pretend to even guess at what it feels like, to have gone through what you have endured." She turned toward Shudojo. "But I think you're wrong. It *does* matter. You can't go back, and neither can I. Because I *do* have somewhere to go. I can't honestly explain where that somewhere is, but I believe it's real. And I know I have to reach it." She touched Shudojo's arm, and this time her hand was not knocked away. "I have to believe that you're here with me for a reason. We don't have a lot of things in common, but we do have at least one: we're here together, and we know the road for us lies ahead, and not behind. Let's start with that and see where it leads us."

Shudojo didn't answer for a while; she just sat and looked into Mikasama's face. The Princess could feel those pale blue eyes searching, questioning, wondering.

At length, the Sister stood up. Looking down at Mikasama, she said purposefully, "Well? Are you just going to sit there? Let's go try to find some food." As she turned and made her way back up the bank, Mikasama grinned; the old reliable Shudojo had returned. She rose and followed the Sister back to the road.

25

As the great stone gates of Tejinashi swung open, Toshi-hito dismounted from his horse. Shiko and Nakama followed suit, the Deshi apprentice taking the reins of his Master's horse. Itachi signaled to Donaku to come forward with the Hikari. To all appearances their delegation looked much the same as when the pilgrims had approached the Yutakashi and the Shukyoshi.

To Shiko, though, it was hard to mask the conflict and turmoil just below the surface. How far, he wondered, could they rely on Itachi's judgment? Would the Kojuro's brother jeopardize them all in the pursuit of his own ambitions?

The apprentice tried to set aside his concerns, however, as he gained his first glimpse of the inside of Tejinashi. The vista that appeared before him, as the huge gates completed their inward arc, was impressive. Stretching ahead of them was a wide lane bordered on either side by structures built from the same glittering green stone as the walls and towers. The stonework was precise; every mortared joint appeared perfectly smooth. There were no signs or banners anywhere, nothing to mar the ordered appearance of the street.

The craftsmanship and neatness of the city, though, were less on Shiko's mind at that moment than his first sight of the people of Tejinashi. Just inside the area of the gate stood a small contingent of soldiers: three columns of men dressed all in green of a shade similar to that of the building stones. They were armed neither with swords nor with bows, each man carrying but a wooden staff. Before them stood a single figure cloaked in a white, hooded robe.

As Toshi-hito and Itachi walked forward, Shiko could see that the hooded figure was a woman. She did not move, nor did the soldiers behind her. Toshi-hito bowed to the figure in white, as did Itachi after a precise interval that could have bordered on rudeness, but not quite. The Deshi Master spoke first. "Greetings, High One. We come on a pilgrimage at the behest of our sovereign, the Kojuro. We seek audience with the Zaitan."

The woman did not return the bow of either man. Ignoring Itachi entirely she looked only at Toshi-hito, replying to his request in an acrid tone. "You have been away many years, Toshi-hito of Hajimeshi. Much has changed since last you were permitted inside Tejinashi." She glanced with a disparaging eye over the members of the pilgrimage. "Whatever concerns you bring with you, they are not the affairs of the Zaitan. Leave now, and return to your…farms."

Toshi-hito responded with a short bow of his head. "Your advice is most appreciated, High One. Nevertheless we are obligated by the oath to our sovereign to pursue the object of our pilgrimage. We would be most grateful if you could arrange for us to speak with the Zaitan."

If the woman was offended by Toshi-hito's intransigence, she did not show it. She turned her gaze past him. As it lingered on Shiko, standing just behind Toshi-hito's shoulder, a haunting feeling gripped the Deshi apprentice, as if a cold wind suddenly blew directly against his bones. It made him shudder. Then the woman looked away and the feeling left abruptly.

The woman glanced over her shoulder at one of the soldiers behind her. "Take them to the guest quarters." The man, evidently an officer from the sash he wore across his tunic, bowed smartly. He motioned to his men, who spread out on either side of the Hajimeshi contingent. The woman then raised her voice and addressed all of the pilgrims. "You will have no need of weapons while in our city." She lifted a hand and waved it casually through the air in a simple gesture.

Itachi felt a vibration at his side where his sword was belted around his waist, and instinctively he reached for the hilt. As he put his hand on it he found that it felt stiff, unnatural. He tugged on the sword and discovered that it was somehow jammed in its scabbard. Furiously he yanked on it, but it was as if sword and scabbard had been fused together. The sound of oaths from several of his Guards behind him suggested that he was not alone in his frustration.

The robed woman looked at Itachi with condescension. "The steel will return once you leave our city's boundaries. You will have no need of it until then. The City Watch will escort you." With a final glance toward Toshi-hito she turned and walked away, leaving the pilgrims with the Tejinashi soldiers.

The City Watch officer walked up to Toshi-hito and Itachi and bowed. "If you will follow me, please."

Itachi was seething. To take away a man's sword was the greatest of insults to a warrior. No one but the Kojuro had the right to tell a man to remove his weapon. Were his men able to draw their blades, Itachi knew they could dispatch these stick-wielding 'soldiers' in less time than it took to draw three breaths.

With an effort he controlled his impulse to fight. He reminded himself of why he had come here: to get inside Tejinashi and find its true rulers. The gates now stood open at his feet, conveniently opened for him by the actions of the meddlesome Deshi. He could afford to wait; revenge upon those who tainted his honor would come soon enough.

He motioned to his men to follow the Tejinashi officer.

As the officer led them away from the gate and into the streets, Shiko turned his head this way and that as he tried to take in everything around him. The buildings to either side soared in graceful curves, arching up in ways that made the apprentice wonder how they stood up at all. Atop most of the buildings stood pointed towers. Shiko could tell from their delicate design that the towers could not possibly have been designed for defense, but rather must have been purely decorative. High above the street, many of the towers were linked by long curving bridges. Nearly all of the windows in the buildings had curved tops, matching almost precisely the arc of the bridges above. There were few variations; other than a building's height, or perhaps its number of windows, most of the structures appeared almost identical.

As the pilgrims walked down the wide paved lane between the rows of similarly tinted buildings, Shiko also studied the inhabitants of the city. There were far fewer people on the streets than in Yutakashi, despite Shiko's impression that Tejinashi was much the larger city of the two. Unlike the teeming, frenetic activity of the mercantile city, where the streets had been full of busy, jostling people, here the few city dwellers that Shiko could see seemed to wander slowly, in no particular hurry, as if on an evening stroll.

The citizens seemed unconcerned, indeed nearly oblivious, to the presence of the foreigners among them. Shiko noticed a few casual stares but little overt interest, and that only in the Hikari lantern that the pilgrims carried in their midst. The people were all well clothed; the apprentice didn't see anything resembling the poverty of the lower classes of Yutakashi. With the streets so quiet and deserted, the apprentice wondered if perhaps the Hajimeshi had arrived on some sort of holiday.

The pilgrims and their escort entered a large square. At its center stood what Shiko at first assumed was some sort of monumental statue, but as they walked closer he realized it was something else entirely. He slowed his pace as they neared it, finally stopping altogether to stare at it in sheer amazement.

The object was a massive sphere, as large as a house. The apprentice could see sunlight glinting off its surface, as if it were made out of metal. The sphere appeared to be floating on the surface of a pool of water, and spinning very slowly. As he looked closer Shiko saw that the sphere was actually hollow: it was an intricate framework, densely constructed of small bars crisscrossing one another in elaborate patterns within the sphere's structure. Shiko could see through the gaps between the bars straight out to the other side.

Toshi-hito sensed his apprentice's interest. "It depicts the time," he explained. "The sphere revolves in a complex pattern, balanced on the water; the Tejinashi use it to gauge the hour of the day."

Itachi made a show of being unimpressed. "I can look up at the sun and tell that," he grunted. Yet even he stopped to gaze up at the magnificent sphere as it slowly rolled atop the pool.

Shiko was fascinated by what force could possibly move an object so large and unwieldy in such a delicate, precise manner. He could make no sense of the detailed patterns etched on the surface of the sphere. Glancing at his fellow pilgrims, the apprentice saw that all of them save Toshi-hito also appeared astonished at this strange sight, something so outside the realm of any of their experiences. It struck him as well at that moment how provincial they all must have looked, huddled together like...well, like the 'farmers' the woman had called them.

"This way, please," said the Tejinashi officer politely, as he waited for the outsiders to comprehend what Shiko presumed was, to him and to other Tejinashi, a routine sight. As the pilgrims left the square, Shiko thought about the magical bridge outside the city and how Toshi-hito had known how to raise it—or rather, as the Deshi Master had put it, how the pole had 'recognized' him. He recalled too how the woman at the gate had clearly known who Toshi-hito was. Yet in all of Shiko's studying with Toshi-hito, and the Master's discussions of his travels, he had never mentioned that he had been inside Tejinashi...

As they walked behind the City Watch officer, Shiko spoke softly to Toshi-hito. "Master, who was the woman who spoke with us at the gate? Have you met her before?"

"It would be more correct," replied Toshi-hito, "to say that I know *of* her. She is a member of the Zaitan." He chuckled softly. "It is quite unusual for a member of the Zaitan to welcome outsiders at the gate. If, that is, you would call such a greeting a welcome."

"You called her High One. Is she the leader of the Zaitan, the Kordaijan?"

"No," smiled Toshi-hito. "No, the Kordaijan would not come out to the gate. This one was probably the most junior of them. All of the members of the Zaitan are called High Ones, due to the strength of their magic. Each has a particular skill, inherited from mother to daughter. The one who spoke to us obviously has a skill of transformation," as he glanced back toward the Guards and their now-impotent weapons. "It is as a result of such skills that the High Ones demand, and receive, a great deal of respect."

He was forestalled from saying more as the City Watch officer stopped. "This is the House of Welcome," he said, gesturing toward yet another of the green buildings. To Shiko, it appeared indistinguishable from all the rest. "It is maintained by the city," the officer went on, "to honor invited guests...and, other guests as well," he quickly amended. He bowed and turned to go but was stopped by Itachi.

"When will we speak with rest of the Zaitan?" demanded the Hajimeshi general.

The officer fixed Itachi with a disdainful stare. "When you are summoned. Until then, you are free to go about the city." He looked over the Hajimeshi soldiers. "I would suggest you keep out of the taverns frequented by the City Watch. It might be best to avoid any...incidents." He turned on his heel and left.

Fast on his departure, the proprietor of the inn emerged to greet the pilgrims. He was a small, wiry man wearing an elaborately embroidered apron. "Please, please, come in, esteemed pilgrim guests," he wheedled. "Rooms have already been prepared for you, and baths to soothe tired feet..." As Shiko watched the man bowing and smiling, he was reminded of Toshi-hito's warning: that the Tejinashi would have been observing Itachi and his men for some time while they had been encamped across the moat. Clearly the House of Welcome had anticipated the pilgrims' arrival, even though the Zaitan magician had tried to turn them back. Perhaps, mused Shiko, not all of the Zaitan were of the same mind with regard to the Hajimeshi pilgrims.

The innkeeper motioned them all to follow him inside. The sumptuous entrance hall to the House of Welcome managed to surpass even the Audience Hall in Hajimeshi Castle in its opulence. The walls, fashioned from wide planks of light-colored wood, bore intricate carvings from top to bottom: geometric shapes and complex patterns, repeated with unvarying precision across the entire length of the room. The floors were covered with thick rugs, woven in swirling patterns of color. Along the walls stood small pedestals, surmounted by amazingly realistic sculptures of people carved in pure, gleaming crystal. Each figure was captured standing rigidly at attention, gazing out expressionless at the viewer.

It was unlike anything the Hajimeshi Guards had ever seen. The soldiers huddled together like schoolchildren afraid to touch anything for fear of breaking it. The innkeeper herded the pilgrims upstairs to show them their rooms, and here it must have seemed to the Guards as if they had stepped into a dream world. Instead of sleeping mats on the floor there were actual beds; soft rugs everywhere; and even running water, which gurgled straight up out of strange-looking metal pipes. There were rooms enough for each man to have his own.

Itachi scowled at the innkeeper. "We have no intention of paying for a brothel," he said rudely. Shiko cringed at the man's crudity.

Their Tejinashi host only smiled obsequiously. "No problem, no problem, honored sir. The city pays for the cost of the inn. You are all welcome to stay as long as you wish. Or until your business with the Zaitan has been concluded."

Itachi nevertheless demanded that the Guards double up in each room. "I am wary of strange places," he said, "and so far this city has done nothing to allay my concerns." He looked coldly at Toshi-hito. "Be sure you do not conveniently forget, Deshi, to keep me informed when these Zaitan see fit to 'receive' us." He turned away, entering the room that he and Bokusa were to share.

If he were at all concerned by the lingering menace implicit in Itachi's comment, Toshi-hito disguised it completely as he led Shiko into the guest room that the two Deshi would share.

Having seen all of his guests off to their rooms, the proprietor wrung his hands on his apron. His smile faded as he returned to the entrance hall. Clucking with concern, he stared down at the muddy tracks the soldiers had left all over his rugs. He snorted in disgust, wondering what interest the Zaitan could possibly have in such rustic boors.

*   *   *

Shiko and Toshi-hito ate a light meal prepared personally, said the innkeeper, for his distinguished guests. They then spent the remainder of the afternoon in meditation in their shared room. The Deshi Master did not expect the Zaitan to summon them for some while and, as he told Shiko, it would be a good time for them to center themselves in preparation for what might come.

So the two Deshi sat, legs crossed, facing one another in silence. Eyes closed, each entered the meditative trance that had been taught to Deshi ever since the founding of the priory in Hajimeshi. Shiko, though, found that he had trouble concentrating. It was almost as if the soft rug beneath him, while it removed the discomfort of sitting on a hard floor, at the same time dulled his senses. Without any discomfort to focus on, and to isolate, his mind tended to wander. His thoughts kept coming back to Sekai monastery and what had happened to Toshi-hito.

On the long ride down from the monastery the apprentice had wanted to ask Toshi-hito so many questions: who the Brothers really were, and why they seemed to have such distaste for magic. And how Toshi-hito had been healed, if not by some magical means. Surely ordinary medicinal herbs could not have cured him so quickly.

But once they had reached the gravesite that the Brothers had created for Ryori, and had stopped to pay their respects, Shiko had found himself feeling pensive. It had not been the time to pursue questions with his Master, and so the trio had proceeded on their way in silence until they had sighted Itachi and his men camped before Tejinashi's moat. Now, even though he sat alone with Toshi-hito in a comfortable room, Shiko found he was having trouble feeling at peace.

"Master," whispered Shiko, eyes still closed.

"Hmm?" answered Toshi-hito softly.

"Who exactly are the Brothers at Sekai? Did they come from Tejinashi?" He opened his eyes to see Toshi-hito slowly open his own, returning from his trance to focus on his apprentice.

The Deshi Master did not answer right away; he merely stared at Shiko in a way that slightly unnerved the apprentice. When at last he did answer it was with a question of his own. "As we walked through the city," Toshi-hito asked, "when you looked about, what did you see?"

Shiko pondered, trying to recall all the things he had observed. "I saw many magnificent buildings, the great time-keeping sphere...a handful of Tejinashi walking the streets."

"What did you notice about the buildings?"

Shiko furrowed his brow, thinking again about the structures of the city. "They are all green, of course; the Tejinashi certainly seem to like this green stone."

"What else?"

"Well..." said Shiko, frowning harder. "The buildings all look much the same. Each is different in little ways, but they all seem to have the same basic appearance."

"Exactly," said Toshi-hito. "That is the clue to the thinking of the Tejinashi: regimentation. The Tejinashi can build many things, but once they settle on a 'right' way to do it, then there can be no other. There is no improvisation in Tejinashi society."

"And the Brothers? They were unhappy with such regimentation?"

Toshi-hito pursed his lips. "It is more than that. The men and women of Sekai have a deeper conflict with those who rule Tejinashi."

"Magic?" asked Shiko softly.

"Yes," answered Toshi-hito, "although that is only part of it. The Brothers have renounced magic, but not necessarily because of anything sinister about magic itself. It is in how that magic is used."

Shiko was not sure he understood, and his confusion must have been apparent for Toshi-hito continued. "You have seen the type of magic the Tejinashi are capable of. Grand devices such as the time-keeping sphere, and the monumental stone gates. They have no need to farm the land, as they have been able to make their own food by magic." Again changing topics, the Deshi Master asked, "What was your impression of the Tejinashi you saw in the street?"

"They didn't seem in any hurry to get anywhere," answered Shiko. "Certainly I didn't feel like I was about to be run down by someone dashing about, as I did when we were in Yutakashi!"

"And why," said Toshi-hito, leaning forward, "do you think there is that difference?"

Shiko knew, from years spent studying with the Deshi Master, that this was the point that Toshi-hito wanted to make. As frequently happened the point was not obvious, but Toshi-hito was a patient teacher and he waited while Shiko came to his own conclusions. At length it came to the apprentice, and he began to understand what the Sekai Brothers were doing, isolated up in their forbidding mountain environment. "The people in Yutakashi behave as they do," he said, "because they *have* to, in their environment, in order to prosper, or even to survive. The Tejinashi do not need to do these things, since the magic provides it all for them."

"And?"

"And the Zaitan control the magic upon which the Tejinashi are now dependent. The people of the city no longer have farmers to grow their food; they probably wouldn't even be able to open the gates if they did not have magic that could do it for them." Shiko turned his head, visualizing past the wall of the room, seeing the cold stones of Sekai, and an old man running his fingers through the soil. "The Brothers want to live without magic, so as to be able to provide for themselves."

"Which," said Toshi-hito, "makes them what?"

Shiko had to pause only briefly. "A threat to the ruling powers of Tejinashi."

Toshi-hito smiled. "Yes. The Tejinashi, as you know, are ruled by the Zaitan, who are the source of the magic. The people have no incentive to work, or to learn, for the Zaitan have carefully provided for their needs. Which makes for a complacent, and docile, society over which to rule." He pursed his lips, a clue to Shiko that Toshi-hito was about to shift topics once more. "The Zaitan," the Deshi Master continued, "resemble in many ways a guild. The magicians vote as a body to allow new members within their ranks once they have served an apprenticeship. The skills of the magicians are hereditary, and only a few privileged families are allowed to intermarry and carry on the talent." He looked sharply at Shiko. "What would these things suggest to you?"

Shiko considered. "A conservative society. Those in power have a vested interest in maintaining their positions, and have the means to control how change occurs."

"Very good. Yes, and that has certainly been the case with the Tejinashi. It is a rigid hierarchy with the Kordaijan, the most senior of the Zaitan, at the top, with the rest just below. Then come a series of stratified apprenticeships, forming a ladder of exclusivity down to the lowest level. No one from outside this circle has ever been able to progress beyond the simplest of the apprenticeships."

Shiko nodded, but inwardly something still nagged at him. Then he realized that Toshi-hito had diverted his inquiry away from the monastery. While he did indeed want to know more about the Tejinashi, there was still one piece of the puzzle that did not add up, and it was the one thing that had bothered him the most about their entire stay with the Brothers.

"But Master," he asked, "what happened back at the monastery? How could you have been healed so quickly, if not by magic?"

Toshi-hito's smile faded. "That, I'm afraid, is not something that I can explain to you."

Shiko was dumbfounded. Never, in his many years with Toshi-hito, had the Deshi Master ever refused to answer a question, no matter how trivial the inquiry or how complex an explanation was required. It was, after all, the entire premise of the Deshi way of life: to gain knowledge and to share it with others. All Shiko could do was stammer, "I—I don't understand, Master."

"I know you do not understand, Shiko," replied Toshi-hito. "That is precisely why I cannot explain it to you." Seeing his apprentice's continuing look of confusion, Toshi-hito went on patiently. "What it is that must be understood is not something that I can provide in words. It cannot be described; you must come to the conclusion yourself. If I tried to describe it, what you would hear would only be *my* understanding of it. That, in itself, would change it and make it something completely different from how *you* might comprehend it." Once again the Deshi Master went on to another topic. "You spoke with the Abbot at Sekai?"

Still baffled, Shiko tried to keep up with his Master's direction. "Yes. Yes, I did."

"And what did you discuss?"

Shiko thought back, recalling his meeting with the Abbot and how he had felt: at first defeated, dishonored, thinking that he had failed the pilgrimage. Then the Abbot had helped him to see how with a simple change of viewpoint, he could carry on. Shiko had been so focused on having lost the material symbol of the pilgrimage, the Hikari, that he had also lost sight of the meaning of the quest. Now he was back on the pilgrimage once more, still seeking the Kotaishi. "We talked about the pilgrimage," he said. "I—I had been discouraged, but he helped me to see that I could continue the pilgrimage without the Hikari."

"He may have helped you to see, yes," said Toshi-hito. "But he did not provide the understanding, the *belief,* that you could do it. *That* came from within you. His was the key to unlock the possibilities within you that were already there." He rubbed his arm, where the once angry-red sword wound was now all but invisible. "To understand further, you must do so *without* aid of a key, or the interpretations of others. You must walk the path of your own mind, and find the way."

*   *   *

"I'd say it's unlikely anyone is at home," said Mikasama dejectedly.

The two women stood at the periphery of a village, which had been but a short walk from their riverside resting place. Their only welcome was a loose shutter, banging intermittently in the breeze. Before them stood two rows of forlorn houses, lining a dirt road like silent sentinels whose lifeblood had been drained away. There were fields lining the approach to the village, but the plots were barren. Whatever crops had been growing were long since gone, and the fields lay fallow, encircling the village like an arid moat.

Mikasama could see that the roofs of several of the houses had collapsed. The small yards, even the dirt road between the small dwellings, sprouted tall weeds. There were no people, and no animals. It was a dead place.

Shudojo surveyed the abandoned settlement. "I had been told that many of the Tejinashi farmers had left their villages, since the magicians in the city could feed everyone. It seemed ridiculous to me to abandon good farmland. But obviously the stories were true." Walking over to the nearest house, she pushed on a half-open door that groaned in protest on its long-unused hinges. Cautiously she peered inside, then stepped through the doorway to be swallowed up by the interior blackness.

The Princess, left standing alone in the road, suppressed a sudden shiver. To her it felt eerie, standing in a place that once must have been alive with the sound of children playing, dogs barking, old women arguing. She was suddenly struck by an image of a great flowering tree, chopped off at the base with nothing but a dead stump left behind to mark its former presence. An apt description, she thought, for a farm village that would now farm no more. She shivered again, wondering what was keeping Shudojo. Just when she was about to call out to her, the Sister popped back out from the dark confines of the doorway.

"Nothing," she said. "Just empty rooms. They must have taken everything with them."

Mikasama's frustration welled up inside her once more. Why was it, she thought angrily, that just when it seemed that they had surmounted some hurdle, some new obstacle was always placed in their path? Well, she was not going to just lie down and die of hunger.

"Let's start looking," she said to the Sister emphatically.

"For what?" queried a skeptical Shudojo.

"For anything."

The two women spent most of that day scouring the village houses for anything useful. Not every farmer had been as thorough as the owner of the first house, for a variety of small articles turned up. Some items were stuck in niches in the interior plaster, a convenient storage spot apparently forgotten by their owners. One or two things had been simply left behind, caked now with dust, presumably unneeded wherever the farmers had gone.

When one of the two scavengers found something useful, she let out a holler that brought the other at a run. They began making a small pile of objects in the middle of the road, including a bundle of string, a leaky but still usable wooden bucket, and, most precious of all, a flint.

"I found it jammed into a mantle, in that house down there," said Shudojo. She pointed down the street toward one of the larger structures, surrounded by a tumbled-down fence. "There's enough loose wood there that we should be able to build a fire easily enough."

"If we can find anything to cook over it," Mikasama reminded her. Her stomach was beginning to contract sharply in pain, demanding that it be fed. She tried her best to ignore it and to keep her mind focused. If she started to panic, she knew she would be even less likely to find something edible, and then she really would starve. Think, she kept reminding herself. Just think, and keep searching.

She set off toward another of the houses, as Shudojo returned to the house with the flint to see if she could turn up anything else of value. Entering the musty confines of yet another abandoned residence, Mikasama peered about in the dark, trying to ferret out any small objects, or any food, left behind. Despite her resolve her mind kept wandering. She remembered eating chokai pastries in Hajimeshi, one of her favorite treats. Komori would bake them up special, shooing the cooks out of her way; and the two of them would then sneak off to some quiet part of the castle and eat them all, like two kitchen thieves. Which reminded her of Komori's story about her father and Uncle Itachi, and Grandfather catching them out after they had stolen food from the cook.

Dear Nana-san, she thought to herself. Even now, knowing what I do about you, I wish you were still here. That other life of yours, only spoken of when you had but a few breaths left; it was never real, at least not to me. I can pretend it never was. You loved me, and cared for me, and it was from your heart, I know it was. Perhaps I *was* the daughter you never had, at least in a way.

And what of my real mother? Komori clearly knew more about her than she would tell me, I'm certain of that. And now...now I'll never know. All I have are my memories of Hajimeshi, of father, of the smells of the kitchen, like tochuya root or tanbo...

She stopped abruptly. Tanbo? Now why did I think of that? I don't even like tanbo...

Suddenly her eyes grew wide. Seeing a back door to the house ajar, she quickly ran toward it. Banging her shin against the remains of an old battered chair, she uttered an oath that would have shocked her father had he been there to hear it. Shoving against the rotted wood of the door, Mikasama burst out into the yard behind the house.

There, amid the stands of weeds, tall shoots of hardy tanbo arched up, growing wild out of an untended garden patch. Their distinctive smell, a pungent spice-like fragrance, washed over Mikasama, like an acquaintance once avoided but now welcomed as familiar when encountered in a strange place. Hooting with laughter, she ran back through the house and up the street to accost a startled Shudojo.

As evening fell the Sister started a fire with the flint, and the two women cooked tanbo stalks pulled up from the garden. Mikasama munched eagerly on a freshly baked stalk. "I never thought I would be so happy to be eating tanbo. I always hated this stuff."

"That's the way of things," replied Shudojo. "In times of plenty we discard what we dislike, or what is inconvenient." She wiped her mouth with her hand. "It is when you are in need that you appreciate what you have left."

Such sentiments might apply to more than just food, Mikasama reminded herself. Shudojo had not, initially, been her choice for a traveling companion. As she looked over at the Sister, the Princess realized that without each other neither of them would have made it this far. Who knows what would have happened to Shudojo had Mikasama not forced the Sister to cross, back at the waterfall? As for herself, she would most likely have starved, or been poisoned by some appealing but dangerous fruit, had Shudojo not been along to advise her.

It was then that Mikasama had a glimmer of a thought: was this meant to be? She had felt for some time that, perhaps, it was not an accident that she and Shudojo had been placed together. Was this why, since alone they would not have survived? Just as she started to mull this idea over Shudojo interrupted her.

"Lady," said the Sister unexpectedly, "what is it that you seek?"

Mikasama looked up to see Shudojo staring at her intently. Those inquiring blue eyes had a power to transfix one's attention, to make one want to respond in a way to satisfy their curiosity. All the Princess could do, however, was shrug her shoulders. "I wish I knew," she answered. "But...whatever it is, it's getting stronger the further west we go."

Shudojo frowned. "What is getting stronger?"

Sighing, Mikasama turned her gaze to the fire. The flames leapt up into the night, the colors ever shifting and changing, like the panes of the wall of glass...How to explain it, when she didn't know herself what to make of it? Well if she came off sounding foolish, what would it matter? She didn't think Shudojo would shun her simply for having odd fantasies...

"Dreams," she said simply. "Visions. At first, they just seemed like some sort of nightmares that wouldn't go away. But later I began...seeing things. Not real things, though; things that were...only there in my mind, but that...well, *felt* real. They didn't feel like things I was making up in my head, if that makes any sense." Despite the heat of the fire she shivered, recalling the odd sensations she had whenever the visions came. "In the early ones I saw soldiers, and I saw people wearing blue robes, like yours. But they were soldiers, not Sisters..." She shook her head. "Even before I reached Fumosa, the dreams started coming to me while I was wide awake, just riding or walking. The same ones, over and over. I don't understand what the images show me. I just...*know*, somehow, that I have to go west; that whatever is causing these images is there..." Her voice trailed off, as she realized she was beginning to ramble. She looked over at Shudojo again and was surprised to see the Sister's blue eyes wide open, as if in shock. "What? What is it?" asked Mikasama, alarmed.

"The Goddess," whispered Shudojo. "The Goddess has indeed touched you. She speaks through you." She reached for the shasen around her neck, clutching it tightly in her hand.

Mikasama, relieved that nothing was wrong, sighed with relief. "Well, I don't know about that. If this *is* your Goddess she's not been very clear about it. I certainly can't figure out what I'm supposed to make of it all." She noted that Shudojo was breathing shallowly, eyes still wide. Concerned that the Sister might yet again fall into that catatonic state that had paralyzed her at the falls, the Princess reached over and touched Shudojo's arm. "Are you sure you're all right?"

Shudojo nodded, then looked away. Quietly she said, "All my life, I have wanted to believe in the Goddess. How could one not, when one is raised to accept her, without reservation?" She looked down in embarrassment. "But always, always I had a kernel of doubt...and doubt is the one thing faith will not abide." She closed her eyes. "Do you know how hard it is, to want to believe but to always have that nagging question always looming behind you, the idea that perhaps it all means nothing? Then, when your life is turned upside down, and everything you value is swept away, you have to think, was it that little kernel of doubt? Was that my undoing? Was my faith too weak, and so I am punished?"

To Mikasama's astonishment, she saw a tear slide slowly down the Sister's cheek. Shudojo began rocking back and forth. The Princess hesitated a moment, then slid over next to Shudojo, putting her arm around shoulders that shook gently with sobs. The Sister went on, heedless of the tears, her voice choking.

"I have always tried to be strong, to be someone the Goddess would be proud of. After I...had to leave my village, I resolved to try harder, to truly believe. But I kept hoping, waiting for some sign from the Goddess, to tell me that she knew, and understood." She reached up and sloppily wiped away tears from a face unused to harboring them. "I had begun to think that I had waited in vain. But she did hear, and she did send a sign." She turned her now-puffy blue eyes to Mikasama. "*You* are that sign, Lady. The Goddess has touched you, and guided me to be with you. It has been my own stubborn pride that would not let me see. The Goddess forced us to endure, so as to wear away my conceit." She reached down and took hold of Mikasama's hand. "I knew there had to be some reason behind why we were together. I have no better idea than you what lies before us, but I believe the Goddess is guiding you. And where she guides you, I shall follow."

Mikasama was dumfounded. She didn't know what to say. How to respond to such a declaration of faith, when she had no sense whatsoever herself of being touched by Shudojo's Goddess? Unless, of course, Shudojo was right, and what she was seeing and feeling really was something being sent by the Goddess...

Thinking of it caused her to tremble. If there was a Goddess, then what did she want with Mikasama? Why was she sending such strange visions, and what was Mikasama supposed to do about them? She couldn't make any sense of it, but she knew that it was desperately important. She must get there...wherever 'there' was.

The two women held each other closely as they sat by the fire in the chilled night air.

In the morning Princess and Sister left the village behind them. They had gathered together those few items that might be of use on the road ("Now that we *have* a road again," Shudojo had remarked), and set off shortly after the sun had cleared the hills to the east.

Neither woman felt any reason to linger. Shudojo was displaying a renewed sense of energy, her practical nature turned now toward a definite purpose. The fact that the object of that purpose was less sure, Mikasama kept to herself. The compulsion to keep moving forward, however, was still with her. Whether it was as a result of the Goddess or not, she was determined to find out.

The road, little more than a cart track, meandered across low hills, skirting the steeper slopes and the stands of forest that had been too dense to fell. Where the trees were smaller and more widely spaced, the track simply led right through the woods. As the sun caught up with the two women, then slipped overhead while they walked through one such grove, Mikasama found herself with plenty of time to think. She reflected on how odd it was that one's whole perspective could change, almost overnight. Wandering in the hills before the waterfall, hungry and cold, she had felt doomed to walk about, haunted by her visions. It had seemed a purgatory of sorts: condemned to live with nothing but her own memories, and her guilt over what had happened to Komori, while joined with a silent, brooding companion. Now she was once again walking, but felt greater confidence in reaching her goal, however illusive it might be. Her companion was no longer a stranger, pensive and withdrawn; but someone with whom the Princess felt a bond, someone she now felt she could trust.

Was it, she wondered, the simple act of finding food that had changed her perspective so drastically? Even as she thought it, she discarded the idea. No, that had certainly helped; yet she also felt, in the back of her mind, a trace of that odd sensation such as when the visions came to her. She was certain that *both* she and Shudojo had been touched, even if only so very lightly, by whatever it was that had been driving Mikasama on all along.

Suddenly she was jerked to a halt. Startled, she looked down to find Shudojo's hand holding on to her arm. Before she could speak, the Sister put a finger to her lips. Responding to the question in Mikasama's eyes, Shudojo cupped a hand over her ear, indicating that Mikasama should listen.

Then the Princess heard it. Howling. Dogs? she wondered. No, not dogs; wolves!

She looked at Shudojo in alarm. The Sister was staring off into the trees, trying to gauge the direction of the sound. Here inside the woods the sound bounced around, making it difficult to get any sense of where it came from. The Sister leaned close to Mikasama and whispered. "There isn't enough breeze for me to tell if they are upwind or downwind of us. If they take our scent…"

She didn't need to say more, for Mikasama was well aware of what wolves could do. Even close in toward Hajimeshi, wolf packs occasionally ravaged a lone farmer in his field. She had heard, once, about a man who had—

A sharp intake of breath at her side caused her to look sharply at Shudojo. The Sister's eyes had opened wide, and when Mikasama turned to see what she was looking at, her own heart was seized with panic.

A pair of cold, merciless eyes, set behind a sharply pointed nose, stared back at them. The wolf had walked out from the woods and was now standing directly in their path. Other wolves appeared, silently padding up on either side of them. Mikasama's mind instinctively shrieked at her to run, but the way behind was cut off as more of the wolf pack surrounded them.

The Princess stood paralyzed with fear, as if every muscle had suddenly locked itself in place. She saw Shudojo suddenly drop to her knees on the ground, the Sister clutching at her shasen with both hands, lips moving as she uttered silent words. Mikasama realized that the Sister was praying, presumably to her Goddess.

As the Princess stood looking at the wolves all around them, she asked herself, is this it? Is this all it was for? To die here, food for a pack of wolves?

No, she shouted silently to herself. No! I will *not* die here! This is *not* where things come to an end!

She looked at the first wolf that had stood in their path. She moved forward, directly toward it; first one step, then two. Shudojo remained kneeling, still mumbling her prayers. Mikasama took a third step forward, then stopped as the wolf began a low growl. She stared back at him, as if daring him.

Abruptly Mikasama felt her vision skewing, felt the familiar sensation just at the edge of her consciousness. The visions! Not now, she screamed inside, not now!

Yet instead of the now-familiar images, a different scene flashed through her mind. She saw herself, standing on a trail, Shudojo kneeling beside her...Shocked, she realized that it was how the wolf was seeing her. The wolf turned his head sideways, and Mikasama's vision of herself and Shudojo tilted as well. She felt as if her mind was slipping away from her, no longer under her own control...

The wolf suddenly ceased his growling, and at that same moment Mikasama's mental picture snapped back into her own head. She was once again looking down at the wolf standing in her path. At first he seemed confused, but then he turned aside and started a furious barking and howling at his fellows.

They howled back, and one made a move toward the two women. The Princess watched as the first wolf lunged at the aggressor, snarling, smashing into it. They twisted and fought, while the rest of the pack danced about skittishly. At last, with a whelp of pain the attacker broke off, slinking back into the woods. The leader, his tongue hanging in exhaustion, howled again. The rest of the pack sullenly drifted off into the shadows.

There was blood on the lead wolf's flank where his adversary's teeth had found their mark. The wolf gave Mikasama one last, lingering look, then turned and slowly made his way back to join his fellows, in among the trees.

The Princess stood rooted in place, still in shock, unsure of what had happened except to know that she was still alive. She turned and saw Shudojo, still kneeling in the dirt, staring up at her with an expression of awe.

"Lady," said the Sister in a hoarse whisper, "if anything more could prove that you have been touched by the Goddess, it would not surpass what you have just done."

Confused, Mikasama could only stand and stare back at her. Shudojo rose, and as Mikasama began to shake violently the Sister enfolded the Princess in her arms. After a while, when Mikasama had stopped trembling, Shudojo said softly, "Come, we must go. It would be too much to tempt fate further." Gently she took the Princess by the arm, and led the two of them down the path and out of the woods.

26

Night slipped silently over the towers of Tejinashi, leaving their tops hidden in the darkness. Only the greater blackness of their shapes, obscuring the stars, hinted at their presence high above the streets.

Along one of those streets Shiko walked, restless and alone. His inability to concentrate on meditation had finally resulted in Toshi-hito gently suggesting that perhaps he needed to exercise his body more than his mind. The Deshi Master had recommended that it might be a good time for the apprentice to explore the city and see first hand some of the other magical accomplishments of their hosts. "You may wish," he had said, "to seek out the Night Market. It is a popular place for people to gather, for eating, drinking, and gossip." Assured by Toshi-hito that the city was perfectly safe at all hours, at least as long as he avoided the tavern areas, Shiko had thus set out to examine Tejinashi for himself.

As he walked along streets paved with precisely measured stones, the apprentice found his mind still wandering, unable to concentrate any better than when he had been trying to meditate. It was as if somewhere in the back of his mind there was some kind of restless undercurrent that kept him constantly on edge.

One thing he did notice was the orderliness of the city. It was so different from Hajimeshi, where the few streets that were actually paved used such a haphazard mixture of materials that footing during the winter months was perilous at best. Shiko also remembered how long it had taken him, during his years of growing up at the Deshi Priory, to find his way around Hajimeshi, where the streets turned and meandered in every direction. The Tejinashi streets, by contrast, were laid out in flawless lines, running perfectly straight throughout the city.

With the coming of night the green color of the surrounding buildings had faded into a dull, somber hue, and Shiko wondered when the city lamplighters would begin making their rounds. He was startled when suddenly the street and buildings around him flared into brilliant color. The light came from a series of large glass globes, set atop poles lining the street. Each globe was now shining with a sharp blue light that reflected in a glittering display off the green building stones.

Shiko had seen the poles earlier, and had deduced that they must be street lamps of some sort. He had assumed that when darkness came the lamplighters would bring their flame to each and begin the progressive lighting of the city. But of course, this was Tejinashi, and nothing here worked the way he was used to. As he gazed up and down the street at the glowing line of globes, he realized that the magicians could light the whole city at once, without recourse to human hands and simple flames. A great boon, he deduced, for those living in Tejinashi; except, perhaps, those who had once been lamplighters.

Tentatively he reached out and touched one of the poles. He felt an uncomfortable vibration through his hand, almost as if something were crawling under his skin. Overhead, the blue globe seemed to have increased slightly in brightness. When he let go of the pole the glow returned to normal, the spill of its light just overlapping that of its neighbors in their exact alignment up and down the street. He could only marvel at the things the Zaitan had accomplished. From monumental gates and spheres to even mundane things such as lighting the streets, their magic seemed to reach into everything...

As he continued on his way, striding down the lane between rows of nearly identical Tejinashi buildings, he thought about other aspects of this odd city. With every street the same there were no landmarks, nothing individual that set off one street from any other. The precision, and the craftsmanship, was admirable; but at the same time Shiko found it all rather dull. There was nothing about the city that spoke about who lived within it. Were there families up there, he wondered, behind some of those windows? Were people arguing, or children playing? There was no hint of that sort of life in Tejinashi. Certainly it must go on, he thought; but it all seemed to be carefully hidden away, as if to show a human side would somehow mar the perfection of the façade.

"*Shiko?*" came a small voice at the back of his head. Surprised, he stopped abruptly.

"*'Cha?*" he answered. "*Are you all right?*"

The familiar sound of the chodaka bird slid gently into Shiko's mind. "*Yes, I'm fine. Are you outside? Have you seen any sign of 'Ton?*"

Shiko realized that 'Ton must be long overdue to return. For 'Cha to have voiced a concern she must be truly worried about her mate. Looking about him, the apprentice wondered how a bird would possibly be able to find anything in such a place, where everything looked alike. Then he chided himself; he was thinking like a human, not like a bird. To birds the regimented towers of Tejinashi probably seemed no different than the acres of similar trees within the forests, and they apparently had no difficulty locating one another there.

"Yes, I'm outside, but I haven't seen 'Ton. Is everything all right?"

There was a reluctant pause, and then 'Cha said, "*Ever since you mentioned that we were entering one of your city-places, this...cage...in which we've been kept has stopped creating food and water.*"

Shiko frowned. "Does Itachi know? Has he given you anything to eat?"

The Deshi apprentice sensed something that wasn't a word, but which clearly indicated a feeling of distaste and disgust. "*That one knows. I think something about the outside of the 'cage' began behaving oddly, and he opened the lid, presumably to make sure that I was still in here. He could see that the food and water were gone, so he threw some half-eaten thing in before closing the lid up again. Your kind eats....strangely.*"

Concerned, Shiko looked back in the direction of the House of Welcome, as if he might be able to see 'Cha there, trapped inside her magical cage. "*I can't get near you without Itachi noticing. If I see 'Ton, I will certainly let him know what's happened. I will ask him to bring more food back for you, so that you won't starve on Itachi's scraps.*" But 'Cha's response surprised him.

"*No!*" she said. "*Please don't tell him that anything is wrong with me. He has...things...he must do.*"

Puzzled, Shiko sent an inquiry back. "*I don't understand. What does he have to do? And how could it be more important that making sure you have enough food to eat?*"

There was silence on the other end of his mental conversation. At length, he heard 'Cha's quiet thought. "*'Ton must not worry about me. If he comes back here now, he will just be put back inside this foul-smelling box.*" Shiko had trouble understanding the emotions that underlay her thoughts. With seeming reluctance, she added, "*He needs to be outside, because that is where you are.*"

"*Where I am? Why should where I am make any difference?*"

There was another lengthy pause. Her answer was so soft that Shiko had to strain to hear it. "*I have said more than I should. I should not have asked you about 'Ton at all. Please, if you see him, just tell him that 'Cha is well, and that I await his return.*" Shiko sensed, somehow, that she had severed the dialogue, like someone closing a window shutter to block out the sun.

The conversation left Shiko confused. Why did it seem that the chodaka birds were doing things, things that involved him, and yet they would not talk to him about it? And who was telling them to do it? None of it made any sense. If what Toshi-hito had told him was true, only the Kojuro, the Deshi Master, and now Shiko, were able to talk with the Shizen. Were the Shizen somehow involved in the search for the Kotaishi as well? If so, why weren't they willing to talk about it? And why was 'Cha willing to suffer alone inside Itachi's box so that 'Ton was outside, where Shiko was?

Standing beneath one of the oddly glowing Tejinashi street lamps, Shiko debated what he should do. Should he go back and try to release 'Cha from her magical prison? Perhaps then she would be able to tell him more of what was going on. Or should he talk to Toshi-hito? The Deshi Master, more than anyone, should know if the Shizen were involved in the pilgrims' quest. Either way it made little sense for him to continue wandering the streets of Tejinashi. He turned around to make his way back toward the House of Welcome when he saw something flash past out of the corner of his eye.

Twisting his head, he spied a brief flurry of movement further down the street in the direction he had been heading. Squinting in the unfamiliar blue light, he thought he saw the outline of a bird. At that moment the shape took flight, winging its way further up the road.

It was a chodaka bird! Shiko was certain of it. He mentally called out. *"'Ton! Is that you?"* But there was no reply.

He started running down the street, trying to catch sight of the bird again. Even if it were not 'Ton, perhaps it would have seen 'Cha's companion somewhere. As he came to an intersection Shiko saw the bird fly down one of the cross streets. He ran after it, still mentally calling out 'Ton's name. Rounding a corner, though, the apprentice unexpectedly found himself rushing headlong into a huge open square.

He slowed to a walk, mouth agape. There were scores of people across the vast space. He saw row upon row of merchant stalls, all in neat, orderly lines, marching across the entire length of the plaza. Surrounding the square were ranks of regimented streetlights, their blue globes casting an unnatural glow over the scene.

Shiko realized that this must be the Night Market. He was amazed at first; he had heard nothing until turning the corner, despite the presence of hundreds of people milling about the square. Once he had turned off the street, the sounds of a huge gathering had struck him immediately. Somehow the noise and bustle of so many people was prevented from escaping the area of the square, leaving the surrounding streets quiet and peaceful. Once again, he discerned the hand of the Zaitan and their magic.

In the Market itself, there were more people than Shiko had yet seen anywhere in Tejinashi. He saw no sign of the chodaka bird, but it would have been impossible in any case to spot the small shape of a bird against such a busy backdrop.

The bustling activity and vivid color of the Market both rivaled and contrasted with that of Yutakashi. Couples and small groups of citizens strolled casually in and among the stalls; there was no frenetic activity, no shouting and chaos such as Shiko had seen in Yutakashi. Here the people simply stopped and chatted with the purveyors who sat within the booths. Seeing something that caught their fancy, the citizens appeared to simply take it with them, under the beaming, friendly faces of the stall keepers. No money changed hands at all; how any sort of exchange was conducted was beyond Shiko's understanding. He was struck by the sudden thought that Nusumi would have found the entire thing unfathomable.

The Market felt odd to Shiko in another sense as well. It was almost as if it were the only portion of the city that was alive, where people seemed free to talk, and to laugh. The rest of Tejinashi seemed muted, almost sullen. How much, he wondered, did the Zaitan control how the people behaved within their city?

Toshi-hito had told him that a sizable portion of the population turned up each evening for the Night Market; it was both meeting place and produce market, although the food, like everything else, appeared to be distributed free of charge to citizens of the city. The people gathered, he had said, to see and be seen, in the location where all could satisfy their material needs.

It occurred to Shiko that the dependency this created on the part of the people toward the ruling Zaitan was probably quite intentional. The Rafter woman had told Toshi-hito that her kind could not afford the "fancy foods from the city," so he presumed that the food must be free only for those who lived within Tejinashi. Perhaps, he surmised, the magicians used the gift of food to encourage people to come to the city, where it would be far easier for the Zaitan to control their subjects...

Shiko could hear music, its source lost somewhere in the dark. For all he knew, given the magic that permeated this place, it came from nowhere but the sky. He walked up and down the rows of stalls, searching for any sign of the chodaka bird. Periodically he sent out a query: *"Ton? Can you hear me? Are you here?"* But no answering thoughts came back.

He wandered for some time, trying not to be distracted by the many strange foods displayed in the booths he passed. Try as he might, though, it was contrary to his Deshi training not to want to know about new things. Hence he found himself occasionally stopping at a stall for a closer inspection of some unusual-looking object, while the Tejinashi proprietor would cheerfully offer to answer any questions.

After covering what he thought must have been the entire length and breadth of the market, Shiko's legs began to tire. He was debating whether to give up and return to the House of Welcome when he spied a side street leading off from the square. Down either side of the narrow lane were more booths, presumably an extension of the Night Market. As he gazed down the length of the street he saw a sudden movement high up along one of the buildings.

It was the chodaka bird again! Almost immediately the bird flew off down the length of the avenue, away from the main square. Shiko took off at a run, darting among the wandering Tejinashi who stared at him in consternation as he bowled his way past.

The street was relatively short, and Shiko quickly ran out the end into another, smaller square. Other than its size it was almost a mirror image of its larger neighbor: the same types of stalls filled its open space, and unhurried Tejinashi walked about and met with friends while they gathered supplies. Rather than the usual blue globes, however, this plaza was for some reason lit by torches. They were set atop poles that lined the edges of square, their crackling flames casting an eerie dance of shadows across the surrounding buildings. The flickering, random patterns of light and dark contrasted sharply with the usual orderliness of the city.

Shiko, scanning everywhere for the chodaka bird, wondered briefly why this square should be different from the others he had walked through earlier in the evening. Then he noticed an even larger contrast with the other Tejinashi plazas he had seen. Only three sides of this square were bordered with the usual green buildings. The side opposite the street Shiko had entered backed up to a steep slope. It was the first natural thing Shiko had seen since entering the city. The hill stretched upward into the gloom, its summit higher than the towers of the city's buildings. Short, gnarly trees, their branches hung out like grasping arms, sprouted from the hillside in irregular rows extending from the border of the square up the flank of the slope. The pale light of the torches barely touched the hill's upper reaches. Shiko could make out a huge complex of buildings up there, different in shape and form from all the others he had seen so far.

The Zaitan. It could only be the palace of the Zaitan, he thought. Somehow it did not seem strange that their own abode, alone of all those of Tejinashi, would be different from the rest.

After hurrying into the square Shiko slowed to a walk, having lost sight of the bird once more. If it had flown up the hill toward the palace, thought Shiko, I'll never find him.

The apprentice stopped to catch his breath. A short distance away an old man sat on a chair near one of the stalls, comfortably puffing on a pipe with a long stalk. The wizened, bearded face looked over at him. "Fine evenin'. Say so, would ya?"

Distracted, tired and still hoping to catch a glimpse of the chodaka bird, Shiko nonetheless tried to be polite. "Yes, I'm sure it is." Looking out across the crowd of people, he sighed. "It certainly seems like they're all having a nice time."

The old man enigmatically replied, "You'd think that, wouldn't ya?" Shiko thought it an odd reply, but before he had time to ponder it further his attention was diverted by the arrival of two newcomers into the square.

Not far from the booth where the old man sat, two white-robed figures walked slowly into view. They stopped and surveyed the scene silently, but their presence did not go unnoticed. As Tejinashi citizens passed by, each would stop and bow deeply in the direction of the two Zaitan. The magicians paid no attention to these gestures.

Suddenly a child's scream pierced the calm of the night air. So unexpected was it that Shiko, having been lulled by the quiet murmurs of the crowd and the gentle music, nearly jumped sideways into the old man, who, in contrast, did nothing but calmly remove the pipe from his mouth. Most of the citizens in the square stopped walking and looked around in confusion. An edge of concern percolated into their conversations, heightened when the scream rang out once more.

Shiko looked about, trying to find the source of the child's cry, and then he saw it: a young girl, perhaps eight or nine years old, ran out from among the trees at the base of the hill, her eyes wide in shock and tears streaming down her face. She screamed again, looking over her shoulder with an expression of abject terror as she ran.

Close on her heels, thrashing its way out from the gloom of the trees, came a creature unlike anything Shiko had ever seen. Taller even than Bokusa, it loped rather than ran, using its arms and clawed hands almost like feet as it pounded after the fleeing form of the little girl. It was covered with scales, almost like a fish, which caught the light from the torches and reflected it back in a chaotic, flashing display. The creature made no sound, but from a mouth festooned with razor-like teeth a steady stream of bile drooled, leaving a trail along its path.

It was like something from a nightmare. As shocking and frightening as it was to Shiko, he could only imagine what terror the little girl must have experienced, coming across such a thing in the dark. To his horror he saw that the creature was gaining on her.

Looking over her shoulder again, the girl let out another scream as she neared Shiko's end of the square. The apprentice glanced at the magicians, but they were as motionless as before, doing nothing. In desperation the little girl scrambled up one of the trees that bordered the plaza. The creature was too clumsy to follow her sudden move, and it floundered to a stop as the girl pulled herself up into the branches. It was then that the creature made its first noise: a hideous howl, a sound of frustration and anger that grated like the sound of a hundred coarse rocks scraping against slate.

The Tejinashi citizens around Shiko seemed unable to comprehend what they were seeing. All of them simply stood, watching, as the creature pursued the girl. None of them made any move to help her or to deal with the monstrosity that was roaring up at her.

Alarmed, Shiko saw that the creature was trying to get up the tree. No, not up the tree, he realized; the creature was not suited for climbing. It was shaking the tree, trying to knock the little girl out of it. She began screaming once more, and Shiko could see her clutching on to branches, trying not to lose her grip.

The creature must have been something magical, thought Shiko; perhaps some experiment gone horribly wrong. What else could account for such a hideous thing? Why, then, were these High Ones standing idly by? Surely they could dispose of the creature somehow. Or at the very least, do something to rescue the girl. Yet they only watched, like all the other Tejinashi.

The creature wrapped its long arms around the trunk of the tree and jerked it violently, causing the little girl to nearly lose her handhold. There was no time to think, precious little even to act; Shiko knew he must try to save her. He bounded beyond the old man, running directly past the two motionless magicians and toward the scaled creature. As he neared it he could also smell it: a putrid odor, such as might arise from a latrine pit left uncovered. Casting about desperately for some sort of weapon, Shiko's eye landed on one of the nearby torches. He grabbed hold of it, but it had been shoved deep into the dirt at the edge of the square. He yanked up on it with all his strength and just managed to pull it free.

Turning back toward the tree and its screaming occupant, Shiko advanced on the scaled creature. It had not noticed him, so focused was it on its prey overhead. Leveling the torch like a lance Shiko ran straight toward the beast, and with a sickening thud the torch struck the creature hard.

The force of the blow knocked the creature sideways, and it howled in pain, an even more hideous sound than what it had uttered before. It had not, though, been knocked off its feet, as Shiko had hoped. Instead it turned clumsily, holding its side where it had been scored and burned. Turning its vicious gaze onto Shiko, it spied the being that had hurt it.

Now truly enraged, the beast came toward him, swinging its huge arms. The apprentice retreated, frantically swinging the torch pole back and forth, trying to keep the creature at bay. Some small part of his mind found time to mentally hurl curses at the Tejinashi, who still seemed paralyzed into inaction, and even more so at the magicians, who had not made even a token attempt to intervene.

The line of trees that had provided the little girl's refuge was close by one edge of the square, and the creature's advance caused Shiko to back up nearly to the wall of one of the surrounding buildings. Sensing the wall looming up at his back, Shiko was seized with an idea. The creature was slow; if he could trick it into lurching in one direction, he might be able to at least get around it and back out into the open. He started swinging the torch in a wider arc, appearing to leave a larger opening on either side as he did so. The slow-witted creature took the bait, lunging for one side as Shiko swept the torch past. But the apprentice was ready; he threw himself in the same direction as the torch, and just missed being grabbed by the flailing arm of the beast as it sailed past him.

Shiko ran back out across the square, along the line of trees. Climbing up as the girl had done was clearly not an option; the creature would eventually shake him down too. What to do? He had only seconds to decide, for the creature, slow as it was, would be on him in a moment. Then he had it: the bottom of the torch pole he still carried in his hands ended in a sharp point, which had originally been pounded into the ground. It was a risky choice, but there were no other options. And no more time.

As he came abreast of the tree holding the girl Shiko could tell from the sound, and the smell, that the beast was right behind him. The little girl screamed once more, which told Shiko more than he wanted to know about his own proximity to the creature. He would only have one chance, and if it did not work…

He ran right for the base of the tree but just as he reached it he dropped to his knees at the run, skidding in the dirt, angling the top of the pole toward the tree's trunk. In a plume of dirt and smoke the torch extinguished itself as the head of the pole smacked up hard against the base of the tree. Shiko held onto the pole tightly, angling the tail end up, and just as tightly closed his eyes. He held his breath.

The shock, when it came, nearly knocked him over. There was no sound, other than a faint gurgling noise that made Shiko's stomach churn. Opening his eyes and looking over his shoulder, he saw the creature right behind him, standing unsteadily. The sharp base of the torch pole had impaled the beast before it could stop, only inches from Shiko's back. Slowly the creature began to tumble, and then it crashed heavily to the ground, the pole lurching out of Shiko's hands as it fell.

Shiko could feel the drip of hot liquid on his back, whether from the creature's mouth or it's wound, he preferred not to know. Shaking, he leaned forward to prop himself up; even so, his arms nearly gave out. His breath came in sharp heaves, and his entire body was dripping with sweat.

The sound of two Tejinashi running up from the square just barely registered: a man and a woman, evidently the little girl's mother and father, for they called up her, telling her to come down. She cried out to them, and once she descended the tree they took her in their arms and led her away, soothing her. They ignored Shiko completely, as did the rest of the Tejinashi in the plaza. Incongruously, they all resumed their walking amidst the stalls, albeit in a more subdued manner. The only sign they gave that anything untoward had happened was the occasional furtive glance in the direction of the exhausted young Hajimeshi who sat in the dirt at the edge of their square.

To Shiko it was almost as if, now that the immediate danger was past, they all seemed to want to forget that the whole thing had happened. The apprentice staggered to his feet, gazing down at the lifeless form of the scaled creature. In death it seemed much less fearsome. Its eyes were still open, its surprise at its own demise evident in its sightless stare. Looking about, Shiko saw that no one had the slightest intention of doing anything about the dead creature. The little girl and her parents were now nowhere to be seen.

His anger started to build. What was wrong with these people, he wondered. How could they so heartlessly leave that terrified girl to struggle alone with this monster, without even trying to intervene? And now that the beast was dead, why did they pretend that nothing had happened?

Gazing over to where the old man still sat upon his chair, puffing on his pipe, Shiko saw the two Zaitan. They had not moved from their position, but now were looking directly at him. If anyone had responsibility for acting, thought Shiko, it was these two. The creature was so obviously unnatural it could only have been something created by magic. Why had the two High Ones not made some effort to stop it?

Breath still coming in ragged gasps, senses rattled from his close encounter with death, Shiko marched up to where the robed figures stood in magisterial repose. He planted himself directly in front of the pair, ignoring the astonished stares of several nearby Tejinashi. Bluntly he demanded, "Why did you do nothing to save the girl?"

Underneath their hoods, Shiko could see only a portion of their faces. Old, lined expressions, much older than the High One who had confronted them at the gate, stared balefully back at him. Neither one answered his question; instead one of them spoke, in a grating, raspy voice. "Courage."

"Foolhardiness," replied the other.

They seemed, thought Shiko, to be speaking to one another, although they were both looking straight at him.

The first High One spoke again. "Compassion."

The other responded, "Calculated."

Shiko was annoyed by this conversation, seemingly about him, as if he were not standing right in front of them but was some sort of object. "You haven't answered my question!" he demanded. "One of your citizens, a helpless girl, was almost killed by that—by that thing! You must have been able to stop it. Why didn't you?" Anger and exhaustion overcame Shiko's usual reasonableness. He found the blood rushing to his head, and his vision began to swim. "What good is your magic, if you can't help your own people?" he asked. "Or is it just that none you of want to help, all sitting up there in your palace?" He gestured up the hill toward the buildings that sat watching, silently, over the square. "Do your people mean so little to you?"

The only reply from the first High One was, "Principled."

The second magician replied, "Impertinent." With that, one bony hand emerged from within the folds of her robe, and waved casually through the air.

Shiko saw his vision go cloudy. He stepped back, putting his hands to his head, trying to shake off the feeling of wooziness. All of a sudden the sounds of the square disappeared. Looking up, he saw that all of the Tejinashi citizens in the plaza had vanished. The booths, the stall sellers, all were gone. Shiko had to blink several times until he could make his mind understand what his eyes were telling it. He turned and looked over toward the trees. The dead beast was gone. And more: the torch he had used to kill it, in fact all of the torches, were gone. In their place were the usual blue globes of the city street lamps.

Shiko felt dizzy as he tried to get his bearings. What had happened? Had the magicians somehow made everyone vanish? He looked up the side street, and could see in the distance the Night Market, continuing on as usual. There was no overflow into the side street. Everything he had seen since entering that street was as if it had never been. It had all been some kind of illusion, elaborately played out in this empty square beneath the palace. Empty, that is, except for the two High Ones, and the old man still sitting in his chair, puffing on his pipe.

Shiko turned to the magicians, wanting to ask what had happened, but before he could get out a single word they turned their backs on him and walked away. The apprentice watched as they headed toward a path between the trees, a path he had not seen before, in fact was certain had not been there before. It led up toward the palace buildings atop the hill.

The night air, away from all the people in the Market, suddenly seemed cold. Shiko shivered, although perhaps for more reasons than the chill. The apprentice looked at the old man, still calmly puffing on his pipe, as if he had witnessed nothing more than a casual encounter on the street.

"What happened?" Shiko asked. "Why—why did they do all that?"

The old man took the pipe from his mouth, tapped out some of the ashes, and reached for a pouch at his waist. "Don' know. But likes I said, all those people ya *thought* havin' a good time, wern't havin' no time at all." Looking into his pouch, he screwed up his face in disgust. "Huh. All out. Gotta go get some more." He stood up, bracing himself with a small wooden cane that had been leaning against the chair. Turning to the Deshi apprentice, he added, "Don' assume what ya see, is what *be*, boy. Gotta dig a little deeper'n that. Truth be a funny thing." He gave Shiko a queer look. "Sometime, not so funny t'all."

Just then Shiko heard a shout, someone calling his name. It was Nakama, coming toward him down the side street that led back to the Night Market. "Shiko! About time! I thought I was going to have to walk over this whole damned city. Come on, its time."

Still disconcerted by his recent experience, Shiko could only blink in confusion. "Time? Time for what?"

"For your meeting with the Zaitan," answered the soldier as he walked up. "Toshi-hito sent me to find you; you've both been summoned up to the palace."

Shiko stared up at the hill, the dark shape of the palace looming overhead, hunched over the more delicate towers of the city. On the path he could see two white-robed shapes, slowly making their way up the hill. He turned to say something to the old man but his cryptic witness was already gone, shuffling off across the square. The man's cane tapping against the paving stones of the square made a sharp rapping noise, not unlike the snapping of a twig trodden by a heavy boot.

"Come on," said Nakama, as Shiko watched the old man depart. "We need to go. Toshi-hito sent me out after you some time ago. I'm guessing you don't want to keep these Zaitan waiting."

"No," answered Shiko dully, "no, we don't." With one more glance up at the palace, Shiko turned on his heel and walked up the street, back toward the House of Welcome, with Nakama following.

Up on the hillside, the two robed figures suddenly vanished.

Down in the square the old man kept walking, but the air about him seemed to shimmer and crackle with invisible energy. His shape reformed, and where there had been an old man leaning on a cane there now walked a robed figure in white, striding calmly toward the palace hill. The echoes in the square from the sharp rapping of the cane were replaced by an ominous stillness.

Perched on a tower high above, a chodaka bird overlooked the square, watching all. He spread his wings and leapt off, soaring silently after Shiko and Nakama.

*   *   *

"Another!" roared Itachi.

The serving girl cowered, then bowed rapidly before shuffling backwards toward the kitchen. Reaching the curtained doorway, she spun quickly and ran to retrieve another bottle of wine.

The Hajimeshi general leaned his head against his hand, staring down at the wood planks of the table. He had already drunk too much, he knew. But he was angry, and frustrated, and drink helped calm his nerves. Or at least, so he thought.

Inside the dark tavern the atmosphere was fetid with stale air and the odor of spirits. A pair of guttering lamps near the door provided the only illumination. The windows were sealed, and once past the heavy wooden door any guests rapidly entered a world of gloom. It provided the ideal environment for those wishing to be alone, or to meet unobserved. Or to ask questions.

Such had been Itachi's reason for visiting the run-down establishment. It had not taken him long to seek out the rougher quarters of Tejinashi; even in a city where food was free there would always be those who felt alienated, unbound by the rules that governed others. In a city as rigidly conservative as Tejinashi, maybe more so than in other places.

It was with the expectation of finding such disaffected souls that Itachi had walked through the dark streets where no street lamps cast their blue glow, where the magicians did not waste their magic. There, he knew, would be the most likely place to find the key to getting around the Zaitan. A disgruntled bureaucrat, a rejected lover; the flotsam of petty ambitions always washed up in places like these. Usually such wrecks had only one item of value left: information. They would know who really pulled the strings in Tejinashi, and it was to those people that Itachi had affixed his ambitions.

But now? Now, he thought bitterly, he found himself getting nowhere. He had spent hours wandering in and out of buildings whose green facades, while matching the outside appearance of those elsewhere in the city, masked interiors of far poorer quality. A quiet inquiry here, a few coins laid out there, had brought him...nothing. No one knew about any others behind the Zaitan. The High Ones ruled by magic, and ruled with an iron fist. The washouts Itachi encountered were all bitter, used up; but none could offer him anything that he might use to find a way around the Zaitan. He was at a standstill.

As the serving girl placed another bottle on the table, then quickly skittered away back to the kitchen, he tried to think about what to do. Everything was a shambles. He was stuck on the far side of Tonogato, his troops dispersed, and his idiot brother still sat upon the throne, waiting for some mythical Kotaishi to come and tell him what to do. Fool, he thought. *I could tell him what to do, if he would only listen. But where am I? Stranded out here, about as far from Hajimeshi as is possible, with little hope of doing more than returning with my tail between my legs. Even Bokusa is beginning to look doubtful, although the stupid lout has just enough sense not to say anything.*

He reached out and uncorked the wine. Foregoing the cups on the table, he swilled it straight out of the bottle. Not for the first time Itachi wondered if his brother was perhaps craftier than he appeared. After all, there he sat, comfortable on his throne, while Itachi was hunched over a table in a filthy pigsty of a tavern, alone and drinking bad wine.

[He is pathetic. Once I had thought him like me: a force of power who would wreak havoc on those who would oppose the Great Ones. But he is nothing, just a weak little man hiding his insecurity behind a mask. For in here, I can see far more of his mind. This one is nothing without someone else to guide him.

It is indeed a banishment to be locked in here, having once tasted the power to touch others. It is like being a ghost...]

"Troubles, stranger?" said a voice out of the dark.

Itachi raised his head, squinting to see in the poor light. He could just make out a wiry little shape, sitting at a table in the corner. A shock of unruly grey hair was plastered across his head and his hands gripped a bottle of his own. He gazed at Itachi with sorrowful eyes that looked as if they had seen more than their own fair share of trouble.

Itachi grunted in reply, taking another swig from the bottle in front of him. "Stupid," he muttered. "Letting yourselves be run by a pack of women." He smacked the bottle down on the wood, but the thick glass only let out a dull thud. "Deserve what all of you get," he added under his breath.

If the grey-haired fellow was offended by any of Itachi's comments he gave no sign. He rose from his spot in the corner and shuffled over to Itachi's table. Setting himself down uninvited, he offered his own bottle to the Hajimeshi lord. "Try this'n. Better'n that crap they send out," he said, gesturing toward the bottle Itachi still clutched with his hand. When Itachi hesitated, the man set the bottle down in the center of the table. "Go 'head," he entreated. "Never like t' see a man down. A little a this'll see ya feelin' right fine."

Itachi glared at the man, but reached out and took the bottle, accepting the offer. Taking a good, long drink, he decided that it was, indeed, finer than the sewer water the wench had been giving him. He had it in mind to go back to their decrepit kitchen and perhaps express his displeasure. Yes, that would feel good, he thought; break a few bones, hear a few screams. Terror, he had learned long ago, could be intoxicating. Before he could rouse himself from the table, though, his new friend started talking once more.

"Hajimeshi, are ya? Knew a fellow from Hajimeshi, once. Long ways back. He came 'ere to talk with *them*," he said with a snort, tossing his head in the direction of the Zaitan's palace. "Spent my 'pprenticeship up there, learnin' 'bout groomin', and saddlin', 'fore becomin' a full stableman. Long time ago, now…" His words drifted off, and he reached for his bottle to take a draught himself.

Itachi waited. Not for any longing to hear more about the miserable cretin's life story; it was because he suddenly realized that he probably knew whom the man must be talking about.

"Nice chap, he was," the little man went on. "Spent lotta time with the mistress, so's I saw 'im a lot. I used to walk her horse for her ev'ry day, an' I'd see 'em, the two of 'em. Always talkin', talkin', talkin'; 'bout all kinda things…" His voice trailed off once more, his thoughts wandering as they became lost in their own murky past.

It had to be, thought Itachi in amazement. It had to be his brother, Kimeru, that this fool was remembering.

Itachi remembered that he had still been a boy, just turned seventeen, when Father had sent Kimeru off to Tejinashi. The two kingdoms had not had contact for years, as the power of the Zaitan grew and Hajimeshi's had declined. So Father had devised a scheme to send his second son, Kimeru, as an 'ambassador' to the Zaitan. That effort had failed, of course; Itachi, having now experienced the city first hand, could see what a useless idea that had been.

When Kimeru had returned, the Zaitan, perhaps less prideful than now, had at least seen fit to reciprocate with an 'ambassador' visit of their own. Theirs, however, was nothing but a junior disciple, a direct slap in the face of the Kojuro. Father had been furious, and would have nothing to do with her.

Itachi remembered clearly the day she arrived. She had come with Kimeru, his returning entourage escorting hers to his homeland. The moment Itachi had seen her, he had felt...something. Even after all these years, he still didn't understand what it was that he had felt. All he knew was that she was different from the whores he had been used to. She seemed...radiant. It hadn't been beauty alone, although she certainly had that, and a certain grace that Hajimeshi women lacked. There had been something special about her. When she spoke to him, she had caused him to feel...peaceful, if that were possible for one of his nature. Whenever she had been in the room, he had found himself consumed with a desire to possess her, regardless of what it took.

He knew how to charm, back in those days. As a youngest son he did not have the authority, or influence, he would gain later in life; thus charm was the grease that had smoothed his path. His eldest brother, Fugawari, had been more than happy to teach him the art of how to gain advantage for oneself. Unlike the somber Kimeru, Itachi had accepted Fugawari's tutelage readily, finding in the heir to the throne a gateway to pleasures both sensual and sadistic. He had learned how to manipulate the minds of others, focusing on their petty greed and ambitions. His own ambitions, though, even then, had been set on higher things. Seeing the wasteland of Fugawari's mental landscape, he had determined that he would find a way to displace his elder brother and become Kojuro himself once Father had died. Stodgy Kimeru he had discounted as being nothing but a minor hindrance.

Then *she* had arrived: Yonada, junior initiate of the Zaitan, ambassador to Hajimeshi. And Itachi had suddenly found himself pursuing a different objective, one that required far different skills than manipulating weak-minded courtiers. To him women had always been mere toys, to be used, broken if desired, then discarded. Fugawari had shown him how to flatter, how to make a woman think that beneath his tough exterior there existed a heart of gold. They continued to believe it until Itachi crushed the emotional life out of their souls. But this woman had been different...

So he had turned all his energies to convincing this one woman, this one person who had touched something in him that no one else had, to surrender to him. He had become obsessed with Yonada, hovering about her at court dances and functions. He had composed poems of his own poor verse and sent servants to deliver them to her, all to the great amusement of his brother Fugawari and his retinue of hangers-on.

For what Itachi did not know, what Fugawari had deliberately not told him even though the elder brother knew, was that Yonada and their brother Kimeru were lovers. She had been sent by the Tejinashi not so much as a gesture of diplomatic reciprocity but to remove her from their midst in order to avoid a scandal. All the while that Itachi had fawned over her, and she had politely endured, and resisted, his entreaties, Fugawari and his minions had been laughing at him behind his back. To them it had been a hilarious game, watching the boy they knew to have a soul as rotten as their own pursuing an angel, and an angel already committed to his own brother.

Then she had left. He had been devastated, still unaware of her relationship with Kimeru, so discreet had the pair been. Itachi had lost himself in endless rounds of drinking parties with Fugawari's cohorts, once even breaking down and weeping in his frustration at losing what he had indeed thought of as his angel. It hadn't been until one of Fugawari's retainers, nearly senseless from too much wine, had revealed the truth that he had finally understood. The wretch couldn't resist taunting Itachi, telling him that not only had Yonada been her brother's lover, she had left at last because she was heavy with his child.

At first Itachi had been enraged that anyone would cast slurs on the object of his desire, and the miscreant had been fortunate to walk away only maimed and not dead. So certain had Itachi been, and so deluded by his own thoughts, that he had truly begun to believe that Yonada had been swaying to his purpose. But her abrupt departure had signaled a sudden return to reality, and the truth gradually slipped out.

Everything, he had learned, that his eldest brother's associate had said was true. Yonada and Kimeru had become lovers in Tejinashi, and had continued in secret once the Kojuro's son had returned to

Hajimeshi. Finding himself the laughingstock of Fugawari's band, Itachi had bitterly withdrawn into himself, shutting himself off not only from them but also from everyone else. His rage and resentment had fed upon itself, festering like a putrid wound. It was from that moment that he had begun to keep his mental list of those who one day would find their heads severed from their necks and crushed beneath his boot.

A number of months later Kimeru had appeared at court with a baby girl, Mikasama, claiming that she was his daughter. Itachi, now having proof of his worst fears, at that moment had added his brother, and Yonada, once the subject of his greatest reverence, to his 'list.' Yonada, however, had not returned to Hajimeshi along with her daughter. Kimeru would never disclose what had happened to her, and over the years, with so many more acts of revenge added to his growing list, Itachi had forgotten about her.

Until now. Through the fog of too much wine, a long-buried part of him burst into awareness. *Yonada! This washed-up Tejinashi swine is talking about Yonada!*

The grey-haired man continued on. "She sure was a fine one, better'n the resta that lot…Heard tell she followed the young fella back ta Hajimeshi, before comin' back home."

That was it, Itachi knew. This 'mistress' he had served must have been Yonada. In a low, barely contained voice, Itachi said, "Where is she now?"

The man opposite shrugged. "Couldn't say. I been kicked outta upstairs for a while," as he tossed his head again in the direction of the palace. With a sly look, he added, "May be she be 'round somewhere, one know where to look."

Without warning Itachi suddenly swept bottles and cups from the table, sending them crashing to the floor. The Hajimeshi lord lunged forward and grabbed up a handful of the man's tunic, dragging him halfway across the table. His face scant inches from the stableman's, Itachi hissed, "I said, *where—is—she?*"

The stableman's voice quavered. "Don't—don't know meself, sir; just—just knows someone who might, is all…" The man burst into tears. "Please, sir…don't—don't hurt me…I'm just a fellow needs—

needs to get spare change when I can. The wine..." His voice trailed off as he cast a sideways glance at his bottle, now shattered on the floor. The dark liquid spread across the floorboards, staining the wood.

With a snort of disgust Itachi shoved the man back down into his chair. His temper still barely in check, he demanded, "Where can I find this—someone?"

Hands shaking, the grey-haired man tried to straighten his tunic in a vain attempt to recover a modicum of dignity. "Not—not far from 'ere, sir; not more'n a couple blocks. He got a sign out, says healin' potions." He looked about furtively, but they were alone in the front room of the tavern. He spoke quietly. "He more'n that, though. He be a conjuror." The sorry derelict looked around again quickly, as if the simple act of saying the word might cause unwanted attention.

Itachi frowned. He knew that magic in Tejinashi was restricted to the Zaitan, and that no male was allowed to practice it. "You're lying," he growled menacingly at the stableman. "How could he practice magic in this city run by whores?"

"Keeps a low profile. Doesn't do nothin' big, so's they'll leave 'im alone." The man looked earnestly at Itachi. "He knew my mistress; was 'er tutor, teacher, somethin' like that. Honest, good sir! They used to let a few men teach some things up there, little stuff they thought was harmless. Not no more, though, not no more...If anyone knowed where she be now, most like be 'im." He waited, cowering in his chair, clearly uncertain as to Itachi's intentions.

The Hajimeshi lord stared at the unfortunate stableman, but without seeing him. He was thinking instead of Yonada. What if she *were* here, he thought. What if he could see her again? What would he do?

And then he knew. Whatever it was that she had sparked in him had burned out, many years ago. All that remained was an unquenched ember, an unrelenting burning that seared at his soul. *She* was the cause. His dreams, his plans, were now ruined; everything he had become, this path he had taken, was because she had spurned him. If she was still alive, he was going to find her, and the very first important name on his 'list' would know what it meant to make an enemy of Itachi.

He looked down again at the poor stableman, seeing the cowardly wretch quivering with fright. He fished out a coin from his purse and tossed it to the floor, where it landed amidst the sticky remains of the wine.

With a tentative movement, the man slipped out of his chair and knelt to retrieve it. Itachi took out two more coins and threw them through the curtained doorway leading to the kitchen. Then he strode to the front door and flung it open. The light from the cheap lamps fluttered as the sudden rush of air disturbed their usual shallow glow. Then the Hajimeshi lord was gone, like a sudden gust of wind imperiously sweeping up fallen leaves before fading into nothingness.

The stableman picked himself up off the floor, carefully pocketing the coin in his tunic. Turning toward the kitchen, he waited. The curtain slipped aside and a figure stepped into the room. The stableman bowed low; as he straightened, he said, "Ya never said he'd be violent...Gotta temper, that one."

The newcomer said nothing, merely extended a hand that dropped a small bag onto the table. The clear sound of jingling metal echoed amongst the dark rafters overhead. The stableman picked up the bag, and bowed low again. "Proud to serve, High One," he said quietly. He remained bent over as the silent, robed figure glided past and swept out into the street.

27

When Shiko and Nakama returned to the House of Welcome they found Toshi-hito waiting patiently for them. Also waiting was a girl, perhaps ten years old. She was dressed in a robe similar to the Zaitans' except that hers was all green, like the building stones. She didn't speak to either the apprentice or to Nakama as they came in.

Toshi-hito rose from where he had been meditating on the floor. "We have been requested to present ourselves at the palace. And," he added, looking at their young visitor, "we have been provided with a guide to escort us." He made no mention of Itachi, or of the Hajimeshi's general's request to be notified whenever the Zaitan summoned them.

Wordlessly the girl walked toward the door, and as the three followed her outside Shiko could see that she was heading in the direction of the Zaitans' palace. She never once looked behind her, striding ahead with that same quiet arrogance which, to Shiko, seemed to be the hallmark of the Tejinashi magicians. He presumed her to be one of their acolytes, working her way up through the complex hierarchy of the Zaitan that Toshi-hito had described to him. If the girl's demeanor was any indication, thought Shiko, she was well along the path toward becoming a 'proper' magician. Her presence, though, also prevented him from telling Toshi-hito what had recently happened back in the square.

During their walk back to the inn, the apprentice had not told Nakama about what had transpired with the magicians. He had needed time to think, and to try to understand what the Zaitan were up to. Why had they gone to the trouble to create such an elaborate illusion back in the square? Had the bird been part of the illusion, or had it really been 'Ton? Were the Shizen and the magicians of Tejinashi somehow working together?

There had been so many questions that it had made his head spin. The only answers he had been able to think of had seemed so unlikely, as so many things in this strange city seemed to be. He had decided to wait and seek guidance from Toshi-hito, but had not expected to encounter a member of the Zaitan, junior though she might be, waiting with the Deshi Master. His questions would have to wait a while longer.

The formal approach to the palace of the Zaitan was impressive, leading up a road laid down with intricately carved paving stones. The road curved in precise arcs as it ascended the heights, the way bordered by the same blue globes that dotted the rest of the city. For a moment Shiko wondered if his vision of the small square, lined with flaming torches, had simply been the result of an over-active imagination. Then he looked ahead at the small green-robed figure walking confidently before them. No, he decided; it had all been far too real to just be mental delusions. Whatever had happened back in that plaza, he was certain that the Zaitan had orchestrated it.

After a long, climbing walk, the three Hajimeshi and their silent escort approached the main gate. Up close the palace was a confusing mass of towers and walls, all seemingly placed at random as if they were a child's blocks scattered across the hilltop. It was yet a further contrast with the orderly arrangement of the city over which the palace presided. The arrangement of the towers was clearly not defensive in nature, but for what purpose they were actually intended was beyond Shiko's understanding.

The entrance itself was simply a large archway, with no doors or gates visible. As the girl approached the opening the air within the archway shimmered. She passed through it, and then the shimmer was gone. Shiko hesitated but Toshi-hito, unconcerned, did not break stride and walked through as if it were no more than a simple open doorway.

Shiko and Nakama, with a silent exchange of glances, fell into step behind him.

The apprentice felt nothing as he walked through the archway. It must, he decided, have been some sort of magical barrier, allowing the Zaitan to permit or deny entrance at their choosing. From what he had seen of the Zaitans' power so far he had no doubt that, for all its invisibility, such a barrier was probably more secure than even the strongest door.

The path beyond the archway curved sinuously around the towers. Unlike the buildings of the city, here each tower was completely different from its neighbors. Some were fairly short, while others were immensely tall; a handful were made of large, irregularly-shaped building stones, while some appeared perfectly smooth, with no seams or joints, as if they had been cast whole as a single piece. Eerily, the base of every tower blended directly into the ground, as if they were all gigantic trees that had taken root atop the hill.

Shiko was distinctly unnerved as he walked down the shadowy path, the towers seeming to leer over him and his companions as they followed the Zaitan acolyte. There was enormous power here, Shiko sensed. His skin tingled, much the way it had when he had grasped the pole of the streetlight earlier in the evening. It was an unpleasant sensation, as if something were scratching at him, not enough to hurt but enough to be a constant irritant. The entire place set him on edge.

The path finally led down a series of broad steps, terminating inside a sunken courtyard. The steep, windowless walls of towers looming overhead surrounded the remainder of the open space. At the foot of each tower was a door-less archway, ringing the courtyard like dark, silent caves.

A solitary figure stood in the center of the square: one of the High Ones, her white robe reflecting the ominous blue light of globes lining the walls. As the newcomers approached she pushed back her hood. Shiko recognized her as the same woman who had 'welcomed' them upon their entrance to the city. As then, her face was set in a look of scorn. On this occasion, however, it was directed as much at the young acolyte leading them as to the outsiders. In a sharp voice the woman demanded, "Why did you bring this other?" She gestured toward Nakama. "The Sordaijan wished to see but the two Deshi."

Startled, the girl looked at the three Hajimeshi, then back to the High One. Throughout their walk the acolyte's air of aloofness had been a mirror imitation of the High Ones. Now she was just a frightened young girl, her veneer of confidence stripped away under the accusing stare of her elder.

"I'm sor—sorry, High One," she stammered, bowing deeply. "I—I did not understand. He came back with the other one, so—so I thought—"

"Exactly," snapped the High One imperiously. "You *thought*. Instead of listening to and obeying the instructions given you. Have you not learned that directives are precise? It is not for you to presume to interpret them." She waved the girl away. "I will deal with you later. Leave us." The girl, head bowed, murmured another apology before darting rapidly through one of the doorways.

The High One turned her sardonic gaze upon the three Hajimeshi. "The Zaitan are in session to discuss your...pilgrimage. The Sordaijan has requested to speak with the Deshi. You—" she said, pointing to Nakama with a long, bony finger, "are of no interest to her. You will remain here until the interview is over."

Nakama silently inclined his head in acknowledgement, but pointedly did not bow. The High One, however, ignored his actions completely. She turned on her heel and walked toward another of the doorways.

Toshi-hito said quietly to Nakama, "I do not believe we will be gone very long."

The archer shrugged. "It is all right. I am a soldier. I am used to waiting."

Shiko whispered to Toshi-hito, "Who is this Sordaijan, Master? I thought the Kordaijan was the leader of the Zaitan."

"She is," nodded the Deshi Master. "The Sordaijan is second to the Kordaijan, and the next most powerful of the Zaitan. She is responsible for the day to day running of the city."

"Come!" called out the High One from where she stood in the doorway.

The two Deshi, with a last look at Nakama, crossed the courtyard and followed her inside.

They found themselves in a narrow hallway, its roof arched to match the curve of the doorway opening. The walls, of crude, mortared stone, closed in on them as if they were indeed entering a cave. It was not at all what Shiko had imagined a palace to be like, let alone one belonging to the powerful Zaitan. The passageway was dim, only the occasional blue globe mounted along the walls casting a feeble light.

As their footsteps echoed on the stone floor, Shiko had an impression of great age, as if the buildings and the towers were ancient, much older even than the Zaitan. He felt odd, as if the narrow walls were pressing in on him from either side. It was almost a physical pressure, but one felt only by his mind and not the rest of his body. He thought at first that perhaps it was just stuffy air within the close confines of the hallway causing his discomfort. As they walked along the corridor, though, he also felt something else: a strange resonance, a prickly-feeling that seemed as if it was coming up from below. Far below, Shiko realized; below the level of the tower building, deep within the ground upon which the palace stood. The resonance traveled up through him, not quite a physical sensation but more an impression. He could feel it slowly coursing through his feet, up his legs, across his chest. Suddenly, as it reached his mind, it flared up in intensity.

Anger! Rage! Despair!

Shiko almost stumbled, unprepared for such a sudden and violent assault on his senses.

HATE! REVENGE!

Shocked, the apprentice tried to draw his mind back, remembering the time he had nearly been overwhelmed by the thoughts of the Shizen when Toshi-hito had first shown him how to listen to the animals. This was different, however; these were not the thoughts of animals, yet neither were they human. Whatever they were, they were incredibly strong.

He looked down, searching for some sign of whatever it was that he was experiencing. He saw nothing, only the flagstones of the hallway beneath his feet. The act of tilting his head down, though, combined with the feeling of pressure building on his head, caused a wave of nausea to sweep over him. He glanced over at Toshi-hito walking beside him, but there was no indication that the Deshi Master was experiencing any of the same feelings. *Is this all just in my mind, then?* wondered Shiko. *Is my head creating its own delusions, out of anxiety at being here in the palace?*

If so, it was like no anxiety he had ever experienced before. Up ahead the High One had stopped at the foot of a flight of stone stairs that led off of the passage. Pushing his mind away from the clawing tendrils of emotion surging up from below, Shiko focused his thoughts on her as she spoke.

Her icy expression had not changed. "The Sordaijan's tower is above. You will speak with her there." Her duty apparently accomplished, the High One turned without another word and walked away. Her departure did not lessen the effect Shiko felt from whatever lurked beneath the Zaitans' palace, so he deduced that she was most likely not its cause. *If,* he reminded himself, *it existed at all.* Before he could ask Toshi-hito about it the Deshi Master started up the stairs. Shiko did not hesitate in following.

He could hear Toshi-hito's voice echoing in the narrow spiral stairwell; ever the teacher, the Deshi Master was explaining about the Zaitans' towers. "Each of the High Ones has a tower. It is a personal domain of sorts, where no one, not even her own peers, may enter without her leave. They tend to be rather private about them," he added, looking back over his shoulder. Something in Shiko's expression must have alerted him that something was amiss. He stopped and peered carefully at his apprentice. "Are you all right?"

Shiko was glad of the moment to stop and catch his breath, both mentally and physically. As they had ascended the tower steps the awful, seething emotions coming from below had lessened, allowing him some respite. On the other hand, the feeling of pressure on his head was increasing. Between the two he was hard put to keep his thoughts straight.

Despite the assault on his senses he began forming an image in his head, a clear picture that the towers of the palace formed a type of barrier. It was almost as if they were a lid on some kind of insane cauldron that bubbled far below, in a space not meant for human minds to think about.

Leaning against the walls of the stairwell, he realized that he had no idea how he could come to any such conclusion, given that all he could perceive with his eyes and ears was a plain stone hallway and a series of steps leading up a tower. Between his recent experiences in the plaza and what was occurring now, he did not trust that his mind was being terribly reliable. So in answer to Toshi-hito he simply said, "I am fine, thank you, Master." He squared his shoulders, trying to appear as if all were normal. "Do they each build a tower, then? Would they not eventually run out of space?"

Toshi-hito gave Shiko another careful look, then resumed walking up the curved stairway. "The towers are inherited, passed down from one High One to her successor. The towers themselves are all quite old; the last one was built well over two thousand years ago."

As they neared the top of the stairs Shiko wondered, with such a large hilltop on which to build, why the High Ones should want to live atop a tower? As big as some of the towers were, it still seemed to be a rather small space for ones as powerful as the Zaitan. His question was answered as soon as they reached the landing at the head of the stairs.

An open archway led out of the dark stairwell and into a brilliantly lit foyer. The foyer's expanse was immense, larger even than the greatest of the Hajimeshi banquet halls. Its floor was sheathed in an odd-looking marble, with orange-veined striations running through pearlescent white. The walls were of solid stone, with no joints or mortar visible anywhere. Smaller versions of the blue globes seen outside were stationed at intervals about the room, supported on delicately shaped metal stands resembling oversized flowers. Their blue light spread throughout the vast space, while overhead, massive beams supported a ceiling whose furthest expanse stretched up far beyond the reach of the light. There was no furniture, only a series of thick rugs woven in patterns similar to those they had seen at the House of Welcome, arranged in a circle around the center of the room.

Shiko was awed. How could this huge room possibly be at the top of a narrow tower? Had they somehow turned aside, and entered some other part of the palace?

Sensing his apprentice's confusion, Toshi-hito ventured to explain. "Despite what you see, yes, we are still at the top of one of the palace towers." He gestured around him. "This place does not, itself, exist atop the tower. Once through the doorway at the head of the stairs, one...well, one seems to be 'elsewhere.' I suppose the best way to describe it would be to say that it exists in another place."

Shiko's mind had trouble accepting what his eyes were seeing. It reminded him of another, recent experience in which his reality had been altered. "But does this place really exist, or is it here only in our minds?" he asked.

Another voice spoke before Toshi-hito could answer. "An excellent question."

Both Deshi turned as the speaker, another of the High Ones, entered through a doorway along one wall. This, thought Shiko, must be the Sordaijan.

"But in the end," the woman went on, "does it really matter? Whether the reality is here, or elsewhere, or only in your mind, you are here now. One should always live in the moment. Yesterday's moment is history, and tomorrow's has yet to be born."

Her voice sounded middle-aged, and she wore the same white hooded robe as all the other Zaitan. She walked over to stand in front of them. The Deshi Master bowed. "Most High One, may I introduce to you Shiko, apprentice to the Deshi?"

She turned her cool gaze upon Shiko, and suddenly he felt as if his head were spinning. For the face that he saw beneath the hood was that of the old man who had been smoking his pipe in the square below the palace.

*   *   *

Down in the city Itachi walked an empty street. Not even a single candle appeared at any of the windows that overlooked the silent thoroughfare. The only light was that from blue globes elsewhere in the city, whose leftover glow managed to seep across the sky and filter down into this district of cast-offs and drifters. Here, unlike at the Night Market, when darkness fell the citizens turned inward, shunning one another. The stableman had called this section of the city the 'Dismal Quarter.' It was, Itachi decided, aptly named. Inside the taverns he had found nothing but miserable wretches, those who had long since lost hope of improving their lot, or who had run afoul of the Zaitan witches.

The man's directions proved to be accurate. Coming to a sign so faded with age that he could scarcely read it, Itachi made out the words "Potions: Healing Remedies; Lovers Quickening; Truth Serums."

He snorted in disgust. This 'conjuror' was a charlatan, no doubt. Well, hopefully the information would be more promising than the potions. For if not he would return to find the stableman and teach him the wisdom of 'honesty' when dealing with strangers.

He pounded on the door, the sound echoing loudly up and down the street. Somewhere a dog barked, followed by the shouting of a presumably angered owner, for the barking ended with a piteous yelp.

There was no response from beyond the door, so Itachi pounded again. The old door sagged on its hinges, visibly shaking as Itachi hammered on it. Finally the Hajimeshi lord heard the sound of movement inside and the unmistakable clacking of metal bolts and a lock being undone. With a slow, painful screech the door opened a small crack to reveal a shriveled eye peering out at him.

Without preamble Itachi asked, "Are you the conjuror?" Abruptly the door swung open, and Itachi saw an ancient, ill-kept figure, his hair straggling down his shoulders, wearing a filthy tunic. The man became quite agitated, raising his hands to his lips imploringly.

"Quiet!" he said. "Do not speak of such in the street!" He stuck his head out, turning to look up and down the road.

Itachi, indifferent to the man's concerns, persisted in his inquiry. "I am told you know of Yonada, who went to Hajimeshi."

The old man ceased his furtive glances, and slowly straightened. He looked keenly at Itachi for a moment. "Come inside."

The interior of the man's abode was as dirty and unkempt as he was, and smelled as if the washing of clothes, bodies, or anything else, was but a distant memory. Wrinkling up his nose, Itachi looked around as the old man re-bolted the door.

It was some sort of workshop, although the single candle sconce on the wall provided precious little light with which to see anything. There were worktables, and tools whose purpose Itachi could not discern. Around the walls were jars of varying shapes and sizes containing all manner of liquids and solids; of what, Itachi was certain he preferred not to know.

The old man turned to look at his visitor. "So," he stated peremptorily, "you are one of the Hajimeshi pilgrims."

Irritated that the man had recognized him so readily, Itachi replied gruffly. "Perhaps I am. That is unimportant. I am here for information."

"Oh, information you want, is it?" said the man, as he shuffled over to one of his worktables. "Not a potion? Perhaps a little of this," he asked, picking up a bottle containing some vague green substance. "Something to heighten the sexual act? Hmmmm?"

Itachi glared back through clenched teeth. "I care not one fig for your worthless concoctions, old man. Do you know of Yonada or not?"

"Humph," said the conjuror. "Typical of Hajimeshi farmers. No manners whatsoever."

Itachi flushed. Angrily he stepped forward, prepared to strike the man's head against his own workbench as a lesson in 'manners.' At that moment the old man suddenly raised a hand, and instantly the entire room was bathed in light.

Itachi stopped dead in his tracks. Looking about, he could find no lamps, nothing to account for the sudden light that seemed to highlight every corner, every dusty, disused parchment and jar. He saw a smirk spread across the old man's face.

"My name is Wochu, great lord of Hajimeshi. And do not think that your physical strength can subdue what I can produce. For I could slice your head from your body before you so much as reached for your blade. Oh, but of course, you have no blade now, do you? Only an amalgamation of sword and scabbard. Pity..." With a further wave of his hand, the room was plunged back into its original gloom.

As Itachi struggled to adjust his eyes back to the returned darkness, he heard Wochu continue: "However, I prefer moderation in all things. Such trifling displays tend to...draw unwanted attention. So, if you are prepared to be civil, perhaps we can discuss business."

Chagrined, Itachi nodded his assent. Magic, he thought bitterly. Those who wielded it were mad, as this fellow was mad. Better that they should all be driven out, or better yet, driven underground. Into burial tombs.

Wochu said, "You wish to know about Yonada. I can tell you about her. She—"

"Where is she now?" interrupted Itachi. "Where can I find her?"

"Tut, tut, my good fellow," responded Wochu, sitting down on a stool at his workbench. He picked up a shallow bowl and began methodically crushing something in it with a stone pestle. "So many questions. Yes, I know where she is. What teacher worth his skill does not keep track of where his students have progressed? No matter how far..." For a moment the only sound was the plaintive scraping of stone against stone, a sound that grated on Itachi's nerves and made his skin crawl.

Wochu abruptly set the bowl down and turned back to Itachi. His tone was once more business-like and to the point. "But, unlike your Deshi, I do not give away knowledge for free. If I did," he added, gesturing around him at the accumulated detritus of his workshop, "then no one would traffic with poor Wochu anymore, would they?"

Itachi pulled his moneybag from his belt, holding it up for the conjuror to see. "Name your price, old man."

Wochu laughed. "Your gold is worthless to me, Hajimeshi farmer. I can get all the gold I need from the scum of the Dismal Quarter. No, what I want, only you can provide." His eyes fixed Itachi with a steely gaze. "I want the lamp."

Itachi was confused. The lamp? What lamp? And then he realized. "The Hikari? You want the Hikari lantern?"

Wochu shook his head with feigned patience. "How *do* these farmers ever teach their children to come in out of the rain?" he sighed. "Of course, the Hikari!"

Itachi frowned. He didn't really believe that the Hikari was anything more than a simple hallway lamp, but it was a symbol, and a necessary one, for the pilgrimage. To give it up meant giving up any pretense of trying to become the Kotaishi as a way of displacing his brother. Was he willing to throw it all away, in his pursuit of Yonada? Was finding her more important than his future?

"Well, farmer?" asked Wochu impatiently. "That is my price. Now how precious to you is your information?"

* * *

Shiko's mind tried desperately to reconcile the sound of the woman's voice and the face of the old man. Quickly he bowed. "I am honored, Most High One." When he rose up he was again startled, this time to see the face now looking down at him to be that of a middle-aged woman.

She nodded politely, turning away from him and returning her attention to Toshi-hito. If he, too, had seen the old man's face on her, he gave no sign. The apprentice felt even further adrift than ever. Could he trust none of his senses in this strange place?

The magician spoke, the animosity of the other Zaitan notable by its absence. Yet it was a voice, Shiko sensed, well versed in authority: "Your visit was a surprise to most of the Zaitan."

"But not, I take it, to you, Most High One?" replied Toshi-hito.

The Sordaijan smiled, but did not answer his question. "There were some who wished you turned away before entering Tejinashi."

"Our 'welcome' was, shall we say, earnest, if not cordial."

She chuckled. "Yes. Sutoya is our transformationist. She was one of the more vocal in opposition to your arrival. Although not, I might add, by any means the only one of that opinion." She tilted her head to one side, considering. "Your appearance has caused a great deal of consternation among the Zaitan. There are those who say we should have nothing to do with you, that your concerns are trivial and of no matter to us. A few others disagree. They argue that regardless of your sophistication, or lack thereof, you as much as we form an integral part of the fabric of Tonogato. The debate rages on, down below in the Grand Chamber." She gestured dismissively with one hand. "I have chosen to ignore the...deliberations, and see to the matter personally." She stopped and looked keenly at Toshi-hito, then at Shiko. "Tell me, pilgrims of Hajimeshi, what is it that you seek?"

The pressure that Shiko had felt as they had ascended the tower had been growing steadily; in fact, it had been building ever since they had entered the 'room' at the top of the tower, wherever it was. Now the pressure was also becoming increasingly painful. As the Sordaijan fixed him with her gaze, he felt as if there was something outside his mind pressing in, trying to beat past the mental walls that protected his inner self. He visualized himself inside his own head, with arms outstretched, pushing back, trying to keep the walls erect. With difficulty he concentrated on answering the Sordaijan's question.

"We seek the Kotaishi," he said. "It has been prophesied by the Shizen that he must unite Tonogato against a great Darkness that is returning."

Her eyes did not waver but remained fixed on his. "And will you find what you seek here?"

Toshi-hito spoke. "It may be, Most High One, that our quest will reach fruition here. If not, we can but go on seeking until we are successful."

She looked briefly at the Deshi Master then returned her attention to Shiko. The pressure increased another notch, causing him to wince. His breathing became shallow. The Sordaijan's eyes locked on to his. "And you, apprentice? What do you have to say?"

Shiko felt as if he was being challenged, as if the truth of his words was, somehow, to be judged. But he did not hesitate. After his experiences at Sekai, his path had become clear. He could see now that the path had always been there; he had simply been unable to see it before then. "The light that guided us was placed in my hands. I will carry its spirit until it shines on the Kotaishi."

The Sordaijan seemed to consider his words, her gaze steady and unrelenting on his face. At last she said determinedly, "Follow me." She turned and walked to the door through which she had first entered. When she opened it, Shiko saw that it led outside to a balcony, a stone railing lining its far edge. Beyond the railing, all he could see was the dark of night.

The Sordaijan walked out, and almost at once Shiko felt the pressure on his head ease, although it did not dissipate entirely. As he and Toshi-hito followed her outside, the apprentice was struck by how cold the night air was; it seemed to rush up from somewhere far below the balcony before curling up over the edge of the railing. He shivered.

The Sordaijan walked all the way out to the edge of the balcony. Joining her there, the two Deshi could see nothing in the blackness beyond; no sign of Tejinashi, or even whether there was any ground below at all. Shiko had an impression of an immense void that stretched further than he could even contemplate. It felt oppressive, as if the dark sky might at any moment swallow the balcony and all its occupants.

The Sordaijan spoke in such a low voice that Shiko strained to hear her. "It is safer to speak out here. The closer one is to a tower, even my own, the nearer one is to ears, both those that are real and those that are not. And it is better that they do not hear what I am about to tell you." She stood facing the dark void looming beyond the balcony, leaning against the railing. Its support appeared insubstantial against the black night; if the dizzying height above those unseen depths frightened her, she showed no sign of it. "Would you find it interesting to know, Toshi-hito of Hajimeshi, that I have been an agent of Himitsu since before you first visited the Kingdom of Tejinashi?"

Shiko had never before seen Toshi-hito look surprised at anything, but the Deshi Master's face showed an unmistakable expression of shock. He recovered quickly. "That is…quite interesting, Most High One."

"Yes, I imagine it is," she replied laconically. Her voice took on a hard edge. "You have seen what the Tejinashi have become. The people have grown lax, all of their wants provided for them. No one need work. Skills and crafts, even the knowledge of how to plant and grow, all lost. If, as you say, young Shiko," she said, turning toward the apprentice, "the Darkness is coming, then the people of Tejinashi will be easy casualties." She again leaned against the railing, holding on to it tightly with her hands, almost as if she were holding it in place against the night beyond. "The Zaitan have consolidated their power through the subversion of their own people. They have turned the magic into a tool to further their own ambitions. As a result, the people are now weak and useless."

Toshi-hito said gently, "Such a point of view is…uncommon…among the Tejinashi, I would think. Particularly for one who has become their Sordaijan."

She sighed. "Forty years ago, I too was an apprentice. I had just been elevated into the Illusionist Order. It was then that the Zaitan first began to change the nature of things, to become not just the overseers of

Tejinashi but its undisputed master. Along the way we lost touch with our world—making useless objects, measuring things only for the sake of their measurement. Oh, how the Zaitan love to measure," she said bitterly. "The more we quantify, the more we see how much we do not understand. But that just drives the Zaitan to quantify still further, certain that the ruthless application of magical principles will, sooner or later, reveal the 'truth.' They cannot see that truth is not a number, or some elusive 'unifying spell' that will explain the nature of the world with a simple wave of the hand. Truth can only be found within oneself, and one's relationship with the world."

She exhaled deeply, calming herself. "Such heretical ideas did not come to me, of course, fully formed. It was only after I became privy to the inner workings of the Zaitan, and saw the results of their actions, that I became concerned. When the decision to 'make' food was made I argued against it, but as I was but a junior member in those days my voice was not heard. Then and there, I said, 'this is not the right path.' But I did not know what the right path should be."

With a hint of a smile, she said, "As chance would have it, the then-Kojuro of Hajimeshi, the grandfather of your current Kojuro, had just sent an embassage to Tejinashi." She noted Toshi-hito's raised eyebrow. "Ah, I see that this too is unknown to you. You see, your first visit here was not the only attempt to provide us with a Hajimeshi ambassador."

So, thought Shiko, that was the answer behind Toshi-hito's knowledge of Tejinashi! He had come as part of an embassy from Hajimeshi! But why had he never told me? Even more intriguing, it seems that someone had tried before, and Toshi-hito had not even been aware of it.

The Sordaijan shrugged. "It was fruitless, of course. I suspect information of your people's earlier visit was hidden from you, as failures so often are. But the ambassador sent on that first occasion turned out to be a young man named Himitsu. I was assigned as his guide while he was here. One day by chance we happened to be alone. He took advantage of that time to talk, and I listened. And I saw another way."

Her eyes seemed to glisten, even though there was no light outside to shine on them. To Shiko, they took on the aspect of polished flint.

"Himitsu convinced me that the only way to alter the fate of Tejinashi was to rise to the pinnacle of my order. From there, one would have the necessary…'perspective,' I believe he called it…to affect change. And so I waited, and worked my way up through the hierarchy. It has been long, and hard, all these years…"

She looked down at her hands, still holding the railing with an iron grip. "However," she went on briskly, "you did not journey all this distance to hear my concerns. That I am speaking about this to you at all is due to Himitsu's request regarding the girl Mikasama."

At first Shiko drew a blank, so out of context was the name. Then he remembered what Toshi-hito had heard from 'Ton, that the Kojuro's daughter had set out after the Hikari pilgrims. Was she still lost, he wondered?

"I regret to say," the Sordaijan went on, "that I have no word about the Kojuro's daughter. But it was in learning of her plight, via Himitsu's letter, that I was also informed of *your* quest." She looked at Toshi-hito. "There are many in Tejinashi who would not welcome the advent of a Kotaishi. But the Kordaijan is not among them. As I believe you already know."

Toshi-hito nodded. "So I believed when we saw her."

Shiko glanced over at the Deshi Master. Saw her? What was Toshi-hito talking about? When did we see her?

The magician said, "The Kordaijan will support the accession of the Kotaishi. Obviously, you will have my support as well. Between us, I believe we may be able to sway the prejudices of our brethren. It will not be easy, but the caliber of person shown here has not gone unnoticed." Turning away from the railing and the dark emptiness, she spoke to both of them but looked directly at Shiko. "You must return to Sekai monastery. That which you seek will be found there. But you must not delay. There are forces, dark forces, outside of Tejinashi, and Tonogato, that are gathering to defeat your purpose." Shiko, staring into the depths of those ancient eyes, suddenly felt the pressure again increase tremendously inside his head. The Sordaijan, her voice sounding cold, rang in his ears like the pealing of deep, sonorous bells. "I have waited many years to understand why I was called to follow this path, to rise to be Sordaijan of a people whose ideals I did not share. Now, I know."

With a rush the pressure overwhelmed Shiko's mental barriers, and whatever had been outside suddenly thrust in. It was a sensation not unlike a dam suddenly bursting, with the water, long held back against its will, surging forward to spread itself across everything in its path.

He felt his vision go blurry, and dimly heard Toshi-hito's voice saying, "Shiko?" At the same instant that his external senses ceased to communicate with him, he suddenly found his mind able to 'see' things with perfect clarity. It was as if, all at once, he was able to connect the loose threads that had been hovering in the background of his thinking. Things that had been said, by Toshi-hito, and by 'Ton and 'Cha; the odd behavior of Kanyo and Tanoshi toward him in Yutakashi; the actions of the Sordaijan herself.

It was as if a massive puzzle, that he had only been even vaguely aware existed, suddenly fell into place. Pieces interlocked with pieces in his head, and at last he began to understand.

28

Itachi walked swiftly down the dark street housing Wochu's tattered establishment. Or at least he walked as quickly as a man might while lugging a large bundle wrapped in a cloak. Fortunately for Itachi it was not a part of town where onlookers paid much attention to whatever passed by, if they knew what was healthy for them. Nevertheless he was hoping to avoid any notice; he knew that sufficient coins might loosen any man's tongue. He tried to keep the covered Hikari as inconspicuous as possible.

[*A woman! He is willing to throw everything away, the chance to seize power and crush his enemies, all because of a woman! He cannot fool me, although he is fooling himself. He thinks to kill her, to revenge himself on her, out of spite. But he is deceiving his own thoughts!*

He wants her still, this girl that he knew as a youth. He is blind to everything else! I can see his memories, as clear as if they were my own. Had his vanity not overruled his sense he would have seen that the girl would never be his, not then, not ever. And now he is willing to lose everything in order to track her down. Kill her? He might; he is so confused, he isn't sure what it is that he wants. He probably won't know until he finds her. And I can do nothing but watch him ruin himself...

I must try to do something; try to push, somewhere, anywhere, to see if I can alter his thoughts...]

Arriving in front of Wochu's workshop, Itachi raised a hand to knock on the decrepit door. Then he stopped, fingers mere inches from the weathered wood. He had not risen so far in life without using that cunning for which he had long been renowned. So he stopped to re-consider once more what he was about to do.

When he had returned to the House of Welcome after leaving the conjuror he had found most of his men still out in the city, and the two Deshi nowhere to be seen. Only Donaku had been left behind, to guard the Hikari. For once Itachi had been glad that the stupid oaf could not remain awake more than a handful of hours in a day. It had been a simple matter to remove the lantern from under the Guard's sleeping nose.

Now Itachi stood here, ready to hand the lamp over to a crazy old man. Feeling the warmth through the fabric of the cloak, where the flame still burned within the Hikari, he felt a moment of doubt.

To take the lantern, to 'steal' it from the pilgrimage, would probably end the quest. But what did that matter? he thought. I have no hope of convincing the Tejinashi to side with me. The Yutakashi are swine; my bones will rot before I trust any of them again. And if I return in less than triumph, as anything less than this mythical 'Kotaishi' of my brother's imagination, my plans would probably be discovered before I could marshal my forces again. My activities can't remain hidden from that slime Himitsu for long.

So, what difference if this ridiculous quest ends here and now? I wouldn't put it past the Deshi to somehow 'produce' a Kotaishi of their own, as a means to solidify their position in my brother's court. Better then that they, too, should end in failure.

Itachi held the bundled light away from his body. "Nothing but a stupid hallway lamp," he muttered. He pounded on the door.

"Well," said Wochu, as he led Itachi into the dark workshop, "I see you have decided to meet my price."

The Hajimeshi lord walked silently over to a worktable and set down the Hikari. Without preamble he drew off the cloak, revealing the lantern. Its luminescence spread out across the room, a more subtle, pervasive illumination than the light that had been cast by the conjuror's spell. As soon as it was revealed, Wochu let out a sigh.

"Ah, yes," he said. "Yes. This will do nicely." He approached it gingerly, almost reverently. Reaching out a hand, he touched its metal frame, almost caressing it. "Oh, so pretty, don't you think?"

"It is a lamp," answered Itachi brusquely.

Wochu's forehead wrinkled in displeasure. "Have you no sense of artistry, farmer? Are you blind to the beauty of this magnificent light?" He placed both hands around the Hikari, its light reflecting dully off his dirt-encrusted tunic. "What a joy it shall be to destroy it."

Itachi was startled. "Destroy it? Is that what you wanted it for?"

The old man looked up at Itachi with the eyes of a man long since lost to rationality. "Why, of course, my good farmer friend. Why else did you think I desired it? It has been a long time since I have had the pleasure of obliterating a thing so fine as this." His expression took on a harder cast. "Are you having second thoughts, then? Is my information worth less to you now, when you know my intent?"

Itachi felt something unusual, and unwelcome: a pang of guilt. Destroy the Hikari? Why would this old fool want to do that?

On the other hand, he thought, what difference would it make had I walked out the door not knowing what he did with it? It would have been as good as destroyed then, for all intents. Besides, it's just a lamp..."If that's what you want for payment," he said gruffly, "that's fine with me. Now tell me about Yonada."

Wochu smirked. "Of course. Value given for value received. Always a good way to do business." He wandered over to the front of the workshop. "I hope you won't mind," he said over his shoulder, "if I make a few preparations while I talk?" He moved his hands slowly along the edges of the doorway, stopping to tap the wood every once in a while.

Itachi was puzzled. "Preparations for what?"

"Oh, for the extinguishing of the light, of course. Aside from the fact that I, for one, simply cannot wait, how could I deny to one who brought me such a wonderful specimen the satisfaction of watching it die?"

Itachi shivered. This old fool was insane, he realized; he had best get whatever information he could and leave as quickly as possible.

But Wochu seemed to have other ideas. As the conjuror continued to make circuits around the doorframe, the wood started to shimmer, and then to glow, with a faint bluish light.

"Don't worry," said Wochu, seeing Itachi's alarmed expression. "There is no danger for you. I must seal the door, and ward the room, lest any of what I am about to do should seep out. That would never do, no, no. For those harlots from on high would certainly notice, and then where would poor Wochu be, hmm?"

Beginning to feel trapped, Itachi demanded, "What of Yonada?"

"Yonada," said Wochu. "Ah, yes, Yonada. One of my best students. Presumably the very best, if one considers how far she rose. Created quite a stir among the Zaitan."

"So," interrupted Itachi, "she became a full magician?"

Wochu turned briefly aside from his task. "*I* will tell the story, if you please, farmer." Working his way along the front wall, tapping it gently, he continued. "Yes, she became a magician. Quite an important one, too. But she never did see things quite the right way, at least as far as most of the Zaitan saw such things. She showed the good sense to know it too. And so she left."

"Left? Left where?" asked Itachi.

With a quick flick of one hand the conjuror made a short, sharp motion, and an entire network of blue lines, like some giant, chaotic spider's web, instantly snapped into being across the front wall of the workshop, linked to the blue around the doorway. A soft hum filtered into the workshop from where the lines stretched.

Itachi stepped back, eyes wide. Wochu calmly went over to one of the side walls. "Nothing to fear, my friend. Perfectly harmless. Unless, of course, you try to cross the boundary. That would, indeed, be a very sad thing. For you." He repeated the same steps along the wall that he had performed across the front. "But, as I said, this is not intended for you. Only for those arrogant, overbearing, witches of the Zaitan. Now, where was I? Oh, yes."

"Yonada left," he went on, while performing his arcane motions, "although only the Zaitan knew where, at least so they think. To all others, she is still here, only in 'seclusion.' Well, she is secluded, certainly, but not here, not in Tejinashi. She sequestered herself in a monastery up in the hills to the north."

"A monastery?" whispered Itachi. Was that why the Deshi had been so intent on going to a monastery? Were they trying to get to Yonada? What had that brat called it? Sekan, Sekon...no, Sekai!

Wochu moved toward the back wall of his workshop. "The story goes that she went voluntarily, so as to avoid 'unpleasantness' with the rest of the Zaitan. Which means, simply, that she lacked the power base to defeat them, and she knew it." He snapped his hand again, and the back wall was covered with glowing blue lines. The humming sound increased. "She never was one to falter when faced with a challenge. But, then, I gather you probably know that about her, farmer. Else why would you be seeking her out, hmm?"

Itachi did not rise to the bait. He followed the conjuror as Wochu began tracing his lines along the remaining wall. "This monastery. Is it called Sekai? Off the road along the long lake?"

The conjuror turned, surprised. "Ah, you've heard of it then. Yes, that's the one. A dreadfully cold place, up in the mountains. Not the place for any self-respecting Tejinashi, if you ask me." He began humming to himself as he traced out the last of the lines across the wall.

The general from Hajimeshi felt the emotion surging in him again. Yonada! She had been in that blasted monastery all this time, and those Deshi knew it! That little brat apprentice knew it, and he had the gall to stand up to me! And I chose instead to come here. Here! Stuck in a room with some madman obsessed with a stupid lamp. I must get out, I must get to this Sekai Monastery.

A sudden thought flashed through his mind. What if the Deshi went back? What if they left to go back for her, while he was stuck in here? Angrily he turned to Wochu. "I must leave, now! You have your payment. Open a way for me to get out of here."

Wochu calmly finished the last wall, and as he did so all the lines joined together at their ends, making a complete circuit about the room. Their joined sound rose even louder, forcing the conjuror to raise his voice. "'Tis true, my friend, that I could open a way through, from this side. The outside is as impregnable as a mountain of granite. Alas, though, such a passage consumes a great deal of one's energy. And right now, I want to use that energy. On this!" and he strode over to where the Hikari stood majestically on the table.

Itachi, for once frightened by something that he did not fully understand, stood uncertainly, fingering the hilt of his useless sword. He had no choice, he realized, but to wait until this lunatic had finished with his crazy fantasy.

Wochu gently opened the side of the Hikari and the bare light, unfiltered by the glass, spread out across the front of his dingy work clothes. With no regard for the heat, the conjuror reached in and cupped his hand around the flame that burned inside. Slowly he closed his fingers around the flame. The shadows from his grasping fist jumped across the walls, their black dances seared through by the sharp blue lines that hummed in the background. As Wochu closed his grip tighter Itachi, amazed that the man's hand was not burned, saw the conjuror's expression change. A great smile spread across Wochu's face, and with a final squeeze he closed his hand completely, blocking out the light. The shadows disappeared as the light that gave them birth vanished, leaving nothing but the pale blue strands along the walls. Wochu slowly released his grip. Then, quite suddenly, the conjuror snapped his hand out of the lamp.

The flame had not been extinguished. It flared back up, as brilliantly as before. The dancing shadows returned, as if in mockery of the conjuror's efforts.

"Damnation!" shouted Wochu, the mad smile replaced by a look of fury. "It is more powerful than I thought!" He tried to grasp the flame with both hands, tried again to squeeze it out of existence. Still the light would not die. The conjuror started to sweat, little beads of water glittering across his forehead where the light caught them. He stared down at the lamp, talking to it as if it were alive. "Ah, my pretty, so you want to be difficult...I had not planned on having to work so hard. But, oh, ever so much more satisfying when it is done..."

Itachi, forgotten, sidled as far away as possible within the confines of the workshop. Wochu placed his hands once more inside the glass casing of the Hikari. This time, however, the conjuror began reciting words, some strange incantation that made no sense to Itachi. Wochu slowly brought his hands together around the flame, his voice rising. The flame darted and shifted about, first to one side and then the other as if seeking an escape from the relentless pressure of the conjuror's palms slowly enveloping it. Itachi saw Wochu's arms starting to shake, and then the old man's whole body trembled, as he fought the flame that still writhed between his fingers. The conjuror started to shout, then almost to scream his unintelligible tirade. Itachi was certain the man would collapse at any moment.

And then, quite suddenly, it was over. With a final exultant shout the conjuror's hands met, and the room, save for the steely blue glow of the ward lines, went dark once more. In the dim light Itachi saw Wochu remove his hands from the dead lamp, and heard the man's ecstatic sigh. It was the sound of satisfaction as might come from a man who had just lain with a courtesan. To Itachi, it seemed to echo the madness he had felt ever since encountering the conjuror.

Wochu turned slowly away from the lamp to face Itachi. "Was that not," he said softly, "the most wonderful thing? A rare experience, my friend, a truly rare experience..."

Itachi spoke carefully, aware that the madman before him might turn on him at any moment. "Yes, very rare. I'm—I'm glad that you 'enjoyed' it. Now, perhaps, I'll be on my way…"

"Yes, yes of course," said Wochu languidly. He moved toward the door. "Fortunately for you, I still have enough strength left to open a brief passage. Otherwise, you might have to spend the night, hmm?" He giggled, a sound that sent shivers up and down Itachi's spine. The Hajimeshi general would rather have spent the night with a bed full of scorpions than share a room with such a crazed old man.

Wochu raised his hand before the door, then suddenly stopped. He turned abruptly to Itachi. "You plan to go to Sekai, don't you?" Itachi did not answer, unsure of Wochu's intent. Would he try to stop the Hajimeshi lord from confronting Yonada? Or did he have some other deranged scheme in mind?

But the conjuror's reasoning seemed simpler. "You will not get in unaided. The monastery is well protected. How could I let a friend, who brought such joy for me to experience, walk so far only to find himself locked out?" Wochu strode past the workbenches to a rack holding hundreds of little jars and bottles. He searched, tapping the lid of each bottle with a fingertip, humming to himself once more.

Eager to absent himself from this asylum of lunacy, Itachi fidgeted nervously. Finally Wochu found what he was looking for, as with a satisfied "Ah!" and a flourish, he picked a small vial from the rack. "This, my friend, is something that may be of use to you. It is a special dust that will render your likeness to be that of another, for a brief period." He handed the vial to the reluctant general, who eyed it suspiciously. "Don't worry, it is perfectly safe for you. Simply toss the dust in the air over your head, and as it settles about you picture that person whose likeness you want to imitate. You should know, however, that the likeness must be of someone already known to the observer. That is how it works, by fooling the watcher, not changing the user." At Itachi's dubious expression, the conjuror's tone became impatient. "Take it, farmer. It is not often that Wochu is feeling generous. But such a gift as this," he said, gesturing toward the dead Hikari, "deserves a 'bonus,' as it were."

Itachi quickly pocketed the little vial, mumbling a word of thanks. Wochu turned away and walked back to the ward lines surrounding the door. With one finger he drew an oblong shape along the wood, just large enough for a man to pass through. Where his finger traced, a new, dark line followed. Placing his hand in the center of the completed shape the conjuror twisted his wrist, and the blue glow disappeared from that portion of the door.

The conjuror stepped back, keeping his hand extended, palm toward the door. "Go now, quickly," he said, with an effort. "I cannot keep it open for long, for I am tired. And I want to keep the wards up, just in case. You never know when those witches might be snooping about."

Not needing any second prompting, Itachi moved toward the door. Cautiously, he reached for the lock, which was but scant inches from the shimmering blue glow. "Hurry!" enjoined the conjuror, and Itachi swiftly turned the key and drew back the bolt. Once outside and into the cold night, he slammed the door shut behind him.

He darted several quick paces down the street, breathing hard. Turning to look behind him he saw nothing out of the ordinary. The conjuror's shop front appeared as it always had, the faded sign still hanging limply in place. There was no hint of the strange power lurking within. With a deep breath, Itachi turned away, forcing himself to walk slowly up the street. Much as he might want to put distance between himself and the insanity of Wochu's workshop, nothing attracted attention so much as a running man. He walked away as if he were the master of the night.

From the shadows across the street, a man dressed in the uniform of a City Watch captain stepped out into the open. He started in the direction of Itachi's retreating back when a soft voice halted him.

"No," it whispered. "Let him pass. He has done what was desired; he is not our objective this night." The captain bowed his head silently and blended back into the shadows.

Inside Wochu's workshop, the conjuror released his hand from its rigid position once Itachi had passed through the door. The blue glow quickly snapped back into place, sealing him off once more from the outside. With a shake of his head at the simple minds and manners of other peoples from Tonogato, he went over to the now-extinguished Hikari.

He placed a hand on its frame, the metal, now cold, looking like nothing more than the simple hallway lamp that was its beginning. "Such effort," he said quietly, "to make you, to carry you this far. And all for nothing, wasn't it? Except to give me joy." He patted the top ring, as one might a pet. "And now you can become my trophy, a reminder of that—" He stopped, turning suddenly toward the door. "No," he said, eyes opening wide in alarm. "NO!" He ran over to the front of the workshop, frantically waving his arms. Additional blue lines appeared, but even as they did so those already in place began pulsating, their color changing. "Keep out, keep *out!*" shouted Wochu, as he swung his arms to the side, drawing in the blue from the side walls toward the front. But as quickly as he reinforced the ward lines they started changing, first glowing red, then orange, and finally winking out altogether. Finally only the door itself remained protected, its surface a mass of clashing colors.

Wochu backed away, stumbling toward his workbench. With a final effort he tried to establish more lines, but with a sudden surge all of the lines vanished. Instantly the rotted wooden door shattered explosively inward, showering the room with a thousand splinters.

A City Watchman ran into the room with a torch, followed by another, and another. Quickly a dozen men had entered the room, followed by the captain who had watched Itachi depart. One of the City Watchmen shouted, "Here he is!"

The captain watched as his men dragged the pathetic Wochu out from beneath the workbench where he had sought shelter from the deluge of splinters. "Bring him here," ordered the captain. As the unfortunate conjuror was hustled over in front of the officer, another person entered from the street. The white-robed figure paused inside the doorway. All but the two Watchmen holding Wochu bowed deeply.

"You have done well, Captain," said the magician.

"Only with your help, High One," replied the officer. "It was your magic that unsealed the way for us."

"Magic!" shouted Wochu at the men holding him. "Pah! Nothing but a lot of silly mumbo-jumbo. Do you think it is magic that makes the street lamps glow? No—nothing more than—"

"Silence!" commanded the magician. "You have not been given leave to speak."

"Why?" rebutted Wochu. "Are you afraid their virgin ears could not stand to hear the truth? That the 'magic' is nothing more than the Zaitan controlling knowledge that anyone could possess?"

The magician spoke softly. "We have been observing you for some time, Wochu. Now you have gone too far. Do not compound your crimes with further heresy."

The conjuror cackled, the laugh of a man who knew he was already condemned. "What difference can it make, oh mighty High One? Dead is dead, is it not?" Angrily, he went on. "You Zaitan, you only see what you want to see, don't you? Aren't willing to look beyond your proven notions, to see things that *can't* be measured. You can't deal with the inconvenient, or the things you can't explain, and so you try to stamp them out!"

The magician replied with barely constrained patience. "Magic is proven. It is observable, and repeatable."

"Observable, repeatable, hah! Nothing more than mindless repetition," sneered Wochu. "If you can't prove that something exists with your precious magic, then to you it does *not* exist. How arrogant! To think that you Zaitan alone can understand reality."

"Your ideas are old wives tales, and heresy," bristled the High One. "They are dangerous and threaten the established order."

"That's what its really about, isn't it?" Wochu shouted. "You're afraid that someone else will find out that there are other ways, better ways, and then what would you all be? Nothing! Nothing but a lot of old women trying to cling to power!"

The magician turned to the captain. "Remove him," she said quietly. "Restrain him if necessary." The captain bowed and motioned his men to take the conjuror away. Wochu continued to shout, even as he was dragged from the room. A sudden muffling of his voice from outside indicated that his captors had needed little incentive to stifle his railing.

The High One said to the captain, "Seal the building. Then burn it and everything in it to the ground." The captain bowed smartly before going out to give instructions to his men.

The magician, alone in the workshop, turned and walked purposefully over to the workbench where the Hikari sat. Pausing a moment to look at it, she tentatively ran a finger over the glass, which had been untouched by the fusillade of splinters from the door. Then she grasped the lantern's top ring and lifted the lamp from the table. With a final, distasteful glance at the shambles around her she took the lamp and left, walking back out into the shadowy street.

* * *

Nakama leaned against the cold stone walls of the courtyard, awaiting the return of the two Deshi. Save for the few brief hours at the House of Welcome, it was the first time he had been alone for quite a while. It had probably been just as well for, as then, his mind started drifting off onto topics that he knew he should not think about. Or rather, onto one topic in particular.

Mikasama.

Just her name alone, as he rolled it over in his mind, sent a strange flood of conflicting emotions through him. Longing, to hear the sound of her voice. Shame, at having overstepped his position, and having endangered hers as well. Pride, in remembering the delight in her eyes when he did something unexpected. And loneliness...

That last, most of all. For once having tasted the sweet fruit of his Princess's affection, life without it seemed both dry and bland.

His Princess, he scoffed bitterly to himself. Listen to me! After all this time I still try to think of her as mine. That part of my life is over; it has to be, for her sake. As unpleasant as it is to be half a world away from her, this is the only path I can take.

The coolness of the stone against his back reminded him of their last time together before Itachi had intervened. Their stone bench in the garden...

Just as earlier, in the House of Welcome, when his thoughts had drifted down into self-recrimination and despair, a Deshi came to interrupt them. Only this time instead of Toshi-hito coming to ask him if he would go look for Shiko, it was both of the Deshi now returning from wherever it was that the magician had led them.

Nakama pushed himself away from the courtyard wall as Toshi-hito, looking somewhat subdued, approached with Shiko. Nakama thought the apprentice looked...well, somewhat green. It must have been a difficult interview. "So," he asked, "will the Zaitan help?"

Toshi-hito answered quietly, "The Sordaijan will. But we have more to do. We must return to Sekai monastery, and quickly. Our horses will be ready for us at the city gate."

Nakama was surprised, but more than willing to undertake anything that took him away from Itachi. "All right. I know the two of you travel light, and I only have a few things. It should only take us a short while to be ready, and then we—"

"No," interrupted Shiko softly. "We must go now, directly to the gate."

Nakama stopped and looked at him. The young Deshi's voice was different; there was an edge to it, an intensity that was firm, as if he would brook no argument. The boy's eyes were staring, though not at anything that Nakama could see. Something about that look was unnerving. Puzzled, Nakama looked at Toshi-hito, whose expressionless countenance did nothing to explain things.

"Well," the archer said awkwardly, "that's fine, if that's what we need to do. What about the Hikari? Only Donaku was watching it when we left. Should we try to take it with us? At the very least," he added, looking up at the night sky, "it might help light our way."

"No," said Shiko decisively, "it is not necessary. I know the way."

Nakama again looked at Toshi-hito quizzically, but the Deshi Master only nodded, a hint of sadness in his expression. "Come," he said, "we must go."

*   *   *

Mikasama and Shudojo stumbled down a steep hillside, through thick brush and brambles. They had lost the trail from the abandoned village some while back. It had become so overgrown from disuse that the two women had frequently gone many yards before finding it again. After one such break they never did find it again, and had resigned themselves to further cross-country walking.

The women had spoken little since the incident with the wolves. On this occasion, however, it was not as a result of anger or wounded pride. For Shudojo, it was simply that her naturally withdrawn nature had re-asserted itself. She seemed to have accepted, without question, that Mikasama was the chosen instrument of her Goddess. When the Princess had tried to talk to her about what had happened with the wolves, the Sister would only say, "I began this journey with doubt and misgivings; but they have been resolved into a clear path." When Mikasama pressed her, Shudojo had answered serenely, "You are on a mission for the Goddess, and it matters little that its purpose is not plain to see. My role is beyond question: I must support the Lady who follows the Goddess' quest." After that she would say no more, leaving the Princess to agonize in silence, with more questions than answers.

Mikasama herself didn't feel as if she had done anything to cause the wolves to break off their attack; it was as if something *else* had, through her. She kept coming back to the question of whether the visions she experienced were the creations of her own mind, or whether they were being put there. And if the latter, by whom, and why? Was it Shudojo's Goddess? And if the Goddess existed, what would cause her to be so interested in a Princess from Hajimeshi that she would compel Mikasama to travel the length of Tonagato?

It still made no sense, but the compulsion to move on, to continue heading west, had been growing stronger with every step they took in that direction. Mikasama had concentrated on that, hoping that once she found whatever was at the end of that compulsion it would answer her questions.

As the day drew to a close Shudojo started preparations for another night in the open, but Mikasama was of a different mind. She insisted that they keep on moving.

"But it will be dark shortly," Shudojo replied. "And we should rest."

Mikasama demurred. "The sky is clear, and we should have a full moon; we ought to be able to see our way. The longer we keep moving that way," she said, pointing in the direction of the rapidly setting sun, "the sooner we will get where we need to be." Shudojo, less inclined to dispute Mikasama since the wolves had spared them, shrugged her shoulders, and the two women resumed their march across the low hills.

Their way led them in and out of small stands of trees, none thick enough to hinder their progress but requiring their careful attention to keep track of the diminishing light. Dusk had long since departed when they crested a small rise to find yet another range of trees stretching across their path. Mikasama, with the urge to keep moving forward pushing continually at the back of her mind, trod on into the woods without pause, Shudojo right behind. In the deepening gloom, the women had to stop frequently and check for the fall of the moon's tenuous glow, to ensure they were not heading in circles. This patch of forest, thought Mikasama; it's a lot bigger that the ones we passed through earlier. Shudojo might have been right; maybe we should have stopped earlier. It could be hours before we can make our way out of here...

Unexpectedly the two women popped right out of the woods. They found themselves standing on a slope overlooking a narrow open stretch that was cleared of trees. Both women recognized it immediately for what it was, and Mikasama whooped with joy as she ran down onto the hard-packed dirt of what could only be a road.

As Shudojo caught up with her, the two wanderers looked where the narrow ribbon of road curved away, out of sight around a bend through the trees to either side. Wordlessly, in relief at seeing signs of civilization again, they turned and hugged one another. Then they set off briskly, the soft glow of the moon reflecting from the little swirls of dust kicked up by their feet.

They had walked for not quite a quarter hour when the road turned. Around the sharp bend a magnificent vista opened up. Both women slowed to a stop, mouths agape. In the distance was their first sight of the city of Tejinashi.

The light from the many hundreds of blue globes caused the entire city to shine in the night, only the tops of the towers lost to the darkness. The water of the surrounding moat shimmered with the reflected light. It was as if the entire city were a single, massive jewel floating in its own ocean. Shudojo whispered, "Sweet Goddess!" and reached for her shasen.

As soon as she saw the city, Mikasama's heart leapt. In a mad rush, all of her visions swept through her head, flittering rapidly across her consciousness. The soldiers, Komori, the waterfall, the glass wall, the blank, open doorway, beckoning her on...She broke out into a cold sweat, and her breathing suddenly became shallow.

This is it, she thought. *This* is where I am supposed to go! I don't know why, or even where this is. But something down there is the source of my visions...

It was almost a physical need, so strong was her desire to rush down the road and make her way toward the glittering city below. It was as if the culmination of weeks of walking, of enduring freezing cold, and danger, was to be had down there, in that strange, brightly shining city. With great resolve, her eyes focused only on the radiance that seared away the night, Mikasama started walking rapidly down the road.

She had gone only a few paces, however, when she stopped, realizing that Shudojo was not following. She turned to see the Sister still standing in the spot where they had first glimpsed the city, frantically pawing through the folds of her habit.

Shudojo heard Mikasama call up to her impatiently, "What is it? What's the matter?"

"My shasen!" answered Shudojo. "I can't find it!" She searched through the folds and pockets of her habit, and checked yet again around her neck for the familiar feel of her shasen, but there was nothing.

Mikasama hesitantly walked back up to where the Sister stood. "Are you sure? Did you take it off somewhere?"

"No, other than when we were at the inn, I have never taken it off. Something must have happened to it while we were walking." Even as Shudojo was speaking, Mikasama's gaze traveled back toward the city below. Unconsciously the Princess took a half step down the road toward it, even as she said, "When do you remember having it last?"

Becoming more agitated by the moment, the Sister replied, "I don't know! Wait, let me think..." She screwed her eyes shut, trying to recall when she had last felt the amulet against her chest. Then she remembered. "That field! The one with the tall grass, just before we entered the large forest, before the road."

Mikasama's eyes were still focused on Tejinashi as she said absently, "The one where you fell down?"

"Yes! That's it. The grass was so high I didn't see the gully until I stepped into it. I remember now, I felt something on my neck; I thought it was a branch, or something nicking me as I fell. It was already getting so dark..." She looked back up the road, toward the wooded hill from which they had come. "It must have been my necklace breaking. I had been holding the shasen just before that, and when I fell I stuck my arms out to stop my fall."

The Sister turned back to look at Mikasama but her companion was not paying attention; she was still looking down at the city, her body turned toward it as if she were ready to go charging down the road again.

Shudojo drew a deep breath. Oh, Goddess, she thought; is this another test? What am I to do? The shasen is my connection to you, the focus for my prayers. How can I abandon it? I did so once, to my cost. But you also sent me a sign, an answer to those prayers: I am to follow this woman as your messenger. Which do you want me to do now?

To Mikasama's back, Shudojo said quietly, "I will go with you to the city, Lady, if that is where you must go."

Something in Shudojo's tone broke through Mikasama's concentration. Turning, she saw the look in Shudojo's eyes, their pale blue reflecting back the similar color of the lights from the city. There was pain there, she realized; a longing as intense as Mikasama's own, but held in check by something stronger. It took her a moment to realize what that something was.

It's me, Mikasama realized. Shudojo is determined to accompany me. That amulet is probably the most important object in this woman's life, and she's willing to leave it behind in order to follow me.

The thought was sobering. Never before had Mikasama experienced the devotion of someone quite like this. With Komori, it had been different. The old woman had been responsible for the Princess first; it was only later, after Mikasama had committed herself to this journey, that the Princess had realized her own responsibility toward Komori.

But Shudojo was following Mikasama of her own free will. This independent, strong-minded person had chosen, for whatever reason, to attach her loyalty to another. And Mikasama realized that this was a responsibility that she could not ignore.

She had never had the opportunity to govern anything. Even her own life, back in Hajimeshi, had been largely ruled by others, either by Komori, or by the demands of court social life. Nevertheless her father had taught her a few things about ruling. First among these was the duty of a ruler toward his subjects. It was they, he had pointed out, who tilled the fields and crafted in the workshops. It was due to their industry that Hajimeshi was a kingdom. Rulers must never forget that, he had stressed, and begin to believe that they themselves, sitting up in their fine castles, were the 'kingdom.' The duty of any ruler was to serve the ruled, and return devotion with dedication.

Now here she stood, facing a person who had chosen to follow her. Mikasama came from someplace Shudojo had never been, and knew nothing about; yet the Sister was prepared to relinquish her most prized possession in order to support Mikasama's quest.

The Princess could feel the pull of the city behind her. It was urging her on, the thought of turning away from it almost making her dizzy. But she steeled herself. Her 'kingdom' might only be a kingdom of one; but it deserved no less than if it were a city of thousands. "We will go back," she said.

Shudojo shook her head. "We can go back later. It will be easier to find when the sun is up."

"No," said Mikasama emphatically. "I don't know what may happen down there," turning her head slightly toward the city. She dared not look at it for fear that she would lose her resolve. "We can't depend on being *able* to come back. We will look now, and keep looking until we find it." She set off resolutely back up the road, toward the hill. It took all of her will power to force her feet to move, to walk away from that gleaming city on the plain. But she was the daughter of Kimeru, the

Kojuro of Hajimeshi, and she was determined that she would not shame that legacy.

The two women climbed back up the slope above the road, and were soon lost to view among the trees.

*   *   *

Down on that plain, the great gates to the city swung open. Silently the stone pillars of the bridge rose up once more from the waters of the moat. Even as they rose, three horsemen emerged from the gates and stepped their horses carefully across. Behind them, the gates swung closed once the riders had passed through.

As the last of the riders came ashore on the far side, the pillars one by one sank below the water, leaving no trace of the horsemen's crossing. The three then rode hard, and in little more than an hour they swept past the curving section of road that had so recently provided such a spectacular view of the city. An observer might have noted that the lead rider was shorter than the other two, but any more detail would have been lost, for in the dark, and at their pace, the riders were soon swallowed up by the trees that hung over the road as it turned north. Only little swirls of dust hanging in the air remained to mark their passage.

29

Mikasama and Shudojo made their way back to the grassy field, finding the gully where Shudojo had tripped during their earlier passage. Aided by the bright moonlight they started scouring every inch of the ditch. Yet after nearly an hour of scrambling through the dirt they found no hint of the missing shasen.

Standing at the top of the gully, Shudojo breathed a reluctant sigh. "It must have become lodged in my clothes after the necklace broke, and fallen out later." She was staring out across the expanse of field they had crossed after the gully: two hundred paces or more of grass that grew to well over knee-height.

Mikasama followed her gaze with dismay. It would take an incredible stroke of luck to find something as small as the shasen amulet in all that. Shudojo, however, showed no signs of giving up. With silent determination the Sister dropped to hands and knees and slowly, methodically, began making her way through the grass, searching the ground as she went. The sight of the Sister valiantly struggling to recover her lost emblem, despite the odds, was a vivid reminder to the Princess of Shudojo's tenacity.

Mikasama's back already hurt from bending over while sifting through the dirt of the gully, but she knelt and joined Shudojo in laboriously pawing through the tall grass.

As the first hint of dawn edged over the hills to the east, the two women finally reached the far end of the field. Hands and knees filthy, both of them worn out, they collapsed in a heap side by side on a knoll overlooking the field. They had found nothing but earthworms and rocks.

Shudojo's voice was weary. "I am sorry, Lady, for leading you on a wild chase. I was certain I had lost the shasen here."

Mikasama, lying on her back, waved a tired hand in the air. "We had to try." She looked at her grass-and dirt-stained palms. "This was a better lesson in insects and soil than anything my old tutor ever taught me."

After a moment Shudojo said, "You must have come from a wealthy family, to afford your own tutor."

It was then that Mikasama realized that she had never told Shudojo who she really was. She remembered that Mother Narisa had only said that she was 'a noble lady,' leaving it to Mikasama to decide what to tell Shudojo. It had seemed so unimportant at the time that Mikasama had completely forgotten about it. She turned toward the Sister. "Shudojo..."

She stopped as an ever-so-brief glint caught her eye. The morning sun had spread across the expanse of grass before them, and the dew was sparkling; but there was something else, something that was more than just moisture on a blade of grass. Carefully Mikasama turned her head again, trying to see the tiny glimmer. There it was! On that bush on the other side of Shudojo!

The Princess jumped up and leapt over the startled Sister. Kneeling down by the bush, Mikasama saw it: Shudojo's shasen amulet, its broken leather necklace still attached, lying tangled in the stems of the bush. Gently the Princess lifted it out. She turned toward Shudojo with a mischievous smile. "I believe you were looking for this?"

Shudojo had sat up after Mikasama had vaulted across her. Now her eyes opened wide as the Princess handed her back the shasen. Carefully the Sister tied the ends of the strap together around her neck and tucked the amulet securely back inside her habit. Getting to her knees, she bowed low to the ground toward Mikasama, her forehead touching the soft dirt of the slope. "You have returned to me the Goddess's gift, Lady. No thanks that I can give can ever be adequate."

Embarrassed, Mikasama reached over and touched Shudojo's shoulder, raising her up. "Come, let's be on our way."

*   *   *

Retracing their steps of the night before, the two women walked back to the viewpoint where the road began its descent to the plain. In the morning light the city was no less spectacular than at night, its green hues sparkling against the blue sky.

Throughout their search for the shasen Mikasama had felt the pull of the city. Seeing it again, she was hard-pressed not to start running down the road, but she knew that to do so would exhaust her long before she reached the shimmering waters surrounding the city. So she settled for a fast-paced walk, Shudojo striding silently beside her.

It was late morning by the time the two wanderers finally, tiredly, approached the moat. They walked down to the edge of the water, looking about with perplexity at the self-contained river lapping gently at their feet. They saw no sign of either bridge or boat.

Mikasama stared across at the tall, green towers, and the massive walls that paralleled the river's course. So near, so near, she thought. There has to be a way across!

Looking down at the swiftly flowing waters, she was reminded of their last 'water' crossing. Here they would find no washer woman's line to help them make it over. "I've never heard of a river like this, that runs in circles. It's so unlike anything I remember from Juyama's lectures on such things. Do you suppose this is Tejinashi?"

Shudojo stared at her. "Of course, Lady. Did you not know?" The Sister gazed across the moat. "I have never been here, but I knew it to be Tejinashi from the moment we saw it last night. Several people from my village had traveled here, before the Zaitan closed their gates to outsiders." In the distance, both women could see the hilltop on which stood the palace of the Zaitan, its irregular towers at odds with the more neatly arranged structures visible elsewhere above the walls. "From their descriptions, I knew this could be nothing else."

"Well," said Mikasama plaintively, "how are we going to get across the river? Did your informants give you any hints? It doesn't look like anybody is about to put out a boat for us."

The Sister shook her head. "Back then, there were many boats, or so I was told. That is how my people, at least, went to the city. But I see no evidence of any boats anywhere on this 'river,' if that is what it is."

Mikasama was so frustrated she wanted to stamp her feet, and would have, if a more rational part of her mind had not restrained her from an act so unbecoming. It was just about all she could do to keep from diving into the water to swim across. One look at the fast current, however, was enough to tell her that she would make no headway trying that route, and would most likely drown in the attempt.

Both women were standing next to the plain, unadorned pole that stood at the edge of the water, as it had been the only unnatural feature anywhere near the shoreline. Mikasama raised a hand to shield her eyes from the glare of the sky, squinting to see if there was anyone on the walls in the distance who might notice them. As she did so she reached out and grabbed the pole with her other hand to steady herself as she twisted her body from left to right, searching. "There has to be a way," she muttered. "We only have to find it."

Suddenly the ground shuddered. Alarmed, both women stepped back. Shudojo pointed toward the water. "Lady! Look!"

One of the great stone pillars broke through the surface of the moat, stopping as before with water cascading off its top; then another, and another, stretching all the way across the river toward the city. The two women, astounded, watched the stately procession until the last pillar had risen into place.

Shudojo turned to Mikasama. "I believe you were looking for this?"

*   *   *

"My dear friend," began the letter. "It has been a long time since last we spoke. I, for one, miss that stimulating mind of yours. I am sorry that the occasion for your correspondence was a troubling one for you."

"I cannot, I am afraid, put your mind at rest about the girl Mikasama, or her caretaker. I have heard nothing about either of them. However, I did receive a visitation from the others you mentioned. And I believe you must consider more carefully their purpose."

"I suspect, from your words, that you consider their pilgrimage unwise at best; and to be dangerous, a distinct possibility. The latter sentiment, it would appear, has certainly been true. But I believe you must re-evaluate this quest, for it is more than you have given it credit for."

"You are a wise man, my learned friend, but you could not know those things that only one who has spent a lifetime among the Zaitan can perceive. The pilgrimage is not only real, but close, terribly close, to fruition. In it lies the future of Tonogato. I have seen the dark that lies in wait, and we are not prepared. If this quest should fail, we will all most assuredly be destroyed. Even should it succeed, it will only be the first of many hurdles."

"I have sent them back to Sekai, where I believe—"

A knock on the doorframe by the tower entrance interrupted the Sordaijan's writing. Slowly and carefully folding the parchment, as if it were no more than a casual letter, the magician turned to face the source of the knock, a young woman wearing a robe of green. The Sordaijan's eyes flashed with anger. "Did I not make plain my desire to be undisturbed, Kurtaya? I am displeased that you should see fit to ignore my wishes." Indeed she was furious, for her correspondence with Himitsu had to be done in absolute secrecy, lest she be discovered and driven out of the Zaitan. Or worse.

But Kurtaya was her favorite, her protégé. The Sordaijan had been training her for nearly two decades, since she had come to the Zaitan as a mere toddler. Thus she did not receive the wrath that the Sordaijan would normally have meted out to any other who had the temerity to intrude on her solitude. The crest-fallen expression on Kurtaya's face made it was clear that disappointing her mentor was probably worse punishment than anything the Sordaijan could actually have devised.

The young woman dropped down and bowed abjectly, pressing her forehead to the floor. "Your pardon, Most High One," she said. "I—I am sorry for failing your trust. But two women have arrived, one from Hajimeshi, another from Shukyoshi. They—they raised the bridge up from the river. Motochi has brought them from the gate over to the palace. Since they have never been to Tejinashi before, we don't understand how—"

But the Sordaijan had already risen from the thick, wooly rugs carpeting her enigmatic 'hall' at the top of her tower. She tucked the unfinished letter into her robe and swept past her student and down the tower stairs.

*   *   *

Mikasama and Shudojo were escorted into a small, low-ceilinged room, devoid of any furnishings and lit only by a single blue globe. "You will wait," said the short, ruddy-faced woman who had led them there. One of the white-robed Zaitan, the woman had identified herself as Motochi but had otherwise refused to answer any questions put to her by the Princess. Having deposited the two visitors within the room, the magician turned and left, closing a pair of doors behind her.

The two women's arrival had caused considerable consternation. Apparently, they should not have been able to raise the pillars that formed the bridge to the city, or at least so Mikasama had gathered from the confusing conversations that had swirled around them.

The soldiers who had opened the huge stone gates had sent for an officer, who had been equally perplexed. He in turn had requested an even higher authority, which had turned out to be the Zaitan woman named Motochi. As Mikasama and Shudojo had stood forlornly in the midst of a crowd of soldiers, the woman had fired off a rapid series of questions at the officer, who had bowed humbly with each answer.

Shudojo had whispered softly to Mikasama, "One of the Zaitan magicians." It was then that the Princess wished that she had thought to ask Shudojo a few more questions about Tejinashi before they had tried to enter the city...

Mikasama could only imagine what the Zaitan woman must have thought, seeing two filthy, bedraggled people, on foot, with only a handful of paltry possessions between them. After a long searching glance at the two wanderers, the woman had ordered the officer to bring them with her. Their entourage had climbed the hill up toward the magician's palace, where it had been more white-robed women, more questions, and answers that seemed to satisfy no one, until at last they had been led here. And now, apparently, abandoned.

The Princess fumed, not amused at the way they had been treated. She was also tired and confused. The great longing that had driven her clear across Tonogato was still there, but now it seemed without focus. Everything around her felt at once both strange and compelling, as if the entire city held all the answers she sought, if only she knew the right questions...

Her exhaustion, both mental and physical, and her longing for a resolution, any resolution, to the visions that were haunting her, made her irritable. Perhaps it was just the effect of suddenly being thrust back into the civilized world again after too long in the wilderness, but whatever the cause Mikasama was in no mood to be treated like an unwanted problem. She strode over to the doors and tugged. Finding them locked tight, she pounded loudly on them with her fist. "Hey! Let us out! If you can't extend even common courtesy to visitors, then let us find our own way!" She paused, but no answer came from the other side. So she pounded again, harder. The echoes rang through the small room. "Can you *hear* me? My friend and I are hungry, and more than a little thirsty, thank you very much!"

No response was forthcoming. Mikasama was working herself up to try and make even more noise when Shudojo cried out, "Lady!"

Mikasama turned and saw what the Sister was pointing at. On the wall opposite them, another door had silently opened. It swung slowly into their room, not a hint of sound from its hinges. In the space beyond, it was utterly dark, and quiet as a tomb.

Mikasama stared, open mouthed. She felt as if her mind were floating, not really there at all. It was the doorway, the one from her dreams! In her visions, after the light from the rising sun had passed through the massive glazed window, like the one she had seen at Fumosa, she had always seen a door leading into darkness. It was this door, she realized.

Only here there was no sunlight in their room, only the dull glow from a blue globe mounted on the wall. Its faint radiance did nothing to penetrate the gloom beyond.

Shudojo still stood in the center of the room. Mikasama, trembling, slowly walked over to join her.

"Lady?" said the Sister with concern. "Are you well?"

Mikasama's mind was a milling torrent of thoughts and emotions. She knew she had to go in there! Yet she also knew, inexplicably, that something would happen once she crossed that threshold, something irreversible. She could not fathom what it was, but it filled her with both dread and anticipation; and bewilderment, for not knowing why she should feel either.

There was only one way to find out, she told herself firmly. Besides the glass wall in Fumosa, this doorway had always been the clearest of the images in her head. If there were any answers to be had, they were in there. Gritting her teeth, she took hold of Shudojo's arm. "Let's go," she said.

The two of them approached cautiously, stopping at the doorframe. They stuck their heads partway in, but still could see nothing. The Princess slipped through the doorway, the Sister right behind, and again they linked arms. Slowly they stepped forward, each with an arm extended, feeling for anything in the dark.

"Hello?" said Mikasama in a quiet voice. "If anybody's here, a little light wouldn't hurt..."

No one answered. The Princess couldn't remember ever being in a room as dark, and as silent, as this one. Outside, in the forest, there was always noise, everywhere. This place seemed so...unnatural.

She felt Shudojo jerk to a stop. "What? What is it?" she asked, but even as she spoke she saw what Shudojo must have seen.

There was a small pinpoint of light, directly in front of them. Had the darkness not been so complete, it would have been impossible to see. Gingerly they both stepped toward it. As they did, the light started to grow brighter. It became a flame, and Mikasama could make out some sort of framework around it. And glass, she realized. The flame was shining through glass.

Then her eyes opened wide with astonishment. She knew what this was! She had seen it before. It was the lantern! The Hikari lantern!

With a gasp, she rushed forward, Shudojo half a step behind. The lamp flared into brilliance, flooding the room with light.

Mikasama stared at the Hikari in amazement. How did it get here? The last time she had seen it, in fact the only time she had seen it, was when Nakama and the pilgrims had carried it out of the gate as they had left Hajimeshi. Why was it here? Was he here then? Was Nakama here?

Shudojo asked, "What is it, Lady? Do you know what this is?"

"Yes," she whispered, looking down at the lantern. "Yes, I know what this is."

From behind them came a commanding voice. "As it, apparently, knows you."

Both women turned to see another white-robed figure standing in the doorway. She stepped into the room, walking toward the light. "I am the Sordaijan," she said imperiously. Walking over to the two women, she stopped in front of Mikasama. "The lantern came to us unlit. You, it would seem," as she stared intently into Mikasama's eyes, "have the power to bring it back to life."

Uncomfortable under the woman's scrutiny, Mikasama shrugged. "All—all I did was walk toward it."

"Yes," replied the Sordaijan. "I know." She glanced at Shudojo, then returned her attention to Mikasama. "This is not, I take it, your original traveling companion?"

"No," said Mikasama softly. "No, Komori—she died at Fumosa Monastery, in Shukyoshi."

"Ah. I see." She turned to Shudojo, taking in the Sister's tattered habit. "That, then, would explain you."

Shudojo bristled. "I wasn't aware that I was a question," she replied angrily. Despite her strong words, she reached up to grasp her shasen.

The Sordaijan raised an eyebrow but did not respond to Shudojo's statement. Over her shoulder, she called out, "Kurtaya!" Instantly a young woman, similarly garbed to the Sordaijan except for the green color of her robe, appeared at the door. "Have food and drink, and fresh clothes, brought at once. And tell the Stable Master to attend me."

"At once, Most High One," answered Kurtaya with a bow, as she hurried off. The Sordaijan turned back to Mikasama.

"You have traveled far, but your journey is not yet over. On you, as well as upon others, rests the fate of many. In the hills to the north of Tejinashi lies a monastery, called Sekai. Your destiny lies there." She looked at the Hikari, its flame dancing behind the glass. "You must take the light with you."

"Why? What's there?" countered the Princess. "Is it Nakama? Is he there, at this monastery?"

The Sordaijan paused. "What you seek, is there." Mikasama started to ask another question, but the Sordaijan raised her hand. "You must leave quickly," she said. "There are other concerns, things you do not know, and some you would not wish to know. You must get to Sekai as soon as possible. I will arrange for horses, and an escort to take you, as soon as you have eaten." Looking down at their torn and dirty clothes, she added, "And changed."

* * *

"Lord Itachi!" Bokusa shook the general awake. Grumbling, Itachi rolled over, exhausted after his nocturnal endeavors with Wochu.

Upon his return to the House of Welcome the previous night, Itachi had been relieved to find that the Deshi's belongings were still there. He had been jumping to conclusions, he realized. The Deshi had already been to the monastery; there was little reason to think that they would have come to Tejinashi simply to turn around and return. And so he had decided to allow himself some sleep, and to slip away from the Deshi in the morning with his men and make his own way up into the hills. To Yonada.

Now that lump Bokusa was grabbing his arm. "What?" demanded Itachi. "What is so important that you have to interrupt my sleep?"

"'Pardon, lord," said Bokusa. "But the Hikari is missing!"

"What? Missing!" Itachi feigned surprise and anger. He knew he must look convincing enough to fool Bokusa. Which, he knew, would not be too hard…"That idiot Donaku was supposed to be guarding it! Did he fall asleep again?"

Bokusa nodded. "Seems so, lord. I took the liberty of making sure it won't happen again. I thought losing a finger'd be a proper reminder about not sleeping while on watch. I don't think he'll be finding sleep so easy for a while."

Itachi tried to stifle a yawn. "Where are the Deshi?"

"Don't know, lord. Their packs are still here, but they don't seem to have come back from last night."

"Well," said Itachi, "perhaps our Deshi 'friends' stole the Hikari." An excellent excuse, he thought; convenient that they were still out.

What Bokusa told him next, though, shattered his complacency. "There's more," said the thick-necked soldier. "On my way back this morning from one of the brothels, I saw Princess Mikasama."

Instantly Itachi's mind snapped into focus. "How could she be here? You must have been mistaken!"

The big man shook his head. "She was with one of those magicians, and a troop of soldiers. Looked pretty ragged, like she'd been on the road a long time, but it was her all right." He grimaced. "When she was first learnin' to ride I had to go once as escort. Stupid waste of a soldier's time."

Itachi was not listening; instead his thoughts were racing. He had given Mikasama up for dead long ago, figuring the pampered girl would have been killed, or eaten, before she had ever reached the borders of Hajimeshi. Now the little bitch was here! And with the Zaitan! Things were happening faster than he had planned. He jumped up from his bed. "Where were they going?"

"To the palace, looked like. Least, they were headin' that way."

"Send one of the men to watch the palace. I want to know as soon they step foot out of there." He started scooping up his gear. "Then get the rest of the men ready. We're leaving."

Confused, Bokusa said, "Leaving?"

"We're going to that monastery the Deshi went to, before we came here." As Bokusa continued to look stupidly at him, he barked, "Just do as I say! Or do I have to get fingerless Donaku to carry out my wishes?" The big man bowed rapidly and left to roust out the men, while Itachi hurriedly stuffed his belongings into his pack.

Something was going on, and it infuriated him that he had no clue what it might be. Now that he was fully awake, he realized that for the Deshi to still be gone could only mean that they were with the Zaitan. He cursed himself. *The bastards fooled me! And Kimeru's little harlot, turning up here, of all places! Too much of a coincidence, for her to appear out of nowhere like this; it must have something to do with those conniving Deshi.*

Well, he thought, *without the Hikari, no one is going to end up as my brother's cursed Kotaishi. So whatever the Deshi are planning, it won't matter. Better that I quit myself of this city of magician-whores and track down Yonada. Once I've confronted her, I can set about returning to Hajimeshi. And then we'll see what becomes of my weak-willed brother.*

Most of the space in Itachi's pack was taken up with the box for the chodaka birds. To his irritation, the magic that had been providing the food had inexplicably stopped working when their group had entered the city. He opened the cage and saw the female bird lying on its side, half dead since it had refused the scraps of food he had been tossing in to it. The male bird had never returned since the last time he had sent it back to Hajimeshi. There was no point in hauling the box around, he decided; the female was useless without the male. He would leave it here to die in its cage.

As he angrily jerked the box out of his pack, a flutter caught his eye. Turning to the window, he saw a bird alight on the sill.

It was the male chodaka, perversely choosing that moment to return. Its belly was large, Itachi saw; it must have brought back food to dispense to its companion, in that disgusting way that birds did such things. He looked down at the female. It feebly lifted its head, apparently aware that its mate had returned. Setting the cage down, Itachi walked over to the male bird on the sill. It sat patiently, turning its head. The bird did not struggle as Itachi reached out and clamped his fist around it.

Stupid, he thought; it could have flown free. Instead it came back here. It deserves to die along with the other one.

He carried it over to the cage and shoved it inside with its mate. As the male gently began regurgitating the food it was carrying into the female's mouth, Itachi frowned. He had paid a small fortune for the birds, an investment not easily discarded. After a moment's indecision, he snapped the lid closed and crammed the box back into his pack.

* * *

Mikasama felt as if she were at the center of a small storm as young acolytes of the Zaitan swirled around her. Several were helping her to change into fresh clothes while another small parade brought in supplies, stuffing them into travel packs. The Princess looked over helplessly at Shudojo, who was enduring the same chaotic activity, and who looked equally uncomfortable.

Mikasama had never had a chance to query the Sordaijan further on why they had to go to this Sekai monastery, let alone ask the woman what she might know about the visions the Princess has been experiencing. Once set in motion, the junior acolytes of the Zaitan had responded rapidly to the Sordaijan's requests to prepare the women for their journey. The Sordaijan having left the two visitors in their care, she had then departed as enigmatically as she had arrived.

The two visitors were brought clothing and food right there in the same room in which they had found the Hikari. The lantern's glow suffused the room with warm light, the shadows it cast across the walls pale and ethereal. Amidst the flurry of robed bodies moving about the room, the lantern alone appeared quiet and unmoving.

The Princess had difficulty taking her eyes off of it. Why, she wondered, had it come alight when she and Shudojo had entered this room? The Sordaijan had implied that somehow Mikasama had done it, but the Princess knew that she had done nothing. At least, not anything that she was aware of...

As a young woman asked her to lift her foot so that she could try on a sandal, Mikasama wondered what the Hikari had to do with her visions. She had never pictured it in her mind, other than to remember Nakama following behind it when she had last seen him in Hajimeshi. But its presence here definitely felt strange to her. It was as if it did not belong here, should not be sitting in this room with her and this busy cadre of acolytes...

Just at that moment her vision started to grey about the edges, and the old familiar feeling returned. The visions, she thought to herself; what will they show me now? Will I finally see why I am here?

Yet it was not the by-now familiar images that ran through her head. Instead, the Princess saw herself walking *through* the black expanse of the doorway, and saw the light that she knew would be the Hikari. Suddenly the scene shifted and she was in a cave. There were a great many people in the cave with her, but the only one she had a strong impression of was a woman dressed in dark robes.

"Lady?"

Shudojo's voice broke through, disrupting the images; everything became a confusing mass of color, and then swirled away into nothingness. Mikasama rubbed the side of her head with her fingers, then glanced over at Shudojo. The Sister was looking at her with concern, a frown across her face. "Lady," she repeated, "are you all right?"

Mikasama looked around her. Everyone in the room had stopped moving, and was staring either at her or at the Hikari. "Yes..." she answered slowly. "Yes, I'm...fine." She glanced over at the lantern, but saw nothing different about it. "What—what happened?"

Shudojo spoke softly. "Your eyes glazed over, and then the flame within the lantern flared up, almost like the sun..." Her voice trailed off in awe.

Mikasama could feel the silence in the room, almost as a physical thing. Hesitantly she replied, "I'm—I'm alright. Thank you..." She kept her gaze on the Hikari, though, as the acolytes slowly, quietly, resumed their preparations.

Almost before she was aware of it, Mikasama found herself and Shudojo being escorted out of the room and into a courtyard. The surrounding towers loomed overhead, seeming to lean over in watchful expectation. There were two horses saddled and waiting for them in a courtyard, with two of the City Watchmen, already mounted, waiting nearby to escort them.

Still disoriented from the rapid sequence of events, Mikasama dully allowed herself to be helped up onto one of the horses. Her mind was still having trouble grasping what was happening to her. Her initial rush of elation at finding the place that seemed to be the source of her visions had been replaced by confusion, as it now seemed as if she had found nothing but more mysteries.

She was obviously still having visions, even here within the city. And yet they still gave her no clear idea about what she was supposed to do. She could recall nothing from her earlier dreams about any monastery, other than Fumosa. She had no idea what the cave represented; it certainly did not appear like a monastery to her. All that remained of the experience of her most recent vision was the Hikari lantern, now carried by Shudojo.

Mikasama glanced over at the Sister, who held the pole of the Hikari firmly in her grasp. After the Zaitan acolytes had found a suitable pole from which to suspend it, Shudojo had insisted that she be the one to carry the lamp. It was the proper thing to do, she had said, to be the bearer for the one whom she followed. Embarrassed, Mikasama had acquiesced, wanting to avoid any more awkward looks from the young girls who had been assisting them.

Following the City Watchmen as they led the way down the hill back to the city, Mikasama tried to calm her mind. She remembered that her tutor, Juyama, in his efforts to instill a sense of decorum in his irrepressible charge, had once taught her some of the meditations used by the Deshi.

Well, she thought, if ever I needed to calm my soul, it is certainly now. What was it that Juyama had said? Something about a stream? Yes, that was it; I was to picture myself as a stream, and then make my worries and cares into rocks. Then I could flow over them and around them, and not let them impede my path...

Diligently she tried to apply the lesson, shutting out the distractions of the strange city around her. She could feel her mind calming, and realized with a start that she had been breathing heavily, in fact had been nearing a state of panic in her uncertainty and sense of helplessness. She could feel her breathing returning to normal as she concentrated on her imagery of the stream, and she shifted her attention away from the city around her. She noticed the unfamiliar feel of the clothes she wore, and the smell of the leather saddle beneath her.

It felt odd, she thought, to be on horseback again. Her muscles, grown unused to riding, were protesting at the sudden change in requirements. As she swayed in her saddle, she reflected on how her perspective about riding had changed. Where once she had looked at being on horseback as liberating and exciting, now she was simply relieved not to have to walk.

Glancing down at the clean tunic she had been provided, she thought of the Zaitan. As the young acolytes had led her and Shudojo out to the courtyard, they had passed a gathering of older Zaitan, arguing amongst themselves as the two visitors had passed by. The Princess recalled the stares and fierce expressions from many of them. She suspected that the Sordaijan would have some explaining to do once she and Shudojo were out of sight. In fact she wished she could be there for it, for she could do with some explaining of things herself.

This city, she thought; it felt so compelling. Other than the briefest recollection of things taught to her by Juyama, she could remember nothing about Tejinashi. And yet here she was, riding through it after having traveled the length of Tonagato; and this city of magic seemed to her somehow...comfortable...

She turned to Shudojo riding beside her. "It's strange," she said. "I get such a peculiar feeling from this place. In some ways, it feels almost like home. But that makes no sense, since it's nothing like Hajimeshi."

Shudojo arched an eyebrow. "Perhaps you are merely relieved to be out of the forest, and back in a city?"

Mikasama pursed her lips thoughtfully. "No, I don't think that's it. It's more a feeling of not wanting to leave, but at the same time...I guess I feel that something's still not right. And whatever it is, I can't stay here until it *is* right." She sighed. "Which, presumably, is why we are having to go to this Sekai monastery. But I wish the Sordaijan would have explained to us what is going on!"

The Hikari, bobbing gently over their heads as Shudojo held the pole, swung in rhythm with their horses. "Perhaps, Lady," answered the Sister, "a monastery will be the best place to find the answers to put your mind at rest." Eyeing the odd green buildings along their route, she added, "Hopefully it will at least be a place of peace and tranquility."

Mikasama sensed the undercurrent in Shudojo's words. "That must appeal to you, to be going to a monastery. I gather that Tejinashi does not suit you."

Shudojo frowned. "I do not know of what faith this monastery is, but it will most certainly be a less strange place than this city."

The Princess smiled. It was, indeed, a strange place, she thought. Yet even so, it still felt oddly comfortable.

✶ ✶ ✶

The Sordaijan, shoulders slumped in exhaustion, entered her tower chamber. The Zaitan were most unhappy with her. They could not understand why she, of all people, had acted so recklessly, and without regard to their consul. This Hajimeshi woman, they had asked; who was she, and by what power had she been able to re-light the lantern? Why had the bridge risen for her? And why was the Sordaijan packing her off, out of the city, before they had all had a chance to examine her?

To none of these questions had the Sordaijan responded. This had occasioned considerable grumbling, although as yet no overt action. She was fortunate that her Zaitan brethren were so rigidly hierarchical, some might say to an extreme. Yet, she knew, this would not prevent them from deposing one in whom they had lost confidence. As the Sordaijan was all too keenly aware...

She rubbed tired eyes with hands that looked older, she thought, every day. The strain of years of subterfuge, of misleading even the most zealous of the Zaitan, was beginning to tell on her. She had caught them all off guard by her out-of-character behavior, but she could not rely on that to shield her from more aggressive inquiry. She had finally set the wheel into motion; now she must follow it down the path, and hope that it did not roll away too fast for her.

Her acolyte, Kurtaya, had accompanied her back to the tower, ready to attend her mistress with anything that was required. The older woman spoke softly to her. "I will need nothing further, child. You may go. And," she added with a slight smile, "this time, truly no interruptions."

Kurtaya bowed deeply, and returned back down the stairs, back to the real world of dark stone passages that honeycombed the palace hill. The Sordaijan knew Kurtaya would stand before the entrance of the tower, letting no one pass, for days if need be, until she had passed out from exhaustion. She will be a strong one, the magician concluded. If she survives. If any of us survive.

The Sordaijan walked out to the balcony, where the darkness had now been replaced by sunlight. Not the sunlight of Tejinashi, which was still nowhere to be seen from this unearthly vantage. Here, the clouds gathered in white cottony balls, drifting above and below the level of the balcony, as if it were suspended amongst the heavens. The wind was cool, the air crisp.

She waited for her visitor. She knew it would not be long.

30

"The girls an' two guards, my lord, tha's all," said the man Bokusa had dispatched to watch the approaches to the palace. "They headin' toward the city gate."

Itachi scratched his chin, thinking. "And you're certain they had the Hikari with them?"

The man nodded emphatically. "No doubtin' it, my lord. I'd know that lamp from anywhere, believe me."

The Hajimeshi general was puzzled. First that harlot niece of his had shown up, when by all rights she should have been dead, and now the Hikari had reappeared. He had seen it extinguished with his own eyes by that crazy fool Wochu. How could Mikasama have possibly come by it?

Or was it perhaps a fake? Was it all part of the Deshi plan, to get someone else proclaimed as the Kotaishi? Those traitors would stop at nothing to put one of their own on the throne of Hajimeshi!

The packs and gear of Toshi-hito, Shiko, and Nakama still lay where they had been since the previous night. Where had the Deshi gone? Back to the monastery? They had gone there once before, and it was too much of a coincidence that Yonada was there also. Regardless, the Deshi had tricked him by leaving their packs behind. All he knew for certain was that his niece had a Hikari, and she was leaving the city. She *must* be involved with the Deshi, otherwise why would she be here at all?

Well he was leaving too, for Sekai, and Yonada. If his niece was scheming with the Deshi it would be a simple matter to force out of her what she knew about their plans. But not here, not inside Tejinashi; he would have to wait until they had escaped this den of lunatic magicians.

"All right," he said, "we follow her."

"What about the others?" asked Bokusa, nodding his head toward the Deshi's unoccupied room.

"Forget them," said Itachi. "We can't know for certain where they are, but we do know where my niece is. Better to follow the one that we've got. You—" he said to the man who had scouted the palace, "follow them, and wait for us by the main gate. Let me know if they stop, or talk to anyone on the way; anything that looks suspicious. Go!" The man hurried out of the room. "The rest of you, gather your gear. We'll get to the gate, and then figure out how to get the bridge up. We may have to knock a few heads, but someone there should know how to raise it."

Bokusa had been looking dubious, but all of a sudden his dull face was creased with a smile. "I think I have an idea, my lord," he said.

Itachi rolled his eyes at such an unlikely notion. "Speak quickly then, or hold your tongue. I don't want to get too far behind them."

Bokusa was looking inordinately pleased with himself. "How about a boat?"

*   *   *

The soft breeze that wafted across the balcony reminded the Sordaijan of the village of Nohanshi. As it was intended to.

She had been born in Nohanshi, and had lived there, happy and without cares beyond those of any other typical child, until her eighth birthday. On that day her parents had told her that they were sending her on a trip. To Tejinashi, they had said; a great city, full of wondrous things. Excited, she had prepared for the great day of leaving, eagerly anticipating all of the magical things her elders had told her about the fabled city. When at last the day came, and all the people of the village had turned out to see her off, she remembered thinking how wonderful it was that they had wanted to share in her excitement. But then, how could an eight-year old have been expected to understand? This was to be no temporary excursion; she was leaving for good, never to return. Certainly she had not understood that. Not then, nor through the many tears that followed. Only later had she come to accept that she would never be going home again.

It had been a day like this, she remembered: a bright blue sky, the clouds dancing aloft, carefree and playful. As then, the clouds now above her delighted in the moment, for tomorrow might bring storms to tear them apart. But that would be then, and this was now; and so they frolicked, unconcerned. She came here often, to watch, and remember.

Behind her there was a soft rumbling sound. Turning to face it, she saw a pinpoint of light appear above the stone balcony. Slowly it expanded into a circle, a round window opening into someplace even further removed from Tejinashi than the magician's illusionary balcony. The Sordaijan stepped toward the circle, waiting to greet her visitor.

The odd sunlight that filtered through the opening reflected off the golden mane of the lioness Shidosha, the supreme Shizen. She looked out at the Sordaijan, and in her direct and unadorned manner, spoke: "*She arrived.*"

Hearing the familiar 'voice' in her mind, the Sordaijan bowed. "*Yes, as you predicted. I admit, I was not so sanguine. But her determination is impressive.*"

The image of Shidosha shifted, almost as if the great lioness were shaking her mane. "*Difficult. It required all of my efforts to influence her. There were many times when she might have turned aside.*"

"*But,*" said the Sordaijan, "*she did not. And that in itself is a testament to her destiny.*" She turned and looked off in the direction that the monastery might lay, had the balcony actually been situated in Tejinashi. "*I have sent her to Sekai, with two trusted City Watchmen. They will see her safely there.*" She added, "*I took the liberty of sending them by the secret way, the sooner to arrive. It seemed prudent.*" Shidosha dipped her head in agreement. The Sordaijan continued, *"The other left last night. He should be at Sekai soon, even though they took the common road."*

"I did not speak with him," said Shidosha. "Since she lacked the knowledge to 'hear,' and so required all that I could provide, I left to others his guidance."

"I can but answer to the result," said the Sordaijan. *"While hers is a path that comes to her by right, his is more, and thus requires more. He was tested, and did not disappoint."*

Shidosha's voice rumbled in her mind. *"His greatest test is yet to come."*

"Yes," she replied softly. "And our future rests with his success or failure."

The image before her rippled, as the window to the supreme Shizen began to fade. Shidosha shared one final thought before slipping back into that place where she dwelt.

"The caterpillar was slumbering, but has now awakened into a butterfly and been set alight. There is no telling where it might fly."

*   *   *

Bokusa signaled, and Itachi and the other Guards stepped briskly across the street. They passed through the opening where the big soldier held open a heavy wooden door. Once everyone was inside Bokusa closed the door quickly, putting an eye to a crack along one edge to look for any signs of activity outside. "All clear," he whispered.

The group of Hajimeshi soldiers stood inside a musty, dark, and decidedly damp basement, located beneath a public shop. The structure had been built against the wall surrounding the city, bordering the moat. Most of the cavernous basement was taken up with a great pool of water: a deep basin containing two rows of wooden boats, bobbing gently up and down. The largest looked capable of holding at least a dozen people.

Beyond the boats, set flush into the city wall, were several large metal doors that extended down into the water. Itachi could recall no sign of any doors when they had examined the city from the far side of the moat; they must have been cleverly camouflaged to blend unnoticeably into the contours of the wall. He could hear the sound of the river moat flowing by outside.

Itachi had to admit he was impressed. When Bokusa had suggested a boat, he had said sarcastically, "A boat, now why hadn't I thought of that? We'll all just wander down to the 'docks' and ask for one. Oh, but of course, there are no 'docks,' are there?..." Thick-skinned Bokusa, however, had ignored Itachi's commentary, and had proceeded to tell him about the boats he had heard about.

Before he had rounded out his night at the brothel, Bokusa had gone gambling, having found a slightly seedy establishment on the edge of the Dismal Quarter. Luck being with him, he had managed to rake in a tidy sum, enough to fund his sojourn with the ladies of the evening. One of the other gamblers, a dowdy little man who had been drinking far too much, had been losing steadily, easy prey for the alert sharks at the tavern. He had accompanied his rising losses with a string of complaints, everything from a shrewish wife to corrupt business partners.

One complaint in particular had stuck in Bokusa's mind. The man had apparently once run a ferry concession before the city was closed to outsiders. All of his boats were still in storage below his shop. He wanted to burn the now-useless hulks, fill in the basin, and use the space for warehousing. The Zaitan, however, had refused to permit it. They had insisted that he keep all of the boats, in case of 'state need;' and so his valuable space was wasted. In his misery, the man had then made an even larger wager. He had lost it all.

From bits and pieces of things the man had ranted about, Bokusa had been certain that he could find the man's shop. Itachi had considered, weighing the uncertainty of raising the bridge versus being able to find the boats. If they tried to force the issue at the gate, there was the possibility that one of the magician witches might be able to stop them. Yet even should they find the boats, it would put them further behind Mikasama's group, which was already on horseback. But from what he knew of his pampered niece, he had suspected her escort would be stopping many times for her to ease her delicate rump. So he had elected to chance the boats.

With all his men now inside the basement dock, Itachi stepped forward and nearly tripped over something. Looking down he saw the crumpled form of a man, lying quite still. A heavy post lay nearby, a glistening stain along one end evident in the dim light. Itachi looked at Bokusa.

The big man shrugged. "The shop owner I met last night," he said in a low voice. "He didn't want to cooperate."

The Hajimeshi general nodded, then waved over the man who had been dispatched to watch his niece. "How far had the Princess gone?" he asked quietly.

The Guard whispered back, "They was gettin' right near the gate, my lord, when Matsugo caught up and brought me back. They was fussin' over the bridge, some confusion it looked like, between the soldiers with the Princess and the ones at the gate."

"All right," said Itachi, keeping his voice down, "you, and you," pointing to two of the men, "go open one of the doors to the river. The rest of you, get in the boat closest to the doors."

The men edged along a wooden walkway lining the basin, and one by one they awkwardly climbed aboard one of the Tejinashi vessels. Donaku, clambering down from the walkway, almost lost his balance as the boat rocked. Trying to steady himself, he made the mistake of grabbing the side with his left hand, which was almost completely wrapped in a thick bandage. He let out a yelp, which was followed instantly by a hiss from Bokusa: "Quiet, fool! Or I'll add your tongue to your list of missing parts!" Fighting back the pain, Donaku silently took his place along the thwarts of the boat.

The two men dispatched to open the doors were confronted with a bewildering array of levers. Not knowing which one to pull, they yanked on all of them. Suddenly, with a loud metallic creak, all of the outside doors started opening at once, sliding sideways parallel to the city walls and to the current of the moat. As the doors opened, light and fresh air suffused the dank space, and the swift-moving water of the moat surged into the basin, rocking all of the moored craft.

"Quickly, you two!" shouted Itachi. "Into the boat! Bokusa, untie the rope. The rest of you, push off!" Itachi leapt into the stern as the men shoved against the wooden pilings of the walkway, and the boat edged out through the doorway. As it floated past the two men who had opened the door, they too jumped in, causing more rocking and the shipping of a considerable amount of water.

As the boat glided out into the river it was caught by the current and turned to parallel the city walls. Scrambling, the Guards hunted for oars, finding them stacked in the bilges. All except the injured Donaku grabbed one and began thrashing madly at the water, churning the space around the boat into froth. Gradually, with Itachi pushing on the rudder bar, they managed to get the boat's head turned toward the far shore. Bokusa, shouting imprecations, and not without a few swift blows, got all of the men paddling in unison, and the boat began to skim quickly across the water toward the land.

Looking back at the city, Itachi searched for any signs of alarm. But there was nothing. They must think themselves secure in their glittering green city behind their cursed bridge, he thought; they had not even bothered to post a rudimentary watch along their walls.

The Hajimeshi paddled their way out, seemingly unnoticed and forgotten.

It took several tries for the ersatz river mariners to find a dry enough patch on which to beach the boat. Once they made their landfall, the Guards abandoned their craft of convenience and set off toward the road. The plain surrounding the city on this side was mostly tall grassland, turning to marsh as it neared the river moat. They plowed their way through the grass, not even the tops of their heads visible above the tall green stalks that swayed in the breeze.

By Itachi's reckoning they would emerge from the patch of grassland a few hundred paces from the flat, open space where the road wound down to the shore, near the pole that raised the bridge. With luck, the Princess and her escort would not be too far ahead of them.

He was startled when Matsugo, the lead man, came doubling back through the grass. He gestured quickly with his hand, palm down. Every man, trained soliders all, dropped immediately into a crouch.

Itachi rushed forward at a low run. Silently, pointing to his own ear, he gestured for Matsugo to speak. The Guard placed his face scant inches from Itachi, whispering, "Grass ends just up ahead. And they're less than twenty paces away! Guess they didn't go back up the road."

Itachi raised his eyebrows and looked hard at the man, a signal for more. Matsugo continued: "Comin' from our right. They should be in front of us," he paused, glancing back to where he had come, "right about now."

The Hajimeshi general considered. An ideal ambush, were his men to rush suddenly out of the tall grass at that moment. All of those on the road would be dead before they could realize what was happening.

[Yes! YES! Finish them! Now! She is your brother's daughter, his only heir. Kill her, and you remove her forever as a concern! DO IT!]

Itachi grasped the hilt of his sword, twisting against the knotted threads that bound the grip. He could feel the sword moving in its scabbard; it was once more free, ready to be drawn, ready to slash at his enemies. He could feel it almost as if it were a living thing. Unnaturally constrained for so long, it seemed now to want to be ripped from its sheath and avenge its humiliation at being held prisoner.

Just as he started to give the signal to attack, a sudden thought caused him to pull in sharply on the reins of his passion. Mikasama's group, he realized; they're not on the road! They're heading somewhere other than the monastery. But they have the Hikari, so they must be going to where the Deshi are, where Yonada probably is. If we kill them now, I may lose my chance to find Yonada. But my niece, ah, my niece! She can lead me to her! Then I can take down all of them, Yonada, the Deshi, and my brother's heir!

Curtly he whispered to Matsugo. "Watch. Tell me when they are just out of sight." The man nodded, and silently moved off in a crouching run toward the edge of the grass field. The remaining soldiers, well versed in battle tactics, waited patiently, frozen into position almost as if they were statues. Itachi drummed his fingertips lightly against the hilt of his sword. Nothing was heard save for the buzzing of insects.

At last the scout returned. "They're into the trees, Lord Itachi," as he pointed back toward the way he had come. "Path they're on turns north right there."

Itachi nodded. "All right, keep them in sight, and we'll follow." The Guard took off at the run in the direction the Princess and her escort had gone. Itachi gestured for the rest of the men to move near him. "The Deshi, and that slut niece of mine," he said fiercely, "have stolen the Hikari. The Deshi mean to make one of their own the Kotaishi, and to rule over us. Us! Soldiers, ruled by weaklings who know nothing but words on paper!" He put hand to sword and half-drew its length from the scabbard, the glint of metal shining unnaturally amongst the stalks of grass. "But this will stop them. I intend to follow these traitors, and surprise them all wherever they have taken refuge. Then the Deshi will see how well words stand against steel." Sharply he slid his sword back, inwardly telling it to wait, to be patient, its time would come. Soon, he told himself, soon I will be able to cleanse from my 'list' one of its greatest, festering sores…

All of the Guards bowed. So intent was Itachi on his purpose that he failed to notice the quick glances shared by several of his men.

Itachi and the Guards moved quickly from the tall grass into the woods, and the dark forest swallowed up his group within moments. The trail was narrow, forcing the Guards to travel in single file. Soon the scout ran back, reporting that the path ahead wound through thick stands of trees and over steep hillocks, so that they would have little difficulty in keeping up with their mounted quarry. Itachi had Bokusa keep the men moving quickly, wanting to remain within striking distance once his niece's party neared its destination.

By midday the Princess and her escort emerged out of the forest and began ascending into rocky, barren hills. Itachi halted the Guards just within the edge of the forest. Trying to remain unseen while following the Princess's group would be more difficult, he realized, now that they were out in the open. But he could not risk getting closer. If the riders ahead became alerted to the presence of the Guards, even in this rugged terrain they would soon outpace his men.

As soon as his niece and the others had ridden behind an outcropping of rock, he waved his men forward. "All right, now move! Everyone up to that rock, then keep out of sight!" The Guards quickly ran up the trail.

Thus the pursuit continued, the pursuers having to wait for long periods before the pursued passed behind rocks and out of view. After several hours of repeated quick marching followed by tedious waiting, the tired Guards found themselves skirting a steep ravine, which deepened into a broad canyon further on. The path continued its ascent, until the men could see mounds of snow dotting the higher hilltops.

Itachi had sent the scout on ahead to keep watch on where their quarry headed, it being easier for one man to hide than a group. As the day wore into late afternoon, the scout rushed back excitedly. "Building...jus' up there," he said breathlessly. He was exhausted from hours of running forward, hiding, and running forward again. "Right onna edge...of the canyon...'Mazed it don't fall right off."

As the man stopped to gasp some air, Itachi realized that the building could only be the monastery. He had not expected this; it must be a back way! He grabbed the man's arm. "How long until they reach it?"

The Guard shook his head. "Can't tell...trail bends around 'fore it gets there...pretty soon, though."

"Right, we all move forward. Now!" shouted Itachi. He led the way, Bokusa fast on his heels, as the men sprinted up the trail. The air was thin, and the men were weary, exhausted from the constant dashing ahead and then waiting while the Princess rode out of sight. Nevertheless they followed dutifully, little clouds of dust forming from the pad of so many feet.

Coming to a sudden turn, Itachi signaled the men behind him to halt. Peering around the corner he saw the monastery, perched as the scout had said virtually on a precipice overlooking the deep canyon. And he also saw the Princess.

Her little group was riding in single file along the trail, the path so faint as to be almost invisible. One soldier was in the lead, then the woman carrying the Hikari followed by Mikasama and another soldier.

Damn, he shouted inwardly; they were already nearly to the walls of the monastery! Too far ahead to catch before they got inside.

Even as he watched, the riders pulled up beneath the walls, and one of the soldiers dismounted to approach a small postern gate. When it opened Itachi could just make out what looked like a woman in a priest's robe. The soldier spoke to her, and she let him in.

Mikasama and the woman carrying the lantern also dismounted. Once the other soldier tethered the horses to a wooden post, he and the two women followed the first soldier in. The postern door closed with a heavy thump, audible to Itachi even at that distance.

He turned away, leaning his back against the steep rock face lining the trail. As his men stood behind, awaiting his directives, he angrily cursed himself. He had miscalculated, badly. He had wanted his niece to lead them to Yonada and the Deshi, never once realizing that the trail they were on was a back road to the monastery. The walls were too high to scale, and they had nothing with which to batter down the postern gate. Across the canyon, there was a bridge that spanned the expanse leading up to the walls, but there was no chance that his men could get across the steep gorge to reach it.

Anger welled up inside him. No, his mind screamed. No! *No No No! I will not be denied! They have taken everything from me! My brother, Yonada, the Deshi, all of them have conspired against me. I will grind them into* dust *beneath my feet!*

[The potion, you fool! USE THE POTION! Oh, why can't his mind hear me? THE POTION...]

Itachi clenched his fist, pounding the hard rock next to him. It did little other than to bruise his knuckles, but it did cause him to shift sideways. As he did he felt something against his side, something hard.

Reaching into his tunic with his hand, his fingers wrapped around the little bottle that Wochu had provided as his 'gift.' Pulling it out into the light, he stared at it. Inside all he could see were little shards of glitter, floating lazily inside the bottle as it moved.

He looked again around the corner of the outcropping, staring at the walls of the monastery and at the postern. When he turned back to face his men, they saw a feral grin spread across his face. He spoke in that quiet, intense tone that all knew to presage his most dangerous moods. "I believe that another City Watchman from Tejinashi has just arrived."

*   *   *

"Some day, young man, you really must choose to visit us at a normal hour."

Such had been Abbot Akiya's greeting the previous night, recalled Shiko. It was about all that he *could* recall, before exhaustion had overcome him. Now, rubbing the sleep from his eyes, he remembered that it had actually been closer to dawn when he, Toshi-hito, and Nakama had arrived at the main gate of Sekai. The old gatekeeper, Tusoda, had let them in immediately, and shortly thereafter the Abbot, remarkably fresh-looking considering the hour, had welcomed them.

It had been a brief greeting, though. The Abbot had taken one look at the exhausted Shiko and had decreed that he and the others must rest, if only for a few hours. They had ridden without respite from Tejinashi, save for a brief stop to pay their respects to Ryori's final resting place. Shiko himself had not slept since they had last left the monastery, and he had endured much since then. Nevertheless the apprentice had protested at the delay, saying that he urgently needed to speak with the Abbot.

But it had been to no avail. The fact that Shiko had to be helped from his horse by Nakama and Toshi-hito had done little to bolster his argument. Portly Brother Numa had even been roused from his slumbers to prepare a potion to help Shiko sleep, but such assistance had been unnecessary. Having been led to the same chamber that he and the others had so recently occupied under rather more adverse circumstances, Shiko had drifted off into an untroubled, dreamless sleep.

Now that he was awake he had to admit that he felt much better for having rested. To one side he saw Toshi-hito sitting, eyes lowered, meditating. Nakama lay next to him, snoring lightly.

The apprentice stood and walked to the door of the chamber. In the hall, waiting to attend them, sat one of the Sekai Brothers, his head bent over, reading a scroll. Shiko touched the man lightly on the arm. As the young Brother looked up the apprentice said quietly, "I would like to see Abbot Akiya." The Brother bowed his head, then set aside his scroll and rose.

Behind him, Toshi-hito stirred as he reached over to gently shake Nakama awake. "Come, loyal friend," the Deshi Master said. "It is time for us to follow Shiko."

* * *

The Brother who had been attending the three Hajimeshi led them through a warren of passageways beneath Sekai. Along the way, Shiko was struck by the fact that none of the other Brothers seemed to be in evidence; the hallways above, and these deep passages, appeared as deserted as a tomb. "Where are the others?" Shiko asked.

"Waiting," replied the brother enigmatically. The apprentice decided to keep his curiosity in check, at least until he could see the Abbot. In any case, it gave him ample time to consider the prospect that he now faced.

He knew that at Tejinashi he had crossed an inner threshold of sorts, seeing for the first time a clear pattern in the events that had surrounded him on the pilgrimage. It had been the Sordaijan's magical touch that had helped him connect his mental pathways, allowing him to see what his mind had tried to keep hidden, even from himself. Having glimpsed what might be, he understood why he might have avoided wanting to see it for himself: it was without a doubt a more terrifying prospect that he could ever have imagined.

But beyond opening that door for him, the Sordaijan had refused to elaborate on what he now believed to be the truth. She had repeated that he must return to Sekai in order to find the answers that he sought. Even Toshi-hito had been enigmatic when pressed to confirm what Shiko suspected: "It is not our place to do so," the Deshi Master had said. "There is one at Sekai who must do that." And thus had begun Shiko's sense of urgency for returning to the monastery as quickly as possible.

As they had departed from the Sordaijan and the palace of the Zaitan, Shiko had once again been able to detect, albeit more faintly, the impression of great anger and hatred that simmered far below the palace. If what he suspected were indeed true, then that seething mass of fury would soon unleash itself on the world above, and as yet there was nothing to stop it.

The group descended what, to Shiko, seemed to be an endless series of stone stairs, and he realized that they must be going deep within the heart of the rock upon which Sekai stood. There were no torches here, their only illumination the soft glow of the lamp carried by the Brother.

Walking down one particularly long and dark hallway, its stone walls damp with moisture, the apprentice found himself shivering. Sekai's heated water pipes did not reach this far below the ground.

The sound of their footsteps echoing eerily against the rock abruptly ceased as they entered a small, round chamber. In an otherwise unadorned face of solid rock before them stood a pair of doors, bracketed by a set of torches. The doors themselves were unlike any others Shiko had seen at Sekai: made of finely wrought metal, their surfaces were layered in complex geometric forms. They were mounted in what must once have been a natural cave opening, for the irregular shape around the doors had been filled in with mortar.

"Please wait here," said the Brother. "I will let the Abbot know that you have arrived." He opened one of the doors and slipped through. Shiko tried to look beyond but was unable to see anything other than a quick glimpse of many candles, confirmed by the scent that wafted out into their chamber.

As the Brother closed the door behind him, Shiko heard Nakama mutter, "Arrived where, I wonder?"

Where indeed, thought Shiko, although he was not certain if such sentiment related to their present whereabouts, or to where they now found themselves in their quest. If what the Sordaijan had revealed in his mind was the truth, there would be precious little time to prepare for the horrendous onslaught to come. Every moment wasted made the task that much more difficult.

He had tried to curb his impatience while following the Brother through the many narrow passages, but now he found it hard to stand still. He paced back and forth across the small chamber, finally stopping in front of the long hallway through which they had arrived. Gazing back down its darkened length, he saw that beyond a few paces it turned black as night. Even though he had just recently walked through it, he could not remember with any certainty what it looked like; he had been so eager to reach the end that he had focused his concentration more on his destination than on his venue. It was therefore with some surprise that he noted a small point of light in the distance, down the hall. Odd, he thought; I don't recall that we had passed any torches along the way.

Gradually, though, it grew larger, bobbing gently up and down. It was a lamp, he realized. And then, with a start, he recognized it: it was the Hikari!

He still distrusted his own senses, given his recent experiences, and he thought at first that perhaps his mind, still befuddled from all that had occurred, was showing him things that he simply wished to see. Then out of the gloom he saw a face emerge beneath the lamp, and he realized that it truly was the Hikari, being carried by a woman.

She was still some distance away, and all he could see in the light was the upper half of her body, but that light reflected off the most amazing eyes that Shiko had ever seen: a brilliant sapphire blue, sparkling like deep ocean water under a noon day sun. Her face was framed with a halo of light from the lantern suspended above her. To Shiko it was as if one of the Guardian Spirits written of in the Tarkinsa Scrolls had come to Sekai, to return the Hikari to him. He stood speechless, watching her approach.

Then he heard another voice from out of the dark, a woman's, that sounded familiar: "Are you sure this is the way the old man at the gate told us to come?" Beside Shiko's walking vision, he saw another figure emerge. "It seems a long way to go to find everybody else."

Unexpectedly Shiko heard Nakama behind him say, "Mikasama?" The Hajimeshi archer stepped next to the apprentice, peering down the hallway. "Princess?" The woman paused momentarily, then she shouted, "Nakama!" The apprentice had to jump aside as Mikasama dashed forward past the Hikari, past him, and then threw her arms around the startled archer. "Nakama!" she cried. "It's been so long, so long—too long! Please, let me hear your voice again." She buried her face in his shoulder. "Say my name, I've heard you say it in my mind so many times, over and over, but it's just not the same…"

As the dumfounded Nakama held her, the woman who bore the Hikari stopped beside Shiko. Up close she was no less striking, even if, as the apprentice now realized, she was but flesh and not spirit. Her iridescent blue eyes stood wide open. "Princess? She's a *princess?*"

"Y-yes," answered Shiko, finding himself unable to look away from those captivating eyes. "She is Princess Mikasama, daughter of the Kojuro of Hajimeshi." The woman continued to stare at the Princess incredulously, while behind her two Tejinashi City Watchmen also emerged out of the darkness of the hallway, stopping uncertainly just short of the small chamber.

Nakama, meanwhile, looked down upon the last person he had ever expected to see in such a place. "Princess...Mi-Mikasama...what—what are you doing here—how did you get here?"

Mikasama leaned back in his arms, absorbing the look of his face, his hair, the way he smelled—it was funny, she thought, how many memories were triggered by such simple things. Smiling up at him she said, "It's a very long tale." Nakama started to speak but she forestalled him by reaching her finger up to touch his lips. "Later," she whispered; and then, removing her finger, she slipped her hand behind his neck, drawing his face toward hers.

Nakama felt Mikasama's warm lips touch his, and in an instant his carefully compartmented emotions, which he had thought locked away forever, were suddenly released. My Princess! his mind exulted. Mikasama! She is here, she is here!

Heedless of what any of the others might think, he passionately returned her kiss, there and then.

Among the onlookers, it was perhaps Shiko who was most surprised. He now realized that the nameless woman to whom Nakama had been writing poetry while they were in Yutakashi had been none other than the Kojuro's daughter, whom he had once met in the Hajimeshi stables!

Toshi-hito spoke softly. "I see that we were remiss in not sharing our knowledge of the Princess's pursuit with Nakama. I did not realize that the reason for her leaving might have been due to someone within our pilgrimage. Such devotion, to walk the breadth of Tonogato!" To Shiko, however, it did not seem so strange, remembering the chodaka birds 'Ton and 'Cha.

At that moment the sound of metal grating on hinges echoed within the small room. Abbot Akiya pulled open both of the doors to the candle-lit space beyond and gazed out upon the tableau before him. "Well!" he said. "I see we have additional visitors. Good," he nodded. "You will all be needed." He gestured into the room behind him. "Please. Come in."

31

There was a knock on the wooden postern gate, and the young female Brother assigned to the watch opened the small sliding view port. She saw a Tejinashi City Watchman, alone, peering in at her. He said, "I have urgent news. You must let me in at once."

She was startled by the sound of his voice, and looked closely at him again. Had she not just let him in a short while ago, along with the others? How could he have gone outside once more, without passing by her?

At her confused look, the Guard went on insistently. "You must let me in, quickly! There is an imposter! One of the City Watchmen is not whom he seems to be. There's no telling what he may do!"

The Brother looked around, but there were no others nearby whom she could turn to for advice. All save her, and old Tusoda at the main gate, had been called away by the Abbot. As she was the most junior, she had been sent to watch the postern.

She chewed on her lip, a habit not yet broken by her months in the monastery. As the man continued to plead, she decided that she had no reason not to believe him. He was, after all, a City Watchman. She reached for the bolts that secured the gate.

*   *   *

When Abbot Akiya opened the metal doors, Shiko had felt a rush of warm air into their small chamber. After the cold of the passageways it came as a bit of a shock, but not nearly as breathtaking as the sight that lay beyond the threshold.

He and the others stood at the entrance to a massive cave, stretching up nearly as tall as a three-story building. Unlike the hallways and the rooms of the monastery above, here the walls had not been fashioned by the hands of man but had been left in their natural state. At the very top of the cave was a nearly circular hole. Through it streamed a shaft of sunlight, forming a narrow tower of brightness in the center of the room. Shiko realized that the hole must travel through a vast amount of rock, considering how far he and the others had walked beneath Sekai.

The interior of the cave was honeycombed with openings, some of them large enough for a man to stand upright in, others little more than small pockets in the walls. Many of the openings near the ground level had projecting shelves of rock, creating an effect almost of balconies lining a stage. Most of the shelves were lined with candles: hundreds of them, illuminating the surrounding rock with a soft glow. The smoke from the candles curled lazily up, converging on the hole in the ceiling high above and forming swirling patterns within the shaft of light.

But the cave was occupied by more than candles. On the floor around the edges of the room sat nearly the entire complement of the Brothers of Sekai: young and old, both male and female. They all knelt in silence, gazing at the newcomers as they entered the room.

Shiko and Toshi-hito, along with Mikasama and Nakama, hand in hand, and Shudojo carrying the Hikari, all entered the cave. The two City Watchmen, taking up station to either side of the doors, remained in the chamber beyond. Abbot Akiya gently closed the ornate metal doors, then turned to bow to the visitors. "Welcome to our most sacred place. This room," he said, gesturing around him and to the beam of sunlight at the cave's center, "was found by the first of us to come to Sekai. It is a place unlike any other."

Shiko was certainly inclined to agree. Beyond the unique structure of the cave and the light that permeated its depths, he could feel a resonance, a sensation that was similar to, but far more pleasant, than that which he had felt in the palace of the Zaitan. There was a power of some sort centered in this cave, although he could not fathom its source or why he could feel it.

The Abbot turned to the Princess and Shudojo. "My name is Akiya. These," he said, waving a hand to encompass the onlookers silently lining the room, "are the Brothers, who have come to Sekai to find a purity of soul. They come from Tejinashi, where magic has corrupted the will to live. They come from Shukyoshi, where blind faith has replaced contemplation and the exploration of spirituality. And they come from Yutakashi, to escape the lust of materiality. Some," he added with a wry smile at Toshi-hito, "even come from Hajimeshi, simply to find a quieter place to study. But they all share a common desire: to someday return to their homes, and make them better places for all. This they cannot do alone, nor while the Darkness threatens to destroy all that they seek to build."

There was a soft rustling sound from the far side of the chamber. A drapery covering one of the larger openings was pushed aside, and a woman stepped out into the cave. Dressed in a Brother's robe, hood pulled up atop her head, she walked toward Akiya and the others. At her approach the Abbot knelt down and bowed. All of the other Brothers within the cave bowed where they sat.

The woman stopped before the newcomers. The bright shaft of light was behind her, outlining her form as if she were a figure set apart from the rest of the cave. She reached up and pulled the hood away from her face, and Shiko was not surprised to see that it was the same grey-haired woman whom he had seen sitting next to Akiya in the garden. He *was* surprised, however, to hear the gasp from Mikasama, standing next to him.

"I know you!" she said to the woman. "I—I saw you, in my dreams! I saw your face, here—in this cave…"

The woman smiled, although it was a smile tinged with sadness. Even the soft light from the candles did not mask the lines of worry that creased a face too young to bear them.

"I am glad that you have dreamt of me," she said. "For I have dreamt of you often, and tried to send my thoughts to you, wishing that you could hear them." Her voice, when she spoke, was instantly recognizable to Shiko. It was the one he remembered saying to him that all would be well, upon his first arduous arrival at Sekai when the Brothers had carried him inside. Now the woman held out her hands to Mikasama, those same hands that had made such an impression on Shiko when he had first seen them in the garden. "My name is Yonada. I am your mother."

*   *   *

Bokusa peered carefully around the rocky corner where he and the other Guards waited, shielded from view of the postern. He saw Itachi, looking just as he always did, standing before the gate and demanding to be let in.

Bokusa himself had little faith in potions or 'magic dust' and so was skeptical of the whole venture, but it was not his place to question his lord's will. Behind him, though, he heard muttering. He could tell that the men were unhappy. He could hear them whispering that Itachi had either lost his wits, standing before the gate pretending to be somebody else; or else had been touched by sorcery. Either way, it seemed to Bokusa that their confidence was shaky.

Looking over his shoulder, he growled, "Next man who speaks a word goes head first into the canyon. Understood?" He was answered by sullen silence. He didn't care, as long as it was silence. It was as close as he came to inspiring men.

Turning back to watch Itachi, he saw the gate open slowly, as if whoever was on the other side was hesitant. In a flash Itachi was through the opening, and the gate closed behind him. Bokusa hissed to those behind him, "He's inside!" Nothing happened for some time, long enough that Bokusa started to worry. Then the gate opened again, and there stood Itachi, his arm around the girl's neck and a knife to her throat.

"Come on!" said Bokusa, and he and the others quickly scrabbled across the remaining length of the trail.

✶   ✶   ✶

Mikasama was thunderstruck. She tried to make her mind wrap itself around what the woman had just said. Her mother? This woman, Yonada, was her mother? Komori had been right then, her mother wasn't dead at all, she had just been sent away. Sent here, to this place in the mountains. But why?

She had so many questions that her mind couldn't keep up, and all she could do was stand weakly staring at the woman before her. Yonada, hands still outstretched, took a step toward her. The movement broke through Mikasama's confusion; eyes filling with tears, she ran forward into her mother's arms.

"I—I don't know what to say," she burbled in Yonada's ear. "I've thought of you so often, I didn't even know if you were alive, and—and now you're here, and I want to call you 'Mother,' but I—it sounds so strange to say it—"

"Hush, hush," said Yonada softly, stroking Mikasama's hair. "I know, I understand...one cannot replace a lifetime of absence with a simple word." Gently she pulled Mikasama away from her, looking into her daughter's eyes. "I want you to know—I never stopped loving you, in my heart, as my daughter. No matter how far you were from me."

"But—but why did you have to leave Hajimeshi?" stammered Mikasama, "Papa—he loves you so much, if you could only see how much it hurts him when ever someone mentions you—"

Yonada dropped her eyes, but not before Mikasama could see the candlelight reflected in her tears. "It saddens me," her mother said, "to know that he has been in such pain. I, too, long for him. I love him as if he were my husband," she said quietly, reaching up to stroke Mikasama's face, "though I have not seen him for so many, many years."

Toshi-hito coughed gently. "Perhaps it would cause less pain if I were to relate the tale, Highest One." Yonada nodded silently in reply.

"Highest One?" said Mikasama, confused.

Toshi-hito nodded gravely. "Your mother, Princess, is the Kordaijan of Tejinashi, supreme among the Zaitan."

*   *   *

Arriving at the postern, Bokusa was welcomed by Itachi thrusting the girl at him. "Take her," the Hajimeshi general said. "Keep her quiet."

The big man wrapped his huge arm around the girl's neck, but not before she let out a small shriek as she looked at Itachi. "You're—you're changing! What are you?" For the man she had seen as a Tejinashi City Watchman was transforming into someone else before her eyes as Wochu's potion wore off.

Her cry was quickly stifled by Bokusa's hand clamping down over her mouth. Drawing his own dagger, he placed it against her cheek. "No more words, pretty little one," he said. "Or not so pretty anymore."

The other Guards had by now all slipped inside, and Itachi closed the gate behind them. "All right," he said. "The Deshi are here; the Hikari is here. And now we are here. But it will be the Castle Guards from Hajimeshi that will carry the Hikari out of this place." He drew his sword. "Let's go."

*   *   *

"Many years ago, Princess," said Toshi-hito, "your grandfather attempted to establish better relations with Tejinashi. He sent two young Deshi novices to investigate opening an embassy there." He clasped his hands behind his back. "It so happened that one of the Deshi novices, during the months he spent in Tejinashi, fell in love with an engaging young woman of charm and grace, who also happened to be an acolyte of the

Zaitan. It was not a match that was approved of by the magicians, or for that matter by the Kojuro. For the young woman in question was the daughter of the Kordaijan, and thus destined to take her place at the head of the Zaitan. It would have been unthinkable for her to be intimately associated with an outsider. And the young man was a son of the Kojuro, training as a Deshi since his elder brother was heir to the throne."

He paused. "This created a situation of some...embarrassment...for the Zaitan. They decided to select the young woman as their envoy to Hajimeshi in order to remove her from public view." He stroked his chin, covering a small smile. "This, quite obviously, did not in the end have the desired effect, for the Kojuro's son and the woman he loved could not bear to be parted from one another. They planned to marry, contrary to the wishes of their liege lords and parents. Some time after their arrival in Hajimeshi, they left secretly in the night, making their way to Yutakashi. There the young man discovered that he would soon be a father, as his bride-to-be told him that she was with child."

"They could not, of course, keep themselves, or their new 'situation,' a secret for very long in a place such as Yutakashi. Soon word came from Tejinashi that, under threat of war, the daughter of the Kordaijan must be returned. Similarly, the Kojuro insisted that his son return to Hajimeshi immediately or be forever banished."

"And so, before they could bring themselves together as husband and wife, your mother, Yonada, reluctantly returned to Tejinashi, while your father, Kimeru, returned to Hajimeshi. Later, once his brother assumed the throne, Kimeru resigned from the Deshi order to take up his responsibilities as heir."

Yonada squeezed her daughter's hands once more. "I did not leave until after you were born," she said. "Kimeru stayed by my side, defying his father, until he was sure that I, and the fruit of our union, were well." Tears welled up in her eyes. "I could not take you with me back to Tejinashi. Already the scandal was such that I, and my own mother, had been threatened with expulsion from the Zaitan. And, my daughter, you will soon understand why I could not let that happen, no matter what the cost to me, or to those dear to me." She reached up and stroked Mikasama's cheek. "But oh, it pained me so, to have to leave Kimeru and the two of you behind."

"Two?" said Mikasama, confused.

"Yes," replied Yonada. "There were two sprouts from Kimeru's seed. You were preceded by a few moments by a brother."

The Princess said, "I have a brother? Where is he? Why didn't Father bring him back to Hajimeshi?"

Toshi-hito interjected. "Kimeru left both you and your brother in Yutakashi for a time, thinking it safer for you until he was able to re-establish his position at home. He placed you in the care of trusted friends who raised many orphan children in their home, where the addition of two more would go unnoticed."

"You see, Princess," he added, "before Kimeru and his Deshi companion left for Tejinashi, they had done the forbidden: they had entered the Sacred Grove. Shidosha, the supreme Shizen, told your father that he would have a son, who one day would be the future Kotaishi. Shidosha said that the boy must be hidden and protected until the time was right for him to emerge and unite the kingdoms of Tonogato against the return of the Darkness."

"Why did Father never tell me any of this?" demanded Mikasama. "Why didn't he tell me my mother was here, or that I had a brother?"

Toshi-hito looked at Mikasama apologetically. "After you and your brother were born, Kimeru knew that he could not safeguard his young son from the intrigues and plots of court politics during all the years to come. As no one had been told that there had, in fact, been two children born to Yonada, he brought you back to Hajimeshi, announcing you as his daughter and making no mention of his son. He hoped that the existence of your brother would remain unknown until the time was right. Only Kimeru, myself, and your foster parents in Yutakashi knew the truth. As much as it hurt your father to withhold the truth from you, he felt it also your only safeguard against the dangers of the court, should the reality ever become known."

Mikasama at that moment was reminded of Komori, and how even one so close to her had been the eyes and ears of another. Perhaps, she reflected her father's caution had not been unwarranted...

Toshi-hito continued, "As you may have guessed, it was I who accompanied Kimeru into the Grove and to Tejinashi. I took the son into the service of the Deshi, and his true identity was kept secret from everyone. Until now."

Mikasama looked at him, still perplexed. "Then who...?"

Yonada took one of her hands and held it out. Toward Shiko.

He had known the moment was coming. He had seen it back in Tejinashi, atop the Sordaijan's tower. It had explained why Toshi-hito had selected him to accompany him on the quest. Kanyo and Tanoshi; they had behaved so oddly because they had raised him there in Yutakashi, at least until Toshi-hito had brought him to the Deshi priory as a toddler. They had, he realized, been his surrogate parents.

'Ton and 'Cha had both known, or at least had known that he was something out of the ordinary. As had the Sordaijan, although he suspected that she had known everything, and probably for some time.

And the Kojuro...my father! thought Shiko. He had placed the Hikari in my hands himself. And this woman, Yonada. My mother...

As if in a dream, he watched himself walk over to her and place his own hand in hers. At the touch of her fingers against his, he felt a definite sensation: power, and energy. He said, without knowing how he knew, "You are a healer."

"Yes," she smiled sadly. "That is my greatest gift, although I have others. The Kordaijan alone among the Zaitan is blessed with multiple talents, and that is why the daughters of our family have held that position for generations." She drew back both her hands and held them before her face, as if they belonged to someone else. "When I came to Sekai, I made a vow never to use magic again. It has so cursed my people that I did not want to aid and abet those who would abuse their positions of trust. Thus I foreswore the use of those gifts I was given. My hands were to be but hands, furrowing the soil in the garden." She glanced at Toshi-hito. "Until one day, I faced a choice. To let my old friend die, or break my vow." She cast her eyes down. "I could not let him slip away, without lifting a hand to aid him."

The Abbot, still kneeling on the floor, interjected quietly, "Your dedication to your vow, Highest One, has been the greatest example to each of us at Sekai. I am sure there are none among the Brothers who fault you for your act of mercy."

"You are very kind, Abbot," she smiled, yet she still held her hands down in front of her, as if they were somehow to be judged for breaking a sacred promise. To Shiko she said, "It was only later, as I saw you in the garden, that I realized that I really had no choice. I had tried to deny what I am; I had thought myself finished with magic. But I came to see that my wishes, my dreams, were no more than grains of sand compared to what faced Tonogato. I could not withhold my gifts; to do so would be to sentence everyone, including those most dear to me, to certain destruction once the Darkness was unleashed."

She looked with sadness at the son standing before her. "I had to let you go, once again; this time so that you might go to Tejinashi and see for yourself what had become of my people. But I knew you would return. And so I waited, hoping for the arrival of both my children." She reached out once more to take their hands in hers. "Now that you both are here, the prophecies will be fulfilled." She looked at Mikasama. "You, my daughter, must accept the mantle of Kordaijan, and guide our people back to what they once were."

Mikasama, still stunned by everything that had transpired, was having trouble thinking straight. She had just found her mother, but now Yonada was talking about Mikasama being the Kordaijan? Why, she wondered; where was her mother going?

But before she was able to form the question into words, Yonada turned to Shiko. "And you, my son; you have an even greater destiny." She reached into her tunic, and pulled out from around her neck a large circular medallion. It was clearly of great age: made of some kind of metal, it had tarnished into a diluted mix of colors. "This has belonged to the Kordaijan for centuries, passed from mother to daughter, ever since the Darkness was last driven back into its evil den." Looking up she said, "You have a honsho, do you not?"

Shiko nodded, and retrieved it from around his neck, Ryori's family emblem still clinking gently against it.

Yonada said, "Your father made that for you, just after you were born; he carved it with his own hands. I never thought much about it, until my mother presented me with this medallion just before she died." Tenderly she ran her fingers across its ancient shape. Then, without another word, she held it out to her son.

A part of Shiko was reluctant to take it, for he knew that accepting it would seal a destiny that he had not, as yet, committed himself to. But that's not true, he told himself. I was committed before we ever left Hajimeshi, the moment I accepted the Hikari from my father's hands.

He reached out and took the medallion from his mother. There was writing on the medallion, around a hole at its center; it was a single word, *tai*. The hole in the medallion was just of a size to fit his honsho. Carefully he removed the honsho from its leather strap and placed it within the opening. The two pieces fit together perfectly with a soft click. So quiet had the chamber become that the sound echoed amongst the rocks of the cave.

He stared down at the medallion, and saw that the two symbols representing his name on the honsho, *shi* and *ko*, lined up in a circle with the word *tai* on the medallion. Thus could it be read differently: Ko-tai-shi.

Shiko felt a vibration from within the medallion. It traveled through his fingers, down his arms, all the way down to his feet. Already it felt familiar: it was the resonance of whatever latent power suffused the entire cave. Moreover he realized now that he had felt such a sensation before. Only then, it had been coming up from below the deep waters of a lake…

As the vibrations gradually diminished, he was amazed to see that his honsho had fused completely into the medallion, as if they had always been one.

The time had come; he could hold the truth at bay no longer. He took a deep breath and hung the now-combined medallion around his neck.

He heard a gasp, and turned to look at Shudojo. She was staring at the Hikari, which she still held aloft. The flame was dimming of its own accord, growing smaller and smaller until, with a gentle wisp of smoke, it quietly went out.

Its purpose had now been fulfilled. The Kotaishi had been found.

Yonada, followed by Toshi-hito, knelt down on the floor and bowed toward him, their foreheads to the floor. Shudojo, after a moment's hesitation, set the now quiescent Hikari down and bowed as well, as did Nakama, and all of the Brothers in the room, including Abbot Akiya. Only Mikasama and Shiko still stood.

The Princess looked at Shiko, her mind still reeling. A brother, she thought; not only have I found my mother, but I have found a brother as well! And of all people, the Deshi apprentice I saw in Hajimeshi! It could not have been a coincidence that we crossed paths then....

At last she realized that everyone else in the room except her was on the floor and bowing toward Shiko. Being a Princess, she was used to seeing others bow; but she realized that this must all be new to him. She smiled at him reassuringly, then joined the others by kneeling down and bowing her head to the floor.

Shiko's thoughts were confused. He felt both relief and awkwardness at the same time. So it was really true, he told himself; I *am* the Kotaishi!

Not so long ago, he had been worried about passing the oral exams to become a Deshi; now he found himself having become a leader of Tonogato. He still half-disbelieved it, despite the evidence before him. The sight of everyone bowing to him was unnerving; he had done nothing to deserve such respect. Then he realized that no one was sitting back up. Quickly he returned the bow to everyone at large.

They all straightened but remained kneeling on the floor, as they might to a sovereign. Awkwardly Shiko asked Toshi-hito, "If you knew I was destined to be the Kotaishi, why did we go on the pilgrimage?"

"It was important," Toshi-hito replied, "that you experience, first hand, the people that you would be expected to lead, and the difficulties to be faced in trying to unite them. The Kojuro knew that the quest presented its own risks. But your success in overcoming them would also prove, to yourself and to others, that in the end you were, indeed, the one to lead us."

"And Lord Itachi?" asked Shiko. "Was he one of those risks?"

Toshi-hito frowned. "Not in the way that was anticipated. He—"

The Deshi Master was interrupted by a shout from the hallway outside, and sounds of an altercation. All heads turned toward the great doors as they were suddenly thrown open, slamming back with a metallic crash against the stone walls to either side.

Lord Itachi strode into the cave, sword drawn, its red sheen reflecting in the candlelight the unmistakable stain of blood. "Did you think you could all hide down here?" he shouted. "Are you all such cowards that you seek to bolt down the deepest hole?"

Behind him, the other Hajimeshi Guards spilled into the room. Bokusa dragged in a Brother, a young girl, with his arm around her neck and a dagger held ready to cut her throat. The other Guards all had their swords unsheathed. Beyond them, two figures lay motionless on the ground beside the doors: the unarmed City Watchmen from Tejinashi, blood already pooling beneath them.

Nobody in the cave moved, frozen into immobility at the suddenness, and the violence, of the intrusion. Yonada, kneeling before Shiko, was almost directly beneath the shaft of light from the ceiling, making her the most visible person in the room. Itachi thus spotted her immediately.

He sucked in his breath. "Yonada!" Striding over to her, his hand flexed against the hilt of his sword.

[She is here, so kill her, as you wanted to. Do not wait, do not think! If you think you will fail. KILL HER NOW!]

Itachi found his mind a whirling mass of emotions. Memories came flooding back. He remembered her as the one person who had meant something to him. Looking down at her, all he could see was that face, that same face that he had fallen in love with all those years ago. More careworn, perhaps; but she was that same compassionate woman who had treated him as if he were a friend, little that he had done to deserve it. In truth, she had never herself made him feel foolish about loving his brother's betrothed; that had been the work of others. She had always treated him with kindness.

Now he stood motionless in front of her, a bloody sword in his hand, in turmoil, while Yonada calmly looked up at him. There was no sound but the lingering echo of the metal doors reverberating against the rock.

Then Itachi noticed that everyone was kneeling. Except one. He turned and saw Shiko; saw the great medallion hanging around the boy's neck, and in an instant realized what was happening.

"No," he said mockingly. "Oh, no! You can't be serious!" He looked down at Yonada, then at Toshi-hito and the others. With a rancorous laugh he said, "This boy? You expect this *runt* of a boy to be your vaunted Kotaishi?" He laughed again; almost a maniacal cackle that echoed among the rocks. "What a pack of *fools* you are! To think a mere child could stand up to me!" With a disdainful look at Shiko, he shouted at his men, "Take him! Drag him outside and throw him off the walls into the canyon."

No one spoke, but neither did anyone move. Itachi tore his gaze away from Shiko to look over at his men.

They stood where they had entered, uncertainly looking from him to Shiko and back again. Bokusa, still holding the female Brother, twisted around. "Did you not hear the general give an order? Move, you pack of dogs!" Still none of the Guards moved.

Then Donaku, hand still bandaged and sword sheathed, stepped in front of the others. He knelt abruptly to the floor and bowed his forehead to the ground. Toward Shiko.

Itachi yelled, "What are you doing, you imbecile! Get up!" But Donaku did not move. One by one the other Guards slid their swords back into their scabbards and followed Donaku to the floor, heads bowed toward the Kotaishi.

"I will execute you for this!" Itachi screamed. "You are traitors, all of you!" He whipped about, facing Shiko. "If they won't dispose of you, then I will!" He raised his bloody sword, ready to hack down at the focus of his frustration and anger.

Shiko stood paralyzed. It was as if every muscle in his body had suddenly frozen into place. Itachi appeared to be moving underwater: Shiko could see the man's arm rise up, so slowly; could see the snarl spreading across his features, flecks of spittle escaping from his mouth; and the sword, rising higher.

Then a high-pitched cry pierced the air. In a movement as fast as Itachi's seemed slow, in an instant Yonada was between him and Itachi, springing from her spot on the floor like a pouncing cat. Itachi's sword blow was already on its way, already committed. He turned it aside at the last moment, but it was not enough. The blade sliced deep into Yonada's shoulder.

Mikasama screamed. As Yonada fell to the floor, covered in blood, the Princess ran to her side. Shiko, too, dropped beside her.

Itachi stepped back, his mind aghast at what he had done, forgetting what had driven him to Sekai in the first place. He stood shaking, sword still held limply in his hand. *Yonada!* his confused mind yelled at him. *I have hurt Yonada!*

[You fool! You should have killed her as soon as you walked into the room! Instead you let your idiotic memories get in the way. I can feel them now, flooding up through you...]

The initial surge of blood from Yonada's wound slowed with incredible rapidity given the depth of the injury, yet still the blood began pooling quickly beneath her. Mikasama tried desperately to staunch the flow with her hands. "Mother! Mother! Can't you heal yourself?" Her mind felt like it was exploding inside. How could this be happening to her? How could she find her mother, after all these years, only to lose her again? "Do I have any of that power? Can I heal you?"

Yonada shook her head. "No, my dearest," she said weakly. "You...do not have it...yet."

Abruptly Mikasama felt something, a strange sensation inside her head. With a start she realized that it was her mother's voice, although Yonada was no longer speaking. *"There is something..."* the Princess heard the voice say, *"...that we must do first..."*

Mikasama felt her vision grow cloudy, as with her dreams. In her mind's eye she could see her mother, uninjured, standing quietly inside a windowless room. Her mother's voice continued to speak inside her head, although the image of Yonada that she saw did not appear to talk. Here her mother's voice spoke strongly, confidently.

"The Zaitan, my dear Mikasama," said Yonada, *"pass their knowledge to their daughters through a complex, some would say rather tedious, series of rituals. But we do not have the time for that, nor for the years of training that should have prepared you for the transfer."* The image of Yonada raised her hand, holding it out toward Mikasama. *"You must take it now, and use it as best you can; you must keep me alive, for there is one thing left we must do, together..."*

Mikasama couldn't pretend to understand what was happening; all she knew was that her mother was hurt, and that she had to help her. She felt herself reaching out and grabbing the image of her mother's hand. The instant she touched it, it was as if she had grasped a lightning bolt with her bare fingers. The shock was tremendous, and yet her hand felt locked in place, and she could not let go.

She could feel something flowing into her, through her hand and up her arm, spreading across her entire body. She could not even describe what it felt like, but through the confusing mass of sensations she could feel the part of it that was connected with healing. Desperately she pushed aside all of the other energy threading its way into her, mentally reaching for and grabbing the tendril that related to healing. As she wrapped her thoughts around it, pulling it away from the others, her mind suddenly snapped back into focus within the cave.

She was looking down at her mother, who was still bleeding profusely. Without knowing fully what she was trying to do, she placed her hands atop Yonada's shoulder, and focused all of the healing energy that she could feel down through her hands and fingers and into her mother's wound.

Itachi still stood shakily. He stared down at Yonada; he saw her blood, saw her clench her teeth in pain. His brain refused to accept that he had been the one to do this terrible thing. Someone else did this, he thought; somebody has hurt my Yonada!

And as his mind redirected the blame and the guilt, his eyes found a likely target.

Him! That boy! He caused this to happen to Yonada! It's his fault she's lying there, in agony!

[Yes! That's it! Forget the woman. This boy is your enemy, you must destroy him! Let your rage go! KILL!]

With an animal cry, Itachi lifted his sword again and sent it slicing through the air towards Shiko's head.

But Shiko had been looking at him, had seen the look of confusion replaced by one of focused anger, and had seen the telltale movement of the blade. He pitched himself backward onto the floor, while with one hand he pulled down on Mikasama just as Itachi's blade swept over their heads in a blinding arc of flashing steel.

Shiko rolled away, certain that Itachi was after him now and would not attack Yonada again, or Mikasama, at least not yet. Quickly he jumped to his feet, just in time to see Itachi leap over the prone forms of both Princess and Kordaijan and come toward him. The apprentice took a step back, then two, as Itachi advanced.

He heard a shout from behind him. "Kotaishi!" It was Donaku, who had pulled his sword from its scabbard with his good hand. He flung it across the floor, where it clattered down next to Shiko's feet. Bokusa, still holding the knife to the Brother's throat, reached out and viciously kicked Donaku in the head, sending the man sprawling.

Shiko dropped to the floor to grab the sword just as Itachi swung at him again. With barely a second to spare, he managed to get the sword up and in front of his face as Itachi's blade crashed against it. The shock jarred Shiko's whole arm, nearly pushing him off his feet.

Bokusa flung the girl aside and advanced toward Shiko's back, dagger at the ready. Shiko heard Shudojo shout, "Look out!" But he could not afford to look behind him, for Itachi was in front, looking for the opening in Shiko's guard that would allow him to thrust his sword through for the kill.

Bokusa raised his arm, ready to plunge his knife into Shiko's unprotected back. Suddenly the big man stopped. He looked down, incredulous, at the arrowhead protruding from his chest, and at the blood that ran off its end. Then he fell, with a crash like an old rotten tree falling in the forest.

Behind him stood Nakama, already notching another shaft on his bowstring. He took aim at Itachi only to find his hand once again pushed aside by someone else. Turning angrily, he was shocked to find that it was Toshi-hito.

The Deshi Master wore an expression of profound sadness. "No. This is a battle that the Kotaishi must fight alone. He has learned how to honor life, now he must learn the other side of ruling—when to take life, when it must be done."

"We are many," insisted Nakama, looking at the Brothers surrounding the room. "We can stop him."

Toshi-hito only shook his head. "The Brothers are sworn to peace. They will not take part in any violence, not even to save themselves."

Itachi, standing in front of Shiko, laughed. "Of course not—all of you priests and monks are weaklings, you have no stomach for killing. Which makes you nothing more than fodder for those of us who do!" He swung his sword again at Shiko, feinting quickly to one side and then slashing toward the other.

Shiko just barely caught Itachi's blade with his own, the sharp ring of steel echoing around the rock walls. He had practiced with wooden staves at the priory in Hajimeshi, but had never handled a real sword. And Itachi was renowned as an expert swordsman. In such an unequal contest, Shiko knew he would last but minutes, if that, before Itachi's blade finally found its mark.

So he turned and ran, dashing for the side of the cave. Running between two of the kneeling Brothers, he sprang up on one of the low ledges that formed the spaces around the cave walls.

Itachi laughed again. "Coward!" he shouted. Waving his sword in gentle circles in the air, he leisurely sauntered over toward where Shiko stood. "Come down and die like a man. Because you *are* going to die, whether you run like a dog or stand in one place."

Shiko, breathing hard, tried to think. He stood no chance against Itachi in a sword fight. And there was no question that Itachi meant to duel to the death, fully expecting that death to be Shiko's. So he needed to find a different kind of weapon. But where, what?

One thing he knew for sure he must do, and that was to keep Itachi talking, for when the Hajimeshi lord was talking he wasn't fighting.

"Lord Itachi," he said, "I am your nephew. I am the Kojuro's son. You cannot kill family."

For just a moment, Shiko saw the consternation in Itachi's eyes, as the man tried to reconcile Shiko's statement with the reality that he knew. Whether he believed it or not, Shiko could not tell, for Itachi simply laughed again. "You fool! Do you think I would fall for a trick as simple as that? You Deshi think to supplant me, with one of your own. But book scrolls are no match for warrior's steel—"

Unexpectedly he lunged forward, his blade aiming to take off Shiko's feet at the ankles on the ledge above him. But the few seconds of talking had given Shiko precious time, time he needed to see out of the corner of his eye where to run next. Even so, he was unprepared for Itachi's sudden attack and had to jump backwards, his head striking the curving rock behind him. As the pain echoed inside his skull, he could hear Itachi saying, "Hah! You'll have to do better than that, 'nephew.' "

Itachi was right, Shiko knew; and so he quickly darted forward and leapt to another nearby ledge, even as he struggled to keep his eyesight clear from the blow he had received to the head. Caught off guard, Itachi swung at him but was wide of the mark.

Irritably, Itachi said, "I tire of this game, boy. If I have to, I can climb after you and cut you down in a stinking cave hole; but," he added mockingly, "that would hardly be a fitting death before all of your 'followers,' now would it?"

That's it, thought Shiko. That's the key! Itachi's pride!

He shouted down at Itachi, "More fitting than that which you provided Ryori! To have him felled from afar as if he were wild game from the ancient hunts. Is that how you portray honor, Uncle? Do you kill all your enemies through others, afraid to strike the blow yourself?"

Itachi's face flushed. "What would you know of honor, gutter rat? You Deshi scum are worthless parasites." He brandished his blade in

Shiko's direction. "We who wield the sword know the true meaning of honor!"

Now Shiko laughed. "Oh yes, such honor there is in a man who would kill his own brother. For that's what you want, isn't it? To kill the Kojuro, to take by force that which rightfully belongs to another?"

He knows! Itachi screamed inside his head. He knows! And if he does, then all of them must know. They've been playing me the fool the whole time—sending me on this pilgrimage as if it were some sort of 'privilege.'

His brother Kimeru, and that old bastard Himitsu; how hard they must have laughed, as he had marched out the gate in Hajimeshi beneath that ridiculous lantern! They had sent him out knowing that they would place this boy at their head. He, Itachi, would be pushed aside, a trifle, a worthless scrap; fit for nothing better than nipping at the heels of a boy who was surely yet to find the right end of a woman.

There he stands, this 'Kotaishi' that they thought would supplant me. Me! The greatest warrior in Hajimeshi! Well, they're wrong! They will see their Kotaishi's head on the end of a pike when I march back through the gates!

[They tricked you, all of them. They deserve to die! Let your blade sing; extinguish them! And him, most of all...]

With a bellow of rage, Itachi leapt toward the ledge upon which Shiko stood and began climbing up it. But Shiko was now ready. He had enraged the bull, now he had to use his head to direct that anger toward its own self-destruction. He waited until Itachi was nearly all the way up the ledge and was committed to pulling himself up. At the last moment, before the soldier could gain his feet and rush at him, Shiko jumped out into space.

Itachi swung his sword, but the tip missed Shiko's back by inches. He saw the boy land on the cave floor, stumble, then run toward the back of the cave, darting behind a curtain and out of sight. Weakling! Itachi shouted to himself. So frightened he runs away, thinking he can hide.

Flinging himself off the ledge, yelling at the top of his lungs, Itachi thought of nothing but smashing the life out of this impotent brat, this pretender. Yonada, Kimeru, Hajimeshi, all of it was pushed aside by a mindless rage. He could hear it clearly in his head:

[*Yes! Kill him! KILL HIM!*]

He pounded across the open space of the cave, kneeling Brothers scattering like stalks of grain fleeing a scythe. With a vicious snarl Itachi ripped the curtain off its support. The sound of tearing cloth echoed in the cave, followed an instant later by another sound, the sound of tearing flesh.

Itachi gaped down in astonishment at the sword buried in his midriff. Directly in front of him stood Shiko, who had waited just beyond the curtain, knowing Itachi would lift his arm to tear the curtain aside.

The Hajimeshi general felt the shock, and the pain, searing through him. He saw the boy release the sword hilt and, as if it had been the only thing holding him up, Itachi started to fall. The last thing he saw before he slipped away into darkness were the cold eyes of the Kotaishi, expressionless. Just like his father's.

And a voice, not his own, screaming in his head, [*"NOOOooooo..."*]

Itachi's body struck the floor, and the lifeless hand released its sword, the blade ringing against the stone. And then there was silence.

No one moved. Shiko, chest still heaving, stared down at the man who had been both uncle and murderer. He looked at Itachi's sword, his mother's blood still fresh on the blade.

I will take his sword back with me, he vowed, to set at the feet of the Kojuro, so that my father will know what has happened in this place. That it was his own son that felled his brother. I doubt, though, that my father will be either surprised, or remorseful, at his brother's demise.

My father. It still sounded strange to him to think of the Kojuro as his father. The thought reminded him of his other parent, much closer to hand. Shaking himself out of his reverie, he quickly ran over to where Yonada still lay, supported by Mikasama.

Brother Numa, having left his spot to attend the wounded Kordaijan, was sitting next to his mother along with Nakama and Shudojo. He looked up at Shiko with a sad, gentle shake of the head.

Mikasama, tears streaming down her face, kept her hands against Yonada's wound, trying to infuse her own energy into her mother's body. Shiko knelt on the other side of his mother, gazing down at the pale face, delicately framed by stray strands of wispy grey hair. Anxiously he said, "Is she—"

Before any of the others could answer, Yonada herself looked up at him and whispered, "Not yet, my son, but soon..."

Looking down into those dark eyes, eyes whose light he could see dimming even as he watched, his heart pounded. The Deshi priory had been the only home he had known. He had no memories of a mother's gentle hand on a fevered brow, or the quiet encouragement of an ever-loyal supporter. Yet a part of him wanted to reach out, wanted the chance to experience with her that love that comes only between mother and child. But that chance was rapidly drifting away...

Weakly Yonada said, "Shiko...You and I, and your sister...we have one more thing left to do..."

Mikasama, eyes closed as she put all her concentration into holding the delicate thread of her mother's life, said in a choking voice, "Mother! I can feel the healing power that's still in you, but you're not using it! Why aren't you trying to heal yourself?"

"Because, child," said Yonada softly, "whatever strength...I have left, must be used...to bring her here."

"Bring who here, Mother?" asked Mikasama, but even as she spoke, she could sense at the periphery of her senses that strange feeling again that presaged the onset of her visions. Yet unlike the last time, the vision did not enter completely into her head. In fact, the vision seemed to be someplace else in the room...

She opened her eyes, looking to one side of the cave while trying to keep her focus on maintaining the regular beat of her mother's heart. Shiko and the others turned toward where Mikasama was looking just as a point of light flashed into brilliance in the candle-lit cave, accompanied by a low rumbling sound. The point of light grew larger, opening into a flat, clear window into someplace well beyond the cave, and well beyond Tonagato. Through the opening sunlight spilled into the cave, casting across the figures of Mikasama and Shiko where they knelt by Yonada.

Beyond the window stood the Shizen lioness, Shidosha.

The Brothers of Sekai, and Toshi-hito, all bowed to her. Shudojo gasped in wide-eyed amazement. "The Goddess! The Goddess has come to us!" Clutching her shasen in front of her, she too bowed her head to the floor before the image of the lioness.

Yet Shidosha did not speak, as she gazed through her window at the trio before her.

"Quickly, my children," whispered Yonada huskily. "It is time...for the task that only the three of us...can complete." With teary eyes she looked up at Mikasama. "You must keep my spirit alive, dearest Mikasama...until Shiko can tap into that power I have left. My son," she said to Shiko, "...you must bring her through...you must bring Shidosha through into our world. Join with me...quickly..."

Shiko had no time to think about what she meant. He could sense Mikasama's desperate efforts as his sister struggled vainly to cope with power she did not understand, trying through sheer force of will to bend that power toward saving her mother. *Their* mother. But he knew that Yonada could not last much longer.

Without waiting for understanding to come, and knowing as little as Mikasama about the mental forces involved, he simply acted. Closing his eyes, he focused all his thoughts on Yonada. He tried to picture her just beyond the door that led to his conversations with the Shizen. As he pushed the door open he could sense her presence in his mind, but it was weak, ethereal; he could not quite find it within his mental landscape.

He reached out with his hands and placed his fingers on either side of his mother's head, hoping to strengthen their bond. He knew that when he had learned to speak with the Shizen the key for him had been visualizing in his mind the door that had to be opened. So he tried creating a mental image of what he needed to do now. He pictured himself diving down into Yonada's soul, as if it were a vast pool of clear water.

It worked; her presence coalesced within his mind, and he could sense his own thoughts 'flowing' through his fingers, down into her, merging with her thoughts like a waterfall splashing into a river.

As he mentally 'swam' up through her thoughts, his head broke through the surface of the 'water' in his image of Yonada's mind. He found himself floating just off what appeared to be the entrance courtyard to Tejinashi, before the great stone gates.

He could see Yonada, standing in the courtyard. Mikasama stood facing her, and the two were holding each other's hands. Their eyes were locked on one another, oblivious to him or their surroundings. Shiko climbed up from the river and 'looked' around, trying to see what it was that he was supposed to do.

He felt as if he were walking through some sort of dream world. The river moat flowed past slowly, the water moving as if it were a sluggish, solid mass. On the far side of the moat Shiko could see Shidosha. She sat patiently, waiting, by the edge of the glacially moving water.

"*She must come across,*" he heard Yonada say in his mind.

"*But why, Mother?*" he heard Mikasama say, her mental voice sounding calm and even. "*It will take so much strength, it will kill you.*"

Shiko turned back to them. They stood as before, looking at each other; their lips did not move, but their voices were as clear to Shiko as if they had spoken aloud.

"Yes," answered Yonada, "*the power needed is great. That is why all three of us, of like blood and spirit, are required.*" Shiko saw the image of Yonada squeeze Mikasama's hands more tightly, and he inexplicably felt the gentle pressure as well. "*My life is but a small payment, measured against the greater need of Tonogato. Shiko cannot bring the kingdoms together without Shidosha's help; her knowledge and power are vast, which the Darkness knows all too well. It will try to cut her off from us, trapping her in her other realm. It is not yet strong enough to seal the passages, but soon, far too soon, it will be. We must act quickly to bring Shidosha here, to Tonogato, if she is to aid us and her own subjects.*"

Another, rumbling voice came through in Shiko's mind. It was Shidosha, speaking from the far side of the moat. "*Kotaishi,*" she said, and Shiko felt himself slowly turning to face her, across the moat.

"*Kotaishi,*" she repeated, "*you are the one who has the power to unite the six kingdoms.*"

Six? wondered Shiko.

"Yes," answered Shidosha. "*Hajimeshi, which you will soon find your own. Tejinashi, which will fall to your sister. Yutakashi and Shukyoshi, which will challenge you. The fifth is Sabakushi, across the far desert.*" Ah, Shiko remembered now, Toshi-hito had told him about Sabakushi before they had left on the pilgrimage.

Shidosha pawed the ground before her. "*The sixth kingdom is that of the Shizen, the animals of Tonogato, which I bring to you.*"

Shiko sensed the urgent need to act, but what was it he was supposed to do? He could see nothing in the courtyard other than Yonada and Mikasama. He walked toward them, then around them, his feet feeling as if they were floating, not really touching the 'ground' at all. He stopped with the gates of Tejinashi at his back. He looked past the women, back toward the moat and Shidosha on the far side. What should he do?

Here, in this strange world of the mind, Yonada's shoulder was undamaged. He reached up and touched it gently with his fingers. She did not respond, her attention still focused on Mikasama before her; but Shiko could feel something when he touched her. He grasped her shoulder more tightly with his hand, and felt a surge of energy up through his arm.

This must be it, he realized. A connection of some sort...

With his other hand, he reached out and touched Mikasama's shoulder. The link suddenly came alive, as a tremendous flow of energy passed between the two women and into him. He was aware at the edge of his mind that Mikasama was concentrating on pouring strength out through her own hands and into Yonada's, sustaining that spark of life still burning inside their mother. Yonada, for her part, was sending all of her energy to Shiko.

He could feel it: a massive wave of power, as if his mother were channeling to him every shred of her being. Which, he realized, she was.

But there was no time to reflect on it. He could sense its fleeting nature; in a moment, it would begin to fade, along with her life. Shiko focused on Shidosha, and on the river that separated her from them. How could he bring her to their side?

The bridge! he realized. I must raise the bridge!

He sent his thoughts down, down into the depths of the thickly moving water. He found the stone pillars of the bridge, far below the surface, in a place where little light ever penetrated. He focused on the nearest pillar, visualized it rising, rising up and through the surface of the water.

It was difficult, like pulling a knife through thick cheese. It was as if the pillar resisted his efforts, wanting to remain below in the dim confines of the moat. Then he realized: something else was pulling down on it! Below, in the blackness at the bottom of the moat, he could sense the Darkness, grasping at the pillar, trying to pull it back.

Shiko re-doubled his efforts, heaving on the pillar to bring it up. He felt the Darkness losing its grip, felt the pillar respond to his own force.

At last the pillar broke through the surface of the moat, the thick water plopping aside from its top.

Quickly Shiko moved on to the next pillar, and again he felt the Darkness clawing at it, wrapping its tendrils around it, in an effort to keep it pinned to the bottom of the moat. But the Darkness could not withstand Shiko's efforts. The Deshi gripped the pillar with his own mental hands and dragged it up to the surface. Losing its grip once again, the Darkness sent forth a deafening screech: a hideous, bone-shattering howl that rocked through Shiko's mind. He slammed closed mental doors and windows, blocking the sound out, and methodically moved on to the next pillar.

One by one he slowly raised them, each an exhausting struggle against the forces buried deep beneath Tejinashi. At last only two pillars remained.

He felt a drop in the power flowing from his mother; she was fading. *"Hurry,"* she said, even her mental voice now sounding weak. From his other side Shiko heard Mikasama say, *"Hold on, Mother! Please, hold on!"*

Shiko pulled harder. Raising the pillars was exhausting him, even with Yonada's power. The second to the last one broke through the river's surface. On the far side, he could see Shidosha poised, ready to leap as soon as the final pillar was in place.

It was the hardest of all. Shiko heaved mightily, gripping the shoulders of the two women as if they were the embodiment of the pillar, and he was trying to pull them both up. It moved, slowly, so slowly. The Darkness clung with an insane tenacity, as if it were sucking up the entire bottom of the moat to wrap around the pillar and hold it down. Shiko heaved, and the Darkness heaved back, the pillar held fast in a stalemated tug of war.

He felt his mother begin to slip, her power ebbing. He heard Mikasama sobbing through their mental link, while she still tried to hold on to Yonada. Taking a deep breath, Yonada said quietly, *"I love you both, my children."* And she sent a final, sudden surge of power through the link to Shiko.

He grabbed it, held it, wrapped the final pillar with it. With a single massive pull he ripped the pillar free of the black anchor restraining it. The pillar rose, splashing up into the air. With a roar, Shidosha leapt, bounding across the bridge. And Yonada collapsed.

In an instant Shiko was back in the cave, still where he had been kneeling beside the prone form of his mother, Mikasama across from him. The sound of a roar echoed around the walls, and brother and sister turned to see Shidosha leaping through the window from that other place, her four padded feet landing on the stone floor of the cave. The window snapped shut in a shower of sparkling light.

At that same moment, a cloud, unaware and unconcerned about the tableau being played out far below it, passed between the sun and the hole that pierced the roof of the cave. The shaft of light suddenly dimmed; then as the cloud moved on, the light returned brightly. The sudden change drew Shiko's eye. He saw the wisps of smoke from the candles curling up through the light, on up into the sky, and at that moment he knew that his mother was gone.

Mikasama finally sat back, her hands no longer able to provide sustenance for the mother she had barely known. Nakama drew the sobbing Princess into his arms as her tears flowed unchecked. Shudojo sat next to her, providing what comfort she could.

Shiko, too, sat by the still form of his mother. He looked down at her face, a face that only now seemed to be at peace. Toshi-hito, his stalwart friend, came and sat beside him. Shiko reached out to brush a strand of loose hair away from his mother's face. He leaned over and gently kissed her forehead.

32

"I have sent them back to Sekai, where I believe—"

And there the sentence stopped, as if the writer had been interrupted. Perhaps, thought the reader, who was ever vigilant to such subtleties, such would account for the off-center crease of the parchment. The writer may have had to suddenly conceal the letter to deal with the intrusion.

The words, however, continued on, only now they began again with a new paragraph. "I find," wrote the sender, "that I was premature in my pronouncement regarding the Kojuro's daughter. She has indeed been found, and on my own doorstep. She is quite well, if perhaps a bit worn about the edges from her travels. However, I am not entirely certain that such has been a bad thing. She has, I believe, developed into a young woman of remarkable character."

"She too, I hasten to add, is an integral part of that greater plan concerned with the survival of Tonogato. I have therefore sent her on to Sekai, there to join with the others. I am certain that you, and her father, will hear from her in due course. If things proceed as I suspect, do not be surprised to find her circumstances vastly altered from what they have been."

"I must now conclude this letter, old friend, with news that I would rather not impart, although you will have undoubtedly already guessed its substance. Mikasama's caretaker Komori died in Shukyoshi, a victim of the plague. She was tended to in her final hours by her own charge, who, I understand, stayed by her caretaker's side until Komori had breathed her last. I am told that her words at the end were that she still loved you."

"I regret that I cannot share your pain; that, unfortunately, must be yours alone. But I can grieve for your loss. And on the strength of the miles, and the many years, between us, rest assured that I do."

"Take care, old friend."

Himitsu crumpled the piece of parchment. He squeezed his hand until he could no longer feel the fingers holding that harbinger he had dreaded.

At last, knowing he could not crush it away, he released his tormented fist. With a contrasting tenderness, he gently placed the parchment on the coals of the fire. He watched as it caught, little sparks of light flying from its surface as the flames took hold. He watched, and waited, until it was no more than smoke. And then he watched the smoke waft about the room until it found the window, his favorite window with the bench seat. As the smoke drifted out through the opening and into the sky beyond, he went and sat, gazing out.

Time, he had always told himself; there would always be time later. But now later had come, and gone.

Outside it was morning, the sun just now rising and glittering off the walls of the castle where a shower had fallen the night before. A sight that usually cheered him, as he sat here in his window. But today, watching the people who stirred below, going about their daily chores, one day to the next; today, he found no joy. The sun glittered off one more drop, one not left behind by the evening rain.

* * *

That same sun rose over the quiet courtyard of Sekai monastery.

The silent dawn was just slipping over the snowy hills as a group of Brothers, led by Abbot Akiya, and accompanied by Shiko, Mikasama, and Toshi-hito, made a solemn procession down into the canyon below the monastery. There, brother and sister quietly placed their mother beneath the burial stones, to rest and to further nurture life as she had done throughout her own. As the last of the stones was placed, Toshi-hito erected the small marker flag over her that would signal to the Fates that another soul lay ready for its journey along a different path. The Brothers did the same for the two unfortunate Tejinashi City Watchmen.

Abbot Akiya turned to the siblings and spoke quietly. "Yonada's spirit shall always remain with us at Sekai, no matter the path she walks with the Fates."

Shiko and Mikasama both bowed their appreciation. Shiko said, "We could ask for no better guardians of her memory." With a troubled look he added, "I regret that our presence here has caused the intrusion of so much violence, and so much magic, into your refuge."

Akiya waved his hand. "No, no, do not worry for that. Violence is always deplorable, but as long as man walks the world it is unavoidable. Only a fool would think he could escape it completely by running away to a mountaintop. As for the magic, well," he sighed, "it is not the tool that is at fault, but how it is used. We refuse magic here more as a rejection of those in power in Tejinashi, and their ways of using magic, than for any particular distaste for magic itself." He looked keenly at his two visitors. "Can I not persuade you to remain at Sekai a while longer, at least until you've had more time to rest?"

Despite their fatigue, both brother and sister declined. "Thank you, Abbot," said Mikasama, "but we dare not delay further."

Shiko nodded his agreement. "Weariness is the least of our concerns, considering the road that lies ahead of us now."

Despite the shock of the confrontation with Itachi, and the heart-wrenching loss of their mother, both Shiko and Mikasama had been forced to set aside their exhaustion and emotional turmoil. The previous day the Brothers had removed the fallen from the great chamber and ushered everyone to the monastery above. Shidosha, Shiko, and Mikasama had been left alone to confer, sovereign to sovereign. The two siblings had spent much of the night sequestered with the supreme Shizen.

When at last brother and sister had emerged in the early hours of the morning, neither would divulge what Shidosha had said to them. But their expressions had told all: difficult times were ahead, and there would be little rest for any of them in the troubled days to come. They had permitted themselves only a few brief hours of sleep before rising to join with the Brothers in honoring their mother's remains.

While those from Hajimeshi paid their respects in the canyon below, Shidosha stood serenely by the main gate. She had waited many years for this course of events to unfold, and had long since learned the value of patience. The Brothers, and the Guards from Hajimeshi, remained a respectful distance from her, as they would for a human sovereign. Only Shudojo, confronted now with an embodiment of her Goddess, was bold enough to approach the lioness. The Sister knelt before Shidosha in silent supplication, any prayers that she offered unheard by those who observed from afar. But they noted Shidosha looking down at the Sister kneeling before her. When Shudojo rose up, the face with the odd blue eyes carried a contented smile.

The wind chimes along the wall, which the day before had been silent, rang softly in the gentle breeze as the Abbot and the others returned to the monastery's courtyard. The Hajimeshi Guards, under Nakama's direction, were preparing the horses provided by the Brothers. Each of the Guards had flipped over his cassock, and in place of the subdued grey each man now sported blazing white, indicative of a completed pilgrimage. Looking at the preparations of the Guards, Akiya asked, "Where shall you go now?"

Without hesitation Shiko replied, "To Tejinashi. We must confirm Mikasama's succession as the Kordaijan."

"I miss my father terribly," added the Princess. "I desperately want to go back to Hajimeshi to see him, especially since he is so ill, but this is a responsibility that cannot wait. I think Papa would understand." She frowned. "From what I saw at Tejinashi, and from what Shiko and Toshi-hito have told me, I know it will be a struggle. I have no training in whatever magical arts I inherited from my mother, and the Zaitan will certainly not take kindly to the suggestion that an 'outsider' is the heir to the Kordaijan. But," she concluded firmly, "it will be done."

The Abbot noted the determined look in her eyes, and took pity on anyone who would stand in the way of this young woman once she set her mind to a task. "And you, young man?" he said to Shiko. "Yours is a terrible responsibility. How does one go about unifying kingdoms so unlike one another?"

Shiko pursed his lips. "In truth, Abbot? I don't know. Unfortunately, along with becoming Kotaishi, I was not also blessed with a ready-made plan for accomplishing what must be done." He glanced at Nakama and the Guards. "As soon as we have escorted Mikasama to Tejinashi, I must return to Hajimeshi and see my father. We will have to deal with any remnants of Itachi's disaffection there before we can decide what to do about Yutakashi and Shukyoshi. As for Sabakushi—" He stopped as he saw some of the Brothers carrying bundles across the courtyard. Those standing with him were startled when he suddenly shouted, "Wait, please!"

Hurrying over to the Brothers, Shiko saw that his guess was correct: they were carrying Itachi and Bokusa's packs, which had been left near the postern before the attack. He opened Itachi's pack and withdrew the box holding 'Ton and 'Cha. Carrying it back over to his friends, he touched the box's seal. He was unsurprised to see that he was now able to cause its colorful transformation himself.

Mikasama, wide-eyed, asked, "What is it?" but before Shiko could answer the lid suddenly sprang open. The two chodaka birds immediately dived out, sweeping up over everyone's heads and into the clear mountain air.

"Those poor birds!" gasped Mikasama. "How could they have been cooped up inside that little box all this time?"

Watching the exuberant flying of "Ton and 'Cha, Shiko said quietly, "A wise person once told me not to assume that what you see, is what truly is." He glanced with some sadness at his sister. "I suspect we will have to take careful heed of that advice, once we reach Tejinashi."

'Ton and 'Cha flew down over Shidosha, commencing a furious chatter, which only increased when Shidosha lifted her head and uttered a low, rumbling roar in their direction. The birds circled the lioness excitedly, while Shidosha wore an expression of bemused indulgence.

The birds alighted on the wall above the gate. They ceased their usual chatter for a brief moment while peering directly at Shiko. Inexplicably the former apprentice suddenly burst out laughing. The two birds jumped aloft once more, winging in circles and spirals overhead, until they flew out of sight into the trees across the canyon.

Toshi-hito, who had not sensed any of the conversation between the birds and Shiko, asked, "Did they speak with you? What did they say?"

Shiko smiled. "A conversation best left unspoken, I think. However, you might consider what you and a mate might want to do as soon as you were free once more to be yourselves."

"Ah," nodded Toshi-hito. Mikasama blushed.

Nakama walked up at that moment and gave a short bow to Shiko. "We are ready, Kotaishi, whenever you wish to leave."

Shiko returned the bow, still not quite at his ease but learning quickly the behaviors expected of a leader. "Thank you," he said. "We had best start now. The tasks ahead will not become any easier for the waiting." Nakama nodded and signaled to the men to mount their horses.

The pilgrims from Hajimeshi bowed to Abbot Akiya, expressing their gratitude once more. He waved them on their way, saying, "All we have done here is but provide a small stepping stone. Glad as we are to have done so, there are yet higher steps that await you." He held out his hands, in a gesture to encompass the entire pilgrim group. "May the Fates watch over you. Sekai will always welcome you, whether here or in your hearts."

As the pilgrims set themselves atop their horses and organized themselves into traveling order, the old gatekeeper, Tusoda, pulled open the main gate. He stood and watched as Shiko rode out and onto the bridge, paced by Shidosha striding beside him. Behind them, Mikasama and Nakama rode side by side, followed by Toshi-hito and Shudojo.

The Guards of Hajimeshi brought up the end of the column. Last in line, and now the highest position of honor, was Donaku. He bore the quiescent Hikari on its pole over his shoulder, which along with the reversed cassocks was the traditional sign of a pilgrimage successfully completed. Trailing after the pilgrims, it served as guide to those who might choose to follow the same path.

As the group made its way across the bridge, Tusoda, staff in hand, walked partway across after them. He had not seen such excitement at the monastery in many, many a season, and it brought a spring to his step. As the pilgrims made their way across to the far side he saw the two birds diving and circling above them. Tusoda leaned on his staff and watched in wonderment.

Overhead, the same rain cloud that had visited Hajimeshi earlier now passed by. It began a gentle spring shower, and Tusoda held out his hand to catch some drops. As the pilgrims rode out of sight the rain increased, drumming softly on the wooden boards of the bridge.

Humph, thought Tusoda; no point standin' out here and gettin' wet.

He turned and walked back to his gatehouse, where he knew a warm fire waited.

About the Author

Kevin Radthorne and his wife Lise live just outside Seattle, in a little house in the woods (sort of). They are periodically visited by the neighbor's cat, as well as by a family of crazy Russians. Kevin amuses himself during the day by working as a computer programmer, primarily exchanging emails with his friend Sofia and occasionally cutting code. The rest of the time, his mind is busily dreaming up more stories to tell.

The Road to Kotaishi is Kevin's first novel. A sequel, The Sands of Sabakushi, is currently fermenting beneath his fevered brow.